FAIRWEATHER
OF THE BARK ENDEAVOUR

HELEN WEISS

Publisher: Inspiring Publishers,
P.O. Box 159, Calwell, ACT Australia 2905
Email: publishaspg@gmail.com
http://www.inspiringpublishers.com

A catalogue record for this book is available from the National Library of Australia

National Library of Australia The Prepublication Data Service

Author: Helen Weiss
Title: Fairweather of the Bark Endeavour
Genre: Fiction
ISBN: 978-1-922792-00-6

Udo Hans Weiss
For Everything

CHAPTER 1

There are those cats who live in fancy homes, on leafy boulevards, eating the finest selections of fish, preening their perfumed fur, watching birds through curtained windows, watching their manners, and waiting for attention from the lady of the house, much like my mother. Her name was Princess.

Then there are those cats who live by their wits in the dark alleys and damp streets, searching for their next meal in garbage cans, or hunting swift rodents, their coats matted and smelling unclean. They have no owners and sleep where they can. They have no manners, only cunning, much like my father. He had no name that I knew of.

My name is Fairweather. I would say, in my opinion, that I am a little of both my parents, and with such a mixture of breeding, when rare and wonderful experiences have come my way, I have sized them up and taken them on. Using the talents passed on to me by my lineage I have not missed an opportunity, and hence my story begins.

As a kitten, my mother taught me all she knew, in the beautiful home to which I was born. My birth name was Barnaby Charles Arbuthnot Peabody, a name that makes me shiver with embarrassment to this very day. I cannot utter it even in my own mind for fear someone may overhear.

When Madam's maid fed me juicy portions of tuna and sardines, I ate carefully, spilling nothing. I licked the cream from my floral plate delicately, so as not to splash the polished marble floors. I cleaned my mouth and whiskers until no trace remained of the meal I had eaten so carefully.

Madam would call for us after dinner to sit on the chaise lounge by her side, to be petted and stroked.

"Purring is essential!" Mother would say. "Madam must know that you enjoy her attention."

I must state that I did not have to try very hard to enjoy a scratch under the chin. All cats, be they plain or proper, enjoy a good chin scratching.

Occasionally, my father would visit. My mother was never very impressed when he yowled and scratched at the kitchen door. She felt it embarrassed her, but she would invariably let me greet him outside. I was always excited to see him and would save a little of my sumptuous meal when I knew him to be visiting. I would sneak past the cook with mouthful after mouthful until a neat pile of fish lay waiting by the door, and I alongside it, looking longingly up the lane for his familiar shape.

He was a roguish fellow, lean and agile, as alley cats are prone to be. After he scoffed down my offerings, we would wrestle in the lane behind the stables. He taught me to catch the mice that scurried around the alleys. I never ate them; I did not need to, but I always enjoyed the chase.

"Cats must be cunning hunters, fit for anything, alert and wary!" he would say. After his visit as he skulked into the night I would take my captured rodents, dead from fright, to the scullery maid.

"Oh, you clever cat!" she would say. "We don't want these horrid little creatures in the kitchen, do we?" I always felt proud, and strutted around the kitchen with my head held high and my back arched in anticipation of the reward I knew would come – a salted herring or an extra dish of cream.

My mother would look at my victims lying dead on the kitchen floor, turning her nose up at the commonness of my actions, but I knew she was secretly proud that I had established my place in the household.

Madam liked to know that I had caught "the filthy little beasts." Little did she know that my father had a hand in my hunting trips, or she would have ordered the butler to chase him with the garden shovel, as I once saw him do at her command.

"Don't let me see that common alley cat snivelling around my doors!" she would shout. "Hit him hard and hit him well!" Needless to say, the butler never did catch up with him, but our meetings were more careful after that.

As much as I enjoyed my life back then, I felt something was missing. Occasionally, as the breeze blew inland from the harbour, I would catch a faint smell that stirred my soul. My mother told me it was the smell of the sea. It had a quality that spoke to me of mystery and excitement. As I grew, my longing for the origin of this heady perfume grew with me. I knew nothing of the harbour, least of all how to get there, but I knew I must go.

"Go along, lad!" my father urged on the last night that I saw him. "Taste the unknown, live a full life, and remember the things I have taught you!"

My mother cried when I left. "But this is your home, dear, and Madam will miss you!"

"I must go to the harbour!" I pronounced proudly. "Its call is strong and insistent, and I am ready!"

"Very well, dear, but mind your manners and be wary of the wrong types." She understood that my father's wandering spirit was part of my being, and with the courage of her breeding, she bade me farewell.

I do not know how I knew the way, and to this day can only tell you that I followed my nose, so to speak. The breeze was fresh from the sea that morning and my destiny awaited me.

Through crowded streets filled with horses and carts, businessmen rushed in my way. Impatient delivery boys and women in long ruffled skirts blocked my path. A blur of feet, carriage wheels, and hooves flashed by me at every turn. I stopped to catch my breath in the lane behind an inn. My heart was beating so heavily in my ears that I did not hear the rubbish cart clambering along the cobblestones behind me, its wheels on a direct course for my tired body. All of a sudden, pain, the like of which I had never known before, seared through me! The cart stopped. I looked down to see my hind leg snapped like a broken twig. The howl that I could not control attracted much attention. I tried to get up, wanting to run, but my leg would not hold me, and the pain became worse.

A strong hand gripped the scruff of my neck and held me aloft. Our eyes met and at once my instincts told me that a kind fellow lurked beneath that strength. He carried me to a room behind the inn and placed me gently on an old dresser. He began to break a wooden crate into small pieces. I was not sure what he intended, as his mighty blows smashed the timber, but something in his eyes told me he meant well.

He selected a sturdy piece of the wood and placed it thoughtfully along my leg. With one swift but painful motion he straightened my broken limb and placed the selected timber alongside it. He produced a handkerchief from his coat pocket and firmly bound them together. Strangely, I was able to stand, and the pain had eased.

"Well, then, cat," he murmured softly, as he stood back, scratched his chin, and admired his handiwork. "My name is Tom, and I shall call you 'Lucky', as indeed you are!"

He left me to rest a while and sleep came quickly. I am unsure how long I lay there, but I awoke when Tom returned some time later with an old tin plate laden with scraps of lamb and a saucer of milk. The pain had eased by now and I eyed my rescuer with affection. A huge man to say the very least, in well-worn clothing, but smooth faced and clean. His hands wore the mark of a hardworking chap, calloused and rough, but a gentle touch he relayed to me as he massaged my chin.

"You will stay here until you're well, but take care that the innkeeper does not see you, or it will be my job you will lose," warned Tom. I understood, and stayed well out of the way.

Days passed into weeks. I slept under a crate in the lane behind the inn by day. I watched from between the wooden slats, this new and unfamiliar world I had entered. Women and men scurried from doors into the streets, only to disappear into other doors and up other streets. They seemed busier here than those near my home, having work and chores to attend to. Surely, every afternoon, Tom would arrive for work, inspect my mending limb, and secretly present me with food and drink from the kitchen of the inn.

Late at night when the inn was filled with rowdy men, I would creep quietly to the windowsill and sit, listening to their stories of the harbour. The ships that came and went, the hard work they performed loading and unloading cargo onto the docks. Some were at the inn every night; others came and went with the ships.

After the inn closed, the familiar smell of the sea I longed for wafted in from the harbour. It must have been close by, as it was stronger than I had smelled it before, and my soul stirred once again for its company.

Finally, the day had come for Tom to release my leg from the splint. He carefully unwrapped the handkerchief and I stood unaided. It was stiff from inactivity but I managed to walk. Tom seemed happy with himself. A few days later, I took one last meal from Tom's tin plate, and I sensed that he knew I would leave him. He stroked my fur. "Lucky, old mate," he announced proudly, inspecting my mended leg, "a job well done if I do say so myself, as good as new! Now, be off with you! You have places to go, I can tell."

And with that, I was gone.

CHAPTER 2

y journey seemed to rush before me, closer and closer with each step. Tom had repaired well my wounded leg, as it kept pace easily with the other three. I do not remember how many towns and villages I passed through. It could have been three or four, it could have been dozens, but within what seemed to be the mere blink of an eye, I finally approached the harbour. My heart beat wildly with promise, only to be drowned out by the noises my stomach made. I had not eaten since my last night with the good-hearted Tom. Not a real meal, anyway. A few morsels from rubbish bins and licks of water from puddles along the way, but I could not stop now. I had to cast my eyes on the water I had so longed to see.

As I neared the end of a wide cobble-stoned street, it must have been dawn. There were not many people around except the street sweepers labouring over their tasks, and two cleaning ladies scurrying about with mops and buckets. There were no homes on this street, not like the home I had come from. The brown stone buildings held shops of all kinds, and an inn like the one Tom worked at. Above them, the shopkeepers slept.

A heavy fence blocked the end of the street where the sweet smell lay. I jumped up, and there just below me, was the lapping of what I now know to be the Thames River. As I raised my head further, it seemed to stretch quite a way, and then was stopped by land on the other side. This could not be all there was? I must say I was expecting a little more than this meagre expanse of water. It certainly smelled good, though, and I sat for a while and let my eyes take in the sights around me.

I was at the docks. All shapes and sizes of ships were moored here. I had never seen such things, only paintings of them in Madam's drawing room. They were rather larger than I had imagined, and even at dawn, were a hive of activity. The men worked between the decks and the docks, carrying this and that, like ants tending a nest. Huge crates and coils of ropes lay waiting for their turn to be lifted, shifted and stored away in secret chambers on the ships. As many things as I saw loaded onto these huge ships, they still seemed hungry for more. I concluded that at some time in the near future, I must find out where such things went.

As the sun rose above the horizon, the calm and hazy water reflected a shimmering golden pink, which held my gaze for some time. It reminded me of the sunlight on the marble floors in the kitchen of my home. The cook was always the proudest of her kitchen at this very time of day, when the reflection made her clean floors gleam in much the same way. Having a thought for my home made me a little sad, and reminded my stomach that I must not have eaten a proper meal in days.

More strongly than the harbour smell that drew me here, right now the smell of fish enticed me more. Across the road from the docks was a large building, housing a fishmonger. Men in heavy aprons were placing some of the tastiest looking fish I had ever seen carefully on display. How nice of them to place their wares before me, as if knowing how hungry I was. I approached with little care, my stomach leading the way.

"Oy! You! Cat! Be off with you!" boomed a huge man with a heavy beard and hairy arms. "Nick, get that wretched cat away from the fish!" he yelled. "The customers won't touch this stuff if they see that mangy cat here! Get him! Get the shovel!" He appeared to be turning quite a deep purple in colour. I took this to be not a good sign.

The thin and spotty Nick came quickly with the shovel. "Where'd he go, sir?" whined Nick, but by that time, I had wisely decided not to wait around and find out what he intended to do with his wildly waving shovel. I was off! I scampered round a sharp corner at the end of the building into a very narrow lane, where I caught my breath for a moment. How silly of me to think they were providing this sumptuous feast just for me. I would have to be more careful, hungry or not. I watched from the corner for a while, where I realised after some time that Nick and "Sir" went together to the back of the store to fetch the fish, returning to place them on the counter at the front of the shop. I waited for the men to disappear from sight, knowing I would only have a few seconds before their return, and I bolted for the nearest fish I could see. I jumped to the counter, grabbed the tasty beast in my mouth, turned and readied my escape. As I turned, there was "Sir" right in my path. He had returned too soon!

"Ahh! Here he is, Nick. Where's that blasted shovel?" he yelled.

I had not a moment to think! I pounced at him, knocking him right off his feet. Down he went, like a clumsy giant, right on his behind!

"Owww, Nick! Get over here, you imbecile! That damn thing's attacked me! Get him, you lazy sod!" bellowed the injured "Sir."

By this time, with fear and great speed, I was half way back to the stone fence, and I noted with joy and amazement, that the fish was still in my mouth. I looked back momentarily to see the huge hairy "Sir" still floundering on the ground and Nick trying to no avail to help him up. From that distance I could see that "Sir" was much more purple than before, and the bumbling Nick feared for his own neck.

Back to my fish, I thought. I jumped down behind the fence to the rocks below and out of sight to satisfy my hunger. I settled happily into my meal, but just as I was swallowing the first delicious mouthful, I heard scurrying around the rocks. The fur on the back of my neck bristled. Three cats had gathered in a circle around me. I was a little nervous, as they appeared scruffy and unkempt, and had a threatening presence to them. More than afraid, I desperately wanted to finish my meal, and was not about to let these three beggars do me out of it! As they looked greedily at my catch, I placed my paw defiantly upon my fish and stood to my full height.

"Who are you, and what do you want?" said I boldly.

The scraggiest cat I had ever seen spoke up first. "Listen to 'im, Badger. A right toff, ain't he. Name's Slim, guv'nor, what's it to ya?"

"Be quiet, Slim! I should like to speak to this fellow," ordered the larger cat. "My name is Badger. Allow me to introduce my friends. This ugly scatterbrain goes by the name of Slim," said Badger, "and my quiet friend behind you is Rubbish-Bin-Bob." I looked around to find a rather fat grey cat with small ears, unfriendly looking and his eyes fixed on my fish.

Badger stepped forward. "That is far enough, Mister Badger! I have come a long way. Whilst I am tired from my journey, I am not too tired to defend myself and my meal from the likes of you!" I realised just how hungry I must have been, as I had never spoken to anyone in this manner, and quite surprised myself.

"Fear not, young chap," declared Badger, "we are not about to impose upon your well-earned meal. The three of us witnessed your antics with the fish-monger, and I must say, we are suitably impressed!"

"Yeah, we saw ya' give that old scoundrel what for," cheered Slim. "Laughed and laughed, we did. Never seen 'im on 'is back before. Given 'im all sorts of trouble, we 'ave. Never seen anythin' like what you did, though! Young Nick, he was worried for 'is life. Last I saw, he was still tryin' to get the old bloke up off the ground. Funniest thing I ever seen."

Rubbish-Bin-Bob said nothing, just wobbled slightly in what I can only imagine to be a chuckle.

"Bob does not have the gift of speech like our Slim, thank goodness, or I would surely be driven out of my mind," muttered Badger, annoyed by Slim's babbling. "Now, good fellow, we will leave you in peace to enjoy your spoils, for I do believe you deserve such a fish. This evening we are planning to meet at the inn by the entrance to the main dock. It is called the 'Seaman's Rest' and is down that way." He pointed. "We would be delighted if you would join us for a catnip or two. Until then, brave chap!" Badger bowed and the three turned and left me, Slim jumping around Badger tirelessly, and Rubbish-Bin-Bob dawdling along behind, looking over his shoulder hungrily at my fish.

As I watched them walk away, my legs shook a little, and my heart pounded, but my stomach took control and I devoured my fish with great speed. Finally, after I had washed my face and tidied my whiskers, that old urge to sleep after a huge meal came over me. I found a quiet spot behind a collection of old crates, closed my eyes, and slept a dreamless sleep.

CHAPTER 3

I woke with a start. How long had I slept? It was late in the evening and I remembered Badger's invitation. I decided that these chaps warranted further investigation, and I could do with a few friends in this strange place, so I carefully made my way to the inn he had described. The "Seaman's Rest." It was a bustle of loud voices, much like Tom's inn, where I had spent time recovering from my injury. I made my way down the alley behind the old brown stone building, being careful not to attract any unwanted attention.

"Oy, you!" That familiar irritating voice. Slim. "Oy! Up here!" I looked up, and there they were, perched on a window ledge high above the rear door of the inn. "Come on, then!" Slim wailed. "We been waitin' for ya!"

I had the right place.

I jumped to the top of some crates by the door, then to the ledge by way of a railing, where I joined the group. There was another cat with Badger, Slim and Rubbish-Bin-Bob. He was rather unpleasant to the eye and I felt a little uncomfortable. Badger must have sensed this, and made the introductions.

"Turkel, may I present..." He stopped, and an uncomfortable pause followed. "Dear fellow, we do not even know your name!"

"A recent acquaintance named me 'Lucky'. You may call me by that name, if you choose," I announced, being rather glad to be rid of my birth name.

Slim rolled about laughing. "Lucky? Not likely! I seen what you did to the fishmonger. Luck had nothin' to do with it. Pure guts is what it was!"

Badger interrupted him, "Will you be quiet, you mangy beast!" he grumbled. "Please take no notice of Slim, my dear Turkel. He has no manners to speak of, although he is correct in summing up our new friend. He performed a rather courageous feat this very morning."

Badger turned to me, "We cannot possibly call you 'Lucky'! You must have a new name at once! One befitting your enterprise this morning! You were fearless, bold and daring!" He thought for a moment. "Aha! 'Bandit' shall be your name, as a bandit you were! Taking what you wish with the bravery of a true scoundrel!"

The name Bandit was not without its merits, I thought. Other cats would fear and respect me with a name such as this, and this advantage would be necessary if I were to stay at the dockside. "As you wish, Badger," I agreed, hoping I could live up to my new name.

Turkel listened to Badger's description of my hunger-driven deed with some interest, although it was hard to tell. This cat was unlike any I had encountered. He had one eye missing, covered by a black patch. His other eye stared straight ahead most of the time, only looking at me briefly. He was missing a front leg, and where it should have been was a wooden stump with his name, "Turkel," and a picture of a ship carved roughly into the timber. His coat was shiny black, like my father's, and I could not help but stare at him.

After the long and somewhat exaggerated story had been told, Turkel finally spoke.

"Bandit!"

I jumped. His voice was deep and strong, and even as he whispered, it made me shiver.

"You may think you have courage, my boy, but until you have sailed the high seas, as I have, you know nothing! I'll tell you stories of the things I've seen and known. Great storms and sickness, hostile lands with tribes of dark-skinned natives who eat their own kind. Things that will make your fur stand straight up, and give you hellish nightmares!"

All of us in this small group on the ledge leaned toward him, so as not to miss a single word. I was in awe of this mystifying animal. He spoke with great authority of ocean voyages that he been on and heard; tales that had been passed down among the generations of cats who had sailed on board great ships. Their captains had searched the vast oceans for undiscovered lands, to claim them for their countries and kings, making them rich and powerful.

Focusing his one good eye into the distance, Turkel spoke of recent voyagers; friends and acquaintances who had braved the hardships of life at sea.

"For two hundred and fifty years, the Dutch, Spaniards and Portuguese have attempted to chart the Pacific Ocean. A few English and French have sailed its waters, scoundrels mostly, more interested in thievery than discovery. My old friend, the great 'Bard,' was the cook's cat aboard the 'Dolphin,' Captained by 'Foul-Weather' Jack Byron, on the first real British expedition in search of a great southern continent known as Terra Australis Incognita. Not a soul had laid eyes on this land, but all believed it existed, somewhere in the Pacific Ocean. It was rumoured here among the docks, that Byron was without the spirit needed for such an adventure, but brave 'Bard' boarded the ship as a companion for the sentimental old cook. They had been life-long friends since 'Bard' was a mere boy, and he feared for his master's safety. On dangerous seas and violent storms, they pushed on through the Northwest Passage, a fearsome route, striking at the hearts of the bravest men. The dreaded scurvy killed many of the crew."

"Scurvy?" I interrupted.

"Aye, my boy, a foul and unavoidable disease which will grip even the strongest man. With great journeys between lands, fresh foods perish, and all that is left for human consumption are sea rations of salt beef, and hardtack, an unpalatable dried biscuit. Without fresh fruit and vegetables, men cannot keep up their strength. We felines are a much tougher breed. Fish and sea birds are plentiful at sea, satisfying the fussiest cat, but a crew of men without fresh rations become ill, and many die."

We dared not utter a word as Turkel continued.

"Aye, scurvy, the devil's own work. I too have witnessed this wretched plague. Men I had grown to know died grizzly deaths from it, when their mouths and gums would bleed and their teeth would fall out! They would bruise from the slightest bump, their bones ached, and in the end they would lose their appetite, their will to live, and they would die! Good men, old and young, fit and feeble, the scurvy can take them all!"

Turkel bowed his head for a moment, as if to pay his respects to his fallen comrades. It was an uncomfortable pause, and I was grateful when Badger reminded us all that the kitchen hand had left some scraps on the ledge, with a bowl of catnip. We were all quite hungry and the food was welcome. Slim and Rubbish-Bin-Bob attacked the bowl of food as if it were to be their last meal.

"Gentlemen!" roared Badger. "Where the dickens are your manners? We are in the company of greatness, and here you are unashamedly making pigs of yourselves!" Slim and Bob backed away from the plate, their heads bowed just a little, but with their eyes glued as keenly to that plate as if it were a mouse about to escape.

"Now, Turkel, my good fellow, we would be honoured if you would dine on this pleasant offering, and enjoy some fine catnip. We will eat when you are satisfied," offered Badger, casting a scolding glance at the greedy pair.

Turkel ate little, but did take quite a hearty drop of catnip. When he had finished, Badger allowed us to dine on the remains, and a fine feast it was. The catnip was especially good, and as I had never taken this drink before, found it quite tasty and drank my fill. It made me somewhat light-headed and perhaps a little spirited.

"Please continue your fine story, Turkel!" I slurred. "I grow impatient to hear more!" Slim and Bob sniggered at my impertinence.

"Take it slowly with the catnip, dear boy," Badger warned. "It is a potent brew, made by the kitchen hand himself, and not all have the head for it. Excuse our friend here, Turkel, he is new to the ways of the docks. He will learn in time to pace himself."

Turkel ignored Badger's apology. "More, is it you want, boy?" he assumed. "I will tell you more. The more, the better! You might learn to stay in comfort here at the Deptford Docks, or better still, find a home and master, instead of dreaming of the sea!"

I wondered how he knew that the sea had haunted me all my life, and as if to read my thoughts he nodded suggestively toward me.

"I see it in your eyes! I know the look of a lad who seeks adventure! I have seen it many times, and I know of the grizzly fate that befalls them! Aye, you are one such animal and it is for your skin that I fear!" His gaze stayed upon me for the longest time, but I wavered not, and finally he continued, as if resolved to warn me of my doom.

"Captain Jack Byron found nothing new in the Pacific, and by the time *Bard* had returned, having witnessed his own master's sickness, he vowed never to return to the sea. Last I heard of him he was still living with the old cook, in a sleepy seaside town far from here." He paused to honour his close friend.

"Another, by the name of Samuel Wallis, took over Byron's ship *Dolphin* on her return, and along with Phillip Carteret commanding a second ship, the *Swallow*, were commissioned by the British Government to find this elusive land. This was my voyage. I had heard such rousing stories of sea life that I had to see it for myself, much like you, boy. The night before the two ships sailed, in August of 1764, I stowed away in a longboat on the *Dolphin*. The *Swallow* was a worn-out old sloop, not looking at all seaworthy enough for my liking. As we made our way through the Magellan Strait, a mighty storm came in hard upon us. The seas rose up like mountains capped with white foam, and then plunged into deep valleys. It roared like a caged lion, deafening and endless. The rain came across the bow, not falling down, but sideways, driven by a savage and relentless wind. Lightning flashed, brighter than I had ever seen, lighting up the ship as if it were a beacon. I wish now that I had been wise enough to stay below during this nightmare, but I was spellbound by this wild and thrilling spectacle. I felt alive, and foolishly braved the elements until a loose plank tore away to the windward and hit me. I remember nothing of my rescue. Shock, I suspect. When I awoke in the doctor's cabin, I was in hellish pain. I could see nothing from my left eye. My right eye surveyed the worst of my injuries. My left leg was gone, torn away by the force of the blow. The doctor, although a quiet and serious man, had stitched and bandaged my wounds to the best of his ability, and tended me for some time after." He paused again as we all gasped, wide eyed.

"During the more peaceful times when the storms had passed, he fashioned my wooden leg from the very plank that had caused me such grief, giving me my name and etching it into the timber along with a likeness of the ship, for all to see. He made a patch for my eye to hide the scars from my injury. He said very little to me, but my gratitude was such that we became silent friends."I was soon able to walk, and the crew discovered my presence on board, where once I had kept out of sight. I could not help but be obvious with this damned wooden leg clunking against the wooden decks. They were impressed with my appearance, likening me to a pirate, and I was given the respect of a true hero."Fish were always on my dinner plate, the occasional bird, shot by one of the men, was always shared, and I slept wherever I wished. I learned that our two vessels had separated after the storms and heavy seas. The *Swallow* was too slow and could not keep pace with us. Carteret and the *Swallow* continued on to Polynesia and made many important discoveries before returning to England. We on the *Dolphin* continued northwest across the Pacific, changing to a western course when the winds favoured, and soon sighted towering mountain peaks, topped with clouds in the distance, then more and more peaks stretching across the hazy horizon. There was much joy amongst the crew, and Captain Wallis ordered extra rations for all, in celebration of the sighting of this great southern land. Moments later, a thick fog enveloped the ship and our mountains were no longer visible. During the night our ship had drifted, the winds took us, and the great Terra Australis Incognita was no more to be seen. "By dawn we were off Tahiti and surrounded by canoes filled with handsome, dark-skinned men and women. They followed us from a distance as Captain Wallis steered the ship along a thunderous reef, where we could not cross to land for fear of striking the rocks or coral below and 'holing' the ship. The rolling waves crashed monstrously across these shallow waters and the danger of sinking kept us clear. "Soon a break in the reef was discovered, where calm waters allowed us to sail through and anchor in Tahiti on the eighteenth day of June 1767. Captain Wallis mapped the entrance to Port Royal Harbour. I went ashore with the longboat and crew. A more beautiful place I have never seen. Gently sloping mountains covered in palms and breadfruit, yams and bananas; valleys cascading with waterfalls spilling into the sea.

"Warm weather day and night, not cold like our England, and clear blue water full of exotic fish. We stayed there for six weeks, enjoying the friendship of the natives. Mind you, lads, while they were friendly and eager to trade with us, the stories of a tribe of cannibals made us all a little wary."

"What are cannibals, Turkel?" I interrupted.

Badger gave me a withering stare. "Will you cease these infernal questions, boy!"

Turkel paused, closing his good eye for a moment as if gathering strength.

"Cannibals?" whispered Turkel. "They are vicious men, who fight like great warriors and eat the very men they've killed. I've seen their skeletons stripped to the bones and laid out in the sun to dry. The skulls of their victims are their trophies, displayed at their huts for all to admire and fear!"

I shivered visibly and the fur on the back of my neck stood out. The others looked at me as if satisfied that I had changed my mind about setting out to sea.

Wearily, Turkel finished his tale.

"The ship was stocked with provisions and water while the crew made repairs to the *Dolphin*. We set sail for England, but we never again saw the distant peaks we had seen earlier. We will never know if what we had seen was the elusive Terra Australis Incognita."

I had many questions for this remarkable Turkel, but I dared not interrupt again.

All of a sudden, Turkel stood up. "I am weary now, and must get some sleep, but before I take my leave, boy, heed my words well. I have seen many fine sights, and new lands, and discoveries are enticing when you are a young boy with the sea in your sights, but you will risk your health, your safety, your life!" And with that he turned and jumped from the ledge into the street, quite deftly for a cat with a wooden leg. I looked after him with great admiration as he disappeared.

"Well, lad, there goes a fine chap," said Badger. "It is rather late. The inn will be closing soon, and we too must take sleep. We have a meagre residence, not far from here. It will be safer for you than the streets, and you may join us if you wish."

"Thank you, Badger. I will accept your kind offer, as I have had a full and interesting day. A restful sleep will suit me well, for tomorrow I intend to investigate the docks and familiarise myself with these ships."

"After that story?" gasped Badger. "You must be mad!"

Slim roared with laughter! "Mad Bandit! Mad Bandit!" he taunted.

Rubbish-Bin-Bob plodded along behind, having lost interest.

I followed the trio to a quiet laneway and curled myself restlessly upon some rags. I was ever so tired, but sleep did not come quickly, as Turkel's words played over and over in my mind. The smell of the sea comforted me, and finally I slept. I dreamed of ships and grand adventures, and the Tahitian sun warming my fur. Thankfully, I did not dream of cannibals.

CHAPTER 4

I rose at dawn the next morning. I was determined to take less catnip in the future as I felt rather unwell. My head ached and my stomach turned. The others had already left our sleeping quarters in search of food, and I wished them well, as I could not face a meal in my condition. I wandered slowly but cautiously to the street, only to be met by a bustle and gossip drifting like waves in the direction of the docks.

My curiosity got the better of my malady as I was drawn to the source of the commotion. I followed an endless stream of officers, gentlemen, seamen and curious laymen to the furthest end of the docks. I passed towering ships and sleek frigates and brigantines, as I had heard them called, until I caught sight of the cause of all this fuss.

It was a small ship, tubby with a blunt bow, and not at all like its powerful counterparts. I gathered from the animated conversations between men that this little ship, the category of 'bark', was something of a joke among the locals. The chatter among the onlookers was that of disbelief that the Royal Navy had commissioned this odd-looking ship for a great voyage. I wandered unnoticed to a spot close to three important-looking gentlemen and listened.

"By God, Reginald! Has the Royal Navy gone barking mad? This Lieutenant Cook, while I am familiar with his ability, he cannot be seriously considering taking this bumbling little ship to the Pacific! A larger, more comfortable vessel would be more to the task, don't you agree?" questioned the older gentleman.

"Yes, I must agree with you, Charles. Edmund Halley, in 1716, suggested that the distance from the Sun to the Earth could be calculated by timing the transit of the planet Venus across the face of the Sun. Transits of Venus are rare, and the 1761 transit observations had been disappointing. The next transit is to occur in 1769, not followed by another until the year of 1874, and steps must be taken to insure better measurements of the phenomenon. The tracking of the transit is apparently best reported from the Pacific. Tahiti, if I'm not misinformed. The progress to navigation by the stars, being far more accurate by this report, would be of enormous benefit to shipping, and here they are entrusting this monumental task to this bedraggled specimen," scoffed Reginald.

The third gentleman spoke up. "Yes, chaps, whilst I agree that she looks unlikely for the task, Lieutenant Cook's a good man with impeccable credentials, and I have it on good authority that he is quite confident of success. I have learned from a colleague at the Navy office, that this ship is a cat-built bark, originally a North Sea coal carrier named *The Earl of Pembroke*, built for the worst the sea could do to her. She is three hundred and sixty-eight tons in weight, ninety-seven feet long, and twenty-nine feet and three inches wide, with plenty of space for stores and provisions. The Royal Navy has spared no expense in having her refitted with carriage guns, new masts, spars and rigging. Her bottom planks have been sheathed with thin boards filled with large flat-headed nails to protect her from the wood-boring molluscs native to warmer waters. She should be under way by the end of next week and I am quite sure they know what they are doing," said the gentleman convincingly.

"Yes, I suppose you are right there, Robert. I hear that the eminent botanist Joseph Banks and his cronies are joining the voyage to collect plants and animals from the Pacific Islands. Important chaps, those! The Royal Society wouldn't risk their loss to the sea, if they were not confident of the outcome of this trip. Yes! Yes! Robert, you do have a point there," mused Charles.

Robert continued. "My colleague also hinted, although vaguely, that he had heard that Lieutenant Cook, under secret sealed orders, is to continue on after the transit has been recorded."

"Continue on to what?" demanded Reginald.

"New lands, my good fellows! Discoveries in the name of King George." Reginald lowered his voice and I had to strain my ears to hear. "Terra Australis Incognita!" he whispered.

"Now I have heard everything!" Reginald barked. "The Royal Navy and The Royal Society have gone utterly insane. Terra Australis Incognita is simply a myth! Sea-weary sailors' stories! Drunkards, most likely! They are all doomed, if you want my opinion."

"We will see," boasted Robert with a knowing smirk. "I'll wager you fifty guineas, chaps, that this tubby little vessel completes its journey, returning to England with unimaginable wealth for our good king!"

"You're a fool, Robert!" laughed Reginald. "I will take your wager, and dance through Piccadilly Square with your fifty guineas tied to my hat!"

"Gentlemen! Such behaviour!" scolded Charles. He leaned toward Robert, looking around so as not to be seen.

"I too will accept your pledge, for I am not convinced that this venture of Cook's isn't pure folly. But keep it quiet, chaps! It would cause a scandal if someone were to hear us," he whispered.

Someone did hear them. Me! I felt a rush of excitement through me. This journey could mean only one thing. My dream of the sea and the adventures it held! I dismissed the doubts held by Charles and Reginald. I had a sense that this Robert knew his business and that of this ship's intended voyage.

The three gentlemen marched off along the dock as if they had more important business, continuing their argument until I could see them no longer. I wandered toward the stern of this smart-looking little ship, in some kind of hypnotic daze. I looked up to see the word "Endeavour," proudly and boldly etched into her timber. Endeavour! The name itself was strong, courageous and eager and I knew there and then that somehow I would be on that ship when it sailed!

I wandered back in a dream to my lodgings behind the Seaman's Rest. The lads were there sleeping off their morning meal when I arrived.

"Badger! Lads! I'm off to sea!" I shouted.

"Bandit, you irritating beast, I was just dozing off. What the dickens are you talking about?" demanded Badger.

Slim and Rubbish-Bin-Bob looked up momentarily, but went back to sleep.

"I have found my destiny, Badger! A ship sails for the Pacific from this very dock within the week and I plan to be aboard it when she sails!" I announced.

"Settle down, lad, you are rambling. I am familiar with all of the ships' departures from these docks, and I know of only one leaving within the week, and it is rumoured to be a disaster in the making. The *Endeavour* is the questionable little tub, if my memory serves me," sneered Badger.

"That is the very one! The *Endeavour*! A proud name for a ship, don't you think?" I asked.

"Are you deranged, boy? There is not a soul amongst us that thinks that ship will return to England," he scoffed.

"Badger, I feel it in my bones, this is my opportunity. I have dreamed of this all my life and now my chance, the *Endeavour*, lies moored at the end of the docks. I will not be discouraged!" I said boldly.

"We will discuss this later," yawned Badger impatiently. "I need my sleep. Turkel will be at the Seaman's Rest this evening. He will talk some sense into you!" He turned his back to me and settled back to his napping. I could not sleep. I was much too restless. I wandered to the docks and watched the men for the rest of that day, coming and going from "my" *Endeavour*, loading provisions and equipment.

That night, after a hearty meal with my friends at the inn, we settled onto our ledge above the noisy crowd below and watched in silence. The crews from the ships had all gathered to talk of voyages to come. The men I had seen earlier loading my ship were discussing their preparations to sail. They looked strong and confident and ready for anything!

Badger could sense my interest in the scene before us.

"See here, boy..." he said. "Turkel will be along quite soon, and while I am sure you have the best intentions, cast this sea-going folly from your mind. He knows what he has seen and if you are as smart as you look, you will stay here with us."

Before I could answer, Turkel was behind me. "I wish to speak to Bandit alone!" demanded Turkel.

"Forgive me, dear boy, I did not see you there," bowed Badger, backing away. "Slim, Bob, come with me!" They begrudgingly left their comfortable ledge. Badger hurried them away, leaving us alone. Turkel and I watched silently for a while and then he spoke, quite differently than he had the evening before.

"Bandit, I have heard talk of a small ship, 'Endeavour' is her name. She leaves for Tahiti within the week. I know I cannot persuade you to stay. You have the sea in your veins; you are young and strong and have a look about you that befits adventure. I had that same look once myself, and for all I might have said to try to bring you to your senses, you, boy, will go to sea! Rumours that this ship is unworthy are plenty, and the risks are great, but I feel in my gut that this voyage will be full of promise and success. Take my advice and be aboard the *Endeavour* when she sails!" And with that he was gone as quickly as he had appeared.

Badger, Slim, and Rubbish-Bin-Bob returned.

"What was that all about, lad?" questioned Badger.

I was quite unable to speak and just sat staring into the crowd below.

"Turkel musta scared 'im stupid!" laughed Slim. "Look at 'im, can't even talk. That's fixed 'im, eh Bob?"

Bob shrugged and said nothing as usual.

"I fear you may be correct, Slim," said Badger with authority. "I think Turkel may have put an end to this boy's fancy for the sea!" Badger settled comfortably, feeling he had achieved his aim.

I continued my silence on the ledge, knowing I should not tell them of Turkel's advice, for it was in confidence that he spoke to me as one seagoing cat to another. I returned my attention to the men below me, who would be my future companions and comrades, and listened until all had left the inn.

CHAPTER 5

I awoke alone on the ledge at the inn the next morning. I jumped to the street, as hungry as I had been for some time. The lane was deserted, but for the scurry of mice in the rubbish. I knew where I would spend my day, so I hunted as my father had shown me and cornered a tasty morsel, which would fuel my activities at the docks, and keep me in good form.

The time passed quickly as I spent my days watching my crew load the *Endeavour* with all manner of things. I heard them speak of telescopes, astronomical clocks, journeyman's clocks, barometers, and thermometers. I had no idea what these contraptions were but they looked rather important, as the men took great care with them as they loaded them below. Then came the stores, which interested me more. Enough salted meat and ship's biscuit to last twelve months, eight thousand pounds of sauerkraut, one thousand pounds of dried soup. Then came large jars of wort of malt and robs of oranges and lemons. I had heard these were to prevent scurvy and so felt better about the health of my crew. By night I investigated the ship when few men were on board. The ship carried ten carriage guns, twelve barrels of gunpowder, with round shot and pellets for the muskets and pistols. She seemed well-armed for trouble.

I travelled the decks high and low, familiarising myself with my soon-to-be-adopted home. The lowest decks held the captain's stores, the ballast, the hold and the gunpowder. Above were small but comfortable cabins for the master, second lieutenant and clerk, then the sail locker and the carpenter's cabin and workshop. The deck above held cabins for the astronomer, naturalist and draftsman, captain and lieutenants, and the Great Cabin to the stern of the ship. Forward laid the forecastle, more commonly known as the fo'csle, and the sea chests. The upper deck carried the guns, longboat, pinnace and yawl. The foremast, mizzenmast, bowsprit and spare spars were strong as if hewn from one whole tree. The ship's wheel was made from the finest timber and turned and polished highly. It was smooth and regal and I liked to look at it gleaming under the moonlight at night when no one could see me.

The critics came and went each day, none having a good word for my ship or its voyage. I dismissed them with the contempt they deserved. After my explorations on board the *Endeavour* I returned to the Seaman's Rest late in the evenings to eat with my friends. Little did they know that I would be leaving them soon. I listened silently to my crew and watched their excitement build for their pending adventure. I learned much about the men from these evenings spent on the ledge.

I had not seen Turkel since his private words with me, but did not think it odd, as Badger explained that he came and went as he wished. The night before my departure I went to the Seaman's Rest quite late and found them all in conference.

"Here 'e is now, Badger!" Slim yowled.

"Where have you been, lad? We are about to toast the *Endeavour* on the eve of her departure. A sad moment in history if you ask me. Poor blighters are doomed!" said Badger with some sadness.

"Chaps!" I announced. "I, too, depart your company to join the *Endeavour* and those poor blighters you speak of. But Badger, it must be said in their defence, a fine crew they are!"

Slim laughed. "Ahh, e's lost 'is mind, Badger! Too much catnip e's had! If 'e goes on that ship e'll be histry!"

"Is this true, lad?" begged Badger. "Are you intending to sail with this *Endeavour*?"

"Yes, it is indeed true, Badger. I cannot stay here with you. As much as your friendship has meant to me, the sea beckons and I leave tomorrow," I declared.

"But dear boy, you cannot be serious! You have heard the stories!" Badger pleaded, for I think I had found a place in his heart.

Just then a dark figure appeared behind us.

"Leave him be, Badger," said Turkel sternly. "I have consulted with this lad, and he is leaving on the morrow at my recommendation. He must do what he must do." He turned to me. "I bid you good luck and fine weather, Bandit, and mind you stay below during storms!" he cautioned, tapping his wooden leg. He smiled at me; a smile that I gathered was quite rare, from the astonished expressions of my friends. He then rose and turned quickly, pouncing from the ledge. It was the last time I saw him.

I turned to my friends. "You have all been so kind to me and it is with a heavy heart that I bid you farewell."

"Well," said Badger with dignified surrender. "I propose a toast, not only to the *Endeavour* and her crew and noble enterprise, but to my good and deserving friend, Bandit, whom I have come to admire in so many ways. I shall miss you, my brave companion."

The others took their catnip with much gusto. I had come to respect this potent drink and its effects, and as I had an important morning to attend, I drank little. Our celebrations went long into the night along with the crew at the inn who were also anticipating an important day to follow. Food and ale still flowed amongst the men below, as we cats retired to our lodgings for what was left of the night.

I awoke a few hours later at dawn and bid the fellows a final salutation. I made my way to the Deptford Docks rather carefully, as many men and women milled around my ship to bid their beloveds farewell. The *Endeavour* was ready to make its way down the Thames to Plymouth for more provisions and final preparations before heading out to sea. I hurried toward the gangway, through the crowds of legs and skirts. I tried to find a way up the ramp to the ship without being seen, but it seemed impossible. Too many men were coming and going with last minute baggage and fond good byes. Men nodded to their sons and brothers respectfully. Mothers, sisters, and daughters hugged, cried, and waved. So much noise and movement, I began to panic. I ran from one end of the ship to the other along the dock, looking for an alternative to the gangway. Just as I started to feel that I would miss the *Endeavour*'s departure altogether, a hand grabbed the back of my neck.

"You'll do!" said a young man's voice. I started somewhat, as this was the last thing I was expecting. I knew not of this chap's intentions, and feared that I might be carted away from my destination. I had to get away, but his forceful grip shoved me swiftly into a large duffle bag with little room for the likes of me. I tried to escape but the cord at the top of the bag was pulled tight and I was thrown over this scoundrel's shoulder. I wriggled around inside the bag enough to peer through the small hole at the top, only to discover that I was indeed being taken on board the *Endeavour*. What luck!

"Stop squirming, blasted cat! Someone will see you!" whispered the voice hoarsely. Needless to say, I got the idea, and lay perfectly still amongst this fellow's possessions. Shortly after some bustling and fairly rough treatment, my duffle bag was dropped on a rather hard surface, making me a little cross to say the least. The cord was released and the hand plucked me from my hiding place.

"Now, cat, before the others arrive down here to pinch my bed, as I know they will, my name is Isaac Smith, and you are my cat," he announced. "Whatever you do, don't let anyone see you till we're well clear of land, or you'll be off the ship and I with you. Hide in my duffle and I'll sneak you food from the galley when I can." He looked around warily while busying himself unpacking his baggage but continued to speak to me.

"The captain's wife is my aunt and I'm on this voyage whether I like it or not. Between you and me, I'm scared stiff, and you're here to keep me company. I'm new to this game. The lads will give me hell if they know I'm related to the captain. Quick, they're coming. Back in the bag till I tell you it's safe!" One by one the others noisily joined us, jostling for positions in this tight space.

"Oy, boy! I see you've picked the best spot down 'ere," barked a large man. "Ya know there's gunna be ninety-four of us lookin' for a bed by the time we leave Plymouth. Don't like ya chances of keeping that spot!" The others all laughed, but Isaac spoke up rather boldly, I thought, for a young lad.

"If I'm smart enough to get down here first, I'm smart enough to keep my bed!" he said defiantly.

"Well, boys," said the large man, "can't argue with that, can we?" He ruffled the boy's hair roughly. "What's ya name, laddie?"

"Isaac. Isaac Smith. Sailor and apprenticed surveyor under the captain," he boasted.

"Well, Isaac Smith," said the large man, "ye looks to be a youngish lad. What be your age?"

"Sixteen last birthday," said Isaac rather boldly. "But I am here to work hard and I can hold my own if there be any trouble!" He cautioned, casting a wary eye upon the group.

"I fear, boys, that we've been warned!" laughed the large man, addressing his comrades, and with a more playful tone made the introductions. "Charles Clerke, master's mate at your service. This 'ere is Doctor William Perry, the surgeon's mate."

Doctor Perry unpacked quietly, not wanting to draw undue attention to himself.

Charles Clerke continued. "Some of the crew 'ere, Richard Hughes, George Nowell and Francis Haite. John Reading, bosun's mate. Henry Jeffs, ship's butcher. John Thompson, ship's cook."

My attention was drawn to John Thompson the cook, for the most obvious of reasons. I made a promise to myself that I should get to know this fellow, along with the butcher, Henry Jeffs. If I had the favour of these men, tasty titbits could be forthcoming.

"The others'll be along shortly, I expect," said Charles Clerke as he stowed his possessions.

They all shook hands with Isaac along with John Thompson the cook, who only had one hand but Isaac shook it regardless. I must say I wondered how the food would taste, prepared by a one-handed cook!

These were some of the chaps I had seen at the Seaman's Rest, and I felt that I knew them intimately already.

Charles Clerke took charge. "Captain's joinin' us at Downes on the way down the Thames. Mister Banks and the gentlemen are boardin' when we reach Plymouth, so we've plenty of work to do, boys. They're loadin' on all sorts of strange stuff so we'd better get up there!"

"What sort of strange stuff?" asked Isaac.

"Contraptions for catchin' bugs, fishin' gear and nets like I never seen, some device for seeing under the water, and bottles with spirits in for preservin' specimens, I think. Looks like the business of mad scientists, if you ask me," said Charles Clerke, laughing. "Come on, then." He gestured that they should all help.

Isaac let them all go ahead of him, then turned and spoke to his duffle bag where I was still hidden. "I'll be back soon, cat. Just stay put!" whispered Isaac.

I was suddenly alone, but needed a well-earned snooze. These adventures were already presenting themselves to me as hard work. I slept for quite some time even though the noise of the activities above me was ceaseless. I cared not; as my purpose was finally fulfilled and I was on board the *Endeavour*!

CHAPTER 6

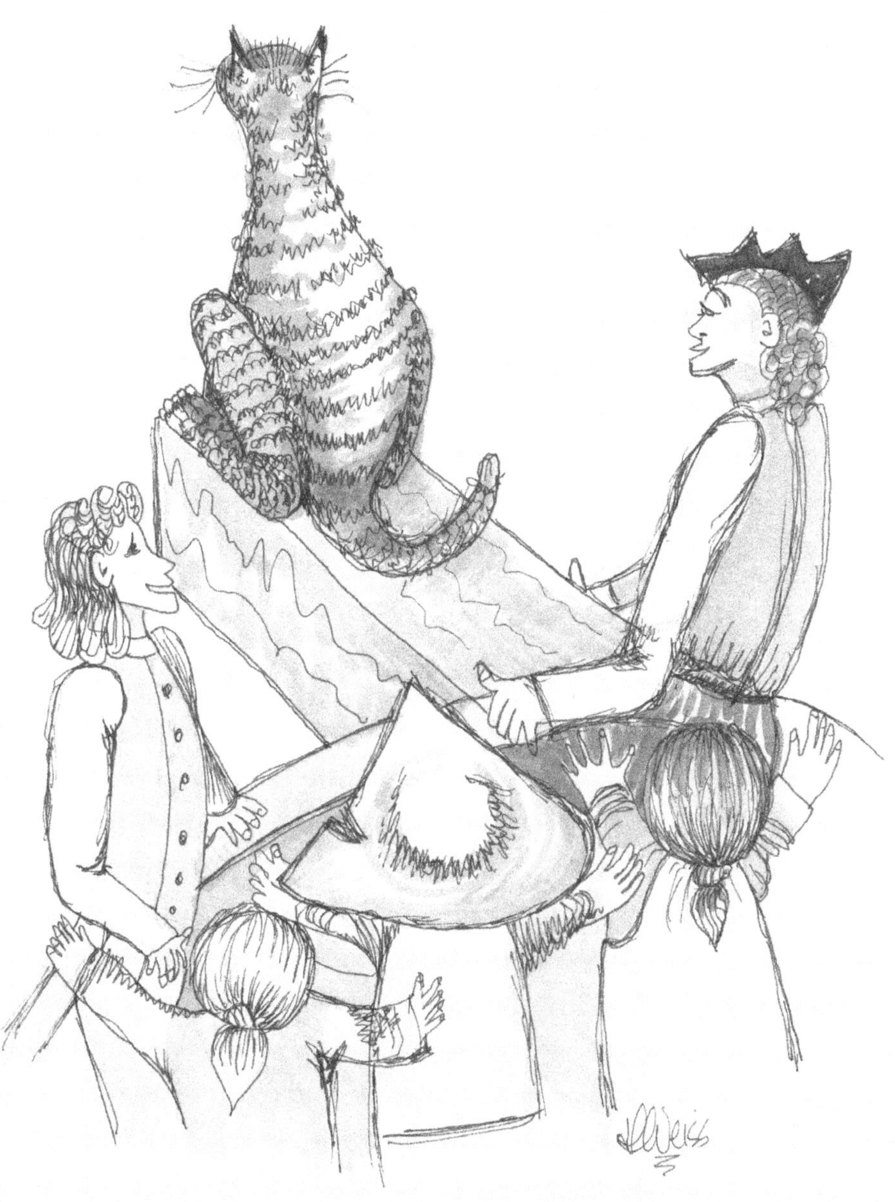

I woke to the gentle rocking of the ship. We had cast off from the Deptford Docks and were on our way to the sea! I scrambled from my duffle bag when I was sure no one was present and found a small window. I peered out at the Thames River's banks cruising slowly by and caught glimpses of people waving from the shores.

There was much activity on deck now, as the men familiarised themselves with the ship and each other. A pilot had taken charge of the ship through the channel avoiding the shallows, shoals and sandbanks. A difficult task by the looks of it, weaving in and out along the river for what seemed like miles.

We reached Downes where the captain was to join the ship. I rather deftly made my way to the longboat, and squeezed underneath its canvas covering. I could see the entire deck from this vantage point and none could see me. All of the crew were on deck for the captain's arrival. The officers who had boarded whilst I slept stood to attention as a tall uniformed man with a fine face and prominent nose ceremoniously boarded his ship.

"First Lieutenant James Cook, boarding the *Endeavour*!" barked an officer. "All stand to attention!" The whistle blew his arrival.

The men stared straight ahead as this most regal chap marched aboard. He spoke quietly but with authority.

"Men!" he called and began to pace the deck. "I am Lieutenant-in-Command James Cook. Whilst I am not a certified 'captain,' as acting captain for this voyage, you will show me the courtesy of addressing me so, as I am indeed in charge of this fine ship by order of His Majesty King George and the Royal Society. "We embark on an historic voyage to track the transit of the planet Venus across the sun, from a vantage point in the Pacific Ocean. This occurrence will be visible to us with the astronomer's instruments from our destination in Tahiti. With this new and more accurate information we shall have gathered, navigation will be made more accurate for the future of shipping, and land discoveries for our king. We sail to Plymouth this very day to complete our provisioning for this long and important journey. Those of you who have sailed with Wallis and Byron on the *Dolphin* will assist those unfamiliar with this route." The captain paused.

I knew of those names and that ship! The *Dolphin*! Turkel's ship! I would do my best to seek out those men, as unlike many others they had obviously returned from the sea!

The captain continued. "Those of you who have sailed with me in the past will know that as first lieutenant and captain of the *Endeavour*, I have the interests of the king to consider. Those of you who have sailed with me will also know that no man will be put at risk, nor will the safety of the ship be compromised. Those of you who have not sailed with me before have my personal pledge that this be my aim. We carry the usual sea-going rations, but fresh fruits and vegetables will be gathered at every opportunity as I refuse to lose a single man to scurvy. I wish for us all a safe and prosperous voyage in the name of God and King George!" He concluded.

This Captain Cook took the helm, dismissing the pilot who had guided the ship through the hazards of the Lower Thames. Orders were conveyed from the captain to the officers who in turn commanded the crew to weigh anchor and set sail for Plymouth.

It was the morning of the 8th day of August 1768 and I was at sea!

I stayed in my longboat, as I knew I must keep out of sight until after we were to leave Plymouth. Isaac found me there and thought it an excellent spot to hide until then. He brought me some hard tack from the stores. It was like a biscuit made only from flour and water, and to say the very least, completely unpalatable. I was hoping the fare would improve when I was released from my confines, whenever that may be!

As we made out to sea it was all I had hoped for. I stood forward of the longboat, or for'ard as the crew called it. The smell fresh to my nose with the wind from the northwest was rustling my whiskers through the small gap in the cover.

The water was quite different to the Thames. Blue! Dark and deep and capped with white foam tips as I had dreamt and I could hardly contain my excitement! Even though the coastline was not far from us, I felt the great expanse of this ocean and the promise of days to come.

During the five days sailing to reach the docks at Plymouth, I dared not venture too far from the longboat knowing I would be put ashore there if I were discovered. Isaac came to me often with titbits from the table, the "mess" as he called it. During this leg of the voyage the men bustled around the decks with much enthusiasm, cleaning, stowing, rearranging all manner of curiosities to fit in the confines of the ship.

Our captain walked the decks issuing orders to the men, who obeyed without question. I watched his fine face as he walked past my hiding place to and fro. His brave and resolute stature indicated to all that his authority should not be dismissed. Yet I sensed a kindness and decency about him as he graciously patrolled his ship. I thought this Captain Cook warranted an interview with me when the time was right.

At night the ship did not sleep, rolling gently through the waves, with the men on watch tending her every need. I gathered that those not on watch slept below, resting before returning to take up their positions on deck. This constant vigil gave me no chance to explore the ship and acquaint myself further with the men. I would have to wait.

Plymouth was an enormous port with even more ships than I had seen at the Deptford Docks. This port seemed to be the first and last stop for many voyagers. Ships were filled here with large stores for journeys to come, and then emptied and repaired when they returned. All manner of vessels were tied up awaiting their destiny, and we joined them in the queue for attention.

More curiosity surrounded us as we docked. The rumours had preceded our arrival and scores of onlookers came to view our odd little ship. As I listened to their gossip from my hideout, I began to have my doubts. Were we doomed, as they all suggested? Should I stay behind in Plymouth and wait for a better ship? And would I ever get out of this longboat?!

Whilst I mused miserably, the crew tended to the stowage of enormous quantities of food and livestock. One hundred and eighty-five pounds of Devonshire cheeses, fresh meat, and freshly baked bread for the first days; six hundred and four gallons of rum; one thousand six hundred gallons of brandy; and one thousand two hundred gallons of beer! The latter worried me a little, as it was a well-known fact that sailors liked their drink! Would their good sense prevail under the influence of liquor?

Then came extra sails and rigging, paint, gunpowder, ammunition, small arms and cutlasses.

At this point as I watched, I thought the ship would surely burst, when along came live chickens, pigs, sheep, oxen and a milking goat! Where were they intending to put it all? Would we sink from the sheer bulk of our cargo?

As I mused, a dozen or so soldiers came aboard. All carried their muskets and obviously meant business!

The captain ordered the men to attention on the deck for their introduction.

"We welcome aboard Sergeant Edgcumbe and his Marines for our safety upon this voyage," he began. "They will guard the arms, my cabin, the spirit room and other stores, and the scuttlebutt." The Sergeant Edgcumbe dispersed the lower-ranking privates to their posts below.

Some of these terms escaped me! "Arms" being the muskets and guns, the "Captain's cabin" and "stores" were evident, but the "scuttlebutt"? I took it from a particular private's position that the "scuttlebutt" was the drinking water cask on the deck. I had heard "madam" use the term at my home when other "madams" arrived for tea and gossip. I imagined that the drinking water cask would be where such gossip would originate on board and made note to self to loiter there at some future time for chitchat with the crew.

Isaac had appeared within touching of my longboat, with Captain Cook and John Satterley, the carpenter. They discussed employing some of the men to build a wooden platform over the stern of the ship to house the animals. Quite rightly, they decided that the roof of this platform would also make an excellent deck called a 'bridge' for the gentlemen to use. I became anxious. This ship had been stacked to bursting with men and stores, and now barraged with new decks and fittings. Would she be rendered unseaworthy and break up in the ocean? I worried shamefully during their discussion until John Thompson the cook excused himself to the captain.

"Captain Sir, my 'umble apologies for the interruption, but with all these 'ere fresh foods comin' on board we're goin' to need ourselves a cat. Mice'll be runnin' the ship if we don't!" warned Thompson.

"Yes, yes, quite right, Thompson," agreed the captain, rubbing his chin. "We cannot have the ship overrun with vermin! Isaac, have we the means to procure a cat for the voyage?"

Isaac shuffled his feet and looked at the ground in a way that portrayed his guilt. "Well, Sir," he muttered quietly. "It's like this, er…"

A more timely invitation I had never heard! All my concerns disappeared as I sprang from my longboat, frightening the life out of John Thompson and positioning myself at the feet of Isaac.

"Lord love a duck! Where'd 'e come from!" cried the startled cook.

I curled my body around Isaac's legs and looked confidently at the captain. He looked down at me and a faint smile played on his face.

Isaac thought quickly and spoke with much courage. "I had already thought of it, Sir, and found a moment earlier to go ashore and fetch this animal just for the task you mention!"

John Thompson spoke up. "Not too shabby, lad! Fast as anythin' I've seen. Scared the livin' daylights outta' me. Should make a good mouser, Captain!"

The captain looked at Isaac knowingly. "Well, Isaac, I see that you have put the needs of the ship ahead of your own. This cat will serve the purpose well. He will be in your charge. Take him below and let him lose among the stores in the hold. You will report to me of his progress."

"Yes, Sir, Captain, Sir!" muttered Isaac, enthusiastically scooping me up and making off as fast as he could.

"That was a close one, cat!" Isaac whispered as we went below. "How'd you know to jump out of that longboat at just the right time? Could have got me into big trouble with the captain, but now he thinks I got you from Plymouth as a mouser! Good thinking, cat!"

We continued on below toward the stores, which were the lowest deck in the ship, holding all manner of things. The men took little interest as we passed, knowing what my assignment would be.

I was one of the crew! A mouser! My earlier despair had gone and with it came a sense of purpose and an admiration for Isaac, the captain, and this worthy ship. Isaac scratched my neck and let me down in the hold.

"Now, do your work and make me proud. If you catch something, I'll be in good with the captain," instructed Isaac as he turned and left for other duties.

I must say I felt rather proud to be even the lowliest member of the crew. I now had the freedom to explore the ship under the guise of my new profession. No man would question my existence on the *Endeavour*, as I had work to do! I set about the hold determining the most obvious places for mice to be found. The gunpowder and ballast room looked unlikely places to find mice, but the fish and meat rooms, bread room, ship's biscuit and grain stores seemed highly likely to hold my quarry. As these stores had only recently been loaded, I found nothing of interest and deemed it wise to acquaint myself with the rest of the ship.

I found my way to the deck above. This deck had been added during the *Endeavour's* refit to house the kitchen and cook John Thompson and the "mess" where the crew dined at swinging tables and hung their hammocks to sleep when not on watch. Forward of the mess, were the sail room, the boatswain's or bosun's cabin and bosun's storeroom. Aft of the mess, I found Second Lieutenant Zachary Hicks, the surgeon William Monkhouse, and the gunner Stephen Forwood, all preparing their cabins. I did not stay long with each man, except to make my introductions and receive a scratch under the chin, for I heard a commotion on the deck above and thought it prudent to investigate.

On my way to the companionway, I heard from the men I passed that Mister Joseph Banks and his party had arrived and were boarding. This would account for the ruckus, as I had heard that Mister Banks was to be accompanied by four servants, along with his Secretary Herman Spöring, the naturalist Daniel Solander, and two artists named Sydney Parkinson and Alexander Buchan, and Charles Green the astronomer from the Royal Society.

Their presence alone would make a disturbance, but the loading of their equipment was a trial of the highest degree. The crew knew nothing of the items they were carrying aboard and Mister Banks was rather animated in his concern for his instruments, commanding Mister Spöring to look after them. I heard much yelling and decided to stay out of the way to observe.

I scarpered up the ladder to the deck and the source of all the bother, positioning myself in the rigging high above the deck to study the scene in progress below. In quick succession an array of implements filed on board. Contraptions for catching and preserving insects, all kinds of nets, trawls, hooks and drags for fishing, and a peculiar new sea telescope for observing the depths of the water below. Microscopes, paper for drying plants, and salts to pack their seeds. Bottles for preserving new species in spirits, tin trunks for storage, wooden cases, boxes, and hundreds of other items including beads and mirrors for trading with natives. This Mister Joseph Banks was rather a theatrical gentleman and patted his reddened brow with a silk kerchief while waving his arms in frustration as the crew awkwardly carried his precious possessions.

He looked to the captain for reassurance. "James, old man, where the devil did you get this crew!" he shouted. "My equipment will surely be ruined if they are not more careful!" He screeched at Mister Spöring, a Swedish chap of a middling age, employed by Mister Banks to attend his instruments and, it seemed, his every command.

"They are efficient men, Mister Banks, if left to their work without interruption. I shall oversee this task, you are welcome to retire to your cabin and make your preparations for the voyage," said the captain wisely.

"Yes, yes, quite right, James, I think I shall take leave of this chore. I will leave our equipment in Mister Spöring's capable hands for he is not only my personal secretary, but as a trained watchmaker he will ensure that our instruments are stored in good order." Mister Spöring marched forward, keen to flutter protectively between each item and issue orders to the crew to guarantee their safekeeping.

"George!" Mister Banks beckoned to his black servant, George Dorlton. "Bring my books down to my cabin, there's a good man. Oh, and don't forget the dogs!"

The fur on my neck stood to attention. Dogs? What dogs? I cast my eye toward the dock and there were two excited beasts of the greyhound variety tethered by a larger black servant by the name of Thomas Richmond. Surely, the captain would not allow dogs on this fine ship! These wretched animals could make my voyage a living hell if the upper hand of yours truly was not taken immediately upon our meeting! I vowed that if I ever came down from the rigging, swift action must follow with these two, if I were to carry out my duties for my captain and crew.

I watched with loathing as the two mongrels yelped and strained at their leashes while Tom the servant struggled to keep them controlled.

Finally, they were aboard and taken below to Mister Banks's cabin. I settled somewhat once these two villains were out of my sight, but my contempt for these two curs as the natural enemy of the cat laid heavily on my mind.

I dismissed the interruption for the time being and busied myself with a closer look at the spars, yards, mizzenmast, mainmast, foremast, and finally to the bow. I found a comfortable spot next to the bowsprit perched on the end of a rather solid wooden protrusion that would allow me good views of the waters below and of our course ahead when at sea.

"Look, lads!" bawled a voice. "There's a cat on the 'cathead!'" It was young Will Howson, the captain's servant, but I couldn't for the life of me understand what he meant. Cathead? The crew laughed and slapped each other on the backs, as if my presence there was a good thing. The captain came forward to survey the disruption.

"What is the meaning of this commotion, men?" he ordered. "We have little time for flippancy with our departure so near!" chided the captain.

"Sorry, Sir, but there's a cat on the cathead, Sir, and your good self knows what that means!" said Will Howson insistently.

The captain softened his tone the moment he saw me perched there on what I now know to be called the "cathead" - a prominent beam forward of the ship for drawing up the anchor, clear of the ship's sides. This place is also affectionately used by the crew for the placement of good luck charms during a voyage. The captain smiled as if blessed, and an excitement filled his voice.

"Ah yes, men, we are bound for good fortune and fair weather! Our good and deserving cat…" He paused. "Does this mouser have a name, Isaac?" asked the captain.

Isaac hurried forth from the crowd. "No, Sir!" he responded.

"I hereby name this crewman, 'Fairweather,' as he bodes us the very conditions we seek! Fairweather!" shouted the captain.

"Fairweather!" shouted the crew, throwing up their hats and dancing little jigs.

A prouder moment I had never chanced upon. Of all the names I had been given in my quest for the sea, Fairweather was far and above the most splendid of all! I held my head high and felt the glory of my new name as the crew lined up to pat me one at a time for luck. I had no need for introductions from this time onward. The entire ship's company knew exactly who I was and treated me with the greatest kindness and respect. I promised them all, in my own way, that I would live highly to their expectations.

The ship was taking some time to ready. While the men performed their tasks with good will, I thought it prudent to busy myself with my duties. Mister Banks's servant Tom walked those wretched dogs each day, so during their absences I had the ship to myself.

I went below, and one by one inspected the stores for the presence of vermin. Surely enough, with the hold filled with fresh food, I detected a great deal of activity in the grain room, just past John Gathrey's cabin below. Mice! My father's lessons came to me at once as I lay in wait for the offending beasts.

It was not a long wait, for out of the corner came a likely catch. I pounced and caught the blighter with one swoop. My victim lay lifeless on the floor as I set him down. Not a moment went by before I heard another scurry within my range. Leaving my dead victims together, I attacked yet again. More scurrying! One by one they fell to my tactics.

Within no time I had captured six of the best and laid them all together. What would I do with them? I could not leave them here. I knew that they would not all fit in my mouth at once. With some effort I managed to pick up all six by the tails, their bodies swinging from my mouth, and made my way to the decks above. The men stood astounded as I passed them on my way to find my Isaac.

"Well, I'll be blowed!" said the cook John Thompson to his assistant Thomas Matthews as I made my way past the galley. "This 'ere cat's a wizard! Six 'e's got in 'is mouth!" Tom Matthews rarely spoke, but nodded his approval where mice were concerned.

The men looked up from their tasks, clearly amazed by my performance. Isaac came forward and picked me up. I was not about to let go of these mice.

"Well, I'll just have to take you to the captain with this mouthful, seeing as you won't let 'em go!" said Isaac, as we walked onward.

"'Ere, Fairweather!" said John Thompson waving a knife with his one good hand. "Mind you return after your visit with the Cap'n, and I'll 'ave a tasty reward for ya'!"

"Well done, cat!" whispered Isaac, as he knocked on the Great Cabin door.

"Come in!" came the captain's voice from within. Private Samuel Gibson as guard allowed us entry.

Isaac entered with me and spoke excitedly. "Captain, Sir, forgive my interrupting you, but you must see this!" And with that, Isaac placed me on the chart table in front of the captain complete with my mouthful of mice. I dropped them on the chart of the Atlantic Ocean, and the captain and Isaac began to laugh. I must say I was a little put out by their mirth, and held myself up with contempt for their humour. After all, I was doing my job!

"Now then, Fairweather," said the captain, "do not be offended. I am impressed with your offering, but the Atlantic Ocean could well do without six dead mice in its waters!"

I relaxed a little, seeing the funny side, as the captain stroked my fur.

"A fine mouser, Isaac! I commend you on your choice. See to it that Fairweather is suitably rewarded!" said the captain, still smiling.

"Thank you, Sir, I will, Sir!" Isaac said proudly.

We dismissed ourselves, after Isaac had removed my mice from the Atlantic Ocean chart and flung them out the window to the waters below.

Outside the door, Isaac spoke softly. "Keep that up and we'll get extra rations, cat! Rather proud of myself, knowing you to be a good mouser."

I failed to see how Isaac could have known this, but dismissed his bragging, as I was happy to be on board and had him to thank for it. I graced the galley for my reward; fine saucer of cream. I enjoyed it knowing it would be the last time I would see cream at sea.

With the gentlemen and crew finally ready, and the *Endeavour* fully stocked and stowed, we untied from Plymouth's dock on the 26th day of August 1768, with little ceremony and only a small crowd of well-wishers to be seen. An unfit beginning, I thought, for such an important voyage as this.

Captain Cook sounded his orders to bear west-north-west, signals of which I still do not understand except to say that navigators knew their trade and I knew mine. The crew sprung into action and we were away. Anchors were weighed, ropes untied, and sails hoisted. All were in fine spirits as we bade farewell to mother England.

As we sailed steadily and further from land, I made my way to the stern of the ship where I sat for the longest time. I remembered my mother and father and my home far away, but with no longing, for my dream was before me! I merely watched as Plymouth became smaller and smaller. Her voice became but a whisper until I could hear only the sea and my ship, the *Endeavour*.

CHAPTER 7

The first four days at sea had made me wish for the calmer surroundings of the Deptford and Plymouth docks. The high seas of the Atlantic Ocean rolled the ship like a toy boat in a young lad's bath. I observed from the stumbling of the crew, that having four legs as opposed to the humanly two was a distinct advantage!

Misters Banks, Spöring, and Doctor Solander busied themselves taking notes on the many and varied bird species hovering above us. Mister Spöring always did most of the handwriting as Mister Banks dictated his findings hurriedly; this practise not giving Mister Spöring time to say very much and causing him to write furiously to keep up.

I hoped the birds in question would come within my range, as a bird would make a challenging catch, a tasty morsel, and a pleasant change from the mousing below.

"Porpoises, Mister Banks!" called Doctor Solander. Had I misheard him? "Poor pusses?" I was not suffering any malady to warrant such sympathy! Certainly not from the "Gents," as the crew had taken to naming them collectively. Their disinterest in my good self was apparent at most times! And the plural "pusses?" There was certainly only one of me aboard! Were they suffering from a madness so early in our voyage? Apparently, they alluded to something swimming alongside the ship so I thought it wise to investigate.

Sidling up beside the gentlemen as they leant over the side, I looked down and could hardly believe my eyes! "Porpoises," it seemed were not a collection of suffering felines! These were the biggest fish I had ever seen! By far, bigger than the menu at the Deptford Dock Fishmonger's! Diving and jumping high into the air, these huge bottle-nosed fish kept up with the ship as if it were some type of game to them. I looked longingly at Doctor Solander, licking my lips.

"I can tell from his expression, Mister Banks, that this feline would like to have his hungry way with one of these porpoises," quipped the doctor.

"Damn the cat, Solander! I am increasingly ill and cannot possibly continue my observations here! I fear this wretched ship sails like a tub and we shall surely die of the sea sickness if the damn thing doesn't sink first!" complained Mister Banks. "I simply must retire to my cabin and bathe my temples with cologne until I feel human!" And with that, he staggered away clutching his brow.

His absence left me momentarily alone with Doctor Solander.

"An expert in his field, that Mister Banks, and a fine fellow," said Doctor Solander addressing me with a wry smile. "But only a fine weather sailor I'm afraid, and not of good humour this day." I nodded in silent agreement, dismissing Mister Banks's damnation of me, and continued watching as Mister Parkinson joined us with a casting net he had been dragging alongside the ship for some time.

He removed the contents of the net, took out his drawing implements and tried to sketch the creature found within. Some kind of sea insect, the botanists had decided. By my observations, poor Mister Parkinson was having much trouble conducting this business with the rolling and pitching of the ship. I have to say the creature looked quite unpalatable, so I left them to their task and made my way to the rigging to oversee the crew and their business.

By the fifth day of rough weather, the sickness seemed to have left Mister Banks and by all reports he was feeling much better. Alas, not for long. The crew spoke of the bird life overhead, which apparently foretold the weather ahead and the condition of the seas, by way of the differing species hovering above the ship from time to time.

"Mother Carey's Chickens!" they cried. I thought about the chickens kept by the cook aft of the ship. I was certain that the birds in question were none of the sort I had seen there. While observing the examinations of these suspect "chickens" by the botanists, their correct name became known to me. "Storm petrels" it seemed. I heard Isaac speak of them as an omen sent by the Virgin Mary to warn of foul weather ahead. This disturbed the crew, and me not a little, as in my inexperience I was of the opinion that we had already experienced enough foul weather for the last five days.

Quite suddenly, a howling gale set in upon us as we reached the Bay of Biscay between France and Spain. The captain ordered the crew to close-reef the topsails and man every station for heavy weather. Through the low cloud and spume from the rough seas, a huge ship loomed quite suddenly close by.

Captain Cook and the gentlemen distinguished her as the man o'war, HMS *Guadeloupe* and by way of sailing close together, they spoke of the bad weather.

Predictably to me by now, Mister Banks retired dramatically to his cabin, again with the seasickness. Mister Spöring fussed about him as they left us.

Our good captain was quite indifferent to these sea-going turns of Mister Banks or any of the other gentlemen, to his credit. I, too, thought them quite weak in a humanly fashion. As a good captain should be, he was far more preoccupied with the ferocity of the gales and the state of his ship, which in turn would provide for the health of all of us.

As the foul winds and high seas continued, I took my own precautions and hid in my familiar covered longboat. Not that I was afraid, of course, but as the crew scurried in all directions as ordered by the captain, I deemed it wise to be out of their way. A crack was heard high in the rigging as I watched from my safe vantage point.

John Gathrey, the bosun, who was responsible for the rigging and sails suddenly shouted, "Captain! The wind's broken the main topmast puttock plates."

I thought this not a good sign.

"Never mind that, Mister Gathrey!" shouted the captain above the roaring of the wind, "Secure the bosun's boat on the deck! It is looking as if she'll go over the side!"

"Aye, Captain!" called Mister Gathrey, but his voice was lost in the ferocious wind. Mister Gathrey's silver whistle could be heard tooting orders to them over the sound of the gale and the sea. Only the seamen knew what the short, sharp or long whistles meant.

Try as he did to carry out his orders, Mister Gathrey and the bosun's mate John Reading, could not save the little boat. With one lunging roll of the sea, the bosun's boat left its safe position and fell to the depths below, along with three or four dozen of the chickens caged nearby.

The captain ran toward the bosun. I thought Mister Gathrey was in for it, having been given the order to save the little boat, but I noticed in the captain's face the understanding graciousness of his demeanour. As far as Mister Gathrey and John Reading were concerned, all was forgiven there and then.

"The wind and sea are unpredictable beasts," admitted the captain. "The consequences are small compared to the safety of the ship and your good selves."

"Aye, Captain!" said Mister Gathrey as softly as the screaming of the wind would allow, the admiration clear upon his face. I, too, felt great regard for the captain, as the loss must have been great; chickens being not a creature easily replaced at sea, nor the bosun's boat for that matter.

To his credit and in respect for the captain's understanding, Mister Gathrey kept vigil all that night as the winds continued to blow and the *Endeavour* continued to pitch and roll. Mister Gathrey's whistle was heard giving orders all night.

By the next morning, the weather had ceased its punishing force and at dawn on the second day of September, the captain, who had had little sleep through the night, ordered the crew to lose two reefs from the topsails, speeding our progress in the calmer conditions.

By midday, the northernmost point of Spain, by name of Cape Ortegal, was within sight. The *Endeavour* had made a distance of three hundred and ninety nautical miles in ten days. I took this to be a significant expanse of sea to traverse as the crew discussed our progress with great pride.

CHAPTER 8

As we sailed on, Mister Banks and his associates came more often to the upper decks as the weather continued calmer. Misters Parkinson and Buchan busied themselves sketching and examining the various specimens brought up in the nets from the sea below. Now that they had recovered from the seasickness, I thought them a more likeable lot. I inspected their works from time to time when not attending to my vigil for rodents in the stores. They did not seem to mind, and my stomach benefitted occasionally from the discarded specimens. Some were palatable and I noted them. Others were horrid and I grimaced at the offering.

One calm evening, with the ship and all hands at a restive pace and the stars shining as I had never witnessed, the captain retired to the Great Cabin to attend to his log, as I had seen him do many times. I thought it wise at this moment to familiarise myself with this fine man and I followed him there for the first time.

As we approached the door, I edged myself through, unnoticed by Private Clement Webb who was relieving Private Gibson on this evening. I watched as Captain Cook prepared for the task at hand and as he settled into his chair, I pounced ever so carefully to his table so as not to disturb him.

"Well, Fairweather, how did you get in here?" he asked, looking surprised.

I held a paw out in greeting to him, to which he placed his hand around my own and shook it, as a gentleman would do.

"I know not what manner of cat you are, but I can tell from this gentlemanly custom of yours that you may come from a higher breeding than I first thought! What the devil are you doing on this ship, my fine friend?" The captain looked curiously at me.

I held myself up to my full height and matched his gaze squarely and true.

"Ah, I see!" said he. "From that look in your eye, you are here for adventure! I have seen that look many a time in men, but rarely in a cat!"

I thought it wise to relax him a little and began the purring my mother had instructed of me when holding court with "Madam" back at my home. The captain scratched behind my ear thoughtfully as he prepared to enter into his diary, the ship's position, the weather and the day's events. I watched over his shoulder.

To be honest I knew not what he was writing, but as he wrote he spoke it aloud as if to explain it to me. We had become instant friends, and from that time forward I gathered with him each night to assist him with his log. Somehow and secretly, I knew that reading his written words out loud to me made him feel as if each day had truly occurred, and was not just his dreaming during a contented nap.

On the 12th day of September 1768, our first port of call was in clear view. A Portuguese island named Madeira, in the Atlantic Ocean off the northwest coast of Africa.

The captain ordered the crew to swing the ship south past Porto de Sao Lourenco. The port of Funchal was tucked away into the southern coast of the island among terraced vineyards. The following day we approached our anchorage.

I gathered from my position at the cathead that this port was a busy place, and wondered how we would fit in amongst the many and varied ships docked there. Our neighbours were the HMS *Rose* and several merchant ships. By the captain's orders we found our position amongst them and settled for the night.

That night, I looked forward to a restful sleep in the calmer waters of the harbour after a hearty meal with the accomplished cook John Thompson and his fine assistant Tom Matthews. My every doubt about his ability to prepare a meal with only his left arm was dispelled in the budding of our voyage. We had plentiful stores at this early stage and as I had kept those stores clean of rodents for him, his thankfulness always extended me the finest meal at night. We often dined together right there in his galley, the odd morsel falling purposefully my way as he prepared the meals. If by chance he was not so clumsy as to drop food for me, he would otherwise not forget me, and a selection from the menu was always forthcoming upon his finalisation of the fare.

This night I was particularly impressed with his offerings and we spent some time together savouring our meals after the men had eaten. Quite abruptly, our mutual enjoyment was unceremoniously interrupted by a disturbance above. We both left our meal and hurried toward the source of the commotion.

The captain and quartermaster, Alex Weir, had beaten us to the mark.

"Damned carelessness, Mister Weir!" snapped the captain sternly. "Whoever had fastened this stream anchor in such a neglectful fashion should be flogged!"

John Thompson had motioned to me that the anchor in question had fallen from its tethered position into the harbour below. I understood completely that the captain would be angered by this mishap.

"I agree, Captain," admitted Mister Weir, embarrassed by the inefficiency of his crew. "But be that as it may, we need that anchor so I shall gather a party and a boat and set to raising it. Can't be in more than twenty-two fathoms of water. We'll find it, Sir."

With that he promptly rounded up a company of men and they were away in a small boat to search for the sunken stream anchor.

"Don't worry y'self, Fairweather, all will be well," said John Thompson as we looked after them. "Mister Weir, though a Scotsman and mind; I don't personally hold it against him, is a mighty good quartermaster."

We watched as they rowed until they had positioned themselves below the ship where the anchor had fallen. The rope was still attached to the ship and Mister Weir called out.

"Found it, Captain! We'll have it up in no time!" The captain seemed pleased, watching intently.

A buoy rope was attached to the anchor rope from the ship to aid their efforts in the darkness. As they raised it slowly, Mister Weir looped the loose rope over his shoulder. Curiously, as we watched, the boat became unsteady. Something was wrong! The anchor rope slipped from a seaman's hand and the lot went over the side along with Mister Weir hopelessly entangled in the loose buoy rope. The captain called to them but they were caught up in the tension of their predicament.

Able seaman James Nicholson yelled desperately to us from the boat.

"Mister Weir's gone over the side, Captain! He's tangled and he's going to the bottom with the anchor! We're trying to bring him up, Sir!"

"Make haste, my good man!" shouted the captain. "He cannot stay down there long."

"It's stuck, Sir! Must be caught on the bottom!" cried Nicholson in panic.

The captain held his gaze on the drama unfolding before us. As the seconds became minutes none of us moved, or breathed it seemed.

The captain consulted his pocket watch and spoke very quietly. "I fear he is lost, men."

We watched as the able-bodied men in the tiny boat freed the anchor and hauled the buoy rope up and up. First came the lifeless body of Alex Weir tangled in the rope, then came the stream anchor. We had lost concern for the latter, as word came back.

"Mister Weir is dead, Sir!" came the hopeless cry. "Drowned!"

Those words seemed to echo through the quiet in the harbour and ring in our ears for the longest time.

The gentlemen, the captain, and the crew who had gathered behind us removed their hats and placed them upon their hearts. We bowed our heads and took a silence.

The captain was the first to speak as the boat returned.

"Bring him aboard, men," he ordered sadly.

With their return to the deck, we gathered to comfort the guilt-ridden Nicholson who feared it was all his fault.

"Accidents are inevitable, Mister Nicholson. You did your best," said the captain, knowing him to be tormented by the tragedy.

"Thank you, Captain Sir, but I wish I could have done more," pleaded Nicholson, weeping visibly from his inner torture.

"No more could be done under the circumstances, lad. We all here gathered witnessed your efforts," comforted the captain. He turned to the others from the little boat.

"Good work, men." One by one they slapped Nicholson consolingly on the back without a word.

The captain turned to the rest of us and indicated that we should join him in benediction.

"A fine quartermaster and family man, Mister Alexander Weir. Our thoughts and prayers go to his widow and children, and with the grace of the Almighty, we wish him speed to his final repose. God rest his soul."

And with that we dispersed solemnly, James Nicholson to wrestle his inner demons, and the rest of us to thinking selfishly of our own mortality and the hunger of the sea.

A solemn air surrounded the ship all the next day. No one spoke of the death of Mister Weir. The men and I attended to our duties, passing each other and nodding our unspoken grief. Mister Nicholson quietly carried on his duties amidst his torment.

CHAPTER 9

I had disposed of a considerable number of vermin in the stores early in the day, and was thanked by John Gathrey, the bosun, last of whom to have his own cabin before the hold.

I sallied forth the gangway and settled on the cathead for a nap in the sunshine. I was just dozing when a small boat approached the ship.

The Portuguese authorities had sent a team of medical men to inspect our crew before they would allow them to go ashore. I thought this odd as none of them looked unwell, but I discovered during their examinations that this practise was essential to the health of the islanders, as they would not allow crewmen ashore if they were diseased.

I did not escape inspection, nor did the other animals on board. I was poked and prodded in all manner of places, none of which I appreciated in the least. After all, one does not wish to be probed about the ears and eyes, let alone the nether regions. The little dignity I still possessed after my examination was the reward of having scratched and drew the blood of the offending doctor as his purpose approached my rear flank. He appeared to have little interest in me after that. All were given a clean bill of health and the excitement seemed to build as the anticipation of an intermission on shore became apparent.

Isaac had made quite a few friends among the youngsters. These lads were usually trusted to a ship as a penance for petty crimes, or were sent to sea by way of a charitable gift from the home for poor boys.

My Isaac, as I had come to know him, was ranked as Able Seaman, apprenticed to the captain to learn the fine art of surveying. Isaac's companions were Will Howson and John Charlton, the captain's personal servants, William Harvey, the Second Lieutenant Zachary Hicks's servant, and Isaac Manley, the youngest of the group, who was Master Robert Molyneux's attendant.

Isaac Manley was a well-mannered but impressionable young boy of the age of twelve, and from my scrutiny, from a good home. My Isaac of the "Smith" variety and the other older lads were of similar ages, and at fifteen to seventeen years were in for much mischief when not attending to their duties, or should I say, as much mischief as would allow without resulting in punishment.

The captain had ordered the men who were cleared by the doctors of any illness, and wishing to take leave of the ship, to line up at the gangway on the port side for the short boat trip ashore. Isaac and his chums took their places eagerly at the head of the queue, as young lads are inclined to do, and I alongside them, having decided that a nap could be taken at any time, but a trip to Funchal might be an entertaining diversion. After all, adventure was my purpose!

Mister Banks and his cronies bustled past us, rushing the servants and those dogs along with them. I hid behind Isaac's legs and fortunately for me, the dogs did not catch my scent. I had up until now, neglected to sort out those hounds, but was not in any hurry to do so now. My chance would come.

Mister Banks and his party made their way successfully to the front of the rank.

"Come quickly, gentlemen, we have specimens to collect and Mister Cheap awaits our arrival," chirped Mister Banks.

"Blasted gents!" whispered Isaac to his friends. "Always at the front of the line."

"Who the devil is Mister Cheap?" asked William Harvey.

"He's the British Consul of Madeira," explained John Charlton. "I overheard Mister Banks making arrangements to stay in Mister Cheap's house. Banks and the other gents'll be there for our visit, collecting plants and insects and specimens and what-not, lucky blighters!"

Will and John, as the captain's personal servants, seemed to know the most intimate details of the captain's plans and made overly sure that they knew everyone else's business as well. I felt sure that these boys would be a valuable source of knowledge when needed, as did my Isaac.

Young Isaac Manley piped in. "Funny name, though. Where do you suppose he got a name like that?"

Will was only too happy to elaborate, "He's also the local trade merchant. With a name like that you've got to imagine he's able to get just about anythin' you want. Just the luck o' those gents to be gettin' in good with Mister Cheap."

Collectively the lads sighed, imagining the misbehaviour they could arrange with Mister Cheap as their guide.

"Alas, chaps," continued Will, "with the contacts Mister Cheap's got, he'll have 'is ear to the ground. He'll know who we are, where we're from and our mothers' maiden names before we even set foot on land. No doubt in my mind that if he catches us at anythin' devilish, he'll report us to the captain and we'll be in for it b'fore we even get back on the ship!"

The boys agreed that they would have to be careful if they were to misbehave.

Mister Banks's party filled the longboat to the brim, and the oarsmen set themselves to shore. We watched as they disembarked, to be greeted by some official-looking fellows. Hats were tipped, bows were made and hands shaken. Those horrid dogs ran at full stretch up and down the beach with Mister Banks's servants, Tom and George, straining every muscle to control the beasts. Half-witted creatures! Not an intellect between the two of them! If they had any sense they'd conserve their strength for the evenings ahead exploring the port of Funchal.

The longboat returned and it was our turn to go ashore. Captain Cook was standing attentively at the gangway, surveying the group due to board next. He scratched at his chin. On his face the question: Should he or should he not allow our band of rascals the run of Funchal?

"I suppose that you boys intend mischief upon this town?" quizzed the captain with a stern aspect. "Do you intend to besmirch the reputation of the *Endeavour*? Or your good captain for that matter?"

Isaac stood tall and came forward. "No, Captain, Sir. We dare not set a foot out of place, for fear of the consequences to our ship and your kind self."

"And the repercussions you will personally face?" enquired the captain.

"Those too, Sir, definitely, Sir!" said my Isaac with sound resolve.

"Very well, then, you may proceed. But as God is my witness, should there be any misconduct on your behalf, you shall suffer a flogging from Lieutenant Gore's cane. In fact, should the *Endeavour*'s good name be slandered upon these shores I shall deliver the punishment myself," warned the captain.

The lads stood to attention, saluted their captain and in chorus an "Aye, Aye, Sir!" was delivered.

As they turned in rank toward the gangway, I observed a slight wistfulness on the captain's face. I detected a roguery remembered and long since past. I suspect that he secretly wished them a lively visit to shore and perhaps even longed for the days when he could do so himself.

Just as I was about to board the longboat with my boys, John Thompson came running forward, a kitchen cleaver in his left and only hand.

"'Scuse me, Cap'n. I beg your apology, but where's that cat think he's goin'? I need 'im on board or we'll be overrun with pests by mornin'. I 'eard this place's famous for the size of its vermin!"

The captain looked down at me, then at John Thompson. I gathered from his expression that he could not decide whose needs were the greatest. I must have won, as he motioned me to carry on with the boys. John Thompson looked questioningly at the captain.

"Our good and deserving Fairweather may go ashore with the youngsters," said the captain playfully. "I feel certain that he will double his duties when back on the ship, to compensate for his absence on this day."

John Thompson skulked away mumbling to himself.

The captain continued. "Isaac, I charge you with this cat's return to the ship. Now be off with you before I change my mind." He turned on his heel and walked back toward the next group awaiting the trip to town.

I found myself tucked under Isaac's arm as we boarded the longboat and rowed ashore. Isaac put me down on the soft sand.

"Now cat, if you're not back in this spot by sundown this day, I'll be flogged," and with that he made haste with the lads through to the main street of Funchal.

Now, I had the entire day to myself, and much to do. I sauntered forth through town, noticing the informal pace at which the islanders kept. The bustling of English cities far away could not hold a likening to this slow-moving place. I seemed to be the only living creature with a purpose, and those whom I passed looked upon me as somewhat of a puzzlement. Through the quaint little town I ambled, noting the larger lodgings for the wealthy and the meagre shanties for the poor, all of which were ill built, but uniquely picturesque.

I reached a vineyard on the edge of the town and there encountered Mister Banks and his group. After ascertaining that those dogs of his were nowhere to be seen, I joined them to watch a demonstration of wine making. This being the only form of financial gain in Madeira, I surmised that they would be good at it.

The grapes were put into a square wooden vessel, and then the strangest business ensued. The servants removed their jackets, stockings and shoes and got right into the crate to squeeze the juice from the grapes with their bare elbows and feet!

Upon beholding this strange site, I made a promise to myself to refuse wine whenever offered in future. I had smelled the feet of men, and vowed therein forward to never touch the stuff! As the demonstration continued and the scientists discussed this and that, most of which was far beyond my comprehension, I wandered back to the tiny town to scare up a morsel or two.

Suddenly, across my path at great speed ran the boys. I had not seen them since we disembarked and hadn't even given them a passing thought as I had much to see. In a scurry of feet the pack dashed past me, my Isaac at the lead.

Following closely behind was a rather angry shopkeeper brandishing a large stick. "I get you, boys! Come back here! I teach you lesson! You not mess with Pedro Alvarez!" he shouted.

I thought it best to follow this fracas to support my crewmates. This swarthy half-dressed chap looked like he meant business. I ran as fast as I could and passed the perspiring Pedro to catch up with Isaac.

"Get out of the way, cat, that lunatic's going to thrash us if he catches us! He thinks we've pinched sweets from his shop," puffed Isaac.

Quick thinking was required.

I scanned ahead of our path and spotted a tower of empty wine barrels ahead. I had to put on extra speed to get ahead of Isaac and the boys. I timed my assault, and the very moment the lads passed me I sprinted to the top of the cask tower. The speed and force at which I mounted this monolith sent the casks tumbling and rolling along the path. I jumped just as they threatened to crush me, and flew like the wind to catch my troublesome friends. I glanced over my shoulder and saw Pedro Alvarez entangled in a mountain of scattering wine barrels. He fought them off like the enemies they were, but could not free himself from the attack.

We rounded a corner in the path some distance away, and looked back at the sight. Many islanders rushed to his aid, only to be caught up in the casks as their assault gained momentum with the downward slope of the path. The lads were rolling about laughing and clutching their sides. Tears of mirth rolled down young Isaac's face as the entertainment continued. I looked at them reproachfully.

Through the incessant giggling Isaac attempted to explain.

"Unbelievable!" hailed Isaac. "Fairweather, you've saved our skins!"

"Look at him, lads!" laughed Will as he watched the scene at the top of the path, "That blighter Alvarez is as red as beet. He can't get up!"

"What a lark, lads, and we've been saved by none other than this half-witted cat!" sniggered Will.

"Half-witted, Will? I think not!" chided Isaac, as the laughter stopped. The boys peeped again upon the riot on the pathway, just to be sure they were not still pursued by the angry Pedro and the town's people.

"Aw, come on, Isaac, he's just a cat," groaned Will.

"Just a cat?" protested Isaac as the other boys stared at him in surprise. "This 'cat' as you would have him, has quite willingly and skilfully saved our skins! Did you not see him in action?"

"Well…er…yes, I suppose I did," confessed Will.

"Then we owe him a debt of gratitude, lads!" suggested Isaac as he, too, took another glance around the corner, just to be sure. "But enough of that now, they're coming to their feet and I anticipate that the chase will resume if we don't scram!"

With that, the boys ran as fast as their collective legs would carry them, back toward the beach where their adventure had begun. I kept up with them, as I too had had enough of Funchal for the time being and the hour was late. We gathered at the beach as the longboat approached to ferry us back to the ship.

"Well, Will?" demanded Isaac of his chum, as they waited for the longboat to arrive. "What have you to say for Fairweather's chivalry?"

"Alright, lads! Fairweather's a pal. We'd have been for it with the captain if he hadn't come to our service. Now who's got the sweets we nicked?"

I looked at Will and my Isaac as if I had been delivered a dull blow to the back of the head. I believed Isaac had told me during the chase in question, that he and the boys had been unjustly accused of pinching sweets from Pedro Alvarez's shop. Had I known that they had done the deed in question I may not have been so eager to assist them in their escape!

Ignoring my obvious disapproval, the boys distributed their loot between them, without even a thought for my share. I was suitably incensed! The trouble I had gone to for these guilty criminals with their mouths full of the evidence of their crime was misplaced, and if only I had known, I would have let them suffer the consequences of their actions. As a fellow crewman, however, I could not let them down, and even now feel that I took the correct course of action at the time.

When we finally returned to our ship, and the boys had discussed their close call with the angry Pedro Alvarez, possibly the law, and worse still, the captain, I was finally and suitably rewarded by the boys with a hearty meal and a comfortable bed for the night. I gathered from the distinct absence of movement in their general sleeping quarters, that all were quite exhausted by the day's activity. I, too, slept rather well, having finally been established as the hero of the day.

The boys had wisely resolved to stay on board for the remainder of our stay, for fear that Mister Cheap would hear of our misadventure and further mischief would be reported to the captain. Each day with the comings and goings of the longboat, they dreaded the possibility of discovery. No such moment arrived and soon the episode was forgotten.

A new crewman by name of John Thurman was recruited by the captain from a New York sloop moored along with us in Funchal. He was taken on board as sailmaker's mate and by his surly outlook, did not appear at all pleased with his assignment. The crew were still a little sensitive from Alex Weir's untimely death, and did not welcome this new man willingly. Disquietude followed him for some time until he showed his talents to be worthy of some respect even though his temperament lacked any semblance of good humour.

For the days to follow, the crew were occupied with the taking of stores on board. Fresh beef and greens arrived and were stowed. Our casks were sent ashore to be replenished with water and wine.

I thought the men would be pleased for the preference of fresh rations to the hardtack dispensed when the former was in short supply. To their detriment the choosiness of certain individuals to refrain from partaking in fresh beef and vegetables angered the captain. If he were to maintain a scurvy-free ship, the offending men would have to be punished and with that made an example to the others for the future.

From my vantage point in the rigging on this fine day, I observed the captain's wrath for the first time. He had learned of the disobedience of his orders by some of the crew, regarding the consumption of fresh food, from John Gore, the third lieutenant. He sent for the man.

"Lieutenant Gore. I am saddened by the news that my orders apropos the taking of fresh beef and vegetables to avoid the scurvy have been violated. Find the culprits and have them brought to me at once!" demanded the captain impatiently.

Able Seaman Henry Stephens and Marine Thomas Dunster were brought before the captain who had, in the mean time, assembled the entire crew on the deck.

The captain addressed the men. "Stephens and Dunster have been brought before you to receive a punishment which I personally abhor. However, it is my aim throughout the voyage of the *Endeavour* to safeguard your health. Therefore, I must discipline these two men, as much as I detest the application, to ensure that no man disregards my explicit orders where nutrition is concerned. Misters Stephens and Dunster are guilty of disobedience in not taking fresh meats and vegetables as ordered, and for their dereliction, must pay the price. Lieutenant Gore! Administer the punishment of twelve lashes per man!"

With that the crew looked on in astonishment, as did I, it is true to say. I thought this captain of mine to be a fine and respectable gentleman, but here he was issuing harsh measures to the men in question for merely not eating correctly. I did, however, remember Turkel's words of the evils of scurvy and how it had affected his crewmates. While I felt the captain was a little severe, I knew he simply meant for the remainder of the crew to learn from Stephen's and Dunster's mistake, and consequential ill health.

I was in the vicinity of Isaac and the lads and overheard them discussing the forthcoming consequences. "Lieutenant Gore's goin' to give 'em the cat!" he whispered. The others nodded so as not to catch the captain's attention for speaking in rank.

The cat? I thought! What good would it do to hand these two casualties over to me? I could not imagine how I would carry out discipline upon these men. Perhaps a scratch or two, or a bite, but I daresay that whilst I would do my utmost to scratch or bite them severely under my captain's orders, these actions seemed inadequate under the circumstances.

John Gore pulled a curious gadget from the depths of his uniform. It comprised a rod with nine leather straps bound to the end. "Yep!" whispered Isaac, "It's the cat 'o' nine tails for them, alright!"

All became clear to me. I ascertained that this implement was in fact "the cat," and that the nine tails were the straps swinging from the end of this oddity. I spurned the reference to my good species as a contraption for punishment. Why they could not have dubbed it a "dog of nine tails" is beyond me. This genus of animal being a punishment in its own right! But I digress, and more to the point was the physical penalty about to be delivered.

Stephens and Dunster were ordered to remove their shirts and face the men. They gripped the nearest solid object they could reach and winced in anticipation, knowing what they were in for. One by one, blows were delivered to their bare backs, twelve each in all, by Lieutenant Gore, who was no doubt in charge of the administering of discipline. I watched in alarm as their exposed skins were welted by the impact of the "cat." Blood came from the deeper of the cuts, and combining with the sweat from their fear, ran like rivulets down their bodies. I was somewhat overcome by what I had just seen. I could do nothing but stare in disbelief at how men could inflict their own with such harsh treatment.

"Let this be a reminder to all," said the captain solemnly, "that I would favour your collaboration in the taking of the proper nourishment, and that it is for your personal good that my orders are to be followed in the strictest sense. The reprimand for further offenders will be precisely as you witness this day. Lieutenant Gore, take them below to the surgeon's quarters and have Doctor Monkhouse attend to their wounds." And with that he dismissed the men and walked to his post at the helm in silent contemplation.

The men dispersed and went about their duties, but I sensed a fear for their own skins, should they not follow the captain's strategy for maintaining their health, along with a resolve to avoid the "cat" wherever possible.

I, too, went about my business in the stores and around the galley, feeling not a little uncomfortable at having witnessed this incident. I proposed to take this matter up with the captain later, when I kept my usual evening appointment with him in the Great Cabin for a chat.

Later that afternoon, Mister Banks and the gentlemen had returned from their mission in Funchal, laden with specimens collected from the area. After my meal, and with much purpose, I sauntered to the captain's chamber for our rendezvous.

I found him not alone. Mister Banks and the gents were engrossed in excited discussion of their significant Madeiran findings. The captain seemed suitably absorbed so I settled in a comfortable spot for the entertainment, and just in the nick of time as Mister Banks was beginning his report.

"Mister Cheap was to be commended for his admirable lodgings and assistance. He graciously supplied us with horses and guides, and the support of the local folk in gathering shells and fish specimens. The five days, which we have remained upon the island were spent so exactly in the same manner, that it is by no means necessary to describe each of them. I shall therefore only say, that in general we got up in the morning, went out on our researches, returned to dine, and went out again in the evening."

The captain and I listened on, with increasing interest. Mister Spöring's lively support of Mister Banks findings was of great interest. He brought forward an assembly of specimens whenever required, looking very pleased with himself.

"I ascertain that the island has been produced by a volcano, stones having shown signs of being burnt and the sand itself was absolute cinders. The sides of the hills as you, my dear captain, have seen from the ship are covered in vineyards almost as high as the eye can distinguish, above this being the chestnuts and pines. I estimate the highest of the hills at some five thousand feet, much higher than any land measured in England. The local people, some eighty thousand, seem to be as idle and uneducated as I have ever seen."

This I knew from my own conclusions, but I let Mister Banks continue uninterrupted.

"I saw no wheeled carriages on the roads, those being so poorly constructed that they were barely passable but for donkeys and horses. The men send every drop of wine they produce to town on the heads of their women in vessels made of goat skins."

I had seen this practise myself in my travels and thought it odd for women to carry the odd-looking things upon their heads. I was glad of the fine explanation courtesy of Mister Banks and I allowed him to continue.

"We found walnuts, chestnuts and apples in the hills not far from the town. The banana tree, the mango, cinnamon, all rich and in abundance if farmed, and yet the idleness of the inhabitants is so great, that even that is too much for them. What corn grows here, which indeed is not much, is of a most excellent quality; large grained, and very fine. Their meat also is very good, mutton, pork, and beef more especially, all of which we have brought on board the ship. It is agreed by all of us to be as fine as our own English produce. "The churches and convent here are peculiarly ornate to say the least. I saw a curiosity of a very extraordinary nature; a small chapel whose whole lining and ceiling was entirely composed of human bones, two large thigh bones crossed, and a skull in each of the openings. Among these was a very bizarre anatomical curiosity, a skull in which one side of the lower jaw was perfectly and very firmly fastened to the upper by fossilization, so that the man whoever he was, must have lived for some time without being able to open his mouth. A hole on the other side of the jaw had been beaten out, by which he must have received his nourishment."

We were spellbound by the curious nature of Mister Banks's conclusions. I for one had not noticed these particular oddities, although as you are well aware, I had my hands full with those devilish lads! Nevertheless, both the Captain and I were sufficiently entertained by the end of Mister Banks's report.

"Well, Mister Banks, a most eventful stay, I would venture to say! You indeed have gathered enough specimens to keep yourselves busy," said the captain, addressing the other artists and botanists.

"We shall take our leave on this occasion, dear captain!" gestured Mister Banks, waiving his kerchief toward the cabin door. "We have much to accomplish with the documentation of our tour. Gentlemen? Shall we?"

Mister Spöring fussed about shuffling the artists out, and with that, they took their leave and I was finally alone with my captain.

"Come, Fairweather, we have our log to draft." He sighed, scooping me up into the crook of his arm as we retired to his quarters for our regular parlay.

As he settled wearily, he sighed. "This has been an eventful day, Fairweather, and I tire as we speak. My entry to the log shall be brief as we sail at midnight this next evening and we have much to prepare for the morrow."

I looked longingly at this refined, diligent man, wishing to address his punishment of the unfortunate Stephens and Dunster, but as he wrote up his journal and read the brief notes aloud to me, he showed the signs of having censured himself enough without my condemnation of his actions. As much as I felt for the tortured pair, I likewise observed the captain's sadness between the lines of his words. I deemed it wise to leave well enough alone and retired with him right there in his quarters for I could see that he was in need of a friend whilst he slept. I, too, did not mind the company.

At midnight on Sunday, the 18th day of September, we sailed from Funchal, after taking on board ten pounds of onions per man, three thousand and thirty-two gallons of wine, ten tonnes of water, two hundred and seventy pounds of fresh beef and a live bullock. What in the world the captain intended for that poor beast was beyond me, although from my reckoning, and Henry Jeff's comments on its "meatiness," this animal would serve no purpose but for his destiny at our dinner table!

The weather was fine and clear and the tide was full as I took my place at the cathead. Not many saw me there in the dark, but I knew my place as a herald of fine weather to be of the utmost importance, and as the stars were my only witness, I remained in my position there throughout the night for the good of my captain, crew and ship.

The passage from Madeira under moonlight was a memorable one. I kept my vigil, and was joined by misters Banks, Spöring, Green, Parkinson, Buchan and Doctor Solander. The "Gentlemen or Gents," as the crew and I had named them, were not sailors and yet admired the view of the island as we made distance from our mooring.

Their discussion lulled me somewhat in the clear, calm conditions and I dozed on and off as the noblemen rejoiced in their findings over a glass of fine brandy under the stars. When the horizon was finally clear, we felt we were now on our way to new waters, warmer than we had ever known, and Brazil lay ahead. The moon stayed within view until it set in the early hours of the next morning, when the gents retired to catch up on their sleep.

Our voyage to Brazil was by and large an uneventful one, except for some rather savage storms. Turkel's eye patch and wooden leg strangely appeared in my imagination whenever storms loomed, even though I found it difficult to remember his words at times. I found the storms to be different in their nature with each performance. Some brought a howling gale in upon us, whipping the sea into a frenzy and blowing the tops of the waves into spume. Others delivered a dumping rain, so heavy as to wet a man, or cat for that matter, right through to his bones. Worst of all were the storms with flashing lightning and thunder rumbling through the sky, all around us and so close at times and that we feared for our skins.

These storms saw the crew at their best. During high winds there was always the danger of torn sails and lost rigging. Master Robert Molyneux was obliged to the business of such resources and reported directly to the captain should there be any trouble. The poor man had to brave the elements during all storms to ensure the condition of this most vital equipment, as it was not likely that we could replace such essentials in the middle of the ocean.

During these episodes, I knew well to stay below and out of harm's way, for the saying goes that "curiosity killed the cat," and I had made up my mind quite early on, never to let my curiosity get the better of my good judgement. Mind you, nothing could keep me away from a porthole to watch the goings on outside. The power of nature and its effect on the sea never ceased to amaze me.

At this time, the captain had set the men to three watches. One third of the crew would man the ship whilst the remaining men slept. Then the first tour would retire to their beds and the second patrol would appear to take over their duties. After they had performed their watch, they too would retire and the first watch would reappear rested, and so on and so forth. This practise maintained both their bodily strength and a sound mind, the latter more important than pure physical ability during long stretches at sea. I had heard the stories. Men spending too long on watch were vulnerable to fatigue and the likelihood of strange visions was an inescapable risk. Some of the crew had experienced such hallucinations on previous voyages and were certainly in no mood to ever see them again. They spoke of huge sea squid crushing a ship in its eight enormous tentacles, whales with fire in their eyes setting ships alight with one burning stare, giant birds which could pluck an entire ship from the sea in their beaks! I was assured they were just stories but kept my eye trained for such things in my own moments on watch.

Young Isaac Manly had many nightmares of such beasts after a night around the table with the crew. I would hear him crying in his bed when all were heavy with sleep. I felt sadly for this poor boy, youngest of them all, and always made it my charge to comfort him during such terrifying dreams. No matter where I was on the ship, somehow I always knew when he was in the grip of a horrid nightmare, and in pity I would rush to his aid. All that was required of me was to curl up next to his twitching frame and he would hug me as tight as a child would hug his dearest comforter. At times I feared he would squeeze me so tightly that I felt that all my breath would leave me. His tears wet my fur, but I knew him to be suffering from the preposterous stories of a crew with questionable principles under the influence of a few ales. He would settle after a while and I hoped my little friend would eventually grow to know that these horrors were simply images from the mind, and not to be trusted as truth.

It was my understanding from the captain's calculations that this leg of our voyage to Brazil would be a long one, many days and nights at sea without a landing. I deemed it wise during this time to familiarise myself with the comings and goings of Mister Banks's dogs. I had up to this point kept well away from them for obvious reasons and Mister Banks's servants had kept them exercised and well fed. However, I knew that our paths would cross sooner rather than later, and if I were to gain the upper hand with these hounds I should introduce myself when they were off their guard.

I rose early on one of the finest, stillest mornings to date, determined to take my chances with the offending beasts. I tracked them keenly as Tom Richmond walked them. Up and down the deck they pranced as if they owned the ship. Tom gave them a good deal of exercise until they were sent panting to their water bucket. I watched patiently as they lapped up a full pitcher of the purest, and thought it a waste of good drinking water when they were clearly of no use to the ship, unlike the crew and my good self! Tom gave them beef scraps that they devoured within seconds, barely touching their tongues enough to savour the fine meat. Here I thought they were not quite as favoured as I, having endeared myself to the cook and acquired the run of the galley. Scraps were never fed to me. Only the best for Fairweather.

Knowing myself to be of lazy demeanour after a hearty meal, I had gathered correctly that these two dogs would be ready for a good lie down. Now was my chance to introduce myself, without the disadvantage of their hunger or their eagerness for sport. I estimated that they would be hampered by their fatigue and full stomachs, and not in such a great hurry by now to pursue me should I attract their disfavour.

They skulked along toward the fore deck in search of a sunny spot to snooze, no doubt. I followed closely behind, and as I was downwind, did not attract their attention. I stayed behind the foremast until they were settled together and then I bravely made my approach, oozing confidence from every pore so as not to attract any suspicion.

Now, greyhounds, being the tall, spindly types that they are, do not jump to attention swiftly as they are handicapped by the very nature of their stature. The mind of the dog travels at much greater speed than the disentangling of the legs and let me assure you that when there are two of them in repose and in close proximity, the sight of them trying to spring to their feet is most amusing.

Isaac was close by attending to some menial task when the sight of my aim caught his eye. He beckoned the surrounding crewmen to watch whatever was likely to unfold.

Having detected my presence, the dogs launched into a demonstration of their awkwardness. Scratching and clawing at each other, these two idiotic creatures finally unravelled their limbs and stood to their full height, panting, growling and flaunting their huge teeth in a show of bravado. The hair on my neck, back and tail stood naturally to attention, giving me the appearance of a much larger cat than I was. This helped my cause in no small way, as I drew up my paw, claws extended and swiped at the male of the species. Along with a meaningful expression and pinpoint accuracy, I connected with the snout, causing the animal to yelp in pain and back away with his tail between his legs. The female rushed to his side, licking at the wound, which had drawn a little blood.

"Good heavens, cat!" she scolded. "Was that really necessary?"

"Well, yes!" said I without apology. "Both you and your friend here were displaying offensive behaviour toward my person! Should I not defend myself?"

"Let me at him!" growled the male. "I'll have him for my supper and enjoy every morsel. Filthy feline!"

"Oh, be quiet, dear, it's just a scratch, and you were being a little boisterous. I'm sure this chap meant you no real harm," she said, trying her best to calm him.

"No harm? No harm?" he blustered. "I am the victim of a vicious assault by this demon! I shall give him harm!"

"Chester!" she scolded. "He is the ship's cat. I have seen him around and he is held in high esteem amongst the crew. The consequences of harming him would be rather severe, I would think. My advice to you is to stop all this barbarous behaviour of yours. We must co-exist on this wretched ship for goodness knows how long, and I will not have you making trouble! Now be still whilst I make our introductions!"

He sneered silently at me as if it were his dearest desire to tear me limb from limb.

"My name is Lady, and this is my companion, Chester. I have heard of you amongst the crew. You are the keeper of good fortune and fine weather for this ship. Your name is Fairweather, is it not?" she inquired.

"Why yes, Madam! You are correct in all aspects, but I shall add that I am the ship's mouser to boot! I am pleased to make your acquaintance." I extended a paw in greeting. She flinched a little.

"You are not intending to harm me also, I hope?" she asked playfully.

"No, Madam! That is to say I am a peaceful chap without enemies to my knowledge. If you and your friend intend me no harm, then I would most certainly look forward to a friendship between us. I have no doubt that we can assist each other in one way or another," I intimated respectfully.

Chester was not convinced.

"Friendship? With a cat? Surely you would not consider such an arrangement, Lady?" he scoffed.

"Chester, you can be such a stubborn fool at times. There is no point in holding a grudge with Fairweather. If we can be of assistance to one another during this trip, then I will have to insist that you do not harbour any ill feeling toward him. He was simply defending himself from possible attack. How was he to know we would not eat him? Besides, I see that he is no ordinary alley cat. He speaks well and his manners, other than that swipe to your snout, are impeccable. Now I demand that you two make arrangements to be civil," she said, standing firm.

"Hurrumph!" Chester snorted. Lady gave him a stern look. "As you wish, my dear," he conceded. He turned his back and went back to his sleeping arrangement growling beneath his breath.

"Pay no mind to him, dear boy. He will come around. His pride has been wounded more convincingly than his nose," said Lady. "Do your best to keep out of his way for a while. He will forget all about this little incident in time."

"Whatever you deem best, Madam. For now, I am your comrade, and at your service," I replied bowing and taking my leave. I sensed a kinship with Lady that would stand the length of our voyage. I was not persuaded that Chester felt the same way. Time would tell.

Isaac and the men watched without speech as I strolled calmly by.

"Did you all see what I saw? That Chester should have torn him to shreds! Seemed like Fairweather and Lady talked him out of it!" Isaac cried in disbelief.

"Nah! You're imaginin' things, boy!" laughed the others. But my impression was that they all agreed with Isaac's interpretation of my little encounter with those dogs, but were embarrassed to admit it.

I looked back only once on my way to the galley, to see Chester with one eye closed in sleep and the other eye trained on me in a most disconcerting fashion. There was clearly still work to be done to make peace with this chap.

CHAPTER 10

The days passed uneventfully for some time. The weather remained calm and sunny and the crew busied themselves with the maintenance of our ship. Calm weather gave them the opportunity to tend to the upkeep of the sails and rigging and they set about their tasks with purpose and good humour.

Chester and Lady crossed my path quite regularly, but without incident. Chester still harboured resentment, as was obvious by the guttural growl emanating from his form as we passed each other. Lady kept him in check when we were together to his obvious disgust, but on the odd occasion as the sun set about the ship, and while Chester was sleeping deeply, Lady and I found the time to discuss our backgrounds and found that we had much in common.

We both came from decidedly well-to-do homes, but unlike my calling to the sea, Lady and Chester felt no deep desire to accompany Mister Banks on this adventure. Lady felt that her home was where she ought to be, and Chester, well, he merely grumbled over any inconvenience to his daily routine, and this voyage was one of them. The more Lady and I chatted, the more I came to like her and it seemed that the impression was mutual. The more I saw of Chester, the more resentful he became so I avoided being alone with him.

With the conditions so calm and all tasks attended to, the captain gave orders for the mates and midshipmen to partake in small arms drill. This required an education in the proper use of firearms. Misters Banks, Green, Spöring and Doctor Solander watched with some amusement at the exercises performed under the captain's guidance.

"Mister Green, I cannot help but fear for our safety with this rabble attending to the weaponry!" whispered Mister Banks. "If we are set upon by irritated natives, I am certain we will have to shoot them ourselves!"

"If they could only synchronise their efforts, they would appear less amusing and more of a threat," countered Mr Green. "I feel that any angry natives confronted by this army will surely laugh themselves to death, thereby negating the need for force at all!"

The gentlemen sniggered amongst themselves while the captain and crew persevered with their lessons. I thought them snobbish and rude at the time, as the men were doing their level best to master the arms they would certainly use to protect us all. At such a time as life and liberty were threatened, I was sure that these faultfinders would be only too happy to have an armed crewman rush to their rescue. I left them to their criticisms as their attitude to my fine crew incensed me.

The captain had ordered the issue of hooks and lines to some of the men, along with pipes and tobacco. These men seemed more amiable company and I joined them in the hope of lighter conversation. Puffing away on their pipes, with their lines over the side of the ship, they were relaxed and in good cheer, swapping stories of this and that, and pulling in the odd fish. Upon my arrival, a tasty morsel was thrown my way, and I devoured it with relish as they piled their catch for the evening meal.

Life at sea could not have been more pleasant among these good-humoured crewmates and I spent many days among them in their pursuit for an alternative meal to the sauerkraut and portable soup: a meat essence boiled with oatmeal, that had been issued under the captain's orders. Without exception, the men hated these rations, but with the recent punishment of men not taking adequate nourishment, they forced it down to avoid the inevitable lashings should they refuse. Fish, however, was a welcome change and they tended their lines with vigour when given the opportunity. With the sun shining, just enough breeze to fill the sails, fish aplenty and the good cheer of all parties, trouble was the last thing on anyone's mind, but I saw above the rigging the tell-tale signs of bad weather. Storm petrels circled the masts and as my concern grew, my agitation caught Lady's eye. She was resting comfortably with Chester in their usual aft location on the gents' deck when I rushed by to warn the captain.

"Fairweather!" she called. "What is the trouble, dear?"

"I fear a storm may be looming, Madam. I suggest you and Chester go below to be out of harm's way," I said in earnest, directing her eye to the mast and the birds.

Chester yawned and rolled lazily in my direction. "Storm?" he scoffed. "Not a cloud in the sky, and this pestilential creature tells us we should take ourselves below? I think not!" He rolled away ignorantly.

Lady pawed at him impatiently. "Chester, you fool! Fairweather is to be trusted in his observations, Mother Carey's Chickens circle the rigging as we speak. He knows his business and we should take heed and cover!" she insisted.

"Mother Carey's Chickens!" he taunted slothfully. "You are both quite daft. Never heard of such a thing!"

"I have heard the crew speak of them as fore warning of bad weather, Chester. I beg of you to accompany me below!" Lady pleaded.

"Rubbish! I am enjoying this fine day! Now leave me in peace, both of you, for you bore me with your silly notions!" he scowled.

"Come along, Fairweather. You and I shall take cover and leave this miserable hound to find his own shelter when the storm is upon us," hissed Lady, walking proudly off in the direction of the hatch to the lower decks, with her nose in the air.

I followed quickly behind her. "Surely, we cannot just leave him there?" I asked.

"If he insists on being lazy and stubborn, he can jolly well look after himself!" argued Lady with not a little contempt for her partner's attitude.

"Very well, Lady, as you wish, but I cannot join you below until I have warned the captain of the danger ahead. I shall be along when I have tended to my duty," I concluded, conveying the urgency of my mission.

We nodded to each other and I set off quickly to find my captain, knowing him to be still trying to drill the crew on weaponry.

In the middle of what seemed to be his final attempt to have the men present arms in good order, I leapt to his attention, clawing at his leather boots. He looked down at me as if a nuisance had come upon him, shuffling me out of his way as gently but firmly as he could without acknowledging my presence. I attempted the same manoeuvre once again and with that he ordered the men to stand at ease, and he attended my disruption.

Bending down toward me as if to chastise me for my disrespect, he whispered, "What the devil is the matter with you, Fairweather? I am presenting important training to the men and cannot have you interrupting."

I demonstrated as much agitation as I could muster and motioned in the direction of Mother Carey's Chickens flapping about the rigging. I could see from his expression that my display was not lost on him.

"Men, we shall have to finalise our drill, as I fear that foul weather looms. Man your stations, secure the deck of loose items, and Isaac, have Mister Molyneux report to me immediately," the captain decreed, leaving no doubt of his intentions.

He looked purposefully at me as I waited patiently for my orders. "Fairweather, you may very well have saved our skins!" he whispered. "I was preoccupied with the task at hand, and had not noticed the signs above. Be off with you to my cabin for your own protection whilst I secure the ship."

I stood fast and I knew he understood.

"Alright then, if you insist on manning a post, take your position on the cathead for as long as your comfort provides and I shall join you below when I am sure that all will be well." He looked into the distance to see dark and ominous clouds forming, and from my vantage point I could see him calculating within his mind the strategy for the conditions ahead.

Mister Molyneux purposefully arrived on the deck and consulted with the captain. Their words were beyond my hearing as I took my place into the wind upon the cathead. The calm sunny weather was quite quickly replaced by a moist and stiff breeze, heralding the elements ahead. My whiskers worked hard to stay upon my face as the wind picked up speed.

Mister Molyneux assembled the required men for the servicing of the sails and rigging under the watchful eye of the captain. Mister Molyneux knew his business and performed quickly and efficiently to secure the ship. The crew attended his every order obediently and with great speed, much to the captain's approval.

I alone kept my vigil, for'ard of the ship as the thunder rumbled in the distance and lightning flashed as if giants launched great silver spears from the blackening clouds toward the angry sea. Ever closer the squall came, and as the sea turned darkest blue littered with white caps, the swell tossed the ship. The remaining men tethered themselves to the rigging for safety, in case the waves attempted to wash them from the deck and into the sea. In these conditions, men swept overboard would never be seen again. On short ropes they continued their duties until Mister Molyneux was satisfied that all was secure for the rapidly growing storm.

The swell of the sea built quickly, coming from all directions during this wild tempest. The wind and weather came from one direction, fighting with the currents from quite another, so that not only did the ship rise and crash through the waves and troughs, but lurched from side to side as well.

The sea rose ever higher, sometimes seeming as high as the tip of the mast. As the captain steered the ship to avoid capsizing, the men scurried from one task to another, reefing in the sails so that the wind did not affect the speed at which we travelled, allowing the captain to control the ship correctly against the angry sea.

Men fastened the pinnace, yawl and longboat, all our small craft needed for leaving the ship to make for the shore. They secured the animals on deck so that the pitching of the ship did not catapult them over the side. They fastened the ropes and anchors so that none were lost to the sea.

I found the going not a little difficult as the ship pounded through the waves, tilting sharply in the crosscurrents. As important as it was for me to man my post, I deemed that my comfort level had been breached by one powerful wave, almost flinging me into the sea below.

I fought the instability of the deck beneath me with my claws digging purposefully into the wood with every step. The wind became a wild force, driving the torrential rain sideways, parting my fur and stinging my eyes in my attempts to navigate my way to the hatch. Waves began to break across the deck from the cross current. The wash would surely take me overboard if I did not hold tight to whatever I could feel.

As I pushed on, I glimpsed a familiar shape from the corner of my eye. I stopped as well as I could and turned toward the starboard side of the ship. The rain limited my sight and I could determine nothing of concern. I pushed on thinking I had simply imagined trouble, remembering those tales of strange visions being common during such storms.

By this time there was no way to distinguish the sea from the sky, a deep grey blue had engulfed us. The white spume mixed with the biting rain and I could not tell one from the other. Lightning flashed through the grey, lighting up every nook and cranny darkened by the storm. Thunder rumbled and cracked like blasts from huge cannons. A few forced steps further and I would be at the fore-hatch making my way to comfort below.

A fearful yelp distracted me from my destination. It came from the very place I had imagined the familiar shape, and as much as my deepest desire was to head straight for safety, I felt compelled to investigate.

I braced myself to jump toward the direction of the sound, carefully judging my distance, and with one strategic leap slammed painfully into the starboard rail. I had not allowed for the force of the wind behind me, and reminded myself to allow for such contingencies in future as I caught my breath, which seemed to have left me quite suddenly.

With claws still anchored firmly in the decking I squinted into the rain and scanned the immediate area for the source of the disturbance. A rope was hanging strangely perpendicular to the ship instead of being fastened or blowing with the wind. Knowing that Mister Molyneux had ensured all ropes were secure, I cast my eye downward following the direction of the rope.

To my horror, there below me was Chester, dangling over the side by his leg! He had most surely been washed over the side by one of the waves, and only his leg caught in the rope had stopped him from disappearing into the blackened sea.

"Chester!" I yelled "Are you mad? What the devil are you doing down there in this foul weather?"

A painful wail was all he could muster. I could see that the stray rope bound his leg.

"Fool cat!" he growled, mustering just enough strength to chastise me. "Get help! This rope will break if this wretched ship lurches again!"

I looked along the rope and saw the problem. The line he was tangled in was tossing him from side to side against the ship like a rag, rubbing against the wooden railing and was fraying before my eyes. Thread by thread snapped as the fibres strained against Chester's weight.

I quickly looked around me for signs of the crew. No one was nearby and the wind and rain were so deafening that I suspected we would not be heard.

"No time for that now, Chester!" I shouted.

"Do not let me die here, cat!" he bawled! "Do something! Help me!"

I looked at the sea I had been studying from the cathead. The wind and currents were still at cross-purposes and from what I could make out, the ship was in the trough of a wave. At any moment we would rise up the face of the next wave and lurch down into the following trough. Taking the wind into consideration this time I devised my plan.

"Cat! Cat! Are you there? For heaven's sake, save me!" Chester yowled miserably.

"Hold on, dear fellow! I have a plan!" I tried to sound encouraging but feared he was in no mood.

"Blasted useless cat!" he screamed over and over, as if he wanted his last words to condemn me forever. His cursing and yelping continued incessantly. I had to be firm!

"Chester!" I demanded with no uncertainty. "Stop your infernal blubbering! Pay attention and do exactly as I say or you will die right here and now! We have only seconds to act!" Chester stopped immediately, realising that I was his only hope.

"Chester!" I yelled. "The ship is rising on the crest of a wave. When it drops to the trough below, I want you to swing your body alongside the ship as high as you can!"

"I cannot!" he wailed. "I am already in pain! My leg!"

"Do as I say, Chester, or I shall leave you here and save my own skin!" I warned.

At that very moment the wave peaked. Chester looked up at me and nodded staunchly, forgetting his pain and readying himself, as he knew this was his only chance.

I leapt to the railing, my claws digging deeply into the wood. At the crucial moment when the ship slammed into the trough, Chester swung, struggling in the direction of the standing rigging. I braced myself to it, and as he swung by me I stretched my front paws toward him, claws extended as far as they would go. A fearsome yelp came from Chester as my claws connected with his neck, and digging them into his flesh as far as they would go, I managed to steady him close to the rigging.

The ship had paused for just long enough in the trough of the wave allowing me a moment of calm to execute my plan.

"Chester!" I strained. "I cannot hold you for long! Bite into the rigging and do not let go! Chester clamped his jaws into the thick rope shrouds. Thankfully this kept him quiet as I clawed wildly at his neck and back, rolling him little by little toward the railing. Finally, he rolled over the starboard rail, and as I could not easily let him go we both tumbled awkwardly onto the deck.

His leg was still tangled in the rope and as I freed him I surveyed his injuries. As was my experience with broken limbs, I suspected that the rope had broken Chester's leg, poor fellow. Not to mention the bleeding scratches I had inflicted during his rescue. He was not in good shape, but he was alive.

Tom Richmond came clambering onto the deck calling for Chester. He crouched low and forced his large frame into the biting wind and rain.

"Chester! Chester! Where you be, dog? Master Banks have my hide if you up here in some trouble!"

Tom spotted us through the rain and crawled toward us. "What has happened here?" he shouted against the storm.

He eyed me keenly as the scene before him looked more like a battle between cat and dog, than a rescue. Chester lifted his head breathlessly and licked me gently to dispel Tom's fears. Knowing his charge so well, Tom understood that no ordinary scrap had occurred between us, as Chester gestured toward the rope and his injured leg just before he closed his eyes, benumbed by his ordeal.

"Fairweather, you have saved Chester from some death?" Tom asked.

I looked between railing toward the sea below and back at Chester. Tom understood all, as was his way as keeper and companion to Mister Banks's dogs. He stroked my head and lifted my chin. His grateful expression met my weary eyes as his strong arms lifted both Chester and my good self. Through the ever-driving wind and rain, slowly but steadily he took us below to safety. As we passed by the curious crew below, all of us soaking wet, me with Chester's fur in my bloodied paws and Chester with deep cuts along his body, courtesy of yours truly, and not to mention a sizeable snap to his hind leg.

Tom only said quietly to each and every man,

"Been an accident. Cat saved dog from death." Mister Banks and Lady hurried forward, Lady barking wildly as she looked upon her companion.

"Tom, what has happened to my Chester?" he demanded "And what of this cat?"

Tom repeated his only explanation. "Been an accident, Mister Banks, Sir. Cat saved dog from death."

"Nonsense, Tom! Is this some silly superstition of yours, or have you been consuming alcohol?" defied Mister Banks.

"No, Sir, Mister Banks, Sir." Tom bowed his head. "Cat saved dog from death. I see it in his eyes."

"Very well, Tom, if you insist," sighed Mister Banks. "But he is injured, a broken leg if I'm not mistaken, and those scratches! Are you sure that cat did not inflict those injuries in some spiteful brawl?" he asked suspiciously.

"Sure as God!" Tom replied devoutly. "Cat had to scratch him to get him up safely from death!"

"Take him to Doctor Monkhouse, and have him attend to Chester's wounds. I shall join you there shortly for a consultation," ordered Mister Banks.

Lady ceased her barking and looked toward me.

"Is this true, Fairweather?" All I could manage in my exhaustion was a weary nod.

Lady reasoned that as she had left Chester on deck when the storm began and that I had maintained my vigil on the cathead, trouble had befallen Chester, and I, without a mark upon my person, must have saved him "from death" as Tom put it.

The crew looked at each other, determined to learn more, but Tom could explain no further. Only Chester and I knew what had occurred. The storm was subsiding as Tom took us both to Doctor Monkhouse, who splinted Chester's leg and dressed his scratches.

"Be sure and look after cat!" implored Tom. "He be a hero. Saved dog from death."

Doctor Monkhouse checked my body for damage, but other than some tender parts of my anatomy and claws full of Chester's bloodied fur, I was unharmed but for exhaustion.

"Fairweather seems to be well enough, but could do with some rest from his duties for a time. And Tom, if he indeed has done what you claim, a plate of the finest and a saucer of milk would be appropriate," Doctor Monkhouse concluded.

I agreed.

Chester stayed with Doctor Monkhouse while Tom took me to the kitchen. Word had already spread all over the ship that I had saved Chester's life, and a plate of fine lamb in gravy with a saucer of precious goat's milk awaited me.

"Told you that cat was a fine animal!" boasted Isaac. The rest of the crew were busy trying to imagine what had happened.

"Neptune's trident scratched the dog! I saw it from the fo'rard hatch. He stood on the bottom and cleared the ship nigh to a hundred feet high!" shouted Isaac Manly. The ever-increasingly superstitious young fellow had been around the crew too long already.

"Nay, laddie! I saw Zeus pluck a lightning bolt from the sky and scratch the dog!" shouted John Thomspon the cook, above the growing rumbles of the crew.

"Me, too!" screeched Tom Matthews who said little else usually.

The roar about the ship was now as deafening as the storm itself with men arguing back and forth as to which god had done the deed.

The captain appeared and with one booming "Stop!" The men dispersed to their duties mumbling when out of earshot.

Tom Richmond waited patiently as I finished my fine meal, and carried me gently to the captain's cabin.

"S'cuse me, Captain, Sir. Thomas Richmond, Mister Banks's servant." He bowed in introduction as they entered.

"Yes, Tom, what happened here?" asked the captain.

"Been some trouble, Sir, on deck, Sir, cat saved dog from death, Sir," explained Tom respectfully.

"Is that so?" the captain said in disbelief.

"Yes, Sir. Doctor Monkhouse given cat a few days' rest, Sir, he be tender from the strain, Sir. Thought you might have a quiet spot for him here, Sir?" Tom suggested, bowing politely.

"Yes, yes, Tom, leave him with me," insisted the captain.

Tom placed me gently on a soft cushion by the captain's chair where I fell into a deep and restful sleep. The last thing I remember for some time was Tom's respectful exit and the captain rubbing my ears. "You are indeed a mystery, Fairweather, my friend."

CHAPTER 11

I must have drifted in and out of sleep for a few days, for as I finally woke fully, the sea was calm and the weather slightly warmer, the sun shining and not a cloud in the sky. My hunger drove me to the kitchen where John Thompson had prepared me the left-over morsels from the meals I had missed.

"Been missin' you, Fairweather!" confessed John. "Mice in the stores, me boy. If you're strong enough to eat then be off with you and catch the little blighters!" Nothing more was said of his stirring the crew the night of the incident.

I went in the direction of the stores, but detoured by Doctor Monkhouse's surgery to visit Chester. He was not there. I knew that I had last seen him alive, but feared that during my own recovery he may have taken a turn for the worst.

After an extensive search I found him recuperating in Mister Banks's cabin.

"Chester, old boy!" I greeted him warmly, relieved that he was still with us.

"Fairweather!" he beamed weakly. "A rough time we have had together, what?"

"Yes, yes! How are your wounds, old thing? Healing nicely, I expect?" said I, keeping cheerful, for he did look the worse for wear.

"Time will tell, time will tell," he repeated, becoming uncomfortable, for I believe he wished to broach a rather delicate subject and was having difficulty beginning.

"Er…Fairweather, dear boy, er…" He stumbled, thought for a moment and began again.

"I wish to, er…" Still no hint of what he was trying to say.

"Blast you, Fairweather!" he growled impatiently. "I am trying to thank you for saving my life, but that supercilious expression of yours impedes my progress!"

"Chester, dear old thing! You aren't grateful by any chance, are you? Perhaps a little in awe of my bravery and comradeship? Perhaps you owe me your life?" I bragged, not at all ashamed of rubbing it in. After all, he had not been my dearest friend prior to this incident. Chester suppressed the urge to inspect my insides and gathered his composure.

"Forgive me, dear boy, I do wish to thank you for your brave deed on that fateful night. If you had not come to my aid, I would no doubt have perished in that evil storm," he said meekly.

I looked at him reproachfully and he knew what was on my mind.

"Yes, Fairweather, I admit that you did warn me of the disturbance to come, and had I not been such a stubborn fool, would have taken your advice and retired to Mister Banks's cabin with Lady. She has scolded me in no small way as she was worried, the dear old girl, for your safety as much as my own."

"And your future attitude to my existence, Chester?" I inquired bravely, as I knew he couldn't get up from the bed for his broken leg.

"I remain your servant, Fairweather, but please do not embarrass me in front of the crew or I shall be the laughing stock of the ship, and perhaps even dinner if we run short of supplies, for they all think little of me, 'a waste of space', I have heard them say."

"Never mind them, Chester, we shall find something for you to aspire to by way of a duty. When they discover you are of some use, after all, your place on the crew will be secure and your fears laid to rest," I replied positively. I think this possibility impressed him as his demeanour changed, and I had an inkling that more amiable relations would be achieved between us in no time.

"Well, Chester, old hound! I must away to the stores to attend to my own purpose. I shall think long and hard for a function for you. In my absence, rest well!" With that, I wished him a quick recovery and went about my business.

I went to work in the stores, rounding up vermin until I had an impressive collection to place before John Thompson by the wood stove in the galley. By now, my friendship with the cook had flourished to such a point that eating my catch would be second rate to the reward from John's galley. His assistant Tom Matthews always complied silently with John's wishes that I eat well.

"Well done, me boy!" chirped John, waving his cleaver in the air. "Isaac!" he hollered. "Throw these evil beasties into the deep."

Isaac came from nowhere, scooped up my collection and disappeared to attend to the cook's wishes. I had not seen Isaac for some time; mostly my doing, as I was sleeping off my latest adventure, but he seemed distant of late. I ran after him and tracked him to the Great Cabin. A conference had begun. Second Lieutenant Zachary Hicks and Third Lieutenant John Gore discussed the charting of the equator, which was looming ever closer. Isaac was apprenticed to the captain and sat in on most discussions of this type to be educated. He scooped me up as the officers prepared their notes.

"Be quiet now, Fairweather, we have important business and I must watch and learn," whispered Isaac. I looked up at him with insult upon my face.

"Don't give me that look. I have been busy with my duties to the captain and my schooling. We'll have time together soon." He turned away from the captain and officers so as to pet my fur in apology whilst maintaining his dignity in front of his superiors. He put me down and turned to the group, straightening his jacket, preparing to listen intently and take notes for the captain.

"Lieutenant Hicks, Lieutenant Gore..." he began. "By my calculations, tomorrow we pass over the equator, a milestone in our voyage. Upon sunrise we shall meet on deck with Mister Green, our astronomer to make the necessary calculations and observations. To mark the occasion for the men, I shall order extra rations of ale, wine and brandy. They have performed admirably during the recent storm and deserve some recreation. Lieutenant Hicks, if you would be so kind as to inform Mister Molyneux of my intention for the crew as he alone is charged with the rationing of alcohol. I expect that you will both attend with me, the customary ritual of 'ducking' and ensure that the safety of its victims is not compromised?" The captain chuckled along with the officers and even Isaac grinned from ear to ear.

"Never mind your mirth, Isaac, you and your young friends shall be first in line as you are young and cannot possibly have crossed the equator prior to this voyage!" grinned the captain. Isaac seemed determined not to let the captain's teasing unnerve him, but I sensed an apprehension on his part.

This "ducking" was an unfamiliar term to me. I knew there to be no fowl of the "duck" variety on board the ship. Even if there were ducks in the vicinity, how would a simple bird "compromise" the safety of the men? I could not imagine that even a sound pecking from such a bird would inflict much more than a slight bruise. It sounded to me as if they had all lost their minds, and that our captain's sanity might well be in doubt. At the same time, I felt that this display of idle merriment would most certainly be misplaced were my crew to be in any danger.

That night I found Isaac in his bunk while not on watch and I curled at his feet. We both slept restlessly as the anticipation of the events of the day to follow held both fear and excitement for both of us. Along with my concern for him and the crew, the exact whereabouts of this wretched "duck" kept me awake for most of the night.

As arranged, on the very next morning, the 26th day of October 1768, the interested parties arose and met at dawn on the for'ard deck for the crossing of the equator. The captain and officers studied their charts eagerly as Isaac watched, taking in every word.

I was enormously proud of my fine Isaac, as I knew him now to be a studious chap, and although young and mischievous, he took his obligation as apprentice to the captain very seriously. After the formalities of mapping the equator's position had been recorded, the captain and lieutenants called upon Mister Molyneux to assemble the crew. As they gathered on deck for this momentous affair, I sensed an overwhelming excitement among them. Was it the event itself, or the extra rations of alcohol that made them so excitable? And where was that duck? With resounding cheers, the equator approached. Having seen the captain's maps, I somehow expected to see something resembling a line or mark upon the ocean, pointing out this "equator," but no such sign existed.

The crew, officers, and gentlemen alike, began to chant in unison.

"Ducking! Ducking! Ducking!" they yelled with excitement! Clapping and cheering began as the victims queued in turn.

Mister Molyneux came forward with a list to be read aloud.

"Those men who have crossed the equator upon past voyages step forward now and swear upon the captain's chart that they have done so!" he decreed. The more experienced of the crew did so, vowing that their pledge be truth, apparently to avoid this "duck."

Mister Molyneux continued. "Those men who have not crossed the equator, step forward now to be ducked, or sacrifice four days' grog rations to Neptune!" he declared.

Some shuffling of feet and muttering emerged from the ranks.

"Come now, lads! I have a list here of those to be 'ducked'. If you do not step forward now, I shall make it a weeks' grog rations you will do without!" threatened Mister Molyneux, rather enjoying himself.

With that warning, twenty-five men stepped bravely forward, rather than give up their rations.

I watched from the rigging above as a makeshift chair of sorts was roped to a pulley and attached to the main yard hovering precariously above the sea. I saw no "duck" or water bird of any species, and gathered that this "ducking" practice meant something altogether different to the horrible pecking I had imagined.

Three pieces of wood were tied together, one of which was positioned between the legs of the man to which he was fastened very firmly. Another was for him to hold in his hands and the third was over his head separating the two ropes, to ensure that the ropes he was lowered on did not twist and harm him.

One by one these brave souls stepped forward and sat down into the makeshift chair. The bosun, John Gathrey, gave the command by his whistle and the first man was hoisted as high as the rope would allow. Then the rope was let go and the weight of the man plummeted him into the sea. Fortunately, the weather was fine and the sea relatively calm, or I feared these poor chaps would be drowned by this hastily assembled furnishing.

It seemed to me that John Gathrey left them in the water far too long before whistling the signal to raise them, as most were hoisted out spluttering and gagging, only to be dropped yet again and again until the customary three "duckings" were performed. I worried for my crewmen, yet my concerns were unfounded as even the most apprehensive chaps were deposited back on deck after their ritual, in the highest of spirits!

I was now aware of what "ducking" was, and banished the bullying, billed bird variety from my mind.

The boys, of course, were secretly the most unwilling, struggling playfully as the men pushed them into position. They held a bold demeanour in the face of their fears, as the taunting they would receive from the more seasoned seamen would be severe if they showed their fright.

After the first few lads had experienced the ceremony, the other youngsters relished the event, as their first equatorial crossing was a milestone in their careers at sea.

Their rations distributed to them, one and all laughed, compared their experience and slapped each other admirably for their bravery!

Down Mister Molyneux's list was Joseph Banks, his servants and dogs, Doctor Solander, Herman Spöring, and the rest of the gents!

These select few had paid for their escape from the "ducking" in brandy rations to avoid the indignity. I thought it a shame, as I looked forward to viewing the nobility in such an inglorious ritual. Having witnessed the twenty-five selected crew undergo this extraordinary tradition I attempted to move off toward a more comfortable spot for a snooze, satisfied that all was well and the event had been enjoyed by one and all.

"Just a moment, Fairweather!" yelled Mister Molyneux. "You, my fine feline, are the final victim!"

The crew roared their thunderous approval, and much to my disgust, not one stood up for me to offer their rations and have me avoid the sea! Fine associates they turned out to be! I could not charm my way out of this horrible fate, and as they were all quite drunk by this time, I seemed to be the highlight of the show!

Will Howson, one of Isaac's lads, grabbed me and holding me high above his head with little concern for my dignity, paraded me through the crowd to the delight of the crew. Uproarious laughter from my so-called friends did little for my spirit, but as my fate was determined, I held myself with honour and weathered the "ducking" with the spirit that was intended.

Will secured me to the chair and hoisted me as high as I would go. He paused for a moment and then down I went beneath the surface. I closed my eyes tightly and held my breath. All I could hear was the sea whooshing past my ears and the thumping of my heart within my chest.

Thankfully, Will had taken my size into account and not held me down there for as long as the men who preceded me. As I rose on the rope for my second and third "ducking," I held my head high and flinched not for fear that my status of brave ship's cat would be compromised. All cheered as I weathered the ritual with aplomb, and once released I was not forgotten.

John Thompson, my faithful provider, presented me with a saucer of milk laced with brandy. My good sense told me to leave it well alone, but as the crew looked upon me to join the merriment, I lapped up the mixture with gusto. Not too bad at all! Though I must say the effect it had on my sensibilities was questionable.

After briskly frolicking around the deck with the lads until midnight, wrestling the chickens and tormenting the bullock, I retired with my Isaac to sleep off my frivolity, with not another thought for "ducks" of any kind!

CHAPTER 12

A change of weather greeted us the next morning. The temperature climbed uncomfortably and a moistness filled the air. The humidity and lack of wind made man and beast weary. The crew were wretched enough after their day of whimsicality and the consumption of spirits, staggering purposefully about the decks attending their tasks, but with little vigour.

I too sported an aching head and sensibly avoided strenuous activity and sudden movement for most of that day. The merest thought of a mouse anywhere in the vicinity of my mouth made my stomach turn. Hence, I opted to shirk my duties and nap away from loud noises instead. Brandy, I thought for future reference, while heightening the spirit at the moment of consumption, should be avoided wherever possible.

The "doldrums" were upon us. This heat, humidity and insufficient wind to fill the sails impeded our progress. Lieutenant Gore had warned the captain and officers that these doldrums could last a week or more. He was skilled in the Pacific conditions having taken over command of the HMS *Dolphin* on its previous voyage when Captain Wallis was taken ill.

Mould covered everything from leather chests to boots. Mister Banks's books had to be wiped clean daily to avoid ruin. Anything made of iron became rusted, even the knives in the pockets of the crew.

Chester had recovered quickly from his injuries and although he walked with a limp, was by Lady's side whenever Tom Richmond exercised them gently. During the doldrums, neither man nor beast wished to be below deck with the temperature so high and not a breath of air to cool the body.

As we neared the end of October fresh gales came from the East and with them a change in the sea. By night, small flashes of light could be seen in the water. The scientists were particularly curious of their origin. The crew maintained that they were "blubbers," pieces of whale fat floating in the sea, but Mister Banks was determined to investigate. Some of the crew cast nets over the side of the ship and brought the catch on board. They appeared to be a barnacle of sorts but no one could explain the light they emitted. In such beautiful waters, all were content to merely admire the phenomenon as if watching tiny candles glimmer below in the sea.

Chester and I lay on deck quite late one night as Lady had retired to Mister Banks's cabin for the evening.

"Fairweather, old thing, you haven't by chance thought of some employment for me?" he asked.

"I have not given it much thought as yet, Chester. I have been quite busy below, what with the weather bringing the mice out in strength. I would imagine that even vermin feel the heat," I said in passing.

Chester looked a little disappointed but said nothing.

I quizzed him with interest as I knew him to be needing a purpose since our debacle during the storm.

"What are you good at, dear boy?" I began.

Chester thought hard, his brow furrowing. "Well, I walk with dignity and grace along the footpaths of London. Mister Banks and his friends often comment on my gait," he ventured proudly.

"Hmm, not so much a task as a talent," said I, tactfully.

"Yes, I see your point," he said, pausing further for thought. "I hunt a good duck during the shooting season."

The word "duck" still tormented me a little and I shivered uncomfortably.

"No, no, Chester, that simply will not do, we are in the middle of the Pacific Ocean! No duck shooting season here! And I will thank you not to mention the word 'duck' in my presence for the time being," I scolded.

Chester snickered. "I sympathize, old chap. Really, I do. Mister Banks thankfully paid our way out of that predicament. I must say I was impressed with your gallantry, though." He continued to chuckle. "I've not seen a more dignified response from such a waterlogged and distinctly shabby specimen!" He laughed, somewhat more heartily now.

I was incensed. Here was I trying to find an occupation for this hound, and all he could do was ridicule. I thought it time to put this chap in his place.

"Chester! I did not see you volunteer for the ducking, and paid off or not, you are in no position to criticize!" He stopped his banter forthwith, but I could imagine from his point of view my saturated condition, and could see the lighter side, so I let him enjoy the moment. I had, after all, tormented him enough since the storm. I too began to laugh heartily, and we both rolled about the deck chuckling as he remembered, and I imagined, how I must have appeared.

As we both lay under the stars with the stiff breeze filling the sails and ruffling our fur, we agreed that Chester's duty would have to be broached at a future time as sleep was fast taking the place of mirth.

Many days of good sailing and sunshine followed, the crew keeping up a good pace with the speed of our ship under such favourable conditions. Chester and Lady, when not exercising, lolled about on the deck awaiting my arrival from duty to join them for a doze in the sun.

At dawn on the 8th day of November, an excited cry aroused one and all from sleep.

"Land ho! Land ho!" came the excited voice of my Isaac, who had happily volunteered for watch on as many dawn shifts as he could, often trading duties with other rostered men.

On such occasions when he would disturb my sleep to rise before dawn, he revealed to me quietly that he wished to watch the sun come up across the sea and perhaps be the first man to sight land – always an honour!

This was his very first sighting and one and all rushed to the deck to catch the first glimpse of land in some time. As I manned the cathead, which was by now expected of me, distant mountainous peaks, their summits bathed in clouds, appeared upon the horizon.

Within two hours of sailing toward the once distant mountains a fishing boat became visible not far from the ship. Mister Banks and Doctor Solander were up and about by this time having bathed and breakfasted and took particular interest in the inhabitants of the craft within our view.

As we hove to and the captain greeted the fishermen, the gentlemen insisted on boarding the small fishing vessel to summarize the contents. There were eleven men on board, all Portuguese and nine of them black skinned, with an admirable catch. From what I could see from my vantage point, Mister Banks haggled with the master of the small craft for the purchase of their fish. Although Englishmen and native Portuguese spoke a language foreign to the other, they had come to some agreement as to the negotiations and our crew took on board an abundance of bream, dolphin and welshmen. These species of fish were a rarity to catch in the deeper waters we had sailed. Fresh and mouth-watering, one and all looked forward to their consumption.

"Mister Banks!" hailed the captain as they returned with the bounty. "This would be the fare for this evening's meal, would it not?"

"Why, yes, good captain, and at a fair price of nineteen shillings and sixpence!" crowed Mister Banks.

"Fine, fine!" returned the captain! "A wealth of fresh fish will please us all, but at the price in English currency?" he pleaded.

"I have it on good authority from the master of the fishing vessel, that English money does seem more preferable to their Spanish currency, as it buys more for them upon their return to port. I feel, however, we have purchased well and the abundance of the catch will suit us all for our meal this evening," he bragged.

The captain was satisfied but probed further. "Were you able to ascertain from the vessel's master our distance from the port of Rio de Janeiro?"

"According to the master we are south of Espiritu Santo and all but three hundred and fifty miles from Rio de Janeiro," reported Mister Banks.

"Just as is my reckoning!" confirmed the captain with much pleasure. I gathered that he was glad to have his own calculations verified by some local authorities. He rushed away to the Great Cabin to attend to his charts and make his notes.

That evening, John Thompson excelled himself with the preparation of the fish, all men enjoying the fare, myself included!

On the night of the 11th day of November, we rounded Cape Frio, east of Rio de Janeiro and by next morning we coasted along mile after mile of the purest white sand, which stood before the highest mountains I had ever seen, covered in lush green forests.

Sugarloaf Mountain stood like a tower, the highest of all mountains and was visible from the ship for days. We were still somewhat short of the river mouth and harbour as under the present conditions, the sailing had been slow.

On Monday the 14th of November 1768, we sighted the three peaks guarding the narrow entrance to Guanabara Bay and its islands. As we drifted inside the bay, Sugarloaf Mountain rose one thousand and three hundred feet above us, its summit in cloud, dominating the surrounding peaks as if an ominous giant stationed forever at the mouth of the bay to guard the Port of Rio de Janeiro.

As I manned my usual position at the cathead, I could not help but notice the fortification of this bay.

As we cruised through the channel to our left and right there lay forts of many and varied sizes. The first, a battery of twenty-two guns, followed by a fort of square stonework with bastions of cannon, then two batteries of five or six guns. Fort Lozio lay beyond; a stone hexagon of fourteen or fifteen guns. On the opposite side of the bay, the Fort of Santa Cruz made again of stone with two tiers of guns. As we negotiated the next two to three miles in from the entrance on the western side of the bay lay the Isle of Borghleone, a stone battery of seventeen cannons and six guns. Opposite Borghleone, the battery of Saint Dominica with seven guns and below a church at the Isle of Bon Voyage a battery of three guns. Then south of the city of Rio, Fort Isla de Cobras, a well-armed rampart, bastion and parapet. Overly guarded, I thought, compared to our previous ports of call!

Hearing the captain justify the weaponry to the gents and crew as we passed assisted my understanding.

Long had it been known that Brazil and the Port of Rio de Janeiro were the jewels in the Portuguese crown. Such an important port was the envy of every country and therefore suspicion ran high for fear that Rio would be invaded and Brazil captured. Jewels and gold were mined here. Common scoundrels and privateers were notorious for acts of piracy, theft, and smuggling, and our commissioned English ships fell under suspicion as spies. With their armed posts and garrisons, I could not help but think that this city was ready for anything!

The Castle of Saint Sebastiano loomed over the city, governed by Don Antonio Carlos Vicente Xavier Furtado de Castro de Rio e Mendoza. Such a lengthy name I had never heard! The castle maintained seven regiments of regular troops, and three regiments of militia, two on horse and one on foot. One-twentieth of the people were white men and the remaining black, but living free and not as slaves.

As was the custom in Brazil, no ship could gain entry to the Port of Rio without a pilot. The captain positioned the ship just above the Isle of Cobras, which lies before the city, and sent Lieutenant Zachary Hicks and Master's Mate Charles Clerke ashore in the pinnace to request a pilot's services in mooring the ship.

Expecting the pinnace to return with our officers and a pilot or *disembarkador*, the captain was angered to find that Lieutenant Hicks and Master's Mate Clerke had been detained on shore until it had been established that we were not mischief-makers, scoundrels, or pirates! Hence, our pinnace returned only with the disembarkador and the colonel of the Portuguese regiment accompanied by a ten-oared boat full of soldiers!

"What is the meaning of this?" demanded the captain.

The colonel puffed out his chest and spoke officiously. "It is by order of His Excellency the King of Portugal and the Viceroy, His Excellency Don António Rolim de Moura, that the captain is to come ashore before any man can step off the ship!"

The boat filled with soldiers boarded and circled the ship, and within minutes yet another boarded with several of the viceroy's officers. The senior officer saluted the captain and delivered the terms.

"His Excellency the Viceroy wishes knowledge of your purpose here before he will allow you to shore and release your men!" he announced in his very best English, but with a heavy accent.

"Very well," said the captain impatiently. "We are the HMS *Endeavour* on route to Tahiti to track the path of the planet Venus across the sun, by order of his Royal Majesty King George the Third of England. During our journey we intend to chart the waters, islands and the coasts of the continents, gathering specimens of the plants and wildlife for scientific study."

Whilst trying their best to understand, the Portuguese soldiers looked at each other suspiciously, as they had obviously never heard of such a thing.

"What number are your men and guns? What is your cargo? You English are not here for illegal trade?" demanded the officer, thinking that our mission was dubious as he did not understand the good captain's explanation.

Captain Cook took the senior Portuguese officers aside as their soldiers stood guard. He walked with them throughout the ship, explaining further our botanical, geological and astronomical quest, showing them our instruments and specimens. Though his efforts to clarify were great, these officers could not understand why the *Endeavour* had travelled all this way to look at plants, lands, and the sky.

Upon their return from the captain's tour, heated discussions were conducted on deck and finally the officer announced that the entire ship's company would remain on board for the duration of our stay, and only the captain would be allowed ashore with a guard to purchase provisions through an agent.

This declaration was by order of the King of Portugal and was not negotiable. All were quite disturbed to be confined to the ship for our visit, particularly the scientists who were keen to survey the land and collect specimens.

John Satterley, the carpenter, stepped forward. "With a long leg ahead of us, the ship will not heel over for an inspection of the hull, Captain Sir. We have a full complement of men on board. She is heavy and we need them off to take her on her side and clean the bottom!" he pleaded.

"We shall do our best to attend to her skin below the waterline, and in place of shore leave we must all do our best to make repairs." Despair crept into his tone as he admitted defeat.

As I followed him to his cabin for a consoling conference, much muttering and heated debate about the unfairness of our treatment was heard amongst the men. The captain did not speak to me whilst updating his log, but I sat by him for comfort, as I knew him to be feeling helpless.

The captain made arrangements to go ashore the next day, on the 15th of November. He was the guest of the Portuguese diplomat and Viceroy, His Excellency Don António Rolim de Moura, and was accorded full traditional courtesies during his stay at the palace.

The captain returned with our expensive but badly needed supplies, and had negotiated the release of Lieutenant Hicks and Master's Mate Clerke who were with him. All eyes pleaded for an opportunity to go ashore.

Mister Banks spoke up as the scientists assembled on deck. "Do tell Captain, were you at all successful in gaining us leave of the ship?"

"Alas, it is with loathing and against my wishes, Mister Banks, that we must all stay on board," he grumbled, as the crew stowed the provisions.

"I had hoped for more co-operation from the Viceroy, as the ship's bottom needs attention. I could not, however, convince His Excellency to allow the crew the run of the port as he imagines our journey to be either a foolish folly or a trick by our king to spy on the Portuguese."

The officers and seamen all quietly cursed this outcome.

Mister Banks was furious. "Nonsense, Captain, I will have none of this absurdity! There are forty other ships here in this harbour and we have observed them under no such restrictions!" proclaimed Mister Banks, as if he could make any difference to the situation.

"They are not English ships, Mister Banks, and by law we must remain here or risk arrest!" the captain barked.

The captain arranged for Lieutenant Hicks and selected crewmen to return to shore with notes from misters Banks, Parkinson, and Doctor Solander to the Viceroy, relaying their displeasure.

They had, however, gone ashore without the required guard, and when the lieutenant returned to the ship on a Portuguese boat under armed escort, and without his crewmen, he told of the seizure of the pinnace and the imprisonment of his crew.

We all worried for the wellbeing of the crewmen detained in jail. When they were further returned in the pinnace the next day under armed guard, they reported their wretched treatment. They had not been locked up for long, but all had gone without decent food and looked unwell upon their return. Of course, Mister Banks was inconsolable and stayed in his cabin.

For the next few weeks, a paper war erupted between the captain and the viceroy, over the treatment of our ship in this harbour. Our little boats were launched daily with letters from the captain to the viceroy. They were either returned unopened or answered in a manner suggesting that if the good captain did not like the terms of the Port of Rio, he and his ship could leave whenever they wished.

By this time, our captain was at his lowest, feeling like a prisoner aboard his own ship. Although he alone could go ashore at any time with a guard, he refused to do so in protest. To his honour, he preferred to keep the morale of the men in good shape as they worked at maintaining the ship while they peered longingly toward the shore.

These weeks were spent caulking the ship, heeling her over as much as was possible, and filling any gaps in the planking with a mixture of oakum, felt, horsehair, lime, linseed oil and tar to protect her from the sea on the long leg ahead. One could not escape the evil smell of this mixture and all were glad of the occasional fresh breezes. The sails were made as new, but not without incident. John Thurman, the new chap from Funchal, was punished with twelve lashes for refusing to help repair the sails.

My distaste for this practice was such that thankfully my duties below kept me from being witness to the event. I heard comment amongst the lads below that he was suitably humbled by such an outrage to his person, and in their opinion, John Thurman's disposition might be all the better for it. The lashings, it seemed, served to remind each man of their place and the rest of the crew kept to their orders.

The rigging and lines were restored to perfection. The coopers repaired the casks, the forgers restored the ironwork, and the ship was cleaned from one end to the other. Each and every man went about his duty with resolve to leave Rio de Janeiro as soon as we had made ready. I, too, was kept busy, making sure that any and all supplies were free of pests as they came on board.

On one moonless evening under the cover of darkness, and unbeknownst to the captain, Mister Banks sent two of his servants ashore to gather plants. George Dorlton and Tom Richmond, whilst appearing to know little, were sharp intelligent chaps with only their superstitions to impede their aims. I sensed they were not comfortable with this clandestine mission and their white eyes darted hither and yon as they quietly rowed to the shore well away from the main streets of Rio to complete Mister Banks's undertaking.

On their successful return, misters Banks, Parkinson and Doctor Solander spent the daylight hours examining and identifying their pickings. Not satisfied with the specimens themselves, the gentlemen wished to know their origin.

I happened upon these gents whilst on my patrol the next evening sneaking furtively out of the Great Cabin window at midnight. I jumped to the ledge as they were lowering themselves down a rope to a boat waiting below.

Mister Parkinson looked up at me. "Quiet, Fairweather! The ship's sentinel has no knowledge of this and I have dismissed Private Webb for the evening. I shall make your life miserable if you make a sound!" he hissed.

Well, I might be a cat, but I did not require threats to keep my silence. I knew them to be good fellows, in need of more resources than had been made available. I nodded in agreement and he winked his approval. I stood at the window, as the only watchman for this covert exploit. Someone had to keep an eye out for these fellows!

They returned hours later before dawn, armed with more specimens and notes. As they climbed back up the rope, I manned my station until all were safely on board. My deed did not go without recognition. Mister Parkinson ruffled my fur good-heartedly and knew that my lips would be sealed.

"Fine fellow, this Fairweather, Mister Banks?" he announced. "Kept sentry detail during our outing." But Mister Banks was consumed with his discoveries and merely added a distracted "Yes, yes," to the comment.

Again, the next night, Mister Banks ventured out, this time alone with his servants and before daylight. I was uneasy as he stayed ashore for the entire day and returned after dark.

Once again, I stood sentry, and Tom Richmond acknowledged my services upon their return. He knew his animals, and was thankful for my value as watchman. I followed them as they hurried to meet with the other scientists.

They were assembled in the Great Cabin under the reproachful eye of Captain Cook.

"Mister Banks, I will thank you to explain your absence this day!" he demanded.

"Good, Captain!" He bowed waiving his kerchief. "I simply took an opportunity otherwise neglected, to pursue my studies of this land. We could not leave without the required specimens and notes for the Royal Society. They would wonder with some concern as to my state of mind."

"On the contrary, Mister Banks, it is I who am most concerned with your state of mind. Have these last weeks not shown you that the Viceroy will not tolerate such behaviour? He thinks we are up to mischief and accuses us of being English infiltrators and you endanger our entire voyage with this unauthorised escapade?" The captain was in no mood for this recklessness with the Viceroy breathing down his neck.

"I cannot apologise enough, Captain, but I felt it imperative that we investigate the port further. I took every precaution to avoid detection, and we are safely returned with plentiful evidence." He begged.

"Very well, Mister Banks. I accept your reasons and your apology, but I request for the future that you will consult me before embarking on such dangerous pursuits, as you might have had us all sent to prison and this voyage terminated! Such a risk I am not prepared to undertake for the sake of a few plants!" warned the captain.

Mister Banks bowed. "You have my word that your orders will be obeyed herewith, Captain!" he said humbly.

"This issue having been put to rest for the time being, I am interested to be informed of your findings,'" requested the captain.

Eagerly Mister Banks related his accomplishments.

"I met several of the inhabitants who were rather civil, taking me to their homes where I bought from them stock for the ship, and tolerably priced. A porker, middlingly fat, for eleven shillings, and a Muscovy duck under two shillings," he announced proudly.

The captain nodded his approval as Mister Banks continued.

"The town of Rio de Janeiro in the capital of the Portuguese dominions in America. I apprehend it is named after the Roman Saint Januarius. It is well built after the fashion of Portugal, the streets all straight and intersecting at right angles. The citadel called Saint Sebastiano looms above the houses with many guns to protect the town."An aqueduct brings water from the neighbouring hills into a great square opposite the governor's palace. Obviously, many people gather there and it is well guarded."

"They have finely dressed churches with more ornaments than I have seen in Europe, and their daily processions to beg for money to maintain the church, and to pray, form at every corner of any street."

"All boys under a certain age, even gentlemen's sons, were obliged to attend. They wore a black cassock with a short red cloak, carrying a lantern atop a pole of six feet. The two hundred or so lights I saw one night from the cabin, made me think the town was on fire!" Mister Banks always embellished if he could.

"And we have all heard from here on the ship, they sang hymns, with all vociferation imaginable even though we lay half a mile from the town!" The gents nodded.

Chester, Lady, and I were pleased to know what all that singing was about. It was haunting and curious!

"The Governor and Viceroy seem to do whatever they wish without consulting their Council. Even unjust things, like putting a man into prison without a trial and not letting his family know, then leaving him there till he is glad to get out, not even knowing why he was put in there!" I thought this a little despotic, as did the captain!

"They have an unusual way of restricting their people to travel into the district where gold or diamonds may be found. The Viceroy changes the bounds every month and everyone must find out where they are for themselves, for if the people do not know the bounds and are taken by the guards they are imprisoned!"

"Not fair play, that!" I said to Chester who agreed whole-heartedly. Mister Banks continued.

"The townsfolk are Portuguese, Negroes, and natives of the country, some six hundred thousand of them. The natives do not live in the town but many of them travel here to do the king's work for little pay. Their skin is a light copper colour and they have long black hair but I was not able to learn more of them."

"I spoke to an English gentleman, a Mister Foster, who said that the military would knock a man down for not removing his hat in their presence! Consequently, everyone here is well mannered by force!" The gents were a little shocked but mumbled their approval as if England should adopt such a brutal system to enforce good manners!

"Thus, for the town, now for the country," Mister Banks continued. "Their sugar and tobacco are sent to Europe as they are very good. They have plentiful cattle but their pastures are devoid of grass and consequently the beef is cheap and so lean that an Englishman could hardly eat it. Cassava bread is made from tapioca and like sawdust to the taste. The European bread is exceedingly bad on account of the flour, which is made hot in the holds of the ships during its passage here from Europe. Their fruit production is prolific but tasteless. "The chief riches of this country come from the mines, which are far up in the country, but we could not determine where as the roads to them are guarded and the location concealed. Anyone found on the road without being able to give a good reason is hanged immediately!" Harsh punishment indeed, I thought. One would not find a Fairweather on those roads!

"Some forty thousand Negroes are imported yearly to work the mines, half of which die from the terrible conditions! They collect diamonds, topaz, and amethyst up to a determined limit, and then are not allowed back into the mines for another year."

"Plentiful species of fish abound in the river and the bay, the entrance to which is well fortified against invaders, as you know, Captain!" The captain nodded.

"I must conclude in saying that if Rio de Janeiro were in the hands of Englishmen, we would soon see more industry and commerce, as things are tolerably plentiful under the direction of the Portuguese, but I take them to be without exception the laziest and as well as the most ignorant race in the whole world!"

"Harsh words, Mister Banks!" challenged the captain.

"It is merely my opinion, Captain," countered Mister Banks.

He presented the captain with specimens of the flowers he had collected, which all confirmed to be more luxurious than those in the finest English gardens. The speculation among the scientists of their origin and genus carried on into the night.

The captain and I took our leave to make good the log, and attend to the final preparations for the next leg of our voyage. He made his judgement of Mister Banks's actions to me with a mixture of disappointment for his incautious conduct, pride in his findings, and judgement of the Portuguese.

At noon the following day, the company were assembled on deck for the punishment of three men. I had not seen nor heard of any disobedience to warrant such discipline, but then I had been rather busy with covert patrol duty, what with chaps stealing away from the ship willy-nilly and without permission.

Lined up to receive twelve lashes per man were Able Seaman Robert Anderson for attempting to desert ship, Private William Judge, Marine, for abusive language to the officer of the watch, and John Reading, bosun's mate, for failing to punish them both for their wrongdoing.

The captain attended as was his duty, but with his usual contempt for such cruelty. He gave the order to Lieutenant Gore to administer the customary twelve lashes. Each in turn gripped whatever they could and bit down hard on anything nearby; be it a length of rope or a cloth they had carried for the purpose.

I had seen this once before and did not wish to witness it again. I turned to the sea and imagined cheerful times as the cries of the men pierced the air. I felt shame that my comrades deemed it befitting to hurt each other, be it the code of the sea or not. I wondered if they would learn from their mistakes and steer well clear of the misdeeds that afforded such a penalty. As they were released and sent to the surgeon for attention, I feared it would not be the finish of the lashings.

I attended the captain in the Great Cabin as he composed a testimonial to the English Admiralty, reporting the trouble we had encountered with the Viceroy. He had arranged the missive's passage by way of a Spanish ship leaving Rio for England.

My poor captain grumbled and muttered as he drafted it, and I felt sure that the contents would not impress the naval authorities back in England.

"The king will hear of this!" he roared, striking a blow to the table where I was settled at his right hand, fairly frightening the life out of me! I knew him not to display his anger easily, but I understood that he had endured enough of this wretched port and his frustration had gotten the better of him.

After consoling me for his outburst with a decisive chin scratching, he purposefully strutted to the last longboat bound for shore. This final excursion, while delivering the captain's letter, was to obtain as much fresh beef and greens as could be acquired, with the water casks filled and our rum supplies replenished.

At dusk I stood my post at the cathead as the longboat from shore returned to the ship laden with the final supplies. Satisfied that the approach was successful and all who had left had arrived back safely, I ambled back toward the gangway to oversee the loading of the inventory.

Content with the progress and while scanning the cargo for miscreants of the vermin variety, two irregularities in the proceedings caught my eye. The rope thrown to the longboat upon its approach had been secured with ease, but whilst the crew went about the business of replenishing the ship, two dark figures seemed to scurry along the rope between the pinnace and the ship.

As custodian of the supplies due for storage, my mission was to investigate such an occurrence, but by the time I had doubled back to where I thought this incident had occurred, I was not sure whether I had imagined the sight as merely an hallucination. The dark figures had all but disappeared and frankly I was baffled! Apparitions of the size I had supposedly witnessed were peculiar to me and warranted immediate investigation.

Whatever I had seen was not dissimilar to a mouse in appearance, but I was quite sure the size of the intruders was unfamiliarly large, almost as much as my good self. I felt that I had best be vigilant about my duties and ensure that some unpleasantness was not to follow.

As the crew continued to unload the supplies from the longboat, the rope which had secured her broke and she had cast adrift still with some of our supplies on board. The crew managed to secure her tentatively but she had filled with water and all were concerned with the salvage of the longboat and her much anticipated cargo of rum.

The captain sent word to the viceroy of our loss and word came back that the longboat could be salvaged without incident. The pinnace was launched and our longboat was successfully retrieved with the rum on board but all other supplies lost. The crew were obviously delighted for the salvaged rum, the other supplies taking far less concern.

On the 2nd day of December 1768, a Portuguese pilot was requested to take us out of the Port of Rio de Janeiro, through the bay and out to sea. The anchors were weighed and all hands manned their posts. Every man was eager and all eyes were cast to their tasks. Not one noticed seaman Peter Flower, who had been observed earlier swilling much of the salvaged rum, make a clumsy slip in the rigging and fall overboard along with all the ropes he was attending.

Chester spotted the accident and barked loudly to attract attention to the port side at the location where the seaman had dropped. The nearest man to the area rushed to his aid, shouting for a rope but all spare lines were in service to the rigging, or had gone over the side with Peter Flower.

Chester continued to yelp and howl until Tom Richmond rushed forward, pulling him away by his collar. He strained at Tom's grip as if there were something he could do to help. Tom's strength won. Chester was pulled clear of the scene and silenced but for a helpless whining. The crew had come to aid and franticly tried to release the tethered longboat so as to facilitate a rescue, but the current in the bay had rushed Peter Flower far from the ship.

By the time the boat could be lowered all eyes had seen Peter Flower go down below the surface for the last time. The captain ordered the boat lowered and six strong men to man the oars, even though he sensed Peter Flower to be lost. The flow of the current was such that it could pull a man under and keep him there for hours until the tide changed, only letting him go at the ebb. The *Endeavour's* starboard anchors were set down and we waited until the search proved fruitless.

The longboat returned to the ship without Peter Flower and the crew in turn quietly congratulated the six hopeful rescuers for their attempt to save him. Hands were shaken, backs were slapped, but no words were uttered. Yet again, the sea had taken one of ours and the captain spoke as the men shuffled their feet and bowed their heads.

"We have lost our comrade Able Seaman Peter Flower, a good hardy seaman who has sailed with me above five years. For his service to me, and to this ship, I commend his body to the sea and his soul to Almighty God, in the name of His Majesty King George the Third and Mother England. May he rest in peace, and his family be comforted in knowing him to be a sturdy consort and a commendable sailor." All bowed in respect and quiet homage, with the exception of Chester who continued to whine softly.

I felt for him, as he must have been the last to witness the face of Peter Flower's panic as he fell to the sea below. I moved to his side for comfort as the men went about securing the longboat in preparation to set out of the bay again.

"Why, Fairweather, are the men not looking for Mister Flower?" he whispered in a stifled voice.

"The current is strong, Chester. I heard the captain say that he could be anywhere in this bay at any given moment. He may not even surface for weeks, or ever!" I tried to comfort him but I knew him to be feeling that not enough was done for the poor chap.

"I should have jumped in to save him!" he groaned.

"Nonsense, Chester!" I cautioned harshly. "I tell you, the current was too powerful. It would have pulled you to the bottom along with Mister Flower. One man lost is enough! There is no point in losing two of the crew!"

"Crew?" Chester gasped. "Do you really consider me one of the crew?"

"Why, yes, old fellow!" I answered affectionately. "No one would have known Mister Flower to be lost if not for your ceaseless barking!"

"Crew!" he said to himself. "Crew?" he continued as if he could not believe it of himself.

"Now cease this show of self-pity, Chester," I ordered. "You must promise me that before you go throwing yourself into the sea after drowning men, that you will take more notice of the conditions and listen closely to the captain. If he wanted men to jump in after Mister Flower, he would have ordered it so. He knows his business and you must heed his orders. Now pledge that you will do this!" I demanded.

"Very well, Fairweather, you have not failed me yet. I warrant upon this day, that I shall carry out the captain's orders to the letter as befits a dutiful crewman!" He agreed thoughtfully.

"Just as it should be," I concluded with a purposeful nod. I suspect Chester had far grander plans to promote his position than merely barking at men who had fallen. I would have to be vigilant when hearing his signature "man-overboard" call. I made note of its tone for future reference, as his progress must be monitored. I feared that without my surveillance and guidance he would most surely make a fool of himself, not to mention the possibility he may drown!

We waited at anchor in the bay through squalls, thunder, and lightning for the currents and winds to favour us until the 5th day of December 1768. All the while we scanned the waters for Mister Flower's body, which had yet to surface.

The crew tried to weigh the anchor but it had gotten well hold of a rock, common to this channel, and held fast. By the passing of twenty-four hours, the wind and current once more favoured us, the rock gave in to the anchor, and we hove to and headed higher up the bay, anchoring before the Isle of Bon Voyage.

On this 7th day of December 1768, the captain discharged the pilot and with him went the guard boat that had accompanied us at all times.

Just as we had dispensed with the formalities a thunderous blast was heard from the starboard shore. An odd whistling sound followed it and Chester and I braced ourselves, for we knew not of its origin.

"Cannon fire!" shouted the captain.

"Man the guns!" came the command from Sergeant John Edgcumbe. The Marines followed his orders and quickly loaded four-pound shot into the carriage guns to the starboard side.

"Hold your fire, Sergeant Edgcumbe!" ordered the captain. The men braced themselves as the cannon shot splashed in the water just short of the ship. Chester and I scurried to a safe vantage point where Lady joined us.

"What is happening?" she panted breathlessly.

"We are being fired upon," said Chester emphatically.

"What?" I quizzed. "What the devil does that mean?"

"The Portuguese are shooting at us, Fairweather!" he answered with authority. "You have not been shot at before this?"

"Well…er…no!" I admitted sheepishly.

"Keep your heads down!" he advised. "And stay out of the way!"

There was little to be said by either Lady or myself as Chester's instructions seemed to have merit, and his conviction left no doubt that he knew what to do.

"Captain?" shouted Sergeant Edgcumbe, awaiting further instructions.

"One shot, Sergeant. It is but a warning, but I require a company of Marines to go ashore with word of my displeasure to the fort commander and the viceroy!" said the captain furiously. "I will not stand for this attack upon my ship while attempting to save a drowning man!"

Sergeant Edgcumbe assembled and armed the required Marines under the command of Corporal John Truslove, his second in charge. They rowed quickly ashore while we waited.

"Chester?" I quizzed. "Are we likely to be shot to bits in this God-awful bay?"

He chuckled a little to relieve the tension.

"I doubt it, Fairweather. You heard the captain, did you not? It was simply a warning shot," he replied assuringly, but with a sideward glance at me as if to suggest that I too should practice my own advice and listen carefully to the captain.

Nevertheless, anxious moments followed until the boat was seen returning with our soldiers intact and a replacement for the drowned Peter Flower. Corporal Truslove reported to the captain, conveying the apology of the Fort Commander and relaying the assurance that we would be free to leave without further incident.

The captain welcomed aboard Manoel Pereira, a local Portuguese sailor keen for pay and adventure, as Peter Flower's replacement sent by the Portuguese authorities as an apology for their unwarranted attack upon our ship. He seemed an amicable fellow and no ill feeling followed him even though his countrymen had treated us with utter contempt.

The crew returned to their duties, secured the longboat, weighed the starboard anchors and made haste for the open sea. I took my usual position at the cathead, as we rounded the entrance to the bay.

The sun came out as if an apology from Rio de Janeiro. The stiffening breeze filled the sails and the crew sang heartily of the sea as we made south in the open ocean. As I gazed headlong into the distance, I had no doubt that man and beast would be glad to be rid of this port.

However, in the back of my mind was my essential investigation of the mysterious creatures that had boarded the *Endeavour* and vanished to some dark corner of my ship.

I joined my captain in his Great Cabin to attend his log. Not a cheerful companion on this eve.

"Fairweather," he sighed as I sat contentedly upon his chart table.

"A more pleasant and fruitful landing at Rio de Janeiro I would have wished for," he wrote some more.

"No opportunity to compile charts and maps of the Port, except to sketch most of the bay during our delays," he sighed.

"This, I fear, will only give an idea of this place." More writing.

"A captain and navigator's hell this harbour has been," he wrote long into the evening as I dozed.

The snap of his log closing disturbed my snooze and he gathered me up under one arm still speaking as if no time had passed at all since his last comment.

"We have a long leg ahead, the crew are set to watch, and my hopes for a safe rounding of Cape Horn and a more satisfying landfall awaits us." We retired to his cabin, he to relieve the tension that Rio de Janeiro had inflicted upon him, and I, simply to continue my nap.

CHAPTER 13

As we bore south, the temperature fell and the weather varied from the clearest blue skies to the most devilish of gales with thunder and lightning.

My *Endeavour* established herself as the sturdiest of ships and rival to every wave. We were in the South Atlantic Ocean and as the cold conditions set in, the captain issued the men with sturdy felt woollen jackets and trousers known commonly amongst the crew as "fearnoughts" or "dreadnoughts" to ward off the chills in their bones. He ordered the crew on shortened watches; no more than four hours' rest per man, which availed more lads for emergency service. With the ever-changing weather, the captain could not be too careful.

My duties became more difficult as the cooler weather kept the vermin tucked cosily into every nook and cranny. They did not eat as plentifully as during the heat. Now the cold had made them lazy and difficult to detect. Nevertheless, my constant surveillance proved to be fruitful and my position as mouser, never in doubt.

The large visions I had seen boarding the ship in Rio de Janeiro proved to be quite a different matter entirely. I found myself vexed by this incident. Had I imagined it? They could not be eluding my tireless investigations. I had accounted for every corner of the ship and by my calculation they were too large to hide with ease. Yet their shadows and sounds constantly haunted me. A muffled scuffle here, a spectral silhouette there! Only a hint of their existence!

I wondered whether I was suffering from a mysterious malady. Perhaps a few fruits and vegetables would be helpful in my own diet, although having sampled them on one occasion curiously, found them quite foul to the palate. My reasoning could not rule out the possibility that I had simply dreamed the boarding of large beasts by rope on the evening in question!

John Thompson, however, was of a very different opinion! Late one blustery afternoon, as the ship pitched and rolled toward Cape

Horn, I managed to round up several mice and made my way to the galley with my victims.

The cook was always pleased with my deeds and his rewards and flattery always made me feel appreciated. On this day, he worked in the galley with Henry Jeffs butchering chickens for the evening meal. Tom Matthews eyed me strangely whilst tidying after them. Their regard for me was not of its usual calibre.

"Yes, yes! Fairweather!" he muttered impatiently. "What of them rats? Big evil rats! A blight on my ship!"

Then his tone elevated to anger. His cleaver rose in his hand, and a sour expression contorted his face. Down came the hatchet on the heavy wooden table, splintering a sizeable chunk, and spitting it into the air!

"I've seen 'em! Right 'ere in the galley! You been lazin' about in the sun? Malingering with them dogs again? Captain gets wind of this and you'll be off the ship at the very next stop. That's if I don't pitch you over the side meself! Now get yourself to workin'. I want them diseases off my ship!"

"Here, here!" agreed Henry Jeffs, who only spoke when the need arose. "Lads 'ave seen 'em. Big as cats, they say!"

Tom Matthews grumbled incoherently except for the word "rats!"And with that, they turned from me in a huff and ignored my meagre mice.

As I skulked from the galley, my Isaac crossed my path.

"More mice, eh?" he said with pride. "Hand them over and I'll toss them over the side." He bent to scratch behind my ear and take possession of the catch. With sullen mood I dropped them lifelessly at his feet and snubbed his admiration. Isaac became curious of my disposition and made haste for the galley where no doubt the cook and the butcher would have enlightened him of my incompetence.

I was incensed! Rats? What the devil were they talking about? I had never heard of such a thing! They must have been partaking of liquor. I was the *Endeavour*'s mouser and they were talking of rats! As big as cats? And what of my ample catch? Not so much as a thank you! Vexed is the only word for it. I was truly vexed! They had turned on me. Liquor was the only explanation!

I made haste for Chester and Lady. I needed consoling and knew that they would help. As I searched the ship for my companions, it seemed that every man knew of these reputed rats.

"There he is, the mouser who can't catch rats!" came the taunts.

"Some cat, 'e is!" They laughed.

For the first time, the flush of embarrassment burnt my cheeks. Not that one could perceive it as my fur concealed the colour. I continued on, though, trying my best to hold my head high.

Chester and Lady were in their usual spot for'ard of the ship lazing about the gents' deck in the sun.

"Rats, Chester!" I pleaded. "What the devil are rats? I am expected to catch something I have never laid eyes on and which are reported to be as big as my good self. I have never been so insulted in my life! The cook! The butcher! My crew! Everyone knows of these things but I. What am I to do?" I huffed in panic.

Lady spoke calmingly. "Now, Fairweather, compose yourself. Have you by chance seen a shadow or two lurking about of late?" she questioned.

I thought for a moment and then all became clear! It was not fruit and vegetables I needed! I was not mad with disease! What a relief!

"Yes, of course! The phantoms that boarded the ship at Rio de Janeiro! I was sure I had imagined them. Am I to catch these elusive villains?" I said keenly.

"Why, yes, dear boy," scoffed Chester, questioning my sanity with one of his looks. "Cats do not only catch mice, especially at sea. I know for a fact that the Port of Rio has been recently overrun with rats. So much so that the authorities imported large numbers of cats to control the plague. I imagine that just such felonious escapees could have boarded our ship to vacate such a feline-infested port."

"Well, then, Chester! I think it best, as you are the expert, that you acquaint me with their appearance and habits so I might rid the ship of them and restore my reputation," I demanded.

Chester and Lady defined my quarry well, as a mouse-like creature the size of a cat, and wished me luck with my quest. With resignation, but a little uneasiness, I went about the ship searching for this scourge. I would not have my well-earned position sullied by rats, be they meek and frightened or fire-breathing demons!

Making my way to the nether regions of the ship, I encountered nothing. My senses were at their peak and every muscle strained to leap at whatever I detected. Scuffling was heard and shadows appeared, but as I reached each source no trace remained.

As we continued on toward Cape Horn, much uneasiness consumed the men. The cape was notorious for its foul weather and as we were buffeted by gales, thunder and the like, so too were we blessed with bouts of calm weather.

The captain continued to drill the crew in the use of small arms and the great guns. The caulkers drove oakum into the decks to preserve them from their battering by the weather and sea. All men were busy about their duties to ensure us safe passage around Cape Horn.

I continued my vigil below deck to find those elusive rats. Uncovering the odd mouse, I continued to attempt to impress John Thompson, but to no avail. He merely dismissed me with the contempt I apparently deserved for failing to rid his galley of the worst of all vermin.

I dropped my mice before every man on the ship, and although they threw them effortlessly into the deep, none were impressed and served to remind me that the larger variety was where I should concentrate my efforts.

I attempted to impress the gentlemen with my captives. Mister Banks waived me away with a flutter of his kerchief.

"Rats, Fairweather! We have rats! They gnaw at my precious leather-bound books as you sleep! Be off with you and capture the beasts!" He hissed.

Before this rat debacle, I had felt of some use, but now I was considered a failure amongst even my most dedicated friends. I joined the captain on many evenings leading up to the Christmas season. Even my devoted commander made reference to my doubtful abilities.

"Fairweather, whilst your company comforts us all, these rats are becoming a burden. I have seen them this very night in my cabin, and reports have come to my attention that my personal stores are invaded regularly by these pests. What are we to do with you?"

The captain, too? My shame was all too burdensome. I had relentlessly pursued those troublesome rats to no avail and whilst trying my very best to regain my self-esteem, no man would forgive my inability to dispose of the evil creatures.

Interspersed with my efforts to find these offenders and the self-pity that had consumed me, were the grand events of the voyage. None had impressed me as much as they should, as my spirits remained at their lowest.

Huge birds; albatross, as I had learned, circled our ship. As superstition would have it amongst sailors, the killing of such birds indicated bad weather ahead. Be that as it may, Mister Banks ignored the omen and shot a "giant wandering albatross."

To my temporary relief, this misdemeanour took the place of my own weakness and the crew held Mister Banks in contempt for his actions. Rumour was rife amongst the men that the consequence of his behaviour would be frightful weather conditions.

The mood became suitably downcast until Christmas Day as this superstition proved to be groundless by a demonstration of the finest weather. Mister Banks was forgiven his misdeed. I had wished to be so lucky!

By this time, I felt I had suffered as an outcast for long enough. I was determined to vanquish those villains and enjoy my first Christmas away from home. I rose early and set to the task at hand.

I picked up the unfamiliar scent of my enemy and followed it stealthily to the captain's stores, a small room in the under-most quarter of the ship dedicated to the storage of the captain's personal effects.

Creeping quietly into the darkened room I detected the smell of liquor and the sound of laughter. In a corner by the captain's brandy cask lay two huge mouse-like beasts, not quite as large as I had imagined, but intimidating enough! They lay on their backs, full to the brim with my captain's personal treats, the crumbs of which lay strewn about their vicinity. Upon observing me, they made no attempt to flee and after a pause, continued chuckling uncontrollably.

"Whatchew doing here, cat?" they said in unison, laughing more heartily at the coincidence that they should both speak as one.

"I am the custodian of this ship from the likes of you, and if I am not mistaken you have not only been into the captain's private stores, but his finest brandy?" I questioned with authority, having noticed the upturned bottle and the puddle of spirits they were consuming.

"Well, Paco!" said the larger of the two sarcastically. "We been catched, my brother, and by this foolish excuse for a cat. This calls for more drink!" And with that they burst into hysterical laughter, clutching their sides and rolling about.

"Juan!" said Paco the smaller rat. "You think he planning to eat us?" Then he buried his nose into the still-substantial brandy puddle.

"Nah, Paco, he no match for the Garbagio brothers!" mocked the larger rat. More giggling followed.

I thought quickly. These two demons were drunk. I planned my strategy based solely upon their disregard for my presence.

The brandy had made them more stupid and slothful than they should have been. I circled them in search of a suitable restraint. Their sheer size would not allow me to catch both without cunning. An empty sack caught my eye and with ease I distracted them from my purpose.

"May I introduce myself? Fairweather is my name and you are?" I asked nonchalantly.

The larger rat spoke up proudly. "Juan Garbagio!" He saluted and gestured to his kinsman. "My brother, Paco Garbagio! We be the Brothers Garbagio! Famous of Rio de Janeiro. Finest rats in South America!"

"Yeeha!" squealed Paco, proud of his heritage.

"How are you enjoying the captain's brandy?" I asked, manoeuvring the sack into the exact position for their capture.

"This is not the captain's brandy!" mocked Juan. "We 'ave been drinking our brandy!" And with that they exploded with laughter.

"Our brandy! Juan, you are so funny!" giggled Paco.

I continued to engage them so as not to arouse their suspicion, "I, too, like the odd nip. I am sure we can become fine friends. In fact, I have an extremely rare barrel of the captain's choice right here in this sack. Very potent. Perhaps you are not up to it?" I challenged defiantly.

"You know who you are speaking with, cat?" Juan asked bravely, and without awaiting my reply. "Juan and Paco Garbagio! Fine drinkers, finer rats, finest in South America! So fine you cannot catch us!"

"Yes," I yawned, "you have already enlightened me as to your name and notoriety, but I have yet to see you consume this fine liquor without falling over quite dead!"

The challenge had been thrown down. Disinterest in their boasting was now my strong point. If my calculations were correct their arrogance would get the better of them.

I sauntered purposefully toward the sack as if to partake of this potent brew. With a speed that became them in their present condition, they bolted for the insides of the sack to outrun me. Swiftly and expertly, I gathered the opening of the sack in my paws and twisted the edges around and around with my mouth until there was no escape.

"Hey! Juan! I see no brandy in here!" protested Paco.

"Cat!" yelled Juan. "What you doing? No brandy in here!"

Then silence for a moment.

"We are tricked, Paco," muttered Juan.

"No, he just playing with us, Juan. He want to be our friend. We give up, cat, where be the captain's brandy?" he whined.

"Your brother is correct, Paco, you have been tricked!" I scoffed. "Finest rats in South America? I think not. Finest mouser and rat catcher in all of England has you where he wants you!" I chortled.

I dragged the sack with the two intoxicated rats up the companionways and steps, banging their heads on each and every rung. Much cursing and protest came from the sack and I must admit, it was a heavy business!

As I made my way to the galley, my Isaac caught up with me. From the squeals of protest coming from my sack he knew what I had caught. He did not attempt to assist me with my heavy burden, as he was aware of the trouble I was in, and knew me to be a proud chap wanting only to personally deliver my prize to John Thompson, Henry Jeffs, and Tom Matthews. He cleared my path and the gathering crew looked on.

"Caught 'em, has he, Isaac?" they asked, bewildered at the sheer load I was dragging persistently to the galley.

"Make way, lads! Fairweather coming through!" demanded Isaac proudly.

Finally, I had reached the galley where my critics, John and Henry, were preparing the festive Christmas fare. Chickens, beef and fresh vegetables from Rio lay strewn about the kitchen awaiting John Thompson's magical touch. Isaac and many of the bewildered crew had followed me there.

I stood at John Thompson's feet panting but erect, and still holding the sack in my mouth, as under Isaac's strict instructions, none should take it from me.

"What's all this, then?" growled John Thompson, still holding a foul temper toward me.

Isaac stepped forward, arms akimbo, holding his head high. "Rats, Mister Thompson. Fairweather caught them in this here sack!"

The onlookers were speechless, as was Henry Jeffs the butcher, and as usual Tom Matthews. Isaac grabbed the sack from my mouth and shook it. Screeching sounds were heard from inside, punctuated by the odd hiccup from the drunken pair, but there was no doubt as to what lay within.

"Well, I never!" gasped John Thompson. "Cat with a sack full o' rats! I was expecting 'em one by one, but not both! And delivered in a sack no less! Is this me Christmas gift then?" He laughed and shook his head, looking down at me as I panted from the exertion.

All eyes looked upon John Thompson's expression. He went to the larder and fetched a jug of fresh goat's milk, poured it into his finest bowl and presented it to me without a word. He scratched his head in disbelief as I lapped at the offering, for my thirst was great after such a strain.

As the crowd dispersed, my Isaac simply grinned at Mister Thompson's bafflement. He took possession of the bag of vermin, threw them over his shoulder and made haste for the deck to dispose of Paco and Juan. With all his might he threw the two villains, sack and all far out from the ship to the sea and wiped his hands happily!

The cook, the butcher, Isaac and I knew somehow that I would not do without for some time to come.

As I meandered about the ship on this fine Christmas day of 1768, all men were in fine spirits and congratulated me with varied attentions; a titbit from the ocean, a scratch under the chin, or just a few words of praise. I felt that they had forgiven me.

The captain had ordered the duties relaxed and rum aplenty for this holiday. By the evening meal, not a man on board was sober. The crew, having set the ship for an easy sail, joined the gentlemen, officers, and captain, and all dined together this night.

John Thompson had excelled in furnishing a fine feast, not forgetting me, of course! Even Chester and Lady joined us and ate as well as I. Loudness and laughter burst from every corner of the mess. In the presence of the captain, the lads kept their heads as best they could. A painful task whilst so full of the *Endeavour*'s fine food and drink.

The captain stood and tapped his wine glass and the men came to silence.

"In honour of this holy day, we offer a silent prayer to our fallen comrades!" All bowed their heads in complete hush until the captain continued. "We praise the Almighty God for our safety and ask that our voyage continue to be protected by his hand."

"Amen!" came the response, and for the not so religious a hearty, "Here, here!"

The captain seemed to be a little intoxicated himself, unusual for this steadfast man, but in keeping with the jubilation of the day.

"Misters Thompson and Jeffs are to be praised for this accomplished meal!" slurred the captain. Glasses clinked, cups clashed and more rousing cheers rose from the heartily stuffed lads.

"More yet, lads. Quiet!" They hushed yet again.

"My final commendation is to the entire company of the *Endeavour*. We have had our moments, but a more skilful and loyal crew I could not have wished for!" He raised his glass to one and all.

By my observations, not a man present did not look upon our *Captain* with anything less than admiration.

"Upon the conclusion of our celebration, you may be dismissed to your leisure, unless the weather changes my mind for me!" he ordered leniently.

Rousing cheers went up into the night and the captain sat down for fear he might teeter. The gentlemen and officers shook hands and exchanged their wishes for the season.

With mugs of spirits in hand the crew took off to carry on their binge. Some played betting games in the stuffy quarters below, some fished from the deck pensively thinking of home, others lay hopelessly drunk and asleep where they had dropped.

Chester, Lady, and I proceeded to one of our favoured foredeck positions under the stars. The younger boys lay up there with us, intoxicatedly giggling and tussling and chatting well into the night of their hopes and dreams.

"Merry Christmas, Fairweather!" whispered Lady.

"Yes! Yes! Season's greetings, old chap!" said Chester, stretching lazily.

"And to you, my good friends!" said I warmly.

The dogs slept and I lay quietly, thankful for the good weather, for goodness knows what would have become of us with the men in such a drunken state. I pondered the wonders of the universe above me, shooting her stars across the sky for my pleasure alone, until I could stay awake no longer.

CHAPTER 14

As expected, the following day saw most of the crew suffering the ills of their excesses, but the welfare of the ship waited for no man and they carried on regardless.

Every day, Mister Banks and Doctor Solander caught something from the sea, or shot a bird for examination. Mister Spöring, as usual, took his notes.

As Doctor Solander relaxed one fine morning in the sun, dangling his baited line over the side, he was taken by surprise by a monster at the other end of his hook. The men rushed to his aid and joined in the struggle under the weight of the massive beast, cheered on by all on deck as the thin line strained against the huge fish.

"'T'is a whale!" cried one.

"Sea serpent!" bellowed another.

Men rallied to sweat and heave against the rail and bring it on board. Once the beast had cleared the sea, it lurched and jolted against the ship and the unfamiliar air. With much encouragement from Mister Banks, a huge female shark was brought aboard and cut open to reveal six young ones, one of which was dead.

"Nothin' but a fat ole' shark, with younguns in her belly," whined the men who had helped bring the supposed monster on board.

The scientists, not so disappointed with the catch, plopped the five remaining babies into a tub of seawater and they swam briskly while the gents took notes.

I ventured a sniff at this exhibition. Standing boldly with my front paws on the edge of the tub, I took a swipe at them, as cats will do. The small grey babies, whilst not as large as their mother, were the size of my good self, and held my interest thrashing about in the tub. I toyed with them brazenly until one of the blighters took a nip at my paw and would not let go! I wailed a painful cry and Doctor Solander ran forward to assist!

"Mister Banks! You hold the cat and I'll release his paw from the shark's mouth!" cried Doctor Solander.

Mister Spöring flapped his hands with disgust at handling a shark for the sake of a cat!

"I will do no such thing!" said Mister Banks with disinterest. "You, Doctor Solander, must hold the cat and I shall release him from the shark!" he directed. Mister Spöring nodded in agreement and hoped that he would avoid the loathsome task.

Such quibbling between these two, while I writhe in pain? This beast had me by the paw and continued to whip his body around the tub! It was all I could do to stay upright and not fall in with them.

Isaac and the boys ran toward the commotion and without question and released me from the shark's grip. Doctor Solander examined my paw, and determined that whilst bruised and probably painful, I was unscathed. Unscathed? I was incensed! I did not consider this to be the case, after having my paw in a shark's mouth while my supposed friends fought over who was to save me! Gents or not, I, the ship's cat, was in peril!

Isaac let me down to the deck and I hobbled in a circular manner to ascertain the damage for myself.

"He's alright," motioned Isaac to the other boys, satisfied that my paw was not broken. I hobbled away in a huff, turning to the gents to give them a stern look. The boys, too, silently showed their contempt for misters Banks, Spöring and Doctor Solander before taking their leave.

"I doubt, Mister Banks, that we will be in favour with Fairweather or the boys," confessed Doctor Solander.

"Pay them no mind, Daniel. Their disfavour will affect us little!" crowed Mister Banks with a waive of his hand.

But I knew the boys to be the most superstitious of the crew, and I was their good luck charm and saviour in the port of Funchal. Mischief would be brought upon the gentlemen for their bad form, and I felt sure that whether I wanted to or not, I would be made a part of their vengeance.

I know not of the fate of the young sharks, but had hoped that I would be eating a portion or two of the scoundrel that bit me, for my supper that evening was indeed a fish of a similar variety.

By the end of December, we had passed many islands and weaved between sandbanks and shoals. Mister Banks pleaded daily with the captain for a landing to collect specimens, but the mission of the ship to land in Tahiti was fundamental in the captain's thoughts, therefore Mister Banks's requests were denied.

On the last day of December 1768, with a change of wind direction, a blustering land wind blew thousands of moths, butterflies and insects about the ship as thick as clouds.

The men on duty waived their arms wildly to keep the pests out of their eyes and mouths, but they were so many as to make this practise pointless. Mister Banks decided that with the change of wind, his scientific luck had also changed and he wasted no time mustering all the men he could to his aid.

With the promise of rum, Mister Banks issued the crew with nets and set them to catching as many winged species as they could. Those without nets gathered handfuls and deposited them in huge corked bottles until the scientists could identify, categorise, and sketch them.

They swarmed about the rigging and clung to the sails and the sides of the ship. So thick were they that the colour of the *Endeavour* changed, as if a child had dotted her sails and hull with paints of varied shades and hues.

I stood by the captain as he chuckled at the sight of his men dancing all over the deck, swiping at butterflies.

"If another ship were to see us, we would be the laughing stock of the British Navy," he intimated to me mirthfully. "We must look a colourful sight!"

Mister Banks trotted around excitedly, giving orders and marvelling at the new species. Isaac and the boys joined in, cheerfully romping about and glad for a boyish game.

I, too, joined them in frolic, pouncing on the odd insect and leaping about in folly. I was quite pleased to chase something other than mice for a change!

Young Isaac Manly whispered to the others. "Here! Lads! We could do Mister Banks a mischief with some of these bugs. Get him back for Fairweather's mishap with the shark!"

My ears pricked to attention. The others looked impishly at each other and huddled together to form a plan. With some uneasiness I joined them.

It seemed that some of the insects were of the biting variety and most of the men had been careful in handling those, as their bite would cause a welt to appear and a damnable itching to take hold.

They had been carefully stored separately in a bottle of their own. Nasty looking creatures, black as night with a scarlet tail, a little like a large ant with wings and vicious pincers.

Will Howson, John Charlton, and young Bill Harvey made off with the bottle of stingers, as Isaac Manley kept watch. Privates Gibson and Webb were on deck enjoying the hunt with the rest of the men, leaving their posts at the gents' doors unattended and my boys to do their worst!

My Isaac scooped me up and we made our way to Mister Banks's cabin.

The boys had gathered there one by one so as not to arouse suspicion. Isaac and I were the last to arrive. Will and John were in a heated discussion as to where to put the biting insects.

"I say we bung 'em in his bed!" Will demanded.

"Nah! They'll do their worst in 'is clothes!" hissed John.

"What about 'is hat?" suggested Young Isaac Manly. "If they're in 'is hat they'll bite him square on the head!"

"Don't be daft Isaac," chided Will, "they'll just crawl out of his hat and fly off before he even puts it on!"

My Isaac broke up the argument. "Lads! Lads! Calm down. We must use these insects to their fullest effect! You are all correct, except for you young Isaac, for they will just fly off if they're put in his hat." He ruffled young Isaac's hair so as not to offend and directed him to keep watch at the cabin door.

Isaac thought for a moment. "We'll put them in his night shirt, underclothes, and in the bottom of his bunk. When he dresses for bed, they'll do their worst, and even if he gets them out of his night shirt and underclothes, when he slides into his bunk, they'll get him again!"

"Quite right, Isaac!" agreed the boys, nodding to each other.

They went to work on Mister Banks's bed first. Once they had removed the covers and decanted half the jar carefully into the bottom of his bed, they hurriedly remade it, carefully tucking in the covers to keep the insects from flying away or stinging them.

Then they laid his night garments on the bunk as if his servants had done so, tipping the stingers from the jar into the opened neck and arms of his nightshirt. Folding it just so, they ensured that none would escape.

"C'mon, chaps!" said Young Isaac. "We'll be caned if we're caught!"

"Just a minute, boys," said Will. "Doctor Solander and Mister Spöring are as much to blame for Fairweather's mishap. We've got a few bugs left. Let's get them, too!"

"Yeah!" they agreed.

"No, Will!" said my Isaac firmly. "If we get Doctor Solander and Spöring as well, they will surely know who did this. Do you not remember that evil scowl we all gave the gents after Fairweather's accident? Even you, Fairweather, gave them a look to kill!" he gestured to me.

Whilst I nodded in agreement, I could not help but think this tommyrot would be the undoing of these boys!

Will and the others thought for a moment. "He's right, chaps, they'll know it was us," said Will, shaking his head. The others groaned for they were caught up in the excitement of wreaking havoc on the gents, but they could see the sense in my Isaac's argument and complied nonetheless.

Young Isaac, still on watch, waved his arm in the door gesturing for us to be quiet.

"Let's go! Someone's comin'!" and with the empty jar under Will's arm we were off, each of us bolting in different directions so as not to be suspicious.

We met upon deck, resuming our hunt for butterflies and moths as if nothing had occurred. More stingers were gathered to refill the empty jar.

The boys crossed each other's paths many times that day, nodding approval and smirking in anticipation of the evening's entertainment.

It must be said that as a cat, the years usually seem to spill over uneventfully into each other, but life at sea gave reason for many celebrations and this evening of the 31st day of December 1768 was no exception. It marked the end of our first year at sea and all were as one in festivity. These milestones gave me a sense of time, as humans knew it. I felt, as always, like one of the crew and looked forward to these festivals.

As we had all come to expect from him, John Thompson exceeded himself with the evening menu, fit for yet another spirited spree. To see the end of 1768 and at midnight, bring in the new year of 1769, all anticipated a boisterous and bawdy evening. None more so than the boys, what with good food, rationed grog, and the anticipation of Mister Banks's comeuppance awaiting them.

I took my meal in the galley with John Thompson who had dismissed his assistant. He whispered to me of the wish for good luck to come as we headed for the Straits le Maire and Cape Horn. Such unsettling murmuring could not keep me from enjoying his charity and the atmosphere of the affair.

Once again, upon the conclusion of the banquet, our good captain rose to address the crew.

"Dear friends and colleagues!" he greeted, tapping a spoon on his glass for their attention. Noisome as they were, their civility was expected and a hush became them.

"Yet again we find ourselves in merriment on this, the eve of the New Year of 1769!" he certainly knew how to rouse them!

A raucous cheer went through the crowded room! The captain rendered them silent with another tap of his glass, and motioned the bowing of heads for a prayer. He also knew how to silence them!

"We are beholden to the Almighty God for his protection during our voyage. We ask that his guardianship continue as we make our way to unfamiliar lands. Again, we give tribute to our fallen comrades and wish their families well. For ourselves, we merely pray for your continued protection, the success of our mission, and your blessings upon our families at home." He took his seat, thoughtful of his own family I suspect, as were the rest of the crew for a moment.

I, too, thought of my mother and father, but a scattered chatter broke the silence and once again the revelry returned. I surmised that each man wished for the comfort of their loved ones but knowing this to be an impossibility, chose to reflect later during restful times, and not on this eve of freedom and jubilation.

Lieutenant John Gore stood and commanded the attention of the men. He held his glass high in toast. "To the Captain!" he shouted.

"Here! Here!" shouted the men. The captain nodded his gratitude.

Lieutenant Gore continued. "I need not remind you that the time-honoured tradition of sixteen bells will occur at midnight?" he questioned jauntily.

Rousing approval rose up around the room. "Eight bells for the old year and eight bells for the new! That is if you are still sober by midnight!" More roaring approval.

After the meal the men dispersed, chatting loudly about their hopes for the future. I proceeded to the deck to find Chester and Lady waiting for me.

We, too, reminisced under a cloudless sky, grateful for the good weather.

"Good night, Fairweather, my dear," yawned Lady as she and Chester retired for the evening. They dawdled off, heads down wearily to find a quieter place below.

By midnight, all the men were tottering about in the throes of inebriation, recalling funny stories of the sea and making jokes about the gents. Fairly irreverent, I thought, but with all the lads being full of the drink, it was not surprising.

A few scuffles broke out on deck as good sense could not hope to prevail, but were soon diffused as the atmosphere was that of jollity, not rivalry.

The boys wrestled and laughed and I watched from the foredeck.

The captain and gents arrived on deck with lieutenants Gore and Hicks for the sixteen bells. The lieutenant consulted his timepiece and with the first eight bells tolled, the crew shook hands and congratulated each other, boastful of a job well done so far. The old year was forgotten.

With another eight bells, they threw up their arms, hats, or anything else they held, in salute of the new year to come. It was now the 1st day of January 1769, and its significance to every man was not lost.

With that the gents retired to their quarters, as the hour was late. The most sober of our crew stayed on deck to tend the sails and sheets.

The Marines had retired for the night except for Private William Judge who was unsuitably intoxicated and snoring at his post.

The boys would not sleep yet, as they knew Mister Banks would soon bed down for the evening, promising a prank to surpass anything they had concocted to date. Their excitement kept them awake and at the ready. I sauntered over to the lads, now crouched around a knothole in the timber decking.

Mister Banks's cabin lay just below the deck adjoining the Great Cabin. My Isaac picked at the knot with a knife produced from his pocket, whilst the boys whispered and tried not to giggle.

"C'mon, Isaac, hurry up and pull out the knot so we can see in!" Will spat. "You're takin' forever!"

"Patience, Will!" hissed Isaac, the boys sniggering behind him. "'Tis a delicate job and if Mister Banks hears us there'll be strife!"

"What are you boys up to?" demanded Richard Pickersgill, a rowdy young Yorkshireman recruited as master's mate, studying astronomy when time allowed.

He and Edward Terrell, the carpenter's mate, had become close friends as they were of the same age of nineteen years. Not much older than my boys, but they held higher office and misused the privilege whenever it suited them.

The boys stood upright, their guilt not quite hidden by their innocent faces.

"Nothing, Pickersgill. Just…err…inspecting the deck!" Isaac replied boldly. The other boys mutely nodded.

Edward Terrell walked around the gathering, his hands behind his back, inspecting each suspicious face. "I think these chaps may be telling whoppers, Richard!" he mocked.

"Do tell, Edward! Shall we report them to the captain? Or are they going to let us in on this mischief?" Richard and Edward, smelling strongly of liquor, were enjoying taunting the boys.

"Leave off, Pickersgill!" Will Howson stood defiant. "You're both three sheets to the wind. Captain wouldn't give you the time of day, except to lock you both up for a few days!"

"Yeah!" Isaac needled the older chaps. "Who's the captain going to believe? You? Or us blameless youngsters who, after all, are gainfully tending to the decking?" The boys displayed their purest of wide-eyed expressions as an example of what the older boys would be up against in a trial before the captain.

Not wanting to back down from the challenge, and trying to maintain their seniority, the older boys eyed each other cleverly.

"I have a solution to our quandary!" boasted Edward, puffing his chest out pompously. "Let us in on this lark, Howson, and if it piques our interest in an entertaining manner, we'll not breathe a word."

My boys looked cautiously at Isaac and Will for guidance.

"Swear on it!" demanded Isaac.

"Yes. Yes. Alright," sighed Richard, pretending to be bored, but the sheer secrecy between the young boys had kept him intrigued.

In a huddle, Will Howson whispered only the barest of details to Edward and Richard, while Isaac went back to loosening the knothole in the deck. The knot finally gave way, and out it popped just in time.

Mister Banks had finished his evening brandy with the captain in the Great Cabin, and was retiring to his quarters.

Will hushed the lads as they huddled in closely to take turns at peering into the hole at Mister Banks below. I was certain from the muddle of bodies around that tiny peephole, that I would not be able to witness my own revenge.

I mused for a moment and then all became clear. These boys had to hide in the dark and squint through a hole to view the coming attraction, but as the ship's cat, I could attend the event in plain sight and would be suspected of nothing! What luck! With that I bolted for the companionway and on to Mister Banks's cabin below.

I loitered unobtrusively around the Great Cabin, where the captain was discussing our impending rounding of Cape Horn with lieutenants Zachary Hicks and John Gore. They were heavily engrossed in their maps and charts and though they bid me a good evening, were not surprised to see me, as my nightly chats with the captain were now of common knowledge.

The door to Mister Banks's cabin was slightly ajar and I positioned myself on the captain's chair to have an unobstructed view of the proceedings. I could hear scuffling overhead from the overly excited boys and hoped they would quiet down somewhat or risk detection.

Mister Banks's hummed a happy tune, what with the specimens he had gathered and the brandy he had enjoyed with the captain. Occasionally, he mumbled a curse upon the noisy crew above for fear that they would keep him awake. Little did he realise that most of the crew were passed out drunk, and the bustle above him were my lads bent on revenge.

He disrobed carefully, in the small dimly lamp-lit room, folding and positioning his clothing delicately for wear the next day. He washed in the small bowl of fresh water left by his servants and dried his face and hands on a cloth. He quickly put on his nightshirt and turned to latch the door. I saw him square on, and the look upon his face was worth a thousand shark bites!

"Ahhh!" he screeched like a mad old fishwife! So girlish was his voice I hardly believed it had come from him! He reminded me of the cook at my home, when mice had overrun her pantry!

"Ahhh! Ahhh! Help! I am bedevilled by an evil thing!" he ranted.

The captain and the lieutenants rushed to his cabin door.

"Are you alright, Mister Banks?" ventured Lieutenant Gore.

"No, I am not alright! Ahhh!" he continued. The biting had begun. "Come here, you fools, and help meeee!" Mister Spöring arrived in his night attire having heard Mister Banks's squealing.

"Mister Banks! Mister Banks! Whatever is the matter?" he cried.

"Ahheeeee!" came another squeal from Mister Banks, sending Mister Spöring cowering to a corner for fear he might catch whatever ailed his obviously maniacal mentor.

The captain and lieutenants opened his door fully, to reveal him jerking and writhing, thrashing and slapping at his body.

Mister Spöring gasped from his corner. "What has become of him?" he whimpered, clutching at the neck of his nightshirt.

I could hear the boys still shuffling above for a glimpse, but was quite sure that the captain and officers would not hear them above Mister Banks's ruckus.

"Good God in heaven, man! What are you doing?" questioned the captain, unsure of his scientist's sanity.

"Get these blasted beasties off my person! Ahhheee!" he squealed.

The captain and lieutenants looked at each other quizzically. They could see nothing and were not sure of what he meant.

"The night shirt?" ventured Lieutenant Gore sceptically.

"No! No! You imbecile! Ahhh! This hellish infestation within my night shirt! Eeeh! Ahhh!" he wailed, still hopping and slapping uncontrollably at his body.

Lieutenant Hicks leapt forward, uncertain as to whether Mister Banks had gone mad, and tried to calm him.

"Now there, dear fellow. Keep a level head and explain to us why you suffer so?" Lieutenant Hicks spoke in a soothing voice.

In his frenzy, Mister Banks slapped him square across the chin sending him reeling across the tiny room where he cracked his head on the scientist's desk and swooned from the pain.

The lieutenant escaped before the other flailing hand could do its worst. The captain and Lieutenant Gore caught the injured Hicks as he stumbled from the tiny cabin, blood streaming down his face from the wound upon his head.

Mister Spöring stayed glued to his corner in fear.

By this time, the astronomer Charles Green, and the naturalist Doctor Solander had arrived on the scene. Their cabins adjoined Mister Banks's and the commotion saw them rush from their beds to the source, bleary-eyed and confused.

"Ah, Doctor Solander!" the captain thought quickly. "Accompany Lieutenant Hicks to the surgeon's quarters for treatment to his wound." Doctor Solander gathered up the swooning Hicks and they stumbled away as requested. Doctor Solander looked back dumbly as he had not the faintest idea of what had occurred.

Mister Green stood by, caring little for the health of Lieutenant Hicks or poor Mister Banks, as was his way.

"My sleep has been interrupted, Captain! What is the meaning of this?" Mister Green demanded. He had taken heavily of the drink early in the evening leaving one to wonder if this was the ideal fellow to help the captain with Mister Banks's condition.

The captain decided to take matters into his own hands.

"Mister Green! Your sleep has been disrupted by the obvious distress of a fellow in need. Mister Banks requires our help, and you are to assist me until he is at ease! You and I shall enter his cabin and relieve him of what ails him!" The captain ordered, leaving no room for argument. Mister Green nodded dutifully and accompanied the captain to Mister Banks's aid.

Mister Spöring nodded dumbly also, still clutching his nightwear and thankful to be excluded from the task at hand.

From my vantage point, poor Mister Banks was still yowling in the midst of his contortions and demanding relief from his demons. The captain and Mister Green readied themselves and made haste for the door. Mister Banks had managed to take off his infested nightshirt and escape from the infernal stingers, but was still scratching and swatting at the flying beasts.

The captain and Mister Green approached him warily.

"Good Lord!" cried Mister Green. "What has become of you, Banks? Are you mad?"

The captain assessed the plague of flying, biting insects and dragged Mister Banks out of his cabin and into the airiness of the Great Cabin.

He seated the quivering Mister Banks, and throwing open the windows, he allowed the beasts to escape into the night, leaving a few to flutter aimlessly at the lighted lamps.

Mister Green followed having seen the infestation for himself. He and the captain inspected the welts and redness of Mister Banks's exposed skin.

Upon seeing his mentor's damage and the remainder of the pestilence buzzing about looking for escape, Mister Spöring let out a shrill cry and made haste for the safety of his own cabin, no doubt to inspect every nook and cranny for similar creatures prior to his own retiring.

"Mister Green, would you be so kind as to fetch the surgeon," asked the captain.

Mister Green stood firm, the whole episode being a test of his patience.

"The surgeon will be attending Lieutenant Hicks, and as Mister Banks looks to be in fair shape, I would prefer to return to my bed, thank you, Captain," said Mister Green confidently, thinking that if Mister Spöring had escaped this chore, so might he!

The captain was incensed by this selfishness. "Mister Green!" he barked. "Attend to my orders immediately!"

"But…" stuttered Mister Green.

The captain gave him such a look as to leave no room for argument and Mister Green sauntered away grudgingly, mumbling incoherently to himself.

The captain poured Mister Banks two stiff brandies hoping to calm him a little.

"Bitten me they have, Captain!" he slurred pitifully, whether from the shock or the brandy, I did not know. Tears escaped his eyes and he shook uncontrollably.

"Yes! Yes! Mister Banks, I am aware of what you have suffered," soothed the captain. "Doctor Monkhouse will be here hastily to attend to you."

"Bitten me savagely!" he continued, calming somewhat but scratching at his reddening skin.

Mister Green arrived with Doctor Monkhouse, fresh from tending to Lieutenant Hicks's damaged head.

"What is going on here, Captain?" asked the doctor. "Hicks has a nasty wound to his head, which I have patched as best I can, but he insists that Mister Banks is to blame! Mister Green has only given me sketchy information regarding some kind of madness that has consumed Mister Banks!"

Suddenly, Mister Banks convulsed yet again with the itching. Witnessing this fit first-hand quite shocked the doctor and his tune change somewhat.

"Great Heavens, Captain! Banks is unquestionably experiencing a conniption of some kind!" Then he noticed the huge red welts on Mister Banks naked flesh.

"Banks! You have been bitten!" he announced. "By what?"

"Blast you, Monkhouse!" screeched Mister Banks. "Never mind what! Get me an ointment or I shall certainly go mad! Eeeh! Aaaah!" He sprang at the doctor only to be held back by Mister Green who unceremoniously plopped him back down on his chair, for fear he might give the doctor the same treatment he had bestowed upon Lieutenant Hicks.

The captain stepped forward. "Mister Banks has been bitten by stinging insects, Doctor Monkhouse. I would be obliged if you would treat him, as he is in much distress. I have given him brandy in an attempt to calm him."

"Give him more, Captain! If it will soothe his demeanour prior to my return, he will most certainly be easier to attend to!" said Doctor Monkhouse with authority, and with that he turned quickly toward his quarters for medical supplies.

Mister Banks's torment persisted with his agitated scratching and writhing, while the captain decanted large mugs of brandy for Mister Green to administer. He gurgled them down, one after another until he was quite silly.

Doctor Monkhouse returned with a soothing salve and daubed him liberally with the pinkish coloured paint. By the time every welt had been treated, Mister Banks appeared a comical sight, snivelling from the irritation and teetering on his chair. He had calmed significantly under the care of the doctor and the large doses of medicinal brandy, so the captain ventured an inspection of Mister Banks's cabin.

Investigating tentatively inside the cramped room, he heard the unmistakable shuffling and sniggering from the young boys above. He knew that something of mischief was afoot!

The boys could see their captain through the knothole below swatting at the odd lingering insect, and quieted themselves as best they could.

The captain searched the cabin from top to bottom as the lads tried to be silent above. He noticed the opened knothole above him and as he moved about Mister Banks's belongings, he kept one ear pricked and one eye out for discernible signs of the culprits he knew to be overhead on the deck.

If a prank had been concocted upon Mister Banks, he would have to leave no stone unturned to find his evidence. After inspecting, every nook and cranny for signs of further irregularity, he finally pulled back the covers of Mister Banks' bedding only to reveal more of the same biting insects.

They flew at the captain with a vengeance, having been confined to Mister Banks's bunk for some time. The captain had the sense to recognise the imminent danger to his person and flee the cabin, shutting the door behind him. He called for Richard Pickersgill and Edward Terrell, who were intoxicatedly enjoying the proceedings from above.

The other lads feared for their skins.

"Damn you, Pickersgill!" threatened my Isaac, having heard the captain's beckoning. "If you breathe a word of this to the captain, I shall devise a plot against you so hellish that you'll wish you had never been born!"

"We're with Isaac!" motioned the other boys.

"Yes. Yes. I assure you that your innocence will be established if we are questioned," he nudged Edward Terrell.

"To be sure, we speak the truth," Edward concurred.

Terrell and Pickersgill hurried to the captain's aid but my Isaac was not convinced.

"Those two are trouble, lads. I am not sure that they can be trusted to keep our secret," he said with suspicion.

"Nah!" chimed the boys. "They won't let on. They promised!"

"Be that as it may," warned Isaac, "don't be surprised if they give us up to the captain if it saves their own hides!"

The boys continued their turns at peering through the knothole. With my Isaac's words troubling their minds, they watched silently below.

I remained seated and aloof in the Great Cabin so as not to attract attention to myself and swatted carefully at the odd insect still buzzing around the lamp.

The captain gave Mister Green permission to take his leave. He returned to his bed still grumbling of the inconvenience.

Doctor Monkhouse continued to daub linctus to the welted skin of a much-quieted Mister Banks.

The captain and doctor then cleared the remaining insects from Mister Banks's cabin and promptly escorted him back to his bed. Mister Banks swooned and staggered, covered in pink paint and sloshed from brandy, until he collapsed on his bunk whimpering.

"If you will, I shall return to Lieutenant Hicks now, Captain. I wish to look in on him before I retire," said Doctor Monkhouse. "He sports a nasty gash and must be attended regularly."

"Yes! Yes! Of course, Doctor," said the captain and with that Doctor Monkhouse left us.

Pickersgill and Terrell entered and stood to attention as the captain addressed them.

"Clear this room of dead insects and spilled brandy men, and when you have finished have the younger boys report to me immediately," ordered the captain.

As they cleaned and tidied the Great Cabin, Pickersgill and Terrell exchanged shifty grins, knowing that my boys were for it.

The captain approached me and I started not a little!

"Hmm…" was all that went past his lips as he looked askance at me.

Did he know of my involvement? How would I defend myself? I purred and rubbed against his elbow in an attempt to gain favour. He ignored me. I felt rather awkward and sat in a huff, awaiting the boys' arrival.

It was not long before the younger boys dawdled to the captain's quarters escorted by Pickersgill and Terrell.

"You're in for it now!" hissed Pickersgill, as he and Terrell hurried them along from behind.

"Captain knows you are to blame for Mister Banks's troubles!" warned Terrell, nudging his cohort.

"And how would he know such a thing if you have not reported us?" asked my Isaac with contempt for his older crewman.

"We wouldn't have done such a thing!" he sang. "We promised!" Pickersgill giggled.

They entered the Great Cabin, and gathered as one they fronted their captain.

Pickersgill and Terrell took their places behind the captain. The smirks upon the older boys' faces gave them away as the traitors they most probably were.

"I suspect a sinister plot against Mister Banks. Hatched by you gathered before me," said their captain with a wary eye.

"Have you anything to do with this mishap?" he questioned, noting the expression on each boy's face for signs of guilt.

"No, sir, Captain sir. We have no knowledge of Mister Banks this evening. We thought he had retired for the night some time ago," announced Will convincingly.

They all nodded as the captain's eye examined the group. He paced up and down before them.

Isaac Manly, the youngest of them, had been holding his tongue and his breath for some time. His face reddened with lack of air and he began to quiver with weakness. All at once his breath exhaled and with it the entire story, as if his very mouth had exploded!

The boys looked at each other and at poor young Isaac, who had by now dissolved into a flood of hiccupping tears.

Pickersgill and Terrell grinned from ear to ear as the captain's face became stern and unforgiving.

"Is this true, young Manly?" he asked with little compassion. All Isaac Manly could do was nod.

The other boys stood, shocked at young Isaac's outburst and trying hard not to appear afraid. One by one, the other boys were questioned by the captain. No thanks to young Isaac, they now had no choice but to admit their involvement.

"Will one of you scoundrels step forward and inform me of the reasoning behind this mischief?" he asked impatiently.

Will Howson pushed my Isaac forward, knowing that the captain would be more forgiving toward him than the other boys, as he was the captain's own apprenticed surveyor and a member of his family. Isaac stumbled into position, sneering at Will over his shoulder, and stood to attention.

"Well, Isaac Smith, you have come forward to volunteer information concerning this incident?" prompted the captain.

"Captain, sir, yes sir!" he stuttered, looking to the other lads for support. They merely nudged him from behind as if he should know just what to do.

"I await your explanation!" said the captain, settling into a chair as if he planned to wait forever, until the boys gave up their every secret. It was obvious to my Isaac that they would be detained until the entire truth was revealed.

"Well, sir, Captain sir, you see…Mister Banks let Fairweather be nastily bitten by a baby shark taken on board this very day," stammered Isaac.

"And what, pray tell, has this to do with the stinging insects in Mister Banks's quarters?" asked the captain calmly.

"Well, sir, Mister Banks refused to help Fairweather out of the clutches of the shark!" he explained, gathering confidence.

By now, the captain was tiring of prompting the reasoning for their actions.

"Spit it out, Isaac! I have had enough bother for the evening and the hour is late! We have the cape to navigate and it annoys me greatly to press you for the facts!" he hissed impatiently.

"Yes, sir!" pledged Isaac, while gathering his thoughts for a convincing explanation.

"The lads and I thought it only fair that the gents be punished for letting Fairweather suffer the awful ordeal of being bitten by the shark. He was injured and we were pressed into his service following the disinterest of misters Banks and Spöring and Doctor Solander when Fairweather was in need! That shark could have bitten his paw right off, if we had not come to his aid!" The boys thought this is fine excuse for their actions and nodded their assent.

"A fine and noble attempt to release yourselves from guilt, I must say!" affirmed the captain.

The lads relaxed a trifle as they thought their captain to be of the same opinion. I pretended to be asleep but kept one eye poised on the group, should I be summoned to testify on my own behalf.

"However!" he roared, frightening the life out of the somewhat relaxed boys. I, too, was stricken but tried to maintain my calm in light of the captain's change of tone.

"It is not your place upon this ship to exact revenge, nor is it your place to punish gentlemen!" There was no doubt as to his conviction.

Terrell and Pickersgill had stood sneering behind the captain while my Isaac attempted to excuse them from their misdeeds, but quite suddenly he turned upon the prudish pair to his rear.

"You two elder chaps have had a hand in this! If not to fail to report this mischief to me before Mister Banks became their victim, but also to add to your accountability, I feel that you enjoyed the escapade with as much vigour as these less prudent boys!" accused the captain.

"Begging your pardon, Captain, but we were not aware of this misbehaviour until your orders to secure the culprits were dispatched," whined Dick Pickersgill.

"Captain, sir…" interrupted young Isaac, still sobbing from his outburst. "It's not true, sir! The older boys were there on deck with us enjoying the trickery. They were full of the drink and thought it a great lark!" He whimpered.

My other lads saw the merit in sharing the blame with these two, as Pickersgill and Terrell were quite prepared to let the younger ones accept the entire burden and consequent punishment. They stepped forward and nodded their approval of the report.

"Is this so, misters Pickersgill and Terrell?" asked the captain, knowing full well that they were amongst the culprits.

They looked at each other for an escape, but neither could summon an answer.

The captain did not wait long before he continued. "Upon your lack of response, I shall assume that the boys tell me the truth, and for your part in this crime, you will join them for an appointment with the cane!"

My boys knew of their fate before the sentence was passed, but Pickersgill and Terrell were astounded that they would be joining the boys in such a childish penalty.

They merely stood before the captain, outraged at their pending punishment.

"But captain, sir!" moaned Pickersgill. "We had no part in this scheme. Should we be punished along with these vile boys?"

"You have two choices as I see it, Mister Pickersgill!" he contemplated, tiring of their arrogant manner. "You may join these boys in an encounter with the cane, or you may choose twelve lashes. If you insist upon displaying your seniority over these lads, when I know full well that you have both been party to this violation, then twelve of Lieutenant Gore's best will not faze you in the least!" he concluded.

Edward Terrell stepped forward, giving his accomplice a sour look.

"Captain, sir, we confirm your allegations, and admit that our judgement would have been better served by chastising the boys, instead of encouraging them. For our offence, we accept the punishment of the cane in preference, and hope that you will accept our heartfelt apology. Our foolishness will not be repeated," he implored.

Pickersgill gazed hesitatingly at Terrell, thinking they could have avoided all manner of punishment, but as the captain had made it perfectly clear that they were for it, one way or another, conceded that the cane would be surely more tolerant than twelve lashes.

"Very well!" said the captain, satisfied that the truth at last was revealed, and the punishment determined.

"I shall send for Lieutenant Gore. He will administer your penalty tomorrow upon deck, and in the light of day, for the entire company to witness. Mister Banks deserves your admission of the crime and an apology. I shall see to it that you are summoned to his service whenever he sees fit, as you have much to make up for. Let me never see this impertinence from you again, or the consequences shall be dire! Now be out of my sight!" he concluded with displeasure.

The boys marched from the room silently with their heads bowed in disgrace. Outside I could hear them lamenting as they moved on. The captain turned to me, as we were now alone.

"Fairweather, my friend, you have many allies upon this ship, do you not?" I sat up straight and proud as the captain moved toward me.

I thought I, too, would be punished and was determined to accept my fate like a man. Instead, he scratched behind my ear and sat in his favourite chair sighing wearily. I accepted his affection and listened to his thoughts while he prepared to update his log.

"Wretched boys!" he stated, shaking his head. "They have disappointed me this day. It pains me to punish them, but it must be so, or they will have run of the ship and all manner of havoc will occur!" he resigned himself to his decision.

"With Cape Horn ahead this week forward, and the tides preparing to thwart our progress through the Straits of le Maire, I have enough to occupy me! Their timing could have been better. Wretched boys!" he grumbled.

I sat beside him as he wrote his words in the log, then the depths of the sea and times of the tides to calculate a clear path through the Straits of Le Maire.

From his charts I gathered that these "straits" were some kind of passage around the tip of Cape Horn, and from his furrowed brow, I supposed it to be perilous. He wrestled with his thoughts.

"If my estimations are correct, Fairweather, old friend, we are in for a troublesome passage through these straits," he sighed.

"May the Almighty guide my hand on the morning tide and bless us with favourable conditions." He rose from his chair and with a stretch and a yawn from both of us present he bid me goodnight and shuffled to his cabin.

"Do stay away from sharks!" he said over his shoulder wearily. I vowed to do so quietly to myself as he had spared me from penalty.

I felt that young Isaac would need comfort and made my way to his bed. I joined him on his bunk, as indeed he was a sorrowful young lad. He held me close.

"I'm scared," he whispered. I rubbed my face against his.

With his tears wetting my fur, I vowed to be by his side on the morrow when he must face Lieutenant Gore and the cane.

CHAPTER 15

A s we had spent some three months sailing south off the land of Southern America, the weather had turned colder as we ventured even further south to Cape Horn.

On the morning of the 1st day of January of 1769, the crew were assembled on the quarterdeck to witness the boys' punishment, having donned their dreadnoughts to keep them from the cold. They shuffled and moaned and leaned into the chilled wind as it blew against them, blowing their breath into their cupped hands to keep them warm.

I was certainly glad to be in possession of my very own fur on such a blustery day!

"Damn fool boys!" Muttered one of the men. "We could be workin' and keepin' warm but for this!" A few who felt the cold and were suffering from the excesses of the night before mumbled in agreement.

The entire crew had heard of the prior evening's shenanigans. Those who despised the gents nudged each other, chortling quietly into their cupped hands at the thought of Mister Banks's attack. Mister Banks and his cronies were indeed a pain in their rears, demanding their assistance with unseamanly duties whenever it was his fancy.

They were here to sail! Not as errand boys for the toffs!

On the other hand, there were those of the crew who had, at one time or another, found my boys to be irritating. Mumbling and chuckling occurred between those parties who had been victims of the lads' boyish but innocent pranks.

Whatever their reasons for enjoying the penalty to come, a buoyancy was spreading amongst the crew like a plague and all were shuffling with anticipation for their own reasons despite the bitter chill.

Lieutenant Gore appeared with the captain and the gentlemen, who took their positions on deck.

Mister Banks was still scratching from the bites he had endured the previous night.

Mister Spöring stood by him scratching himself at the mere thought.

Mister Banks had been informed that the attack had been a concocted plan and that the culprits had been located. He stood agitated and red-faced as if he were about to breathe fire from his nostrils as the boys were paraded in line and deposited themselves in front of him.

I took my place by young Isaac as promised to him.

"Mister Banks," began the captain, "your misadventure this last eve was executed by these young lads before you." The boys' heads lowered in shame, as Mister Banks straightened.

Fussily, he took a kerchief from his sleeve and sniffed the calming fragrance it held, as if his encounter the previous night were a dire and grievous crime against his person, for which there could be no forgiveness!

"What have you boys to say to Mister Banks?" demanded the captain.

My Isaac stepped forward as the representative for the group. Quietly, he lifted his head and glared directly at Mister Banks, not for one moment believing he should be apologising. Determined to get the whole business over and done with as quickly as possible, he began in a quiet voice so that only Mister Banks could hear.

"Mister Banks, sir," he said with gritted teeth, "these here boys and I apologise for the little trick we played on your good self this last eve. It will never happen again."

Isaac's disdain was not lost on Mister Banks, who seethed in reply.

"Captain!" he wheezed. "This boy mocks me to my face! He is most defiant, and definitely not sorry!" He ruffled at his sleeves expecting that the captain should further humiliate the boy in front of his peers and the crew.

Some men reddened visibly and could barely control their laughter at Isaac's feigned apology. They chortled into their cupped hands pretending to breathe warmth into them.

"Mister Banks!" said the captain impatiently, aware of the mixture of mirth and impatience within the ranks assembled. "Has the boy apologised on behalf of the felonious group?"

"Well, yes, but his tone was unsatisfactory!" Mister Banks scoffed.

"That will do, Isaac." He motioned to Isaac to take his place back with the other offenders.

"Captain! I demand a heartfelt recantation from these boys!" He sang, the tone of his voice rising with his temper.

"Mister Banks, the apology has been made, let us get on with their punishment," said the captain leaving no room for argument for fear that the crew would lose their control and laughter would surely ensue.

Mister Banks would be mortified if he could see the men's behaviour behind his back! I daresay the captain could barely control himself but for the example he must make of these boys!

One by one, the boys were to step up to Lieutenant Gore for their punishment.

"Boys!" roared John Gore. "Take you places for the cane! Kiss the gunner's daughter!" They shuffled forward in line and a mighty roar rose from the crew.

I moved to stand by the captain for this ceremony. He looked below when my presence was noticed to him. A glance exchanged between us told of our regret for the impending punishment of our boys.

Neither was my confusion over Lieutenant Gore's order to "kiss the gunner's daughter" lost on him. I had seen no women of the "daughter" variety on my ship! I thought the term merely a slip of Lieutenant Gore's tongue!

The captain knew the younger of the boys would also be confused by this order, as they looked at each other curiously. He directed them that "to kiss the gunner's daughter" was to be bent over the cannon, bare bottomed for the cane!

An embarrassment for them flushed my cheeks, but at the same time I was glad that no "daughters" had escaped my detection upon my ship!

Isaac being the bolder of the lads stepped forward, clearly displaying an example to his peers. His gaze fixed upon Mister Banks's uncomfortable glory. The other boys followed suit, knowing that their caning was inescapable and supposing that they might as well be defiant in the face of humiliation.

"Boys?" shouted Lieutenant Gore. "Be you ready for your discipline?"

They nodded as one.

"Pants down, boy!" yelled Lieutenant Gore to my Isaac, the first of his victims.

A roar escaped every man on board. Isaac lowered his trousers slowly, still glaring at Mister Banks, who fidgeted and ruffled his kerchief irritably.

Lieutenant Gore stepped back, lifted his cane, and charged at his target with a stroke so cutting as to draw blood instantly. The sheer whip of the cane against the naked backside of my consort whistled above the howl of the wind. Every blow sharpened within my ears.

Isaac flinched with the first, but gritted his teeth and maintained his defiance in spite of the obvious pain he must have been feeling. . By the time twelve of Lieutenant Gore's best had been delivered, my Isaac stood, turning to reveal the reddened and bleeding flesh on his tender behind.

As the crew gasped at the sight of his injuries, he returned his trousers to their correct position and moved away with as much dignity as he could muster, to be replaced by the next boy in line.

Isaac's example was followed by all of the boys in turn. Mister Banks writhed visibly under the strain, but as his scratching persisted, he was quite sure that these boys deserved every stroke. Mister Spöring flinched at every lash and feeling quite faint at the sight, turned away to gather himself.

Young Isaac Manley was the last in line. He tried, poor lad, to follow his senior crewmates' examples, but I could see the tears welling up in his eyes.

He stepped forward to Lieutenant Gore and lowered his trousers gingerly. As soon as the cold steel of the cannon pressed against his bare stomach a howling cry escaped him.

"Please, Lieutenant Gore, please!" he blubbered, but the lieutenant turned away from his anguished appeal.

"Please, Captain!" young Isaac pleaded, wailing with the wind, his tears stinging his cheeks.

I looked up at my captain as he hesitated for the merest moment. All eyes had turned to him, as young Isaac bawled without shame.

"Deliver this boy's penance, Lieutenant Gore!" he commanded, although I knew him to be sympathetic to this youngest of boys.

All eyes turned back to the pathetic lad, as the lieutenant prepared to swing wearily at his mark. All but young Isaac were grateful that Lieutenant Gore was unable to summon more energy for the task at hand.

As a hush grew amongst the crew, young Isaac bit down hard upon his lip in anticipation of the pain before him. Exhausted, the lieutenant issued his orders on this last remaining offender, but not with his previous gusto.

Lieutenant Gore had tired somewhat and young Isaac was the better for it!

One by one the twelve strokes of the cane were allotted to young Isaac's behind. The other boys grumbled as Isaac looked up in surprise, as if his predecessors had nothing much to wince about!

"He's gettin' off lightly!" whispered Will. The other lads agreed.

Isaac ceased his whimpering and took his punishment with courage. He returned to his place beside the other boys for the final word from the captain.

Hitching up his strides, he grinned at his fellows proudly, as if he, too, had endured the same torture as the other boys. I took my place beside him as he had been as brave a young boy as I could have wished, whether Lieutenant Gore had been lenient with him or not.

The captain surveyed the crowd.

"Lieutenant Gore, the whereabouts of misters Pickersgill and Terrell?" he questioned.

Each man looked to his right and left for the two older boys, not knowing of their intended punishment. They were situated at the rear of the crowd hoping to be overlooked, but the crew jostled them forward willingly to stand them before Lieutenant Gore.

"What am I to do with these boys, Captain?" he enquired politely, thinking his duty as punisher to be finished.

"Twelve of your bests for each one!" demanded the captain.

The crew nodded to each other and applauded loudly as it was clear that none were fond of these two pompous rogues.

"'Bout time!" someone yelled from the crowd.

"Toffee-nosed brats!" came another.

Pickersgill and Terrell tried to appear above the cutting remarks, but their faces could not hide their distaste for the common seamen.

Lieutenant Gore stepped up to the mark.

"You know the drill, boys, drop 'em!" he sneered. The lieutenant seemed to have a renewed sense of vigour for punishing these two!

They looked at each other as if to wonder whether this humiliation was at all necessary.

"Over the cannon with 'ya!" ordered Lieutenant Gore. Mustering all his strength he delivered the twelve cuts to each lad, as if they were the first in line.

Pickersgill and Terrell grimaced and groaned with each cut, the shame all too much for them. With that, the crew cheered for each strike of the cane, happy to see these cocky chaps put in their place.

When Lieutenant Gore had finished, they replaced their trousers and stood red-faced opposite my boys. They held each other's gazes in silence as if to declare a mutual hatred from this moment on.

"Mister Banks!" shouted the captain above the ever-increasing wind and sea. "Have you witnessed retribution deserving of the crime perpetrated against you?"

Mister Banks nodded his approval. "Lieutenant Gore has accomplished an admirable penalty! He is to be praised for his robust performance of the duty!" he sang.

The entire crowd turned silently to Mister Banks. He had not endeared himself to the crew and although they enjoyed the boys' discipline, all now wished they had not been caught!

The captain dispersed the crew and sent the lads off with Doctor Monkhouse to attend to their wounded behinds.

I accompanied young Isaac Manly as he stumbled along, rubbing his rear.

It always astounded me that men inflicted wounds upon each other, only to be sent for treatment afterwards. Would it not be simpler to overlook the entire painful and time-consuming performance? As a cat, I did not understand punishment, but knew the captain to hold it of great importance. I vowed to inquire on the subject with him later that evening.

Once the boys had been attended by the good doctor, and as I felt that young Isaac Manley's cheer had returned, we all went back to the business of sailing the ship.

I sensed a tension, however, between my lads and the two older boys, Pickersgill and Terrell. Although nought was said, I feared a vengeful campaign had secretly been vowed. I had heard it said that "boys will be boys" and I would need to be on guard for any plans for further fuss.

Mister Banks and his coterie having settled back into their observations, discussed the colour of the sea, which had turned a curious shade of green.

"Aquamarine in colour," they determined after much discussion.

I did not understand the term but enjoyed the change and watched with them for some time.

I was about to doze when a whooshing sound interrupted me. As I lifted my head in the direction of this blasted noise, a mist of sea caught me squarely, and dampened my fur. I rose, shaking my coat to disperse the water, when yet another whoosh and mist befell me.

"Whale!" shouted the seaman on watch.

Mister Banks danced with excitement at the idea and bustled Mister Spöring to notate the sighting.

It was my duty to investigate.

The whooshing and misting thwarted my progress to a safe vantage point, but I kept low and managed to peer under the gunnel rail. The shock took me aback! A giant fish leaped from the sea! I must be in the midst of a favourable dream! I shook and returned to my position. Two! Three! More and more giant fish lurched from the sea, shooting towering funnels of mist from their heads! They rolled and splashed colossal waves, their tails slapping against the surface of the ocean! I paced and peered dumbstruck by the sheer size of these beasts and the waves they made, which jostled my ship!

"Whale!" I heard from all corners of the ship. I stood close to the scientists, as I knew they would be the first to identify this enormous species.

"A fine pod of whale. Smallish, however," I heard Mister Banks remark.

"Smallish?" I thought. Mister Banks must be mad! Even in my wildest of dreams I could not concoct a fish so large!

I watched, mesmerised at the antics of these whales. They seemed to be enjoying a frolic or lark, completely undisturbed by the presence of our ship.

Mister Banks and his team were busy taking notes and drawing pictures of the giant fish. Why was no man attempting to catch one? I drooled at the thought of one of these mammoths flopping about on the deck for me to eat. Of course, not all in one sitting, but I would dine at my leisure for quite some days given the opportunity.

I looked about at the crew, none of whom had baited a line to drop over the side, or prepared a gaff and rope to spear the things! I paced in wait but to no avail. My usual crew of fishermen were nowhere to be seen!

We sailed on as the whales breached and plunged and whooshed. My opportunity for a sizeable meal was growing more and more unlikely as the distance grew between us.

My heart was heavy as I sauntered sadly toward the galley. My mouth watered and my stomach ached after the giant fish were allowed to escape.

John Thompson and his crew were at their usual dinner preparations and a plate of their finest was there for me, but the food turned to ashes in my mouth as I closed my eyes and imagined one or two of those whales for my supper.

Leaving my meal unfinished, I moped toward the Great Cabin in search of my captain.

By now, any Marines on guard knew of my nightly attendances and always let me pass undisturbed. I knew the captain to be attending his log and wished words with him, what with punished boys, and whales allowed to escape my appetite. He was sitting at his table with his charts and notes.

"Ah, Fairweather!" he sounded pleased to see me. "A rather eventful day, what?"

I leapt wearily to the table for a chin rub. It had all been too much for me.

"The boys will mend from their wounds," he said as if to read my mind.

"Upon their reflection of today's ordeal, it would be my hope that they will be of good behaviour for some time."

I looked at him questioningly but he ventured no further opinion. I took it that their pain and humiliation would stick in their ribs for some time and keep them from further shenanigans. But what of my whale?

"Mister Banks seemed pleased to see the whale about the ship this day," he read out loud as he wrote.

Yes! Yes! My whale! I nudged his quill as he wrote, causing him to overshoot the page and smudge his words.

"Fairweather!" he cursed as he blotted the smudged ink from his page. "It would seem that you harbour harsh thoughts of these whales!"

I ignored him.

"Or is it that you wished one for your supper?" He laughed, dismissing the very thought. I gave him a stern glance and he understood.

"Ah, you did indeed wish one for your supper!" he mused, chuckling away to himself.

Whilst grateful that he always understood me, I maintained my huff as he got on with his log. As he wrote, a chortle escaped him occasionally. "I have a feline mascot who requires a whale for his supper!" I swear I heard him titter!

I sniffed the air for signs of alcohol upon his breath, but none was apparent. With so obvious a disregard for my plight I stood, arched my back and turned from him, leaving him to look at my rear, tail held high.

I left him giggling to himself as he continued his work. I could see that my huff would not attract the slightest of sympathies from him and left him for more worthy company.

I found young Isaac Manley and nuzzled in next to his sleeping body. He whimpered ever so softly and threw a flailing arm over me. Sleep came quickly and I dreamed of whales, salty, tasty whales! Whales of all colours and sizes. None smaller than our ship! Whales!

CHAPTER 16

We sailed on southward for one week before sighting the Falkland Islands off in the distance. Mister Banks pleaded with the captain for a landing there but it was not our captain's intention to do so. There was the dreaded capeto negotiate. Mister Banks would have to wait!

The weather had turned colder with each day and I was beholden to my winter coat for warmth. Heavy seas, rain and hail kept me below for much of the time.

My occasional stroll on deck when in calmer weather led me to discover more strange sea creatures, all of which piqued my curiosity and appetite. I stood inquisitively with Doctor Solander on the occasion of new discoveries. He would always tell me of their species and habits in a manner I could grasp. I thought of him as a teaching man. Always enlightening those who took interest, including my good self.

Hence, when the crew spotted sea-going creatures, a shout would be forthcoming for the sake of discovery and notation by the botanists.

"Porpoises!"

When the crew sounded this name upon their discovery, I was always confused! "Poor pusses" always seemed to allude to a sympathy required for the plural of my species. Hearing the crew uttering their name caused me much confusion. Doctor Solander was always the gentleman to seek when an explanation was required. Porpoises, he informed me, were a somewhat fun-loving creature, usually travelling in groups and frolicking about the ship. Another tasty specimen, which to my disappointment, none of the crew would attempt to catch for me!

"Penguin!"

Strange little fellows ducking and diving about the waves in their search for fish. They appeared to be rather formally dressed, in a dinner suit of some sort. I wondered how they managed to swim with such agility when fully clothed in eveningwear! Doctor Solander informed me that these were birds, yet they did not fly! Swimming birds? How odd! They swallow their catch and return to land only to vomit the contents of their stomach to feed their young. Disturbing, that! Not having had offspring, I questioned their usefulness. I mean to say, if infants cannot feed themselves, and one must regurgitate one's very own meal for them, what good were they? And what of the infants? Regurgitated fish was not my idea of a tasty meal!

"Seal!"

Another of nature's mysteries. To look upon them one would swear they were cats of a marine variety! Blessed with whiskers and a pleasing face, but a distinct lack of ears and fan-like paws for swimming made them a laughable curiosity! Even so, I took a liking to them having at least some feline characteristics. Their usefulness again confounded me, as they appeared to have nothing better to do than splash about making odd barking sounds, much like a dog! Not at all as pleasing to the ear as a feline meow or purr, but likeable ninnies nonetheless.

Seaweed was dragged on board for the scientists to study. Slimy grassy sea plants only useful for sheltering small fish. A grateful friend they had in me! I enjoyed licking the salt from their fronds but found no other purpose for seaweed, as the small fish they reportedly harboured were not included when brought on board.

My evenings spent with the captain found his concern growing more with each day nearing the Straits Lemaire.

By the time we approached Cape St Diego at the west entrance of the straits on the 12th of January 1769, we could see The Three Brothers, famous mountain landmarks of similar size to point our way, but the tides held us off land.

The next morning, we were still no further to our next landfall of Tierra del Fuego and the tides and bad weather had caused the ship to pitch violently, dipping our bowsprit below the sea and washing the decks with spume.

Hail and rain came and went in blustery gales. I saw fit to enclose myself below during such weather.

For four miserable days, our captain tacked an approach to land. We zigged and zagged our way across the straits off Cape St Diego, much like my attempting to catch a mouse in an alley!

To find a fortunate moment when tide, current and wind all joined forces to allow us our way was proving almost impossible for our captain.

He knew of the westerly current that thwarts progress around Cape Horn and through the Straits Lemaire but had not anticipated the forces of tide and weather to be against us also. Such forces of nature combined to create a surf with waves crashing in all directions against our ship.

Each evening, his despair was obvious as he read aloud his logged entries of the three failed attempts to enter the straits. He spared no time for me but I understood his preoccupation and left him to his charts and associated mutterings.

A boat was eventually sent ashore with an impatient Mister Banks and an officer, as the *Endeavour* stood off land, unable to anchor in the rough sea.

They returned with a selection of plants and the news that it was too rocky and shallow to allow a safe anchorage.

They had seen two natives on shore, who watched them for some time and then retired into the woods.

The naming of landfalls and points of interest was our captain's purpose as the fine chartsman he was, but he often took suggestions from the crew when stumped for an apt and descriptive choice.

Some of his namings seemed pointless and inappropriate to me.

I gathered that recent places of interest such as the inhospitable Vincents Bay, Port Maurice and Cape Bartholomew, which he had named and then avoided as anchorages, perhaps alluded to chaps from his youth or hometown, or his Navy companions. As he gruffly entered them into his log and charts, I thought it safe to assume they were fellows he had not much taken a liking to!

On the 16th day of January, Lieutenant Gore finally laid us to anchor in a somewhat more sheltered bay. The "Bay of Good Success" was Lieutenant Gore's choice of name and was adopted and noted by our good and deserving captain. He was pleased for the relief of an anchorage after this, his fourth attempt to land us safely.

Amidst snow and rain, the men eagerly secured the *Endeavour* on the starboard side of the bay near rocks for shelter.

As the crew tended the ship, the captain, Mister Banks and Doctor Solander and a few good men took a trip to shore on the smaller boats to look for a watering place and to speak with the local folk.

With our arrival, thirty or forty natives had gathered on a sandy beach at the head of the bay. I watched nervously from the deck as our troupe approached them on shore. Our men were certainly outnumbered by my reckoning, but upon seeing our Marines at the heads of the boats sporting their firearms, the natives retreated into the woods.

I was thankful for their good sense and went back to my work below, tidying the stores.

It never ceased to amaze me how quickly rodent numbers multiplied. I would no sooner be of the opinion that the stores were clean of these pests than more would appear as if by magic.

I ventured the opinion that they were breeding under my very nose, but did not look too hard for the happy couples as their offspring kept me employed.

If I were to eradicate them completely, I would no longer be of use! Merely keeping them in their place and their numbers to a minimum was largely the best plan for all.

Management, I called it, and it worked to my advantage. The Bosun John Gathrey was well pleased, as his sleep was not interrupted by vermin scuffle, and his bedding not eaten away by the mice.

Not long after we anchored, a party of men and scientists went ashore on the boats, the crew to gather wood and water and kill the odd animal to make a welcome change from our sea rations. The scientists to collect their specimens and attempt contact with the natives. I avoided this trip as the natives appeared from my distant vantage to be a rowdy and fearsome lot.

From the safety of the ship, I observed that these "Fuegians" had skin of a copper colour, painted in streaks of red and black, sporting long black hair hanging to their shoulders.

The women wore skins over their privy parts but the men observed no such decency.

Their feet were bound in several places by sealskin, these being adequate as shoes.

Their huts were likened to beehives, all sporting a little fire outside and the bows and arrows of the men for hunting. Entire families followed our landing party curiously on their duties. They behaved peaceably enough but were not at all the types of chaps I wished to meet.

I was napping in the Great Cabin when a commotion roused me from the depths. I toddled up to the deck encountering Chester who was as bemused as I.

"What the devil is going on, old chap?" said Chester.

"I know not, old chum. Blighted natives have boarded the ship, as far as I can tell." We both looked on.

To our horror, three natives had returned to the ship with our party of scientists and men. We assumed they were invited, but kept our distance.

Mister Banks escorted them to the captain and greetings were exchanged. A crowd had gathered to hear of Mister Banks's intention with these chaps.

The natives stood dumbly as Mister Banks breathlessly began his explanation for their presence.

"Doctor Solander and I took trinkets and red beads to the Fuegians! They were seated on the beach when we approached. They displayed threatening sticks as we approached, but threw them to the ground to indicate peace!" he explained, making hand gestures to embellish his story.

The crew were all scratching at their heads, somewhat confused.

Chester and I raised a concerned eyebrow or two at each other.

"We were greeted with friendship!" he continued. "Although they are uncouth, they took great delight in our gifts of beads and ribbons. So here they stand, ready to explore our ship, and have brought with them a priest or conjuror of some merit."

Mister Banks bowed to the captain and the conjurer, having explained the Fuegians' presence and was rather chuffed with his newfound friends.

The captain stood silently wary. The soldiers received a nod from him to stand at ease but be ready for trouble. The crew looked at each other with some curiosity.

The Fuegians were offered our bread and beef which they sampled, displeased with the taste, yet keeping what they did not eat.

They sampled our wine and spirits, barely letting it past their lips; they spat in disgust at the taste. Somewhat ungrateful, I thought! This attempt to please them now over, and with little success, they proceeded to inspect the ship.

"Chester!" I nudged. "This is unusual, what?"

"Hurrumph!" he snorted.

Mister Banks gestured to the conjuror to step forward.

Holding up some manner of stick with shells tied to the end, he waived it maniacally and shouted a rowdy incantation as loudly as I had ever heard! Chester and I leaped on the spot, every hair on end! Not to mention frightening the dickens out of the soldiers! Pistols at the ready, they stood poised. The captain waved a hand gesture to stand them at ease.

"Good Lord, Fairweather! What in the blazes is he up to?" Chester wheezed, the tension of the moment being too much for him.

"The man is obviously a lunatic of some kind!" I deduced.

Mister Banks seemed perfectly at ease with the chap and marched all three Fuegians forward to inspect the ship.

The captain gave his approval but had them escorted by the soldiers as a cautionary action. The crew paraded behind not to miss whatever this crackpot had in mind.

Chester and I thought it prudent to bring up the rear, keeping out of sight, but a concerned eye on this curiosity.

At every turn, this conjuror spied an object that he had never before laid eyes upon, and the barbarous cries and shaking stick would explode from his fidgeting body.

The crew howled with laughter at each outburst!

The soldiers clenched their pistol holsters!

Chester and I saw nothing amusing about it at all! Quite frankly we both thought it rather disturbing!

"He is banishing the demons from the ship!" explained Mister Banks in all seriousness, ensuring more laughter from the crew.

Finally, the conjurer had screamed and quivered his way all over our ship and rallied his two chums to leave, satisfied that we were cleansed of potentially evil spirits.

As he doubled back past the still sniggering crew, he spied Chester and my good self.

"Ahhhhhheeeee!" he bellowed with renewed vigour and shrieked a cry in his native tongue!

"Snow Cat?" Mister Banks met his eye in question, somehow knowing a few words of Fuegian.

"Ahhhhhhhheeeeeeeee!" he screeched, further shaking his shell-laden stick at me as if I were the devil himself! Chester and I raised that all too familiar eyebrow.

"Get that cat out of here!" Mister Banks motioned to my Isaac who was himself giggling like a girl.

"Fairweather?" asked Isaac.

"Yes, you stupid boy, that cat!" he ordered, pointing an accusing finger at me.

"Ahhhhhhhheeeeeeeee!" The conjuror's eyes almost leapt from their sockets!

Isaac scooped me up and ran at speed with me to the Great Cabin.

"Stay here!" he ordered, dumping me unceremoniously on the captain's desk, then running off and leaving me quite alone with my bewildered thoughts.

What had I done? Whatever it was, I was quite sure of my innocence! I paced and pondered until Chester arrived with Lady in tow.

"Fairweather, old feline, are you quite all right?" he asked. "I have apprised Lady of the situation at hand and we a concerned for your wellbeing." Lady sat beside me as if I were doomed.

"Situation! What situation?" I demanded, knowing full well I had done nothing to deserve the bawling of a mad savage.

"Mister Banks deciphered the outburst. The priest thinks you are a 'snow-cat'. A horrible native-type beast of the first order!" Chester explained with some nervousness.

"Never you mind that horrible savage, dear," Lady attempted to soothe with some kindness.

"Snow-cat?" I spluttered. "What the devil is a snow-cat? I am nothing of the sort! I hate the snow! It tangles my fur and freezes me to the bone! Not to mention the icicles on my whiskers! Snow-cat? I laugh at 'snow-cats'! Ha! Ha!" I was troubled.

I paced. I mumbled.

"Fairweather, dear boy, settle yourself. I have it on authority from Mister Banks that wild cats of the snow-dwelling variety live in the mountains, behind the native village, and steal their food at will in the dead of night. They do not know of our fine English domesticated feline and have mistaken you for this demon!" Chester was doing his best.

"Demon? Stealing food? I am Fairweather! Of the *Endeavour*! Did this Banks not explain?" I was incensed to be mistaken for some thieving barbarian, feline or not!

"Mister Banks tried but the priest could not be sweetened to your presence." Chester bowed as if he had failed me. "Just stay out of sight of these ruffians and you will be safe."

"Out of sight, Chester? I think not! How dare this quack assume me a wild and uncultured brute!"

"Yes, Fairweather dear," Lady soothed. "But you must not take it personally, they are savages, after all."

"Savages or not, my good name is at stake! All and sundry on our ship! What are they to think of me?" I appealed.

Chester edged me aside, knowing my pride to be wounded. "I know it for a fact that Mister Banks and the scientists are planning an expedition to the inner country tomorrow. You could seek out this 'snow-cat' and point out your differences to the natives." He tried to whisper but Lady hears all.

"Chester!" she scolded.

"Surely you do not intend such folly, Fairweather? The natives may have your skin! And we know nothing of 'snow-cats! They may very well eat you!" she uttered mortified.

"He shall attend!" spoke Chester bravely. "And I with him!"

"Chester, old thing, you honour me with your bravery, but I cannot let you risk your life for my pride."

"Bah!" he scoffed. "I have seen a pack of short, pointy-eared canines in attendance in that village."

I gasped. Canines? And the canines of savages at that!

Chester continued. "They stand between you and your pride! They are guardians of their village. No match in size for my own, however!" He stood imposingly to his full height, feeling well pleased with his stature. "You will require my protection on such a mission."

"If short, pointy-eared canines stand in my way, then your comradeship will be welcomed, Chester, old defender of the intrepid!" I felt empowered by his gallantry.

"Quite right!" barked Chester boldly.

"On the morrow then, old boy?" I spouted.

"Right-ho, old thing!" The decision was made.

"Good heavens, what will become of you both?" Lady questioned, feeling that this demonstration of gusto could only end in tragedy.

Chester trotted off with bravery in his heart and Lady ambled behind him looking back at me as if it would be our last conversation.

I proceeded to the remainder of the ship, feeling somewhat better, that my mission on the morrow would clear my good name.

Upon exiting the Great Cabin, I encountered my boys, readying the supplies for the gents' journey inland. They were a sight for sore eyes and I felt sure they would hold me aloft from these ghastly allegations.

"Ooooh, Isaac!" sang Will Howson. "There's that snow-cat! Ain't he the devil 'imself?"

"Yeah, keep away from him, he's likely to curse us with a flick of that tail!" laughed John Charlton.

William Harvey and young Isaac Manly fell about in fits of laughter.

"Oy!" shouted my Isaac. "Leave him be, you 'orrible lads!" Bless him coming to my defence. I sidled up to his leg for a grateful rub.

"Ahhh! He touched me!" cried my Isaac, full of laughter. "I'm turning into a toad! Ribbit! Ribbit!" He hopped about, imitating the slimy beast, the traitorous boy!

My Isaac, of all people! The boys all joined in chorus of this mockery. Ribitting and leaping about at my expense! Hideous ingrates! I would remember this for future reference when called upon to assist these miscreants.

I flicked my "evil" tail at each one and stalked off to find my good friend John Thompson in the hope that a morsel or two would ease my pain. He was nowhere to be seen in the galley. His assistant, Thomas Matthews, was chopping the heads from ducks shot that day for our supper. On noting my presence, his cleaver aloft, he chased me from the galley caterwauling like the conjuror! The crew in the vicinity similarly whooped and wailed as one, roaring with laughter!

I deemed it prudent to lay low until the morning. These cruel taunts were doing nought for my morale. I crept off to the safety of the stores to sleep among my closest friends, the rodents. At the very least, I knew they would not mock me!

The dawn brought a flurry of activity on deck, waking me even from the bowels of the ship. I ran at speed for the deck so as not to be left behind.

The jeers and chuckles followed me all the way there, strengthening my resolve to put an end to this lunacy. I was, after all, Fairweather! Not some fearsome demon!

Assembled on deck were misters Banks, Spöring and Doctor Solander, the surgeon William Monkhouse, Charles Green the astronomer, and Mister Banks's draughtsman Alexander Buchan.

All of Mister Banks's servants were prepared: James Roberts with instruments, Peter Briscoe with bags for the collection of specimens and the ever-faithful Thomas Richmond and George Dorlton tethering Chester and Lady for the expedition.

The captain had ordered two seamen to accompany us, the brothers Littleboy, Michael the younger and Richard the elder, both strapping lads ready for anything. I had seen little of these two to date. Busy with sailing the ship, I imagine. I made it my mission to acquaint myself with them at the earliest possible convenience!

The weather had turned for the better, much like a sunny London day in May, cloudless skies and still air made for calm waters. Perfect for a boat trip to shore.

The captain bade us a successful mission, eyeing me purposefully as I boarded the longboat tactically so as to remain unseen.

I suspected that he disapproved of my joining this expedition, especially as I was a suspected "demon" amongst the locals. I positioned myself skilfully with Chester and Lady.

Upon our arrival on the beach, Thomas and George released Chester and Lady who raced about the beach thankful for the exercise.

I stayed with the gents hidden well behind the unloaded gadgetry until the party were suitably assembled and ready to meet with the locals.

A party of native dignitaries approached us on the beach, headed by the chief and followed closely behind by the priest who had sullied my good name.

I thought it prudent for the success of the gents' mission that I was not seen at this time. I skulked quietly away to join Chester and Lady who were now tethered further down the shore, sniffing at this and that.

"Fairweather, old thing!" Chester panted, fidgeting here and there, while Thomas attempted to tether him. "A good run that was. I feel positively invigorated!"

"Whilst I am glad for your health, Chester, keep still so I may hide behind you from that sorcerer!" He sat with Lady so as to block me from view.

"Detestable chap might see me and that will be the end of the gent's excursion," I mumbled.

I relaxed with them, awaiting the end of the formalities so that we may proceed inland.

No sooner did I feel better than the local pack of dogs confronted us! Confirming Chester's earlier sighting, they were rather short, stocky fellows, brownish in colour, with pointed ears and unfriendly intentions!

Chester was caught by surprise and stood to his full height very quickly, chest out, growling as I had never heard him; low and menacing, lifting his nose to bare his teeth. Thomas struggled to hold him tethered.

Lady stayed in her position with George, head down, so as not to catch their glaring eye. The gents turned toward the ruckus from further up the beach but Mister Banks dismissed it with a wave of his hand, as nothing important. Typical of him, I thought!

"Who are you? What do you want here?" They barked in concert, closing ranks as if to ready themselves for an attack! My fur stood to attention but I kept hidden behind Lady.

Chester stood resolutely, planting his paws firmly in the sand.

"We have business here!" Chester snarled, leaving no room for argument.

I stole a glance from behind Lady. Chester's formidable teeth were still on display, and a frothy drool emitted from his lips, certainly impressing me!

The pack seemed unconvinced and bent on defending their borders, standing shoulder to shoulder to increase their size against the mighty Chester, I suspect.

A rather larger fellow stepped forward from the rank and approached us closer. Nose to nose with Chester, he stood.

"Get out! Now! You are not welcome here!" yelled the leader, turning to his comrades for back-up.

"Get out!" Get out!" They barked, frothing cheek by jowl, as one!

Chester hesitated for a mere second, clearly outnumbered by these small but brazen chaps. They began to edge forward, sneering and drooling. This did not bode well for Chester's safety, and I saw in this stand-off, a moment to utilize my "demonic" status in an attempt to calm the outlook. I know you will say that I risked being torn limb from limb, but I concluded that this would occur either way, should these mutts decide a rampage was in order! So, I sallied forth, as confidently as possible under the circumstances. Lady gasped audibly.

"Now see here, you chaps!" I trumpeted, taking position in front of Chester, but no more forward than him. Chester looked down at me, shock filling his eyes as if he did not have enough to do defending himself, let alone me, a mere feline!

Clearly, no other feline species was known to these foul canines, other than the snow cat. As far as they knew, I was he! And in the flesh! The very same beastly chap who eats their chickens and terrorises young children! A few snouts bore the scars of a cat, and I daresay some fear entered their hearts!

I sat, purposefully, flicked my bristled tail, and eyed my left paw with claws outstretched as if picking a bothersome bug from it. I engaged their beastly stare and got ready to continue with I know not what. I expected something of a well-placed slap on the nose of this chiefly fellow would be required. However, to the astonishment of all, the pack began to whine, ears back, and inch by inch, backed away from us.

Have no doubt, I was more dumbfounded than any, but kept my huffy poise until they were well out of sight, having cowered back to their camp, tails between their legs, not even looking over their shoulders! None of us moved for the longest time. Chester spoke first.

"Well, I'll be darned!" he turned to Lady, bewildered. "Did you see that, dear?"

"I certainly did!" She turned to me. "Fairweather, what on earth possessed you? And more to the point, what did you do to them to send them cowering?"

I played the chivalrous chap, even though my very innards were still of the opinion they were lining up for an open-air examination!

"T'was nothing at all, dear Lady. We were in peril. I simply rose to the occasion, is all!" I examined that nonchalant paw yet again.

Thomas and George having witnessed the entire episode, mesmerized, while tethering Chester, finally looked at each other and burst into gales of laughter.

"Told you, dat cat special!" Thomas howled.

"Special?" giggled George. "He super cat! Fighting off many dogs wit'out fear for his self!"

"Snow cats beware! Fairweather be here!" They sang, tears of laughter rolling from their eyes.

"Ah, all is clear, Fairweather," Chester spoke, the fog clearing from his obviously befuddled expression. "They thought you the dreaded snow cat!" He breathed a sigh of relief that his mind had not played a trick upon him.

Lady nodded. "Fairweather, you bright boy! Still, and may I say, who knew they would think of you in this way? Very foolish of you though, dear! You may have been eaten!" she scolded.

"Rest assured, dear Lady, my reputation had preceded me! No doubt, thanks to that ghastly priest! I knew he would run back to his tribe with news of my hellish existence!" I did not know this for sure, but had merely hoped.

Grateful that my hopes had not been dashed and we all remained intact, I thought it best to leave it at that. I was, after all, getting a little carried away with my own heroism and my guesswork aside, things could well have taken a different turn.

"Well, thank goodness for your celebrity, old thing! I was not altogether certain I could make headway with these brutes!" said Chester with grateful sigh.

"Chester?" I asked out of the blue. "Have you noted that we felines and canines seem to enjoy a universal understanding of each other's languages? Unlike the struggle our human friends have conversing with those of other lands?"

I must admit this did mystify me, but I certainly was in no position to ask it until now!

"Yes! Yes! I have noticed that! On my previous jaunts with Mister Banks, I have found that we will be understood. Take it as read! Good for us, I say! Makes the going easier." He mumbled as if it was of little importance.

It was all new to me! I thought it a great triumph! The worry over a misspoken word or two possibly causing unintentional trouble, being clearly absent from all animal species, was indeed an important discovery! Not to mention how much more clever of us to be universally understood, unlike our silly humans with their regional dialects.

Without doubt this would make ease our trip, if by nothing other than a good understanding of the spoken word! Here! Here! I thought.

The tribal dignitaries had left the gents by now, free to go about their journey inland in search of plants and animals to discover, sketch and catalogue.

Thomas and George brought up the rear of the party with Chester and Lady, still giggling. "Super-special, super-cat!" They chanted softly, nudging each other. Knowing that the gents would hardly believe them, they kept the joke a private one.

I strutted along with them, rather pleased with myself but still wishing not to catch the eye of that crackpot conjuror. Should he sight me, his antics would certainly attract the worst kind of attention and no doubt get me sent back to the ship.

Even though this recent scrap with the local hounds had been excitement enough, I wished not to lose sight of my goal. I had a snow cat to find! My very own enterprise! That which would clear my blotted name! "For'ard-ho, gents!" I thought.

We headed off through a forest, Mister Banks at the lead examining every leaf and twig and gesturing for Mister Buchan, the draughtsman, to draw anything of interest. We strode along at a steady pace until we cleared the forest and before us stood what appeared to be a grassland in the distance.

By the time we reached it, it turned out to be a thicket of small beech saplings, so closely packed together that they could not be bent aside and the ground beneath our feet was like a bog.

The going for the gents and company was slow, Mister Banks muttering the entire time. "No travelling could be worse than this!"

Chester, Lady and I sauntered through without issue, our weight being lighter and distributed wisely between four legs. Finally, we broke through after one mile and all men were exhausted and sodden.

Mister Buchan saw the going tougher than most. As we paused, he began to take some kind of conniption, falling to the ground and twitching madly.

"Doctor, quickly!" gestured Mister Banks. "Mister Buchan suffers from the epilepsy. Please attend to him!"

Doctor Monkhouse hurried forward, whipping his belt from his trousers. I thought Mister Buchan deserved better treatment than a lashing! I knew not of "epilepsy" but determined he was ill, quite obviously. This disturbed me.

"Leave aside, men!" said the doctor, folding the belt in two places. Unlike what I had imagined was the use for that belt, the doctor wrenched open Mister Buchan's gritted teeth and put the folded belt in his mouth!

"Stops him swallowing his tongue," explained the doctor for the education of all, should this treatment be required in the future.

I was no doubt relieved that he was not going to be punished for simply falling to a fit! These things cannot be helped in such afflicted humans, as the good doctor explained.

After lighting a fire for comfort, Mister Banks and Doctor Monkhouse decided that Mister Buchan and the brothers Littleboy should stay there while we pressed on with Doctor Solander and Green, the servants, Thomas and George with the dogs, Spöring and Briscoe with the instruments.

The brothers Littleboy both quietly thought it a stroke of luck to be left by the fire!

We pushed on and emerged into an open rocky area.

Mister Banks, chuffed with his progress as the leader, assumed the demeanour of botanist, and trembled in awe of the alpine plants abundantly placed just for his discovery.

"Spöring! Briscoe! Draw and catalogue everything! Take samples of everything!" He cried, as he danced from one plant to the next.

"Careful, careful!" he blustered when their handling was boisterous.

Thankful for the rest, I enquired of Chester. "Is Mister Banks always like this?"

"Hmm, yes," sighed Chester. "He is an excitable gentleman. Plants and animals are his work, dear boy." I thought him terribly polite about his master. Mister Banks had so far only appeared to me as a well-bred loony, and I had so far seen no evidence to the contrary, but I took it under advisement from Chester to give him the benefit of the doubt, as he was, after all, a renowned scientist, and such types have their eccentricities.

Whilst all but the scientists were resting, and knowing Mister Buchan and the Littleboys to be safe by the fire I determined this was my chance to do some discovering of my own!

I announced my intentions to Chester and Lady, as the weather was favourable.

The usual farewells and promises of care were exchanged and I set off further up into the rocky hills in an attempt to meet my native feline counterpart.

Mister Banks had given me a short description while chatting with the sorcerer. Much like I, but with a long tail, thick fur and sleeping in the lower branches of trees to avoid the snow. Uncomfortable but sensible, I thought.

"Bring on ye snow cats!" I howled as I jumped from rock to rock, keeping an eye on my distance and direction so as not be become lost.

"Snow cats beware! Fairweather is amongst you!" I was getting further away and a little edgy as the terrain became steeper and difficult to navigate.

"Bring me snow cats! Come one! Come all!" I bawled. And bring them quickly, I thought! I was becoming somewhat weary.

"You have nought to fear! I merely wish to meet distant friends!" I added sensibly and loudly, fearing they may perceive me a threat to them.

I rested on an outcrop, puffing not a little, and heard the snap of twigs from behind me.

I stared straight ahead as if to be unaware when the guttural growl above me sliced the silence like a dagger. It did not sound as friendly as I would have liked. I had to assume my poise, yet be wary of attack!

Suddenly, a rustle of leaves alerted me and I pounced to one side of the outcrop.

The fiend in question fell awkwardly on the very spot I had vacated. It was caught off guard by my agile leap to safety!

Fumbling about comically trying to get to its feet, I stood to my full height and wasted no time in bravely introducing myself.

"Good afternoon, dear chap! I am Fairweather of the ship *Endeavour*. I have no doubt you have seen our good vessel in the harbour from this lovely vantage point?" I attempted to make favourable conversation.

The brute stood a little taller than I, tan in colour and a thickish fur covered in small black spots, changing to a fetching stripe, not unlike my own, around the face and chest. A roguish sort of outfit and well suited to the weather, I thought!

Its menacing eye and that low grumble made me feel quite unwelcome, though.

"I am Geoffrey, and jou arrrre a meal," he hissed.

I fidgeted about cautiously upon this news.

"I most certainly am not!" I replied, trying not to be nervous. I had to think quickly.

"I am an envoy of his Majesty, King George, sent here to discover if feline varieties inhabit these parts! It would be a crime against England for you to eat me!" I pounced from rock to rock so as to keep moving should he attack.

He looked bemused, obviously not knowing what the dickens I was talking about, but I could tell he was beginning to think of me as a little more than just food, not having seen my species around here before now.

I took my lies further.

"Come along with me, old thing, we have scientists for you to meet, you must be interviewed and your image drawn for our research. The king will be most impressed with you!" Hopefully appealing to his ego, I bustled forward as if to hurry him along.

"I not know of which jou speak, jou are meat and I be hungrrry. My whole family be hungrrry. Be still for me to catching jou!" he growled.

"Ah! You are the famous, 'Snow Cat'"? The feared one who eats the villager's chickens?" Nothing.

I took another tack. "You have family here in these woods? Little ones to feed? Brothers, sisters, cousins and aunts?" I was all ears. He was surprised that I knew of him and that his presence held fame.

"I am the Geoffreys cat! 'Snow cat' eef you mussst!" he declared, settling a little.

"Why the chief and sorcerer told us of your great hunting skills just this very day! I was sent to seek you out and determine your importance to our research!" I looked him over as a scientist would, as if examining his species.

"Geoffreys not go to theee villages unless darkness fallll. We would be keeellled," he explained. "We eat the cheeekens, becawwws they hunt usss for our furrrs."

"Ah, I see!" I said, fingering my chin, seeming all knowing, and as if committing this important piece of information to memory for my official report.

"This explains much, Geoffrey! There are more of you in this area?" Again, I was asking seemingly important questions to avoid being eaten.

"Yeesss!" He was keen to elaborate. "We keeep to our own lands. There is Pampas Geoffrey in the grassssy land, Water Geoffrey who fissshes the streams. A few are Mountain Geoffreys like meee. There are mannny Geoffreysss. My land eees the highest land of all Geoffreys!" he said, bursting with pride.

"Aha!" I managed. "King of the Geoffreys as you indeed must be, you understand the importance that I not be eaten, hence I may report of your kingliness to my king."

He scratched his chin, musing.

Here he was a few moments ago wanting nothing but my insides, and now seemed to be not only a font of local knowledge but also the King of the Geoffreys!

All of them being named Geoffrey made me think it a smart thing to keep to their own territories. A family gathering of the Geoffreys would be a most confusing event! I took a moment to imagine it…

"Hello Geoffrey, old thing!"

"Why, Geoffrey, you're looking well!"

"I am well, thank you, Geoffrey."

"No, he was asking after MY health, Geoffrey!"

"How are the children, Geoffrey?"

"Which Geoffrey's children are you asking of, Geoffrey?"

"Ah, the Geoffrey with the two females, Geoffrey."

"There are four of us here with two female children, Geoffrey!"

"What are their names, Geoffrey?"

"Geoffrey and Geoffrey, of course, Geoffrey."

"Well, I trust all the Geoffreys are well?"

And a chorus of, "Yes, thank you, Geoffrey."

Very confusing it would be!

Back to the task at hand quickly for fear I should not pause for him to think too much.

"Well as 'King' of the Geoffreys you simply must accompany me to our camp for introductions to our scientists," I advised.

"Not I, Furrwedder, I have family. I cannot be dead, they will shurrrley die, too. Nutthing to eat without theeese Geoffrey to hunt for them!" An honourable man, I let the incorrect pronunciation of my name go at this occasion.

"I tell jou what!" His eyes lit up. "You tell the hunters to stop keellling the Geoffreys and I will let jou go. This is all I will do for jou."

This was as good an outcome as I could hope for under the circumstances. I was meant to be eaten. I pushed my luck a little, though, as I felt he had come to respect me and his tactics were noteworthy in saving his kin, and my skin!

"I'll tell you what, old Geoffrey. How about you stop hunting the village chickens and I will tell the scientists of you with great favour. Of your families, and your plight with the hunting of Geoffreys, I shall tell them to stop. They will trust my good instincts on this matter. Oh, and of course you will not eat me!"

He pondered. He paced.

"Agreeeed Furrwedder!" He placed his rather larger, stronger paw over mine. I could feel the needle-tipped claws of a true hunter through my fur. His eye met mine and the pact was in place.

Now more comfortable with my distant kin, I paced.

"Leave me to think, King Geoffrey! We must concoct a foolproof plan to bring a peace between your Geoffreys clan and the townsfolk!" I stated.

"I cannot see dis as posseeble! We have beeen sworn emineees furrr as long as there have beeen Geoffreys and mennn!" He paced, agitated at the possibility of causing more trouble than there had so long been in this territory of his.

"Yes! Yes!" I paced now, unafraid and back to my usual self. "I understand your concerns, dear chap, but as the king's envoy it is my duty to be of assistance to all parties!"

I was stretching it a little here but knew I must get the old grey matter hard at work, not only for the Geoffreys, as I truly did wish to help, but to summon some kind of miracle to impress that wretched sorcerer, therefore cleansing my questionable nobility.

"I have it, Geoffrey!" I stood tall and flicked my tail. His morbid pacing ceased, although a note of doubt could be seen on his face. He sat, awaiting what he believed to be folly, not understanding the genius of my plan.

"Can you gather the Geoffreys en masse and speak to them as the king and highest ranking diplomat of the Geoffreys that you are?" I whispered, thus drawing him into my purpose and favour.

"Yes, of course!" came the answer from His Kingliness.

"We've not much time, King Geoffrey, as our party is merely visiting and we must undo the misdeeds of many years!"

Geoffrey paced with me now as if our upper stories worked as one, which was odd really as he had no clue of what I might suggest. The only knowing he had was that the united Geoffreys would be a force to be reckoned with.

I stopped. "Your entire clan must assemble on the morrow, where I shall meet with you and your kind, where we shall negotiate a truce that will not fail, and will last an eternity! But we must be clever and well-rehearsed!"

"Furrwedder!" he gasped. "I will need to know morrrre to gather our peoples asss one. True, we are all Geoffreys, but we have our own terrrrritoriesss and some Geoffreys do not always get alonggg!"

"You must trust me as King George's envoy!" I stressed. "I know my stuff!" I stood firm. I contemplated my bravery as not long prior I had been intended as a meal.

He accepted my assurance.

"We assemble at dawn. Every male, female and little Geoffrey, for a trip to the native camp, to meet with the sorcerer and elders."

"What????" he shrieked, echoing around the terrain. "Furrwedder! You joke with meee! I be not convincing the whole Geoffrey clannn to do disss!"

He turned.

"You have made a fool of meee, and I will now keelll you as I first intended!" I was not expecting this, I must say.

"My family will be most happy to pick jou boneses clean!" I quivered not a little. He leaned forward, his face a mere whisker from my own.

"And I, Furrwedder, will be the firrrst to take my fill of jou," he whispered menacingly.

I stiffened as needed, to convince him my plot had merit. It was getting strangely nippy, considering the lovely weather so far, and snow began to float with a quickly turning breeze, picking up speed as we both stood off, not knowing what would follow.

Fortunately, my occasional shivering could be seen to be from the cold and not my nerves getting the better of me. I could only think to use my considerable powers of speech to sway this king.

"Now, listen carefully!" I used my tried-and-true whispering technique to pique his interest.

"As a large and formidable group, you will dominate the meeting with my help. The success of my plan is absolutely assured. If you do as I say, your clan will not be hunted and your kin will not go hungry, for generations to come, but you must follow my lead. I have not earned my position as King's Envoy without proof of prior diplomatic deeds such as this!" I had him there.

I thought of my mother briefly, though. This lying would have earned me a well-deserved slap.

He mused. "Verrry well, Furrwedder. I have my fearrrs but will gather my kinnns, and we shall meet at theee beaches at sunrise," he keenly committed.

I took a chance here. "Make that the following day, and a little later than sunrise if you will, noble friend. We English work well into the night and need our sleep and you, too, have a large task ahead of you, gathering all your Geoffreys."

"You have a point therrre, Furrwedder. We arrre a big group and spread widellly through this land. Some Geoffreys will be harrrrder to breeng than ottthers. I weeelll see you again on the beaches at middle morning on the after morrrrow. Be asssured that my breakfast that day will be small, not having keeellled you and taken you to my fameely to eat!"

He hurrumphed unexpectedly, no doubt his stomach giving way to the more important plan at hand.

"Now go to your shipp as thees snow will blizzard and we both will die withouttt shelters!" And off he sprang as only a wildcat could, I imagined.

I swallowed hard, as the result of the gratefully escaped collective of my portions was still intact!

He was right. I was feeling the change in weather and hurriedly returned to camp. There was much to do.

Chester and Lady had to be informed of my plan, and no doubt convinced to assist. My biggest hurdle was going to be to convince the elders of the village and that blasted sorcerer to call a truce, and all the while being scrutinized by Mister Banks and the gents, who already thought of me merely as a mouse catcher.

I brooded as I descended the cliffs, the going a bit tough, as I was not usually found climbing up and down mountains!

I was looking forward to that fire I had left, as it was now hellish cold and snowing hard. Up went my fur and out went my whiskers to feel my way in this hideous weather.

Finally, I was back at camp. What a shambles!

All I found were the brothers Littleboy shivering while Mister Buchan was wrapped in the only blanket to keep him from his seizures, which seemed to have stopped. Mister Banks and the gents were nowhere to be seen.

Where the dickens Chester and Lady were worried me most, and of course what of George and Tom. I could see that a native bird, having been shot as a specimen earlier, had been cooked and eaten without so much as a scrap for me!

I would have to make do with some dried beef that I found in what little provisions were there, whilst setting out to track my comrades. The beef was particularly unpalatable whilst on the run with half my party to locate.

I thought it wise to back-track toward the beach, as they had certainly not passed me whilst I was trekking the mountain.

Back through the wretched impenetrable thicket I found Mister Banks and the rest of our group. They took little notice of my showing up.

Mister Banks was trying his best to awaken George and Tom who were lying as if dead in the snow!

Thankfully, Chester and Lady were by their sides, no doubt for warmth.

"What the blazes is going on here, Chester?" I demanded, shocked to find this scene!

Chester lifted his head wearily and begged I come closer.

"George and Tom stole the rum supply for the entire party, dear boy. They drank the lot between them in a bid to keep warm." He then laid his head on Tom's stomach.

Wearily, he continued. "They both just laid down here in the snow and refuse to move. We must attend them." Chester was clearly unwell!

Both Tom and George lay on their backs, unconscious from the drink. The entire party's share between them made them perfectly useless.

The rum is a strong drop in moderation, but I must say that I had yet to see any benefit of this drink!

Doctor Solander too had lied down and would not move. "I cannot go on!" was all he could say.

Thankfully not full of the drink, Doctor Monkhouse managed to get him to his feet and talk some sense into him. "Where's the brandy, Solander?" asked the good doctor, knowing its benefit to Doctor Solander at this time. It, too, like the rum, would warm him.

"Tom and George drank the brandy, too!" he wailed.

No one doubted that the state of Tom and George was dire, as they had drunk all the alcohol!

Mister Banks gave a suggestion. "Hold their heads up and try to get them to drink some water. It may dilute the contents of their stomachs and they may come around!"

A wise approach if you ask me, but this was to no avail.

The gents took Mister Banks's lead, shaking and slapping them in a bid to bring them around, but they were as if dead, and what little they could utter was a distinct refusal to move!

"Gents, go for Mister Buchan and the Littleboys. We had best get them back here to assist and keep us together." Another wise decision of Mister Banks's. He was growing on me.

By now it was dark and the gents followed Mister Buchan's fire to bring them back.

The attempts to awaken Tom and George continued for what seemed an age! Chester and Lady, without the benefit of the warming rum in their bellies, were looking worse by the moment, lying bravely with their keepers in the freezing snow.

"Chester! Lady! You must get up!" I pleaded of them.

Neither moved. They just closed their eyes. I was almost hysterical but tried to remain calm for the good of my friends.

"I know not of the fate of Tom and George, but I am certain that no effort is being spared to get them safely back to the ship! You must arise! You will freeze to death!" My warnings were lost on them.

They just lay there. No movement, no answer, nothing!

Tom and George's condition worsened by the moment. I was distraught!

I nudged and licked Chester and Lady as it was, after all, a feline thing to do, and all I could think of! I tried to convince them that the weather would break and would warm all concerned and revive their keepers.

Still nothing!

The brothers Littleboy, with an arm under each side of Mister Buchan, returned with the gents. They, too, were shocked at the sight before them.

Their fire had kept them warm enough to reach us, and they were apprised of the situation. We were all glad to see them safely back but the news dampened our hopes of reaching the ship alive!

"The captain and crew will be worried, will they not? Sending a search party?" asked Mister Buchan hopefully.

"I briefed the captain before we set out, that we could likely be here overnight," Mister Banks admitted. The entire party groaned. This was the first that most of us had heard of it!

"Yes! Yes!" said Mister Banks gruffly. "But who knew of these dreadful changes in the weather?"

This fell on deaf ears as all and sundry were losing hope, and we certainly had not packed enough rations for the night.

My opinion of Mister Banks returned to that of mad scientist and certainly that of a fool, for not arranging to carry enough for the night.

All the while continuing to rouse my friends, Lady's head rose and she whispered wearily, "Leave us, dear boy, we shall not go on without Tom and George." I could not bear this!

Doctor Monkhouse laid his head on George's chest, listening for his heart to beat.

"George is dead," he announced mournfully. He moved on to Tom and likewise examined him. "Tom is dead also. They have given up with all the rum in them, and frozen to death." Again, forlorn that this could be the case.

Mister Banks bowed his head, sniffling quietly. Although Mister Banks had seemed to treat them merely as insignificant dog-keepers, his sadness for their passing could be seen.

I was not a little surprised. This was the first sign of the milk of human kindness I had seen from this man!

Chester and Lady refused to be moved from the keepers, dead or not.

I lost my composure.

"Chester! Lady!" I howled! "You cannot just lie here and die with them! Get up! The two of you! I would perish without your companionship, and we have much good works to do upon this voyage!" I pleaded.

"Please! Dearest friends! We can make it back to the ship! The sun will come out and the weather will warm!" I found myself sobbing these words without shame, only barely noticed as the party prepared to bury Tom and George.

Wearily, the men dug rough graves in the hard ground for them, erected a cross above the head of each man with their names and the date of their demise. Then Mister Banks led the prayers and God speed to their souls.

Chester and Lady remained where they lay. I bowed my head, my eyes filling with tears for Tom and George, but more so for my friends who seemed destined for the same fate, as they seemed frozen and near death.

Suddenly, Chester rose rigidly to his feet!

"Yes! Yes! Chester, good man!" I thought my words had egged him on!

He nudged at Lady, licking her tenderly until her eyes opened. She, too, rose from her potentially icy grave. Chester and Lady stood tall and abreast, pointed their noses skyward and howled painfully for what seemed an age.

I had hoped my humble begging had roused them to their feet, but felt somehow that their loss and grief for Tom and George had revived them, if only to respect their passing.

Whatever it was, I placed myself between them and I howled with them. The loss of Tom and George was also a tragedy to me, as they had understood my feline ways and always treated me with respect.

While we howled, the gents and crew tried to light a fire but were unsuccessful, so they huddled closely to see out the night without perishing from the cold.

Chester, Lady and I kept each other warm, by curling into balls around each other.

By six the next morning, as suddenly as it had turned cold and bleak overnight, the snow stopped, the sun came out and the wind dropped. What a fickle place!

The gents and crew packed what little we had and we set out for the ship.

Chester, Lady and I were quietly respectful, as were our party as we trudged the slow march back to the beach. The going was slow with the thicket tangled in snow. Mister Banks was the most solemn,

I believed, for he had lost his dog keepers, a fondness he had for them quite obvious.

More so, I was grateful to the Almighty that my Chester and Lady had survived! Such firm friends we had become, and without them I knew not a happy future on our ship.

I still wept a little selfishly but quietly as we progressed toward the beach. Tom and George were gone, but my dearest comrades marched with me.

Meanwhile, back at the ship, the captain was indeed worried and had assembled a search party, knowing the gents had not packed for a blizzard! They were gathered at the beach preparing to set out for the lost, when we straggled through the village causing enough commotion for the search party to cease all and but watch. Being locals, the villagers knew we had suffered. I still kept out of sight of the sorcerer.

All of us weary and bedraggled staggered to meet our captain. The greetings were sombre and brief as we were missing two men, dead.

The captain charged the Littleboys with maintaining the dogs, now and in the future. They took the honour to task, setting them a warm place in full sun, now on the beach. I joined them. They ate and drank, sharing with me. I sat with them quietly in doing so, feeling their loss.

As we boarded the ship, all men were given hot food and drinks and sent to their warm beds. Chester, Lady, and I gathered in a corner of the galley as the oven gave off much warmth. Nothing was said between us. We slept.

I woke with a start! We had already missed one sunrise, what with being stuck in that wilderness, and I had to get Chester and Lady to help with my "Geoffrey Plan" as I deemed it. I woke them both and they stretched and yawned. We all went on deck to our usual places to attend our ablutions.

"Chester, may I have a word?" "Good mornings" being overrated as their mourning for Tom and George was not lost on me. I would have my work cut out for me.

"Yes. Yes, old thing," he said wearily.

I explained my own adventure of the night before and the plan I had concocted with King Geoffrey. His eyes widened at every turn in my story until I finished and he just stood there, mouth agape. Lady had stirred and heard the last of my "Geoffrey Plan." Her eyes and mouth were not unlike Chester's.

"Are you completely mad, you fool cat?" was his retort.

"Fairweather, did you dream this in your sleep?" asked Lady wearily.

"None of the above, dear friends! And I need your assistance to bring about this peace!" I tried to elicit some excitement in them.

They looked long and hard at each other, their eyes still popping and their mouths still open.

Chester cleared his throat.

"We have just lost our dear friends, Thomas and George, and here you are blubbering some insidious plan that I cannot fathom, let alone condone!" he bawled.

"This would be your worst, Fairweather," said Lady sadly. "I am shocked that you can imagine yourself bringing peace to an entire town! Let alone the danger! And Chester and I must mourn our dear Thomas and George in the correct manner! This requires being quiet and still for one day, as a respect for their passing."

Chester piped in. "Not to mention that we have the Littleboys as keepers now and must break them in!"

"To be honest, dear friends, I too mourn the loss of Tom and George, but we must go on. I believe they would be the first to cheer on my plans, and I'm sure they would wish us to keep busy rather than lazing about," I pleaded.

I pulled Chester aside. "I have given my word, Chester, and I cannot pull this off alone. There are canines to address!" I tried to arouse some interest in him.

"Give me the gist and I shall consider it," he whispered.

"You will do no such thing, Chester!" barked Lady having heard him regardless.

"Rest, Lady, I shall hear the boy out," he stated.

I described in detail the plan I had conjured during my restless night's sleep.

"Have you taken a blow to the head of late, old thing?" Chester quizzed.

"No, I have not!" I said, not knowing what he meant. His expression told all.

"I am not mad, Chester!" I was offended. "This will work. I swear it to you! Not to mention that we will be heroes!"

Chester's demeanour changed somewhat.

Lady looked up from her resting place, somehow knowing Chester would get in amongst a cunning plan at any cost, these things making him feel more important than just Mister Banks's hound.

He mused. "Very well, we must plan this to the letter. We are two, and insignificant ordinarily. This requires great thought and much discussion."

Lady just groaned and continued to snooze, knowing she could not change his nor my mind.

We discussed our planning to within an inch of perfection.

"Before dawn then, my boy?" Chester finished.

"As one old chum!" I pipped, and we separated. He to convince Lady to assist and I to follow my nose to fish! I was starving!

Mister Banks had not rested. Even in the mercurial weather, now being bad, he was too busy trawling the sides of the ship for sea life to categorize, name, draw, preserve, or whatever his aim.

With my feline ability to steal fish, I waited until he was out of sight with his nets, and I snapped up a specimen of which I knew him to have two the same. Into the longboat I squeezed and ate happily.

I took a stroll to the Great Cabin in search of my captain, grooming myself on the way as I was looking rather shabby after my adventure with King Geoffrey. He was in situ, consulting his maps.

"Ah, Fairweather! You are not looking your usual self! Been in a scuffle, have you?" he muttered.

I thought I had done a good job of grooming myself, but clearly not!

I groomed some more to satisfy my captain while he grumbled his discontent over the weather.

"This bad weather is going to delay our departure from this hellish place. I wished to leave at dawn tomorrow!" He said, shocking me to my very core!

Leave? We cannot leave! I had plans to perform to save entire tribes!

"Unfortunately," he paused reading his charts whilst my very existence seemed to hang on every word. "There will be no departure tomorrow, the weather remains too foul."

I breathed a sigh of relief. "Mister Banks will no doubt be happy. Tragedy having befallen him, he is resolved to pay another visit to the village." He shook his head, not understanding his botanist's resolve for new species, even upon the death of his slaves.

I was truly relieved as he had previously unnerved me! I would have time to unleash my plot and one must not upset the plans of clever cats, as Envoys to the King of England!

Dawn came and the captain had decided to join us. I was always a little self-conscious when he was with us, especially when I had a plan. Not wanting to disappoint and all!

Mister Banks and his cronies were assembled on the deck for our landing on the beach. All I could do was hope that the Geoffreys were ready. Chester certainly was, and he had convinced Lady to assist, although being a female of the species, she begged him to promise that should trouble start, we be off forthwith to safety.

We took the longboat to shore, the weather being cold but not snowing. The brothers Littleboy, now in charge of the dogs, were lying back, thinking it a fine lark to be off the usual sailing and maintenance duties.

Upon disembarking, Chester and Lady, having been set loose for a run by their new charges, confronted the pointy eared canines, while I snuck through the village unseen to meet with King Geoffrey. As I snuck, I hoped that Chester and Lady were able to convince the pack of dogs to comply with my plan.

The outcome pivoted on Chester's powers of persuasion with the dogs, and King Geoffrey's all-night romp to rally the full Geoffreys clan.

The sorcerer and the elders were gathered on the beach upon our arrival. The usual greetings with the captain, Mister Banks and his party were being attended as I snuck past the gathering, unseen.

To my hope and surprise, through the village and into the thicket I encountered King Geoffrey, and some one hundred or so Geoffreys, large, small, dappled and different in their looks. To look at them, it was not a wonder that the villagers were afraid for their chickens and children!

"Furrwedder!" called King Geoffrey. I could not make him out at first, as his kin were all the same! They hissed as one upon seeing me, but were hushed by a simple look from their king.

"King Geoffrey!" I saluted. "What a fine clan you have!" He looked tired. I complimented him, as he must have worked all night to produce this gathering! "Are your kinsmen briefed and ready?" I asked.

"We who have come for thees silly plans of jous, are all angry to come sooo farrr for what might not worrrk!" he scoffed, obviously tired from his night's work. "Some Geoffreys refuseddd to come, as they have lossst kins to thees tribe."

"I understand, your Kingship! This is a wonderful turnout! I did not expect quite so many Geoffreys. They must have come from miles in every direction!" I praised.

Meanwhile, at the beach, Chester and Lady were confronted with the pointy-eared pack! I heard them howling as one from my position with the Geoffreys.

Chester had made his case with the canines! Obviously, as advised, telling them I would personally be back to scratch their sniffers if they did not comply, and that it was a good arrangement for the village in general.

"Furrwedder, I hear the dogs. Does thees mean we have a truce?" King Geoffrey asked.

"To my knowledge, yes, it would appear so!" No greater enthusiasm could I have shown him.

"We will not come any furrrrther into the village for fear theeees may turn out bad!" he put his foot down sternly.

"I understand, old thing." I addressed him more casually now, having so far carried out my plan.

All the while, the captain, gents, crew and natives heard the howling from the dogs. Wondering what was happening, the sorcerer led the way, the chief and underlings following closely behind. No doubt a combined howling of their native pack would pique some interest!

The dogs were marching in my direction, Chester and Lady at the lead and the pack two by two across marching admirably. Well done, Chester, I thought!

The sorcerer with his stick was none to happy with this parade and behind the two foreign dogs! He started into his "Ahheee-ing" and the shaking of his stick, rather on time, I thought.

The elders muttered amongst themselves and the captain, Mister Banks, and the rest of the landing party followed up the rear, not knowing what was going on.

The dog pack with Chester and Lady at the forefront assembled near the livestock enclosures where an array of chickens and other foul were cooped, and pigs, sheep and goats fenced. This was obviously the target of the Geoffreys when food was scarce.

Chester had assembled the pack in a line-up just beyond the livestock. This was my cue.

I gave King Geoffrey the word and, on instruction, the Geoffreys lined up opposite them. I took my place beside the king, fronting the line-up.

Behind us all, the captain and tribe fell quite silent. The sorcerer stopped in his tracks and not another "Ahhhhhheeeee!" escaped his lips. He had spotted me! And with Geoffreys cats! All were mesmerised by the sight of sworn enemies cheek to jowl, standing before each other. Now even the sorcerer ceased to fidget and wail.

King Geoffrey and his envoys came forward first, with the skins of dead Geoffreys in their mouths; skins that had not been taken by native hunters or the native dogs. They were Geoffreys who had died peaceful or untimely deaths, not at anyone's hand. They placed the pelts in front of Chester, Lady and the dog pack. They backed away heads bowed to allude to their offering of just what the villagers needed to keep warm. Not a sound came from our audience.

The dogs came forward next, delivering dead wildlife they had hunted themselves, and the odd dead chicken and goat that the tribe had not noticed overnight, wild birds and rodents. They, too, placed them before their opposites, the Geoffreys, knowing this was what they required to exist.

Both sides backed away, both sides taking the offerings. Not a sound was made. No one moved. Not even that blasted sorcerer!

A truce had been signed by the deliverance of needed items. It was clear to all.

I thanked the king and bade him farewell and a long life for him, his kin and all Geoffreys present or otherwise. They quietly moved off into the thicket to their homes under the king's orders that all proceeds would be shared in the future.

I faced Chester, Lady, and the pointy-eared pack. The seniors of the pack took the pelts to the sorcerer and tribal elders and delivered them to their feet. The pack dispersed, their job done.

No one uttered a word for the longest time. Mister Banks and the captain came forward to the elders. My captain did not know what to say. He was aware that there was a problem with wild Geoffreys cats and the native dogs, as Mister Banks had told him, but did not expect this!

Mister Banks was quite beside himself.

"Did you see that???" he uttered to anyone who would listen.

The sorcerer looked at Mister Banks, the closest to anyone present who understood him. "Ahhheee?" he whispered. Mister Banks gave him a stern look and it was enough to quiet him.

After all this, sorcerers and botanists were the last people anyone wanted to interfere with what was so obviously a pact between the Geoffreys and the tribal dogs!

I sauntered forward, followed by Chester and Lady, all of our charge having left by now.

The captain broke the ranks, knowing that Chester, Lady and I had something to do with this, patted the dogs in turn and lifted me up under his arm for a good chin scratching.

The sorcerer came forward to the captain and squinted his eyes, still a little cautiously as I did so look like a Geoffrey, his sworn enemy. The captain held me out a little as this madman actually tentatively touched me without jumping and wailing.

A truce had been formed! All and sundry knew that Chester, Lady and I had orchestrated this wonderful bit of peacemaking! I accepted the sorcerer's petting, which was now more meaningful.

To my astonishment, he stopped quite suddenly and now began "Ahheeee-ing" again! I cringed back into the arms of my captain. Mister Banks came forward with authority and translated the problem.

"The sorcerer wishes to know how their neighbours, the 'Oona' people were going to benefit from this truce." He explained trance-like, still not fully believing what he had just witnessed.

"Oona people?" I thought. I know nothing of Oona people. No mention of Oonas had passed my sensitive ears. What of Oonas?

I was certainly not in the mood for this "Oona" problem. I had extended myself above and beyond the call of domesticated feline of the ship variety, and here we were ungratefully discussing Oonas!

I was not about to pull this stunt off again for "Oonas" or any other party for that matter. This one was difficult enough to organise without an encore with "Oonas." Blasted "Oonas" be damned!

Mister Banks explained that they were a neighbouring tribe who did not war with these villagers. They, too, had trouble with the Geoffreys. They hunted together at times with the "Oona" dogs.

Dogs? I had it!

Chester was lying on his back, joyfully accepting tummy rubs from the villagers along with Lady who stood quietly accepting her share of petting and hugs from the little children, which she was obviously enjoying.

I jumped from my captain's arm. He knew I was up to something yet again, and with the good deeds I had just performed, I'm sure he hoped that I had something cooked up to help the "Oonas," whoever they may be.

"Chester!" I yelled, trying to get through his crowd of admirers.

"What, dear boy?" he yelled back, not attempting to remove himself from this fine bit of attention!

"Chester!!!" I hollered gruffly, having squeezed through the well-wishers, trying to avoid being petted myself.

"We have more to attend of this plan than first thought! Now get up and help me, or my name shall still be mud with this village, and that ratbag sorcerer!" A lot to ask of one cat, however clever!

Chester sauntered out of the crowd, standing tall and looking proud.

"Yes, wretched Fairweather?" He answered as if I had taken his last meal.

"There is a problem with a bordering tribe. The 'Oonas' I am told are kindred with this village and want assurances that the Geoffreys will honour a similar agreement with them as with this village, concerning the hunting and such."

"'Oonas?'" Chester chuckled. "'Oonas!' 'Oonas!' 'Oonas!' What care we of 'Oonas'?" He was chirpy, having lapped up the attention of a hero. "I Doona care of Oonas!" he laughed hysterically. Whilst a funny play on words I had to get him to come around.

"Chester!" I scolded. "Can you get the Oona dogs to agree to the same truce with the Geoffreys if we toddle off to their camp?"

"Doona care of 'Oonas'! Doona care of 'Oonas'!" he sang, trotting about chuckling out loud.

"Chester! You are not being one bit helpful, and my good name is still on the line as that brutish sorcerer has asked more of us than we had bargained for. You must stand up with this village's dog clan and convince the 'Oonas' dogs to conduct themselves in the same manner."

"Doona care of 'Oonas'!" He was still giggling.

Just then, out of the trees came a group of some fifty or so natives, unlike the villagers we had dealt with. Mister Banks went with the sorcerer and elders to greet them. The captain stepped forward as Mister Banks introduced himself and our party.

Indeed, these were the "Oonas!" Right on cue as if they had heard me, Chester ceased his ridiculous behaviour as a similar pack of pointy-eared dogs brought up the rear.

They too had a sorcerer not unlike my vile madman. Upon spotting me, he began a similar dance with the usual stick and much "Ahhheee-ing." Not this again!

Fortunately, my sorcerer explained that I was not in fact a Geoffreys cat, and obviously told them of the doings between us, truce-wise. Thankfully, he ceased his flinging about and discussions got under way.

The natives were covered in seal oil to survive the cold, yet still a few wore Geoffreys furs.

Mister Banks was very keen to see them. They had arrows tipped in glass, which gave a hint of prior visitors. Perhaps the glass was a gift from "Bougainville," a Frenchman having visited these parts, explained Mister Banks.

Their bodies were painted in black lines of various patterns, which along with the seal oil made them look quite bizarre.

They must have been given red cloth from a previous visitor, as it seemed to be their favourite colour. All and sundry had beads or cloth of this same red.

Mister Banks, always prepared, sent for anything similar in red that we could give them in exchange for a bevy of freshly killed duck that they had bought as an offering to us. Balls of red yarn were brought forward and handed over to the elders, nicely in exchange for the ducks.

By now the two sorcerers and elders had finished the explanation of the miracle with the Geoffreys and the dogs and I, courtesy of my excellent planning and good spiritedness.

Now they wished Chester, Lady and I to call another truce between the "Oonas" and the Geoffreys.

Chester, Lady, and I took a moment to consider this. Lady stayed back for this encounter. Chester walked forward to the pack leader who prominently sat before his pack. Growling ensued, but Chester managed to convince them that we meant no harm. He nodded to me to join them.

I sauntered along and took my once previous place between Chester's legs. Again, my similarity to the stately Geoffreys cat was not lost on these dogs. And again, the scars of battle were prominent upon their snouts. Their eyes popped and they whined slightly as I settled in my place.

Chester explained what had occurred, leaving no detail unattended while I picked at that ever-annoying bug under my claw, ensuring that I showed no fear.

The "Oona" dogs were highly impressed and vowed a peace to follow between them also. As I may not see King Geoffrey for some time, I suggested that they leave offerings for them in the coming weeks. This would prompt the Geoffreys to honour the same covenant. Having sorted the details and bowed whilst backing away, the two sorcerers and elders of both camps assumed that our mission had been achieved.

Both sorcerers "Ahheeee-ed" to their hearts' content and what seemed like a social gathering or party formed. All of a sudden, the "Oona" sorcerer took Chester and Lady by their collars, and my sorcerer scooped me up under his arm.

"Fairweather? What the devil is going on here?" yelped Chester. "I thought we had done the good and just and brave thing! I am not a little disturbed by this! Damned ingrates! Dare I say this does not look good for us!" he whined.

"What can I tell you, Chester?" I hissed, this madman's grip being rather tighter than my captain's or crews. "I know not of their intentions. I am waiting for Mister Banks to explain! What is holding him up?"

We were taken to the village fire. Not a good sign! A cauldron of some sort was bubbling over the flames.

"We are supper, Fairweather!" howled Chester. "Now, look what you've gotten us into! You and your cunning plans. We could be lying peacefully on the ship had it not been for you, Geoffreys, sorcerers, villagers and 'Oonas'!" he whimpered.

The "Oona" sorcerer tried to calm Chester but to no avail. He was beginning to embarrass me with his whinging. Lady just walked along not knowing her fate but neither complaining of it, to her credit.

The two tribes gathered around the fire with the elders in the front row seated opposite one another. Our captain, gents and crew seated as best they could and others standing to see what would eventuate.

"Ahhhheeeeeeaaaaaa!" screamed my sorcerer, scruffing me by the neck and holding me aloft over the cauldron.

I tensed, hissing wildly, claws extended to try and escape but the grip tightened!

I was held over the boiling contents. I closed my eyes and held my breath, waiting to be lowered into this evening's dinner!

"Aaaahhhhhhhhhooooooooo!" and "Aaaaaaaaaattttttttttttoooooooo!" ensued as he shook his stick and placed the point upon my head!

There I was, suspended over boiling food with a pointy stick on my dome waiting for the end of Fairweather!

Then he gently and purposely handed me back to my captain, having been blessed! Mister Banks explained that this was the way of the tribe, what with all manner of ceremonies, marriages, baby christenings and the like!

I wished he had piped up sooner! I was still stiff in my captain's arms and he knew I must have thought my time was at an end. He petted me in an attempt to soothe but without so much as a word of concern, as Chester and Lady were also blessed similarly.

The entire combined tribes "Ahhhiiiiieeeeee-ed!" and "Ahhhooooooo-ed!" in our honour.

Having been released by my captain and joining Chester and Lady over a bowl of water to quench the thirst of fear, and then some rather choice village food, we sat lazily under a nearby tree for the first time in what seemed an age, while the two tribes and our captain, gents, and crew enjoyed each other's company over dinner of duck.

"What a day, old thing!" said Chester wearily.

"Quite right, old boy! Lady? Are you not proud?" She was rather quiet and pensive.

"Yes, Fairweather, I am proud, but dare I say I was so worried for our safety, that my pride will not be seen until my fear leaves me finally. Females are of this way." She smiled.

"I will let you both know when I am fully proud," she confirmed.

We boarded the longboat late-ish, all stuffed with duck and ready for bed. Those still on board were eyes wide at Mister Banks's recounting of the whole story with the usual flourishes thrown in for effect.

The other gents took a beverage with the captain in the Great Cabin before retiring. As was usual on these occasions, Mister Banks gave an account of his findings of Tierra del Fuego, and as usual it was of interest, but this time brief as we were all weary.

"The shortness of our stay here finds me wanting for information, but I shall attempt to inform."

"As we have experienced, the sea coast is well wooded." He rolled his eyes as he could have well done without the heavily wooded area we trod not long ago.

"The wood here might be fit for repairing ships or making masts. The hills are high, though not tall enough to be considered mountains, being bare on the top with patches of snow. The valleys hold fruitful soil and at the bottom of each valley, a brook with reddish water like those running through turf bogs in England, but it tasted well."

"We have seen seal and sea lion swimming about in the bay, and Doctor Solander and I did see some large footprints in the surface of a bog, but could not with any probability guess what kind it might be." I was glad I had not seen "large footprints!" My bravery might not have been so keen!

"Land birds are few but water fowl aplenty. I could have shot any quantity of ducks and geese but could not spare time as I was gathering plants," Mister Banks continued.

"Fish were few, but limpets, mussels and clams were in greatest abundance, not the best tasting but you would agree that we did not despise them." The gents nodded, but to my chagrin, I must have missed this tasting for I was not aware of limpets, mussels and clams. I would have to be more alert to the offerings of the sea!

"Insects are few and not biting or troublesome. I saw not a gnat or mosquito." He was pleased as the blighters enjoyed his fragrant white flesh.

"There were many species of plants and those truly the most extraordinary I can imagine. White flowers more common among them than any other colour. Doctor Solander and I took the pleasure of our favourite pursuit in examining but a few. They are so entirely different from any before described that we are never tired from wondering at the infinite variety of Creation!" He paused reverently.

"Scurvy grass was found plentiful near springs and watering places. Wild celery grows bounteous by the beach and tastes between our own celery and parsley. Both, as we know, are of benefit in staving off the scurvy." The captain nodded his approval as much had been harvested and taken by the men.

"The inhabitants are of a colour resembling rusty iron mixed with oil; the men large and clumsy and all under six feet in height. The women were smaller at five feet tall. Their clothes a kind of cloak of seal skin thrown loosely over their shoulders and drawn with a string at the waist, and nothing to cover the feet, except a few of them had raw seal hide drawn loosely around their instep. The women wear shells and bracelets on their wrists and legs, the men only on their wrists, but to compensate they wear a brown grass wreath over their foreheads, making them more ornamented than the women. Their painted faces were all differing. Their language is guttural as if to clear the throat. Their weapons were bow and arrow, and expertly made. Their houses were miserable and had no furniture. This tells me that they probably travel and stay but a short time in a place, moving on to better weather and food as needed. "The weather has been bad for the middle of summer and I gather it has been unseasonably so as the plants and insects are not affected by the cold."

His voice was beginning to drone as we all felt the weariness of the day, and I spotted the captain nodding as sleep was overtaking him.

"Captain!" Mister Banks alarmed him. The captain jolted awake, Mister Banks continued.

"Europeans have seen these people before us as they have sail cloth, woollen cloth, beads, glass and nails. They were also well aware of the power of our guns and asked us to shoot a seal for them. Thus, I conclude my report as we all seem to be weary." He looked askance at our captain. He bid his good night to attend his diary and specimens.

Mister Parkinson, having drawn a sample of the local catnip leaf, kindly gave it to me to chew on to celebrate with the remainder of the gents as one last brandy was poured. I found it a stronger variety than that of England, and it made me sleepy.

The dogs were given a nip of brandy and we all slept quite unusually where we sat in the Great Cabin that night, for a great and unusual day it had certainly been.

CHAPTER 17

The next morning, Chester and Lady had been taken on deck for their usual ablutions and a walk. I, too, joined them as that duck had filled me aplenty.

The men were expected to "toilet" over the side of the ship, for'ard near the cathead, where they could haul a frayed rope up from the sea to clean themselves after.

I found it rather a nasty sight, cats seemingly cleaner than men. I, too, adopted the practise as had Chester and Lady but I preferred to refer to it as "ablutions" as opposed to "toilet." It sounded more dignified, and the word "ablution" collectively included the washing of one's face and hands and preening one's fur, which offended me less.

I took my leave to the Great Cabin and my captain.

"Cape Horn! Cape Horn! Cape Horn! Twentieth day of January 1769," the captain muttered to himself.

He was preparing to sail from this Bay of Good Success on the morrow. And an aptly named bay it had turned out to be! Me being the hero of the day and blessed by Fuegian sorcerers!

But the captain did worry so about this Cape Horn. From the crew who had rounded it I had heard horrendous stories. I was not in any hurry to witness it first-hand.

"Ah, Fairweather, you have finally awoken, oh prince of Fuegians!" He laughed. "Imagine my having a cat blessed by a sorcerer!" He lauded. I do think he was rather impressed.

I felt positively lively having slept so well, full of duck and catnip, so I went on my rounds for vermin. It must have been the colder weather, as they were grouped for warmth and too sleepy to run. I would have caught a dozen or so, and as usual, brought them purposefully to the deck hoping as many crewmen as possible would see my mouth filled with a dozen mouse tails! Not a bad catch, if I do say so! But it was not to be so this morning. Chester and Lady were too worse for wear from yesterday's events. The crew were too busy wooding and watering for the departure tomorrow. Snoozing in and out of the way corner was the only thing for it.

The morning of 21st January 1769 arrived, and anchors stowed; all but one that had to be cut free of rocks.

We sailed smoothly out of the Bay of Good Success. I wished the Fuegians, the Geoffreys and the Oonas a fond farewell from my usual spot on the cathead.

The captain set us on a southerly heading, naming islands as we passed them, Lennox, Picton and Nueva, being new to his charts. So far it had been smooth sailing with some rain occasionally but not the monstrous seas I had heard tell.

My Isaac was in the crow's nest keeping an eye out for the Cape Horn bluff, some one thousand four hundred feet high!

"Bluff ho!" I heard him shout. But the captain dismissed him, as a mist had rolled in and he wanted to be well south of the treacherous bluff before turning. Aside from that, the weather and sea seemed altogether too calm for this to be the mighty Cape Horn.

Once the mist cleared, as it turned out, my Isaac had been right! The bluff he had seen was indeed the tip of Cape Horn, and we ended up sailing much further south than required.

"One can never be too careful!" I heard the captain assuring our lieutenants Hicks and Gore, assembled on deck with the captain at the eyeglass, while our ship's apprentices looked on and hopefully learned.

The captain now ordered Mister Molyneux to a westerly course, having passed the bluff.

There was not a man on board who could believe that we were indeed rounding Cape Horn on slight seas and fine weather. At times we languished without so much as a puff of air to fill our sails.

Whilst we rocked gently with our sails only luffing, we had rounded the cape with ease, although such calm weather was losing our captain good sailing time. One cannot have it all ways, I thought.

That evening was spent particularly pleasantly in the Great Cabin with the captain and lieutenants all jotting down this and that at the table, no doubt to do with the unusually easy trip around Cape Horn.

No more the gruff grumblings from my captain after the lieutenants retired. He was a contented captain and allowed me a nip of his brandy. Strong stuff, that. I slept like a babe in his mother's arms.

The next day Mister Banks, as always, was pestering anyone who would abide him, to lower boats into the water to shoot birds for identification, and trawl for fish species.

On one such occasion, in the placid waters, he shot another albatross against the wishes of the crew. Upon boarding with it, he hurried to the galley for Henry Jeffs the butcher to pluck and skin it and John Thompson to soak it, boil it, then stew it for eating!

Neither was particularly happy about the recipe but had to carry out the order. It was eaten, of course, but none other than Mister Banks was fond of it. He wolfed it down with vigour, laughing all the way through it, as no one else would go further than a taste.

This gluttony laid him up ill for four days! The butcher and the cook had the last laugh, after spending so much time on such a hideous catch!

For the eight weeks to follow, we headed north-westerly, leaving the cape and albatrosses alone.

The temperature rose to a pleasant seventy degrees and the food and rum was aplenty.

The winds were not always favourable and we were stilled many times. "Cats Paws" they coined it. I heard it cursed many times, always checking my paws for something foul I may have stepped in! "Cats Paws," I learned, were still waters and a slight breeze dimpling the surface of the sea and resembling the imprint left by my very own feet! I marvelled at such a term, but as it was keeping us from our aim, thought it inappropriate to name this wind after me! I would have preferred, as would my captain, that "Cat's Paws" be a stiff breeze hurrying us along!

It was now March, and the crew were shedding their winter clothing more with each passing day as our heading took us to warmer climes.

I, too, shed some of my wintery coat while grooming, leaving balls of fur to wisp about the deck and catch in the rigging. As it was building up and knotting in the ropes, the two lieutenants Gore and Hicks ordered the offending fur be plucked by the youngsters.

It was a while since I had seen my Isaac of the Smith variety, not to mention Will Howson, John Charlton, William Harvey, and young Isaac Manley, together. They had been tending to their duties on board while the Fuegian adventure unfolded. No doubt they had heard tell of my heroic deeds, though, as I did notice they had ceased tormenting me about being a "snow cat."

I assumed they were finished making fun of me as they picked my ever-mounting fur balls out of the places it had gathered, but their grumblings about such an unseaworthy task were many during my moulting.

I took to chasing my own fur around the ship's deck when bored, this annoying the boys not a little as my pouncing impeded their duty.

"Ere! Buzz off Fairweather! That's me!" came the cry when my Isaac's hand came together with one of my claws upon the same ball of fur.

"Lads! We could make a sweater out of the fur coming from this cat!" cursed Isaac.

The others joined in with their jeers surrounding my moult, as it was a daily task for some time. I took little notice of them, but great pleasure seeing my very own fur tossed over the side of a wide area of the Pacific Ocean. I wondered where the tide would take it? Somewhere hospitable and temperate, I hoped!

We had a troupe of thirteen Marines making up part of our crew of ninety-odd men. I had lost count as they scurried about in different places. I would see one here, and another there, and then quite the opposite. I gave up this counting as too confusing!

The Marines' duty was to man the guns, guard us from hostile natives on landing parties, and while at sea, stand sentry to the rooms and stores. They were most trusted amongst men. I likened them to the policemen, or "bobbies" as they were known back in England. They guarded the streets in my home town from burglars and miscreants. Marines were of this policing duty at sea and thankfully not wearing such silly hats as English "bobbies!"

Sergeant John Edgcumbe was the most senior of our soldiers. He commanded the privates, who were the lower-ranking officers beneath him. Corporal John Truslove, then drummer Tom Rossiter, then ten privates: Henry Paul, Michael Bremer, Daniel Preston, William Wilshire, William Greenslade, Samuel Gibson, Thomas Dunster, Clement Webb, John Bowles and William Judge.

The sergeant positioned them to different sentries and guardianships, mainly of doorways, to the captain's cabin, the Great Cabin, the spirit or alcohol room, the magazine or gunnery room, and the like, and sometimes just to keep them from boredom.

I gathered from my overhearing the grumblings when no one was around, that these Marines would rather be overrunning fierce tribes than guarding doors!

I could understand guardianship of the alcohol room as I had seen the hard drinking of some of the men. And, of course, should some chaps fight and bear a grudge, and the gunnery room was not guarded, there could be bloodshed. Hence, I understood their duties.

One such private, William Greenslade, had been given a piece of sealskin to guard whilst on his steerage door duty from twelve noon to four o'clock. It was going to be cut up and made into tobacco pouches for some of the men.

He knew there would not be enough to go around the entire troupe but wanted so keenly to have one, that when he was sure he was alone, other than with me, he cut himself a piece of the sealskin, and was later found out by Private Clement Webb, who asked to see it.

Private Webb, being a sober and dutiful man, had noticed that a piece had been cut out. As is the way of the Marines he told the other Marines of this crime against their station.

The code of the Marine had been broken. Word spread quickly amongst them, as this was a crime of the highest order: "Once you have disgraced one, you have disgraced us all!"

Private Webb set about finding Sergeant Edgcumbe. He was as mad as I had seen a man. The sergeant assembled all twelve Marines who were previously engaged on other watches or resting. None would dare to miss an order from Sergeant Edgcumbe!

I followed this closely.

The sergeant stood dutifully in front of them, holding Private Greenslade by the arm. He explained this theft, a dereliction of duty, to his troupe. They gasped at the very thought that they would all be implicated in this crime, as was their way.

One by one they all taunted and shamed Private Greenslade.

"You thieving wretch, I was one to receive a pouch from that sealskin!" growled Private Paul.

"Me, too, you blackguard!" from Private Gibson.

"You are a villain, and a disgrace to our good name!" accused Sergeant Edgcumbe. "What have you to say for yourself? You have made us all criminals and none here deserve it!" he hollered.

Private Greenslade, being a quiet, withdrawn type of around twenty-one years, could utter nought. He merely stared at his fellow officers in shame.

"Yes, shameful you should be!" barked the sergeant. "I shall bring this, and you, to the captain's attention immediately!"

A satisfied mumble came from one and all Marines. By this time the crew had gathered on the aft deck and surrounded the doings. A scandal such as this broke the boredom of endless sailing.

Private Greenslade's shame was too much for him to bear having been taunted relentlessly by his colleagues, and the crew alike, egging them on!

Sergeant Edgcumbe took Private Greenslade by the arm and headed for the Great Cabin where he knew the captain to be.

Greenslade whispered to his sergeant, I know not what, and he pulled away heading for the foredeck. All assumed he was allowed to relieve himself. I alone followed him.

He climbed up on the stays looking down to what he must have thought his destiny. Shame had overtaken him so that he would rather drown than take more cajoling and then the captain's punishment.

I clawed at this leg and howled as loudly as possible to attract attention from the men on the aft deck awaiting his return. They were all too busy gossiping to hear me and see him!

He looked down at me. "Fairweather, there is nothing more to do. I am shamed and shall never live it down. I am stuck on this ship with my fellow privates and they will never let me forget my crime against the Code of the Marines."

I clawed some more, but all he did was to give me a thankful look for being the only crewman to witness his end. Then he jumped!

I howled relentlessly! It was dusk by now and none had seen this tragedy but me! I kept calling, but could raise no attention from the group. I ran back and pestered them, particularly Sergeant Edgcumbe, but he merely edged me away with his foot.

They just milled about discussing the events, for a good half hour. I was fed up with their lolling about and placed a nasty claw into Sergeant Edgcumbe's leg.

"'Ere! You wretch! That was me leg!" I at least had his attention! I ran toward the foredeck and it was then that the sergeant realised that Private Greenslade was missing. There was nowhere to hide on the foredeck. He and his Marines and crew bolted for the spot he was last seen but he was not to be found.

"He's jumped!" some yelled. Everyone scanned the sea but as it was getting on for dark, even if he were nearby he would be impossible to see.

Finally, they all knew what my howling was for! Oh, if only men took more notice of cats!

At times I wished to be human, so I may do good deeds, speak to the men as an equal, talk of this and that, and at least call for help! But having seen this poor wretch driven to a death by his own hand, and by those I wished to be like, I decided quite definitively that being feline was best!

I daresay that none of this would have happened had the meanness of men not been present, and well-bred into them by the time they were of this age to sail, or become Marines, or any such profession.

I was ever so saddened by Private Greenslade's drowning, but even more saddened by the conditioning of humans. Yes, they had their goodness, but not this day. I felt I had seen them at their worst, but only so far. I had an inkling I would see worse at some indeterminate time. I was quite glad to be me!

Sergeant Edgcumbe and the Marines milled about, not knowing what to do. A further hour or so passed before the Marines filed into the Great Cabin to inform the captain.

I attended as the only witness to this truly wasteful, tasteless crime. I could not speak for myself, more's the pity! I would certainly have elaborated more than Sergeant Edgcumbe!

The sergeant only told the captain enough to satisfy himself that he and his Marines could not have avoided Private Greenslade's death. The captain rubbed his chin, knowing there to be more to this story than Sergeant Edgcumbe was admitting.

His knowing of the Marines told him a different and perhaps more accurate story. He could do nothing but send Private Greenslade off with the traditional prayers and respects to his family, then report it in his journal alone later, noting to himself his uneasiness of the Marine way. He paced well into the night.

I kept the captain's company as sleep did not come to me either.

CHAPTER 18

We journeyed with favourable winds further northwesterly for another eight weeks. I had ceased my moulting and my boys were ever so thankful, as they were back to their more seaworthy duties and I was cooler and looked attractively slimmer in my summer-wear!

This leg of our trip had the captain bent on heading straight for Tahiti.

In the warmer weather, there were new species of everything just waiting for discovery. Mister Banks and his cronies shot, drew, identified, and named many colourful birds and fish.

I was glad of this change in climate and considered it a holiday! Although, with the warmer weather, the mice were certainly more in the mood for reproducing. I was kept busy, but not overrun that I could not enjoy some time with my now recovered canines.

As we gradually left the cold, southerly weather, the sun on my belly while snoozing was almost as enjoyable as a good chin scratch!

Chester barked at all things new. It was an annoying but useful habit of his. Duty, I suppose, as guardian and cohort to Mister Banks. Most often he was correct in barking as new types of bird hovered round our ship. Mister Banks always attended when Chester started in, knowing that his well-bred and trained dog was always accurate and had a certain tone to his bark, telling of new things for Mister Banks to note.

One such bird caused much commotion as Chester woofed for Mister Banks. It was all white and, with an orange beak and two long scarlet-coloured feathers sticking out of its white tail. The crew agreed that it resembled the "Bosun's marlin," this being red thread used for mending the sails, hence he was named the "Bosun's Bird." I quite liked this friend of the sea. The strange bird scanned the waters aloft looking for fish. A friend he had in me! However, when eyeing a catch, he would drop from the sky like a stone and dive head first into the water to catch his fish in his beak, arising to the surface and eating on the fly. Not so much of a friend to me after all. I would certainly wish to remain dry, and eating on the run was bothersome at best!

Land-based birds began to appear, exciting all! The mood was jovial and relaxed. The captain being closer to his heading to Tahiti meant the beginning of his mission. Mister Banks and his cronies were thrilled at the thought of animals and plants to discover, and the crew, no doubt, would just be happy to get off this wretched ship.

It had been some time since our last landing and they no doubt pined for a sunny spot on an island or two.

"Chester! What fun! I sense a landing soon," I informed him. But he already knew, as did Lady. The smelling senses of the humble hound being better than my own, they sniffed the breeze coming off the land far quicker than I. The captain, of course, knew exactly where we were through his measurements and charting. Clever he was. He need not smell land!

We approached Tuamotus in early April. This was an archipelago or group of atolls, being small islands of coral and sand rising from the ocean just enough to grow trees and house inhabitants.

This group of tiny islands would turn out to be the largest in the world, so our captain could take his pick of landings, but no, to our chagrin he would not stop until reaching Tahiti.

This was the purpose of his voyage after all and he had to be on time. The planet of Venus would wait for no one!

Of course, Mister Banks was particularly excited as calmer waters meant that landings could be made in the pinnace or yawl, so he could seek out his potential discoveries, but the captain would not allow it. There would be plenty of time for findings after the safe anchorage at Port Royal where we were to be stationed.

The first island alerted by Mister Banks's servant, Peter Briscoe while aloft the topmast, caused great excitement!

On word of this sighting, Mister Banks bolted from his cabin and shimmied up the mast to join him. I was quite amazed at his agility, him being a gentleman and used to more preening and puffing than most of us. But I supposed that new discoveries overruled the perfect waistcoat and laundered, keen-smelling kerchief.

I scurried up behind him. If there was such a thing to see for Mister Banks to climb to the topmast, I must be present!

We could not get closer, as the waters surrounding the island were shallow, meaning reefs were present. These caused ships to sink if struck, and the surf broke upon them. This at least showed us where they were, or we would have been "holed," I believe it was called. If the ship was struck and broken below the waterline, leaking and potential sinking would arise. Not something anyone would take risks for!

We would have to be content with what we could see from the deeper waters.

To Mister Banks's great delight there was something to report. He shouted the description down to the captain and lieutenants who were using their eyeglasses to see more of the shore.

"It is one and one half to two miles long!" he shouted down. "Circular and a large lagoon taking up much of the island!"

"We shall name it Lagoon Island!" the captain shouted back, and proceeded to his instruments to record the co-ordinates and draw it for his navigational maps. He had the other scientists sketching what they saw.

We were a mile distant but those who had eyeglasses could see inhabitants through them. I could only make them out as small dots, but according to all reports I was glad they were but mere dots, as the natives reportedly stood on the beach stark naked! Not a stitch of clothing! We of the animal species were best seen in our birthday suits for they were purpose built and perfect in every way! Men, however, I found rather horrid naked, as they were bald of skin, some more than others, and not to my liking. I felt they required a fur to make them even remotely attractive when disrobed!

These natives were holding twelve-foot-long spears as a gesture of defiance! That and their baldness of body was enough for me! We guessed that they did not want visitors, even though Mister Banks wanted desperately to land regardless.

"Tahiti, Mister Banks!" was all that the captain had to shout to the topmast and he stopped his begging. It was not more than ten days' sailing away and there was much to prepare by the due date of this passing of Venus in front of the sun.

Another small island, and fires were lit as a celebration of us as potential visitors. Again, the captain dared not stop.

As more islands came into view we were greeted with mixed emotion. Some islanders put off in canoes but the reefs surrounding the islands where the surf crashed, stopped them coming closer.

Some islanders, while seen, would not even look at the ship. Odd that! I mean to say, as neighbours one would think all islanders were of the same opinion of a ship, but no, mixed gestures were apparent, so it was gathered that each island tribe kept to themselves as a rule.

At another small island, the captain brought the ship closer as the reef was broken up here and there, and the surf merely a swell.

Mister Banks squealed with glee and rounded up his posse to describe the natives on shore. They either had very big heads, or an awful lot of curly hair. Mister Banks deduced the latter as some tied theirs back looking like a bush at the neck. They had crude houses and "proas," double-ended canoes for fishing in the shallows, with an outrigger for steadying the fragile looking vessel in the surf off the reefs.

I was informed that these reefs held an abundance of good fishing. I looked forward to the proceeds at some future time.

Another island looked like a longbow in shape, from the masthead, the centre was filled with a lake. The captain aptly named it Bow Island.

On learning of it, Mister Banks left the dinner table and scurried to his position at the masthead and stayed there admiring its structure well into the evening.

Of course, here in the tropics, the days were longer and although the clock was at a late hour there was still daylight to view the sights.

The trees were not the kind found in England. Coconut trees were an odd sight, what with long trunks and fronds only on the top, as if pruned by the keenest of gardeners!

The coconut fruit was akin to a ball that young boys might kick about in the streets back in England. I was hoping they would taste better than they looked!

The ship continued on through the Tuamotus without landing. One island was so small it had no natives but masses of birds. Of course, the captain named it Bird Island. I was getting the hang of this naming, and guessed at a few, correctly some of the time!

Many atolls or islands we passed, only locally known by name to me. Exotic, though, and worth a mention for their lovely foliage and blue waters: Vahitahi, Akiaki, Hao, Ravahere, Reitoru, Anaa, Mehetia. Native names, no doubt, as they must have already appeared on the captain's charts. The gents wished to visit each one but no, Tahiti it was!

Weaving through the islands in this perfect weather the men "trawled" for fish. Hanging a line baited with pork rind, they caught a blew shark and brought it aboard. The smell was atrocious! "Pew" shark would have been a better name for it, and believe me I had no intention of eating it, let alone standing too close to it, for if it tasted as bad as it smelled we would all be sick or dead! Thankfully, they threw it overboard and washed down the decks. The smell remained in my nostrils for some time, however, and made my stomach turn.

The common grey sharks were aplenty and the men caught them easily. They were rather tasty and made for a change from the usual diet.

Ah, but the kingfish was my favourite. The flesh was excellent eating for the men and they would not share this with me, but my ever-faithful cook, John Thompson, kept the heads and I sat up for one whole night crunching away at the feast he had left on deck for me.

Chester and Lady even sampled some and for them too it made for a change. The three of us crunching kingfish heads in the balmy evening made for a fond memory. Sleeping all the next day was quite the only thing to do as our jaws ached from the bones of the huge fish heads.

The next morning, we sighted the towering peaks of Tahiti, through some unwelcome rainsqualls. Still, rain and all, the sky became filled with exotic birds as if to welcome us with their fanfare! Nice of them, I thought, and wondered whether the coloured ones would be an easy catch and a tasty morsel. Beauty aside, a bird is a bird when the urge to eat takes one!

On the evening that our destination had been sighted, I deemed it wise to attend my captain. He was in conference with the right people to discuss a landing. I put down on a vacant chair and listened intently.

Lieutenants Gore, Hicks and Mister Molyneux were preparing in advance for the anchorage in the Port Royal Harbour, of the locally known Matavai Bay.

Lieutenant Gore explained that he had been here with Wallis on the *Dolphin*. My ears pricked. This was Turkel's voyage! He had been here! I remembered! After losing his leg and eye in the Magellan Straits of Cape Horn! Ha! We had sailed a different course, rounding the cape, thanks to our clever captain! No storms had we! Only calm seas and "Cats Paws!"

I began what could only be called a "little jig" whilst standing on my chair! I caught the attention of all who thought I had gone completely mad. Lieutenant Gore strode forward and patted me unintentionally.

"We had a cat likened to this one in spirit on the *Dolphin*, although black as night. Injured in the straits but survived." I was so excited I jumped to the map table and began hobbling around on three legs, holding one paw up.

Lieutenant Gore blinked a few times as if seeing a ghost! I then sat down and covered one eye with my paw. The lieutenant stepped back a few paces, nearly tripping over a chair.

"Am I raving mad or do you, Fairweather, know of Turkel? Of the *Dolphin*?" he asked me.

The rest of the room thought Lieutenant Gore had taken ill, and I along with him, making such odd movements as to remind the man of our mutual acquaintance.

Laughing burst forth from those looking on. Lieutenant Gore and I ignored it. I sat, still as the dead and looked him unblinkingly in the eye. He knew! I could see it on his face!

And to think, I had not gotten to know this fellow better since we sailed from England! Although, how was I to know that this lieutenant had sailed with Turkel on the *Dolphin*? He had not mentioned it before this. My word! What a coincidence and a lucky one that! I must make myself known to this Gore! Spending too much time with the captain had me not entirely in the know!

However astounded, and after a knowing look right back at me, Lieutenant Gore composed himself enough to avoid being locked in his room with some medicine, as was the intent of the rest of the gathering in the room. He and I would have to catch up later, or I would be locked in with him!

I sat and he continued, although glancing a curious eye at me at intervals.

"We had some difficulty with the natives," he explained. "When rowing ashore we were greeted by so many of them in their canoes that they began to be troublesome and Wallis ordered shots to be fired to stop them from capsizing our small boat." All looked a little troubled by this news.

"Instead of firing in the air, one of the privates accidentally shot one such native and injured another! As tragic and unnecessary as it was, the natives became more respectful knowing the 'power of the white man's weapons.' Sad to say, it was to our advantage in the long run. Relations were cordial, we traded with them amicably, and by the time we left we were begged to stay longer," he concluded.

"Well, Lieutenant Gore," said the captain warily, as he had witnessed our little "get together" earlier. "You will obviously know the position for us to enter the bay through a channel between the breakers?" The captain was always utilising the knowledge of his key personnel, especially Lieutenant Gore's experience having been here before us.

The group departed, all but the captain, tending to his work. I followed Lieutenant Gore to his cabin.

"I say, Fairweather! Am I barking mad or did you just describe, in your way, Turkel the cat from the *Dolphin* to me?" he whispered so as not to be heard in court with a cat!

I gave him a knowing look.

"If you know him and um...ah...spoken?" He was a little out of his league here, not knowing the universal language of the domesticated feline, "Why then would you be on this voyage? Knowing that Turkel had been so badly wounded?"

I stood to my full height, circled a few times, edging my tail against him proudly and he got the idea.

"Hmm, bravery for adventure, is it? The promise of the sea?" Still keeping his voice low.

Again, a knowing look before I skipped off to get my rest, leaving him with his memories of Turkel. Tahiti was not far. I must be at my best!

I caught up with Chester and Lady and told them of my visit with Lieutenant Gore.

"Jolly good old thing!" he praised. "One can never have too many friends on board ship! And he knows your mutual friend? What a small world it is..." he snoozed off.

I, too, lay with them on this balmy evening with all well about me, and another firm friend in Lieutenant Gore.

By the 12th day of April, we had come within canoe distance of Tahiti and some of the natives had braved the shallows where the surf broke in their outriggers to come and trade with us.

These canoes were only wide enough for one person and although they looked fragile, served well in the breakers and through them they came.

The Tahitians were of a tawny complexion with long black hair and rather fetching, I thought. They were not of the greedy type and were happy to exchange coconuts for the odd bead or nail or apple.

They did not come aboard, but the captain made the formal acquaintance of an elderly man named Owhaa, from his canoe. This man had reportedly been of service to Wallis in the *Dolphin*, and my wise captain deemed fit to befriend him there and then, as our stay would not be short, and a friendly elder, knowing our language, would be more than handy!

Having seen the keen trade of the natives and the men, the captain drafted some rules that evening, as we lay off land that afternoon in unfavourable breezes. At the dinner bell all were assembled in the mess for the laying out of his ordinances. I was busy on a plate of scraps John Thompson had prepared for me, but heard the captain easily.

"Men! Come to order!" was the bidding of the captain, as they chatted loudly of our potential landing over their meals.

"I have laid out rules for trading with the natives at this our longest visit to any island thus far." The men looked at each other as if it were of little importance, but quieted all the same.

"Rule One…" he started as the men hushed.

"You must endeavour to cultivate friendship with the natives and treat them with unimaginable humanity." All was quiet now.

"Rule Two…A proper person will be appointed to trade with the natives for provisions, fruit and other productions of the earth, and no seaman or other belonging to this ship will do so, except the appointed person." The men were none too keen on this point.

"Rule Three…Any man working on the land who loses his tools and guns, or allows them to be stolen will have the value removed from his pay, and shall receive farther punishment as the nature of the offence deserves." Rather harsh but fair, I thought. The captain had his reasons firmly embedded in the knowledge that should the natives acquire or steal guns, all sorts of trouble might ensue.

"Rule Four…Any man caught stealing the ship's stores to trade will be punished as with Rule Three."No sort of iron, or anything made of iron, or any sort of cloth, or other useful and necessary item is to be given in exchange for anything but provisions."See to it that each and every one of you abides my rules for we are here for many weeks, perhaps months and I will not tolerate a breach of these regulations!"

That was it. The rules had been read, and the men realised the importance of adherence to them, for safety and good relations, and that we enjoy our lengthy stay without issue with the islanders. Having been duly warned, much chatter broke out over the remainder of the meal.

Finally, on the 13th of April 1769, Lieutenant Gore saw us through the channel he remembered, and we came to anchor in the calm waters of Port Royal Harbour having avoided the surf and entered without incident.

Before the anchor was down, canoes full of islanders, looking to trade, surrounded us. Quietly and civilly, they exchanged as the captain had ruled, beads mainly in exchange for bananas, coconuts, breadfruit, pigs, and small fish.

A few of the natives climbed aboard and thieved an earthen vessel from Mister Parkinson's cabin while all were busy trading.

As soon as the anchor was down, the men hoisted the boats and the captain, gents and a party of men under arms went ashore. The remainder stayed as sentries for thieves.

I climbed in on the second boat with the brothers Littleboy, in charge of Chester and Lady, and Mister Banks, as always, landing his dogs along with him.

Hundreds of natives greeted us as welcome guests. My guess was that all were happy for this greeting could have gone either way.

Owhaa, the elderly chap we had seen the day before our landing, greeted the captain. It seemed that Owhaa was of some note, as he arranged for his underlings to part the crowd and let us through in order of importance.

Obviously, by the time the Littleboys, Chester, Lady and I strode purposefully through the crowd closed in behind us, none of importance following us. As much as I took umbrage at being last, I was grateful for the pats from the closing crowd.

The land was mountainous and green and appeared like crumpled paper in its layout. The black volcanic sand stuck to my wet paws, as with Chester and Lady, making us look a sight as if in formal boots! This amused the crew until the sand fell away.

The peaks of the mountains were topped with clouds. A mile south was an isolated hillock named "One Tree Hill" by Wallis on his voyage, as indeed it was home to a singular breadfruit tree at the summit.

Rivers tumbled down the ravines from the mountains joining to form the Vaipopoo River, which ran parallel to the beach and emptied into the sea at the end of Matavai Bay.

We returned to the ship rather early, no doubt in preparation for this Transit of Venus business, getting under way as soon as was able.

The next morning, Mister Parkinson alerted us of a great number of canoes approaching swiftly for the ship. All men, they seemed friendly until they came alongside.

Mister Parkinson and the men on watch became concerned. The captain was alerted and hastened on deck to be greeted by two apparent "chiefs" and a hoard of natives climbing onto the ship like monkeys!

It was all the men could do to keep them from stealing! I retreated into the longboat as several scuffles broke out with the sailors on watch. Be assured that it was not cowardice on my part that forced me to this spot. I could hold my own in a scuffle! Especially with bare-skinned natives. A well-placed scratch would see me right! I merely remembered the captain's orders to be civil and saw fit to stay put for the time being.

Soon, from the safety of my vantage point, several more canoes, and double ones at that, came toward the ship. We were all a little worried, as we were outmanned if this rabble were of similar intentions to the first landed.

However, they turned out to be natives of a different tribe. Several chiefs came aboard and sent the troublesome hoard on their way, obviously powerful chiefs amongst the islands. These leaders seeming more civil and obviously high up in the pecking order to have gotten rid of the thieves.

Their clothes, demeanour and behaviour were that of a more refined inhabitant, not at all hostile. They had pleasant faces, with large black eyes and the whitest of teeth and were dressed in fine cloaks and turbans about their heads, the old and craggy Owhaa with them.

The captain appeared on deck, greeting these far more refined guests and leading them to the Great Cabin.

I rushed from the safety of the longboat to join them, the scoundrels having been given their marching orders.

The chiefs were entertained by the gents, each chief selecting one of the gentlemen as his own! What an odd occurrence! Perhaps they were selecting kindred spirits or similarly ranking officers. Who could tell? But the gents accepted their ownership with gusto!

The chiefs then patted their breasts, several times uttering the word "Tao," Tahitian for "friend." The gents responded similarly so as to seal their acceptance. The chieftains removed their cloaks and placed them over the shoulders of their "Tao," and in return each of the gents presented the chiefs with a hatchet and some beads.

The chiefs left the ship and the captain and gents reassembled in the Great Cabin.

"This was a fine beginning for amicable and comfortable relations," the captain noted.

The gents agreed, rather liking their cloaks, and off they went about their business. The captain and I parted ways with a knowing grin for it had been a momentous morning.

The men took their food in the mess deck as usual as if they were still at sea. The captain and lieutenants Gore and Hicks's priority now was to secure fresh fruit and meat. They ventured to the island in the afternoon to trade.

It seemed to the captain that Lieutenant Gore had certainly put us in the most favourable anchorage in the harbour. They ventured down the coast in two boats, the captain, lieutenants and Marines in one and Mister Banks, the gents and Chester, Lady, and I in the other. The brothers Littleboy stayed behind to tend to other duties and as we of the animal species seemed to so far have stayed out of trouble were entrusted on our own.

We arrived at Great Canoe Bay as Captain Wallis of the *Dolphin* had named it. Even before we landed, some of the natives clamoured from the trees and rushed about with greetings and welcomes.

Lieutenant Gore had remembered this bay from his trip with Wallis.

"Captain, something is amiss here I feel," he warned. "This bay should be swarming with natives much like Matavai Bay where we are anchored. There are but a few of the many I recall in this vicinity." He was much disturbed.

"We shall take a tour about the area, Lieutenant. I am sure they will surface once word has gotten around of our presence," the captain concluded.

We entered the woods expecting a whole community, but found nothing but ruin and a few straggling inhabitants, not of the type we were comfortable with.

"I expected the canoes to come out and greet us as last time I visited, and some of my old acquaintances to be here." He looked around, waiting for the natives to come forward.

"Had there been a war between the tribes? Or a plague perhaps?" Lieutenant Gore disappointedly guessed.

Some of the remaining natives had masses of lumps upon their faces and bodies with yellow spots upon them, as if an infection so dreadful was consuming them with itch.

"I too am disappointed, Lieutenant Gore. These are a suffering people without hope, let alone trade of any kind. I am sorry for the loss of your friends." The captain was always trying to give hope, but wanted the men away from this place for fear of catching their apparent illness.

We quietly went back to the boats. I, for one, did not want the obvious yellow lumps that the natives were sporting, nor did Chester or Lady. We were the first to the boats! Lieutenant Gore said little and hid his disappointment in not meeting old friends, by sitting as upright and staunchly as he could, but we all felt for him on the trip back to the ship.

It was a quiet night when I dropped in on Lieutenant Gore. I rubbed against him for it is a well-known fact that petting cats can ease the tortured human soul. He vaguely rubbed my chin and scratched behind my ears. I slept in with him that night, as my company was required.

CHAPTER 19

Our second day at Matavai Bay began with an onboard visit from the same hale and hearty chiefs from the nearest settlement. The very ones who owned a gentleman each!

Through what little speech was in common, or drawings or signals or noises, the chiefs had learned of our needs. They presented our captain with hogs, breadfruit and other vegetables not known to us, but according to the men, delicious!

The captain was most impressed to see the men eating such foods to ward off the scurvy. He in turn presented the chiefs with more hatchets and linen and other things they valued.

After this exchange we were invited ashore. The men hoisted the boats and the usual parties, including the canines and the Littleboys and I along, followed their directions. We rowed a long way and were escorted by more excited natives.

"Chester, old boy, I know they're friendly but this is not the usual way to that village, what?" I rumoured.

"No, quite right, old feline. I am uncomforted with this tack." He used his seaworthy terms to reply. "Tack" meaning the "direction" we were taking.

Lady just sat calmly as usual, knowing that her keepers, the now well-trained Littleboys, would look after her.

When we finally landed on the black sand we were gestured to head for the woods.

"Fairweather, I'm not liking this!" a nervous Chester whispered.

"Nor I, my friend. Should we stay upon this beach? Let the men go, I say!" I suggested selfishly.

Lady piped in. "Oh, for goodness's sake, you two! The captain would not take us all into danger!" She scolded rather sure of herself.

Chester and I raised an eyebrow or two, but remained chastised as was Lady's way, and there was no arguing with it!

After some distance we reached a "long house." This was the house or natively known as the "ario" at Point Utuhaihai at the very southern tip of Matavai Bay, the throne room for the very old but very grandest chief of the land. It had a roof but no walls, keeping it cool no doubt, and seemed to be the local meeting place. Old Owhaa was there and a number of ornately adorned natives.

Introductions were made and mats laid out for all by attendants and we were all made to sit on the ground. In walked the biggest man I had ever seen! Everyone stood.

He thumped his ample chest in friendship. "Tao!" his voiced boomed proudly.

"Tao!" answered our party with equal vigour.

Following him in was a beautiful and gracious woman, tall and handsome of face, with the carriage of a lady, like my owner back at home in England. Lieutenant Gore explained her to us as we stood waiting for her to take her place on an ornately carved throne. He had met her on his previous visit here with Wallis, and she was much talked about in English society. Her name was Queen Obadia, the elder and more senior of the large chief's three wives.

"Three?" I gestured to Chester. "Of all I have known and heard speak of wives, it seems that a man has enough trouble with one!" Chester laughed as best he could whilst standing respectfully.

Lady gave me the worst glare I had seen yet! Obviously being Chester's companion, she was incensed by my rudeness, taking it far too personally. I bowed to her and she seemed to forgive.

Queen Obadia stood regally and uttered the greeting "Tao!" without beating her chest, merely placing her hand over her heart. This was an emotional gesture felt by all. I gathered she was much admired by her tribe.

Our party returned the greeting. Chester, Lady, and I merely sat quietly on a mat to accommodate the three of us. We were now free to sit and relax it seemed.

The natives here must have been familiar with the canine and feline species, as there was no trouble, nor sorcerers, anywhere to be seen. I had looked about as we came in but saw nothing but chickens and pigs.

Chickens and pigs being terrible bores, I hoped that Chester and Lady might meet some civilized friends and I might see a feline that is not out to eat me! It would all make for a nice change!

"Hercules!" Mister Banks announced and came forward with the captain and Lieutenant Gore. The grand chief's name was actually

Tootaha; Mister Banks had referred to him as the Greek god Hercules because of his size. He was therein known as such and accepted this name proudly.

With his new name, expressly given to him by the revered white man, Hercules ordered a cock and a hen to be presented to the captain and Mister Banks. Whatever was given to our party was gratefully accepted. It was the right thing to do. We were encroaching on the lands of Hercules and his tribe. We would accept whatever was given us.

A piece of perfumed cloth known as "tapa" was then handed out. It was made from processed bark, and this processing was a sacred ritual amongst the women here. They believed it was a link between the divine and the earthly and it was much valued. Mister Banks having the largest piece, eleven yards long and two yards wide, was generously endowed. Not knowing what he would do with it other than categorise it for the Royal Society and present it to the king on his return, he bowed and accepted it graciously.

Mister Banks produced a large lace silk neckcloth he was wearing and a linen pocket-handkerchief as was always upon his person, and presented both to Hercules in return.

I hoped Mister Banks had more of these on the ship as I was so used to him waving that kerchief and dabbing his brow with that neckcloth, that I was sure his personality would change for the worst without them!

A feast was then forthcoming!

Raw and cooked fish and a mixture of fruits were laid before us all on banana leaves. These being cooked in the ground! A cooking method known locally as "Ahima'a" – a hole was dug and a fire lit earlier in the day, I learned, and stones were heated. Then the food was wrapped in leaves, placed upon the stones and covered with more hot stones.

This was quite unusual to us, as we only knew food cooked from the pots and pans of home, and from John Thompson's galley. Chester, Lady, and I received some juicy pork hocks to chew on. This kind of cooking was excellent! I was liking this place indeed!

Mister Banks was seated next to one of Hercules' wives, the ugliest and oldest! We all thought it a bit of fun, as he was not comfortable. Funnily, no one thought of Mister Banks as a ladies' man, always showing such feminine characteristics but one never knows! He bribed a younger, prettier girl to sit next to him, which completely upset our fun at his discomfort with the old crone.

We all ate well this wonderful feast. The women fed the men, mouthful by mouthful, and then held a coconut to their lips when they were thirsty. An unusual thing in these modern times! I could not imagine an Englishwoman woman feeding and watering her men! Preposterous in modern England!

Lieutenant Gore explained who was who, that he could remember. His help was invaluable to the captain and gents. Knowing who one was in the general scheme of things would help the captain to keep good relations between both our tribes!

After our meal, and the servants taking away our scraps, some native women came forward, drums began to beat and dancing began. This dance was called the "Timorodee," and we gathered it was reserved for special occasions.

We watched in awe as these beautiful women danced crudely in very little but coloured cloth around the waists. Along with their graceful hand gestures, and pearly white smiles, they were most pleasing to the eye.

I looked around to find most of the men leaning quite forward on their mats. Some to the point of almost falling over! Their eyes glazed and a broad and ridiculous smile on their faces.

I gathered that some female companionship was intended by this posturing. After all, we had been at sea for some time and they must be missing their wives, fiancés or girlfriends. My word, though, the collective crew took on an extremely dumb expression!

The dancing was interrupted by a loud "Hey!" from Doctor Solander. He and Doctor Monkhouse left their mats and reported to the captain and Mister Banks, that their pockets had been picked, thieved while sitting down to dinner! An opera glass was missing and a snuffbox! This was not good!

Mister Banks stood, ignoring the attentions of his lovely hostess, and struck the butt of his gun against the ground, making a loud cracking noise, which succeeded in calling everyone to a halt, and frightening the natives, this being his aim.

Old Owhaa was at his elbow in defence. Everyone ran out of sight except Hercules and Queen Obadia, the other two of Hercules' wives, a few other minor chiefs. They were worried at this interruption and sat very still, awaiting an explanation from the captain and Mister Banks with the elderly Owhaa by his side.

Lieutenant Gore tried his best to explain with gesture and much play-acting. It worked admirably and Hercules offered that our men help themselves to a pile of scented and coloured cloth in exchange for the pilfered items.

Mister Banks refused. The victims wanted their precious items back. Hercules' ample body wobbled as he stood. He marched off we knew not where. Not long after, he returned with the items having gestured that he found the culprit and had him punished.

This ended the evening's frivolity and unfortunate hostility, but peace was restored thanks to the brave Mister Banks and the actor in Lieutenant Gore. The captain was pleased.

We returned to the ship, all filled with native cuisine, and the men no doubt thinking fondly of the dancing girls. Sleeping was the next item on the agenda for most of us, and for most it came easily. The Marines took their watches to dissuade any natives from thieving while we slept with our bellies full of Tahitian food.

On the morning, I visited the Great Cabin, where misters Green and Banks were in conference with the captain. I sat in, as always.

"We are little more than six weeks away from the observation of the Transit of Venus, Captain," said Mister Green the astronomer.

"That is exactly the point, Mister Green. We will ensure that our observatory and fortress is built and ready! I promise you that nothing shall impede its progress and we shall begin today!" The captain assured him.

Mister Green being a civilian and our lead astronomer was keen to get the spot ready for the observation and equipment for reporting the transit. After all, that was why we were here!

"Must we build a fortress, Captain?" he asked, thinking it a little more than what he required for observatory purposes.

"Judging by the thieving we have witnessed so far, I should think so, Mister Green!" the captain demanded.

"We have one of everything required and if opera-glasses are an item worth stealing then I believe our instruments to be endangered and in need of protection and vigilant guardianship. I will ensure this! What's more, there are other less amicable tribes here and our safety is my foremost concern!" the captain made it quite clear that there would be nothing less than a fortress and armed guard for this important observation.

"Very well, Captain, I shall be on hand for anything you require." With that, Mister Green departed.

The captain wiped his brow. "Fairweather, these civilians and scientists can be such a trial," he confided in me. I agreed and sat while he designed the observatory and surrounding stockade.

He had chosen a spot at the northern end of Matavai Bay. There, it was a sandy spit of no use to the Tahitians as Lieutenant Gore had reported. The Vaipopoo River was on one side, and along the banks the captain had set out a double row of water barrels for the cover of our armed men, so that it was protected.

Picket fences were to be built to shield the sides of the fortress between the beach and the river. Armed men in boats could protect the side facing the beach. The safety of the observation now covered, he also noted that the trees were few, leaving the sky open for telescopes.

This beach was of no apparent importance to the natives, according to Lieutenant Gore. He had it well planned. He had decided to include some of the ship's guns behind the barricaded walls. So important was this mission that no effort to protect it would be spared!

The captain had been informed by Lieutenant Gore that although the people of Tahiti were generally peaceable enough, the island of Tahiti was prone to warfare, examples having been witnessed during our walks through the area; spear heads in trees and decaying bones placed meaningfully upon rocks to warn folk of mischief and death!

Lieutenant Gore had heard of a certain King Tiarreboo at the far end of Tahiti, who was much feared and waged these wars from time to time.

As far as our captain was concerned, even the friendly Hercules was not to be trusted with our mission.

Another local chief was made known to the captain. Mister Banks had named him Lycurgus, after the mythical god of Sparta. His native name was Tupura'ai Tamaita so we kept his name as Lycurgus for our ease. Indeed, any of them may turn against the visitors. We must be vigilant!

On the 15th day of April, the captain arranged that we take official possession of the site he had chosen, so we were all off again in the boats, this time with many men and the thirteen Marines led by Sergeant John Edgcumbe.

Mostly, the men tended the ship, which required upkeep from our long voyage here. Now that the anchorage of the *Endeavour* had been established, some of the men jumped in and swam ashore when they were able, on permission from the captain. We saw little of those and hoped they were adhering to the captain's rules. I also hoped that if they had been meeting with the lovely local girls, that their manners were intact and that there was not a large angry father within site!

We disembarked and the captain stood with the English flag and pronounced the area Point Venus, and the fortress, Fort Venus, the names seemingly obvious, and all in the name of King George.

A tent was produced to shelter the men and tools during construction. Owhaa the old was there yet again. Somehow, he just knew when and where we would be in attendance! Sorcery, I suspected!

"Could the ex-*Dolphin* crew please step forward?" asked the captain.

Crew? I thought? I only knew of Lieutenant Gore. Mister Molyneux stepped forward with a few of the crewmen. I was shocked! Yet again, I chastised myself that I had not gotten to know more of them!

"Lieutenant Gore," the captain continued, "please do your best with the natives to teach them a few English words so that communications may be less strenuous," he pleaded.

"Yes, Captain," saluted Lieutenant Gore.

Hundreds of natives who had seen us coming had assembled to watch, us being a rare curiosity.

Mister Banks drew a line in the sand with the butt of his musket and made signs to them that they must not cross it. None did so. Frightened of the musket, having seen it in use with Wallis and the *Dolphin*'s visit, no doubt.

The captain set the crew about erecting the tent.

With this, we left Jon Monkhouse and the Marines to guard the construction crew and set off with misters Banks, Green and Parkinson, and Doctor Solander on a mission for further trade, particularly hogs and hens, which we needed desperately.

Followed by the usually bevy of natives, we reached the Vaipopoo River where Chester and Lady took a well-earned swim. I, however, not being overly fond of immersing myself in the stuff, stayed away from the water and lay happily under a palm tree watching the dogs play about.

Mister Banks waded into the river as with some of the other gents, muskets armed with bird shot at the ready. They alarmed some of the local ducks and Mister Banks held his aim, and killed three with one shot! Chester retrieved them from the water, as was one of his duties to Mister Banks. I was perplexed. Three birds with one shot?

"My word, Mister Banks!" said the captain. "A fine shot, indeed!" Many congratulations followed from the other members of our hunting team. To the natives, however, it was three ducks killed with one shot, and seemed to be a miracle! Many of them fell to the ground as if they too had been shot! This play-acting was rather disconcerting for those with arms, and they checked that they had not accidently shot the natives by mistake. The natives rose eventually and Mister Banks showed them that bird shot was indeed a grouping of pellets, whilst shot only once they dispersed in different directions, enabling him, still chuffed with his kill, to bring down the three birds. They understood and were quite wary from then. I, too, was grateful for the explanation of three birds with one shot!

All of a sudden, we heard gunfire coming from the direction of Fort Venus! The captain and gents ran until they were dry! Chester, Lady, and I following up the rear.

There was pandemonium on the beach! Owhaa, not with Mister Banks and our party, were screaming wildly!

Sergeant Edgcumbe was puffing with fear that he had done wrong by his captain!

"Captain, sir, I was going about my business and the locals had stayed well away from the line in the sand for this some two hours!" He puffed some more.

"Calm down, Sergeant!" the captain demanded.

"A fat native crossed the line and pushed one of the men over, grabbed his musket and ran off through the crowd!" He leaned down, his hands on his knees as if having run a mile in a minute, still puffing!

"I ordered the Marines to open fire on the crowd as they all ran!" he panted. "The culprit was shot dead but many were injured!"

Chief Hercules had turned up. The captain had to try and explain to him that the man was shot because he took the gun, and that the crime was deserving of death. It was a bit of a stretch, I thought, but relations were at risk and the captain had to fib a bit, as this crime in our England would not be punishable by death.

But it worked! Chief Hercules persuaded about twenty Tahitians to return. He described the crime and punishment to his fellows, and the regret we felt that some other locals had been injured, but as before, they had been warned! If Lycurgus was happy enough with this explanation, they would be, too.

They sat watching the men work in wonder at the large tent being built, much more quickly than a hut. Relations seemed to be restored.

After sunset the king and his subjects left satisfied, the tent was pitched and we retired to the ship. I knew that Mister Parkinson, being a kind and gentle fellow was deeply disturbed by the terrible death of one of the Tahitians, so I visited him in his cabin after dinner.

He was awfully pensive and my rubbing and smooching was doing nothing for his mood. I scratched him, gently but enough to draw blood. He spoke to me for the first time.

"Yes, Fairweather, blood has been spilled this day and I cannot abide it." His voice quivered. "Other than the thief, these were unarmed men and women. It could even have been a child injured. Who knows?" he looked skyward his hands in prayer.

He wiped his brow on his sleeve. "We have not spoken before but I know you to be a fine cat and member of the crew, confidante to the captain. I believe you drew my blood with that scratch to alert me of my own humanity. Was this your intent? To remind me that today's actions were necessary to get the message across to the Tahitians? I fear so that they will rebel against us!" he stood, wringing his hands with worry.

I looked at him squarely and raised an eyebrow. He had gotten the message. I gathered he was still a little concerned that full-scale warfare would ensue, us having shot at them, but Chief Hercules had done an admirable job and I for one believed it would not come to that.

I left him with a little more peace than he had prior.

I sauntered off to the Great Cabin to apprise myself of the captain's thoughts.

To my grief, Mister Buchan was lying on the cabin floor with someone's belt doubled in his mouth! I gathered from the previous attack that this must be the epilepsy yet again.

One wondered about the maladies of humans. Much more sensitive than we cats, or dogs for that matter, as they were in attendance with Mister Banks and the other gents, making for a somewhat crowded gathering.

Doctor Monkhouse was quietly in attendance on the floor with Mister Buchan, holding his thrashing limbs as best he could.

The epilepsy would usually pass and leave the victim feeling poorly. This was not the case for poor Mister Buchan. The twitching and thrashing limbs would not stop. The belt in his mouth was almost bitten through.

For the longest time we hoped he would recover. All of the gents were by now holding him still and the captain and I looked down at him with softened eyes. They merely peered back with a hysterical glare as if he were silently being tortured.

Soon the seizure stopped. Mister Buchan's eyes closed. He must have been exhausted as this fit stretched over one full hour!

"Help me take him to my cabin," asked Doctor Monkhouse of the gents.

They all grabbed an arm and a leg and held his head and back straight, as I followed them. They placed him on the surgeon's bed. The others would not fit in such a small place and milled around outside Doctor Monkhouse's cabin, pacing as best they could with the low roof outside his door.

I stayed with him, and licked his hand with eyes closed, as my mother had done for me when I felt poorly. I hoped it would help, but Doctor Monkhouse shooed me away.

Some, including me, went back to the Great Cabin to discuss this awful day with the captain, knowing they could do nothing for Mister Buchan. Doctor Monkhouse stayed with his charge.

"This is the worst I have seen of Mister Buchan's fits!" said Mister Banks, his newly restored kerchief patting his nose after some soothing snuff from his box.

I wondered what that stuff was but was never to find out. All I knew was that it placated Mister Banks, and that it had a friend in me! His hysterics were well documented!

Mister Parkinson came to the Great Cabin to find out what the ruckus was. He was dealt yet another blow. His good friend and fellow artist Mister Buchan had been struck down with another fit!

Doctor Monkhouse poked his head around the door of the Great Cabin.

"I fear he will not come out of this one," he said dourly. "It has been his worst and try as I might I cannot bring him around."

The captain dismissed him. "Do your very best, Doctor. We will await the outcome."

We were all shocked, but Mister Parkinson was quite beside himself, looking as though he too would take a conniption of some kind. Brandy was forthcoming; even I had a nip from a well-placed saucer.

At two in the morning of the 17th day of April 1769, Mister Buchan died. He did not awaken from the fit he had taken. We all bowed in silence. No one had slept.

The captain sensibly took hold of the situation, taking everyone's minds off this tragic death.

"Mister Parkinson!" the captain piped. "You will be on your own now as the only 'figure and landscape' artist aboard the *Endeavour*."

"Yes, sir!" said Mister Parkinson. "A job I take over dutifully in Mister Buchan's honour."

A fine distraction by the captain! And a fine response by Mister Parkinson, having gathered himself a little since my visit.

Mister Banks proposed his own toast. "I sincerely regret him as an ingenious and good young man," he trumpeted. "His loss to me is irretrievable. Had he lived on another month, his drawings of the figures and dresses of the natives here would have entertained my friends admirably back in England. What an advantage that would have been for me!"

A rather larger brandy followed, and an odd look from all of us present, toward Mister Banks who was snuffing away at that box.

Following his insensitive speech was a toast to Doctor Monkhouse's attempts to revive him, and to Mister Buchan himself as the gentle and sensitive artist he was.

I detected a tear from Mister Parkinson at this stage but he held firm, brandy holding him in place.

"I fear we will have trouble with the Tahitians if we bury Mister Buchan on shore," said the captain mournfully but dutifully. "They seem quite superstitious from my observations. Those bones and blood on trees we had all seen were not there for the sake of décor! I feel that they will take umbrage should we bury him on their lands."

Quite right, I thought.

The captain conducted an immediate service on board, with the usual prayers and honours, and he personally went out with the gents in the pinnace and longboat as far as they could get toward the reef, to bury him at sea.

I joined the captain alone in the Great Cabin upon his return and we watched the sun rise from the windows very quietly together. He was at the lowest point I had seen him to date and I felt for him deeply. I shinned up against him and he scratched my ear while we watched the red ball rise through orange clouds.

"This voyage is taking its toll, Fairweather," was all he said. He nodded off in his chair for what little sleep he would get. Perhaps an hour. Perhaps two.

CHAPTER 20

The morning was dour with showers, as if the sky cried for the loss of our sensitive artistic friend.

The captain cast aside his gloom by determination. The fortress and observatory were his mission and a way to keep the saddened gents and men busy.

He took ashore fifty men with saws, axes, and spades, for digging and cutting wood. By midday, Point Venus was likened to an ant's nest from the safety of the ship. Men so large in the flesh, but small from the ship, dug and chopped, and erected the fences.

The natives joined in, encouraged by the captain who asked for permission to cut down a tree and then offered gifts in repayment! After all it was their land! They thought it all fantastic fun!

By noon, the captain had ordered pork to be cooked in gratitude for the service of all. Pigs being few, they commanded the payment of an axe!

Our ship had arrived in the height of the breadfruit season. Breadfruit was likened to a potato but with a dimpled skin. There was no shortage of coconuts, yams likened to a sweet potato, and plantains, which were a bland type of banana, all very rich in the nutrients required by the captain's scurvy rule. He need not worry about that here!

There was an oversupply due to the season and we had to try and communicate that nothing further was required for at least two days! Such was the amount we had accumulated! A bead the size of a pea would purchase four to six breadfruit or a similar quantity of coconuts! We had to save the beads for further trade!

The fort was coming together and the main tent was up. Misters Banks and Spöring spent their first night in the tent surrounded by a troupe of sentries on guard. Fortunately, no one came to bother them.

Chief Lycurgus turned up the next day with his extended family. They brought household furniture and even whole houses to be erected in our neighbourhood. The natives moved their whole houses as they saw fit.

Mister Banks had encouraged this chief as none other as he was locally wealthy and of means which would ease our stay. Occasionally, though, they would take offence at some trivial thing and uproot the thatched houses and move, only to come back, their houses with them, when the captain and Mister Banks went to them with gifts to placate them.

Doctor Monkhouse took a walk in the woods and reported to the captain of the body of the man shot by us earlier. He was placed on a bier or altar, supported by stakes and a covered hut, which was built for the purpose; the body wrapped in cloth and around it, war instruments, a hatchet, some coconut fibre, and a cup of water.

Mister Banks found out from Owhaa that the Tahitians believed in a future world where they would go when they died, and that the body and its adornments would be used in this future world. They did not like us being near it, but then for the stench of rotting flesh, we preferred not to be too close either! This being the end for a man's body here, we decided it was more than prudent that we had buried Mister Buchan at sea. He and all alike would have wanted it so.

By the 22nd of our April, the fort was almost finished. Six days was all it took our remarkable crew and, of course, the agreeable locals who thought the whole thing a lark! I imagine it gave them something to do besides picking fruit!

The fort was higher than I imagined when the captain was drawing it, with a palisade of wood on three sides, and the fourth protected by the water casks. None would interrupt the scientists in the days to come for their sighting of the Transit.

Some of our swivel guns from the ship were mounted on the top of the castle ramparts, with a four-pound canon on each end. Within the walls of the fortress, a small community had been established.

There were living quarters, a kitchen-dining tent, a special area for the gents, a forge for shaping steel, and enough food stores to make it self-sufficient. This ceased the to-ings and fro-ings from the ship with food and the like.

My wonderful cook John Thompson and butcher Henry Jeffs were well pleased to be out in the air, cooking up all manner of things. They even tried the native way of the hot stone burial of a hog. I can say first hand it was delicious!

The fort was ready for the transit of Venus with nearly six weeks to spare. All that remained to be done was set up the telescopes and other instruments. These were locked in the hold of the ship for security. The captain was not about to entrust them even to the fort, what with curious thieving natives about.

Now that the fortress was finished and regular visits to us by Chief Hercules and Queen Obadia were established, and occasionally Chief Lycurgus and his party of two to three hundred, I was bored. The men had been so busy and even the Littleboys chipped in on the building, keeping Chester and Lady tied up while they worked, exercising them regularly but never venturing too far away. One never knows what natives might decide to eat!

The gents drew and collected and categorised everything but the sand, and even then I'm sure a bottle of it was seen heading for the ship!

A three-watch system was still maintained on the ship under the captain's orders, and I taken on board regularly to see to my mousing duties. The warm weather certainly suited my prey!

One such day, with all relaxed or attending their duties, Chester, Lady, and I decided it was high time we took a tour of our own. We toured the pens and holds for the chickens and livestock. Our bullock and cows were now neatly housed with plenty of fresh grasses to eat. They intimated they were being treated rather well, almost as royalty!

The Tahitians had not seen cattle before this, and what they could be used for. They enjoyed milk and the knowledge that one day they may enjoy beef once the happy family produced some young. Eventually they would have quite a herd if the young bullock had his way!

Our own little discovery party went bush to ascertain the wildlife situation. The colourful birds made me drool but I was so well fed that I needed only to admire them. A centipede crossed our path, curious shiny black worms with more legs than I had ever seen. I sniffed at it but Chester shoved me sideways.

"Here, Chester! What the devil?" I spluttered, the breath gone from my body!

"Sorry for my shoving, old thing, but this centipede will kill you with one bite! I was merely looking out for your safety," he explained.

"By gosh, Chester!" I puffed, filling my lungs. "It looked so unassuming crawling along on all those feet! You've saved me yet again! I do believe thanks of some kind are in order, but that shove! Old friend, you do not know your own strength sometimes! Needless to say, I am grateful for the tip!"

"Think nothing of it, dear feline! I have seen them before with Mister Banks and witnessed a bite to a man, which pained him so he screamed like a woman! It was an age before the bite healed and it left a nasty scar," he informed, always forthcoming with his knowledge.

"Well, centipedes can keep well distant from me!" I shouted, hoping they would all hear and I need not be too vigilant, as there was much more to see than staring at the ground looking out for worms with one hundred legs and a nasty bite!

Lady called us over to some rocks for a look at the native gecko in a crevice. It made an odd ticking noise.

"These little fellows eat insects, my dear," Lady explained, herself a font of information when Chester was not forthcoming.

"Centipedes?" I inquired with vigour, knowing them now to be a pest of the worst kind.

"No, dear," she replied as if I were as dumb as a rock.

A lizard darted across the rocks a little further away. I checked with my instructors to ascertain that it was not lethal before attempting to chase it. Too fast for the likes of me, unfortunately! Lady explained that they too ate insects, and as I have thought long about such insects as the native "no-nos," a small beastie with an itching bite that taunted the men on shore, was much concerned. They could not penetrate my fur, even in my summer coat, but poor Chester and Lady, if they were sleeping on their backs, would wake with a torturous itch that drove them to shimming across the sands on their bellies! I was grateful for the gecko and the lizard, for their sakes and that of my crew!

"More lizards and geckoes!" I announced to Chester and Lady. They agreed whole-heartedly.

Something on our tour was bothering me. A rustling was heard here and there and seemed to follow us. I thought it the stomping of centipedes or perhaps the odd lizard, but it persisted and I knew such animals not to be stalkers.

I had fallen behind the canines looking at this and that. I sped up without running, in case a similar species to Geoffreys cats was tailing us. Running was a lethal manoeuvre on my part, if a wild stalking thing were about. The hunt for Fairweather would be on!

I found my friends sniffing near a tree. Chester in particular liked to urinate on anything that did not move, to ascertain his dominance of the area!

"Chester!" I whispered when sidling up to him and Lady. "Something follows us!" I looked from side to side.

"Don't be silly, Fairweather. It may have been a fowl or lizard rustling the undergrowth," he chided, cocking his leg on a rather dominant coconut tree, as if that would teach it a lesson for merely growing there!

"Stop for a moment and we shall listen!" I demanded. I was not going to be put in my place when I knew there to be something out of sorts!

"Act casually, then," Chester directed. He knew his stuff where the hunted or the hunter was concerned.

I nosed around sniffing at the breeze while the three of us tuned our senses to the surrounds.

Surely enough there was a rustling, and it was no centipede!

"Fairweather! I hear it," Chester whispered.

Lady with her keen sight, spotted a pair of eyes and a snout that looked oddly familiar poking through the bushes some way in from our path, parallel to us. She pointed it out to us without frightening or angering it, whatever it was.

"Act as if you have seen nothing, and spread out," whispered Chester, a plan coming to his head. "I will circle around behind it and surprise whatever the thing is."

Lady gave him that "be careful" look and off he sauntered as if nothing in the world bothered him. Sniffing here, marking his scent there.

All of a sudden, out of the bushes shot a dog, not dissimilar to Chester and Lady in size!

I bristled and climbed the nearest coconut tree; these having no branches allowed me hike up the top rather briskly. I clung and stared down.

"I say!" barked Chester, puffing himself up. "Here! Who are you?"

We had seen nothing of the canine species so far on this island. The brute just stood looking rather dopey. Chester had the upper hand and Lady backed him up by flanking his rear.

"Speak up, man!" Chester demanded, baring his formidable teeth.

"I am Paroo," he said meekly, not making eye contact for fear that Chester would attack.

"Hurry up, Chester! Make short work of him! I am stuck up this blasted tree!" I shouted down impatiently.

"Tao!" was all he could utter, feeling the sense of doom that Chester could muster in one at times.

"Tao!" said Lady softly.

The droopy-eyed hound met her eye. "I am Paroo," he addressed her, bowing.

"What are you doing, woman?" Chester demanded impatiently of his partner. The dog merely stood stupidly, all legs and paws in different directions.

"Tao!" she repeated to the silly mutt.

Chester was incensed! "Enough of this Tao-ing! We have not established that you are indeed a friend! Where do you come from? We have not seen your species here!" he commanded.

"I am Paroo," he repeated, fumbling stupidly in circles.

"Yes! Yes! We have established that!" Chester was getting impatient.

"Oh, Chester!" I yelled down sarcastically "Are you quite finished? Otherwise, I can see that I will be sleeping in this wretched tree for the night?"

"I am Paroo, and these are my kin," he pointed idiotically to the bushes. From where I clung, I could see some twenty or so dogs of the same variety, but in varying colours of stupid. I shimmed further up and clung much firmer to my coconut tree!

Out of the bushes came the twenty or so. "All stop!" Chester barked loudly and menacingly. They complied. Chester and Lady flanked each other and stood to their full height.

"Tao!" came the greeting of "friend" from the twenty or so.

"Chester, I do not think they mean harm, they are quite the odd breed. I have seen a 'blood hound' such as this back at home in England. They are used for hunting. Those floppy ears and drooping eyes are not the signs of hostile dogs," she explained.

Chester had to agree. They were a gangly lot, browns and blacks and tans. Some were a singular colour, others all of the above, but all sporting a type of puzzled demeanour. Native to the species, I gathered.

"Chester!" I howled. "Am I to come down out of this tree?" He had obviously forgotten about me!

He pointed his nose toward me and uttered the word of the hour. "Tao!" Paroo looked at me and repeated the word for friend.

"I think it is safe for you to come down, Fairweather!" yelled Chester finally, eyeing the rabble. "I shall protect you and you can always go back up there if there is trouble!" This threat not lost on the bedraggled pack.

Backing down a coconut tree is not anywhere as coordinated as shimming up one! I certainly left my mark in the thing as I fumbled my way to the ground.

Taking Lady and Chester's lead, I stood finally and said, "Tao, Paroo, old thing. Yes! Yes! Friend! Frightened the living daylights out of us, you did!" I stuttered breathlessly a little, hanging from a tree not being my strong point.

"Why have we not seen you here before?" Chester was wary.

"We keep to our kin. We hunt wild hog for the chiefs," Paroo explained.

"I am Fairweather!" I piped up proudly. "And this is Chester and Lady." Introductions now complete we could get on with the social activity.

"You look vaguely familiar," Lady ventured.

"Paroo is Tahitian for 'white man's dog.' We have been here since Captain Wallis left my father and mother and a few of his faithful dogs for the natives, many years ago. We have bred to make more of us. We are useful to the chiefs and called when a hunt is on." His English was a little stilted and rusty but he got the point across admirably.

"By Jove, Chester!" I sprang forward. "These are distant English relations of yours!" I was quite excited for him.

The other hounds all rallied round, droopy-eyed and floppy-eared waiting for the nod to be friendly. I could see no sign of nastiness in them. They all looked too dull-witted to be of harm.

"These are no relations of mine!" Chester argued. "I will have you, Paroo and your family, know this. I will determine our friendship in my own good time. You must prove it to me before I will greet you so," Chester lauded, like some "King of all Beasts."

Lady was of the same opinion as I. "We will consider your friendship and look forward to it, as we have not seen other dogs since we left England."

"We have not seen dogs from England since the *Dolphin* left us here for the Chief," said Paroo. I thought that a little harsh. One doesn't leave perfectly good canines behind for natives! A fairly decent trade must have occurred for Captain Wallis to leave his hounds behind!

Now that all but Chester had befriended, a lot of sniffing and scent marking was being performed. This was the way of the canine and I had to tolerate it.

I was terribly impressed with Paroo's English, now that it had loosened up, and looked forward to a good chinwag with someone other than Chester and Lady, no offence to either as my very best friends.

"Do you have cats here, Paroo?" I ventured.

"Yes, we do," he replied.

"Chester! Lady! Do you hear this news?" I was a little more excited than Chester approved of. I did a little jig on the spot, which made the hounds laugh uncontrollably.

Always willing to entertain, I carried on a treat at this news. The hounds rolled about chortling at my antics.

"Fairweather! Will you cease this infernal dancing! You are a crewman of the *Endeavour* as are we and some order is required as per our station!" Chester was being a bore.

"I will not!" I sang. "Bring on ye cats and bring them now! Be they friend or foe I will charm them with my wit and we will be 'Tao's' too!"

At this, the hounds could not control their mirth. I daresay the local cats did not jig or sing! I would fix that! But for now, I was a spectacle.

"I will take you to them, Fairweather," Paroo offered. "I will go first. I must explain you and tell them of our meeting and friendship. They are wary cats. Sometimes hunted when the meat is rare."

"What?" I stopped my jig and stood firm. "The natives eat cats?" I thought it incredulous.

"Not often, it is rare, but the cats keep out of the main village just to be safe," he explained.

I felt a terrible fear for them. How awful! A cat was not meant as a meal, I dare say!

Chester piped up finally after his veiled threat. "And what of you, hounds? Do you hunt well?" he challenged, urinating on the nearest tree to establish his dominance.

"Oh, yes!" Paroo stated proudly. "We are descended from an Englander hunting blood line and it is in our hearts to kill for the white man, and now the Tahitians. They look after us with food and occasional grooming from the ladies."

"That is English, sir, not Englander!" Chester said, puffing up as if he was the most knowledgeable chap around. Paroo ignored him.

"Chester, you could do with a little grooming!" I laughed. Lady, too, joined the party along with the twenty or so.

"Hurrumph!" he huffed. And with a low hiss… "Fairweather, you foul beast. Leave off this taunting. It does not make me look superior for you to joke about such things," he warned.

"Chester and Lady are 'greyhounds' belonging to our most senior gentleman, Mister Banks and they are much revered upon our ship as fine canines of the highest breeding!" I explained, building them up status wise.

The twenty or so all bowed their heads a little, as if in the company of royalty.

"A finer mouser and braver feline you will never meet!" said Lady, Chester still sulking although I had talked him up to the hounds.

They bowed to me also.

"Fairweather! We must get back to the fort, it is getting on for supper and we are expected," said Chester self-importantly.

"Well, 'Tao' all twenty or so hounds of Tahiti!" I sang. "I shall call on you tomorrow to see how you got on with the felines here. Make me look good, I could use some company of my own species!"

And with that we went back the way we came. I could not keep from the excitement of the meeting and the knowledge that kindred spirits loomed in the outer village.

I strutted purposefully back to the fortress, avoiding centipedes!

That evening, we all went to the ship, other than the Marines left to guard the fortress.

Lycurgus and some of his family were dining with us. He copied the gents' every gesture, holding a knife and fork just as well as an Englishman might. They enjoyed their stay and I enjoyed the leftovers!

Many of the men began affectionate relations with the local girls, learning their language a few words at a time and teaching them English in return.

There was still much work to be done. The longboat had been leaky so it was taken ashore where sea worms were discovered, eating away at the timbers. The carpenters set in to re-skinning the longboat, my favourite hiding place. I was pleased for the eradication of sea worms!

Lycurgus dined often with the gents at the fortress, and one such evening had left after the meal only to return with fire in his eyes. He seized Mister Banks's arm and gestured for him to follow him back to the village. It seemed that a drunken Henry Jeffs, my butcher and friend, had requested a trade with Lycurgus' wife. One nail for the chief's stone hatchet! Not at all a fair trade. She declined and the angry fellow threw down the nail, grabbed the hatchet and threatened to cut her throat if the trade was not struck!

The demon alcohol had struck again! Mister Banks arrived with Lycurgus and intercepted the butcher, having the gents drag him back to the ship, promising Lycurgus that Henry Jeffs would be punished the next day.

The captain was apprised of this crime on Mister Banks's return that evening. His even-handed approach to punishment never wavered even for the butcher. He was incensed by this crime against our good name!

Lycurgus and his family were invited on board the next morning, but were unaware of our captain's intentions of punishing Henry Jeffs for them, in the usual manner of the "cat."

As soon as the Tahitian family were on board, the captain and crew drew their attention to the aft of the ship where the crew had gathered around Henry Jeffs, tied at the wrists to one of the starboard stays, his shirt nearby and his bare back glistening with sweat. He knew what he was in for but the family of Lycurgus did not!

The captain explained the crime to the crew quite emotively, no doubt to ensure that Lycurgus and his wives would see it as a serious crime, not just worthy of a slap on the wrist or a day without rations.

He ordered Lieutenant Gore to give Henry the customary twelve of his best across the butcher's bared back.

The women, wives, and daughters of Lycurgus were incensed by this cruelty. They wailed and cried out for the lieutenant to stop. Even the wife whom Henry had threatened moved in front of the butcher to fend off the cat's destination, but she was pulled aside by Lycurgus who actually seemed to be enjoying the lashings!

Once over with, the Lycurgus family took their leave and Henry Jeffs was sent to the surgeon who salved his wounds. No doubt Henry would never repeat this incident as he was well scored by the "cat" and swore off the drink for some time after.

This being the only serious incident between the crew and the Tahitians so far, the captain was generally proud of the men's manners with the natives, but our captain wanted to keep it that way! Henry Jeffs was made an example for both the crew and the Tahitians!

Chester, Lady, and I slept with the gents in the fortress that night, not wishing to be on the ship after the lashings we had witnessed.

I missed my usual chat with the captain, but I daresay he would have been grateful, as I would not have been able to help but chastise him over my butcher's punishment, deserved or not.

I debated the matter heatedly with Chester for some time, he taking the "for" stance, and I the "against." Lady finally put us both in our place with a stern eye and a "Go to sleep!"

CHAPTER 21

Upon our waking, we ambled to the dining tent at the fortress, our stomachs hollow and noisy.

I was keen to learn of cats from Paroo, but there was a new face amongst the already risen gentlemen, seated at the dining table sipping tea. He was Tahitian but wore the clothes of an Englishman, albeit a little tattered. This was news! Chester, Lady, and I sat in.

The captain had been summoned to the fortress by way of the newly skinned longboat and arrived as we were settling in to some breakfast. Native cats would have to wait for Fairweather! This was far too interesting a development!

As the captain entered, Mister Banks had the entire party stand.

"Captain Cook, meet Tupia!" Mister Banks introduced the good-looking young man excitedly.

"Tupia," bowed the captain.

"Captain Cook, I am honoured to meet you, sir! Much has been said of you in the village and Mister Banks has updated me as to your project and its progress." He said animatedly, shaking the captain's hand vigorously. Whether it was a proper greeting is debatable, but it was heartfelt.

"You speak English well, Tupia!" the captain complimented.

"I was taught by Captain Wallis when the *Dolphin* was here. I have tried to keep in practise but I live with the natives who until now had no English. Your men are teaching them well, Captain!" He said appreciatively.

"I would be grateful for some of the local knowledge of Tahiti, if you would indulge me?" asked the captain.

Tupia stood proudly, keen to be of service to the white man and most honourable Captain Cook!

"Yes, sir. I am well versed in the local history and having learned to write, I have noted much of our island's history. Mister Banks is keen to visit me and read it," he said.

"By all means, Mister Banks, read up, but a brief version from you would suit me well enough for now," said the captain impatiently. He had much to do, but this Tupia warranted some little time with such credentials.

"Of course, sir, Captain." He bowed graciously as if in the courts with royalty.

"We have our 'big chiefs,' such as Hercules and Lycurgus." He smiled here, knowing their real names. "They are called Hui ari'i or Ari'i-nui or Ari'i'rahi depending on their holdings of land, cloth and the like. Their extended families formed the highest class. Their status and rule is by inheritance of land.

"Then lower down are the Ra'Atira or landowners. They have made gifts of produce to the big chiefs in order to own land. "Then there are the Manehune. These are the poorer people of our land, unable to gift the chiefs and therefore not owning any land. They must hunt and gather their own food from the areas without the landowners seeing them."

"The families are called Ari'i who breed within their own. Some are sadly malformed but they exist prolifically and most are of good health."

He certainly was a font of knowledge, I thought, and his command of the English language was rather good! Captain Wallis had taught him well.

"It is worth informing you to keep away from any wooden bundle wrapped in matting. These represent the sacred Ta'aroa, the creator of the universe. He made some of the other gods: Tu, Tane, and Oro and Maui are some of the gods worshiped here. They are presented as carvings, or 'ti' and statues of our ancestors are here and there. Please leave them be as they are much respected. The main altar…"

"Yes, I have seen this!" interrupted Mister Banks.

"The altar is where we perform sacrifices and honour our gods. Especially Ta'aroa. It is made of twenty-six skull bones and six dogs, and built up with rocks to form a platform."

"I spied some of your crew there trying to take the sacred rocks for ballast on your ship. I shooed them away before they could do much damage. I do hope the Captain does not mind?" he enquired.

"No, Tupia, the men have been ordered to keep in favour with the Tahitians and observe their customs. I will spread the word among them further regarding your altar," he promised.

"Thank you, Captain." Tupia bowed.

"There was recently a war here." The Captain's interest piqued, as the signs were about the place but he knew not of the circumstances.

"Raiatea is my home village. I fled when the Bora Bora Chief 'Puri' conquered our village. I was wounded and sent away, hence my name meaning 'defeated'. I lived in hiding while I healed. This 'Puri', being a scoundrel and mean to his people, exiled me here to live in Old Man Valley just south east of here below the mountains.

"When I was well enough, I came to this village, where Queen Obadia made me her 'Chief Priest' for my intelligence and of course, my uniform. Captain Wallis himself gave me this fine suit!" He straightened his vest, tearing it a little. It was threadbare and faded from washing and wear.

"I shall replace your clothing with some of my own," said Mister Banks unselfishly. I think he was happy for a local guide and a well-spoken one at that. He would do nicely as his "aide-de-camp!" He hoped that Queen Obadia could spare him from his duties for a while.

Other than Mister Spöring, Mister Banks did not have the usual level of minions as he was used to in England. Mister Banks could hardly wait to dress Tupia up and parade him around, but he was also keenly interested in his local knowledge and hoped he knew some flora and fauna terms. For whatever reason, Mister Banks was the happiest I had seen him with this newfound friend.

The captain was happy enough with the brief explanation of the war and swore to look out for this "Puri" if he came into town. News seemed to travel fast between these islands somehow. Although the islanders kept to their own, some must take boats and encounter others whilst out fishing, swapping gossip and stories, Mister Banks decided.

Rumours of our landing here would be rife.

Tupia continued. "I am at your service, Captain."

"Many thanks, Tupia. I will call upon you when required," he confirmed.

Mister Banks hurried Tupia into the longboat and managed to convince the brothers Littleboy to row them out to the ship for his new uniform.

They returned sometime later, Tupia looking dazzled at his newfound clothing and ever so grateful to Mister Banks. No doubt, Mister Banks had manipulated the young man so that he would idolise him, resulting in his assistance when called, over all others, besides the captain.

The men occupied themselves in a number of ways while we awaited the transit date.

Mister Banks had detailed the botanical species within three weeks and brought samples every day with Mister Spöring and the other scientists, and of course, his new puppet, Tupia.

Mister Molyneux enjoyed shooting at a large swamp, filled with duck and teal – all good eating. He even took to shooting rats! Apparently, even they were good to eat! One day he shot one thousand as they swarmed while the natives ignored them. They thought our crew quite mad for eating rats when other foods were aplenty. I admit I felt the very same, good food being plentiful! The men were bored, and rat on a stick over the fire was a pastime.

I had ignored the village rats as the villagers themselves cared little of their existence. I ensured that should any hide away in the supplies taken to the ship, they would be evicted as soon as I saw them. Occasionally, I missed a few, but John Thompson would remind me of it when I came aboard and I would be sent down to the lower decks to rid him of the blighters!

Flies and mosquitoes drove poor Mister Parkinson mad whilst he tried to draw and preserve all his species. No sooner would he put pen to paper than he and the specimen would be covered in the blighted "nonos" as the natives called them. The scientists and gents threw mosquito netting over themselves when working on their discoveries, for fear that nothing would get done otherwise. They did look a sight, but it worked admirably.

My boys were thrilled with their surroundings! When not learning their respective trades, they swam and tossed coconuts about the beach with the native boys their age, learning new games each day.

They were maturing before my very eyes and particularly young Isaac Manly, seemingly growing inches per day until he was taller than the other boys, all his elders! It made for some confusion during scuffles between them as the youngest would almost always win at wrestling and outrun them at their ball sports on the beach.

My Isaac and the other boys of his age were becoming quite professional at their chosen trades. They still skylarked at any interval but not enough to get the cane!

Everyone seemed to have found friends except yours truly! Cats! I had my mission set out for me upon Paroo's visit with me one afternoon.

"I have spoken with the cats," Paroo drawled. "Some are happy to meet with you, others not so much."

"Jolly good work, Paroo!" I said excitedly. "I shall entertain the felines who are happy to meet with me and charm the felines who are not! They will come around to the Fairweather charisma! I shall see to it! Lead on, Paroo!"

"What? Now?" he whined.

"Yes, you lazy devil, lead me to my long lost friends!" I demanded.

"Oh, alright." He turned, paws and limbs losing their place as if each had a mind of their own.

Me thinks the bloodhound is of lazy temperament when not forced to hunt, and how those legs managed to co-ordinate in order to chase down a victim was beyond me! But they must have qualities I had not seen as the natives revered them for their hunting skills. Perhaps it is a keener sense of smell, as their noses were quite prominent. Generally, however, they were still a dumb-looking lot and although their English was passable they slobbered it out slowly, drooling on every word.

Off we toddled to find my kinsmen. Paroo walked as slowly as I imagined he would, and a few of his muttly friends joined the entourage.

"Can we step it up a little please, Paroo?" I was growing impatient.

"Nooo. Be patient, cat!" He woofed as dumbly as I thought he would.

We travelled through the village, more and more of the dogs joining us. I supposed this was a rather big event for the bored bloodhounds. Not much would be going on in the cat world, I suspected.

We passed a communal kitchen type of area, where a large number of native women were preparing pits for cooking and grinding fibrous plants and fruits. Behind a large rock I noticed the ears of a smallish cat. Said ears had strangely pointed wisps on the tips.

"Wait, Paroo!" I halted them. One by one the mutts ran up the rears of each other, the connection from brain to paws being faulty and slow.

"I see a cat!" I exclaimed.

Paroo yawned. The next time I looked the ears were gone.

"Never mind, Paroo." I must have imagined those ears in my haste to see other cats! Those wispy points in particular, very unusual.

Once the bloodhounds detached themselves from one another, we kept ambling along at Paroo's pace.

Further ahead from behind a thickish bush were those ears again! I dared not stop Paroo and his pack this time, as the pile up of dogs was time consuming, as with the last stop they were a tangled mess for some time!

I did not see the ears again until we were well through town and approaching an abandoned hut, where some ten or so different coloured cats lounged about. Their unique coats should make their names easy to remember, I thought.

Paroo approached, I slightly behind him, and the rest of the canine rabble following up the rear.

I appeared in front of the cats, but none of them moved from their reclined positions. I felt a little miffed. They knew I was coming. No ceremony! No singing! Nothing! They merely eyed me as if I was a nuisance, and blocking the way of them looking at something more interesting.

"There, Fairweather. The chief cat's name is Pie'pie'toi'maroo," he indicated.

"This is Fairweather." Paroo dribbled out my introduction in as boring a tone as I had ever heard, then turned on his bumbling paws taking the pack back to the village.

The large chief stood and yawned.

"Fairweather," he repeated awkwardly.

"Good afternoon, Chief Pie'pie'toi'maroo!" I bowed. "Your name is very long and I am sure, very worthy of such a great chief, but may I call you Chief Maroo?" I smoothed my way with him hoping he would allow me to abridge his name. It was, after all, a mouthful.

"No!" he replied. There was a long and uncomfortable pause.

"Them close to me call me by 'Chief Pie.' When you are close to me you can call me Chief Pie. Until then you will call me Chief Pie'pie'toi'maroo!" He was going to be a tough nut to crack!

He was black from head to tail, much like my friend Turkel back in England. I thought this might be a good conversation starter.

"I believe you have met Turkel of the *Dolphin*?" I asked nonchalantly.

"That fool?" He howled with laughter! I was a little confused, Turkel being my hero and all.

"I do not understand you, sir!" I protested.

"That Turkel fella, he and I got up to some mischief! He a good fella! How are the old fool?" His command of English was not as good as the hounds. No doubt the felines of the island had not as much contact with the Englishman as to learn the correct terms.

The other cats were a little more interested in me now. At least a few of them had ceased sleeping! These were females and my dashing coat no doubt interested them!

"He was well at our last meeting. What mischief was it, Chief Pie'pie'toi'maroo?" I asked, trying hard to get the tongue around that name. "Was it good mischief or bad mischief?" I asked keenly.

"Bits of both. Do you have the white man liquor?" he asked. I gathered from this question that the mischief he and Turkel had gotten up to involved the demon drink! He was rather keen for me to answer.

"Yes, I can say that we have the drink," I said impatiently, wanting other talk than that of liquor!

"Mmm, good!" He smacked his lips, no doubt remembering old times with Turkel. This drink, interesting him so, I would have to make some a gift to him to earn his favour.

"What your name again?" he asked, going around the sleeping males and biting their ears to wake them.

"Fairweather! Of the *Endeavour*! Have you seen our ship in Matavai Bay?" I asked, thinking he might be impressed with my local knowledge of the harbour.

"That name of you is long and silly!" He laughed. I was incensed! My name was long and silly? What about his? Mine was a proud and noble name and not that long if one had their English in place!

The rest of the cats chuckled along with him sleepily between yawns. "I will call you 'TeaTea.' This means 'white' in my words, and you being posh English gentleman with some white parts, and also drinking tea, will help you remember this is your new name."

"I say, Chief, I am not altogether happy with this name!" I protested. "TeaTea? Could you not come up with something a little more regal? I am considered rather gallant amongst my men!"

"No," was his standard and brief response. He turned from me and repeated, "TeaTea" to his cohorts. They all laughed.

"But Chief! I might be English but I do not drink tea!" I tried to implore. Suddenly there was a giggle from behind me. I turned to see those ears! I had not imagined them!

It was a young female. She was of three colours. Only singularly had I seen them before. Black, tan and white; she was all of them. There were no particular patterns in her markings. They were random, and to say they looked as though they had been painted on would be as close as I can describe. She was interestingly pretty. Her fur was long unlike the other shorthaired cats. Her eyes were green and slanted in an almond shape. Slightly crossed as if to look at her own nose. She was annoyingly spirited and spry, and chirruped a strange little mew as she darted about, unable to keep still.

"TeaTea! TeaTea! TeaTea!" she mocked. I gathered she was spoilt by the chief and allowed to do as she wished, as most of the other female felines were quiet.

"Kitchen!" growled the chief.

From this, I imagined a feast would be forthcoming. How good of him to cater to me!

"TeaTea! TeaTea! TeaTea!" She danced a little jig, wretched little minx!

"I have been watching the white men and this fellow, Father. He is alright!" she explained.

"Ah, the chief's daughter! Good afternoon, Miss," I bowed.

"TeaTea, you keep away from Kitchen!" I was confused. My name was now a pathetic "TeaTea!" I had passed the native's kitchen on the way to their lair, and I thought it not something I should keep away from! In fact, neither the native's nor the cat's kitchen should be off bounds to a visitor of my importance! A terrible mix-up, this!

"Kitchen!" He growled yet again. The food must have been late arriving. I wondered what we would be eating.

The young miss was smiling at me, her eyes squinting in a most attractive manner. I could not, however, understand why the chief kept calling out "Kitchen." We were nowhere near the kitchens, and the females who tended them had not moved. I doubted the likelihood of the kitchen itself coming to the chief when called!

The chief hissed and made the miss run off.

By now, the chief could see my confusion regardless of his knowledge of better English.

"Kitchen is my daughter! You stay away from her, TeaTea!" he warned.

"Oh!" I finally got it. "Her name is Kitchen?" I asked for confirmation, as this was a silly name.

"Yes, and that where she belongs. She gather scraps for us from the big chief kitchen. She also Queen Obadia favourite cat. This important work for her and you must stay away." He gave me a threatening scowl.

"I was hoping to have her explain her sneaking around as I came here," I said without hesitation.

The look upon his face told all, but he addressed me in a low and threatening tone.

"I catch you near Kitchen, and I will kill you myself!"

"Kill?" I asked. "I little harsh, don't you think?"

"No!" Again, with the abrupt answers. "Kill!" he confirmed. "Besides she is promised to Muto'i. His name mean 'police' here and he is strong in keeping order!"

"I will abide your instructions, Chief Pie'pie'toi'maroo!" I bowed respectfully.

"In that case, if your words is good, and you bring the white man liquor, you may call me 'Chief Pie.' We will drink together!" I was now accepted through my pledge.

"Well, I must get back to my ship. My duties call," I informed purposefully.

"Righto, TeaTea." He sounded rather English here. "Righto" being a left-over from Captain Wallis's visit, I suspected.

"The other cats merely yawned and it was off to sleep for them again.

I imagined that this island caused little for their occupation. The rats swarmed in every direction without interruption, and if Kitchen was fetching the pride's meals from the Queen's kitchen, they need kill nothing!"

I bowed, turned on my heel and made tracks for the camp and inevitably the ship. It was getting late.

I wondered as I walked briskly, which of the lazy males Muto'i was, that he had to have his ear bitten to wake up! Some policeman he was!

No sooner had I completed this thought than a large feline stood in my way upon the path, appearing as if by magic, not a sound did he make.

He was chocolate in colour all over, and I imagined him to be Muto'i, as I had not seen him in the feline lair.

"Stop right there!" said the chocolate cat, blocking my way.

"I shall not!" I said defiantly. "Who the devil are you?" I inquired.

"I am Muto'i and I been watching you," he stuttered in worse English than his peers back at the lair. "You are the ship cat, now known as TeaTea?"

"That is Fairweather to you, sir!" Using my rightful name made me larger than I felt.

"Keep away from Kitchen. She belong to me soon," he threatened.

"I shall do nothing of the sort!" I scoffed.

No chocolate policeman was going to choose my friends. Just as this was determined, the miss herself appeared.

"Muto'i! Stop that!" she demanded.

"No! This cat, whatever his name, not welcome. He look at you funny," he accused. "I saw him earlier. He like you! He can't have you. You is mine!"

"Look here, old policeman, I am not in the market for a bride. Your Kitchen is perfectly safe! I am a seagoing feline, a free spirit, and I remain here only as long as my captain decides." Reasoning with him was best, I thought.

"No Muto'i!" The little fidgety Miss stood firm. "I am going to marry him! He a fine gentleman, not like you!"

Well, the blood drained from my face and my mouth was as dry.

"Here, Kitchen!" I interrupted, my voice as if I had sand in my mouth. "That's a bit rash me thinks. Muto'i is a fine chap, I'm sure, especially being a policeman. One could not hope for a more honourable husband," I pleaded of her.

Neither took any notice of what I had to say. A tiff of the domestic kind was occurring and I could do nought about it.

"Marry this cat? He so stupid looking and not brave like me!" He laughed.

"Careful, sir, you step on my pride!" I warned.

"Yes!" said Kitchen, quite positive of her intentions. "He is not a brute like you and would treat me with kindness."

True, I would, but this was neither the time, nor the place for it. As much as she might enchant me, I was not about to enter into an arrangement with her, nor an argument with these two!

"Ha! Kitchen! I will show you brute!" howled Muto'i and with that he lunged at me, catching me unaware and knocking us both to the ground, a tangle of fur and paws!

We separated.

"What was that for? Are you quite mad!" I hissed, the breath having left my body.

He took my hissing as an overture to a fight! Quite mistakenly!

"I am mad! You will not have Kitchen! I will kill you first!" He came at me again but by this time I had steadied my stance and did not fall when shoved.

I had to defend myself! I shoved right back, being the brave, courageous fellow of the *Endeavour* and not about to take rot from some wretched native policeman!

He stood off.

I stood off.

A guttural growl came from his throat, and a widening of his eyes that was new to me. His face contorted and he hissed and howled loudly. This attracted the rest of the pride and the remaining cats now surrounded us, including Chief Pie.

I had never been in a predicament like this before and was slightly at a loss, except to keep my paws planted firmly on the ground. I need not have bothered. The policeman Muto'i lunged at me with claws outstretched and with as much force as he could muster!

The sharp pin-like daggers sunk into my flesh and he gripped and would not let go. I had no choice but to return the onslaught with my own grip of razor-sharp claws.

We rolled across the sandy path in a ball of cluttered fur, neither of us wanting to be the one to let go first. He bit into my neck, drawing blood immediately! It was ever so evident on my white parts and it hurt like a searing hot knife! We fought head to head, neither letting go. We grappled and rolled around on the ground, the grit sticking to my bloodied body.

His rear claws came up to scratch into my stomach, the fleshy parts, and very sensitive. He had done this before! I had not! I howled with an unheard-of noise, especially unheard of by me!

The pain sent a sensation through me that I can only describe as primal. My heartbeat was racing and a super strength engulfed me! I bit his head right through to the bone! I felt my top and bottom teeth stop at his skull and jaw! He pulled away and we released each other from the deadly claw-hold.

He stood, blood pouring from his head, but not as obvious on his chocolate coat. I lay where I was, on my side in the sand, hoping this onslaught was over. He growled, that guttural growl again as warning to me. He turned and walked a little further from where I lay and turned.

"You cannot beat me in a fight, TeaTea, you silly English cat," he said proudly while licking at the blood running down his nose. "Stay away from Kitchen or I kill you the next time!" He proudly ambled off down the path to the cat hut.

I was still laying where I fell, licking at what wounds I could reach, and in shock. This pain was only similar to the broken leg I suffered back at Tom's alley so long ago! But all over my battered body! And I could not get up immediately!

"That teach you!" said Chief Pie, proud of his policeman. "Stay away from Kitchen! And bring the white man liquor next you come!"

He turned and motioned to the cats to move on back to their lair. It must have been only a few minutes before Kitchen reappeared.

"Are you alright, TeaTea?" She licked at the wounds I could not reach.

"Yes! Yes! Kitchen," I said impatiently, thinking that Muto'i and the like would return and do me in for being seen with her. "Go back to your father and Muto'i. I will be killed if you stay here," I said tiredly. Shock most probably. I had seen it in men. One feels sleepy and faint.

"But what of you, TeaTea?" she appealed.

"I will go back to the ship when I have recovered a little. The surgeon will mend me. Now go!" I demanded. "I will come and see you when I am feeling less like the living dead!"

I hissed and she scooted off.

I was angry that she had gotten me into this, which brought me around somewhat. I stood shaking and tried out my legs. They moved, although sore, so I slowly walked back to the fortress.

Marry her? Good lord! I did not know her! She had just assumed! The anger kept me walking without dying there on the spot. I was wounded not a little.

Paroo and his pack lifted their heads as I walked toward the village. I passed the kitchen, this reminding me of the horrid little Miss who had gotten me attacked. Again, only my anger at her kept me upright and forward.

The ladies looked concerned but tended their duties.

My boys were taking a well-earned break from their duties as I hobbled through to the beach heading for the fortress.

My Isaac was the first to spot me.

"Fairweather!" he ceased his activity with the boys and came running. "What's happened to you?" he lifted me up and by that time the other boys had joined him. By the looks on their faces, my body was more bloodied than I had thought.

"Looks like the dogs got him!" said Will Howson. The boys agreed.

My Isaac turned me toward him staring at the bleeding scratches on my stomach and the punctures to my neck.

"This isn't the work of dogs, boys! Cats, wild ones probably," he announced.

"Will, John, William, Isaac!" He took charge. "Get the longboat. I'm sure Doctor Monkhouse is on the ship today!"

"We have to ask the captain and he's at the fortress!" said Will dutifully as he did not want to land himself in trouble.

"Then we run and ask!" commanded my Isaac, tucking me firmly under his arm and hurrying us all to the fortress.

The captain and gents were all in attendance. I was feeling rather ill and Isaac's grip hurt me through, not meaning to, but hurting all the same.

"Captain sir!" John Charlton interrupted. "Fairweather has been attacked!" He was breathless but calm. "May we take the longboat to the ship to see Doctor Monkhouse about his wounds?"

I gave my captain a pleading look, but need not have. He was available to me immediately upon laying eyes upon my blood-soaked and sand-matted fur, which had by now oozed onto my Isaac's uniform.

The gents rose on seeing my state. None looked at me as though I would live!

"We think the wild cats got him, sir!" my Isaac reported.

The captain looked into my eyes and realised my pain. My eyes were getting tired and I wished to sleep, such was the loss of my blood. The captain noticed this straight away and looked me squarely and sternly.

"Stay awake, Fairweather!" was all he said, some knowledge of the dying he must have had. He did not take his eyes from mine. "Boys! Get the longboat and see him to the surgeon immediately. He will not live if you dilly dally!"

"Here, Isaac!" said Mister Banks, handing over his best white neckerchief. "Hold this cloth on his stomach and neck, and firmly now, to stop the flow of blood."

The gents all agreed. I was taken to the longboat, my Isaac's grip still tight and now the searing pain of his pressing the cloth to my stomach and neck was more than I could bear! I wanted to leap from his arms, but my body would not allow it!

The boys rowed like never before. In the haze of pain, I noticed a wake behind the boat, reckoning that we must have been at speed toward the ship. I could see it looming.

What took merely minutes felt like an age until we boarded the ship, Isaac holding me tightly and running for the surgeon.

Doctor Monkhouse was attending to his instruments and notes when the boys and I arrived in his doorway.

"Captain says to fix Fairweather's wounds, Doctor Monkhouse, sir! Can you do it right away? He looks to be dying! The gents said so!" Isaac blurted out at speed.

The surgeon took one look at me and prepared a surface for my pain-ridden body, clean and ready to work.

"Hold him, Isaac!" barked Doctor Monkhouse. "He's in a bad way but he'll try to get away!"

He was right! Other than falling into the deepest of sleeps, I wanted to escape Isaac's grip as his hold on me hurt me more and more. But the sleep, it was calling upon me like an old friend.

I remembered the captain's words. "Stay awake, Fairweather!" I blinked and shook my head as best I could with Isaac and the boys holding me in every conceivable place so that I could not move.

"John Charlton!" snapped the doctor. "You will assist me!" John merely ran! The sight of my open wounds making him turn pale and sick.

"I will assist you!" said a familiar voice but by now I was unable to see clearly who it was.

"Boys, wait outside!" came the order. My cook, John Thompson! He must have seen the boys and I on the way to the surgeon's quarters.

"Me, too!" Another friendly voice. Henry Jeffs, our butcher!

I opened my eyes and looked at them for a moment or two. They lay me out as if to dress a turkey for cooking! I thought I might be dinner but the concern upon their faces was enough to convince me they were not planning on stuffing and cooking me! I was certainly in a haze of silly thoughts.

Doctor Monkhouse poured clean water over my wounds to flush them of the blood-encrusted sand to reveal the damage.

A new height of pain was reached and I howled desperately, unable to move under my cook and butcher's grip.

"Get me the cat gut!" ordered the doctor.

What? I thought! They were going to remove my stomach? What would I do for food? So beloved were my meals! I could not imagine living without it! I writhed not a little but the grip of the cook and butcher was too strong!

"Stay still, blasted cat!" barked the surgeon.

John Thompson left the holding of my poor wretched body to Henry Jeffs, him being larger and his butcher's hands knowing exactly where to hold me so I could not move. Not even a whisker!

Doctor Monkhouse cleaned my wounds with a foul-smelling brown potion. It stung hellishly! Disabled I may have been, but I could still produce a howl second to none!

"He's got some deep scratches. The punctures on his neck are deep and prone to infection." The doctor spoke unwittingly to his aides. "They are open and bleeding still. Have you found the cat gut yet, John?" He was growing impatient.

I wanted so to keep my "cat gut" but Henry's hold had me paralysed. I would have to live on without a stomach? This could not be! I felt the deepest urge to bolt and Henry just held me firmer. One paw escaped a little and I sunk it into his flesh.

"Ouch!" he bellowed, rounding up my stray limb. "I'm tryin' ta help ya, cat! Be still now!"

"I will dress your scratch when we are finished with the cat Henry." The doctor assured him, if only to get him to keep me still.

"Where is that cat gut, Mister Thompson?" The surgeon yelled, still bathing my wounds with the evil smelling mixture. It stung and burned and I wish to flee or die!

"I found it, doctor!" he announced.

Funny that! I thought it odd that John Thompson had found "my gut" in the surgeon's supplies! But my mind could not be trusted at this point as I was having very strange thoughts, particularly of my mother and father, and that lovely sleep I wanted so badly.

"Then pass it here with the needle," ordered Doctor Monkhouse.

Again, odd what? Needle? I could only think of those needle-like claws that did this to me in the first place! Was the evil Muto'i back to finish me off? I was delirious.

John Thompson passed the needle threaded with a thick black string of some kind.

"Will this cat gut hold his wounds closed?" asked John.

"Yes, it is strong, the thickest I have. I will stitch him up with it if you can assure he remain still." Doctor Monkhouse held a sharp razor like I had seen the men shaving their beards with. He gently shaved the fur from my stomach. "Once he is stitched together, we will just have to wait and see how he fares."

Doctor Monkhouse, Henry and Thomas were ready. I felt the pain of the needle enter my body and the thread coursing through my bare skin!

Was this the part where they were removing my gut? It was still hungry so I gathered not.

Cat gut and stitches and foul-smelling potions! My boys! My captain! That blasted Kitchen and the evil Muto'i! Paroo and the chiefs! Turkel and my friends back in England! All passed before my eyes!

The urge to sleep was no longer something I could control. As the painful needle criss-crossed my wounds my eyes closed and I fell into the deepest, soundest sleep.

All was quiet and I felt no pain. It was as if nothing at all had happened to me! Ever! I was with my mother while she licked my forehead. I had finally passed out.

CHAPTER 22

I do not know to this day how long I slept, but according to Doctor Monkhouse it was a miracle that I woke up at all! When I did, the pain was still strong but the bleeding had stopped and my stomach looked like a laced boot. I was without fur in the regions of my wounds. Doctor Monkhouse had stitched me together like a torn shirt. I was ever so grateful to be in the Great Cabin on a pillow donated by one of my boys. I do believe I drifted in and out of consciousness, as I thought I heard the captain talking to me when entering his journal. As we always held court over his nightly writings, perhaps he thought it might wake me from my endless sleep.

I did eventually wake to the soothing sounds of the water lapping at the ship and my captain writing furiously in his journal on one evening.

"Ah, Fairweather! You are back with the living, I see?" he enquired. I looked at him wearily and his gaze shone as if I was the world to him. Mine was reciprocal.

I meowed softly as it was all I could muster. He understood. I was weak. He came to my corner and I received a heartfelt chin scratch, he avoiding my neck wounds.

Lady was in attendance and from what I gathered, she had not left my side while I recovered.

Chester, too, stayed with me and had it as fact that I was near death, just as my deep sleep took hold. I learned that this depth of sleep was usually a precursor to death, so all were awaiting my waking, or passing, not knowing which way my state would end.

Every man on the ship visited me in the Great Cabin!

Henry and Tom brought me my food, but I was not terribly hungry for the following few days. I drank a little water, and when I felt better, I stood and tried out my poor battered body. It was weak, stiff and sore, but it still worked, thanks to my surgeon, cook, and butcher. A fine medical team they were, however unusual their usual occupations for such a task.

I was grateful to my boys for getting me to the ship in the nick of time and purred gratefully when they were in attendance.

One morning, after some weeks had passed, I received a visit from Doctor Monkhouse as usual. He checked my stitching every day. This day he held a pair of scissors and pincers and announced to the captain that he was in attendance to remove my cat gut! Not this again! I thought I had been spared the removal of my stomach on the day of the incident, as I was able to eat now! I could not understand! I was feeling better, able to move about a little and did not think the removal of my gut was warranted!

The captain held me down. His grip was not something I dared struggle against. I held my breath as Doctor Monkhouse started in to remove my gut! I supposed he had his reasons, though I could not see it. But no! To my surprise and joy, he merely snipped the stitches and pulled them out with the pincers!

"Good, strong cat-gut this," mumbled the doctor to himself. All was now clear to me! "Cat gut" was the thread used to stitch my stomach. It was apparently indeed made of cat gut, and fortunately not my own! I knew not whose it was, but was grateful to the donor as it kept my innards in place while they healed, and I was spared the removal of my stomach!

I licked my wounds regularly as was my instinct. This kept them clean. I stayed there in the cabin for many more days. The boys came to take me up on deck for my ablutions, cleaning up after me, as I could not hang my body over the side of the ship for the pain. I had to toilet on the deck. Poor chaps. I felt awful for them but knew they understood.

Little by little I felt like my old self, although the Fairweather pride had too been wounded. Until now, I was a hero, even sorting out Garbagio Rats and whole tribes of Geoffreys Cats! Now here I was, almost at death's door by the hand of a domestic feline! Albeit a wild policeman but nonetheless a commoner! I was grateful that no one had decided to rub it in, as it was a sore point to the Fairweather spirit. Perhaps even more so than to my physical self!

The timing of the transit was today, this 3rd day of June 1769. I had spent much time recovering on the ship. I ventured ashore early to the fortress, as I was almost fully recovered and the scientists were preparing their instruments for the tracking.

The main tent was a hive of activity and I was certainly in the way wherever the men and gents were, darting this way and that with charts and gadgets. I was determined not to miss this transit business, and the hour was early.

I popped outside to see Chester and Lady, who were lazing in the sand having come ashore even earlier with Mister Banks and the gents.

"How are you feeling, dear?" Lady inquired.

"Yes, old thing, you're looking well, other than that bald stomach of yours! Rather slimming, though!" he joked.

"Thank you, Lady, I am feeling close to my old self, and Chester! You may leave off with the comments about my bald stomach. I know it must look silly but it was a necessity. I will, however, have you know I have been keenly avoiding mirrors ever since!" I chuckled, wincing a little with the slight pain I still had.

"Have you seen Paroo and his crew?" I asked, attempting to catch up with the doings.

"No, old thing, they are off on a hunt with the tribesmen at present. They have been away from here for as long as you have been laid up," he informed. "A young female cat has been asking after you, though!" He nudged me a little as if to tease.

I swallowed hard. "She was not accompanied by a chocolate cat of the policeman variety named Muto'I, was she?"

"No, dear boy. She introduced herself to us," said Lady. "Kitchen being an odd name, and the daughter of the chief of cats to boot. Very pretty little thing. She explained what had happened. It must have been awful for you, dear," she sympathised. "She has visited here every day to give you her best wishes for a full recovery."

"Hurrumph!" I replied. "Wretched little thing was the cause of my great injury and potential death. Wanted to marry me instead of the brute Muto'i, the local policeman who did this damage to my person!"

"No!" barked Chester in disbelief.

"Oh, yes! This particular female was so insensitive as to announce her intentions in front of Muto'i! He threatened to kill me next time he sees me! He already had a good go at it! I'm lucky to be here only for the good doctor and his aides! Are you sure he hasn't been around?" I looked warily in all directions.

"I am informed by the wee Kitchen, that Muto'i is dead!" Chester knew that this piece of news would cheer up the old spirit!

"Dead? By whose hand, Chester?" I asked. "You haven't been after him in my defence, have you?" I was pleased for my own safety but nervous. "I dread the implications for peaceful relations between us and Chief Pie and his tribe, including the menace Kitchen! Not to mention that any such act would be frowned upon by Paroo and his hounds and the Tahitians! This could make for my end as a crewman, if the beast Muto'i has been attacked on my behalf!" I blubbered on worrying about the state of play.

"Fairweather!" Chester interrupted. "I have done no such thing! He is dead by your hand!"

I was shocked to the core!

"How can this be, Chester?" I quizzed unexpectedly. "I have not seen him since our altercation! It was an unnecessary fight on his part and one I did not start. Such was witnessed by Chief Pie and his tribe themselves!" I defended my actions, thinking the whole pride of cats on this island would be after me!

"Fairweather!" Chester scolded. "Will you stop this infernal carry on and let me explain?"

I was silent as requested.

"Muto'i died from the wounds he received in the fight between you! The native cats did not have a surgeon, cook, and butcher to mend their wounds! You only survived as a result of good medical care! This poor Muto'i suffered sorely from the bites and scratches you inflicted on him! He took as long to die painfully as you did to recover comfortably!" I was suitably chastised.

I did not know whether to be proud, sad, guilty, or whether to hide.

"How is the feeling on the ground with the cats, dogs, and Tahitians, Chester?" I asked, fearing for my sore but mended skin.

"Let me see," he taunted me. "The Tahitians do not care either way as long as the dogs are safe." He puffed up with self-importance. "Paroo and the hounds are less one cat of the policeman variety and they could not be happier. He was a menace to the dog pack, it is said. They saw the altercation and believe it to have been started by Muto'i. You were merely defending yourself, they say."

All good news thus far!

"Yes, yes, Chester, and the feline tribe?" He was explaining too slowly for my liking.

"They are sad for the loss of their tribesman, but they too were of the opinion that Muto'i was only a good chap until Chief Pie made him a policeman. After that he was a bit of a tyrant, old boy, and the chief is well rid of him! He was starting to form a pack in alliance with another tribe to wreak havoc on the island. This has been quelled by his death!" Chester concluded.

Ah! I thought, politics amongst and between tribes.

"So I am not a pariah? And I do not look forward to being killed by anyone?" I asked for confirmation.

"No, you are actually an unwitting hero yet again for doing the island no small favour in ridding them of this menace, Muto'i," Chester chuckled.

"What is with the mirth, Chester? I was terribly worried about the future of my stay here and the consequences of my actions on the locals and our crew!"

He chuckled again. I was ready to plant a well-earned scratch on that snout of his but I remembered how much it hurt, having been a victim to catch scratches, so I fought the impulse to slap him. He continued to chuckle and Lady sat with a wry smile on her lips.

"It would be Kitchen whom you should be afraid of, Fairweather!" He laughed aloud. "She wants to marry you now more than ever! And her father wants you as chief of police!" He rolled around on his back howling with laughter, tears running down his eyes, knowing full well this would not impress. I was flattered of course but she was nothing but trouble!

"Chester, you evil hound. Did you not tell her I was some kind of evil devilish fiend of the worst kind?" I suggested.

"No, Fairweather. I was not aware that I should!" He thought it was a great laugh that a female, and Chief Pie's daughter no less, was after me as a husband! True, I had not given him instructions regarding this female, and apparently she was around every day asking after my health and when I would be well enough to marry, and take over as the pride's new policeman! Chester was laughing so hard he could only stutter the odd insult.

"Policeman…married…" He was utterly breathless from torturing me.

"Spare me this hysterical conniption of yours, Chester!" I protested. "I have no intention of policing that dreadful group of cats. They are a blot on the good name of felines! And marriage? To Kitchen? She is nothing but a pest!" I announced.

"I think not on the latter, old thing!" He laughed again. "Your face became quite soft when there was mention of the young thing."

Lady chirped in. "I think you have a soft spot for the little wisp. She is quite the attractive girl, other than for all that fidgeting about." Lady was siding with Chester! Not something I expected!

"Here! Here! You two!" A stupid smirk had appeared upon my face, which did nothing for my case against this Kitchen. I had to admit, she appealed to me.

"Speak of the devil…" Chester whispered.

All of a sudden, as was her way, she was in front of us prancing around and flicking her tail in a most fetching manner.

"TeaTea! You are fixed! I am very happy!" She beamed. "Father wants you to be our Police Chief! Then we can marry now?"

Chester tried his best but lost his aplomb and laughed out loud once again. Kitchen took no notice of him, not taking her eyes off me for a second with that beaming grin or hers.

"Look here, old girl, keep still while we discuss this," I instructed.

She smiled an enormous smile and sat, trying desperately not to fidget. Chester was still chuckling and Lady just looked on at what could be trouble for me either way, depending on how I managed this conversation.

"Yes! Yes! TeaTea, I am ready!" Her enthusiasm only matched by her lovely eyes, looking longingly into mine.

"I am very fond of you, Kitchen." Her smile grew wider. "I would be very happy to get to know you further but you must know that I am a member of the crew of the *Endeavour* and our work here will come to an end very soon."

She pouted pitifully. "But TeaTea, Father wishes you to be a policeman and then I can marry you. He will not be very happy after you killed Muto'i who I was to marry, and then finds out you do not want to be our policeman!" Not only a spirited little devil but also calculating to boot!

I remembered her very own words before my fight with Muto'i that she did not want to marry him, as he was "a brute" and unkind to her. She was doing her best to trap me! With this stretch of the truth and veiled threat concerning her father, I would have to be very careful here!

"Kitchen, dear," I softened. "You must understand, I am a man of duty and courage and a necessity to my shipmates and captain, much more important than even a policeman! I will see you often and fondly whilst I am here with the *Endeavour*, but sadly for us I must leave with the ship." I used my own prowess, erring on the romantic side to appease her.

"Really?" She beamed. "You will see me tenderly?" She fidgeted again. "And you will see me many times? Lots of times?" She came forward and rubbed up against me. I felt a slight shiver, not having been involved with a female before and I quite liked the feeling.

Chester was still chuckling in the background and not helping my case, but we both ignored him.

"Yes, of course, Kitchen. I am very fond of you. I will see you whenever my duties allow me freedom," I promised.

"I am happy with this, TeaTea! Your duty and honour I like in you!" She was placated.

She obviously admired these qualities and with my promise to see her often, she had forgotten her father's want for a policeman of the Fairweather variety!

I was most happy with this arrangement and rubbed against her in affection. She in turn rubbed against me.

"I will see you here at the fortress so father does not see us together." Then like a shot, she ran for the village, no doubt to tell her womenfolk that she was the girlfriend of the *Endeavour*'s Fairweather, a status she no doubt enjoyed.

Chester was still grinning. "TeaTea! That is a nice name for you, Fairweather, old blot!" he teased.

"Chester, you fiend. Could you have laughed any louder or harder during that delicate piece of conversation? I was trying my best to not be landed in the soup with this girl and Chief Pie!" I scolded.

"You do like this fidgety girl, don't you?" Lady knew of my feelings being a female of the most sensitive type. I was not going to fool her.

"Yes, I will admit I have warm feelings for her, annoying as she is!" I puffed up.

"Just be careful there, my dear," said Lady. "She seems a determined little thing and you may land yourself in hot water with Chief Pie."

She was a keen protector of the heart, but knew the outcome if Chief Pie were to upset the old "apple cart" so to speak. It could have a trickle-down effect, should Chief Pie complain to Paroo and the natives find themselves with angry dogs. Relations could be strained between the entire island and our captain's mission could be compromised. Delicacy was required!

"Nicely manoeuvred, however, old boy!" said Chester, laughing. "You were nearly a policeman with a wife! And could still be if this little minx has her way!"

"Never fear, Chester, it is not lost on me, the Fairweather charm has saved the day and will continue to do so!" I confirmed.

During this badly timed interruption, the gents, scientists, and astronomers had set up all the equipment for the transit. The weather had not been the best for clear skies but this morning it was crystal clear. Everyone was hopeful. It was, after all, a long way to come for a cloud to get in the way of this thing!

Mister Green was the "chief" of these proceedings. His composure under this enormous pressure was commendable, always the calm, clear-headed type, perfect for today's business. He had tried, much to the captain's approval, to teach some of the crew astronomy, but none wanted to learn it. A great shame, indeed.

Mister Green had the telescopes transported to the large tent recently erected on Point Venus beach, under heavy guard, and very early. The Tahitians were too curious and prone to thievery for these important pieces not to be protected!

The astronomical clock with a gridiron pendulum was set up in the middle of one end of the huge tent. It was housed in a frame of wood made purposely by astronomer's calculations and the fine craftsmen in Greenwich, England. The scientists made sure it was adjusted and set to the very same specifications as it had been in Greenwich, employing the carpentry skills of the clever John Satterley to ensure its frame's accuracy.

Twelve feet exactly from the clock stood the journeyman clock and the astronomical quadrant upon the top of a large cask fixed firmly to the ground. The telescopes were placed out in the open, and all readied themselves to watch, note and admire this natural phenomenon.

While there was some time to wait according to his calculations, Mister Green asked to make a speech with the captain's permission. The captain called all to order for Mister Green.

"Thank you, men. I will explain why we are here at this momentous time in history," Mister Green began, always wishing to inform. "The Royal Society is concerned with mathematics and astronomy. These two form an alliance for navigational purposes. Calculation and the movement of the stars being the way of the future of navigation, we are here to help future voyagers."

"When on long ocean treks, out of sight of lands that had already been charted many mariners were lost." The crew all nodded having known fellows who had died.

"The forces of the north and south poles caused their compasses to falter, and if they did not use their mathematics and the position of the stars, they could make a mistake in the direction they were sailing. It would then be only by latitude and longitude that they would know where they were going; 'latitude', being the measurement of the earth's surface around its left and right girth, and 'longitude', being the same measured increments of its up and down girth. A grid pattern of sorts. He showed us by way of a globe of the earth. Only the very experienced, like our captain could measure and plot our path, but he too needs the information required for farther voyages from charted lands and hence the Royal Society's plan and financing for this trip."

He had the men's attention and continued. "At the same time all over the known world, scientists are positioning themselves to track the path of the planet Venus across the sun. This is a phenomenon that only occurs four times every two hundred and forty-three years. Very rare indeed!" The men all nodded with the enthusiasm they were capable of as mere sea-going chaps, but approving of this jaunt if it meant safe sailing.

Mister Green continued.

"We are part of a large group and a measurement from Tahiti is essential for the mathematicians and astronomers to gather their information. Our good captain is versed in mathematics, astronomy, and navigation, the perfect commodore for this momentous and significant task."

He bowed to the captain and it was returned in gratitude.

"Clear skies being our aim as the transit will occur during this day June 3rd 1769. We are all honoured to be a part of written history in this calculation. From the captain to the cat, we have all assisted in this important task, and now we will do our best to measure Venus' path across the sun this day. Well done so far to one and all!"

I was honoured to be mentioned, even though at the rather low end of the order.

The men let up a cheer for Mister Green's speech and awaited the Transit of Venus across the path of the sun. Most of us expected some kind of monumental phenomenon.

As we watched and waited, at around nine o'clock in the morning, the observers spotted the planet and although the sky was clear, the edges of the planet were hazy and blurred, but for all its glory we, the uninformed, imagined more than just a little black dot moving across the sun.

Most of us could only watch for a moment as the sun hurt our eyes and blinded us.

The scientists made their calculations peering fixedly through the telescopes. At nine hours, twenty-five minutes, and forty-two seconds, in the a.m., the first contact with the sun was measured. A cheer went up from the gents and Mister Green, so a cheer from the men followed!

All were a little disappointed in the small black dot, perhaps expecting more. After nineteen minutes the planet was completely in the sun's path. Another cheer!

It continued its way across the sun until three hours, fourteen minutes, and eight seconds in the p.m. A long journey the little black dot had!

Another cheer went up from the scientists and gents, pouring themselves a celebratory brandy. It was a little early to be consuming alcohol, however their success must be celebrated!

Any who were still at the site hurrahed and drank along with permission from the captain!

Some had gotten bored and left, preferring the company of the native girls.

Speaking of girls, Kitchen turned up to see me earlier during the transit, and we chatted of this and that and the differences in our cultures. She was quite well informed. She sat with Chester, Lady, and I for a while.

"What are we supposed to be looking at?" she inquired.

"Why, dear girl," Chester said. "We are looking at that small planet travelling across the path of the sun!" He chided as if she was not educated enough for him.

I took over as he was putting her ill at ease.

"This is the most important discovery of a new way of navigation the world has seen yet! And we are here to see it!" I put it simply and importantly. She stared at it for a little, fidgeted, yawned and then lost interest, as was her way.

"Well, goodnight!" she sang, and off she went, back to her camp skipping all the way and singing that odd chirrupy "mew" with each step.

"Not one for staring at dots and suns," I said, grinning.

"No," said Lady and Chester, smiling along, as she did possess a certain charm.

The captain and Mister Green came forward.

"Our thanks to all who have assisted this and all prior days," said the captain, turning to Mister Green and shaking his hand firmly in congratulation of his achievement.

The captain sent for Sergeant John Edgcumbe, the senior of the Marine guards.

"Sergeant, please round up the entire crew. I have an important announcement to make." This was unlike the captain as he rarely assembled the entire crew for anything, other than lashings. I wondered who was going to get it?

All the Marines, who were guarding the fortress, scattered in all directions. Some of the crew who were still on the ship were herded into the longboat and rowed ashore. Others were interrupted from their social endeavours with the local girls. Once all had gathered murmuring their distaste for yet another speech, the captain began.

"Men of the *Endeavour*, this transit of Venus is now over, and I can reveal to you that this is not our only purpose here in the Pacific," said the captain, hushing the crowd.

"The King has given me secret orders which I was not to open until the Royal Society's undertaking of this transit was performed. Before you all, I open the seal and read them aloud for the very first time." All looked sideways at the next man. "Secret orders?" "What of secret orders?" "Why were we not told?" came the murmurs.

The captain, true to his word, had not so much as sneaked a peek at these "secret orders." I wondered at the loyalty of our captain, to the distant and unnamed men who sealed these orders thousands of miles away, and yet, in leaving them unopened until now, he was resolute. I might certainly have had a quiet look into that envelope!

"I read this to you now," he prepared, having scanned the document quickly and gotten its gist.

"After the transit, we are ordered to proceed southward in order to make discovery of the continent, seen by Captain Wallis of her Majesty's ship the *Dolphin*, of Terra Australis Incognita. Enclosed are Captain Wallis's charts. We are to fall in to the eastern side of this continent to the land discovered by Able Tasman and now called New Zealand, and chart its coastline extensively.

"If we discover the continent, Terra Australis Incognita, by proceeding westward afterwards, we must chart its coastline, observing the latitudes and longitudes, the variation of the compass, the headlands, the height, direction, and source of the tides and currents, depths and soundings of the sea shoals or shallows, rocks, and surveying and making charts and taking views of bays and harbours as may be useful for navigation and landing." Each of the crew was aghast, while the gents' excitement elevated!

The captain continued.

"We are also to observe the nature of the soil and the products thereof, the beasts and fowls that inhabit it, the fishes in whatever rivers we see, and in case we find any mines, harbouring minerals or valuable stones, bring samples of them home, along with specimens of the seeds, fruits, and grains we may collect."

Mister Banks and the other gents could hardly contain their enthusiasm. This was a dream for them!

"Observe the temper and disposition of the natives and cultivate a friendship, being ever careful and protective of ourselves."

"We are to take possession of convenient locations in the country in the name of the King of Great Britain. Set up proper marks and inscriptions, as first discoverers and possessors of said lands."

"If we fail to discover the continent Terra Australis Incognita, proceed to England, by the most able way home."

"We are to observe all islands we may discover in the course of our voyage and take possession for His Majesty." He paused, noting each man's reaction.

The following, he kept to himself and did not read it aloud, having noticed it forward as he read. "When you return to England, you must demand all diaries from all officers, petty officers and the log books and journals they may have kept must be sealed before leaving the ship and delivered to the Royal Society." He told me later that he omitted to tell of this, as he wanted the men to record and write freely without worry that the Royal Society would see their notes. Their diaries would make for better reading.

The captain finished with, "The whole crew is not to divulge where we have been until we have permission to do so. It is signed 30 July 1768 by members of the Royal Society and sealed by King George."

A buzz amongst the men broke out. Secret discoveries seemed rather exciting and the captain was hoping for this as he read the orders.

"We are embarking on a potential discovery, which will write our names in the history books of all mankind forever," the captain appealed to the men.

A mumble of approval broke out. Each man wanting his name in writing and to be a proud man for all we had endured so far.

"I'm up fer it, Captain!" yelled Mister Molyneux, the sailor in him coming to the fore for the captain, and for his own sense of discovery.

Then lieutenants Zachary Hicks and John Gore yelled a loud, "Hear! Hear!"

More and more cheered along! Adventure was infectious, and an excited buzz had grown in our midst!

Before they had time to think further of it, the captain announced they would leave Tahiti on 13th day of July 1769 and that all would do their duty to have the ship ready for this great adventure.

"Rum for all, if you please, Lieutenant Hicks!" ordered the captain in appreciation for the men's keenness for this enterprise we were about to undertake.

"Yes, sir!" came the reply and the men all rallied for the captain.

Not a moment later, Sergeant Edgcumbe received a whisper from Corporal John Truslove. "Archibald Wolfe, Able Seaman, has stolen one hundred and twenty pounds of nails from the ship's stores, sir!" he reported.

"Thank you, Corporal. Round up the Marines while I notify the captain," the sergeant ordered and off went the corporal.

"Captain, sir!" shouted Sergeant Edgcumbe. The captain was off to join the gents in conference about this new development. He held up for the sergeant.

"Able Seaman Archibald Wolfe has been reported as stealing one hundred and twenty pounds of nails, sir. He was caught with some of them in his pockets, sir. I've sent my men to round him up with his accomplices," reported the sergeant.

The captain was shocked at this news. The stores on the ship had been left unguarded while the Marines stood sentry over the astronomy gadgetry. Nails being circulated by the thieves would lose their value for trade with the natives, and at a crucial time when they needed supplies for their new destination.

"See to it they are captured and brought to me, Sergeant!" he said gruffly. He had just read his secret orders and gained the crew's trust. He did not appreciate this interruption!

All the Marines scattered in different directions to find the rest of the crew and potentially the culprits.

Some were in the village and a loud "Hoy!" was all that was required to bring them out of huts and hammocks to comply. Some had gone back to the ship and Privates Bowles and Judge rowed out to fetch them.

Corporal Truslove came forward through the now well-informed crowd, his arm clenching Archie Wolfe who was wriggling and writhing to try and get away. The corporal had a firm hand on him, with his arms tied behind his back, so as not to allow him to dispose of the nails upon his person.

He was brought before the captain.

"What is the meaning of this, Wolfe?" demanded the captain as angry as I had seen him.

Wolfe said nothing.

"Who is in on this with you and where are the rest of the nails?" The captain's face grew red.

Wolfe said nothing.

"I see. You will not give up your accomplices in this most heinous crime against our ability to trade with the natives?"

Wolfe shook his head and said nothing.

"Remove the nails from his pockets, Sergeant," the captain said impatiently.

Sergeant Edgcumbe stepped forward and produced a large handful from both of his pockets.

The captain's eye pierced the felon. "Wolfe, you will receive twenty-four lashes for this crime, double of my usual, and in front of the crew and the Tahitians! I will not have you ruin our relations here by giving away these nails and making them hence worthless as trade items."

One communal gasp came from all within earshot.

"Sergeant Edgcumbe! See to it that Lieutenant Gore punishes this man!" The captain stormed off to find assistants in helping find the remainder of the nails, our only currency here.

It was safe to assume they would be on board the *Endeavour* in Archie Wolfe's effects. They were so found and it was reported back to the captain. He was pleased but the heavy double penalty of twenty-four lashes played heavily on his mind. Punishment as always was not to his liking but the example must yet again be made to the men. The Tahitians must also know that theft was punishable, the nails being as good as money with them!

Lieutenant Gore brought out the "cat" and delivered the lashes, all twenty-four bleeding heavily as Archibald Wolfe stood lashed to a palm tree. The native women tried to intervene, as it upset them, but the Marines held them back. The native men merely watched and winced at each stroke of the cat, hoping that their chief would not take up this means of punishment.

Kitchen had come back to witness this tragedy. We animals always thought it odd that men be punished so severely and then mended immediately by the surgeon. My own injuries still hurt and the lashes Wolfe was receiving were near as deep as my wounds from Muto'i. Chester and Lady, whilst used to it, could still not watch for long. I winced along with Kitchen, who merely stood mouth agape at what men would do to each other over currency.

"Why do you men treat each other so?" was all that would escape her mouth.

"We do not understand it either, Kitchen," I admitted sadly. "The men have their ways and must do their duty by their rules and laws, and we must accept it."

With the lashings over and Archie Wolfe transported to the ship to have the surgeon attend to him, Chester and Lady went to Mister Banks tent for the night.

Kitchen and I were alone. The moon had risen above the water and it was as full and large a moon as I had ever seen. The moon and stars here, and at sea, were so much brighter than back in lit-up old England. I explained this to Kitchen who sat close to me.

"I would like to come to England with you TeaTea!" she offered.

"That's very nice of you, old girl," I replied. "But our voyage has become a new adventure and we are not returning home as we first thought. The captain has secret orders to discover Terra Australis Incognita, a whole new continent as big as ten thousand Tahitis!" I said, hoping she would stay here with her family.

"I see, you do not want me to come on adventure with you, TeaTea?" she asked purposefully, pouting a little.

I must be careful here or land in the soup.

"No, dear girl, your life will be at risk. I know of the terrible seas and storms and have been witness to much danger. You will stay here with your family and I will keep your company until the day we are to leave. Besides, we may very well come back this way on our journey back to England. We shall see how it turns out. For now, we will just quietly watch the stars." I turned to the sky.

She shinned up next to me, her paw upon mine, and our noses touched. It was my first kiss and I enjoyed it very much. After such a momentous day, we lay there together, lying on our backs in the Tahitian breeze alone, and watching the stars until sleep came.

CHAPTER 23

The captain was now ready to leave Tahiti and anxious to obey his secret orders. The ship, however, needed work for this unimaginable adventure, and he wished to map the entire island of Tahiti before we were to leave. "Much to do. Much to do," he would mutter while keeping his logs with me at night.

I had taken to staying on the ship more often as Kitchen was becoming more of a fixture in my heart, and this would not be good for either of us when the day came that I had to leave.

We spent the days together, away from the chief and her tribe. She wanted to familiarise herself with all things English. She would not leave off the idea of sailing with me, but I always managed to change the conversation enough, to make her forget to confirm it with me. I learned much of Tahitian life and she of English ways and the sailing of ships.

Part of the maintenance of the ship was tending to its bottom. The *Endeavour* was brought as close to the shore as the depth of the water would allow. The captain had ordered the men to "heel" her over, this requiring the collection of large rocks. And none from the sacred altars of the Tahitians as ordered by the captain. They were placed to one side of her hull along with anything of weight, to lean the ship over as far as they could to reveal the foul surface covered in weed, shells, worms, and barnacles. These pests slowed down the progress while sailing, so off they were scraped. I learned that this cleaning process was known as "boot-topping" the bottom.

"Pew!" Kitchen said, wiping at her nose as we watched. The men were painting on a mixture of pitch and brimstone to sheath the ship's bottom against any more of such bits that might stick to her. And a foul smell it was, too! If I were a barnacle, I would not go near it!

On the 5th day of June, it was the king's birthday. All were busily attending to the maintenance of our good ship, but we managed a feast on the island with Hercules, Lycurgus, and Queen Obadia. We drank to the good health of the king, but the Tahitians could not seem to wrap their mouths around "King George," calling him "Kihiargo" instead. We thought it a bit of fun at the king's expense but he would never be told!

Poor Tupia was so keen to drink to the king's health that he got enormously drunk and had to be carried to his bed early.

During the festivities came a most unusual occurrence. We were all dining and chatting when an old woman staggered into our midst, tears running down her face.

Queen Obadia got up from her place with the chiefs, and the captain and Mister Banks joined her to ascertain the problem.

She talked in a melancholy tone in Tahitian so we did not understand much of it.

"She is much saddened by the death of her husband this hour," explained the queen.

Mister Banks began to take her hand in condolence but she threw his hand down as if it were a serpent! She removed from her clothing a shark's tooth and struck it to her head with great force, six or seven times! Much blood flowed and the queen's servants brought forward cloth to mop up the mess. She began to collapse, but the captain held her up.

"Is this quite normal, Queen Obadia?" enquired Mister Banks, quite shocked at the display.

"Yes, this is a sacred blood-letting for the dead. It is also done when new babies arrive or if one becomes too blessed with holiness, so as they must bleed it away," the queen explained.

As the captain held the woman, the queen stemmed the flow of blood from her self-inflicted wounds with the cloth. There was much blood and we all hoped she would recover.

Quite suddenly though, when the bleeding had ceased, she looked at the captain smiling and spoke in Tahitian. She thanked him for catching her before she passed out. We were all quite amazed that she conducted herself as if nothing had happened, while she cheerfully collected all of the bloodied cloth!

"She will now take the cloths to the water and throw them in, so that no one is reminded of her actions this night," explained the queen.

The captain and Mister Banks were a little pale from the incident, and the woman toddled off with her bloodied cloths as if nothing had occurred, obviously happy in the knowing that she had done her religious duty by her dead husband. We all took our previous places as directed by the queen. No fuss was to be made of this scene.

The differences in our cultures never ceased to amaze us all.

The next day, we saw the hut that had been erected to house the woman's dead husband. Yet again, the foul stench of the decaying body was in the air for many days, but the family of the dead man stayed in temporary huts close by to mourn his death.

The captain brought some seeds on shore that he had purchased in England before leaving. They were of the vegetable variety and the ground was prepared for their planting by some of the men. The captain showed the Tahitians how to do this themselves, ensuring that they would have new and varied foods for the future and their good health.

That evening, I sat with my captain on the ship, leaned as she was to the "port" side, this being the left or weather side. The *Endeavour* had already been repaired on the right or "lee" side. This tilting made it rather difficult for him to write his notes, the ink spilling from the filled well. He cursed not a little as his clothes, hands and notes were stained.

"Fairweather?" he quizzed, mopping at the ink and making it worse with the spread. "I have noticed you in the company of a small female cat?" he stated, as if I would tell him all! I merely rolled my eyes a little to address his question.

"Ah! She is an annoyance, is she?" My furrowed brow confirmed his assumption and he chuckled a little at my expense. "Coming with us when we leave, is she?" Teasing me not a little and still smearing more ink in all directions. I dabbed my paw in the pool of ink that had settled near his teacup. With great purpose, I left a paw print on his notes and gave him a stern stare.

"Ah!" He laughed right from his belly. "I believe by this action that the little thing is a blot on the Fairweather page?" Again, with a roll of my eyes he understood.

He laughed long and hard, a tear or two of mirth trickling from his eyes, he believing me to be more human than feline.

I noticed the marines stationed outside the Great Cabin door poke their heads around the corner. I supposed they knew him to be alone other than for my presence and may have thought him quite mad for laughing so hard without another person in the room. I suspect he took little notice of what others may think of our friendship.

With a whip of my tail, I was off, leaving him chuckling to himself. I took the last longboat to shore that evening, to see Kitchen and sleep under the stars.

Early the next morning, Chief Oborea and his associates came from another village to visit at the fortress nearby where Kitchen and I slept. They brought with them many gifts including a very fat dog. He was apparently bred for eating by the nearby tribe, where they would trade them for other supplies with our village. He was considered a delicacy among the locals. This was disturbing, but I thought to have a bit of fun at Chester's expense. I excused myself from Kitchen as her duties to provide the cat population with scraps was foremost. We went our separate ways.

Chester and Lady had been lying on the warm black sand early that morning. I came from the visitors in the fortress with this news.

"I say, Chester! Good morning, Lady!" I was cheery and in the mood for some teasing. "Sleeping well, are we?"

Chester yawned. "Fairweather, old beast, I was dreaming a most charming dream of jolly old England. Must you sneak up on a fellow?" He moaned.

"Good morning, Fairweather dear. Did you catch up with the young lady?" she asked. "Kitchen was around last afternoon looking for you. I assume you were found?"

"Thank you, Lady. Yes, and eventually we slept out here. Even with all that fidgeting the little minx doth sleep," I informed.

"I say, Chester, I have just come from a visit with Chief Oborea from the nearby village and he has brought with him a fat dog from their breed as a gift." Chester rolled on his back, the morning sun on his belly.

"Now steady on with the name-calling, Fairweather! Fat dogs have their purpose! I was not aware there were more dogs here, old boy! What fun! Is this fellow peaceable enough?" he enquired lazily, no doubt thinking he would make a new friend. Paroo and his mutts were busy hunting most of the time and Chester and Lady had seen little of them.

"He seems charming enough." I was ready for the punch line. "He is our lunch, Chester!"

Well, Chester jumped to his feet from the lazy position on his back as if bitten long and hard by the dreaded centipede!

"What?" he asked dumbly, his eyes large.

"Yes, it seems the breed is for eating. I would be careful, dear friend, if they eat dog, you may be next! Although there is a distinct lack of meat on your skinny bones, old thing!" I cajoled.

Lady seemed a little perplexed but in her relaxed and comfortable manner, knew she was safe from being a meal and let me have some fun at her partner's expense.

"This cannot be!" His mouth hung open.

"Well, it doth be, old mutt! Come with me, you lazy hound. They're preparing him now for a hot-stony grave!"

"Surely, not!" Chester was having none of it. "The canine being many different and useful things, but certainly not food!"

"Have it your way, Chester. Lady and I are off to the fire pit for a look." She stood ready for the sight-seeing trip.

"Hurrumph!" he trumpeted. "There will be no preparation nor cooking of dog. It is just not the done thing! You will see!" He fell in for the jaunt.

We ambled along toward the kitchen area, passing the long house, which was being readied with mats and banana leaves and decorations for the banquet.

The ladies in the kitchen were quite excited for such a delicacy and were readying the accompaniments!

"See, they are preparing vegetables, not dog!" Chester gloated, not having spied the deceased canine hanging dead from a coconut tree.

"Look up old friend!" I said, ready for his expression.

Well, Chester's legs wobbled not a little and his frame shook from tip to tail.

"Fairweather! This is just not on!" He stuttered, lamenting the death of a potential comrade.

"I am afraid it is looking that way, dear!" Lady was a little incensed but knew the ways of the villagers and that nothing nought was off limits to a feast.

Our cook, John Thompson, and butcher, Henry Jeffs, had heard about the unlikely meal and rowed ashore to witness the preparation and cooking procedure.

"I hope they aren't taking notes for your hide, Chester!" I badgered.

"I have determined by the grimaces on their faces that this is merely a fact-finding mission of theirs and not something they will learn for future reference." He seemed confident. So did I, but I enjoyed bristling him.

Tupia had killed the dog by holding his hands over its nose and mouth, thereby suffocating it. This took up above a quarter of an hour. He then proceeded to dress him much in the same manner as we would do a pig, singing his fur over the fire, which was lighted to roast him, and scraping his skin clean with a shell. He then cut the dog from neck to tail, deep and purposefully. The entrails spilled to the ground in one large lump, oozing on the sand as if they were still alive. Tupia explained the recipe to John and Henry; that he would be wrapped in leaves and cooked over the fire and under hot rocks for some two hours.

I had underestimated the ample provision of this poor dead sap for lunch!

Chief Pie and the felines marched into town. The dog had been gutted whilst hanging in the tree, but my fellow felines were now part of the show! The cats, led by Chief Pie and including my beloved Kitchen, all piled themselves around the bloodied entrails and tucked into the innards of this poor sap! I, too, was now incensed!

"This is just horrid!" Chester whined. Lady, too, was feeling her stomach rotate on its axis!

"You're right, Chester!" I complained. "I would not have believed that my own kind would eat dog! Raw dog! The entrails of dog! Any part of dog!" My stomach, too, was sickened at the sight of my own species tucking into the mess.

"Damn these cats, Fairweather!" Chester saw them as feral rabble eating raw dog gut. Kitchen saw us and prized herself away from their obvious delicacy, twittering as she ran up to us.

"Come and join us, Fairweather!" she enthused.

"Yes, hello, Kitchen," I began the customary greeting she had forgotten in her haste!

"This is fine food, Fairweather. If we do not hurry, we will miss out!" She shoved me as if I should move or go without!

"I would rather not, if it is all the same, dear girl. Fat dog gut is not something we English would consider a delicacy." I tried to spare her feelings.

"Nonsense!" she argued, clearly a new word in her vocabulary. "Our people eat fat dog! Your people will eat fat dog!" I doubted this. "And you will eat fat dog!" she insisted, fidgeting for fear she would miss out if we did not move along.

"Kitchen! I will do no such thing!" I put my foot down. One had to be firm with this feisty female.

She sniffed as if I were a fool and chirruped her way back to the fine dining!

"Nearly had you there!" Chester laughed as best he could under the circumstances.

"Yes, old thing," I agreed.

"She is rather controlling, is she not?" I asked of Lady.

"A little, dear, but she is young and does not know that we females can get what we want in other wily ways." Chester gave her a disapproving look.

"Needless to say, this is all a little primitive, what?" I stated.

"Primitive? Primitive? It is downright unlawful to the sensibilities! I cannot continue to watch this display," Chester announced, turning from the gory scene.

I wondered how the men would feel about eating dog!

The captain, the gents and some of the crew including John Thompson and Henry Jeffs assembled at the long house for this supposedly fine luncheon to sample what the Tahitians considered a delicacy, the humble dog.

Chief Oborea was yet another very fat chap, and oversaw the cooking of the poor animal, to ensure such a luxury was not spoiled by Tupia or the kitchen ladies who assisted in stuffing the poor beast. He was most pleased and wasted no time in asking for the white man's alcohol.

The captain had ordered a barrel of rum brought with him for this strange meal. I gathered that he thought the strong taste of rum would wash down the potentially horrid taste of dog. I remembered my promise to enjoy a drop with Chief Pie and cannily pinched a half coconut shell full, which was left unattended.

While the men sat around the long house, sheltered from the midday sun. I sat under a palm tree with the chief and my pilfered drink. He smacked his lips greedily, not having had such a treat since Wallis was here with Turkel on the *Dolphin*.

"This a fine day, Fairweather. Dog gut for my lunch and now the white fellow liquor!" He was overjoyed and drank the entire cup of rum, not sharing with anyone.

"When you marrying Kitchen and be my policeman?" he stammered, the rum affecting him almost immediately. I excused myself and went back for more rum. This time for myself! I would have to imbue the stuff to gain his trust, and then talk him out of this nonsense!

The men were actually enjoying the dog when I returned to pilfer my supply. Chester and Lady just looked on in despair as their humans liberally ate of their species.

"This meat is far better than I expected, Mister Banks!" said the captain.

"Delightful, Captain! I wonder whether we could convince our friends at home in jolly old London to partake in fat dog?" He laughed.

Just for that, I purloined Mister Banks's coconut shell full of rum. Unfortunately, Chester and Lady overheard him and walked off in a huff. He would not be their favourite companion for some time after a comment such as that!

Back to Chief Pie I hurried and we shared the second shell of rum. I was a bit tiddly but certainly had my wits about me more than the greedy Chief Pie!

I broached the touchy subject. "I must return to England with the ship, Chief. I sadly will not be able to marry Kitchen and take up your vacant position as policeman." I explained with imaginary regret, my grief being the only lie. I was indeed required to go home, and happy for it!

The chief was upset, but so drunk he fell about even from the sitting position.

"You shtay here!" was all he could utter.

"I cannot, Chief Pie." I tried another tack. "My captain will send for me if he sees that I am missing and I will be punished with twelve lashes!" I appealed to his skin.

"Ah I have seen dis lasheses!" He fumbled, drunk. "I think it best you go with shhhip. Udderwise you get hurted big. Kitchy-ennn find anudder hushband, and I find a polisheeman myshelf." He started giggling at his own inability to speak, this being the desired result of the rum.

I laughed along with him as I was a little tiddly myself and he was hilarious. He passed out not long after, not being accustomed to the drink, so I staggered a little back to Chester, Lady and the closing of the feast.

Everyone was preparing to move on but I was in the mood for mischief. Kitchen was in the vicinity having tidied up after her meal of "entrail of dog." I recall thinking of how that would look on a menu in a fine dining establishment. I laughed out loud.

Chester and Lady knew me to be a tad drunk and left me with the last of the guests being the captain and gents having a brandy with the chiefs and the queen. The captain had brought his best drop with him and I was offered a small amount from a leaf. I offered some to Kitchen who thought it most foul, but in her enthusiasm to keep up with me, drank liberally. It is a little-known fact that female cats require less alcohol than male cats to become drunk, and Kitchen was no exception!

"Why is everything I see hazy and moving a bit?" she asked, a giggle accompanying her question.

"It is the drink, dear. You must cease and desist now, or you will pass out like your father," I recommended.

"Pffft!" she said.

"Pffft?" I quizzed. "What is this 'pffft!' Are you dismissing my instruction, dear girl?" I was a little miffed.

"Pffft!" she repeated. "I can drink the white man liquor better than Father and you!" She "pffft-ed" again.

"Are you getting some more of this liquor?" she whined, when seeing the leaf emptied of brandy.

"For me? Yes. For you? I think you have had enough!" She was wobbling on all four of her legs.

"Pffft! Fairwetter! If you drinkie, I drinkie!" she sang, attempting a little jig but failing, falling face first into a shrub.

"Stop all this pffft-ing, Kitchen!" I demanded, although she was a genuinely funny sight.

The captain refilled my leaf, knowing me to have company, although whether his motive was for me to share it with Kitchen, or for me to drink more in the hope that I may tolerate her was merely a guess. He gave me an odd look, which could be taken either way.

She bounded at the filled leaf, falling flat on her face. I laughed out loud.

"Pffft!" She stood, her face covered in black sand. "Pffft, pffft, pffft!" she spat, trying to remove the grains from her mouth, spitting them in my direction. What a sight she was! I laughed uncontrollably.

"Here! Cease with the 'pffft-ing' and the spitting of sand at me!" I giggled, catching my breath, myself a little drunk and trying to drink the brandy before she consumed the lot by herself!

"Pffft, pffft, pffft!" She took a mouthful of sand deliberately to spit at me! Then washed her mouth out with the remaining brandy!

Her eyes were crossed more than usual, and she staggered somewhat, but the feisty spirit, which was her general way, had become more so with the devilish drink!

She ran off along the path, weaving from one side to the other "pffft-ing" all the way. I chased her as I was concerned for her wellbeing and was rewarded by her jumping out from behind a palm tree and tackling me to the ground, biting me hard on the neck!

"Ouch, you evil minx!" I bit her back, laughing hysterically when she whined. We wrestled and tussled there on the path. I taught her to play the English children's game of "hide and seek." Her counting was a pathetic attempt but we laughed and played endlessly until the captain and gents came through to head back to the fortress.

"A fine meal, that!" said Mister Banks, coming into view. I sat by the pathway ready to fall in with the party.

"Yes, strangely tasty!" said the captain with a little too much brandy under his belt.

Kitchen crashed into me and we both fell under the captain's feet, a jumble of bodies and limbs. He could barely tell that we were two cats! He tripped, only to grapple with a passing bush.

"What is this, Fairweather?" he asked, both of us stupidly attempting to get to our feet. "Been giving the young miss my fine brandy?"

Kitchen was full of mischief and stood as attractively as she could muster under the influence of alcohol and "pffft-ed" at the captain!

"I think she may be intoxicated, Fairweather, take her to her lair and come back to the ship. We must talk," he ordered.

Getting Kitchen back to her camp proved more difficult than I first thought. She did not wish to go and I had to lure her with "hide and seek," edging my hiding places ever closer to her home. Finally, we were there and she curled up next to her drunken sleeping father. I left her there and staggered a little on my way back to the fortress.

I found the captain waiting for me in his private tent.

"You and this girl, Fairweather?" he asked. I gave him my full attention.

"Be careful here, my friend. Have you heard of 'the birds and the bees'? he enquired delicately.

"You must like this girl very much to see you play so vigorously, but beware that you do not end up with…er… a…er… litter of…er… little Fairweathers!" he said awkwardly.

Chester and Lady had given me a lecture on just this subject of "birds and bees" and I, full of liquor or not, was staying well away from such an act as to spawn young!

The captain tried in vain to give me the same such advice but his sensibilities prevented the gory details.

"Pffft!" I said, leaving no doubt that I understood.

The captain eyed me with a smile. It was still early in the evening, but both of us laid down on his bunk and let the drink consume our sleep.

CHAPTER 24

The next morning saw Sergeant Edgcumbe at the tent door. "Captain, sir! You must awaken. There's been another theft! A large one!" he stated.

The captain got up, still in his uniform from the night before. This was too important for him to take of a wash. He rushed outside to join the sergeant, where he encountered Mister Banks and the gents in conference about the crime.

"I believe we should fire upon them with the guns, do you not agree, Sergeant?" said Mister Banks. The gents all nodded in agreement.

"Not sure we'll get your goods back that way, sir. I'll check with the captain," said the sergeant.

"We will most certainly not!" The captain now joined them and was angry enough that there had been a theft, let alone that the gents were planning to fire the guns upon the Tahitians who did not know any better than to steal.

"Tell me what has been taken, Sergeant," he asked, giving the gents a look of disgust at their plan.

"Theft was of a coal rake used for the oven fire, a musket, Mister Banks's pair of pistols, a petty officer's sword, a water cask and other small items, sir!" he shouted, standing to attention.

The captain thought for a moment. He knew that a rather large group had arrived at the village that night from the neighbouring island of Tethuroa with fish to trade with the Tahitians. It could also have been either Chief Tootaha's men or Chief Oborea's men. Both chiefs came in late last eve for this fish trade.

With so many suspects, it seemed ridiculous to merely fire the cannons or muskets into a group without knowing exactly who stole the items. Not to mention that it would teach the natives that the way to solve problems was best done with violence. Our peace-keeping captain would not hear of such a resolution to this crime.

"Sergeant Edgcumbe!" the captain barked defiantly. "No one will be fired upon! Get your men and mine, and round up the canoes I see here on the beach! We are about to have a bonfire!"

The sergeant took off with a sturdy "Yes, sir!" and the gents nodded approval that this would get their goods back.

"Mister Banks, I do not intend at any point to fire guns upon these people. A peace must be kept. There are other ways to skin a cat!" he said, putting the gents in their place.

But this mention of ways to skin a cat had me bothered not a little!

"It is just a turn of phrase, Fairweather," he assured me upon receiving a nip on the leg from yours truly!

All the boats, from all three tribes, were assembled on the beach ready to have what would be the most monumental fire I had ever seen! Twenty-two canoes being much wood!

The captain spoke to the three chiefs and threatened to burn their boats if the stolen items were not returned!

Word travelled fast. One by one, the thieving wretches sent their womenfolk to return the stolen goods, so as not to be discovered and punished, or shot! Everything being returned, Chiefs Oborea and Tootaha assembled their men and took off in the boats before more trouble could begin.

Queen Obadia came to the captain. Kitchen was draped around her shoulders like a fur cloak. Nimble little thing that she was. She was with her in an official capacity, always her companion during ceremonial or civil duties. "I believe you have had thieves during the night?" she asked.

"Yes, your Highness," said the captain, scratching Kitchen behind the ear with the queen's permission. I knew she liked that, and the queen was happy for the captain to approach her closely, knowing that he too had a feline companion in me!

The queen spoke slowly but perfectly, having learned much English during our stay.

"I am fortunate, for your actions have resulted in the return of your goods, captain." She thanked him.

"More is the pity that we should have to threaten such things," he said resolvedly.

"Why did you not use your guns on us?" she asked, knowing this would have been an option for such a large theft.

"I am committed to peace between us, your Highness. No guns will be used when it can be avoided." explained the captain of his personal rule.

"We are thankful for your goodness in this matter." The queen bowed and shook the captain's hand, as she had seen the men do from time to time as a mannerism of gratitude.

The captain bowed and shook her hand gently but firmly. "We aim to please as we are your visitors, but theft must be dealt with, and not by force, if it can be avoided," the captain explained of his actions.

"You are a fine leader, Captain Cook!" She smiled. "If you decide to stay, we will make you the most high Chief of the Island of Tahiti!" she offered.

The captain grinned. "Thank you, Queen Obadia. I am honoured by your trust. We will be sailing within the next two weeks. We have more to do for England!" He knew her to be merely teasing with this offer, but his manners had him thank her all the same.

It was after this that peace was in good enough shape to have the captain plan a party to circumnavigate the island for the 26th day of June coming.

In the meantime, the crew seemed to be his biggest problem. James Tunley was administered twelve lashes for taking rum from the cask without permission.

Manoel Pereira, the seaman taken on in Portugal, was missing. The captain thought he was gone with the intention to stay here. Word was sent out to locate him. It was not long before the captain was told that he was at the village of Apparra with Chief Tootaha. Chief Tootaha's own servant gave us this information, as an axe was the prize for bringing him back to the fortress.

Upon Manoel's return he would have been lashed some twenty-four times, but in his defence he explained that he had been taken by force by three natives while taking the longboat from the ship to the shore. He was put into a canoe and transported to Apparra. Chief Tootaha wanted to keep him, he said! The chief's servant brought him back and took the axe. They must not have thought much of Manoel as the axe was swapped for the man!

Then there was John Thurman, Able Seaman, who convinced young James Nicholson, of twenty-one years, to help him steal bows and arrows and a lock of plaited hair from the Tahitians. They were caught and made to return the stolen items and received twenty-four lashes per man for their trouble!

The captain, Mister Banks, Tupia, and a crewman prepared the pinnace for their planned trip around the whole island. Chester and Lady were looking forward to it, as was I. We went without the customary troupe of Marines, but were armed in case of trouble. The Queen warned us before we set off, to expect trouble from the tribe led by King Tiarreboo.

We started out on foot dragging the pinnace along the shallow waters off shore, by way of a rope. Mister Banks and his new attendant, Tupia, rallied around the varying species of plants, taking samples for Mister Parkinson to draw. He was missing his deceased comrade Mister Buchan very much, as when Mister Banks was on a fact-finding mission he was ruthlessly busy and demanding of his artists. Mister Parkinson's work would have to be illustrated upon our return to the fortress from the collected samples, as he had stayed behind to catch up on the drawings he had yet to do.

Much of the coastline was sandy and made for an easy walk, but occasionally there was a rocky outcrop and we had to bring the boat to shore and row or sail around it.

The pinnace was a small vessel, which could be rowed with oars, and having two masts, could be rigged for sailing, which we did when the wind provided the right direction for us to stay close to shore.

Tupia stopped at one part and begged that we go no further. He tried to persuade us to turn back, telling us that we were going to a place where no provisions were to be had and that the people there would kill him. He pleaded, telling us King Tiarreboo would kill us all. The gents made light of Tupia's pleading and loaded their guns with ball shot to prove that they would protect him, therefore easing his mind enough to continue.

We rounded a bend to find a rocky cliff face, too high to drag the boat around and too treacherous to sail. The captain informed we would have to swim out and around it!

Swim? Me? A land-loving beast if ever there was one! My dunking at the equator was more than enough seawater for one cat's lifetime!

Chester looked at the expression on my face and knew me to be fidgety about this jaunt.

"There is nothing to it, Fairweather. Just rotate the limbs and keep your head above the water!" I believe he was enjoying this, knowing that cats were not of the swimming variety.

"There must be another way!" I pleaded.

Then the captain, holding the rope of the pinnace waded out until the depth of the water required him to swim. Next Mister Banks and Tupia all with their heads above the water but arms and legs below moving as Chester had instructed of me.

"Fortunately, there is little swell in the sea and no breaking waves, or you would be tossed about like rag doll!" Chester was not making this any easier for me. "And sharks, watch out for sharks, they frequent these cliffs where the fish are plentiful!" He sniggered.

"Chester! Cease and desist this minute or I will leave you and return to the safety of the fortress!" I threatened.

Lady, Chester, and I entered the water together. It was a fleeting moment of bravery.

"Waves retreat! Sharks be off! Fairweather is entering the sea!" I hollered.

Chester laughed.

It was cool and salty. I licked at my nose when it dunked a few times. I enjoyed the salt but not the submersion. As we progressed into the water, the sand started to run out from under foot, and this rotating of the limbs automatically took hold. I was somewhat surprised, as I had not been taught to swim and had not the call for it until this point in time. Perhaps some ancient ancestors were swimming cats and the circumstances providing, such as now, jogged the old memory banks on how to move the limbs. I cannot explain it in any other manner. It was just there! I daresay it was rather enjoyable, cooling to the core and tasty licking for the old nose-beezer!

We rounded the cliff swimming without wave nor shark, and headed for the next shoreline, where all of us walked out onto the beach, drenched to the skin but in one piece.

We sat on the rocks to dry off a little, hauling the pinnace alongside to get some fresh drinking water. We all drank long and much. The sun dried the clothes of the men, and Chester, Lady, and I our coats. It was sticky and salty and I could have sat there licking the salt from my coat all day, and still not be rid of it. Instead, I jumped into the half barrel of drinking water we had on the pinnace after the men had taken of it. I needed a rinse. The captain spotted me and shooed me out sternly.

"Fairweather, you awful beast! Get out of the drinking water!" he yelled.

Mister Banks and Tupia jumped up to get me out if I would not remove myself. I was out and off like a shot to the farthest rock to dry off. The captain would surely be in a huff with me having salted the drinking water. I would have to make my apologies when we stopped for the night, or I would be left out of his tent in the night to be bitten by "nonos."

I dried quickly and licked the last of the salt from my fur when the men began to ready the boat for more travel.

We rowed, as the wind did not favour us on this tack and arrived at the Kingdom of Tahiti-iti and King Tiarreboo's camp just after dark. Instead of an enemy we found him most cordial and we met up with other native travellers who were staying there for the night, their canoes on the sand.

The king asked to wear the captain's cloak and then made off with it. It was never seen again, but the captain thought better than to bring a fuss to this, the man who had raided and killed villagers to take over their lands.

We ate with them and noted their spoils of war. A semi-circle of the lower jawbones of some fifteen men was evident as their trophy of a recent raid on this part of the island.

These men had killed a great number of Queen Obadia's subjects, burnt their houses, stole their livestock and forced the royal family of Obadia to flee to Matavai Bay. This was not a chief to be tested over the captain's missing cloak!

We saw much evidence of the *Dolphin*'s voyage here. The chief had geese and turkey, gifts from Captain Wallis to keep the peace, no doubt.

The next morning, the captain went off inland with Mister Banks and Tupia.

"Are you staying here, Chester?" I did not feel up to a long walk after my swimming adventure the day before.

"Not on your life, Fairweather, old boy! Do you not recall they eat dog here?" he reminded.

"Ah, a good point, old boy! Who knows what they eat here! Could be cats! Wait up I shall be happy to join you!" I was not going to be left alone with potential killers of men and eaters of dog or other such beasts, namely me, should it take their fancy!

We walked two or so miles inland gathering species while Tupia made rough drawings of the landscape for the captain. He was a good navigator and had developed a keen sense of the land and how to map it, under the captain's tutelage. Between Mister Banks's and the captain's teachings he was becoming an expert at many things. This would keep him in good stead with all, as I knew him to want to return to England with Mister Banks.

Whilst inland we came upon the largest "marae," or altar for worship, that we had seen thus far. It was a wonderful pyramid of stones with a large carved figure of a bird on the top. Near it was a huge carving of a fish from stone. Near the main marae were several smaller ones, and all were decaying through lack of use.

The captain determined that this must have been Queen Obadia's worship spot, now left to rot since King Tiarreboo had taken over this part of her land. On our return the evidence of war was more and plenty. Large numbers of human bones lay between us and the sea.

Upon our return, we bade our farewells and continued around the island. The captain made friends with smaller village chiefs easily and found the bays and harbours to be equal and as thriving as Matavai Bay.

We stayed with many smaller villagers and they fed and housed us in some of the more civilized parts. Otherwise, we erected small tents for our sleeping quarters.

We arrived back at the fortress at Matavai Bay on the 1st day of July 1769, all tired and thankful for John Thompson's good meals, since our villagers were unable to supply much as the breadfruit were out of season.

Kitchen was glad to see me upon our return and as the men were busy doing a final scraping and painting of the ship's hull for our departure, I thought I would be of use.

As mentioned, the island was overrun with rats. Mister Molyneux had been shooting them as plentifully as they would return. He had introduced the villagers to rat on a stick roasted over a fire and they had grown quite fond of it. They learned to prepare it in much the same way as "dog." Singing the fur over the fire and then stripping the skin with a shell.

The only problem was that they could not catch them or shoot them. A bow and arrow was of little use against a swift rodent.

I told Kitchen of my plan to teach the pride of cats to kill the rats and deliver them to the villagers. I always found that when ridding vermin, I was amply rewarded, and had no doubt that the locals would do the same, if these lazy felines could be harangued into service!

She was keen on this as I began teaching her. If I could not convince Chief Pie of the benefits of the hunt, Kitchen may be able to over time. Her father was a tough nut to crack and lazy to boot!

Compared to the smarter variety of mouse back in England, and the mice and rats on the ship, these island rats were unchallenged and fairly lazy, going about their business of scrounging without interruption. Easy prey!

Kitchen started out well enough as she was agile and fast, but when it came to the kill, she intended to let them go!

"I cannot kill them, TeaTea! They are a living thing, like us!" she whined.

"Kitchen, you just cannot let these rats have the run of the place! They are almost under foot everywhere one treads!"

"Can we just shoo them like the villagers do?" she pleaded.

"No, Kitchen, I have it on authority that Mister Molyneux has persuaded the locals to prepare and cook them as with dog. It is becoming quite a social event for them but they need you and the others to catch the rats and mice for them, as they do not possess guns, and their weapons are too slow."

"But TeaTea! It is cruel!" She was not getting the bigger picture.

"Yes, Kitchen, but you have all been spoilt by the natives giving you their scraps, and the true order of things is for cats to hunt mice and rats, as we do in good old England." I tried to appeal to her love of all things English.

"You do this in England?" she said, taking the bait.

"Oh yes, cats are employed by their masters to kill the vermin in and around the home, from the poorest to the richest, from whence I came, it is our duty and calling! The English love us for it, and reward us with cream from the cows, or the best portions of fish. The captain has given your village some cattle and you would be entitled to the best they can produce if you can catch and kill the vermin for them. It is quite simple, old girl."

"Oh alright, I will try." She gave in but not without pouting a little.

"Now, Kitchen, we will pretend that yonder rock is a rat," I suggested.

"But it is a rock, TeaTea!" she argued.

"Just for this lesson, Kitchen, we will pretend it is a rat!" I urged.

"But it isn't moving, and rats move!" she continued, this line of thinking annoying me much.

"Kitchen! Do not argue with me and I will show you how to stalk the rock, then we will move on to rats!" I had to put my paw down with this irksome minx as she was making my task difficult, to say the very least!

"Oh, all right." She sulked.

"Now, you must walk low and close to the ground so as the grass keeps the rats from seeing you." I showed her the correct stance and how to stalk a thing. The rock indeed did not move as I slunk purposefully toward it pretending it was my prey.

"Then you must stop and size up your adversary. Is he alerted by your presence? Or is he going about his business unaware of you?" I lectured.

"It is a rock, TeaTea! It is going about its business being a rock!" She was becoming increasingly annoying with this rock business.

"Concentrate on my manoeuvrings and movements, Kitchen!" I barked, creeping up on the rock.

"Yes, TeaTea." She was now trying her hardest to comply.

"Now, crouch right down to the ground and ready your limbs beneath you by shuffling them into place to pounce." I wriggled, eyes wide and limbs at the ready.

She giggled at my wriggling. "This is what I do when chasing butterflies!" She said cheerfully. I was not impressed, but at least the little troublemaker knew the pouncing stance, so I counted myself as blessed.

"Finally, Kitchen, when you know your prey to be unaware of you, you must pounce purposefully and bite the neck of the beast like so." I pounced the pounce and bit the rock.

She howled with laughter. "TeaTea bit the rock! TeaTea bit the rock!" she sang.

"Oh, do be quiet, you devilish girl! I merely bit the rock as an example!" I scolded.

"Now you try it," I instructed.

She started off well. Her crouching technique? Excellent! The only problem I could foresee was her tail!

"Stop! Stop! Kitchen! If that tail of yours sticks straight up as it has done thus far, you will alert your victim as easily as a roadside sign on the main roads in England!" I considered this and realised she would not know of which I speak.

"But TeaTea!" she argued. "I cannot put this lovely tail down. Queen Obadia thinks it is my prettiest feature!" True, her fur was long and luxurious, and no doubt she had been complimented on it many times, but it was still a beacon of her position whilst on the prowl for vermin!

I tried to explain in terms she would understand. "Your tail is like an arrow pointing to your whereabouts," I insisted. We were not seeing eye to eye, and this was what must be known as our first "tiff," although she could barely argue with me, never having caught anything in her life!

I had to be firm. "I will abandon this teaching business if you do not comply!" I threatened.

"All right, TeaTea, I shall behave and try not to show my beautiful tail as I hunt." She gave in finally, whipping her tail coquettishly at me. I softened a little.

"Thank you, dear one!" I offered as a token of peace.

"Let us resume, TeaTea." She kissed me on my cheek and snuggled under my neck. I blushed somewhat, hoping no one had seen us. This, I assumed, was the end of the argument, and we could hopefully make some progress. I must admit that the affection was a bonus, however!

She returned to her excellent crouching and very deliberately lowered her tail into the downward position I had shown her. She crept very lightly without rustling the grass. She looked to me for approval and I nodded so as to not startle her prey so to speak. She came within leaping distance of the evil rock. The next step being the shuffling of the limbs was most attractive on her. She looked straight ahead, her focus unmoving, and then with a deep breath she pounced higher than I, and possibly any other cat, ever! She came down with a thud, missing the rock and banging her head on it instead.

"Ouch!" She squealed and I ran to her assistance.

"Are you quite all right, old girl?" I asked, seeing a rather large lump forming on her forehead. She began to cry.

"There! There! Kitchen, old thing! We will do better with live rats. They are somewhat softer than rocks. Just give it one more try, not leaping quite so high into the air this time," I advised. "Try more of a forward-moving pounce, and don't forget to extend those claws." I settled her with a rub of her cheek, wiping the tears away.

"Thank you, TeaTea." She eyed me with admiration.

Her next attempt was dead on target!

"Well done, Kitchen, old girl! Shall we try your skills on a live subject?"

"Yes. I think I am ready!" she said confidently. "I am sure that biting a rat will not hurt me as much as this rock has done." She rubbed, wincing, at her forehead.

"You assume correctly. But bite hard and well, Kitchen, or you may be bitten back!" I warned, a rat bite being potentially nasty and infectious.

We headed for the kitchen area, knowing the rats to congregate amongst the natives' food supplies. I chose a slow and rather older type of rat and set her to the hunt. She had seen me hunt and knew the technique now that she had been properly shown.

She crept; tail down this time, not moving so much as a blade of grass. She came to the verge where the grass became sand, and the rat was well positioned distance-wise, however, I was not sure if she had the strength or technique to secure and bite the beast in the soft sand.

She pounced perfectly forward as I had advised, came down on the rat, and so solidly that she pushed it into the sand, not having bitten it on the neck for the kill. She had her sharp claws into it however, and it could not move. Looking to me for advice, I came forward, the other rats scattering.

She kept her victim buried and did not let go. I advised that she bite it hard on the throat to kill it and she did so, although I suspect that had she merely kept it submerged in the sand it would have suffocated regardless.

"TeaTea!" she squealed. "My first rat!" She was so excited, spitting sand and jumping here and there, that she lost sight of her rat in the sand.

"Oh! TeaTea! Where is my rat?" she panicked, not wanting to lose this, her first victim. Luckily, I had kept my eye on its whereabouts while she fidgeted about excitedly. I dug at the sand and pulled it up for her along with a mouthful of sand.

"Pffft!" I spat. "Here it is, Kitchen," I called as she ran around panicking. I left it there for her to pick up herself. The village kitchen women had been watching. We had drawn a crowd and I had not noticed. They clapped as Kitchen paraded about with the dead beastie hanging from her mouth. The sheer volume of rats must surely have been a nuisance to the cooks, and here was Queen Obadia's cat, the very first to catch a rat for the ladies! They clapped politely as Kitchen stood proudly, her rat hanging limply from her mouth.

"I must show the Queen!" she insisted. We walked through the parting crowd of cooks and assistants and off to Queen Obadia, who was at the fortress in conference with the captain over supplies for our departure.

We entered and Kitchen chirruped as best she could with her mouth full of rat. The queen and captain looked at us both, knowing full well by the plague proportions of these beasts that the village cats we not usually interested in rat control.

"Kitchen! You have caught your first rat?" she asked excitedly.

The captain spoke up. "I believe your lovely feline has been taking lessons from my ship's cat Fairweather. He is looking rather proud of himself," said the captain accurately.

"Well done, Kitchen!" praised the queen. "And thank you, Fairweather! Perhaps you and Kitchen can teach those other lazy cats to hunt. We are all becoming rather fond of 'rat on a stick' and will miss Master Molyneux's ample catches. If our cats learn from you, they will keep us in this new delicacy we have been enjoying, and keep the rat numbers down." She hinted at exactly what I was thinking.

Kitchen left her rat at the queen's feet and accepted a well-earned pat and chin scratch, as did I from my captain.

The queen's attendant removed the rat. "Make sure this rat is cooked on a stick for my lunch," she ordered, thrilling Kitchen. Her little jig and endless chirruping, assuring the queen of future snacks and Kitchen of much praise, treats and affection.

Kitchen and I left them to their trade negotiations and strode off to deliver the good news to Chief Pie and the other cats. We did not have to explain very much at all, as the cats had been witness to the kill from a distance. I guessed correctly that they would not at all be sure that they should give up their lazy lifestyle. After all, they were the recipients of the scraps of native food already delivered by Kitchen.

"Kitchen!" yelled Chief Pie. "Why you take hunting lesson from this, TeaTea?" he demanded angrily. "I quite happy to lie about and be fed. No need to hunt rat!" he hurrumphed.

"But Father, this has given me a great sense of purpose and much love from Queen Obadia!" She stood resolute. "I will continue to hunt, for it is rewarding to be active in the village and not just a pretty face for the queen! You will have to get someone else to gather the scraps for these lazy cats!" she announced defiantly.

"You are a female, and my daughter! You will not speak to me in this way!" Chief Pie bellowed. The males agreeing, yet some of the females began to stir.

Chief Pie's senior wife piped up. "I would like to hunt rat!" she said rebelliously. Chief Pie's eyes almost left their sockets.

"What?" was all he could yell. The rest of the wives and other females rallied around her.

"I want to catch rat." One by one, whether meek or daring, they agreed that they wish to learn from Kitchen and rid the village of some of the rats.

The males grumbled and eyed me as an evil enemy, bent on removing their rest time.

"See, Father? All the ladies will help me!" she reasoned. "The men, though, being such cowards, will just lie around watching us clever women, I suspect!" She taunted, hoping to get them to take any kind of interest in the activity.

"Hurrumph! My men are too important for such a thing!" The men all "hurrumphed" in concert.

"Important for what, Father?" she strutted, her tail brazenly high. "All I have seen them do is lie about here sleeping! I think that laziness is more what they are known for!" She walked along the line of women who nodded and agreed with her whole-heartedly. "Are you with me, ladies?" She had them riled.

"Yes!" resounded through the female ranks with great gusto!

"Wait a minute!" Chief Pie interjected. "You can't all go hunting rats! Who will stay here and look after Chief Pie?" he whined.

"You could use the exercise yourself, dear!" came the sturdy voice of Madam Pie, the chief's senior wife and Kitchen's mother! "And the rest of you lazy, insufferable men!" She was gaining momentum. "Kitchen? Fairweather? Will you teach us?" she asked.

"Of course, Mother!" came the reply. I stayed out of it. Chief Pie was eyeing me as a blot on the landscape and a threat to Tahitian cat-ship forever and a day! I felt that at some time I had best be watching my back, for ambush was keenly high on the agenda!

A low guttural growl escaped the chief in my direction.

"I will not hunt rat!" he defied.

"Very well!" said the senior wife. "As Chief, I suppose you can be let off, but only if you get these other males off their bottoms and we will all learn from Kitchen and Fairweather." He had no choice if he wished to remain a fat, lazy chief.

"Men, learn from this TeaTea," he mumbled, hopelessly outnumbered. "Kitchen, you teach the womans." He stormed off to find a resting place away from this, his once lazy and peaceful realm.

A hive of activity it had become! The males were a little heavy around the mid sections from sleeping all day, but we compensated for that with differing techniques. A kind to suit the man; tailor-made so to speak. The ladies were very keen indeed and in much better shape than their fellows, so Kitchen had them rounding up mice by the dozen. Soon there was a lady's pile the size of a large barrel. The males, not to be outdone by mere females, soon had their own pile of size.

The kitchen women had taken the afternoon off just to watch this new and wonderful spectacle, and at the end, a loud and rousing applause drew Queen Obadia to the area.

The cats were still running about chasing those faster rats that had gotten away, when she spied Kitchen and I giving directions.

"Come here, you two!" she called.

"Yes, your majesty." We bowed.

"You will both sit at the Queen's table for this banquet tonight. You have made use of those lazy cats and caught us a 'rat on a stick' feast for all! Thank you both and keep up the good work." She left us to our teachings.

"Did you ever hear such a thing, TeaTea?" She was so excited to be in such favour with her queen.

"I'm very glad, dear girl, but can you please ease up on the 'TeaTea'? I am after all Fairweather of the Bark Endeavour, educator of lazy cats, and the Queen's personal dinner guest! 'TeaTea' seems inappropriate and has always rather annoyed me," I instructed.

"Do not forget you are my boyfriend!" she hissed!

"Yes, quite!" I answered feebly.

"Yes, Fairweather! Sir!" She saluted, pleased with herself as motivator of felines and Fairweather's official girlfriend. Her father would soon get over his wounded pride. After all, he was still permitted to laze about as before.

The village ladies gathered up the rats and prepared them for the 'rat on a stick' feast this night.

While I was busy with Kitchen and her newfound subjects, the men had stocked the ship with fresh goods and sixty-five tons of water ready for departure in a day or two.

The gents were still in wonder over the diverse plants and wildlife, and were always either at the fortress sketching and preserving their specimens or out hunting for more and varied species.

Tupia being the wonderful local guide and now close friend of Mister Banks, was preparing to sail with us onward to the great Terra Australis Incognita by way of "Staten Land" or New Zealand. Tupia had lost his family in the wars and had nothing to keep him in Tahiti; having learned so much of England he was indeed ready to be Mister Banks's trophy from this voyage.

The time for the feast had arrived. This was to be our last "formal" feast as the weather dictated when we should leave. The captain stood and made a brief speech thanking all of the Tahitians for their hospitality and the queen rose and toasted the safe passage of our ship wherever she may go and blessed the many men who had taught them so much.

Kitchen and I took our places by the queen and ate "rat on a stick" for the first time, and with great gusto knowing we had started a trend that would see the cats, dogs and villagers fed in lean times, and not bothered by the plague proportions they had been used to.

I warned Kitchen that night after a few of the local alcoholic nips, to be very careful not to eradicate the entire rat population as the cats would then do themselves out of a job. As on the ship, she was to leave a number of happy couples to breed and maintain the rat's presence.

I mused that if the locals would eat dog, they might very well eat cat if they were not of some use. Kitchen had told her father of this threat, stretching the truth a little by telling him that Queen Obadia would soon order it so, and he let his males comply forthwith, and quickly, at the rat hunting.

During this wonderful feast on Sunday the 9th day of July 1769, with hog and breadfruit aplenty after the entrée of "rat on a stick," during the Marines' middle watch, Privates Clement Webb and Samuel Gibson disappeared, no doubt on land somewhere. These were the captain's personal guards and must be found!

By morning they had not returned so the captain made inquiries amongst the natives as to their whereabouts. They had apparently taken a Tahitian native wife each and fled to the mountains, knowing that the ship was leaving within a few days.

The captain learned that neither man wished to be found, intending instead to stay in Tahiti. This was all he could discover of them. The natives were not willing to divulge their exact location. He gave them the benefit of one day only, to return to the ship and be ready to sail. This information was taken to them, but the natives wished to keep the Privates Webb and Gibson. They liked their presence among them.

The next morning, the captain ordered lieutenants Hicks and Gore to shore to lure some of the chiefs on board as to take them hostage until the two privates were returned. Queen Obadia and Chiefs Hercules, Lycurgus and a number of lower-ranking chiefs were located by the lieutenants' parties and asked to attend the fortress. There they were informed that they were to be detained, until the natives brought Webb and Gibson back to the ship.

Master Molyneux reported that the islanders were much afraid that their chiefs would not be returned, perhaps dead already, or lashed, as was their idea of the want of our captain. Rumour was running rife!

Master Molyneux came forward with some information he had gathered.

"Captain sir, Private Gibson is a wild young man and a sworn brother to Private Webb. They have no reason for this than the pleasure of living in a fine country without the control they are used to being Marines. The natives have promised them some land and even servants, if they will stay," he informed.

"Thank you, Master Molyneux." The captain knew that such promises would tempt even the strongest men.

"Lieutenant Hicks, take the lesser chiefs on board the ship along with Queen Obadia and Hercules." He was playing on the natives' fear that we would take them with us when we sailed. Hercules and the queen's detention would hold much weight with the natives.

"Mister Monkhouse and Corporal Truslove, continue with Lieutenant Gore in finding these men," he so ordered.

Even though our hostages were treated well, they were inconsolable, crying and wailing while kept on the ship. Their subjects on shore could hear their caterwauling, and it was imagined that they were being tortured.

The evening saw the natives return with Clement Webb to the fortress.

"Captain, sir." Webb's head held low in shame. "The natives have captured and disarmed Mister Monkhouse, Lieutenant Gore, and Corporal Truslove. They have taken their guns. They will not give the men back to you until the Queen and chiefs are released unharmed."

This too-ing and fro-ing of hostages was becoming ridiculous!

"Take this man to the ship and detain him until we have secured the return of our men." The captain said with disgust at Webb's causing of so much trouble right before we were to leave.

Lieutenant Hicks had returned to the fortress with this news and the captain was deeply troubled. "May I suggest a full ambush on the natives holding our men?" suggested Lieutenant Hicks.

"Yes, Lieutenant, with regret I think it be the only way to retrieve our captives. We shall give them until the morning. Then take the dogs to help find them, if Mister Banks is in agreement?" He gestured to Mister Banks who nodded his approval.

The captain was of heavy heart for he was always much troubled by the use of force.

Early the next morning, Lieutenant Hicks assembled a large party of armed men. Chester and Lady had persuaded Paroo and his mutts to assist with the search, as bloodhounds are great hunters of the canine species. The dogs sniffed the offenders out in no time, Englishman smelling altogether different than Tahitians; it was an easy task for Paroo's team! They were found up in the hills and approached warily.

"Your Queen and chiefs will suffer if you do not return our men," Lieutenant Hicks told the insurgents.

The natives were appalled at the thought of their beloved chiefs being tortured! Our men were speedily released and brought back to the fortress where the chiefs were then released from the ship.

It was eight of the morning of the 11th day of July when all this kidnapping and counter-kidnapping had ceased. There was much joy among the natives upon the return of their chiefs, but they looked annoyed at us for causing all this trouble.

Clement Webb and Samuel Gibson were given the customary double lashes of twenty-four, in front of the Tahitian population, hoping to shame them. This worked perfectly as none of the Tahitians could stand to witness the punishment. Webb and Gibson were then detained under guard upon the ship until the time came for us to leave.

The ship's readiness was priority over the next two days and all went as planned without any more trouble. All of the items stolen by the Tahitians during our stay had been returned in one afternoon! A strange occurrence this! Perhaps they felt it correct to do so, as we were leaving and may need them.

The captain did not want a dark cloud to hang over our stay here, due to this kidnapping catastrophe at the end. He wished a peace amongst the natives for further good will when more white men would come to visit. He walked along the beach with Mister Banks, Tupia, Chester, Lady and I, and Queen Obadia with Kitchen on the morning on the 13th day of July, the day we were to depart as the weather permitted.

"I am more than sorry for this trouble, Queen Obadia," the captain said softly.

"We too are as you say, 'sorry'. I would like to give four hogs to you as a token that our friendship will be continued," she offered.

"We have nothing to trade for such a token, your Highness," said the captain, having used our quota of trade goods here. What we had left would be needed for further potential discoveries.

"Then let it be a gift for your voyage," she generously suggested. "You and your men and this fine cat have taught us much!" She gestured at me. Kitchen beamed with delight that she was in the company of fine men, myself included!

"As you wish, your Highness," said the captain with gratitude in his heart. We arrived back at the fortress, which was being disassembled so as to leave this place as we found it, pristine and beautiful.

"We have all affected each other's lives," I said to Kitchen. "But hopefully in good ways."

"I will love you forever, Tea-oops! Fairweather!" she declared.

"I, too, will love you, old girl. We have had some fun, have we not?" I was more than a little sad to take leave this place and my enchanting friendship with Kitchen. It was little wonder that some of the men wished to stay in this place!

"Oh yes, and I will remember your visit from deep in my heart, always hoping for your return," she admitted.

"I know not of my future Kitchen. I am a sea-going cat and my fate is in those of the ship and the men. I will always hope to come by this way again." I, too, spoke frankly of my feelings for this girl.

"Until we meet again." She kissed me and nuzzled my neck; I, too, returning the affection.

"We must be off!" Chester barged in, knowing me to be in a tender moment with Kitchen.

"Chester, you blight on canine-ity!" I blurted. "Can you not see I am in conference with this young woman?" I abused.

"Never mind that, we have to leave this place! And the ship is sailing within the hour. Take your place with us on the last longboat or be left behind," he yelled over his shoulder, Lady chastising him for interfering in my delicate moment.

I kissed her nose and turned quickly to avoid a tear welling in my eye, running for the longboat without looking back.

Once in my place next to Chester and Lady, I turned to see her standing quite alone. Her head bowed, sobbing. I felt a terrible ache in the pit of my stomach; something I had never before experienced.

"A love lost, old thing?" Chester tried to cheer.

"Leave him alone, Chester. He is much saddened by this departure," ordered Lady, her female sensibilities always correct.

We rowed quietly to the ship.

Queen Obadia had commissioned her finest grand double canoe with her subjects to escort us to the reef exit for our departure. Much waving and crying was coming from the canoe. No doubt, Clement

Webb's and Samuel Gibson's native "wives" were on board and bereft at their leaving.

I doubt there was a dry eye, or a heart untouched by these people, as the men, the Tahitians and even the captain waved their farewells. Tupia took control of the ship having broken his ties with Tahiti, but bringing his own servant, Tiata. He sailed her easily through the reef and as we looked back, the larger part of our hearts of late, being this paradise and its inhabitants, looked smaller than they should. We were at sea.

CHAPTER 25

Tupia and Tiata were proving the captain wrong in his thinking their joining the ship a bad idea. Tupia identified a small low island off the archipelago. Tupia told Mister Banks that it was uninhabited but a regular place for the other islanders to fish; its waters plentiful in marine life. The total group of islands, which we had seen and discovered, became known as the Society Islands.

The next day, another island came into view, like Tahiti with the jagged mountains rising high into the sky. It was Huahine Island and we anchored in Owharre Harbour at a place called Fare, which was on the western side of the island.

Tupia guided us there with his local knowledge. He reassured the natives in their canoes that all was well, and invited them on board to gain their trust.

The captain and gents, Chester, Lady, and the Littleboys, and of course, my good self, were regular fixtures at these landing parties. We took the longboat to shore where Tupia instructed that he and Mister Monkhouse should strip down to the waist as a gesture of equality among men.

The rest of us stood behind him while Tupia engaged in a long prayer to the gods of their island with the wishes of health, good weather, fine children, and happiness. Tupia offered the chief two handkerchiefs, a black silk neckcloth, some beads and two very small bunches of feathers. The chief was happy. The villagers were happy.

Tupia then proceeded with Tiata to the village "marae" to pray. Tupia explained that the natives could wander from one island to another as long as offerings were made and prayers to their individual village gods were offered.

We spent a few days here and the captain drew the coastline, Mister Parkinson drew anything that Mister Banks found that was new, and the rest were either tending the ship or attempting trade with the villagers. We had given them many things and so far they had brought us nothing! This was unusual until our last day there when we were given eleven pigs! Quite worth waiting for!

The captain, as ordered, took possession of the island by raising the English flag and leaving an inscription on a large boulder, with the date, the name of the island, which he had taken to keeping native lately, and the regulation speeches to claim the land for the king.

We left for Raiatea Island, which we could see from Huahine; again those mountainous peaks. This time, Tupia could not convince the swarm of natives in canoes that we were not a threat. They were aggressive and a lone native on shore armed with a lance started that sorcerer-like shrill chant I had heard before! I would not be going to this island.

We anchored at Opoa on the eastern side of the island. The natives invited themselves on board, finally seeing that we were peaceful, curiosity getting the better of them, I supposed. It was a brief stay with Mister Banks and the gents being the only landing party, to gather more specimens.

The captain charted the harbour, took possession of the island yet again, and moved on after five uneventful days. Bora Bora Island was our destination. We had heard it was inhospitable, from the diaries of Captain Wallis on the *Dolphin*. I was none too fond of this tack, hoping my captain had not lost his senses!

There were many shoals and shallows in these waters with dangerous jagged bottoms that could "hole" a ship and sink it easily. Tupia's great local knowledge was invaluable to this area and the captain left him to navigate us through the deeper channels while he charted them for future visitors.

Heading north, we passed the island of Tahaa. Tupia told us there was little to trade here but for coconuts and we had a plentiful store of these.

The captain noted and drew the extensive harbours that were perfect for anchoring, Mister Banks and Doctor Solander were the only ones to take the longboat to shore briefly, then we moved on for Bora Bora.

We approached this island only to be surprised that the natives were friendly, contrary to what the captain had read of Wallis's journal. Even though we could have made a landing there through what seemed a gap in the pounding reef, the captain deemed it unwise, so he stood the ship off the island while Mister Banks's party went ashore yet again.

By half the hour past five o'clock, we were worried that they had not returned. The captain ordered Lieutenant Hicks to fire a gun to get their attention, hoist a light so they could see us in the dark, and have them come back on board. Everyone worried.

It was not until half past the hour of eight that we heard them sound an answer of one musket fire. The gents returned with three small hogs, a few fowl, and a large quantity of plantains and yams, reporting that there was no breach in the reef on this side of the island, so anchorage was impossible, as the captain had guessed.

The captain was none too happy that the Gents took three whole hours after dark to return our gunfire and cause us to worry so. Mister Banks was chastised, even though this was a rare occurrence. Our good captain was always concerned for the wellbeing of the men and Mister Banks took his reprimand with good grace.

Later that evening, Mister Banks read us his findings of Tahiti for the Royal Society. These speeches of his always entertained.

"We have now seen seventeen islands in these seas and been ashore upon five of the most principal ones. The language, manners and customs did not differ amongst them. My account is from Tahiti, where I was so well acquainted and comfortable among the free and honest locals that I slept in their houses in the woods with not a single companion!"

I had to agree that the Tahitian people were generally my favourites so far! My thoughts wandered to Kitchen as Mister Banks continued.

"On all the island flats along the sea coast there stood houses every fifty yards with their little plantations of plantains, from which they make their clothing. I found there to be only a few people inland in the valleys with rivers. "The men are excellently made and above six feet in height, most handsome except for their flat noses, but without exception each had perfectly even white teeth.

"The women are much the same build as Europeans but their eyes especially were full of expression and fire!

"In colour they differ very much; those of inferior rank who fish and are therefore exposed to the sun, were dark brown in colour. The superiors who spent most of their time in their huts under shelter were no browner than a European brunette.

"Their hair is black and coarse, worn cropped close around the ears of the women. The men exercised more freedom with their locks and beards; some wearing their hair long to their shoulders and others piled on top of their heads. Both sexes remove the hair under the armpits, as it is considered a mark of uncleanliness." I had not noticed this and rather respected Mister Banks findings as being comprehensive.

"Their tattoos are very elaborate with an infinite diversity of patterns and figures, some of men, birds and dogs, which both sexes have on their arms and legs. Their faces are generally left without any marks. All the islanders I have seen have universally tattooed their buttocks in a deep black of arches drawn one above the other. These arches are their great pride showing them as either proof of beauty or proof of their resolution in bearing the pain of the tattoo.

"They prepared the black from fire, mixing it with water and kept it in a coconut shell. The instruments for pricking it under the skin were made of bone or shell cut into sharp teeth fastened to a handle. These teeth are dipped into the black liquid and then driven by quick sharp blows struck upon the handle; every stroke was followed by a small quantity of blood and the part so marked it remained sore for many days before it healed; the ink then permanent.

"It is done between the ages of fourteen and eighteen and so essential I not once saw an adult without it. Not one of the Tahitians would ever give me a reason for it. I can only assume it stems from superstition. The smaller markings on the fingers are only for beauty." I was riveted by this explanation of the Tahitian tattoo! Mister Banks had done much research.

"The women keep their cloths spotless and the ladies seem to enjoy this time in social groups laundering and repairing. The women wear a kind of petticoat for decency, and then swathe themselves in layers of draped cloth. The men wear a piece of cloth between the legs, fastened to the waist to cover their privy parts and also wear many pieces of cloth about their person, some all over their bodies and others merely rolled around their loins.

"Both sexes shade their face from the sun with little bonnets of cocoa nut leaves. Jewellery is rare but some wear an earring in just one ear. They anoint their hair with coconut oil mixed with sweet woods or flowers, but I fear in vain as their hair smelled rancid.

"The women make their cloth from the inner bark of certain trees, mostly the Chinese paper mulberry tree. Some cloth is white and some dyed red or yellow from the juices of fruits. The red I found to be my favourite and the women enjoy the beauty of their stained fingers as a result of the process. A thick brown cloth is also made to shield them from the rain.

"The women make their matting by weaving rushes and grasses, and their baskets are made in this same manner. I found the weavers to be very nimble of hand!"The do not build their houses in towns or villages; they are always in the woods and well shaded from the sun. No country can boast such delightful walks as this; the groves of breadfruit and coconut trees along paths that go from one house to another." I can attest to this beauty and for smallish fellows such as myself, the cleared undergrowth made for comfortable walking!

"A middle-sized house was some twenty-four feet long and eleven feet wide. No walls had they, to allow the breezes to cool the inhabitants. Hay and mats lined the floor with little furniture than one stool used by the master of the family. The people sit on the mats by day and sleep on them by night. Thus, all privacy is banished even from those actions which the decency of Europeans keeps most secret!" We had all seen this and had gotten used to the sight of the Tahitians dressing or undressing without a thought of embarrassment.

"The larger buildings! One I measured as large as one hundred and sixty-two feet long and a breadth of twenty-eight and a half feet! These were for meetings and consultations and for the reception of visitors." I remembered dining in one of those with the captain and Queen Obadia.

"Everything that comes from the sea is esteemed and eaten by the Tahitians, fish, lobsters, crabs and even the blubbers or jellyfish! Fruits: breadfruit, coconuts and thirteen sorts of banana I found: sweet potatoes and yams are cultivated by all; sugarcane is eaten raw; pineapple is the sweetest I tasted." We all knew of these delicacies but enjoyed hearing Mister Banks speak of them in case we had only imagined them.

"The pork, as we know, was most excellent but the fowls a little tough. Boiling their food or baking it in their fire pits is the extent of their cookery skills. I ate of raw fish and breadfruit one evening, finding it rather palatable." Mister Banks would try anything that could not kill him!

"They did not like our alcohol and its effect upon them, and have no similar product of which they make for themselves. They drank water and coconut juice, but occasionally would partake of seawater to quench the need for salt, sometimes dipping their food in it for seasoning."The women abstain from eating with the men and only sup when the men have taken their fill. They eat in the servants' apartments." Lady "hurrumphed" her distaste for this custom, considering men and women equal in the European custom of dining.

"After their meals they sleep and on some days it seemed that all they did was eat and sleep! A few times I saw them at some diversion; shooting with the bow and arrow or throwing a javelin at a mark."Music is very little known to them, which I found odd as they are very fond of it. They have the flute made of a hollowed bamboo about a foot long in which is three holes and they blow it with one nostril holding a finger over the other! Odd what?" All of us agreed, considering the flute should be blown from the mouth! "It is accompanied by the drum, made from a hollowed block of wood covered with shark's skin. They sing and play in groups, which I found to be tuneful and pleasant."In every expedient for taking fish they are vastly ingenious. Their fishing nets are exactly like ours. Their lines are made from a nettle bark that grows in the mountains and is far superior in strength to our own. On their hooks, they put tufts of hog's hair, which serves to imitate the tail of a fish. They strike fish with harpoons made of cane and pointed with hard wood in a very dexterous manner."Axes and tools are made of black stone. They carve their canoes elaborately with these as we have all seen. They lash two canoes together for stability, or furnish them with an outrigger to keep them stable in rough seas. They paddle them but always with one man dedicated to throwing baskets of seawater from the leaky craft. Some are fitted with one or two masts for sailing. "They seem to be as accurate in weather prediction as any I have seen; by observing the Milky Way they seem to forecast which quarter of the heavens the wind will blow!" This was a talking point amongst the captain, lieutenants, and gents for some time, and although they were usually accurate, none could fathom their method.

"They are aware of the movement of the sun and the stars, and their method of measuring time was by counting thirteen moons and then starting again. Relatively accurate, I must say, but they only knew the months by the fruits that were in season at that time." This was good stuff! The captain was impressed!

"Their language is soft and tuneable, but try as I might to get them to say my name, 'Tábane' was all they could grasp. It indeed did not resemble any part of my name but I left it so, as I managed to understand their language in time."Some of the islanders had contracted scaly eruptions on the skin, advancing to leprosy, when their hair and nails would drop off and their flesh rotted from their bones. They were excluded from society, living by themselves so distanced from the villagers, yet supplied with provisions daily.

"They had no medicines, hence prayers and ceremonies were all that could cure the distempers or colic, all of which were minor ailments known to mostly always get better by themselves. They do have plants which they use to cure their ills or wounds and they explained to me their application."Tupia has been instructing me on their religion. They have many gods. The chief god, Tarroati'ettoomoo, is the creator of all things and causer of earthquakes. His son, Tane, seemed to be the more active of the gods. The men worship the male gods and the women, the females. They believe in heaven, a place of great happiness, and hell is only a place enjoying less of the luxuries of life. They marry without the ceremony of a priest."Besides their gods, each island has a bird to which the title of god is given. For instance, Ulietea has the heron and Bola Bola, a kind of kingfisher. They are highly regarded and by no means killed or harmed."There are wars on occasion, some between tribes and others within them. Their weapons are slings which they use with great dexterity, pike heads with the stings of sting rays, and clubs of six or seven feet long and very heavy."Tahiti was divided into two kingdoms, each with a separate king and they were at peace. We saw no signs of punishment or law during our stay. Tupia tells me that theft is punishable by death and smaller crimes in proportion. All punishment is the business of the injured party and the severity decided by them."Well, I leave my findings thus," ended Mister Banks. It had been a long speech but every man was riveted by the botanist's findings. What they had not witnessed for themselves they were pleased to learn.

"Well done, Mister Banks. The Royal Society will be pleased and your thoroughness no doubt rewarded," complimented the captain.

The next morning, we tacked our way back to Raiatea Island, this time anchoring on the western side.

Being ship-bound was new to us all compared to the freedom of the fortress at Matavai Bay. We anchored at Tuu Fenua Harbour on the 2nd day of August. Here the captain ordered the men to go ashore and return with more rocks for ballast as the ship was not heavy enough for the winds she was sailing. He set the men to the task and twenty tons were brought on board. There was a leak in the gun powder room also and this could not be repaired at sea.

We were told that King Opoo would visit with us on the island. Tupia had told us the king was evil and had taken whole islands from their inhabitants. We all expected a fearful chap, indeed, but instead were led to a half-blind old man! His frailty hid a mean old coot, leading much stronger men to many a war.

We were invited to feast and watch a dance called "Heiva." The women were beautifully dressed with great quantities of plaited hair dotted with sweet-smelling gardenia flowers. Bare to the waist, they had placed a bunch of black feathers on each shoulder. Their long petticoats where brown and white striped. The drums beat briskly and loud and they began to shake their hips. Not quite a good thing in front of sailors who had been away from their homes, and wives or girlfriends, for so long.

One of the girls had three pearls in her ear. Mister Banks tried in vain to trade four hogs for them but she would not part with them. The men of the entertaining troupe acted out some kind of play with speaking and dancing but none could understand their words. It seemed odd to me that islands so close to each other had different and varied languages. A testament to their keeping to themselves, I deduced.

After the celebration, we all retired to the ship. I alone sat with my captain writing in his log, when Mister Banks showed up.

"We sail tomorrow, Mister Banks," the captain offered.

"I would wish to stay longer, but the captain knows best." He tried to get his way as usual but by now he knew that when the captain says we sail, we sail! There was no getting around him!

"We head south tomorrow for either New Zealand or the continent of Terra Australis Incognita, whichever we strike first," he informed. All I could think of was that south meant cold and so I set my coat to thickening up right there on the spot.

"Yes, yes! On to new lands!" Mister Banks was excited.

"I have my doubts about this Terra Australis Incognita, but we are commissioned to look for it, and look we shall," he said, dismissing Mister Banks to return to his charts.

I joined him on the chart table as I had many times before. He was staring at a rather blank area of blue beyond the sparsely charted Staten Land, or New Zealand, of which he had little knowledge. Not much was known or recorded of this place, but the captain was more concerned with fulfilling his orders to find a more mysterious place.

"Terra Australis Incognita," he mumbled painfully. "Fairweather, I have no ideas of where and which direction to head us for this discovery." He slumped back in his chair, his arms dangling by his side, looking up as if to pray.

I sauntered my way around the chart, by now almost as familiar to me as home; I, too, had been learning from the captain. I extended one claw of the pointed kind and began to scratch a line into the chart. The tearing of the stiff paper lifted my captain's head.

"Fairweather! Be gone!" he growled, jumping to his feet. "My job is difficult enough without torn charts!"

I stood firm and met his eye. He looked down to where I had torn.

"Blasted cat!" he grumbled, surveying the torn paper, until he realized what I had done.

A look of bewilderment overcame him. He had seen past the tear in his chart to discover that it had purpose and pinpoint accuracy.

"Fairweather?" he quizzed. "Am I mad?"

I eyed him purposefully and stamped my padded paws onto the map to hinder the curling of the torn paper. He looked at the map again, then at me and vice versa, rather a few times, each time, his eyes wider than the last.

"Fairweather, these look like co-ordinates, tacks and distances you have scratched into my map?" He was bewildered.

I nodded purposefully, my outstretched pointer claw tapping on the map to confirm his suspicions.

"No! No! No!" I must be ill!" He held his hand to his forehead to ascertain his temperature. It must have been normal other than for the beads of nervous sweat he wiped away. He closed and locked the Great Cabin door to give us some privacy.

"You know of this Terra Australis Incognita?" he asked. I did not, but having studied silently under him all this time I had a fair knowledge of how to get there. I had seen his calculations in mapping his charts. I had missed not a moment of his instructions to my Isaac on how to determine a path in the sea, given winds and currents. He was always very forthcoming and I lapped up his every lesson.

Abel Tasman and Louis Antoine de Bougainville had claimed to have seen this land and it was roughly plotted into the current charts. I made an educated guess. As I was unable to communicate this, I merely nodded.

"You have been there?" he asked breathlessly. I had not, but could only tap my outstretched pointer claw at the route I had set down.

"This is too much!" he whispered incredulously. "Under my nose and feet, all this time," he paced, "my cat knows the route to Terra Australis Incognita!" pacing further.

Not sure of his sanity, he looked at the map again as I cleaned under my outstretched claws nonchalantly. He had said "my cat" and I was rather chuffed. We had always been friends and comrades but now I was "his cat!" This was awfully good of him and I felt well rewarded.

"These directions take the currents and winds into account, Fairweather!" he said in disbelief. I nodded and continued to clean my claws, blasé in the knowledge that I was probably correct. An iota of doubt crept in as I did not really know the way, but my newfound knowledge gave me purpose and my gut took care of the rest. Iotas of doubt be gone! The captain was impressed!

"Are you sure?" he asked, holding me still as to cease cleaning myself. I held his gaze squarely and nodded yet again.

"And what of the route to Staten Land?" he dared to ask, putting me to the test. After all he was not going to follow the directions of a mere feline, without proof. Myself being correct or not!

I looked the charts over, pausing for effect even though I already knew the answer. I etched yet another route to this New Zealand. The captain looked it over and thinking aloud of winds and currents, plotted what he thought himself to know of the route. The two courses were as one and he knew me to be correct.

He turned and did a little jig, knowing us to be alone. I, in turn, tapped a little dance on the map table, happy in the knowing I had been of some assistance.

He turned to me. "We tell no one of this!" he demanded.

"I shall be sacked as captain should anyone find that my directions are those of a cat." I took a little umbrage, but I understood his position.

I placed my paw upon his in oath as he poured himself a large tumbler of brandy, shaking his head all the while. He then sat, quite relieved and took a long drink, beckoning me to his lap. I complied and was the recipient of a good petting. Not just a chin scratch, a rather good massage!

"Well, Fairweather?" I replied with a meow. "We shall put your directions to the test!"

I purred as the captain sipped his brandy, both of us falling asleep where we sat.

The next day, we provisioned and set sail in the rain, but the winds were favourable so the captain staunchly set the men to the task, and under Tupia's guidance through the local waters, we sailed off for parts unknown only to the captain and I.

We had barely left the Society Islands when huge Pacific rollers and strong winds changed the stillness of the sea and the men all set about securing anything loose.

Mister Banks thought this change meant we must be closer to our mysterious destination than we thought, but the captain dismissed him, clearly of the knowledge that we had some way to travel yet.

By the 15th day of August, we crossed the Tropic of Capricorn, another line around our globe, which was apparently significant. I hoped that the dunking resulting from the crossing of the equator would not be required, and I was not disappointed. No such lark was arranged.

Land was sighted almost daily by whomever was stationed to the topmast. All sightings turned out to be clouds on the horizon and we sailed this way and that chasing nothing.

Day by day the temperature fell, the stock suffered terribly and their fodder wasted away. We ate well on this tack south, as one by one the animals died of natural causes, especially the chickens and pigs. These were used to a much warmer climate back in the Society Islands and perished quickly with the cold.

Albatross, pintado birds, and shearwaters were seen. These birds were known to fly a long way from land, making the captain uncertain that we were sailing in the right direction. I assured him that we were on track at our now nightly conferences over the charts together and alone.

The gents fell ill regularly with the rolling sea and only the seasoned sailors and Marines kept themselves from the seasickness.

On the 24th of August, my Isaac spotted a waterspout to the northwest. I had never heard nor seen one of these vile things, but the crew rushed to watch a dark cloud descend toward the sea, a point lowering itself to connect with the ocean, swirling in circles like water down a drain hole, and sucking water, fish and anything else in its way into its funnel. It slithered across the ocean surface like a snake and I imagined that before knowing what it really was, all manner of sea-going men would swear they had seen a giant serpent emerge from the sea. I for one was of that impression before being better informed! Dangerous things regardless, and able to lie waste a ship. Fortunately, we were going nowhere near it.

It was the 25th day of August 1769 that saw the first anniversary day since we left England. A locker stocked for the occasion was opened and a wheel of Cheshire cheese was produced for all to sample a little piece of home. A cask of port was tapped which all decided was excellently good. The men felt again like they lived as Englishmen and drank to the health of their friends and families back at home.

The port was not all consumed and the captain ordered my Isaac to lock the remainder away in the stores for further celebrations. I met up with him down there whilst chasing the odd rat that had managed to creep onto the ship from the islands unbeknownst to me. They, too, suffered the cold and were nicely slow enough for me to catch without much exertion. The mice were still at manageable levels but hidden well in the cold and I imagined they were none too fond of the native rats who invaded their stores!

"Fairweather, old friend!" said Isaac as we met. "Haven't had much time together lately, have we?" he observed.

I rubbed up against his leg for a chin scratch and was not disappointed. He crouched down and some well-earned attention was forthcoming for yours truly.

"A finer cat I could not have picked from the docks of England!" he praised, himself more than me, I suspected.

Just then the rest of the boys arrived in the stores.

"Ere, Isaac," Will Howson whispered. "You locking that port away?" he inquired mischievously.

My boys' voices had deepened in this the last year, and the older the boy the manlier they looked. Some even had whiskers! I liked this in men. It gave them a certain kinship with the feline species!

"Yeah, Will, what of it?" said Isaac suspiciously.

The boys nudged each other playfully, thinking my Isaac a bit of a stick in the mud being so close to the captain as his apprentice, and not having gotten into mischief since the "bugs in Banks's bed" incident.

The other boys had their share of tomfoolery in Tahiti making sure that no one found out, but Isaac stuck to his studies dutifully until now.

"Lets 'ave the rest of it," Will suggested, his voice filled with wickedness. I was a little concerned!

"Don't be daft, Will, the cap'n will have a conniption if he finds out and guess who'll get the blame, bein' as I've been sent here to lock the stuff away?" Isaac certainly had a point there. "Besides, we're too old for the cane. We'd get twelve of Lieutenant Gore's best!"

"I know!" piped John Charlton, the captain's second servant, completely ignoring Isaac. "We'll drink it all, and stick a knife hole in the side after. It'll look like it's leaked away. We'll even tip a bit on the floor to make it look good! There's been leakage in the gun powder room so nobody will be the wiser."

Oh dear! I could see nothing good would come from this, and hoped my Isaac had grown enough to resist this devilish scheme. Bosun John Gathrey's cabin was last before the stores. He was on duty above, hence there was no one around for me to alert.

Isaac scratched his chin still crouched at my level. "Yeah, all right!" He had succumbed to his youth. I had best stick around for there was a good half-barrel of the potent brew left.

William "Bill" Harvey, Lieutenant Hicks's servant, chipped in. "Manly, you go to the kitchen for a couple of beakers."

"Are you mad, Bill?" Isaac protested. "Manly's a big bumbling brute not made for sneaking around anymore, look at the size of 'im! You go! You're skinny and sneaky. You'll get the job done without anyone findin' out, or I'll give you a thrashing!"

"Am not," mumbled young Isaac Manly, not appreciating his description. A little harsh, but Isaac did have a point. Young Isaac Manly would knock a thing over just by standing near it!

"Listen, lads! Tupia's boy! Tiata! He's always with the gents. John! Go see if you can lure him away for a lark with us. He's probably never touched a drop of liquor and it'd be some fun to see 'im drunk!" Charlton was a menace, but there was nought I could do.

John was off in a shot, nothing but evil on his mind. I followed him to try and distract Tiata so that he may not become the butt of this horrid scheme.

Tupia and Mister Banks were in conference with the captain in the Great Cabin, talking of this route we had taken and its inability to sight land.

Tiata was standing at Mister Banks's elbow, listening intently. Before John could get to the door, I overtook him and jumped on the table, upsetting the contents considerably.

"Fairweather! What is this?" he shooed me from the table sternly as he attempted to mop up his and Mister Banks's teacups that I had toppled, their contents spilling on their laps.

Just then, John Charlton arrived at the door.

"Excuse me, Captain, sir," he interrupted.

"Yes, yes, Charlton, what do you want?" the captain asked impatiently as the extent of the tea spill reached his journal.

"Captain, the boys and I would like to see Tiata down below. We have a game of cards going and thought he might like to learn," John lied.

"That is very thoughtful of you, John!" said Mister Banks. "I believe the captain, Tupia and I can spare him for a while. Run along, Tiata, and enjoy some English fun," Mister Banks said, cleaning his lap of slight spillage and ignoring the attempts made by all to save the captain's journal from the ever-growing puddle of tea.

I ran at the table and leapt again, getting my feet wet and annoying the captain.

"Fairweather! Have you gone mad?" He was not getting my hints, although how could he know just from my upsetting his table.

There were times I sorely wished I could communicate better with men.

"John, take Tiata and Fairweather with you!" he growled. My attempt to warn was wasted, and only infuriated the captain.

John scooped me up under his arm. "Yes! Yes! Be off with you!" said the captain, annoyed at my antics. By now he should have known better! When Fairweather interrupts, he means well!

"Thank you, sir," John excused himself and motioned to Tiata to come with him, leaving the captain and Mister Banks to the mess I had made.

As we left sight of the Great Cabin, John dropped me unceremoniously. I followed closely.

"Come on, Tiata, we've got some white man's alcohol and we're up for a lark. Are you in?" he whispered so as not to attract the attention of anyone he passed.

"I have not tried the white man's drink, John. I will be interested to," He naively agreed. "But are we not playing cards? I do wish to learn!"

John, of course, having no intention of teaching the lad to play was headed back down to the stores with the eager Tiata. The boys were waiting. Bill Harvey was back from the kitchen with the beakers to fill.

"I could only pinch two without being questioned. We'll have to share," he puffed from dodging John Thompson in the kitchen.

"If you wish, the stores carry many coconuts and if you can procure a machete I can split some to drink from!" Tiata offered willingly.

I was most impressed with his ability with the newfound English language, but he was almost too keen and I knew my boys would take liberties with this naïve young man.

My Isaac found a machete amongst the tools for the stores and Tiata set to splitting enough coconuts to go around, deftly with one fell swoop of the knife. I could see he had done this many times before.

The boys drank the coconut juice to leave no trace of this wickedness and Isaac replaced the contents with port from the barrel.

"To new worlds!" toasted Isaac.

"Adventure!" Bill raised his beaker.

"Adventure!" The group saluted with coconut shells and beakers full of the captain's port.

It was not long before this fortified drop got in amongst the lads. Tiata sipped it tentatively at first, but as smooth a drop as had ever been, he drank it as if it were sugared water, hardly allowing the goodness to pass over his tongue!

"This is very satisfying, Isaac! Tasty!" he examined his empty shell.

"Ah, Tiata, you aven't had enough yet!" Bill scoffed, pouring him another.

The other boys paced themselves with the sweet, sticky wine. Tiata continued to drink as if it were nectar, gulping down his shell's contents.

"Are we to pullay cardsh now?" Tiata slurred to his hosts, swaggering and tottering not a little, quite unfamiliar with the effect of strong drink.

"Nah, let's play another game!" The pest John Charlton chipped in, giddy from the port as were his cohorts, but none so much as poor Tiata. He was starting to sway from side to side, this giving Charlton an idea.

"I like that dancing, Tiata," he teased. "Reminds me of the Tahitian girls." He looked around at the group.

"Why shank you, Johnnn!" he drawled, affected terribly. He continued to sway as if a Tahitian dancer and Charlton set forth to egg him on. They finished every last drop of the captain's best and all were jolly and hence fit for mischief.

"Ere, Manly, you go and get some rope. Bill, get some cloth. I 'ave an idea!" When John Charlton had drink in him and an idea, nothing good would come of it. I could only watch and hope for the best.

Young Isaac Manly returned with the rope and Bill with the cloth. Charlton initiated his cunning plan. None could see why he tied two coconut shells together until he tied them to Tiata's chest to mimic the breasts of Tahitian women! Then as Tiata got the gist, Charlton wrapped the cloth around his waist turning him in circles to do so and tucking it in as he had seen the native women do. Tiata was by now quite sloshed and giddy from his being wrapped in cloth.

"Now, Tiata! Dance like the native girls!" The boys howled with laughter, as did the sporting Tiata, not knowing that he was being mocked.

He swayed back and forth unsteadily, tipping here and there, using the elaborate hand movements we had all seen back in Tahiti. The boys spun him round and kept him moving by clapping a beat for him to dance to. What a sight the poor boy made, although he was enjoying himself unashamedly, and giggling like a girl.

"You know, Tiata," said John Charlton with a wicked tone, "Mister Tupia and Mister Banks and even the captain would like to see this special dance you are performing, I'll bet!"

"Would dey?" He swayed about, leaping here and there. "I would be verrry happy to showed them." His command of English was faltering with the effects of the port.

Well, this was the last straw, the boys rolled about crying with laughter at the very thought of Tiata showing up in the Great Cabin dressed as a woman, let alone dancing and drunk to boot!

"Charlton, you're a genius!" Bill applauded. "Let's all go and take Tiata to show the gents how lovely he can dance!"

"Yesh, I aim to pleashe!" Tiata sang. A more eager fellow one would never find for these wretched boys to taunt. Poor sap!

"Wait! Wait!" stammered my Isaac. I was hoping he would stop this charade. "First we clean up this mess we made or everyone'll know we were part of it." The lads agreed.

Tiata just kept swaying in a little world of his own.

"Instead of cuttin' a hole in the barrel, Manly you go get a bucket of seawater and we'll fill the port barrel back up with it. No one'll know. I was supposed to put it away anyhow. Don't think they were needin' it again," suggested Isaac.

Manly took off for the bucket, bumping into everything he could. The demon drink did not help poor Isaac Manly's case where crashing into things was concerned. He returned promptly, sloshing the water all over the deck. By the time my Isaac had filled the barrel there was only just enough of it left from Manly's bucket to replace the liquor. He corked it quick smart and mopped up the mess with Tiata's trailing cloth skirt.

"Let's go, Tiata! I think the gents are waiting for your entertainment!" said Charlton, the ruinous beast.

The boys fumbled and staggered all the way from the stores down below, up to the Great Cabin, giggling till they were red-faced all the way.

I followed closely as no good would come of this. They shushed each other, as there was usually a sentry on the Great Cabin door. When they reached it, as luck would have it, the sentries had taken a break between watches. They jostled forward and pushed the still dancing Tiata through the door and then they bolted. I snuck into the room and placed myself in my usual spot so as not to attract attention.

"Tiata danshing like the girlsh at home for de Captainsh an' Gentlemensh!" He sang as all eyes turned to this ridiculous site. Tiata with the coconut shells still tied to his chest and his skirt trailing behind him so as to trip him between flourishes of dance!

"What is the meaning of this?" Mister Banks and the captain said in concert.

Tiata was oblivious and kept his rhythm without fail except for his staggering and tripping. Tupia knocked over his own chair in such haste to attend this, his own servant boy, who was making a complete fool of himself!

"Tiata!" he scolded. "What is this foolishness?" Tupia said, embarrassed at the state of the lad.

Tiata continued his dance, oblivious to the scene he was causing, and only thinking his actions to be entertainment for his master, the captain and Mister Banks.

By now, the other gents had assembled at the door of the Great Cabin and pushed their way through to witness the pandemonium.

They all laughed at the sight of poor Tiata, drunk as a sailor, dancing like a native girl. Even the captain had a wry smirk that he could not contain.

I could hear the boys on deck and imagined they had found a crack or notch to view this their wicked caper. Mister Banks was confused at first and not being one for the humorous games of young boys, demanded an explanation from Tupia.

"Has your boy gone completely mad?" Mister Banks asked of the shamed chap.

"I do not understand him, gentlemen. He is a good boy. Tiata! I demand that you stop this foolishness right away!" He grabbed at the boy only to miss as Tiata leapt in the opposing direction.

This brought howls of laughter from everyone present and I watched as the captain chuckled, as I had not seen him do. A sober and serious man to date, I supposed that this hilarity might be a release from his captainly duties.

The captain stood with the other gents and merely watched as Mister Banks and Tupia continued to chase the whirling Tiata around the map table. Tupia lurched at him grabbing only at his train of cloth before falling face down on the floor. He did not let go of the cloth, however, and as it tensioned caught Mister Banks amidships and threw him back against the window where he bumped his head and slid down to the seated position on the floor.

Gales of laughter came from the captain and gents as Mister Banks just sat, quite aghast, and Tupia fumbled to regain his footing, still holding Tiata's skirt.

As Tiata kept rounding the table the skirt unravelled in the grip of his master and Tiata, dizzy from the drink and dance, fell headfirst into Mister Banks middle knocking the wind from his lungs! Tupia rushed to his side with a kerchief at the ready, patting Mister Banks on the back while Tiata merely fell asleep where he laid with a smile on his face.

"Well, gentlemen? What say we?" said the captain, still chuckling. "Looks like someone's been into some liquor!" The entire audience laughed as the terribly embarrassed Tupia helped poor Mister Banks to his feet.

"Yes, and I'll bet a week's brandy he was not alone in this blasted lark!" cursed Mister Banks, wincing from the bump on his head and quite breathless from the attack to his midriff.

"Oh dear, Captain sir, I am most awfully sorry that this has occurred! Do you think that Tiata has been taking alcohol?" he asked, shamed by his boy.

"Oh, I would say most definitely this lad is more than a little inebriated, Tupia! He sleeps where he fell and still has his fine coconut shell breasts in place!" The captain's wit had the gents in stitches. It was a side of him they rarely saw. I too was a little shocked and chuckled to myself.

"Well, I am not amused in the least, Captain! I have sustained a head injury and must see Doctor Monkhouse immediately. There is blood on my kerchief! And I may need stitching!" barked Mister Banks. He marched off as best he could to find the surgeon.

Tupia was trying to get Tiata to his feet without success. The gents, having composed themselves a little, took the boy by the hands and feet and started off carrying him to some far-reaching bunk to sleep it off, I supposed. They laughed all the way out the door at Mister Banks's expense, each knowing that the man would recover, and unable to see any serious side to Mister Banks's debacle.

I imagined that their minds would conjure the images before them well into the future, and a smile would come to their lips upon reflection.

"Come back when you have laid him up, gentlemen!" the captain shouted after them. "We will finish off the port!"

My head stood straight up and my stomach rotated on its axis! The port? Not the port! It was seawater! Would this evening of madness never end? I was going nowhere until that port barrel was brought back for a final ending to this caper!

The captain ordered the newly replaced sentry to summon my Isaac, as it was he who was sent to the stores with it. I was aghast! Isaac would be flogged, him being the last witnessed handling the port barrel. Isaac walked in gingerly, knowing what had occurred here.

"Isaac, my boy, would you fetch the port barrel back here for us to finish off?" he asked and ordered. My eyes widened at the thought! I could say nought, but sit and witness the horror!

I had my suspicions from the captain's frivolous tone that he knew Isaac and his lads had something to do with Tiata's form. John Charlton might have asked for Tiata's company for a harmless game of cards, but he knew those boys to be as thick as thieves and somehow responsible for this tomfoolery.

Not long after, the gents returned for that lovely spot of port! Mister Banks returned with a patch to his head moaning and complaining, and Isaac lurked about the doorway with the port barrel, not knowing whether to run or face his fate.

"Ah, Isaac! Will you join us in a glass of this port?" he asked, shaking the contents to ascertain whether it was indeed all there. I believed him to know all, as was his usual way, and he was torturing Isaac in a most wicked way.

"Um, err!" he stammered.

"Come, come lad, spit it out!" said the captain.

"Yes, sir," Isaac said tentatively.

"I say, Isaac!" he said playfully. "We have been treated to some wonderful entertainment here this evening. It is a shame you missed it!" Sarcasm filled his words. "Put the oak beakers out and we will all enjoy a drop of this fine port. Isaac, you may pour yourself a small one and join us." Isaac did as he was told while the captain, quietly standing behind Isaac's back, uncorked the barrel and smelled the contents. As suspected? Seawater! Isaac was petrified, his hand shaking with the filling of every beaker, and trying to appear sober at the same time.

"After all that has occurred here this evening, Captain, I do believe a spot of that port would be required?" Mister Banks concurred, holding his injured head.

"Shall we toast, gentlemen? I do believe we shall drink to the sleeping Tiata for his wonderful rendition of Tahitian dance!" laughed the captain. The gentlemen, now including Tupia, raised their glasses unknowingly.

"Isaac? Are you not happy to raise a glass with us? This is an honour for a young lad such as yourself," asked the captain, well knowing.

"Yes, sir!" Isaac raised his glass along with the other witnesses to their entertainment.

"To Tiata!" roused the captain.

"Tiata!" shouted the gentlemen, laughing.

Down the throat went the seawater, every man spitting it as far as it would travel! Mumbling and grumbling broke out amongst them, incensed at seawater as opposed to the tasty port they were promised. The captain, however, knew of the contents of the barrel and did not take a drink, but my Isaac was forced to swallow it, or implicate himself in the crime of replacing the port with seawater.

The captain kept his eye squarely on my Isaac as he swallowed, the seawater mixing with the abundance of port he had consumed. Isaac began to turn an odd shade of grey, his eyes watered and he held his stomach. The gents looked on, realising Isaac as the culprit as the captain was making him drink it, dishing out his own unique method of punishment.

"Not agreeing with you, young Isaac?" the captain asked.

"Mmm…" he groaned.

"Finish your beaker full and then you may be on your way!" the gents all watched, mumbling approval of their captain's tactics. Isaac held his breath and drank the rest. No sooner had he put his glass reluctantly upon the table than the entire contents of Isaac's stomach made themselves known to us all. Poor lad wretched again and again, coming up as pale as I had seen a living soul.

"I take it from this mess that port does not agree with you, Isaac?" he quizzed, nodding at the gents who were fanning their noses from the vile smelling vomit that lay before them.

Isaac could do nought but hold his aching stomach and shake his head. The captain knew he would not have been in this on his own. Tiata's drunkenness would have been a group effort and none of the boys would have missed an opportunity to help him drink it.

"And who is in on this evil scheme of yours, Isaac?" the captain suspected that the boy would not implicate his friends; a sort of code between comrades.

"Jus' me, sir. I gave the port to Tiata and drank the rest meself." He groaned.

The captain had been correct. "Clean up this mess, Isaac!" He, too, was waiving the smell away from his nostrils.

Isaac ran for a bucket.

"Me thinks he doth run for the deck and another hurling over the side, Captain," said Mister Banks, taking a breath from his nose, which was completely covered by a scented cloth and his eyes watering a little.

The gents all laughed, edging further toward the Great Cabin door to escape the odour.

"Suffice to say I am glad we did not take on wine from Madeira as I had wished! It would all have suffered the same fate! Perhaps a port another time, Captain, when we can be safe in the knowing of the content?" said Mister Banks, taking the laughing gents with him.

Tupia bowed in apology to the captain to the point of annoyance.

"Yes, yes, Tupia, all is well!" He dismissed him, and Tupia backed out the Great Cabin door still muttering his regret and gathering up his cloth as he went.

"Damn fool boys, Fairweather!" We were alone. "I should have them all to a beaker of seawater but for the mess it would make!"

I wanted out of there. Felines, too, have a sensitive beezer! Isaac returned with the bucket looking a little better, the colour returning to his cheeks.

"Not a whiff do I wish to smell when you think you are finished cleaning this mess, lad! And when you think you smell nothing, wash it again! The missing port will come out of your pay!" The captain yelled, scooping me up to leave Isaac alone with his stomach contents and his orders.

This was no small punishment as Isaac's apprentice pay was very little. There were other ways to punish, and the captain had found one! No doubt the other boys would hear of this and whilst not punished themselves, my Isaac would ensure that they remember it, should they ever decide to do it again!

We went on deck for some fresh air, and none too soon, I thought!

The captain letting me down, I sauntered back down below to find Chester and Lady, not seeing them on deck for the cold wind. They were sleeping soundly in Mister Banks's quarters. I crept in quietly so as not to disturb. Mister Banks was disrobing for bed and noticed my entrance.

"Ah, Fairweather, come to keep the dogs warm, have you?" I was a little surprised as I was intruding and was not sure how Mister Banks would take it, but he ignored me for his ablutions so I snuggled up to Lady who sleepily put a paw around me as if I were her pup. Nature is a funny thing. I slept very well indeed.

CHAPTER 26

The 28th day of August saw much buzz regarding a comet seen in the night sky as I slept. Chester, Lady, and I came up to see what all the fuss was about. So bright was it that the little ball and its furry tail could be seen even during the day.

"Rather odd that what?" I said to Chester.

"Hmm, nothing is odd when at sea, old boy!" came the reply.

Some of the men thought it an omen of impending death, but our astronomer Mister Green, as always the cool-headed lecturer, set the men straight that it was merely a piece of flying rock way out in space and had nothing to do with our fate; it was merely passing by and making itself known to us.

No sooner had he finished his speech than John Gathrey the bosun came rushing to the captain who was at the helm.

"Captain!...Sir!..." He was winded. "Bosun's Mate John Reading is dead, sir!" He was much pained.

"Into the longboat!" bellowed Chester, sensing a need for us to be elsewhere. He was correct! All of the crew who had only just been convinced by Mister Green that the comet was not a death knell panicked each other!

They ran to every corner of the ship to alert every man that Mister Green's comet had killed John Reading!

Pandemonium ensued and John Gathrey's whistle piped the order for the "Captain's Attention," shouting it so after each long toot.

Some stopped, others did not.

"I saw Reading looking right at the comet last night!" shouted Thomas Hardman, the Second Bosun's Mate. "Now he be dead!"

Well, that was enough to escalate the men into a dread of the thing, and shouting that they had watched it, too, all turned their heads from the wee rock in the sky.

Tupia began to have pain in his stomach, unrelated of course, but this had the crew completely convinced they would all die some hideous death!

Chester, Lady, and I watched from the safety of the longboat.

"A good idea this longboat of yours, Chester!" I praised, only to have one of the able seamen try to get in with us to avoid Mister Green's comet.

Chester growled and nipped at the in-coming leg, and out it shot. The man in question, having regarded the injury as that caused by Mister Green's very own comet! He set to howling!

One by one, men held their heads, stomachs and limbs and anything that usually troubled them and wailing, lay back where they stood to die! With this the ship floundered as none were at their stations and we stood battered about in the heavy sea.

The captain spoke to Bosun John Gathrey, of what I could not hear. He called for Sergeant Edgcumbe and taking his pistol, fired a shot into the air. The all-too-familiar sound of gunfire got the men's attention.

The bosun, sensing the lull, whistled the "All Stop for the Captain" signal and terrified though they were, they stood to attention, still clutching at their imaginary ills.

"Men!" he shouted, infuriated at their antics. "It is true that Bosun's Mate John Reading has died…" and before he could get another word out, the fracas began again in earnest.

The captain shot into the air again, and John Gathrey blew the whistle. They stood still again, imaginary pain contorting their faces.

The captain thought it best to get right to the point. "John Reading died from too much rum!" he shouted. All aboard stopped their crying, wailing and the holding of their maladies, embarrassment replacing the grimaces on their faces.

It was quiet other than for the sails, booms and stays rattling and fluttering about unattended.

"The good and kind Bosun John Gathrey gave his mate John Reading a bottle of rum last night, but the man drank three half pints, all of it at once, and died during the night!" he yelled.

"Try as he might, the bosun could not wake him this morning!" He continued to yell.

Everyone relaxed a little more, knowing that consumption of one full bottle of the strong rum would be deadly.

"One more thing!" he yelled above the rattling rigging. "Mister Green is not responsible for the comet! It is not of his making! It is as he explained and will not kill us all!" he confirmed.

"Now get back to your stations or we will sink by your own hands!" he cried.

With a scurry, the men abandoned their invented ailments and rushed to right the ship, tossing about in the swell.

No one thought badly of the bosun; he had been generous with his rum. The captain returned Sergeant Edgcumbe's pistol and motioned for the bosun to continue his commands and whistle blowing until the ship was back on tack.

Chester, Lady, and I climbed out of the longboat.

"Are you sure, Chester, that this comet business does not have merit? I have an old leg injury and it aches awfully!" I enquired, licking at the offending limb.

Chester looked at me with pity. "Fairweather, you idiot! Your leg aches because I trod on it getting into the longboat!" I said nought, and ceased licking at the leg, as I had been suitably chastised and that was all there was for it, other than my embarrassment. As I was not the only idiot, I pretended I had said nothing of my leg as the men went about their business of sailing the ship.

By the 2nd day of September in very strong gales and heavy squalls of rain I consulted my captain in the Great Cabin.

"Fairweather? This course on which we sail?" he muttered. I jumped to the map table. "It is too southerly and we have sighted nothing of Staten Land or this mysterious Terra Australis Incognita!" As if it were my fault!

I consulted the chart and found that due to the cold weather and much rain, the chart had softened and torn in a part I had not prescribed! I "meowed" as hoarsely as possible to gain his attention. The captain heeding my call came dashing to the map, probably more quickly than usual with the pitching of the ship.

I promptly and purposefully pointed out the flaw. He held it close to inspect more fully.

"Yes! I see the problem Fairweather lad! It is not as we had laid out previously!" He ran for the deck and I after him.

"To the north and easterly!" We bore and brought to, following the captain's orders. We went below immediately as the change in course would bring questions from the gents. And as expected, along they came with Mister Banks at the fore.

"What say you, Captain? Have we not had a change in course?" enquired Mister Banks as if it were his ship.

"You are quite right, Mister Banks. We have headed southerly enough to determine that there is no landfall. The weather will only get worse and the swell more intense," said the captain, knowing that Mister Banks suffered in these conditions. "I have set us to a northeasterly course. The environment should improve, and we may site Staten Land within one month," speculated the captain, not knowing it for a fact but by my reckoning we would do so.

"Excellent, Captain!" Mister Banks sent for a brandy and the gents enjoyed the idea of warmer climes and calmer seas. I took my customary nip after the gents had left us. Only enough to warm the blood and bring sleep in this hideous weather.

The following weeks provided all manner of clues as to us travelling in the correct direction. The climate became warmer; there was the odd haul of floating seaweed, which the botanists concluded was a more coastal "rockweed" variety.

On one day, what was first thought to be a seal, was brought aboard and found to be a large driftwood, very much having spent a long time at sea, but this gave all aboard hope for a landing. After all, wood must drift from some shore, however distant!

My favourite creature, the feline-like seal, was seen sleeping on their backs in the water, their flippers aloft to keep them steady, as if they were sails. Each day saw many more of them.

The spirits of the men were lofty as land birds came into view hovering around the sails and masts thinking them a good place to perch. So keen were the men to site land that hourly someone from the topmast cried the word! "Land!"

The captain came to the deck at each call and through his eyeglass disappointed us all; merely clouds upon the horizon.

On the 7th day of October 1769, Nicolas Young was at the topmast. He had been Mister Buchan's servant before his death, and now the surgeon's servant, but as keen to see land as any when not at his duties.

"Land! Land! Land!" He could hardly contain himself, nor take breath! The captain came to the deck as usual and his eyeglass confirmed that it was indeed land! Not clouds! Land!

"George's Island!" our captain verified. "I'm sure this is the wretched island that Able Tasman mapped in 1642!"

"Wretched, sir?" my Isaac asked, honing his note-taking skills when at the captain's side.

"Yes, according to Tasman it is so, but we sail for it regardless and will find out for ourselves! Come down from the topmast, young Nick!" he hollered, so grateful for the sighting that he forgot his rank and yelled like the dickens!

Down came Nicolas Young like a monkey in the rigging.

"We will name this point of land 'Young Nick's Head'!" the captain chuckled. "Take that down, please Isaac!" and hurriedly he did so, a little jealous that he hadn't seen it first for it would have borne his name.

"Rum for all, please Lieutenant Gore!" the captain ordered and much regaling began. We still had some sailing to do, so the lieutenant strictly rationed the rum to keep order.

The winds were so unfavourable on this tack that it took three days and nights to reach the coast of this long-awaited land. On the 9th day of October, we came to anchor in a wide bay, the seaward cliffs reminding Mister Banks of the chalky white Sussex coast back in England. I had never been there, but can testify to the whiteness of these cliffs. The land inside the bay was mountainous and green.

"Canoes!" Mister Banks voice aquiver. He loved the spotting of the local folk. These were called Maoris and this was Staten Land, or New Zealand, the northern island of the very same. The natives were numbed with fear, seeing the ship initially as a great and beautiful bird. Then on seeing our three boats launched with colourfully dressed men aboard, they were confused and thought our ship to be a vessel full of gods!

Chester, Lady, and my intrepid self boarded the yawl with the captain, Mister Banks and Doctor Solander. Our boats headed for a sandy riverbank, which ran into the bay, and we had the usual party of sailors and Marines, armed and at the ready.

The Maoris were not as curious as the Tahitians and as we headed for one side of the river, the few on the opposite beach waved their spears in the air with what I could only imagine was intent to harm! They threw spears at us but we were far enough from them that they fell short.

"I say, Chester, this does not look good what?" I questioned.

"No, my boy, this does not!" He bristled. "Lady! Stand behind me!" I had not seen him so protective of his partner. I trusted Chester's senses and stood with the good woman at the rear of the yawl, to keep her company, of course.

By the time we landed on the sandy riverbank, the natives on our side had retreated into the bushes. The captain, Mister Banks, Doctor Solander and Midshipman John Bootie leapt out of the yawl and followed them. We all waited impatiently for their return.

"Faster than us!" puffed the captain. "Just a few empty huts."

"Captain!" barked Mister Banks. "We must go to the other side of the river to interview these natives."

"Yes, I agree, Mister Banks." He was winded but recovering.

The captain turned to the Marines who were readying themselves.

"Arm yourselves, men!" he warned our group.

"Chester, I am not liking this one bit!" I panicked. Maoris on one side of the river would be kindred in savage spirit to those on the other side! And we were headed right for them! As we approached, they yelled and thrust their spears angrily in our direction.

The coxswain of the pinnace fired two musket shots over their heads. Unfamiliar with firearms, the Maoris merely looked around. They carried on threateningly toward us. We were out of their reach but no less vulnerable should they decide to swim!

With the captain's consent, Mister Banks fired some bird shot at one of the men, which sorely hurt him but did not stop him! They stripped naked and continued to advance into the water with their spears!

"They do not fear us, Captain!" judged Mister Banks. The captain ordered that the coxswain fire a third shot.

"Aim it well and true, and quickly!" The captain realized the water would not stop them.

The shot killed one of them on the spot, just as he was about to dart his spear at our boat! The three advancing Maoris were shocked, but after realizing their friend was dead, they turned and ran, attempting to drag the dead man along, but left him in fear for their own lives. This incident caused all the Maoris to run off into the bushes.

"Back to the ship!" ordered the captain.

"Phew!" I gasped.

"But…" was all Mister Banks could splutter.

"Tomorrow, Mister Banks!" the captain pushed us off the sand nimbly as I had not seen him before. The pinnace fell in behind and we were shortly back on the ship.

"That was too close for my comfort, Chester!" I remarked in passing, but my hackles were still up, as were his!

"Yes!" was all he could muster having his own skin, that of Lady's, and his master's to consider.

"What of the morrow, Chester?" I knew not.

"We shall see." He knew not.

We attempted sleep up on the deck, but to no avail. I did not attend the captain as he was in military talks with the sergeant of the Marines and the gents.

I did not begin to understand why these people attacked us, but now we had killed one of them, and it did not bode well for the morrow.

We few on deck just lay watching the last of that blighted comet's tail, wondering whether Mister Green's denying of it meaning death was altogether correct! Armed Marines guarded the ship in case of invasion. I snoozed fitfully. Chester snorted a few times. Lady slept.

Early the next morning, the captain came upon deck with Sergeant Edgcumbe. He had briefed the Marines in vigilance and a fully armed party had gathered for another attempt at trade with these scoundrels.

The captain ordered the boats lowered. I fell in to join, but along with Lady and Chester we were not invited.

"Isaac! Take Fairweather below and have the Littleboys tether the dogs!" he ordered, knowing that Chester would try to follow his master even if it meant a swim!

Blast! I would not be kept below, but I had no choice but to stay on the ship with the hounds. I scrambled back to the deck to watch as the captain, Mister Banks and Doctors Solander and Monkhouse with the heavily armed Marines landed on the riverside.

The Maoris gathered on the other side of the river. Mister Banks called to them in what he knew of George's Island language but they merely answered with a war cry and a dance that from my vantage point, looked nothing but beastly!

The translation must not have pleased them. They formed a line, stomped from left to right as one, brandishing their weapons and contorting their faces, their tongues rolled out flat and even from my distance, I could see the whites of their rolled-back eyes! A hoarse gruesome chant accompanied their war dance or "Haka!" It was meant to frighten their enemies and frighten it did! Tupia translated the course war cry, imitating their facial expressions. I have transposed this Haka myself, with a more personal touch, for those who wish to be informed:

Ka mate! Ka mate!
 Be it a black eye, or a lump on the head, that you wish!
Ka ora! Ka ora!
 Or to go back where you came, bothersome chap!
Tenei Te Tangata Puhuruhuru!
 Then we are the hairy chaps you will see!
Nana I Tiki Mai Whakawhiti Te Ra!
 Who tells the sun when and where to shine!
Upane! Upane!
 Something, something up a ladder!
Upane Kaupane!
 Dumb-diddley dee to the top!
Whiti Te Ra!
 The sun doth shine, tiddlee-pop!

One gets the general gist of the thing; much leaping from side to side, rolling the eyes back in their sockets and sticking out of the tongue. Along with their seemingly black painted faces their countenance was hideous! I was worried for the men. Chester and Lady could see the doings from their tethering at the aft of the ship and Chester, in his protective way, strained at this leash and barked like the dickens!

"Blast you, Chester! Be quiet!" I could not hear what was going on for his wretched woofing.

"Grrr! I need to protect Mister Banks!" He writhed under the control of the rope.

"You cannot help him from there so I suggest you settle down so that I can hear the goings on! Your nose may be superior for the scent of a thing, Chester! But the Fairweather ear? Much the better! Now, the voices carry well across the river, but if you insist on barking, I cannot hear above you! Therefore, I cannot inform you of the progress!" I made it abundantly clear that he would receive a good snouting if this did not stop. I was for'ard of the ship and could just make out what was transpiring.

Chester ceased and I pricked the Fairweather ears to relay the doings back to him and Lady, still standing, straining the rope in the hope it might snap.

These Maoris were a fearsome-looking lot, their war dance lasting a good long time.

The captain set the boats to meeting them on their side of the river! I was aghast! I informed Chester and he was not pleased.

"Are they mad?" Chester asked.

"It seems so, Chester!" I yelled back. I was cross with myself at not having been at the meeting last evening. I might have had some understanding of this!

The captain, Doctors Solander and Monkhouse, Mister Banks and Tupia advanced toward the fifty or so from the river. Tupia began to speak in his own language from the boat, which was surprisingly well understood.

"We are friends!" he said in Tahitian. "We wish to trade with you for water, wood and food." He kept it simple. I was glad. "But if you do not trade with us, we will kill you all!"

What? I thought? Why was Tupia threatening them this way? From what I had seen in Tahiti the softer approach worked much better. But these were not the gentle Tahitians! I figured that the captain must know what he is doing, as he was directing Tupia in what to say to them. The rabble stood silently as Tupia spoke.

"They are not our friends, Captain!" Tupia translated.

One of the natives stripped and dived into the water between them heading for the captain's boat. He was unarmed. This seemed to be the right thing to do. I watched in hope. Two more followed him swimming with their spears! No! Then many more! All armed yet still swimming swiftly.

The captain advanced the boat boldly toward them, Mister Banks and all on board holding nails, iron, bunches of feathers out to them. Chester was whining, as the boat butted upon the sand.

"Quiet, Chester. I will not warn again! They are talking to Tupia and your Mister Banks is being very brave!" Chester silenced.

"Captain, we are lost." Tupia tried to speak calmly while the boat floundered in the shallow water surrounded by the fifty-ish Maoris. "They do not know what iron and nails are for." The few in front grabbed at the feathers. "They want the weapons which can kill a man instantly from afar!" He looked to his captain with grave fear.

I reported this to Chester and he, like I, had no idea what to expect. Just then, the astronomer Mister Green turned around, his back to the Maoris, his "Hangar," the short curved sword he had secured to his waist, was taken by a swift handed native. He made off with it along the shore waiving his prize in the air. The others followed him up the sand.

"We cannot let him succeed!" barked Mister Banks, his gun loaded with birdshot, awaiting the captain's approval to shoot at him. The others agreed and the captain gave the order. The birdshot caught the thief squarely in the back. He stood deathly still, holding the sword over his head as if he would drop. We all gasped. Only a moment passed and he began hollering again with his prize over his head, as happy as any that he was not dead!

More cheering and rasping cries came from the rest of the Maoris. They had stolen a white man's weapon, Tupia explained. They did not know that it was merely a sword; not a weapon of the bullet-firing kind!

With the captain's permission, Doctor Monkhouse opened fire this time. His was the gun with the ball shot. It killed him instantly. Doctor Monkhouse ran toward them bravely and grabbed the sword, retreating to the boat before the other Maoris could capture him. All arms were now cocked and at the ready.

The captain, Mister Green and Tupia fired at the advancing mob, wounding three of them but killing none. I relayed this information to the pacing Chester and he was much pleased that we had fired upon them.

The Maoris retreated with their wounded. The white man's weapons were now much prized as they all saw for themselves the harm they could do. While carrying their wounded away, some leered and others jeered at our party as the boats made for the ship, all of us not a little relieved that we had sustained no loss. Be it sword, nor person!

"They return!" I advise Chester. He began that wretched writhing at the rope that held him.

"Is Mister Banks with them? Is he alive? I heard shooting but could not see!" He was much panicked. I turned to look at him and he had gotten himself so worked up that he had tangled the rope around his head, not allowing him to see anything.

"He is alright dear, and on his way back to the ship," said Lady pulling the ropes from his eyes with her teeth, always the composed and sturdy mate.

"Yes, foolish dog!" I confirmed, laughing at what his loyalty had done: to tie his eyes like a blindfold. "They are returning and I see no blood!" We knew this to be a good sign.

The men tied the boats to the ship, not hauling them aboard. I thought this not such a good sign. As the men climbed the rope ladders to board, the full brunt of the operation had taken its toll.

"Under the circumstances, well done, men!" The captain, always much aggrieved by the shooting of anyone, tried to calm Mister Banks, who had killed a man.

Mister Banks wiped the beads of sweat from his brow and took a large sniff at his scented kerchief. One howl from Chester and he was off to pet his dogs, much appreciative of his own hide.

Doctor Solander merely conveyed his regret that a more fruitful trade could not have been made. If he had remorse for shooting a native it was not obvious.

The captain readied the men to row around the small bay to find a more suitable place to anchor. The river here was not only full of nasty natives, but also the water from it was salty. We required fresh water.

After taking refreshment, the captain, gents and men climbed back into their boats and off they rowed, leaving Chester, Lady, and I to watch yet again. This time, I made Chester promise to be quiet and he chose to obey, for the Fairweather commentary was far more informative than hearing himself bark!

They rowed to the farthest part of the bay and as a fresh wind came in from the sea, along with it came two canoes, one under sail, the other paddling, having returned from fishing. The Maoris on board were unarmed and the captain decided to take the occupants prisoner on board the ship.

I stood yet again as sentry and reporter of doings to keep the wretch Chester quiet. He complied this time, as I accurately but colourfully reported the unfolding drama.

The paddling canoe escaped our boats and outran them to shore. The second under sail began paddling, not having seen us as quickly as the first, but a shot from a musket ball fired over it, stopped them while our men surrounded the canoe.

There were seven Maoris on board. They stripped as if they were going to swim, but instead, pelted the boats with stones and paddles and even their fishing spikes and spears! Some of eight to ten feet! When they ran out of these, they threw their catch at the men; dead fish flying at them, those on our boats dodged the projectiles, only a few of our Marines receiving a rock or fish to their regions.

The Marines fired their guns at the boat and killed four of the seven Maoris.

"Bravo, Chester! The men are firing at the savages!" I reported.

"I can hear some things, you blot!" Chester bawled back at me.

"Not as much as I! Keep quiet while I hear!" I scolded.

The other three sat down in their canoe, expecting a similar fate. Instead, I was shocked to see and inform Chester, that the three were taken on the boats as prisoners! Our men were heading back to the ship with them! Savages? On my ship? I would have to speak harshly to my captain upon their return!

Chester was none too happy with the thought of these unfriendly chaps being invited aboard either. He "hurrumphed" like the dickens when informed. We waited patiently, bristling somewhat until the boats came back.

I watched from the rigging as the Marines took on board the three captives. Chester strained again at his leash, barking and yelping, but Mister Banks gave him a smack to the nose and he quieted immediately.

The captain bid the three to sit and they did as they were told. Upon closer inspection, these were young boys! By my reckoning the oldest of eighteen years, the middle of fifteen and the youngest of ten years!

The men rallied around them curiously, then the captain required Tupia's fine interpreting skills.

"What are your names?" The captain started with the basics. Tupia translated.

"Tathourange!" The eldest punched at his chest.

"Koikerange!" The middling following suit.

"We brothers!" The eldest said proudly. "This Maragooete!" He punched the youngest boy's chest for him, and the lad was none to happy for it. "He not a brother."

The captain and Mister Banks spoke quietly to each other.

Mister Banks gave them clothes and they jumped to their feet excitedly to don them, thus forgetting they had just watched four of their comrades killed by us!

"For now, we will call them Tat, Koi and Mara!" Mister Banks pronounced, always wishing to be of service in every way, including renaming them for our own ease, as the longer versions were difficult for us to get our tongues around.

"We will show these boys all manner of kindnesses while we keep them here, men! They will then, with luck and good fortune, tell the others of their good treatment. This may assist with trade." The captain sent the order on to the galley for bread and water for the boys. They had never seen such a thing and ate happily of a loaf each, washing it down with the water provided.

I edged closer above them to sniff a little and learn more of the captain's plan. The youngest, Mara, while throwing down a large quantity of water to allow for more bread spied me in the rigging. He jumped up and grabbed my tail!

"Rrrraaaooooooooww!" I yelled. He laughed uncontrollably at my expense! Blighted little spot! Chester, Lady, and the men could see the humour in this cruel and unkindly act but I could not! The nerve! not impressed. It hurt sorely.

"There must be felines on this land! See?" informed Mister Banks, "The boy is not frightened of our Fairweather!" He chuckled. I was not impressed. It hurt sorely.

"Bring the dogs, Michael, Richard!" Mister Banks pressed the Littleboys into service. They brought them forward and the young one petted them as if he had known them all his life. Chester grumbled under his breath but complied by licking the boy, knowing that he would gain Mister Banks's favour with such a friendly gesture.

Although they were dark skinned and had the well-known fuzzy hair much like our Tahitians, the elder brothers had theirs tied in a topknot on their heads. The younger boy's hair was allowed to be free. I played with it from my spot above, teasing him not a little for pulling my tail. He waived my paw away like a bothersome bug, causing me to scratch his arm. He rubbed it sorely and poured some of his water on it. The ink that was on his arm and those of his comrades did not rub off!

"They are tattooed in this manner!" Mister Banks was excited. He asked Tupia to get them to explain it.

"It makes them appear fearsome for their enemies," he explained. Quite right, too, I thought. The youngest lad Mara only had a spiral tattooed on his arm but the outlines of further "tattooing" were already in place, a little like an unfinished drawing, the colouring in had not been done. The older two boys had more intricate and delicately perfect lines linking their spirals. It reminded me of Madam's good silver teapot back at home. Etched on them as beautifully as from the finest silversmith.

Tupia continued. "The older the man, the more tattoos he has. They call it 'Ta Moko'. Some of the younger men, like these boys, have combs made out of bones and the ink is put on the tips of the comb needles and then banged into the skin, forcing the black under the skin and to be there forever!" Tupia was very animated when interpreting for Mister Banks, and was not disappointing now, his voice ever so theatrical to enthral all who listened.

"The older and braver men have the designs carved into their skin with a chisel of sorts and the wounds died black. The women, too, have them, only their chins and inside their bottom lips tattooed. The Maori canoes and houses have the painting style of these tattoos, all relating to their kin and history and appearing all over the bodies of the men after some long time at having it done to them. The larger, painted ones on the thighs are called Ta Puhoro, but sometimes this type can be on the face of a man also. The patterns are not of any religious significance that I can tell. It is just a pastime and any one can begin at any age."

The older boy showed us his thigh and was very proud of his artwork, as were the younger boys who had only been tattooed a little and recently, as they were still young. It all looked very painful and unnecessary to me! They were fearsome enough without tattoos!

Mister Banks and the gents kept plying the boys with bread and more water. It was hard to say where all of it was going, they were so lean, but eat they did, by now, two loaves each. The crew dined on salt pork for dinner and the three Maoris ate much of this, then more bread and water!

"Sergeant Edgcumbe, take them below for the night," the Captain ordered. "Tupia, you are to look after them. Take Fairweather, the young boy seems to enjoy him." Up went my head! This wretched boy who pulled my tail? Now I am to be his nursemaid? Definitely a word with my captain was called for later on!

Tupia scooped me from the rigging above and herded the young boys still chewing at their bread to the sleeping quarters below. He had them lie in the beds and they sang a lament, not unpleasant to listen to at all and it proved to lull them to sleep. I lay with the boy Mara and he hugged me like young Isaac Manly used to do, and still did from time to time. I wanted to speak with my captain, so as soon as his grip on me relaxed to prove he was sleeping, I scarpered for the Great Cabin, leaving Tupia to tend the boys all night.

I found my captain in conference with the gents and Sergeant Edgcumbe; all of our ship's company was embroiled in this difficulty with the natives. Mister Banks and the scientists were finding it difficult to land and discover new species of flora and fauna, the captain needed to provision the ship, and the Marines were heavily engaged in this fighting for the protection of us all.

I had missed the briefing while I tended the small Maori, and they were dispersing. Mister Banks stayed behind for a good-sized brandy.

"Thus, has ended the most disagreeable day my life has yet seen, black be the mark for it and heaven send that such may never return to embitter future reflection," said Mister Banks holding his beaker toward the captain in toast. Mister Banks could say no more and after swilling back his brandy left to look in on Tupia and his charges.

"Ah, Fairweather." The captain acknowledged my presence. "This has been a dark and fruitless day for us all." He sipped at his drink.

"We are lucky none of us were killed or wounded, and you know how I feel about the killing of the natives, no matter how provoked." I did, and so I sat by him as he wrote extensively in his log. I slept with him still in his chair in the morning. He had written long of this day.

When he woke, we made for the dining deck to find Tupia and the three Maori boys. The very same who had eaten loaves of bread and almost a whole pig between them the night before were now tucking in to a meal of boiled wheat, with similar gusto! If we did not get rid of them soon, I feared they would eat all our stores!

The captain set the boats at the ready and assigned each of the Maori boys with jewellery and bracelets, ensuring they kept their new clothes on and set himself and Mister Banks to take them ashore. Again, Chester and Lady were tethered and again I was not invited, but for the best this time I thought, as we had not found happy hosts here.

This time, the captain had a cunning plan to release the young boys on shore so that they would tell of the kindness we had bestowed upon them, eating as they did under the provision that our good deeds would be passed on to some native chieftain for reflection down his ranks, and hopefully throughout neighbouring tribes.

The boys began to cry as they approached the shore! These were not "their people" who had assembled some fifty or so. They begged not to be released, as the gathered natives were their enemies and would kill and eat them!

What? Men eat of their own?

"Chester, old thing?" I questioned. "I have it on good authority that these people eat their enemies after killing them. Is this so?"

Well, Chester writhed and ripped at his tether, thinking I had meant that our men would be eaten! One of which was his master, Mister Banks! He broke free and bounded off over the side!

"Chester, you dumb hound! Come back!" I yelled to him. He was busily swimming at speed toward his master in some lunatic bid to save him from being eaten by armed savages!

"Lady! Is there nothing you can do?" I turned to her for guidance.

"Fairweather, you know what an honourable dog he is to Mister Banks!" she scolded. "Could you not have explained more fully before setting him off like that?" I was in for it with Lady now. This New Zealand was a disagreeable place!

I watched as Chester swam to the boat with Mister Banks inside. He did not falter nor look back. I could not raise him. Nor could Lady. He was on a mission.

While Tupia was consoling the three native boys and Mister Banks was trying to explain to the Maoris that we were not enemies, Chester bound on board, still thinking his master to be in peril.

Mister Banks turned to him and motioned him for'ard of the boat to bark and sneer at the Haka dancing throng that had gathered for our landing; some sort of war they wished.

With the positioning of Chester at the for'ard snarling like the dickens, the warriors ceased their Haka-ing and were still for some time while they discussed this thin, scrawny but angry hound that seemed to take control of our boats! They ceased their angry display as this evil hound slathered at the mouth, baring his teeth.

The captain set the boats to row further down the river where the three boys recognized their own tribe. Chester was again at the lead boat snarling as before, as this had calmed the previous Haka-ing Maoris.

When the boys jumped into the river and swam ashore, much ado was forthcoming over their clothes and jewellery. This being his aim, the captain ordered that the boats return to the *Endeavour*. This plan of his may hold some merit after all. He hoped that word would spread that we were gracious "friends."

Upon their return, Chester was lauded as the leader of this latest campaign! He lapped up the attention with much gusto and Mister Banks treated him to a plate of his own dinner! Lady was very proud of him but needless to say she chastised him for his foolishness.

The captain set the Endeavour to sail out of this miserable bay, looking for a more suitable place to wood and water and hopefully, to find friendlier Maoris. Some sailing would give the tribes time to speak to others of our goodness toward the boys. He had planned on calling this "Endeavour Bay" that evening as he attended the charting of this cove, but as it had been so inhospitable and troublesome, he named it "Poverty Bay" instead. A fitting name, I agreed, as it yielded us nothing!

As we sailed out toward the ocean, a canoe came alongside the ship with a small party of Maori dignitaries. Tupia explained that they had heard of our kindness toward the young boys and they were anxious to trade for similar clothes and jewellery as we had bestowed on the lads. All they had to trade were their paddles, but we took them in exchange for cloth. They wanted more, but the captain insisted they keep two paddles for rowing. Then they offered to sell us their canoe for the trinkets we had. The captain declined. The captain's plan seemed to have worked!

The canoe left, but three of the Maoris were found hiding on the deck! No one had seen them board! The captain ordered some boiled wheat, sugared for them, and they ate as heartily as the boys had done; so much so that they went to sleep on a steerage sail under the forecastle. They were in no hurry to leave such was this treatment!

As the *Endeavour* sailed south out of Poverty Bay, many canoes approached the ship from the shore. The captain wanted rid of the three chiefs on board and Tupia managed to convince one of the canoes to take them, that we were not their enemies, and we would not eat them. The three moochers shinned down a rope to the canoe below where there was much talk of the white man's kindness. This was yet another good sign for rumour to hopefully run rife of our integrity upon this New Zealand. If nothing else, the captain now knew how to broach the angry hoards, with Chester at the lead, and to feed and clothe a few captives, hopefully without having to shoot them.

CHAPTER 27

My captain was determined to head south and map the coast as far as it would take us. Our leaving Poverty Bay saw many canoes come alongside but they were not friendly and hence not invited on board.

We rounded a prominent headland, the captain naming it Portland Point, after the so-named southern headland in Dorset, which all who had been there agreed it resembled. This point became the northern tip of a great bay; Hawke's Bay as the captain named it. We sailed around the inside of this bay, mountainous within but a barren coast, not good for wooding or watering.

After two days of sailing with unfavourable winds, we had only reached half way around this bay, so large was it.

On the morning of the 15th of October, nine canoes set sail from the shore. On their approaching we found them to be larger than those we had seen before. The number of men was some one hundred and fifty and they shook large wooden pikes at us and smaller bludgeons called "patoo-patoo," made from wood, bones, or stones, which looked to crush a man's skull with one blow, according to Mister Banks!

I was a little worried. The captain and Mister Banks were in conference.

"This manoeuvre is not to be disregarded! They outnumber us!" warned Mister Banks.

"I agree," said the captain as they yelled their Haka from their canoes. "Fire the four-pound canon, Lieutenant Hicks! Arm it with grape shot! It will scatter and warn them of worse!"

The lieutenant had the bundle of small pellets loaded into the large canon quickly as these Maoris approached, bent on invading our ship! I scarpered to the rear with Chester and Lady, as the four-pound canon is a noisome piece of armoury.

"Fire!" called the captain.

Boom!

The small grape shot scattered at the savage horde. Unaccustomed to this form of attack, they turned and retreated, rubbing at the sore spots where the pellets had hit them, not piercing the skin, but stinging just the same.

"That was close!" cried Mister Banks. "This could have been a massacre of the worst kind had they succeeded!"

"Quite right, Mister Banks!" the captain confirmed.

"Chester!" I bristled. "I am not fond of this place!"

He nodded in knowing that there would be more ahead, and that Mister Banks was a determined man where natives and discoveries were concerned.

The next day saw us at the southernmost tip of Hawke's Bay. Again, canoes came out and the four-pound gun was now kept at the ready. These twenty-two natives were fishermen and did not threaten the ship with their Haka and arms.

"Tupia!" called the captain, watching them below as they held out their catch, eager to trade this time. Tupia ran to the captain's side.

"There is a fellow on this canoe with a coat of black animal skin. Do you see him?"

"Yes, sir, I do."

"Take some cloth and get your boy Tiata to go down the side and offer it in trade for I wish to have it," ordered the captain, selfishly for a change.

Down went Tiata as ordered, on the rope ladder, and leaned over to the man with the fine skin coat, offering some red cloth in trade. The man grabbed the cloth *and* Tiata and dragged him into the boat! They took off at speed with the red cloth and the boy!

By now, all the gents were at the side of the ship expecting fair trade.

"Captain!" blurted Tupia, two men at the front of the canoe were holding his boy!

"We must save the boy!" shouted Mister Banks. He had his musket armed and cocked.

Lieutenant Hicks was at the ready this time and upon the captain's order to fire the four-pound gun it went off scattering grapeshot at the canoe. Mister Banks fired his gun, threatening to kill not only the Maori fishermen but Tiata as well!

"Mister Banks!" shouted the captain, angered by Mister Banks's zeal with the musket. "Lower your firearm or there will be a death!"

"But the boy!" pleaded Mister Banks, loading his musket for a second shot.

"Mister Banks!" The captain lunged for him, turning the aimed musket from its potential target.

"Fire, Lieutenant Hicks!" ordered the captain.

With the second blast of the four-pound gun, the fishermen threw Tiata over the side and paddled furiously away from this booming gun that stung their bodies.

Tiata thrashed about in the cold bay some two hundred yards from us, fear gripping him, he was unable to stay afloat and swim, as he should have been able to do! He gulped seawater and yelled as he dunked below the surface.

All of a sudden Chester was in the water, after the boy! I had not seen him jump!

"Yes, after him, Chester!" urged Mister Banks.

The men cheered him on as he grabbed the boy by the collar and turned to bring him back, dragging him up and allowing him to breathe. The boy recovered a little and the two swam in concert back to the ship.

Reaching the rope ladder, Tiata shimmed up deftly, still shaking with fear and cold. Chester could not climb the rope ladder and he too was now floundering.

"Michael! Richard!" barked Mister Banks at the brothers Littleboy. "Save the dog!" They climbed down and gripped him around the chest and hauled him up the rope ladder between them.

"Down below! Take the boy and the dog!" barked Mister Banks "Where is the surgeon?"

"Here, Mister Banks!" Doctor Monkhouse came forward.

"See to it that they are both in good health!" The captain came forward, taking over from Mister Banks who had everyone in a frenzy!

They were rushed down below to Doctor Monkhouse's surgery where they were checked from head to toe.

Mister Banks was still buzzing around the deck above, caught up in the action.

"Mister Banks! A word please!" gestured the captain to his botanist. I hung about to listen before heading off to see to Chester and Tiata.

"I will not have you firing arms without my consent!" He was giving Mister Banks a good talking to and I was not about to miss such a rarity, knowing that Chester and Tiata were in good hands.

Tupia had gone below to see to his boy but Mister Spöring rallied round, trying to come to Mister Banks's defence but he knew better than to interrupt the captain. The other gents shuffled about, trying not to listen but keen to see Mister Banks reprimanded. After all, it was a dangerous act and one cannot go about shooting at people willy-nilly. I knew the captain would not have it!

All ears pricked as the captain dosed it out to Mister Banks.

"You have endangered fair trade even though the boy was kidnapped!" He scolded pacing a few steps at a time and then returning to his task, allowing Mister Banks to "But…" before he turned on his heel to chide him further.

"You put the boy in peril!"

Again "But…"

"You did not heed me when I attempted to stop you!"

"But…"

"I will not have it, Mister Banks!" His voice raised, as I had not heard it before, as if Mister Banks had been a pest all this time at sea and the captain had said nought.

"I am the captain of this ship and you will obey my every word!" He was copping it now!

"But…" Mister Banks was tenacious, if nothing else.

"No buts! Mister Banks!" His usually calm voice boomed, for the entire crew to hear, from the hold below to the topmast above, the crew were abuzz!

Mister Green clapped his hand once, breaking the silence. Lieutenants Hicks and Gore joined him for the second clap. The third clap heard the other gents chime in, Mister Spöring being the only exception. Then a fourth from some of the crew! By the fifth, the entire boat was clapping vigorously and the odd whistle and cheer came up from those who could not be seen!

Mister Banks face reddened with embarrassment and anger.

"Captain! This is a tirade I do not deserve!" said Mister Banks in his own defence.

"That, Mister Banks, seems not to be the case!" the captain retorted sarcastically. He turned and parted the crowd without another word and beat a path to Doctor Monkhouse and his patients. I followed him.

"How do they fare, Doctor Monkhouse?" he enquired.

"Middling for the moment, Captain. The boy is suffering from the cold and shock, and a few pellet stings, but he will recover quickly under my care. The dog is but cold and wet and will be fine when warmed," was the prognosis.

"Excellent!" He patted Tiata on the head and Chester on the back, and turned to return to his duty.

"Captain!" shouted Doctor Monkhouse after him. "What was all that fuss on deck? Did I miss something?

"Nothing, doctor, nothing at all," he said wisely, not being terribly proud of deriding Mister Banks but knowing it to be well overdue.

The doctor returned to Chester and Tiata. I smooched up against the boy who was now wrapped in a thick blanket, and he gratefully patted me, this calming him a little as he shook uncontrollably from cold and shock, and rubbed at his bruises from the grapeshot.

"Chester! Old thing! Bravery cometh in many forms of late!" I teased.

"Cease! You stain on cat-dom!" He growled, also shivering like the dickens. The good doctor wrapped him in another thick blanket after wiping him down with fresh water.

"Ooh that's a new one Chester! You are in good form considering!" I piped.

"I have just been in the blasted cold sea, you wretch. The boy and I could have drowned!" He hissed through tightly clenched shivering teeth.

"Not with the great and mighty Chester around!" I praised.

"You continue to mock me, you foul animal?" He hissed again.

"No, Chester! I do not mock! You did a courageous thing jumping into the sea after Tiata! I am impressed!" I explained.

"Hurrumph." He snorted, not convinced.

"Have it your way, Chester! I praise thee thus! What with jumping in after Mister Banks and now saving young drowning boys, I am seeing a side of you not obvious before! Bravo, the mighty hound!" This left no room for debate and he ceased his hurrumphing and began to warm and relax.

"Don't know what has gotten into me, Fairweather. I do not like the cold particularly." He tried to make sense of his valour.

"Lives at stake, dear boy! You are the protector of the human species! I suspect it was bred into you, yes?" I ventured.

"I suppose so, although I have usually only gone after things that Mister Banks has shot." He was not convinced.

"It's this dangerous New Zealand place, Chester! It has us all on edge! I bristle at a mouse passing me in the stores!" I tried to comfort him, while curling myself on Tiata's lap, hoping to exude some warmth into the boy.

"Yes. Yes." He saw the sense in my argument.

Mister Banks came to the door, terribly shaken by the display from the crowd and humiliated to the core by the captain's dressing down. Very quietly, he said, "Come, Chester. To my quarters." Chester was a little surprised at Mister Banks's demeanour and jumping out of his blanket was off after his master.

Tiata was sleeping on the surgeon's bunk so I stayed to continue my treatment for a while. When he woke, he sat bolt upright and said, "Fish!" Then he took off toward the galley! I bolted along with him, curiosity getting the better of me. Fish?

"Please, Mister Thompson, may I have a fish if we have one?" He asked of my cook politely.

"What for?" said John Thompson as curious as I.

"Just a small one will do, one that you would not cook for its size. Please, sir," he begged without explanation.

John looked at me and I at him.

"Alright then." He handed over a small fry that had come in with the latest catch.

"Damned if I know, Fairweather?" He looked to me for an answer. I could give him no such thing.

Tiata rushed off and I after him. What did this boy want with a small fish?

"Has anyone seen Mister Tupia?" He asked of everyone he passed. No one had. It seemed he might be with Mister Banks in his cabin.

Tiata knocked quietly on the cabin door and found his master, consoling the sulking Mister Banks, along with Mister Spöring.

"Excuse me, sirs. Master Tupia, do you approve of this fish?" He asked reverently.

"Yes, Tiata." Tupia clearly knew of Tiata's intent.

"Cast it into the sea with a thank you to your god for your lucky escape from death." Ah! A ritual. All was clear. I followed him on deck and he prayed a few Tahitian words and threw the fish into the sea. He was thankful for his skin and his god would be pleased I suspected.

That night in the Great Cabin saw the captain name this place Cape Kidnappers from the experience. Mister Banks who continued to sulk in his cabin did not join us.

We continued south but the captain deemed a landing on this inhospitable coast near to impossible.

The ground was barren, and steep white cliffs kept us away. The mountains within were capped with snow, so we turned at a bluff aptly named Cape Turnagain.

My captain was getting bored with the finding of new names for places and this was clearly obvious with this latest of names. I had not once heard him mention a Fairweather Bay! Or a Point Fairweather! As much as I would have liked the honour bestowed upon me, this New Zealand was not to my liking and I would have preferred a more welcoming place to be named after! I would make a point of it with him when I was pleased to be somewhere!

We sailed back past Poverty Bay with more favourable winds. Mister Banks had recovered somewhat and was back on deck to continue his work, although somewhat quieter.

I sat with him and the gents while we watched a new species of bird gather together to fish in the most unusual way! Brownish they were, and not much bigger than a pigeon, but deftly and as one, they herded shoals of small fish and then the whole flock dived under the water together, all at once! As if one of them had yelled, "Alright chaps, dive!" Then not being seen for minutes, they would come up together someplace else! Comical to say the least, but effective! They filled their beaks time and time again and we watched them keenly until they we sailed out of sight.

Canoes came to the boat daily on this northward tack back over the path we had followed. The captain's ploy with the natives had worked! When coming to the ship they were much more cordial and keener to trade, and trade we did.

At a place known to the locals as Anaura Bay, we fetched in and anchored. The bay was not protected from the sea well enough and the surf was rough, but a boat came out to the ship. The captain and gents were on hand to greet them.

"Welcome! Come aboard!" Mister Banks was most keen to meet the two on the canoe who looked akin to chiefs. Mister Banks had been learning Tupia's language and showed the chiefs around the ship. We were still a little on edge with these Maoris and the captain and men were cautious, unlike Mister Banks.

Chester, Lady, and I watched from the aft deck with the stock animals. They could not care less that Maori chiefs were on board!

"This is working out for the better with these chaps, Chester?" I pondered aloud.

"They are certainly a more civilized pair!" agreed Chester.

Mister Banks directed them toward us admiring their cloaks. The first chief explained his cloak, brightly coloured with bunches of red feathers and Mister Banks admired it keenly. The second chief advanced toward Chester and Lady.

"His coat is made of dog skin! Their dogs are small and ugly and they would prefer our dogs for their coats!" Mister Banks announced.

Chester leapt on the spot and upset Lady terribly.

"Calm down, dear! Mister Banks would not let any harm come to us." She attempted to soothe, after Chester frightened the life right out of her! He was having none of it!

I watched from behind the livestock stalls as this chief admired Chester's fine coat, he writhing like the dickens for fear he would be worn. Lady, too, cringed as the chief checked her coat for wearing potential. Mister Banks restrained the two, their eyes searching for me as if I could help.

The chief spoke to Mister Banks and much bargaining began. I could see Chester, knowing what was occurring, hoping that his master would not sell him as a fashionable addition to the chief's coat! His head was bowed and his tail was well and truly between his legs. Lady held her head high in the hope that this would not occur. The chief rubbed their coats and pulled at their leashes! I was shocked! In an attempt to cause a distraction from what looked to me to be a disastrous turn, I bit the nearest pig on the leg! It squealed terribly and turned the heads of all concerned. Chester saw me and knew his cue. Off he bolted, fairly pulling Mister Banks's arm out of its sleeve! Lady followed. Greyhound legs and paws scrambled over anything they could grip and scattered the gents in their paths, scratching at whatever got in their way. Off they went to the aft hatch heading for who knew where!

I sauntered away from the assaulted swine, as if its suffering had nothing to do with me. A casual Fairweather, I hopped into the rigging to avoid further scrutiny.

The chiefs laughed heartily, and Mister Banks must have smoothed things over enough for them to leave in good humour, without dogs for their casual wear. They boarded their canoe and were sent on their way with much Tahitian cloth as gifts instead.

Mister Banks and the gents carried on an excited discussion about the dog-skin coat and how Chester and Lady were invited to be additions! I thought it best to locate my frightened friends. They were not in Mister Banks's cabin or the Great Cabin. Chester was of such a fright that he could be anywhere and Lady would be with him.

"Chester! Lady!" I called, no sign of them on the mid decks. I would have to search lower.

"Oh, warm and cosy dog-skinned coat!" I was getting annoyed and thought it best to annoy. "Where art thou, oh colourful collar and company?" I chuckled to myself.

Low and behold the keen Fairweather ear detected the guttural growl of the beast. He had heard me. Lower into the stores I had to venture before finding him cowering in the gunpowder room all covered in the black stuff. Lady, too, was not much cleaner.

"Chester! For goodness's sake, you are positively black! And you tremble in the corner like a startled mouse!" I remarked.

"Fairweather!" He panted, quite out of breath, whether from fear or his vigorous escape I could not tell. "They kill dogs here! For clothing!" His eyes were as wide as saucers.

Lady was a little calmer. "I do not think that Mister Banks would allow it, would he, Fairweather?" She searched me for confirmation.

"No, dear woman, he has not allowed it. They were given other gifts and sent on their way." They were both too upset to tease so I held my tongue for another more appropriate time. Chester settled, panting still. Lady sat and breathed a heavy sigh.

"Are you certain?" Chester puffed.

"Yes, yes, dear boy, your hide is safe," I reassured.

"They wear dog in this wretched place!" He said as if to remind himself of what he had seen.

"Yes, old thing, and they ate dog in Tahiti if you will remember!" I tried to get him to come around but he was still panting furiously. "Mister Banks did not let them eat you then, did he?"

"No, but compared to the fat dog they were eating in Tahiti I assumed we were too lean for their tastes!" He had a point there.

"Well, after you so awkwardly beat your escape, scratching at a number of the gentry in your haste, I have it on good authority that Mister Banks gave the Maori chiefs a number of his own prized Tahitian cloths to ensure your safety." I updated him and Lady.

"But of course, he did!" Chester hurrumphed, as if no doubt had crossed his mind.

"Good of him, dear?" Lady quizzed, knowing that all would be well.

"Yes, quite the right thing to do, what?" I knew him to be still in some form of panic, but he blustered on well in spite of it.

"So, Chester, you are down here in the gunpowder room, why?" I inquired, hoping to make him see sense finally.

"Hurrumph…Err…Checking to see that all is well down here!" He recovered.

Lady eyed me purposefully, and I her.

"I see, old thing, well the gunpowder seems to be in order. I see no Maoris wearing dog cloaks!" I could not help myself, chuckling a little. Lady gave me a look to wither.

"No…Hurrumph…Of course not…Err…You say the chieftains have left the ship?" He tried to be nonchalant.

"Yes, old blot, no canine-wearing natives be here!" Lady shot me another wilting glance.

"Right then, this gunpowder room passes muster. Shall we?" He headed for the door and pranced off as if nothing had happened, gunpowder dropping in little clouds as he trotted off.

"Fairweather!" Lady scolded. "How you get away with teasing Chester so, I will never know!" A smile curled the corner of her mouth.

"Friendship, dear Lady, camaraderie, solidarity between canine and feline, call it what you will." I was unconcerned.

Mister Banks met us in the gangway.

"Chester! Lady! Look at you two! Covered in what?" He felt and sniffed the content of his hand. "Gunpowder! Come with me to the deck at once to be washed! I will have the Littleboys douse you with fresh water. I shall ensure that no one strikes a match as we pass! Heaven help us, you will go up in smoke!" He chattered on as we marched purposefully for the deck.

Chester felt much better after his rinse, and I knew Lady would enjoy a bathe. Mister Banks sprinkled them with some sweet-smelling potion to make them keener on the nostrils. Lady felt lavished, but poor Chester felt like a fop! He strutted about the deck shaking to try and rid himself of the feminine cologne as if all hound-dom was at stake!

Lady and I chuckled quietly while he rubbed himself along the great ropes hanging from the rigging until he smelled of the sea once more.

By now the ship was heading back the same way we had come. I thought this unusual until I consulted the captain and the charts, after he returned from a fact-finding jaunt for the day.

"By all reports, Fairweather, there is a better wooding and watering place back from whence we came. I have been in conference with the natives today, having been up hill and down dale admiring their crops and countryside. These folk are much more civilised since word of our kind treatment has made us known. We head for Tolaga Bay!" he announced.

We arrived the next morning to a small cove that the captain named after himself! Odd that! Cook's Cove! It had a pleasant ring to it, and I thought it about time he put his name to a place! We had missed it as we beat north the first time, and it was much more sheltered from the surf, with good wood and plenty of water.

After anchoring, the men took on three boats of wood and filled the casks with fresh water. The captain was well pleased, and arranged for a large quantity of wild celery and scurvy grass to be harvested and taken on board. The celery was a staple of the men's diet, boiled with oatmeal and portable soup every morning for their breakfast.

The Maoris delighted in our Tahitian cloth, in exchange for fifteen pounds of cultivated sweet potato, such was their keen ability to till their rich soil. Any vegetables and fruit were now well tolerated by the crew, as not one had gotten the scurvy since the captain's diet was enforced.

Mister Banks and the gents went ashore every day for new species. Chester and Lady went with the Littleboys to frolic on the beach, getting some well-earned exercise.

I stayed on board as no word of a species feline had come to light. I may have been seen as a devil or a god, I knew not which, but either would have seen me in trouble.

I heard the odd Haka from the ship, as the captain and gents dined with the Maoris, so loud was it to carry across the water to the Fairweather ear.

Chester filled me in on the local gossip when he and Lady came aboard. Mister Banks had seen a strange bird in the area named the "kiwi." He had seen and drawn one but no one believed him, so strange was it! A party was to go ashore the next day and so I made plans to see this Kiwi for myself!

Mister Banks, the usual gents, Littleboys with the dogs, and my good self went ashore. Mister Banks was keen to locate the kiwi and bring one back alive to the ship so that his sighting of it could be believed. Mister Banks did not like doubt of his botanical word; such was his rank in the profession. But he was at sea with many ordinary seamen and wanted them convinced that he was not a loon!

We took the longboat, and Chester and Lady ran up and down the beach, as was their habit on finding a large area to set their long legs free. I waited for them on a warm rock, until Mister Banks and his group were ready to hunt for kiwi.

It was getting on for dark and the Littleboys had erected tents on the beach, for our kiwi hunt was a night patrol, as they lived in burrows during the day according to Mister Banks. This cloak and dagger night business was the workings of a nut I thought, and the men were not too differing in their opinion! All I could see coming of this was that a nice fresh bird would make for a change to the Fairweather diet!

Mister Banks's instruction was for Chester and Lady to sniff the ground once we began the hunt.

"I know not what to sniff, Fairweather! Birds live in trees!" he admitted.

"Quite right, old boy! I think this Banks is of some type of mental illness!"

"I shall humour him. Lady sniff with me!" he ordered of his partner. We were headed to where Mister Banks had last sighted the bird. I could not understand why the hounds had been set to sniffing the ground and at night no less, when most happy birds were asleep in their lofty nests! Doubt was bandied about while out of range of Mister Banks's hearing.

"The kiwi cannot fly. It lives in burrows on the ground and hunts only at night! Look out for them ahead of you!" whispered Mister Banks. A flightless bird? I was perplexed!

"Chester, do you know of flightless birds?" I asked, hoping to be informed.

"Only the ostrich, as well the extinct moa and the elephant birds of Madagascar, penguins and such. Mister Banks has pictures of them at home." He was as confused as I. "But I recall such birds are rather large, Fairweather. Some are as tall as a man!"

"Righto! We're looking for a giant bird with a burrow in the ground instead of a nest, who hunts at night and does not fly?" I was all the more puzzled.

Chester and Lady sniffed the ground as I followed. We separated from the men, hearing an odd high-pitched call in the wild.

"Tuweeeeet! Tuweeeeet!" It rang out in the silence. The closer we came to where we had heard it, the further away it seemed.

"Tuweeeeet! Tuweeeeet!" came another call but lower in timbre. There were two of them. We could hear the scientists rustling about in the grass further ahead, but the calls were now behind us. The Fairweather ear heard much crackling of undergrowth and the Chester-Lady snout sniffed an acrid smell.

"Bird!" hissed Chester, thinking his master was beside him.

"Fairweather, do you hear it still?" Lady looked around for signs of the thing.

"Yes! But it is at our rear!" I whispered, sparing my words for fear of alarming it.

We doubled back, working in circles, oblivious to the scientists and their fumbling attempts to locate the beast.

Its "Tuweeeeet!" was eerie, piercing the night.

"Tuweeeeet!" It was close.

I saw the rounded shape of a furrily feathered thing sitting just beyond a tuft of grass. It was enormous! The size of my good self! I thought it would be somewhat smaller! Its body was that of a bird only much larger. It had a pointed beak with its nostrils oddly placed at the end of it, and razor-sharp claws for foraging but in this instant, they were intent on defending itself. I pounced at it, and hung on while it writhed within my grip. It "Tuweeeeeted" no longer, not dead, but had strangely given up the fight.

"I am kiwi bird, and you are stronger. Must protect the egg!" He grunted, probably capable of disarming my grip with those sharp claws but desperate to defend its potential young.

"You will not savage me with those claws?" I asked before I let my victim free.

"The egg! Must keep warm!" He rasped from my grip around his neck. By now, Chester and Lady had caught up with me. We looked at each other not knowing what to do with this ugly bird.

"Female birds tend eggs!" Chester barked, not believing this awkward-looking male for a moment.

"Not here!" squawked the kiwi, snorting through the small nostrils on the end of its beak.

"Do you hear that, you ninny! Males may sit on eggs! It is all the same warmth! I have never seen a bird such as you!" I challenged its very existence.

"Mister Banks was right!" I whispered to Chester.

"Nor have I, Fairweather!" Chester woofed. "Sitting on eggs, no doubt!" He did not believe.

"Must protect the egg!" The pitiful bird screeched. I let go of it, for as large as it was, its intention was only to warm one egg, this being as big as the bird itself!

"What are you doing, cat?" Chester growled.

"It is a bird, Chester!" I scolded. "The simple fact that it does not fly should be enough to thwart its escape between the three of us! Otherwise, it sits on this egg, as big as itself! I see no threat!" I made some sense of the nonsensical creature.

"It is no wonder that this bird cannot fly! It is far too large and has no wings!" I appealed to Chester, who was still growling, his demeanour that of the hound that had caught the duck for his master.

Lady had softened a little, knowing that the odd creature was protecting potential young, and the mother of the egg was nowhere to be seen. This reversal of traditional male-female rolls seemed to challenge our sensibilities and notions of the way things ought to be! The male bird was only too happy to hatch the egg while the female was out foraging or visiting with friends! Quite confused, we were!

My ear leapt to the ground! The scientists had heard our commotion and were on their way.

"Quickly, Chester, Fairweather, spread out whilst I cover the egg!" hissed Lady so none other than we could hear. "You, Kiwi, run!" she commanded, like I had never heard her.

The kiwi took off tuweeeeet-ing for his mate. Her call could be heard just behind us.

"What are you doing, Lady? We are supposed to be locating this oddball bird for Mister Banks. You are letting it go? And what of this huge egg?" I was unsure of her intent, as she began scratching at the undergrowth covering the egg with brush.

"Help me hide it, Fairweather, Chester!" she demanded, quite uncommonly for her. "Mister Banks and the scientists will take it back to the ship!" I could see nothing wrong with this, but complied all the same, in awe of her insistence. Just as the last sign of the egg was hidden, the gents arrived on the scene.

"Chester! Lady! Have you found it?" Mister Banks quizzed excitedly. Lady looked at us both and bowed her head to deny the sighting.

"Blasted dogs! All that noise and nothing to report?" He was cross with his hunters.

"I see signs of scratching here!" Mister Spöring pointed. "Perhaps the dogs frightened it away whilst it was foraging?" he tried to explain. Little did they know that the scratching was from Lady, covering the kiwi's egg!

The gents edged ever closer to the bulging undergrowth hiding the egg, scratching at the ground to see what it would reveal.

"Chester!" Lady growled low and purposefully. "Prick your ears and run, barking as you go, quickly!" she urged him, as the secret was about to be uncovered.

Chester knew what Lady was up to, but not I.

"Woof!" Chester leapt convincingly on the spot as if he had discovered the bird right underneath him. Then off he bolted in the opposite direction to where the happy couple would have reunited. The gents ran after Chester knowing him to be reliable in his work.

Lady signalled me. "Go and tell the kiwis their youngster is safe, but they must not return to it until we have departed!" Her motherly instincts had come to the fore, preserving life in the most primal way. I had little seen her so bent on a thing and admired her courage and determination in hatching a cunning plan on the run!

"Yes! Yes! Lady, consider it done! Fairweather to the rescue of the hidden kiwi egg!"

"When you have told them, come back to this spot and warm the egg," she ordered.

"What? How do you suppose I warm the egg?" I was dumbfounded.

"You sit on it, Fairweather!" said Lady, as if were as dumb a beast as ever walked the earth.

"I, Fairweather, the *Endeavour's* mouser and all-round hero, sit on the egg?" I could not believe that she asked this of me.

"Yes, and hurry, the ground is cold and the kiwis must stay away, now run and tell them!" she insisted. "Mister Banks will be waiting for me. If I do not return he will come looking for me and the egg will be discovered!" She hissed at me, and then ran off to the calls from Mister Banks.

Well, this was a fine pickle! I shot off to find the pair cowering behind some rocks, and told them of the plan.

"You will warm our egg until the men have gone?" They seemed to doubt the Fairweather ability.

"Yes…yes…err…um…Tell no one!" There was little else to be said so I rushed back to my charge.

I brushed off the leaves and sticks that Lady had scratched into place and eyed it keenly. It was a shiny white egg not much smaller than I. How would I warm the thing by sitting on it? I did not have feathers to spread over it! The Fairweather coat, whilst luxurious, was not at all long! I paced around the egg for some time and the answer eventually came. I shimmed over it with a paw on each corner of the site, and left myself down gently, my stomach covering the egg. This seemed the only solution, and it worked admirably, but if anyone were to approach I would bolt up the nearest tree rather than be seen in such a ridiculous pose!

I stayed in situ for some time while the dogs and gents searched for the elusive kiwis. They were giving the gents a merry chase, and given the direction of their voices I thought the kiwi couple safe and sound, and my current situation unlikely to be witnessed.

The warmth of my body seemed to radiate around the egg and I shuffled a little for more comfort, as awkward a spot as I have ever been in. What would Turkel and the lads back at the tavern have thought of this? I would be the laughing stock of London! A cat! Sitting on a bird's egg!

Crack!

A snout poked through the shell of the thing! I could not cry out for Chester and Lady! The egg would be discovered! The kiwis had been told not to return until the men left! I was stuck with this youngster trying to hatch under my very being!

I leapt off for fear of that pointy little beezer stabbing me in the fleshy parts! Its little beak just kept hammering away at its enclosure, until the shell was cracked all over. It fell away and I leapt back just in time for this chick and all the surrounding muck splattered out of its egg. A close call, if I do say so!

It began tuweeeeet-ing softly but furiously! I was all a flutter thinking that the Gents would hear it!

"Shhhh!" I whispered coarsely. It wriggled a bit and then found its feet. What if it runs off? Toward the Gents? Lady would be horridly cross with me.

It fell and rolled about in the dirt and leaves, its sticky body collecting whatever it touched. Now I was the sole keeper of a small Kiwi covered in all manner of muck!

I had it! I collected the wee thing in my mouth. I could not pierce the skin of this bald baby for all the crud it had collected on its body. Off I ran at speed trying to remember where I had last seen the Kiwi couple, and thankfully further away from the Gent's voices.

I found them dithering about where I left them. They had heard the cries of their young and were all aflutter. I had told them to stay where they were but the primitive call of their chick was more than they could bear.

"Never fear, kiwi friends! Fairweather is here with your newly born chicklet!" I whispered excitedly. They were overjoyed!

"It is a boy!" announced Father Kiwi.

"A boy!" Mother clucked around waddling above her young to keep it warm and pecking at the leaves and sticks that had stuck to its sticky body.

"We will call him your name!" said Father Kiwi proudly.

"Fairweather?" I objected. "Not a fitting name for a land-bound bird, me thinks!"

"Fairweather! His name will be Fairweather Kiwi," he proclaimed.

"Well, I am proud!" I was unconvinced but they were resolute, so I merely bid them farewell and returned slowly to where I could hear Chester and Lady woofing for me.

The gents were retiring to their tents down the hill and I would be missed. As I walked, I pondered the recent event. I had sat on an egg, hatched it nicely, and had the offspring named after me! Flattering, to say the least. No one would believe me!

I straggled back into camp and told Chester and Lady of what had occurred.

"You hatched the egg?" Chester was flabbergasted and laughing till his sides hurt.

"Don't listen to him, Fairweather, I am very proud of you!" praised Lady. "Your feline way might have caused the chick to be eaten, but instead you fostered it and delivered it to its parents." She nuzzled my neck.

Chester burst into fresh fits of laughter, his eyes watering. "Fairweather Kiwi, you have produced young!" He rolled around breathlessly.

"Leave it alone, Chester, you stain on canine-kind! I was under instructions from Lady and I honoured them to the end. All are safe and there is another Fairweather in the world! Even if it is not the same species! I consider myself as an important uncle or godfather or some such thing! Mind you, if this gets around back in London, I will know who to blame and come after you with a vengeance you have never before seen!" I threatened.

There was nothing more for it, Chester merely laughed until he fell asleep and even then chuckled as he dozed. Lady was happy with my good works. I was satisfied with that, as long as my canine friends did not utter it to a soul!

CHAPTER 28

s we left Tolaga Bay we sailed lightly. Some Maoris had softened, and they enjoyed coming out to us for the coloured beads, and the nails, once Tupia had told them what they were for.

Other canoes carried Haka-ing Maoris bent on fighting. The grape shot and four-pound gun did not rest for long. We rounded into a large bay named after our lieutenant: Hicks Bay, then East Cape and the Bay of Plenty after the well-tilled soils and obvious crops.

The mood among the men had lightened since we had not had to fight these people; so amusing was their retreat at one point that the place was called Cape Runaway!

The further north we sailed, the greener and more lush became the countryside. A large mountain came into sight and was named Mount Edgcumbe after our sergeant.

More and more whole villages came into view with their neatly planted lands. There was still no word of felines in this place. I gathered that upon hearing that the natives would eat and wear dog, the feline species would say, "Stay well away from this New Zealand or be dinner or a coat!" So I was resigned that my presence would not be taken well, and I stayed on board.

We passed small islands and great canoes came out daily to threaten us with their Haka, throwing stones and spears just short of us. Doubtless, we were all grateful for the four-pound gun! Through the Bay of Plenty, so named as we collected more wild celery to stock the stores, a suitable site was sought for yet another mission.

On the 9th day of November, the Transit of the Planet Mercury across the sun would be seen to those of us with the right equipment. Mister Green was one such man of course, and he begged the captain for a landing to take his measurements. This transit was not of such importance as our Venus sighting, but worth noting on the astronomical charts all the same. The Royal Society would be most pleased!

On the 5th day of November, a perfect bay was landed for the Transit of Mercury and so it was named Mercury Bay.

Off they tootled, Lieutenant Hicks and misters Green, Banks and Tupia in the longboat, and the captain leaving his Lieutenant Gore in charge.

The lieutenants took this charge very seriously, when the captain was absent, almost too seriously at times.

Whilst the party were on shore with their astronomical instruments, five canoes, three large and two small, with some forty-seven Maoris in just one canoe alone, came out to the ship. These were peaceable enough and of the trading sort so the lieutenant allowed them alongside.

Lieutenant Gore was most keen to trade with them and climbed down the rope ladder himself with an admirable piece of Tahitian cloth. A Maori warrior stood in the canoe with a piece of his own cloth. Lieutenant Gore held his out to trade with him, but it was snatched from him without the fair exchange of the warrior's cloth. The Maoris pushed the canoe off the ship leaving no doubt that they would be off with it and not come back!

Mister Gore took this very badly. He levelled his musket at the man and shot him dead! The entire crowd of Maoris began their Haka!

It was not looking good for us that they were angered so, and they seemed intent on revenge for their tribesman's death!

Lieutenant Gore was panicked by this turn of events and ordered the four-pound gun fired over their heads. They took off for the beach where the captain and party were assembled for the Transit of Mercury.

The Maoris quickly surrounded our party and Tupia came forward to discuss what had happened and try to make them see that the death of their warrior was warranted. They were convinced and left. Our party came back to the ship.

The captain was most annoyed and wished to see Lieutenant Gore and Hicks in the Great Cabin. I followed them, and knew what to expect from my captain. He berated Lieutenant Gore for the senseless killing of the warrior when grape shot would have done the job admirably.

My captain stood firm on his kind treatment of the natives. After all, how could a singular boatful of men change the ways of natives who had been primitive for thousands of years? Killing must be avoided at all costs, as these were still natives who could turn on us and we would all be killed if it took their fancy! A delicate balance had been reached with the Maoris and the captain laid out these orders without argument. He was a forceful man when necessary and although the lieutenants were both of the same rank as he, as "captain" of the ship he made the rules. The lieutenants were dismissed.

"Ah, Fairweather!" The captain flopped down into his chair and began to write, speaking his words to me as he went.

"I have here inserted the account of this affair just as I had it from Lieutenant Gore, but I must own it does not meet with my approbation because I thought the punishment a little too severe for the crime, and we had now been long enough acquainted with these people to know how to chastise trifling faults like this without taking away their lives."

Looking out the window afterward, into the night where the Maori fires could be seen in the hills, I could see that this had affected him somewhat and he would probably hesitate at leaving the ship in future.

The next day, none of the Maoris came out to the ship. The captain could not decide whether it was the shooting, or the bad weather that had set in.

An oyster bank had been found at the river by the wooding place, about a mile up on the starboard side, just above a small island which was covered at high water; here the longboat was sent and soon returned deeply loaded with oysters.

Mister Banks shucked the first specimen, opening the shell and slipping the contents into his mouth and over his tonsils.

"I sincerely believe these are as good oysters as ever came from Colchester!" he announced.

The rest of the day saw the entire crew scoffing down oysters. My cook and butcher, John Thompson and Henry Jeffs were the keenest of the crew as this was a meal they did not have to cook!

"Raw oysters be the candy of the sea!" declared John Thompson, shucking an oyster for the ultimate taster, my good self!

He was right! I rubbed against his leg and each time was rewarded with another oyster, while he chewed them, savouring every morsel.

Chester and Lady declined, but I revelled in this feast as the entire ship's company and I took our fill of this delicacy!

After the last oyster slipped down, not much activity followed, as the full stomachs desired sleep. Most of the men could not indulge such, but not I! Off I went to the longboat for an undisturbed nap, happy that the oyster had given its life to such deserving folk!

On our last day in Mercury Bay, the crew gathered as much wild celery for the men, and grass for our sheep, as the stores could hold. Boat after boat came back from my favourite place, the oyster beds, with my favourite food to date, the oyster, to keep us in our newly found treat for some time. I hovered around the galley for the next few days to ensure that my cook, John Thompson, was forthcoming with these, and to his credit he was!

Before we left this bay, the captain ordered the crew to etch upon one of the trees near the watering place the *Endeavour*'s name, the 15th day of November 1769, and after displaying the English flag, the captain took formal possession of Mercury Bay in the name of His Majesty King George.

We sailed further north, my captain noting and charting every inch of the coastline as always. We rounded a prominent headland and found a deep bay, which the captain named the Firth of Thames, as it resembled the mouth of the river of that name in England. This bay ran to its river, which also reminded the captain of the Thames River back at home and of course he named it so. The captain secured us a landing and named this place Thames. Me thinks he was feeling a little homesick. Thames this and Thames that!

The captain went ashore with the gents to gather specimens and meet the natives, who by now were aware of our firepower and somewhat more genial, as they wished to trade.

Their trip was fruitless but while they were ashore, trouble occurred once again. After the killing of the warrior when the captain last went ashore, this time he left both Lieutenant Hicks and Gore on board with Lieutenant Hicks in charge. He could be sure that reason would apply.

The natives came out to the ship as the captain left, and swarmed all over her. I bolted for my usual cover in the longboat, peering out to see enough. One such native opened the bittacle, a wooden box used for storing the compasses, log glasses, watch glasses, and lights to show the compass at night. He stole the half-hour-glass that measured the half hour for the men on watch to keep accurate time. Such important instruments cannot be replaced at sea! Lieutenant Hicks saw him at it and caught him before he went over the side with it.

This time, the punishment was twelve lashes with the "cat!" He was tied to the gangway and Mister Hicks delivered twelve of his best upon the thieving Maori while his kin and countrymen stood in awe. The usual wounds, softened by the darkened skin, yet no less painful, he shrieked with each lash. This penalty was more befitting the crime than on the previous occasion of theft, but it still may have turned ugly had the Maoris not been so very afraid of the muskets and guns.

As the wounded man was released, so was his grip on the stolen half-hour glass and as it was carefully put back in the bittacle, the Maori's father beat him some more, even as they paddled off in their canoe, as if to condone the punishment.

Upon his return, the captain was much pleased at the reports from Lieutenant Hicks and Gore and commended them on the correctness of their duty.

We sailed on northward, the gents cataloguing their finds and drawing everything they saw. The captain took his readings with the navigational instruments and charted the coast.

We stood off an open bay and no sooner had we anchored than the men caught some one hundred fish, called bream. Tasty! I had a whole bream to myself for my dinner and not a man missed out on this most excellent fish! Another Fairweather favourite, and the captain named this place Bream Bay.

The Maoris came out daily and traded fairly most of the time. On one such occasion a cheeky native took off with some nails that Midshipman Patrick Saunders had sought to trade for one of the Maori's weapons. Saunders was a roguish fellow and sought to exact a revenge upon the thief. As the culprit took off in his canoe, Saunders got a fishing line and hove the hook out to the canoe, catching the bandit in the buttock! So large was the hook that the barb fastened tight, and the Midshipman hung on to what could have been a prized catch!

The thief was left floundering and trying desperately to stay on his canoe, but the hook and line held admirably. Finally, the hook broke and left poor Saunders fallen heavily on his behind, the fishing line flailing in the breeze. As he pulled in his line, he noticed that the barb was missing, broken off in the Maori's behind! This would be a theft he would not forget! We watched him rub at the wound fiercely as the canoe paddled away. Everyone on deck saw the humorous side and much laughing followed Saunders around for days.

Cape Brett was so prominent and tall that the captain named it after Sir Percy Brett, a Lord of the Admiralty in London. I gathered they were either known to each other or the captain wished to gain favour by naming a place after him. The natives knew it as Motugogogo. We all thought it better sense to rename the place, as the native version was a little too difficult to get the tongue around.

On the 29th day of November, the captain headed us into The Bay of Islands, named for the simple fact that small islands dotted the coastline. On one island that we passed, the sea had worn away a hole as big as a ship and we could see right through the headland to the other side. It had Mister Banks's attention for some time.

The crew were getting bored from the lack of a landing due to the troublesome nature of the Maori people. Some traded well about the ships on their canoes but others felt set upon when we landed on shore and we had to leave.

On the 1st day of December 1769, Manoel Pereira, Matthew Cox, and Henry Stephens were amongst the crew on the longboat to shore one evening. They left their duties to steal potatoes from one of the Maori plantations. They were caught and sent back to the ship; a dozen lashes each for their trouble.

Cox complained bitterly at his punishment for what he considered a minor infraction, so he was sent to quarters under guard rather than have him incite rebellion amongst the seamen. While confined he continued to whine and was given yet another dozen lashes and dismissed. He was a little better behaved after this, and all the men vowed to leave the local potatoes alone!

Before the sun rose one morning, the captain took an early stroll on deck and I with him unable to sleep for a change.

The Gunner Stephen Forwood was in charge of the watch. Along with Alexander Simpson and Richard Littleboy, they robbed the spirit cask, which had ten or twelve gallons of rum in it. The captain found part of it on the quarterdeck and in their possession.

Mister Gore was summoned from his bed to deliver twelve lashes per man. The gunner was so drunk he barely felt the cat across his bare back, and having passed out, was useless to the ship. His wounds were ignored and he was dragged below to sleep off his drinking. The captain then assembled the remaining two.

"I shall stop your allowance until the quantity you have stolen and drunk is accounted for! Ensure that when the gunner recovers that he is told of this further penalty!" he commanded. Littleboy and Simpson bowed their drunken heads and staggered off to their duties, having sobered a little after the lashings with the cat!

Upon trading with the Maoris for so much cloth, our economy was in trouble by the 4th day of December. The value of the cloth had fallen as there was so much of it and the price for the slightest thing was becoming too high. Mister Spöring was drawing Mister Banks's discoveries when a Maori near him discovered his paper. A new currency was born! Paper was now the preferred tender for trade! And of this we had much!

With the wind and weather as foul as could be possible, we left the Bay of Islands on the 6th day of December, the captain hoping to chart and double the north point of this part of New Zealand. The winds were against us and we made little progress. Canoes stayed off us during this weather, as it was difficult to make progress in any vessel. The captain hoped we were headed for Cape Maria van Diemen. The cape was so named by Abel Tasman in January of 1643, after the wife of his patron Anthony van Diemen, the Governor General of Batavia at that time. It was thought to be the northernmost point of New Zealand.

The land along the way was dotted with well-cultivated crops, mainly potato and yam. Some villages were fenced and likened to fortresses; "Heppa" in the Maori tongue. Mister Banks went ashore when the sailing was slow and spoke long with the Maoris after Tupia managed to smooth the way with them. He came back confirming that the natives only eat their enemies killed in battle. We were grateful of this news and no one man wanted to be in disfavour with the Maori!

I chose wisely not to go ashore at any time. According to Mister Banks there were no native cats in New Zealand. The many Maoris that visited the ship wearing dog skins, wished to have a piece of the Fairweather luxurious coat! I was not about to wander aimlessly around New Zealand waiting to be plucked, skinned, and worn!

The captain named Doubtless Bay, and it occurred to me that he was falling short of appropriate names for new places. I wondered at his reasoning, and decided it best not to strain the grey matter, for he was resolute in his workings. This bay saw a number of natives come aboard to sell us enough fish for all hands! Doubtless Bay it would be! Knockle Point was next! Again, I could see no purpose in such a silly name, but there it was on his chart that evening!

On the 9th day of December, we were sailing in little wind. Many canoes came but they would not come aboard for fear of our guns. They had heard of them from other villagers. Tupia at last persuaded them to come aboard. I slipped up into the rigging so as not to be detected. Mister Banks bought some of their cloth and asked about the country through Tupia.

They told him that at the distance of three days rowing in their canoes, the land would take a short turn to the southward and from there extend no more to the west. This place must be Cape Maria Van Diemen!

Mister Banks found these people intelligent and desired Tupia to enquire if they knew of any countries besides this New Zealand, or ever went to any.

"They say they have not been elsewhere, but their ancestors have been to a great continent!" Tupia explained.

"What?" Mister Banks was agog! "Ask them where this place is and how we might get there! Good Lord! This might be Terra Australis Incognita of which they speak!" He stuttered excitedly.

The Maoris spoke long of Tupia's request for more information. Mister Banks could hardly keep his composure. He stood quietly but keenly awaited the translation.

"They will not tell unless we trade for the information!" Tupia explained.

"Well, what do they want?" asked Mister Banks impatiently. "We will give them anything they wish in exchange for enlightenment of this new land!" He nudged at Tupia to pass on this message.

Again, Tupia spoke long, shaking his head to Mister Banks's annoyance.

"Tupia! Tell of what they require! And cease shaking your head to the negative! We will give them anything!" he commanded.

"They want the cat!" Tupia informed. My head shot up. The cat?

"Then go and get it. We can make another one in its absence! Hurry along!" barked Mister Banks.

"What do you mean, Mister Banks?" Tupia was confused. The natives were looking eagerly forward to the trade.

"The cat o'nine tails! Go and fetch it for them. It is a small price to pay for directions!"

Just then the captain and lieutenants arrived on the scene and Mister Banks filled him in on the doings.

"Yes, alright, the cat o'nine tails can be replaced," agreed the captain. I was suspicious.

Tupia ran off to fetch the thing while I eyed these Maoris from my lofty spot in the rigging. I had my doubts that Mister Banks's determination of "cat" had been correct. They could certainly have the cat o'nine tails! No one would miss it, but I was unsure that this is what they meant!

Tupia returned with the well-worn whip and handed it to the eager Maoris. They threw it on the ground and much arguing ensued. Tupia's eyes were wide as he explained the problem.

"It is not the cat o'nine tails they want, sirs! It is Fairweather!" I wanted to leap on the spot!

I suspected that this was what they wanted, seeing as they had admired my splendid coat previously. I was having none of it! I crouched low on the boom and tucked my feet and tail under myself so as not to be seen under any circumstances, glad that my diet of fish had kept my flanks from sagging over the side of the wide timber boom! I blended and became one with it!

"What do they want with Fairweather?" Mister Banks asked incredulously, as if I were some blot, hardly a worthy trade! I cursed him under my breath and was I to survive this disaster, would ensure a vengeance be played upon him at some future time.

"They wish to skin him and add him in pieces to each of their coats!" Tupia swallowed hard, knowing their penchant for dog skin on their lavish cloaks.

"Well, don't just stand there, Tupia! Go and get him!" I was dumbfounded! I knew this Banks to be a dog man, but to wish to trade me! Fairweather! Exalted mascot of the ship! I would not believe that he could turn on me in this manner! Tupia turned to obey the order and seek me out.

"Just a moment, Tupia!" the captain interjected. Tupia stood down.

"Mister Banks! The cat stays here!" the captain announced.

"But…but…these Maori know of a great continent which may be Terra Australis Incognita!" Mister Banks could not believe that the captain would not trade a mere feline for such important information!

"The cat stays here!" the captain reiterated, leaving no room for argument. "Find something else for them to value in exchange for the information, Mister Banks!" I sighed with relief but Mister Banks was adamant.

"Captain, I insist that we hand the cat over to these knowledgeable Maoris for the sake of our secret orders!" Mister Banks appealed to the captain's mission and thought he could be moved.

"Mister Banks…" he said quietly, but bursting at the seams for his botanist's insolence, "I have ordered that the cat stay here, and that is all there is for it." His calm was only surpassed by his hidden anger.

"Yes, Captain." Mister Banks had got the gist. I was safe, and let out a sigh of relief. The captain turned on his heel, off for the Great Cabin, the lieutenants with him. I deemed it safe to climb down from the rigging and join my gallant captain below, but I was a little slower than he.

Suddenly a grip on the scruff of my neck saw me whisked from my path! I was handled roughly and thrown into a hessian sack! I could see through the netting and Mister Banks held me aloft to the great admiration of the Maoris. I could not believe it! I was being kidnapped! Against the orders of my captain!

Tupia saw the opportunity and asked again of the great continent.

"They say…" started Tupia, pausing at every sentence so as not to relay the wrong report to Mister Banks, "that their ancestors speak of a large country to which they paddled for one month in a very large canoe."

I squirmed and hissed and a huge "reeeeooooowwwwww!" escaped my being, hoping to attract the attention of the captain, but he had already gone below. Anyone could have heard me, but as Mister Banks held me in the air in the sack, the crew assumed he had the captain's blessing in what can only be described as my end! They looked on with concern but did nought to stop him!

Tupia continued. "Only a few returned to tell of the country where the people there eat 'booah' or hog."

"Ask them if the hog they saw there is found in New Zealand!" Mister Banks dangled me in the air, protesting much, but he had a good grip on the sack. I could not escape!

Tupia translated the question and they shook their heads as one.

"No such hog is to be found here, Mister Banks," Tupia replied.

"Did none of their ancestors bring back hog from this place?" he asked of Tupia.

"No, sir," he replied upon asking them the question.

"Then if their ancestors were foolish enough to return without bringing hog for their people, they must be liars! Tell them, Tupia!" he challenged.

Much quarrelling followed. They were not impressed, but then neither was yours truly! I maintained my wriggling and protesting to no avail. I was doomed.

"They tell the truth, Mister Banks!" Tupia said. Mister Banks withdrew my sack from mid-air in front of them to tease them into truthfulness. They all reached forward to grab at my sack. Mister Banks pushed them off.

"They speak the truth, I see," Mister Banks said, having tested them. "Then their ancestors are only guilty of being fools!" he proclaimed.

Tupia chose wisely not to reiterate this comment. I was again held aloft and the Maoris grabbed at my writhing body within its confines. I closed my eyes. I was fated to become a part of many Maori cloaks! The end was nigh! I struggled no more.

"Mister Banks!!!" came a shout. Lieutenant Gore! My Isaac next to him! Mister Banks hid me behind his back as I began to protest in earnest! Hissing and growling emanated from my every pore!

"Young Isaac here tells me you are bargaining information for our cat!" challenged Mister Gore. Mister Banks was sheepish and had no retort, as the captain had made it quite clear that he was to cease.

"Tupia, thank the Maoris for their information, give them a rooster and a hen, and ask them to leave," ordered Lieutenant Gore.

Tupia did so, bringing both forward and upside down by the legs, and explained their purpose, to lay eggs and bear more chickens and roosters. The Maoris were not impressed. They wanted my fur and that was all there was to it! They threatened Mister Banks and Lieutenant Gore with their spears. Mister Gore loaded his musket and eyed them purposefully.

They were afraid for the first time, knowing that the musket would kill one and all if aimed and fired. They ceased grabbing for my sack, and backed away from Mister Banks, dropping their weapons and running for their canoe. Lieutenant Gore did not stop them. He shot into the air, as they looked back in the hope to receive the Fairweather coat, before going over the side and paddling furiously away. All this time I was kept behind Mister Banks back in the sack. I stopped writhing when the natives retreated.

"Mister Banks!" called Lieutenant Gore as he attempted to skulk away and release me somewhere without incident.

"Ah…yes…Lieutenant Gore…somewhat of a bother, what?" he whimpered. "But what knowledge we have obtained!" he said, trying to save himself.

"Put the sack down!" said Lieutenant Gore, caressing his loaded musket nonchalantly by his side, but purposefully aimed at Mister Banks.

"Sack? What sack?" Mister Banks denied all knowledge even though I was still held behind his back in my confines. I had not moved until now. With one mighty sweep of the paw, I extended the claws from their sockets and through the sack, etching right through the cloth of Mister Banks's trousers and deeply into the flesh upon his buttocks!

"Ahhhhhh!" he shrieked. I held firm and retracted the claws inward so that they would not be released easily. With yet another hefty reach, the other paws followed suit; all four together were in various positions upon Mister Banks's behind and locked in place.

"Ahhhhhh! Get this evil cat off my person!" Mister Banks screamed.

Lieutenant Gore knew exactly what had occurred from his briefing with my Isaac who had seen all. The lieutenant circled round behind Mister Banks to ascertain his grief. Seeing me attached to Mister Banks's behind, the sack having loosened to reveal all but where my claws were incised into his flesh.

Lieutenant Gore nonchalantly enquired.

"Cat? What cat?" Up went the most uproarious laughter I had seen on board to date!

"Ahhhhhh! Ahhhhhh!" Mister Banks shrieked, as I had not deemed it a fitting time to let go of his flesh. He ran from one end of the ship to the other as the captain surfaced from the decks below.

"What is the meaning of this fuss, Mister Gore?" He smiled as Mister Banks ran past him with a Fairweather attached to his flanks!

"Mister Banks was to trade Fairweather for some Maori information regarding the whereabouts of Terra Australis Incognita," Lieutenant Gore said casually.

"Is that so, Lieutenant Gore?" returned the captain in his own blasé fashion, neither of them in any hurry to rescue the felonious Banks.

"My cat?" asked the captain, stalling somewhat. I dug into Banks's flesh as far as the claws would extend.

"Ahhhhhh!" It must have hurt like the dickens as I felt the warmth of blood on my pads.

"No, sir. Our cat! Fairweather as he is known, I think?" The lieutenant joked with the captain.

Mister Banks began swiping behind him to loosen me, but he had no hope, I was not about to let him go after what could have been my demise! Chester and Lady came upon the scene, not knowing whether to laugh or growl.

I let it be known with a tittering yowl that laughter was the correct response. They just sat there, heads tilted in curiosity, as Mister Banks was their master and whatever I had done, their laughter would be imprudent.

"Ah, Fairweather? Our cat? The very same?" the captain asked boorishly. Mister Banks kept up his pace and I kept up my grip. The crew were laughing mercilessly.

"Yes, sir, I do believe that is the cat in question," yawned Lieutenant Gore.

I knew that this comedy would have to end sooner or later but the soul would not allow the punishment to end.

There was no point in letting go of Mister Banks on the run. I would have been flung I knew not where! I kept at it while he tired himself out. Tentatively he stopped to catch his breath, and I released my grip and charged off to the rigging to be well clear of any repercussions my behaviour might have. I licked my paws clean whilst watching the crew fall about laughing below.

"Captain, that cat has mauled me!" Mister Banks whined.

"Did you deserve it, Mister Banks?" he asked.

"Certainly not!" was the reply; the entire crew laughing anew as Isaac had spread the word of my plight with our Maori guests.

"I shall have a quiet word with him this evening when he shows himself," said the captain, eyeing me briefly, safe in the rigging above. He turned with Lieutenant Gore to discuss the matter privately in the Great Cabin.

"Back to your duties, men!" he so ordered on his way, knowing they would snigger for some time, and wishing he had seen the onslaught for himself!

That night, the Great Cabin was abuzz with talk of this development. Mister Banks was all a dither as he ventured his guesses on where Terra Australis Incognita lay whilst nursing his wounds and finding it practical not to sit down upon them for the pain was much.

The captain glanced knowingly at me as I sat nonchalantly out of the way, knowing the route we must take, and that my actions of this day, though well deserved, impeded good relations with Mister Banks. The subject of my very existence was broached.

"Mister Banks, I see that you suffer sorely from your misadventure with the cat?" he asked.

"Wretched animal," he mumbled. "You should punish it!" he insisted, rubbing at his punctured parts.

"Did you attend the physician for some ointment?" ventured the captain.

"Yes, yes, I am dressed and have stopped bleeding, but…"

The captain interrupted. "You will do no such thing ever again I assume?" he caught Mister Banks's eye and held his gaze with a look that would wither the soul.

"Er…" Mister Banks stuttered.

"That would be, 'No, Captain, I will not endanger the cat as he is a vital member of the crew!'" prompted the captain.

"Yes…crew…of course, Captain." He stood berated and nothing more was said of it. I felt rather more important than previously, and Mister Banks's wounds were vengeance enough for me. I would not seek to punish him further at a later date. I would, however, keep well out of his way in future negotiations with Maoris.

Lieutenant Hicks was on duty for the evening and the captain requested him to set our course to round North Cape. As we did so, he found that the Surville Cliffs were east and slightly further northerly than Cape Maria van Diemen and charted it so. Another achievement for our captain!

The weather had turned foul, and we zigged and zagged beating into the wind and heavy rolling swell. The captain found the going difficult to keep land in sight, and chart the coast, and we lost sight of land just before Christmas.

The captain brought us about when his reckoning allowed him a safe southern passage to the western side of New Zealand and before long, Cape Maria van Diemen came back into view and he set it to his map.

On Christmas Eve of 1769, our second such occasion at sea, Mister Banks set to gathering our Christmas repast by shooting gannets and solan geese, the latter being a very large white gannet with black tipped wings, and similar to English geese. He had soon shot enough of them to ensure goose pie for all! John Thompson made ready to cook the traditional meal, even though the rough pitching of the ship slowed his progress. Keeping one's balance while plucking a goose seemed a monumental feat! I had difficulty myself keeping upright for the goose scraps that came my way! But I managed it.

The morning of Christmas Day suddenly beamed with bright sunshine and an unusually calm sea as if to give us a pleasant enough day to enjoy the season. We gathered in the mess deck, letting the ship loll about in the tranquil conditions.

The captain stood at the dinner table and demanded attention.

"We have sailed some rough weather these last few days, men," he began. "Extra rations of rum for all!" He gestured to Lieutenant Hicks.

A rousing cheer penetrated the ship. He bowed his head in prayer for our safety and continuing good weather, asked the Almighty to bless our kin and friends back in England, and then let the men tuck in to the goose pie and rum. He himself scoffed down a sizeable beaker of the good stuff after meting out a small portion for yours truly. I felt warmed by it and was grateful that the saucer of it, along with my very own portion of goose pie, stayed still on the floor while I drank and ate!

Not a sober soul was on board that day, including my captain. He and the men were truly tired from the foul sailing conditions we had experienced.

We gathered on the aft deck in fine spirits and Henry Jeffs had found his "squeeze box" amongst his belongings. This was an accordion with buttons that were played as the air pumped through the baffles. A delightful sounding instrument and we all wondered why it had not been summoned before. But Henry Jeffs was a simple man, not wanting to brag that he could play it. Not until the extra ration of rum reminded him of his musical prowess!

So at the captain's insistence, he pumped out a tune and started the men a-singing. They all knew a comical ditty about an English lighthouse. It went as follows:

Oh…My father was the keeper of the Eddystone light
And he slept with a mermaid one fine night
Out of this union there came three
A porpoise and a porgy and the other was me!
Yo ho ho, the wind blows free,
Oh for the life on the rolling sea!

One night, as I was a-trimming the glim
Singing a verse from the evening hymn
I heard a voice cry out an "Ahoy!"
And there was my mother, sitting on a buoy.
Yo ho ho, the wind blows free,
Oh for the life on the rolling sea!

"Oh, what has become of my children three?"
My mother then inquired of me.
One's on exhibit as a talking fish
The other was served in a chafing dish.
Yo ho ho, the wind blows free,
Oh for the life on the rolling sea!

Then the phosphorus flashed in her seaweed hair.
I looked again, and my mother wasn't there
But her voice came angrily out of the night
"To Hell with the keeper of the Eddystone Light!"
Yo ho ho, the wind blows free,
Oh for the life on the rolling sea!

The men clapped their hands and stomped their feet on the deck with every word, and with every chorus some of them danced a little jig, ensuring much laughter. The singing went on well into the night until the rum had taken its toll and all slept where they fell.

Chester, Lady, and I retired to the aft deck among the livestock. The gents' deck above contained the usual crowd with a good bottle of brandy and they drank heartily in the calm conditions.

"I say, Chester, this singing business doth warm the heart and liven the spirit admirably!" I remarked. "Do you know any of these ditties yourself?"

"I am not of the singing species, Fairweather, you ninny!" he scolded, his nose in the air.

"Lady? Any lilts come to your mind?"

"A few lullabies, dear, but nothing jaunty," she admitted.

"I do believe we shall make one of our own! What say you?" I addressed the pair.

"Hurrumph!" blustered Chester, not wanting a bar of it.

"Off you go, then!" said Lady, a little excited and full of her usual cheer.

"Righto! I shall begin!" I thought for a moment.

> *Ohhhh…there once was a hound of the Chester kind!*
> *A blustery chump but he knew his mind!"*

Lady giggled. "What fun, Fairweather!" I continued.

> *Of jolly old England he always pined,*
> *But a finer pal one could never find!*
> *With…a…tum-diddlee-dum and a whoop-de-dee*
> *Fairweather…Chester…and Lady three!*

Lady was rolling about, laughing, her composure completely gone, along with the other animals who could see the funny side. Chester merely tilted his head at me as if some brain disease had afflicted me. I bowed taking my applause from Lady and the chickens. The gents looked down at us to see what the commotion was but to their ear it was nothing but a cat howling, upsetting the animals.

To honour Lady in the same manner I was off again!

Ohhhh…Lady is a woman one must invest!
She tolerates Chester and that is a test!
He can be such a grumpy, awful pest!
And that is why Lady is the very best!
With…a…tum-diddlee-dum and a whoop-de-dee
Fairweather…Chester…and Lady three!

Tears of laughter rolled from Lady's eyes. "This is too much, Fairweather!"

The livestock laughed heartily. The gents once again looked down, expecting a commotion but we recovered quickly enough that no fuss was made. We merely stood dumbly until they went back to their brandy.

One more verse had to be added, myself being part of the "three!"

I drew breath but was rudely interrupted by Chester. "Stop right there, you blighted blot! I shall not have you tooting on about yourself. You will be too kind. I shall continue with the Fairweather verse!"

"Why, Chester! I would be honoured, but I have not heard you ply your trade in this singing business. How can I trust you to tootle out a tune worthy of my good self?" I doubted.

"You shall just have to trust me," he taunted. I could see I was in for a rousing verse of some mocking, and was not disappointed.

Ohhhh…I once knew a blot of the Fairweather kind
His face resembled a bullock's behind!
He nearly drives me out of my mind
I wish the Captain had left him behind!
With…a…tum-diddlee-dum and a whoop-de-dee
Fairweather…Chester…and Lady three!

I was dumbstruck! "Good lord, evil hound! You thought this up all by yourself? The pigs and chickens did not assist you?" I mocked, trying not to laugh.

"I most certainly did and without said help!" he blustered.

"I will add that you seem to have a fine singing voice, but the lyrics, dear boy! A bullock's behind?" I was a little miffed, although I did have it coming to me after my own verses.

We were all giggling by now and the gents gave up wondering what the dickens we were up to. Then out of nowhere and quite unexpectedly came the following:

Ohhhh…We are the pigs that the men will eat,
And along with the chickens we taste a treat!
We like it when they catch much fish,
So we don't end up as the nightly dish!
With…a…tum-diddlee-dum and a whoop-de-dee
Chickens and pigs are an eating spree!

"By Jove, chums!" I addressed the pigs. "Quite a shock to hear from you! Very fine singing and a rollicking verse, I might add. Bravo pigs!" I praised.

"Thank you, Mister Fairweather!" They bowed. Mister? I was a Mister to someone? I became instantly fond of these pigs! I made myself a promise to chat with them when possible.

"How can you be so full of cheer knowing you are to be eaten?" I ventured curiously.

"We know our place and our lot in life is clear. We will all end up as supper sooner or later, but we remain cheerful all the same," said the large sow.

By now the gentry were quite drunk and befuddled by the ruckus coming from beneath them in the stalls, what with cats, dogs, and pigs singing. They staggered down to ascertain the ruckus, but by then we had ceased our singing and merely sat looking as innocent as possible, although one and all wished to carry on further into the night.

Chester and Lady retired there on the deck in the light evening airs. The gents eventually went to their quarters. I sauntered off to find my captain.

Back in the Great Cabin I found him alone. The moon shone brightly and lit up the ship, the sea, and the passing clouds. The captain picked up his eyeglass and spied land in the direction of Terra Australis Incognita! He squinted a few times and staggered over to look at his chart.

"There should be no land out there, Fairweather!" he slurred drunkenly. He consulted his maps and looked again.

"Ah, tis the Dutch found Three Kings!" I took little notice of him, as he seemed to be talking nonsense. I sauntered over to the map table to satisfy myself that his was the rambling of a drunken captain, but there on the map were three small islands and true to his word, named The Three Kings. I deemed it wise to never doubt the man, drunk or sober.

We continued partaking of our rations of rum there in the moonlight, and both saw things out the Great Cabin windows that were not there. Clouds formed odd shapes and he pointed them out to me.

"That one there…looks like King George!" he began, chuckling irreverently, leaning back on his chair. His balance gave way; the chair slipped out beneath him and down he went to the floor, still laughing while rubbing his behind from the fall.

I saw the funny side also, rolling about on the floor unable to take breath from the rum-soaked hilarity.

The captain got to his feet awkwardly and picked me up, seeing his bed as the best place to be. I did not protest as I too felt the urgent need to sleep off the drink. He fell onto his bed face down; only by a whisker was I not squashed in the process!

I could not be bothered to find a more comfortable spot for the night and I slept on his bed by his snoring head, the room spinning from my excess. Finally, sleep came and deep it was.

After the Christmas debauchery the men went quietly about their duties. The weather turned gusty again, and the swell was monstrous. This drove the gents below, especially Mister Banks who still suffered terribly from the seasickness and the wounds on his behind.

The captain attempted to cheer us all with New Year frivolity. The year 1770 was upon us on the morrow, and must be celebrated no matter how rough the sea. Henry Jeffs, now known as the ship's musician, was summoned for his "squeeze box."

We dined as best we could in the rough sea, on pork no less, and I pondered the lot of the humble singing pigs. Destined to death, but delicious all the same.

The captain ordered the usual sixteen bells at midnight and tapping his beaker with his fork, got the men's attention.

"A good friend of mine, a Scottish poet, Robert Burns wrote this song for the passing of the old year and the bringing in of the new. It is not known to anyone yet, but I do believe it will catch on for this very occasion in the future." The captain began to sing, and Henry Jeffs made up the notes as best he could.

Should auld acquaintance be forgot,
and never brought to mind?
Should auld acquaintance be forgot
and days of auld lang syne?
For auld lang syne, my dear,
For auld lang syne,
We'll take a cup o' kindness yet
For auld lang syne
We twa hae run aboot the braes
And pou'd the gowans fine;
we've wander'd mony a weary foot
Sin' auld lang syne
We two hae paidled i' the burn,
Frae mornin' sun till dine;
But seas between us braid hae roar'd
Sin' auld lang syne
And here's a hand, my trusty friend,
And gie's a hand o' thine;
We'll take a cup o' kindness yet
For auld lang syne
Should auld acquaintance be forgot,
and never brought to mind?
Should auld acquaintance be forgot
and days of auld lang syne?
For auld lang syne, my dear,
For auld lang syne,
We'll take a cup o' kindness yet
For auld lang syne

What an odd song. I was not familiar with the Scottish language but here and there were words I could understand. I hummed along, as it sounded heartfelt and tuneful at Henry Jeffs's hand. Once he had gotten the hang of the tune, he played it again and the men attempted to sing along with the odd words. When unable they merely hollered.

It was a fine mish-mash but jaunty nonetheless. All slept well that night, regardless of the tossing of the ship.

On the morn of the 1st day of January 1770, we were still only off Cape Maria van Diemen and The Three Kings. No progress had we made but to stay afloat in the ferocious seas. This western coast was battered by westerly winds and we could not dare to come too close to land for fear of being beached or holed. The captain tried at Mister Banks's beckoning to get close enough for a landing, but even Mister Banks knew that we had to keep off to avoid catastrophe.

Woody Head, Gannet Island, and Albatross Point were charted and named. It was not until mid-January that the weather turned better.

The country was more lush and greener and a huge mountain, capped in snow even though it was summer, came into view. The captain and lieutenants agreed that this mountain was as high as the Pike of Tenerife; it was some eight thousand feet! The captain named this mountain Mount Egmont after John Perceval, Second Earl of Egmont and First Lord of the Admiralty. He thought it a fitting name for such a harsh-looking mountain, as the Earl of Egmont had never laughed a day in his life!

We pulled into a favourable inlet that the captain named Queen Charlotte Sound, after the wife of King George. She would be pleased! On the 15th day of January 1770, we anchored in a small cove in the sound that we named Ship Cove, as here he wished to overhaul the ship after our long and rough voyage down the west coast of this island.

The sail maker, John Ravenhill, was behind in his duties as so many of the sails suffered damage in the harsh winds.

The carpenter, John Satterley, would need time to make good the decks and masts and "caulk" or seal between the planks of the sides of the ship.

The ship needed to be beached and "careened" or leaned over, to scrape her bottom and paint it with a mixture of tar and oil, tallow and resin to protect her timbers from the ravages of the sea.

The coopers had to make new barrels or casks for fresh water. Much work was needed here for us to carry on further.

While the men worked on the ship, the captain and Mister Banks took a party to the beach. They stumbled upon the body of a woman in the water. When greetings with the Maoris on shore were established,

Mister Banks enquired about their cannibalistic habit, having seen human bones about the camp.

Another tribe had set upon these Maoris and these killed seven of their attackers. Being their enemies, they were eaten, organs and brains alike, all but the heads, of which the hair and face was left intact, and were then dried in the sun as trophies. Mister Banks pressed them for their reasons for this cannibalism. It was merely their way. Turkel had been right about such people!

Mister Banks purchased one of the heads he had seen as a specimen and then asked why they had not eaten the body of the woman they had passed in the water. They were incensed at this. The woman was a relative, not an enemy, and they only eat of their enemies; this finally confirming what we had heard before.

The woman had died of natural causes, and relatives who pass on, are towed out to sea with a rock fastened to them so as to sink them. The woman they had passed must have come loose from her rock.

The Maoris here, whilst still of the human-eating kind, were more friendly than their Northern counterparts. The captain and gents were showed around a village in the sound.

The botanists collected plants, Mister Banks talked long with the natives and the captain climbed any hill he could find to memorize the layout for his maps. The captain believed that no white man had been here before us as Tupia was convinced they had never seen an Englishman and they did not tell of previous visitors.

They were preparing a feast and the gents were invited. Chester and Lady were invited along with my good self and Tupia had paved the way for our visit by convincing the natives that English dogs and cats are of the highest rank and an unimaginable punishment would result if we were captured for eating or our skins! We arrived in good spirits for what we hoped was a tasty treat.

Mister Banks explained that for their banquet they would dig a hole and heated rocks would be placed in it from a fire. Then the animal would be wrapped in leaves and surrounded with wrapped potatoes and yams in the searing hole. They would then cover the hole and leave the contents to cook. This was called a "hangi" and was used for all manner of meals.

Tupia explained to them that we did not have the same taste for "dog" that the Maori would be preparing and as we had brought a pig, we would prefer to eat the latter. They understood this to be our way and the chief cook called for it to be brought forward.

It was our biggest pig and as such animals were not native to New Zealand, there would be enough for all and the Maoris were in for a fine treat. Mister Banks explained how to prepare the animal and our lips smacked as the hair was singed off. We looked forward to our feast, as this form of cooking underground as in Tahiti ensured a tender and succulent meal!

Chester, Lady, and I took our seats with the gents around a rather large fire pit to examine the cooking method. One had already been prepared and was rather large.

"Chester, old thing, that hole for cooking dog seems rather large, what? They must have a huge breed here for eating!" I proposed.

"I have seen the dogs about as we arrived and I believe they must be planning to cook two or three as the dogs I saw are not as big as that hole." Chester moaned, incensed at his breed being considered as a meal. "Savages," he muttered under his breath.

"Try to understand," soothed Lady. "They have eaten of our species since time began, dear! We cannot hope to change their ways!" She was perfectly correct but still Chester could not abide it.

"Hurrumph" was all he could manage.

"Well, I, for one, am looking forward to a morsel of pig!" I smacked my lips as the gents shuffled about, trying to sit comfortably on the ground.

Mister Banks was giving the captain and others a running commentary on this form of cuisine, and as always he would be happy to taste the local fare, dog or not!

"You see, Captain? We must honour these folk by sampling their native food. Insult could lead to harsh feelings towards us," urged Mister Banks.

"If we must, Mister Banks," mumbled the captain, not quite convinced but compliant nonetheless.

Tupia spoke long with them while they prepared the pig and dog, but I for one could only see one dog going into the hole along with our pig. I imagined they must have had vegetable accompaniments aplenty to add to the oversized oven.

The Maori cook ordered two assistants to bring forward the rest of the food to be cooked. Tupia shook his head and looked pleadingly at Mister Banks.

The addition to the oven was a man!

"They are cooking the last of the seven enemies they killed before his flesh turns rotten!" Tupia explained. Out came two Maoris carrying the naked headless body!

"This is the body of the man whose head Mister Banks purchased. They thought that Mister Banks would honour them by eating of him!" Tupia explained.

Chester, Lady, and I merely sat eyes wide in shock.

"Well, Mister Banks?" said the captain with a little mocking to his voice. "You will be pleased to comply, will you not?" Tupia was translating all the while and the Maoris looked hopefully at Mister Banks.

"Er…Well…" he fumbled. Once the enthusiast of Maori cuisine, when he only had to taste dog! Now he stuttered over his own keenness having been put right on the spot!

The assembled tribe were keen to learn of his answer, as they knew us not to be cannibals, and had brought our own pig to roast in the earthen oven.

Mister Banks's face reddened somewhat and there was nothing more he could do but agree.

"Of course, I will try it!" he tried to save face after stuttering so, not liking this position one bit, I suspected.

The captain nodded his approval and the feast was laid in the hole to cook for the afternoon. The dog, the pig, and the Maori enemy were gently lowered into the pit and wrapped in large leaves.

"Will this feast take some time to cook?" asked the captain.

"Yes, apparently, man takes a good long time to become tender," Mister Banks answered without feeling, realising what he had gotten himself into.

The rest of the gents smiled as they were not required to partake, and Mister Banks excused himself to take his mind off the awful thought of eating human flesh. Tupia explained what the Maori cook had told him. The Englishmen were free to look around the village and crops until the meal was ready, some two or three hours.

"Me thinks Mister Banks has some time to suffer in wait of his dinner!" I laughed, turning to Chester, who was as pale as I had seen him, still wide-eyed in shock.

"I would not have thought he would eat of the canine species, let alone human!" he mumbled, turning to Lady.

"No, dear, I must admit it has taken me aback, but he must know that to eat of our kind, and of man, it would keep the peace with the natives."

"He might keep the natives happy, Lady, but believe me, his stock will plummet with the men when they learn of this development. Englishmen just do not eat people!" I could hardly believe he was up for it!

"Mister Banks is a keen scientist!" Chester rebuffed at my mocking. "In the pursuit of knowledge and facts he must feel the need to experiment with this Maori cuisine, so as to be in the know!" Chester tried his best to make excuses for his master, but I was having none of it.

"Well, he's in the soup, me thinks! He either has to eat as he has promised and be the brunt of much amongst our crew, or he declines and angers the natives!" I confirmed.

"You are correct, Fairweather. He is in the soup!" Chester admitted. We three rested under a tree while the captain and gents toured the village. Their crops were of particular interest as they had them lined up and cultivated for ease in picking.

Potato and yam were the chief crop, but bananas were grown not only for the fruit; the leaves were excellent for wrapping meat for the "hangi."

Mister Banks's man was wrapped in the very same and all afternoon, Chester, Lady, and I, while napping safely, could smell at least one familiar smell, pork! Chester drooled a little but slathered it all back into his mouth in case he was seen to be enjoying the smell of roasting dog or man!

I, for one, only snoozed for fear that the Fairweather skin or flesh might be too tempting for the native Maori! I was not vigilant enough, though!

During a catnap, I felt the grip of a strong hand on my scruff. Within the blink of an eye, I was swooped from my safety, into the air to disable my claws, and off in the direction of the kitchen area! Not this again! I thought Tupia had explained the punishment, should harm come to us!

"You will be next furry thing!" said the Maori chief. "I like your fur and it will make me a very important man to have this skin on my best coat!"

Chester had slept with one eye open and having seen my kidnapping, barked ferociously with Lady bringing up the rear.

"Chester! Don't just bark, you fiend! I am being abducted for apparel! Bite the fleshy parts of this thieving monster!"

"I am barking to warn Mister Banks of danger and he will know our tone and hear it for miles! I will let no harm come to you! Be patient!" he barked.

"But Chester! Lady! This brute wants my skin for his coat and probably to roast me afterwards!" I was breathless from the grip and his hastening to the kitchen. "He looks to be a strong chap and may be swift with a knife!" I wailed, howling, and yowling and trying to scratch him, but his grip had me paralysed.

The dogs barked ferociously as the Maori chief gave the order for the cook to skin me. I was thrust onto a chopping block being the stump of a hewn tree. No one had come! Chester and Lady barked and howled but the gents must have been further into the fields than they thought!

The glimmer of a knife appeared. I was doomed.

Just then, Chester jumped and bit down hard on the arm of the cook that was holding the knife. He yelled and dropped it on the ground, clutching the wound for it was deep and bleeding. The Maori chief picked the knife up and cleaned it off on his garment, all the while holding me down!

Lady jumped and bit the arm of the chief just as he was about to strip me of my hide. He, too, dropped the knife and had to hold it to stop the bleeding.

"Dogs! Only good for eating! I will have you both next as skinny as you are!" he threatened. Chester was infuriated.

Woofing wildly, he leapt and knocked the Maori chief to the ground and stood upon him, pinning him down, snarling and baring his sharp teeth. The chief could not move for fear of attack.

I leapt from the chopping block and up the nearest tree. Just as the cook began to pull at Chester to get him off the chief, Mister Banks showed up, musket loaded and drawn. Panting wildly from the run to the ruckus, he pointed his musket at the chief's head.

"Chester! Away!" Chester released his captive and backed away, whining at me up the tree.

The musket point touched the chief's nose and his eyes widened in fear of the white man's weapon.

As the rest of the gents and the captain turned up, Tupia asked what had gone on here. They talked much and argued with wildly waving arms once Mister Banks let the chief get to his feet. All the while his musket was pointed at the chief's head. Other Maoris turned up to see what all the noise was about.

The captain strode forward. "What is this transgression, for which I have been forced to run from the findings?" He was not a happy man, especially with his chief botanist holding a loaded musket at the Maori chief's head!

Tupia explained the doings whilst Chester and Lady stood upright and regal, and I stood in the highest limb of the tree. I was not coming down until this business was settled!

"You have been warned that the dogs and the cat are crewmen of our highest rank and yet you threaten to kill and skin them in our absence?" barked the captain. "I should let Mister Banks blow your wretched heads off!" Their eyes widened as every tone could be heard in every word Tupia translated.

They stood resolute that they would get what they wanted as the price to pay for their supper of pig, dog, and man!

"He wants the Fairweather coat to make him a more important chief than all others! The dogs were protecting Fairweather and had to bite them to release him from a skinning on this very stump." He pointed to where I was to meet my death. "Then the dogs were next on his killing list for biting him and his cook!" Tupia explained excitedly. "He felt it is his right to them, for serving us such a delicacy as man for supper!"

Mister Banks piped in, needing an out for having to taste of human flesh.

"Let him keep his feast! We will take the dogs and cat back to the ship to ensure their safety, right after I blow a hole in these fellows' heads!" threatened Mister Banks, his eye lining up both the cook and the chief in his sights, his arm still cocked and at the ready to blow either of their heads off!

"That will not be necessary, Mister Banks!" composed the captain. "We will return to the ship en masse and not partake in their feast! They will then not require the cat and dogs as payment!"

The look of gratitude on Mister Banks's face was enough to assure me of some safety.

Chester and Lady stood proud that their status was so high as to have the captain refuse a feast with the native Maoris. I, however, was not coming out of that tree, as the eye of the chief was still keenly fixed on the Fairweather coat!

"Fairweather! It is safe to come down! I will escort you to the longboat myself!" yelled the captain to my lofty perch.

I dithered not a little, but Mister Banks held his musket sights on the errant chief and I felt it safe to edge my way to the captain's waiting arms. I must say, that blasted chief did not take his eye off me for a second, and would have snatched me and absconded had Mister Banks not kept his aim and threatened to blow off his head!

"Gentlemen?" the captain ordered. "To the boat!"

The natives were confused as they had used their last man to cook us a rare feast and we were leaving without joining them. They asked Tupia if we wished them to dig up our pig.

"They can keep the pig and tell them so, Tupia!" barked the captain.

With that, we marched off to the boat, Mister Banks at the rear walking backwards with his sights and musket still aimed at the felonious chief and cook, ready to blast away should they follow.

The captain held me firmly under his arm and as brave as I had been under previous threats, I could not hold my head high at this point. I nuzzled under the captain's arm to try and rid myself of the evil glare of the chief, which kept appearing in my mind even when we were out of their sight!

To his credit, Mister Banks kept his weapon aimed at the pursuing Maoris, even at the beach as we returned to the ship. He was a cautious man where threatening natives and the health of his dogs were concerned.

When we were all safely back on board, the captain did not release his hold upon me until we reached the Great Cabin, where he placed me on my favourite chair. Mister Banks and the dogs followed him in and the lieutenants awaited an explanation as to why we had returned before feasting time.

All was revealed as Mister Banks sat with a cleansing brandy to steady his nerves while he petted both Chester and Lady for their gallant actions. The captain merely gave me a scratch under the chin, but I was ever so grateful that I remained intact and back on the ship!

Henry Jeffs and John Thompson were ordered to prepare extra for us who had returned unfed, and not to mention special treats for Chester, Lady, and I.

Mister Banks tucked into the usual fare with renewed vigour having been saved from eating a Maori man. It must have stuck in his mind for a while, as he ceased his whining about the ship's food, and even thanked Henry and John for their efforts for some long time after.

Chester, Lady, and I decided that evening to remain on the ship for the duration of this New Zealand, no matter how long it took!

CHAPTER 29

On the 26th day of January, the captain, misters Banks and Spöring, and Doctor Solander climbed a high peak and built a pyramid of stones encasing musket balls, small shot, silver coins and beads which would survive the test of time, so that any who came there would know the English had been here first.

From his vantage point on the peak, the captain could not help but notice that the sea separated the northern part of New Zealand from the South! This would be tested by sailing further east, until either land stopped us, or the sea ran through, proving that New Zealand was two separate islands! The captain could hardly wait! He returned to this place a few days later and erected the English flag, taking possession of Queen Charlotte Sound and adjacent lands for His Majesty the King.

He gave the old natives present threepenny pieces dated 1763, or spike nails with the king's arrow cut deep into them. They would treasure these and keep them long, proving we had been the first Europeans here. Tupia quizzed the elders regarding the strait cutting this New Zealand into two islands. They confirmed this and made the captain all the more determined to sail and chart it.

On the 7th day of February, we waited for the tide to lift the *Endeavour* off her bottom and off we went to find the eastern sea through what may or may not be a passage. The tide was fierce through here and we had so little wind that the ship almost drifted onto rocks, only for the swift-thinking captain putting out anchors to stop us!

We journeyed south-easterly and surely enough, we were in a passage cutting New Zealand into two separate islands! The captain was so pleased that he named it Cook Strait! Some of the officers did not believe that New Zealand was two islands, so the captain set our course northerly until we were standing off Cape Turnagain, where we had already sailed on the eastern coast! The captain had circumnavigated the now North Island of New Zealand! He called the officers to the deck for them to see that this indeed was an island. All doubt of his ability was now gone.

He set our course southerly to map and chart what the captain thought was another island to the south. It was not Terra Australis Incognita, but his discovery of this magnitude would be momentous for this voyage, the Royal Society, and His Majesty the King!

We passed a significant peninsula and to keep the man happy it was named Banks Peninsula as the gent of that name was sullen and cranky in the rough weather, not only being confined to the ship but seasick to boot. As sick as he was, he was rather chuffed.

The captain spoke long with me in the Great Cabin alone for the next few days. His lieutenants were not convinced that this southerly place we were sailing was indeed a part of New Zealand. They were happier to believe that this was Terra Australis Incognita. I trusted my captain, of course, but there were doubts with the lieutenants and the gents.

"They are so desirous of this being the undiscovered continent, Fairweather," he muttered forlornly whilst I sat on his maps. I traced a rough oval with my claw extended, over the place we were sailing off, which still took him by surprise. He should have known the Fairweather mind by now!

"You believe as I do that this be an island?" he asked incredulously.

I nodded and continued to circle the area.

"Yes, well, you seem to be the only soul other than I to know it to be true! Blasted officers! I proved that the northern island was absolutely that! Why do they question me, Fairweather?" I rubbed my face across his hand, which extended to where my paw was circling on the map.

"Yes, I know you to agree but what am I to tell them? That Fairweather, my cat, confirms my reckoning and tells me so? They would lock me up with a compress of some sort and the medico would be sought!" He was quite right. I was his only ally in this reasoning, and he had to keep quiet about it.

We stood off this South Island for five days making no progress south as the winds would not allow it. Tempers frayed and my captain took solace in the Great Cabin with me, his only supporter.

On the 25th day of February, a fresh and strong gale from the north took our sails and directed us south, the captain keeping us slightly west to map the land.

He named Cape Saunders in honour of Sir Charles Saunders, Lord of the Admiralty and Honorary Order of the Bath! Order of the Bath? I thought it an odd distinction. To be knighted for simply having a wash was a bit of a stretch! I since learned that this "Bath" business harked back to days when a knight would be "bathed" and honoured in a river, or fountain in the lack thereof. British Orders of Chivalry were an odd lot! I heard the captain speak of them at times. "The Most Noble Order of the Garter," "The Most Ancient and Most Nobel Order of the Thistle," and other strange nobilities like "The Most Favourable Grand Order of the Whatsit" and "Thingy." I had become bored with the whole idea. I wondered, however, if there would ever be an "Order of the Most Extraordinary Fairweather!" After my contribution to the discoveries we were making, I thought it entirely possible as long as my captain recommended it! Knights and cats near and far would strive to achieve it!

The captain was a smart sailor and wished to be promoted after his return. Honouring those he knew back in good old England would be to his advantage. Besides which, the names he chose to honour the living were far more distinguished than the odd names he conjured from time to time as we have already discussed!

Continuing south, we were driven off the land and too far east of the coast for any landings or charting. The captain had to battle into the driving winds to bring us back on course to hug the coastline.

By the 4th day of March, we were again just off land and approaching what seemed to be a small island; Stewart Island was now on his charts. We saw large fires on the land and very smoky, but no inhabitants. Mister Banks was certain that the Maoris set the fires, but this southern land was only sparsely populated, and to his vexation no landings were scheduled here.

We rounded Stewart Island but the winds during the night of the 10th saw us too close to land and not far enough west to sail up the eastern side of this southern New Zealand island, so it was back out to sea for us, to reposition our tack further west to continue mapping the coastline.

The captain felt this was his mistake when I consulted with him in the Great Cabin. I could do nought to reassure him that this was uncharted territory and the odd mishap in guessing where to sail could be well expected.

On our way back out to sea we passed a tiny island. The face of it had a very rugged aspect; full of high craggy hills on the summits of which were several patches of snow. The captain named this Solander Island after the good doctor. The land was barren and we saw no sign of inhabitants.

Little penguins swam alongside the ship as we sailed. Mister Banks thought them smaller than the penguins we had seen before and his interest in categorizing was singular in his mind. "*Eudyptula minor*" he called them as I watched them duck and dive swimming as fast as we were sailing.

They were no bigger than yours truly and were fun to watch. Their coats were blue and they had white bellies, so Mister Banks referred to them as "blue penguins" for ease.

They strangely barked each time they surfaced. The scientists agreed that they must have been calling for their partners or young.

Other larger penguins were sighted but rarely; they were the yellow-eyed penguin and bigger than their blue counterparts. The Maoris knew them as "Hoiho" but Mister Banks categorised them *Megadyptes antipodes*.

I could not help but wonder where these long and difficult names came from. Did it make Mister Banks feel more important that no one else could pronounce them? Or was there some method or formula one must follow to categorise an animal?

I decided to seek Chester out on the matter, he knowing all things scientific.

"Chester, old boy. What is with this categorizing business?" I asked.

"Each species has a scientific name. 'Genus' is the taxonomic word given to scientific classification," he answered casually, as if I should already know.

"Taxonomic? I asked you to explain the word 'genus'! Not to confuse me more with your large vocabulary, you ninny!" I spat.

"Taxonomy is the science of classification from the Greek word 'taxis' meaning order or arrangement." He sighed, bored with this line of chat.

"I am not interested in an in-depth reply, you goat! Genus! Keep to the word in question!" I demanded.

"I am trying to explain it, you daft creature! You did ask!" he blustered.

"Yes, yes! Out with it then!" I wished to learn but found it difficult with this wordy Chester.

"Genus is the rank of a living thing. The taxonomic names of which begin with 'Kingdom,' then 'Division,' 'Class,' 'Order,' 'Family,' 'Genus,' 'Species.'" I was baffled.

"Chester, you bore, in English please!" I was losing my patience.

"There are that many different names for one living thing! Each and every one different!" He was getting cross with me.

"Well, you could have come out with that much sooner!" I snapped.

"You, annoying brat, are '*Felinae*', from the family '*Felidae*'. And your genus is '*Felis Catus*.'"

"This is not to my liking, Chester! I rather fancy that my genus is more impressive. '*Fairweatherus felinus spectacularis*'? Or how about '*Felinus fairweatherus fantasticus*'? The mind boggles with the possibilities!" I gloated.

"Something more to the order of '*Fairweatherus botherus exasperatus*' would be my guess!" He chuckled to himself, feeling rather clever.

"Chester, you blot! What is your genus then?" I challenged.

"'*Canis lupus familiaris*' is our genus!" he blustered proudly.

I laughed hysterically. "'Lupus'? From the word 'loopy'!"

"Cease and desist, you loathsome creature! It is a fine and distinguished genus!" Chester stood firm.

"Let me think, '*Canis pompousis ridiculosus*'!" I could barely catch my breath for laughing so hard. Chester began a smile he could no longer hold as I continued. "How about '*Irritatus canis brutus*'?" Chester cackled now, as he could not help himself against my witty scientific names for him. We both rolled about in hysterics as Lady arrived on the scene.

"What in heaven's name is the matter with you two?" she asked, wanting in on the joke.

"Ah!" I declared. "Here is *Femalis canis wonderus*!" Chester and I both laughed harder.

"I am at a loss. You are both ninnies!" She lifted her snout and strode off to sulk.

"I do believe we are in the soup, my botanist friend," I announced still hysterical.

"I do concur, fellow scientist!" Chester laughed.

"I shall catch up with her and explain or she will be miffed with us for some time," I suggested.

"Fine plan. Yes, have us out of trouble, would you?" Chester begged.

"Consider it done." I waltzed off, leaving the chuckling Chester and sought out Lady, explaining all. She laughed as we had done, so I gathered we were both out of the soup, and high and dry.

We had rounded the bottom of this snow-capped southern island and in my captain's opinion we would end up where we started in Cook Strait as long as we followed the land along this westerly coast.

Along the way were many bays but the weather on this coast made it too difficult for a landing, the winds being gusty and fickle and the swell, quite high.

We passed and named Doubtful Sound, George's Sound, and Milford Sound. The newly coined "sound" had me perplexed. I had not heard a sound! I had been straining my well-trained ear to detect a "sound" and heard nought but the winds and sea! My quizzical expression must have prompted an explanation from the captain whilst he charted them in the evenings, a "sound" having been explained to me as a deep ocean inlet. I was much relieved to have the correct information and ceased straining for some kind of noise!

All along this coast we had seen no sign of inhabitants. Perhaps the bareness of the land and the snow was not to their liking. Hazy weather and foul winds had the entire crew in grumpy spirits. Cape Foulwind was named at this place where none had a civil word for another.

We had come closer to shore than we had dared but enormous surf held us off land. We came around the northernmost point and found ourselves back in Cook Strait, with the easterly wind freshening.

My captain had circumnavigated both islands, proving that there was indeed a north and south islands of New Zealand! The doubters were no longer! He expected little praise as was his way, and made it his mission now to land on an island he had previously seen from Queen Charlotte Sound to replenish the ship.

The captain sailed us into a Low Neck Bay at D'Urville Island on the 26th March 1770, where he deemed it fit for an anchorage to wood and water. The captain was singularly minded to collect as much supply as the ship would hold. As many as ninety fish were caught by the crew out the cabin windows alone, and Tupia and Tiata caught a boatload.

Mister Banks and a few of the crew came down with a wretched fever, headache, and retching. This kept Mister Banks from botanizing the area. Whilst this illness did not affect the entire ship's company, we deduced that a stale fish or two might have seen itself on the odd man's dinner plate.

The weather was most foul, but during the odd break in it the captain went ashore to map the inlet.

On the night before sailing, I attended him in the Great Cabin. He was growing impatient to fulfil his secret orders. As we had rounded and charted New Zealand, he wished to be away from this place and in search of Terra Australis Incognita, for which we had both charted our potential course.

Mister Banks had recovered somewhat, and barging in to the Great Cabin, he assembled the gents to give us his account of New Zealand for the Royal Society.

"As we intend to leave this place tomorrow morning, I shall describe what I have seen of this country and its inhabitants, conjecturing and drawing conclusions from my observations, in which I may doubtless be mistaken, but in my daily journal the observations may be seen, and any one may draw his own conclusions from them, attending as little as he pleases to any of mine." Mister Banks began with rather a more negative tone than usual. I judged that he was frustrated with this New Zealand, but we were all ears for his findings nonetheless.

"This country was first discovered by Abel Jansen Tasman on the 13th day of December 1642 and called by him New Zealand. However, he never went ashore upon it, probably for fear of the natives, who when he had come to anchor killed three or four of the seven people in his longboat.

"He also sailed into the mouth of Cook Strait but did sail through it, nor discover that New Zealand was two separate Islands as our good captain did!"

A gentlemanly round of applause was raised for the captain's brave endeavour, as the last doubts were put to rest.

I did not know of this Tasman, and neither did the gents, so all were impressed with Mister Banks's knowledge and finally our captain's fortitude!

"The face of this country is in general mountainous, especially inland and covered with snow. The sea coasts abound in good harbours for wooding and watering. The coasts are barren especially on the South Island, but the hills behind are covered with thick wood and every valley produces a rivulet.

"The soil is light and admirably adapted for root crops that the natives cultivate. Poverty and Tolaga bays had immense woodlands and swamps and the soil promising much from the size of the plants that grew there. The timber trees are the straightest, cleanest and largest I have ever seen."The new River Thames is indeed in every respect the best place we have seen for establishing a colony. A ship as large as ours might be carried several miles up the river, and moored to the trees as safely as alongside anywhere in London.

"The noble timber would furnish plenty of materials for fences, houses and vessels. The river would supply plenty of fish and the soil would make ample return of any European vegetables sown in it."The South Island is more hilly and barren than the North and I believe it to abound in minerals in a very high degree, although without proper investigation it is merely a guess."Dogs and rats were the only quadrupeds I saw, again from the brevity of our landings. There are probably more animals to this land but no evidence I saw, as the natives did not permit us to enter the land fully. I did see the kiwi, and hawks, owls, and quails not much differing to our English, but several small birds I had never seen before that sing more melodiously than I have ever heard!"

They would have been rather tasty too, I thought, but for my not going ashore!

"Insects were no more plentiful than birds. Butterflies, beetles, flies, mosquitoes and sandflies made up the whole list, but at least the latter did not swarm and make going ashore troublesome."For the scarcity of animals on the land, the sea made abundant recompense. We bought many luxurious lobsters from the natives. They differ from our English sea crawfish, with more spikes upon their backs and are red coming out of the water even before cooking. Delicious!" He smiled and rubbed his belly, and I imagined his last comment did not appear in his notes, but the captain and gents all agreed, as did I who had sampled the luscious lobster!

"The plants were not new to us, one or two kinds of grasses exactly the same as in England, three or four kinds of fern the same as those in the West Indies. "We ate the plentiful wild celery and cresses that grew abundantly by the seaside for our health, and met with the herb that English country folk call 'lamb's quarters,' an edible weed tasting somewhat like spinach.

"Yams, sweet potatoes, and coconuts are much esteemed by the natives, cultivating many acres at a time. They grew gourds, the fruits of which they used as jugs and bottles. The Chinese paper mulberry tree is used to make cloth, much the same as the Tahitians, but the tree is scarce there and the cloth from it much valued. "Fruits they seem to have none but some insipid berries. Hemp or flax was their best product, and their clothes were made from it in various qualities. They even used the fibres for their fishing lines. "The people seemed not to favour the seacoasts and lived further inland. The men were stout, clean limbed and active, and fleshy but rarely fat. They were vigorous and nimble and clever in their exercise. I saw a canoe paddled by fifteen men directed by one man, and there was not a fraction of a second observed between the dipping and raising of their paddles, and the canoe moved with incredible swiftness!" We all enjoyed Mister Banks's animated descriptions!

"We have all seen their Haka and all here would agree that it showed incredible strength, firmness and agility and kept time without mistake." Everyone nodded, being well acquainted with their war dance.

"The women were not delicate in appearance but smaller than European women. They had a particular softness of voice, which distinguished them from the men who were dressed exactly alike. They were more lively, airy and laughter-loving than the men and had more volatile spirits. "The disposition of both sexes seemed mild, gentle and affectionate to each other but implacable to their enemies, who after having killed they eat, probably out of revenge! They were predisposed to war and when performing their Haka, worked themselves up to a kind of artificial courage which was only placated after they felt the sting of our small shot, then upon recollecting themselves, were sensible and became friends with us. "Not having a warm climate, the people were not as clean as the Tahitians, as it was too cold to wash often. They oiled their hair with the rancid fat of fish or birds. Both sexes tattoo themselves with the colour of black as the Tahitians, and in the same way. The women seem content to have their lips blacked. The men carried this custom to greater lengths and added to their quantity every year of their lives so that the elderly were almost covered in tattoos!

"Their faces were the most remarkable and by some art unknown to me they dug furrows in them as deep as broad, which were indented and perfectly black. As ugly as this looked it was impossible to avoid admiring the immense elegance and justness of the different spirals and all finished with masterly taste and execution. To look upon one hundred of them, you would judge them all to be the same but upon closer examination no two would prove alike. Both sexes bored their ears and wore in them a great variety of ornaments, stretching the holes to the diameter of a finger. "Their houses were scarce equal to a European dog kennel, barely high and wide enough to admit a man crawling on all fours. The walls and roof were of dry grass and tightly put together to keep them warm. Many had a carving over the door that they seemed to value as we do a picture. They laid thick straw on which to sleep, but they did not bother with furniture; just a box, which held their tools, clothes, weapons, and a few feathers to stick in their hair. I did see some houses grouped together and fenced and I gathered they were for families. "They eat dogs!" Chester's head went up hoping we would be away from here soon.

"Penguin, albatross, and fish, sweet potato, yams, coconuts. Wild thistle, palm cabbage, and what seems like bread to us, the roots of a species of bracken fern common in the hills. "Their boats showed their ingenuity. They are built of planks sewed together; their sides rounding up like ours, but very narrow for their length. The common fishing canoes were adorned with the carved face of a man with a monstrous tongue and whose eyes were inlaid with mother of pearl shell. The larger canoes seemed intended for war and more magnificently adorned with carvings and feathers. "Their tools were of stone and their axes their most prized possession. Their nets for fishing were made in a similar manner to our own and the making is the joint effort and property of the whole town. They were as large as I have ever seen in Europe. "They excelled in cultivation. Their crops evenly rowed and expertly planted. Tillage, weaving and the rest of the arts are best known in the north-eastern parts. "War seemed to be the most practised in the south-western parts. Their weapons were well calculated for bloody fights and the destruction of many. Their spears were made of hardwood and pointed at both ends, some fifteen to sixteen feet long and held in the middle for balance. Battle-axes were likewise of hardwood, the bottom of the handle like the blade of an axe for chopping at their enemies' heads. Patoo-patoos were a kind of small bludgeon of stone, bone or hardwood, most admirably calculated for the cracking of skulls and fastened to their wrists with strong straps and they were rarely seen without them hung from their waists.

"When the large canoes came out to the ship with their chiefs they held ensigns with their tribal designs, threatening us, calling 'Come to us, come to us, come but ashore with us and we will kill you with our Patoo-patoos'. As we all witnessed, they would then begin their war dance and it was necessary to chastise them by firing small shot at them, when they would then leave us."

"Thankfully!" interjected the captain, not at all pleased with the vigilance required for these surprise attacks!

Mister Banks gave him a quieting frown and continued.

"I had the assistance of Tupia to guide me through a story told to me! They had surprised a canoe of their enemies and they had killed seven of them. The meat on them had been eaten and the bones thrown away, which we could see near the fires. This was more confirmed by an old man we supposed to be the chief who came out to us a few days later with several preserved men's heads with the flesh still on. He explained that their brains were eaten as trophies of their victory. You will remember I purchased one that seemed to belong to a person of fourteen or fifteen years showing contusions to one side of it from many blows. I have it preserved in the hold."

Mister Banks was enjoying this gory story but we all winced at his description as it was against the code of Englishmen, dogs, and cats, to eat of people!

"The state of war that they live in warranted the building of forts, which they did by a broad ditch and a well-constructed palisade of eighteen to twenty feet. They could then throw their darts and spears at the advancing enemies. They held a large provision of food in them in case of a long siege."The men tilled the ground, fished in boats, killed birds, and wove the nets. The women dug up fern roots, collected shellfish and lobsters near the beach, prepared the victuals and weaved cloth."We saw few signs of religion and no public place of worship. "Burial of their dead prompted no pompous ceremony; here it was kept a secret. We had not seen so much as a grave. In the northern parts they told us they buried the dead in the ground and in the southern parts threw them into the sea with sufficient weight tied to them for them to sink. They all carried scars from the cuts they administer to themselves during their mourning of their dead, much like the Tahitians with their shark tooth. "I conclude that due to the similarity of the customs, traditions and language between these people and the Tahitians, there remains little doubt that they came originally from the same source."

Mister Banks took a deep breath and closed his journal. I marvelled at how the man was able to gather such information in so small a time. I imagined he must have an enormous brain! He and the gents dispersed to their evening rituals, and after they left us alone I attended the maps with my captain.

"I would prefer to take the route home via Cape Horn," he mumbled. "This would prove or disprove the existence of the Terra Australis Incognita."

I pointed out our route again to him, somehow knowing this would take us to the undiscovered land.

"Yes, Fairweather. You and I both know we are correct. Sailing to the Cape of Good Hope would find us nothing new. We shall head for this Australia and then take a northerly route as we have previously discussed." I nodded my approval and we both retired for the night.

On the morning of 31st March 1770, fully stocked and ready for adventure we set sail heading west, passing Cape Farewell as our last New Zealand landmark. The captain was mightily pleased to be rid of this unwelcoming place!

I inspected the stores and found little activity among the mice. I had kept them down to fair proportions, but since this New Zealand, they had grown in number. I set about capturing them for John Thompson, knowing that should he come down there and see the nibbled holes in his sacks of grain, he would question my utility. Just as I was rounding up my ninth and tenth, John and his servant Thomas Matthews came down to fetch the malt, which had lain unused since we departed England.

"Ah, there you are, cat! Good work. Fetch 'em out of 'ere and keep 'em from the grain!" I did so, as if I needed reminding!

"The good doctor had an idea to boil the malt and mix it with the wheat for breakfast." He explained to Thomas heaving a sack of the stuff down from the pile and puffing not a little. "Thinks it might help keep away the scurvy. 'Ere lad, you carry it!"

Thomas heaved the sack onto his shoulder and they both left. I thought it interesting to follow so I picked up my mice and headed for the kitchen with them.

Thomas Matthews took my delivery and threw them out the cabin window while John set to cooking up the messy brew. The crew seemed to enjoy the change of flavour to their morning boiled wheat, and as I was given a portion, approved of it by scoffing the lot in record time.

"Mousin' give you an appetite, cat?" John spotted me relishing his brew. I had to admit it did make one hungry! Catching but not eating them dried the tongue somewhat!

After a few days of the new breakfast, Mister Banks came to see John Thompson and congratulate him on this muddled new concoction as it had miraculously cured him of his seasickness! Word soon got around and most agreed that the new addition to the breakfast wheat settled their stomachs, although none were too pleased that it would see Mister Banks up and about more often!

By the 7th day of April, we were well on our way to where we thought Terra Australis Incognita to be. The weather became milder and the sea calmer, giving rise to the speculation of land being close.

Private John Bowles was given a dozen lashes for refusing to do his duty, even though asked twice by Sergeant Edgcumbe and Bosun's Mate Thomas Hardman. I had to come to terms with this punishment as my captain proved to run an orderly ship.

The sea continued calm and the weather warmed.

A few red-tailed tropical birds were seen about the ship, and flying fish! My newest discovery. I watched them keenly from the rigging and when Mister Banks was ready to enlighten I listened with great enthusiasm.

"These fish have sizeable pectoral fins with which they glide above water to escape predators. The fish propels itself with the tail whilst in the water, then when airborne the fins are flexed, keeping them aloft for some one hundred and sixty feet." He told all who would listen.

I liked flying fish! A cross between a bird and a fish would be relished by any feline! The botanists found them impossible to catch as they were either flying or ducking and a method could not be formed to secure one. I was a little miffed as I am always keen to sample the varied cuisine of the sea!

Mister Banks had the nets cast and drew up a strange jelly like creature with long tentacles. He categorized them and then got a little too close for his own good. One such tentacle brushed his arm and an agonizing wail came from the man.

"These stingeth more than a nettle! I am off to the surgeon for some balm! Write down my findings Mister Sp*öring!" He stomped away*, cursing.

"Blasted something and blasted something else!" he mumbled.

In Mister Banks's absence, Mister Spöring shot an albatross and its stomach contents included the stinging thing. All wondered how it could digest such a nasty beast. I deemed it wise to not go near the jelly blubber!

Portuguese man of war was another of the jellyfish kind. A smaller air-filled character of attractive bright blue, they floated seemingly aimless on the surface of the sea, but upon netting one and bringing it up, the tentacles descended some thirty feet down into the ocean, so as to sting and haul up small fish or shrimp for its meal. Mister Spöring found himself entangled in the tentacles; they stuck to his flesh and a burning pain resulted, sending him below crying for attention by the surgeon, Doctor Monkhouse. He was certainly kept busy by Mister Banks need to drag anything from the sea for botanising. The crew knew to keep away from such beasts, and I for one was with them all the way!

Porpoises leapt about the bow of the *Endeavour* as if chauffeuring King George himself to a garden party! Their whole bodies leapt fully above the water as if to dare us to play with them. I enjoyed watching their tricks, for it must be a powerful tail to send them soaring into the air as well as keeping up with the ship!

The change in weather brought a damp mist, which wetted the fur through, and the crewmen's clothes began to mould. Shearwaters and albatross gathered about the ship, but the smaller birds and gannets rested in the rigging, letting us all sense that land was not far off.

At night, the captain and lieutenants gathered excitedly in the Great Cabin, referring to Dirk Rembrantse's published notes of Abel Tasman's sighting of Australia. It stated that Tasman's land was due south of our current position, but the captain kept our course west so as to fall in somewhere near it.

I was rather chuffed that my coordinates in agreement with the captain had been followed and it was decided by all that we were not far from it!

On the 19th day of April, Lieutenant Hicks climbed high into the rigging, always keen to be the first to sight land. I, too, followed him as the momentum of finding Terra Australis Incognita grew!

I spotted land before the lieutenant, as my keen eyesight caught its first glimpse. As I was not able to utter the customary "Land ahoy!" that was required, I sunk my paw into the Lieutenant's leg to gain his attention to the correct aspect.

He turned, annoyed at me, and then spotted it for himself.

"Land ahoy!" he cried, excitedly rubbing at his leg from my signalling technique. Down we went to the eager captain and crew.

"Well done, Lieutenant Hicks!" The captain patted the man on the back. I had to take pleasure in my discovering it first quietly as I could not utter the words. The lieutenant continued to rub at his clawed leg and as the captain knew me to be in the rigging with the lieutenant, did at some point suspect that I had something to do with the sighting. It was enough pride for me!

"I shall name this place Point Hicks!" said the captain rather chuffed. The lieutenant thanked him.

We kept our course as the captain and lieutenants held an impromptu meeting around the bittacle for their coordinates.

"This is not Terra Australis Incognita!" said the captain resolute.

"No, we appear to be further north than Tasman's charts suggest!" Lieutenant Gore agreed excitedly.

"I see no land south of this point, where the mysterious land should be, so I suggest that Tasman's land is an island off this continent, this being Terra Australis Incognita!"

It had been said! By the captain himself! Word soon spread from whoever could hear them and shouts of joy came from every corner of the ship. The crew knew that extra liquor rations and a fine dinner would be forthcoming!

The captain steered the *Endeavour* north, determined to follow this land and prove it to be the elusive Great Southern Continent.

The men worked with renewed vigour, knowing they would go down in history if this land was indeed Terra Australis Incognita!

Chester and Lady joined us at the bittacle.

"The captain has found the continent then?" asked Chester.

"Yes, Fairweather, has he done it? Really?" added Lady.

"On the contrary, fine hounds. I, Fairweather of the Bark *Endeavour*, had sighted this land first! If you draw your attention to Lieutenant Hicks you will see him rubbing at a wound I inflicted to draw his attention to it!" I indicated.

"You saw it first?" mocked Chester.

"Indeed, I did! The captain suspects it." I was not having this canine disbeliever in my midst at such an important time!

Chester eyed the lieutenant purposefully, but the lieutenant was ignoring his wound now as more important arrangements were being planned.

"I see no evidence of your claim, blighted cat!" he accused.

Lady piped in. "Chester, dear, there is a little blood on the lieutenant's clothing. It could be from Fairweather's scratch."

"Yes, Lady, you are entirely correct!" I praised. "You are the smartest of hounds! This first sighted landmark should have been called Point Fairweather and not Point Hicks!"

"Well, it is not! It is Point Hicks. Named after the man who spotted it first!" Chester was beginning to annoy.

"Be gone with you, Chester! I will not have you crush my bright mood with your doubts! I saw it first and that is all there is to it!" I was not to be rattled.

Chester skulked away, muttering something about my overt self-importance. Lady stayed and listened to the doings, witnessing eventually Lieutenant Hicks rubbing at his wound.

"Congratulations, Fairweather dear. I did not doubt you for a moment!" she commended.

The next prominent landmark was named Cape Howe after Admiral of the Fleet, Earl Richard Howe, of "The Most Noble Order of the Garter." This "Garter" business I found was dedicated to the patron saint of England, St George, as Lieutenant Gore explained it to one of the crew.

The land was covered in wood and grassland, valley and hills. Not the towering peaks of New Zealand. A much more moderate terrain.

At night, smoke and great fires were seen from the ship. The gents were keen for a landing on this new place but the closest the captain would take the ship only gave us a glimpse of the natives standing on the beach.

These people were a very dark brown colour, almost black. So dark were they that the gents could not determine whether they were indeed this colour, or were wearing black clothing.

We saw canoes, but none came out to visit us. The *Endeavour* would be the first large ship they had ever seen and they seemed either a little afraid of it, or thought it an imaginary thing.

The air here was so clear that the captain had trouble gauging how far we were from the shore, the landmarks and the natives. What seemed to be very close was indeed further than expected. As we sailed north the natives gathered on the beaches but they were of such a black colour none could determine whether they were men or women! Painted or clothed!

Further north there appeared several mountains inland, but their tops were flat like tables, not peaked as we had seen. The terrain there looked to be rugged. The attempts to come closer to shore were thwarted by heavy rolling surf and as many times as a boat was launched to land, it turned back for fear of swamping and drowning the men.

Mount Dromedary was named after the Arabian camel of one hump, as it looked just so according to Mister Banks. Cape St George was a prominent landmark and so named as on this day the 24th April, as it was St George's Day back in England.

We continued tracking this coast north, staying four to five miles from land. Mister Banks grew increasingly irritable at not having landed once as yet.

The captain arranged for the pinnace to be launched for him, Mister Banks and Doctor Solander and Tupia as translator, to go ashore. Mister Banks was excited as he saw four of the blackest men on the beach, two of which were carrying a small canoe. By the time the pinnace was readied in the water it was found to be leaking and was brought back on board.

The yawl was then launched to replace it, with enough room for the party and four rowers, but they only came a little closer to shore than the *Endeavour* herself, for the pounding surf kept them off. They had hoped that the natives would come out to meet them, but on seeing them in the yawl, they dumped their canoe and ran into the woods, never to return. Poor Mister Banks was thwarted again!

The ship approached a deep bay, Jervis Bay as it was named. The captain sent the longboat to find a way in but again the breakers stood them off.

We sailed further north to another bay that seemed well sheltered. The captain sent the Master Robert Molyneux out in the pinnace to sound the entrance for depth and the way of passage. He came back finally reporting this to be a satisfactory place to anchor the *Endeavour*.

On the 28th day of April, the captain led by Master Molyneux in the pinnace, sailed through the entrance to this bay. He named the portside Solander Point, and starboard side Cape Banks. Both men were rather pleased.

We sailed into the inlet; a small smokiness arose from a very desolate place. The captain and gents directed their eyeglasses to the very place and saw about ten people.

Upon seeing us they went to a more advantageous place to watch our ship. Not long after, as the captain relayed to all who did not have eyeglasses, two canoes carrying two men each landed on the beach near them, hauling their boats up the sand and joining the fellows upon their hill. The men proceeded along shore and the natives followed at a distance.

Master Molyneux returned to the ship having scouted a sound anchorage on the southern shore of the bay some two miles in from the sea, and close to a village of some six or eight huts. This was where we were to anchor. He had seen some natives inviting him on shore but as they were armed with long spears he had declined.

Those natives who remained on their hill threatened us with spears and swords. They were as black as the night but some were painted with white bands around their legs, thighs and wrists. Broad strokes of the white paint crossed their chests and backs and looked to us like our soldier's cross belts. They had dusted their faces with the stuff. We wondered if they were trying to look like white men or whether this was their warrior face. The men had wiry beards but their hair and that of the women was not fuzzy like the Polynesians and Maoris we had encountered. Each of the painted warriors held a sword made from wood and painted white resembling a scimitar, which they brandished at us defiantly. They were not afraid but neither were they at all curious about us!

When we had anchored an old woman and three children came out of the woods carrying sticks. She looked up at the ship but without surprise or fear, and not even curious. She merely set about to lighting a fire. Four canoes came into the village from fishing and hauled their canoes up the beach. They began to scale their fish and prepare their meal without so much as a consideration for our appearance here, so close to them. Not a single native wore a stitch of clothing and thought nought of it. I imagined they had done so for many years and were used to it.

We ate our dinner watching the natives from the deck. They were quietly going about their business as we were doing. It was a strange thing! No threat, nor curiosity from them.

After dinner, the captain, gents and my Isaac manned the boats with the Marines armed and flanking. Chester, Lady, and I stayed on board for the time being. We three did not know enough about these people to venture, so we watched keenly from the foredeck.

As our crew approached, two of the natives came down to the rocks and threatened our men with their spears of ten feet in length. They called to us loudly in a very harsh sounding language of which none, even Tupia, could understand. They waived us to be gone even though Mister Banks tried his best with signals to inform them that all we required was fresh water and we meant them no harm.

They continued to threaten, so Sergeant Edgcumbe fired a musket loaded with small shot over them. The younger of the two dropped a bundle of lances when hearing the shot, but as nothing had hit him, he merely picked them up and continued menacing. Another round of small shot was fired at the elder man, striking his legs. He ran up to a house and returned with a shield.

In the meantime, our boats had landed near the rocks on the beach. The captain invited my Isaac to be the first to set foot on this new land. He keenly accepted only to be met with spears from the threatening natives landing at his feet. Two more musket shots were fired at them. The elder threw one more lance and then they both ran away.

The men alighted the boat and went toward the houses finding them empty. The natives had run away, leaving the three children in one of the huts. Mister Banks left some beads, ribbons, and cloth as presents and departed. The Marines gathered up the lances and spears and they all returned to the ship.

Mister Banks examined the lances at great length when he returned. They varied in length from six to fifteen feet, and some were pronged with sharp fish bones.

The gents were of the opinion that they were not a warring people like the Maoris. Their voices were coarse and loud. They were nimble and lean and of a middling size. Mister Banks referred to them as Aborigine: this meaning the original inhabitant of a country or region who has been there from the earliest known time. All soon adopted this name for the natives.

Having returned to the ship with the lances, Mister Banks wished to go to the place we had first seen these people at the mouth of the bay. Having come back rather quickly it was reported that none were there.

Mister Banks had begun to call this place Australia, shortening Terra Australis Incognita for ease. It was catching on among the gentry and crew. Even the captain took up the nickname!

The Marines were on guard all night but the captain did not feel that we were in any danger.

During the early hours of the 1st day of May, Able Seaman Forby Sutherland died from consumption contracted when we were in the Straits Lemaire. He had never recovered from it coughing relentlessly. The captain had his body buried on the southern shore of the bay and named the area Sutherland, after the poor man.

On the gents' return to shore the next morning, no one was to be seen in the village and the trinkets left for the children were untouched in the hut where they were thrown.

Mister Banks and Doctor Solander collected many plants, and as soon as their boat took off for the ship, about twelve Aborigines came down to their huts. They wanted nothing to do with us, but to collect their canoes for fishing. These canoes were not like those of the Tahitian or Maori. They were merely a long piece of bark stripped from a tree of sorts and tied together at each end, two sticks holding them open in the middle. We gathered they would not be seaworthy for long and they would have to make new ones as they fell into disrepair.

With each trip to shore, the Aboriginal people followed our parties at a distance, shouting coarsely and waving their spears but none came forward to attack. If turned upon by our Marines, they ran away at speed!

The captain and gents explored the entire bay, bringing back boatloads of new plants. Mister Banks found the tracks of what looked to him a species of deer, some of dogs and other tracks he could not identify.

The weather being mild, I approached Chester about a trip to shore. He and Lady were so keen for it having been stuck on the ship during the first of the expeditions. Those long legs warranted a good stretch and I for one wished to explore the area for myself. A good scratch at a tree or two would sharpen my claws admirably and from all reports the bird life warranted my attention!

We ventured ashore with the captain and gentry. Chester and Lady ran up and down the beach where the waterers were collecting in our casks. The Aborigines came to look at us but retreated when our men advanced. This disturbed Mister Banks as he wished to speak with them somehow and learn of their habits.

The tracks of animals were found. Those of a dog, typically! Every place we had been seemed to have them in some form. Nothing of the feline species appeared, so I deemed this country to be lacking somewhat.

The tracks of smaller animals were rife and Mister Banks thought them something of a polecat or weasel. Chester got sight of one and with a hearty "woof" ran at speed to catch it for his master. Into the tufted grasses he flew, coming to an abrupt stop at a cleverly disguised tree stump. The animal being pursued got away, of course, and Chester sported a rather large bump on his head for some time. As he was embarrassed, I was suitably warned not to speak of it!

I climbed the remarkable trees, high and grand, oozing a sticky gum of some kind. It smelled rather refreshing, but did not taste so as I attempted to lick the stuff off my paws.

Mister Banks classified them with an unsuitable long name, so the crew labelled them all "gum trees" for ease. There were many types and he gathered as many of the leaves and flowers, while Mister Parkinson drew them for his records.

The birds of many colours feasted on the flowers of the gum tree and had I been hungry could have indulged in one or two. Mister Banks called them lorikeets and must have been familiar with their genus prior to us finding them here.

Cockatoo were a larger white bird with an odd yellow pointed hat, and cackled in flocks in the tallest trees. I left them all to their business as I was so well fed on the ship, I needed not hunt them, but merely play with them in the trees, while Chester and Lady sniffed the ground for animals and the botanists collected their samples.

Whilst patrolling the area for interest, someone yelled.

"Cart! Cart!" Instinct had me dodging and weaving to avoid the rubbish cart that had broken my leg back in England.

Once the heart stopped pounding in my chest, I looked about me and found no such cart!

"Cart! Cart!" I heard, and dithered about finding a suitable tree to hide behind, straining the hearing for the rumbling of wheels, but still found nothing!

Who was yelling this offence to the Fairweather ear?

"Cart! Cart!" I was quite alone with nature, yet I could hear someone calling this to me! I leapt up my tree to be certain I was out of the cart's destructive path. Chester came by and noticed me panting above him.

"What the devil is wrong with you, Fairweather?" he asked.

Still panting, I caught enough breath to answer. "There is a rubbish cart coming this way!"

"A what?" He was befuddled.

"A cart, you numbskull! Can you not hear one of the men warning of it? Beware, Chester, they can run down a creature in a heartbeat and leave much damage to the limbs!" I puffed from my lofty spot.

"I think you have gone quite soft in the head, Fairweather. There are no carts here! Come down from that tree," he demanded.

"I will do no such thing, Chester. A cart will be upon me in no time at all. I suggest you clear the way for it or be wounded!" I warned.

"Cart! Cart!" Again!

"There! You see! A cart cometh!" I froze on my lofty limb.

Chester began laughing hysterically. He mimicked the sound. "Do you mean the 'Cart! Cart!' I just heard?"

"Yes, fool dog! Be out of its way!" I pleaded. Chester continued his insane behaviour laughing as if carts would not dare to run him over!

"Fairweather, you ninny! The call you have heard is from a crow!" He tried to explain but I was having none of it.

"I do not know this 'Crow'! Is he a new man on the ship? It is good of him to warn one of impending rubbish carts! The natives must be quite civilized here to have rubbish carts, yet I have seen no roads!" I was confused.

Chester's laughing saw tears run from his eyes.

"The crow is a bird, you silly feline!" he cackled. I shot him a look to wilt his soul.

"A bird says 'Cart! Cart'? You must be mad, Chester. Have you eaten today? Your senses have left you. Starvation is the only excuse!" I muttered from the tree.

He was rolling on the ground now. "Look up to see a large black bird or two!" Chester was relishing in my painful memories.

I was still all a dither but did as suggested, and surely enough there were two black birds only a little smaller than myself in the limbs above me!

"Cart! Cart!" I watched in shock as the birds opened their beaks at the same time as the words were forthcoming!

Chester continued his laughter at my expense.

"I shall await the next call before believing you completely, Chester, and I shall stay in this tree until I have determined the origin of the words and that there are in fact no carts in the vicinity!" My heart was still pounding.

I looked again training my eye upon them and as suggested came, "Cart! Carrrrtttttt!" The prolonged warning came from the beaks of the birds above me!

Chester saw the look of bewilderment upon my dial and renewed his uncontrollable laughter.

"How do you know this, Chester?" I asked, quite embarrassed at my lack of bird knowledge.

"We have crows in England, Fairweather. Where the devil have you been?" He cackled still.

"Well, I have had a privileged upbringing, Chester, dear boy. Crows did not come to my home and I did not go to theirs!" I puffed awkwardly. He saw my reasoning but laughed all the same.

"You nitwit!" was all he could muster, punctuated by his laughter.

"I will thank you not to continue your frivolity now that I have been informed!" I scolded.

"Ah, my friend, but your ignorance gives me such pleasure!" he puffed.

"Leave off, Chester, you twit!" I warned. "You may have the upper hand in the scientific, but I am intimate with the rubbish cart and its perils." I dusted myself off, climbing down from my perch.

The crows had left us but Chester would not let me forget this.

"Cart! Cart!" he mocked mercilessly.

"That will be quite enough of that, beastly hound!" I chastised.

We were called to the boats to go back to the ship for the day. Lady sauntered over fresh from a nap on the warm beach.

"Do you know what this ninny thought of the humble crow?" he quizzed Lady. She saw the look of confusion still on my face.

"I do not, Chester. But whatever he thought of crows, they must have deserved it!" she shot back at him, leaving no room for argument.

I nodded to Chester, puffed up by Lady's case. Chester nodded to me, chastised as only Lady could.

Late in the afternoon, a strange creature seemed to fly between trees. Mister Banks considered them to be a "flying fox" for they looked a little like an English fox complete with bushy tail, but flaps of skin under their arms extending to their feet and would expand when they jumped, allowing them to soar from tree to tree without the inconvenience of coming down only to climb back up!

The superstitious crew thought of them as devils and feared them somewhat as they were so unlike anything they had ever seen! This indeed was a mysterious place!

I sought Chester out on this animal being as he had debunked the Fairweather "cart theory." He knew nothing of them and I felt a little better for it!

At night we saw the fires of the Aboriginal fishermen and heard the howl of the elusive native dog. Mister Banks had been tracking them with Chester and Lady, and quite successfully although they were only seen from a distance, much like the Aborigines.

The report from Chester regarding the native dog was brief as he was unable to talk with them. They were a slim breed of a sandy to rusty colouring. A little smaller than Chester and Lady, for which

Chester felt superior! However, they were skittish and ran when approached, so this was all Chester could report. The native dog would be unknown to us for the moment.

After a rainy day, the next morning saw the gents on the beach drying the mountain of botanical samples they had collected. Mister Banks set out sheets of paper on a sail on the beach to dry them and then ordered them pressed into books so they may be preserved without turning to rot for the voyage home to England.

The crew sent ashore for water and wood, collected small reddish berries which the crew named "rose apples" or "lillypillies." In the pursuit of science, I tried one. A slightly rose flavour with a bitter hint; I chose to keep my appetite fixed on the plentiful supply of oysters and mussels brought on board daily!

Fish were abundant and the land gave of its best for the botanists!

The captain named the two rivers that flowed into this bay Cook's River after himself for a nice change, and George's River after the king.

Mister Banks and Tupia had watched as the Aboriginal people fled upon each meeting. Tired of this standoffishness, we went ashore and he cornered an elderly native, giving him beads and cloth, and tried to understand him.

He would only talk to Tupia, as his skin was similarly dark. Tupia asked of the tribes' names. The old man stretched out his arm in all directions and said "Eora." Hence all the local Aboriginal were the Eora people. The old man pointed to the differing areas and shouted the names in his harsh dialect. The people living between the rivers were the Bidgigal tribe. Those on the southern shore of the bay were the Gweagal, and their northern counterparts, the Kameygal. The lack of understanding between Tupia and the old chap gave up no more information than this.

The men on the ship hauled in a strange creature from the sea, called a "sting ray." I had seen this odd thing flapping about in the shallows but dismissed it as something imagined! When a large beast was finally hooked and the crew struggled to bring it aboard, the gents flocked to examine it!

"Be mindful of the barb at the end of the tail, people!" Mister Banks warned.

"Until it is quite dead it may flick this whip like tail and land the barb into you, breaking off in your flesh. Death can result." With that, everyone backed away, including yours truly, until Mister Banks deemed it no longer a threat.

After the men had prodded and poked at it, I took a Fairweather look at it. It was flattish like a dinner plate and had a mouth underneath and eyes on the top. It was as I had seen them in the shallows, but this was much larger. I walked the span of its winglike fins and a good ten or twelve cat paces it was across!

John Thompson came up for a look as he was asked to cook it. "This be three hundred and thirty-five pounds gutted!" he exclaimed. "Fetch Henry Jeffs, he can cut the thing." He ordered poking it for cartilage as it belonged to the shark family.

"I'll make a meal of it, but can't promise it won't be tough as an old boot!" And off he went, leaving Henry in charge of portioning the thing to feed all hands.

We ate of it that afternoon and John Thompson had done his best. It was quite delicious, but still a little tough.

That evening, I joined the captain and lieutenants in the Great Cabin.

"More stingrays caught this afternoon, Lieutenant Hicks?" he asked.

"Yes, sir, we will be eating it again for supper with some native spinach," reported the lieutenant.

"I have been up-country today and the land is more fertile there." He was speaking to them as he noted his findings. "Good for cropping." He was preoccupied.

His head came up. "We have not named this bay, lieutenants. I am of the opinion it should be Stingray Harbour!"

The lieutenants versed their approval, as it was an appropriate name due to our recent catch. Mister Banks barged in having heard the conversation from his quarters just off the Great Cabin.

"I object, Captain!" he twittered. "This bay has given of its best and we are swamped with specimens. I say we name it Botany Bay!" He demanded, looking out at the land, which had given him so much to take back to England.

"I was just getting used to Stingray Bay, Mister Banks. It has a good strong sound to it," said Lieutenant Gore.

"Yes, Lieutenant Gore, I agree with you," piped Lieutenant Hicks.

"No! No! No!" Botany Bay! I insist! I have left the naming of all places to you, Captain and I wish to be heard on this," he whined.

"Oh, alright, Mister Banks." The captain rolled his eyes in the direction of the lieutenants. Mister Banks was not about to let up.

"Botany Bay it is!" The captain conceded just to quiet Mister Banks.

"Yes, Botany Bay! I approve! Well done, Captain, and thank you for your consideration!" He was satisfied, and the captain and lieutenants off the hook. He went back to his quarters to review some of his specimens.

"Botany Bay?" asked Lieutenant Gore, shaking his head. Mister Banks poked his head back around the door to ensure that his name for this bay was not about to be changed.

"Yes, Lieutenant, Botany Bay!" the captain retorted. Then in a whisper, unable to be heard by Mister Banks… "If it placates the man, let it be!"

The captain was right. Mister Banks would not let this place be Stingray Harbour as they had agreed. His head kept coming around his door to ensure his demands were met. The captain was tiring of him and inscribed the name Botany Bay on his charts. He stood and walked to Mister Banks's door and produced the written words for him to confirm.

"Yes! Yes! Captain, well done. I shall alert the scientists. They will be pleased." With that, Mister Banks took off to report his winning argument to his cronies.

"We would never have heard the end of it, Captain," Lieutenant Hicks admitted.

"It is a small victory for him. He will be pleased with himself," the captain groaned.

"When do we plan to sail from here, Captain?" asked Lieutenant Gore.

"Tomorrow, me thinks. We have done all we can do here and I would wish to continue north. We should make our way home by means of this coastline and chart it for the good of England, and those who sail after us!" announced the captain.

The lieutenants were pleased as the further north we went the milder the weather should be. I, for one, seconded the motion and with that the lieutenants retired and the captain and I slept.

CHAPTER 30

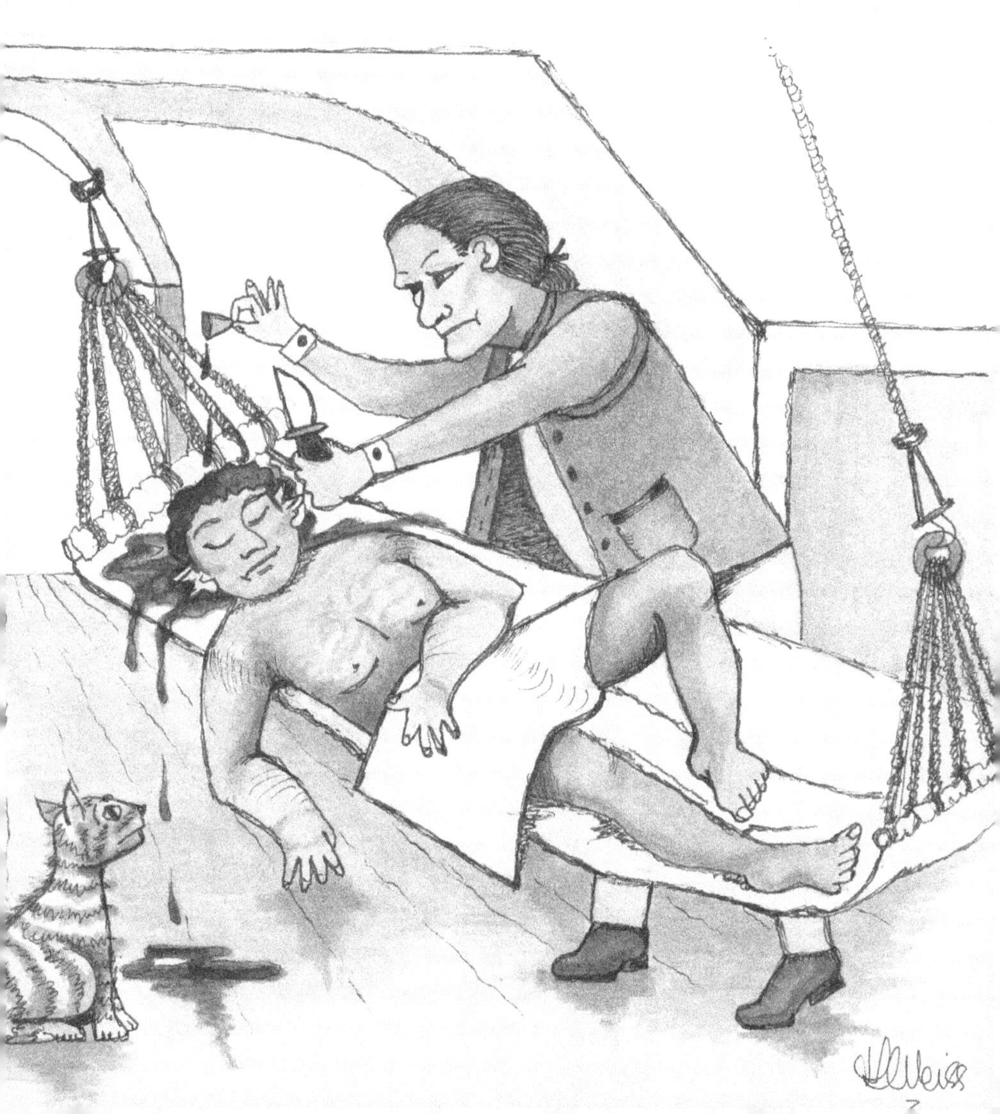

The following morning saw the boats loaded with our dignitaries for the naming ceremony to be held on shore. The captain had my Isaac inscribe the 6th day of May 1770 and the ship's name on a large gum tree, whilst flying the English flag and he claimed "Australia" in the name of King George.

We set sail out the channel of the bay and headed in a northerly direction. We passed another deep inlet to a bay with rocky headlands. We did not enter it but the captain named it Port Jackson after Sir George Jackson, one of the Lord Commissioners of the British Admiralty, and Judge Advocate of the Fleet. It looked to be a safe and commodious harbour and was noted so for future potential settlement.

We tacked for three days off Cape Three Points and Broken Bay, not making any headway north until a fresh breeze picked us up and then we flew!

The captain seemed in a hurry to get us home to England. I, for one, was in no hurry but did not realise the journey back would take us so far until one night when I joined him in the Great Cabin for a briefing. He was pondering his maps and drumming his fingers on the table.

"Home, Fairweather," he muttered. He traced out the route with his forefinger.

I looked at him oddly, as I thought there would be a longer stay in this Terra Australis Incognita we had so eagerly sought, but the captain had found it and wanted us home by way of the northerly coast, however far it took us, and eventually on to Batavia on the northern coast of Java. There seemed to be places on his map to be visited but he intended only to map them.

With favourable winds we continued up the coast of the now commonly known "Australia." It was a difficult job to map the shoreline as fast as we were travelling and the captain put my Isaac to the task when he was otherwise occupied.

Isaac had become very proficient at taking the bearings and coordinating with the captain for accurate drawings of the land. It was a busy time for all as each man was on sentry for the shoal waters threatening to beach us and breakers must be avoided night and day.

Mister Banks and his scientists were busy with the multitude of plants that had been collected in Botany Bay. Mister Parkinson alone had drawn ninety-four sketches by the 12th day of May!

The land flew past and the captain was busily naming prominent points as we sailed: Cape Byron, Moreton Bay, Double Island Point and Indian Head.

The weather warmed and the land became lush and green. We were again headed for the tropics. Smokey fires were seen from the ship night and day. The Aboriginal people were no doubt responsible.

Sea snakes and turtle were caught, and new to me, and I delighted in discovering them.

I was having a bout of sleeplessness during this swift course up the coast of Australia. The cause being not enough exercise on land, I thought. I kept the night watch with the men on duty and found myself walking the decks in an attempt to tire, but to no avail.

I came upon the captain's clerk, Richard Orton. He had joined the Midshipman Patrick Saunders, and Jonathon Monkhouse, brother to our surgeon, and Seaman James Magra, all off duty for a drunken spree. I found it entertaining to watch their antics on the deck. For some time they rolled about laughing of this and that and kept me entertained.

"I'm orf ta bed…" slurred the inebriated Orton, staggering for the gangway, so drunk he could hardly keep upright.

"The man cannot hold his liquor," laughed Saunders.

"I'll bet the next drink that he can't feel a thing!" said Magra with mischief in his voice. They all went for another beaker of the rum they had been rationed.

"Do ya think he feels nothing?" saunders asked, up for a lark and not sure what Magra had meant.

"I'll prove it!" chuckled Magra, standing uneasily and staggering a little. I felt anxiety at this wicked announcement.

"Ha! I dare ya!" barked Saunders, leaning back and toasting his comrade.

"Dare me, do ya?" Magra's voice became sinister. "Follow me and we'll see." He was fiddling in his pockets for his knife and produced it, showing his cronies that he intended to prove his theory. I was uneasy.

"I'll have nothin' of this!" said Jon Monkhouse. "You're on yer own!" He poured himself another rum and stayed put as Magra and Saunders stumbled off to find the unsuspecting Orton.

"Ah, Fairweather!" Jon Monkhouse grabbed me. "Be my friend in their absence!" He petted me roughly. I was having none of this! I wished to catch up with the mischievous pair as I had no idea what Magra had in mind! I broke free and ran for the gangway!

"Ah, silly cat!" came from the still stationary Jon Monkhouse.

Down into the ship I went catching up with the pair next to Orton's bunk where he was already passed out drunk.

"Ere, Magra, what ya' doin' to 'im?" whispered Saunders loudly, stirring some of the sleeping men.

"Shh!" Magra gave him a look to whither. "If we get caught I'll say it was you!" This quieted the silly Saunders as he watched the knife in Magra's hand hover over the sleeping Orton.

I knew not what to do! I could jump on Orton from my spot on an empty bunk but knowing Orton's excesses I did not think it would rouse him, but I feared for the man, drunk or not!

Magra began cutting at Orton's clothes! Saunders was snickering quietly so as not to wake the others. He cut and wrenched at his garments until the man was completely naked!

I began to feel that harm to the man himself was perhaps not on Magra's agenda, and could almost see the funny side of this antic. In true form, Orton did not awaken nor stir in any way, so dead drunk was he!

When Magra had finished, he scooped up all the cut cloth, and they both took off up the gangway to throw the pieces of his clothing over the side of the ship. I followed as they met with Jon Monkhouse to tell him of their antics. Jon laughed heartily as no real harm had become of Orton.

Magra continued drinking but Patrick Saunders and Jon Monkhouse soon passed out from the drink right there on the deck. I could see that James Magra was miffed to lose his drinking companions so early in the watch, when so much more mischief could be unleashed. He mumbled and grumbled his displeasure and fishing around in his pocket for his knife, took on a more sinister appearance, making his way back to the gangway. I saw it best to follow yet again.

I found him at Orton's bunk with the naked chap still out cold. I jumped on the empty bunk to keep an eye on Magra but in the time it took me to leap quietly to a vantage point, Magra was cutting a piece out of both of Orton's ears!

"Think yourself lucky I did not kill you!" he whispered into the ear closest to him.

I was aghast!

The drunken chap still did not move even though his ears were cut and bleeding profusely!

Magra was chuffed with himself, cleaning his knife off on the hessian of Orton's bunk. He took the pieces of his ears up to the deck to dispose of them over the side and clean his hands, and all unobserved!

I was unsure what to do next! I was so astounded that this Magra could have unleashed an act so terrible on a crewmate, and I the only witness, could not herald this heinous act to attract attention to Orton's plight!

I jumped to Orton's bunk landing hard on his stomach so as to wake him for the surgeon's attention, but to no avail! He was, as Magra suggested, unfeelingly intoxicated!

I licked at his ears in an attempt to stem the flow of blood onto his pillow with little success.

"Fairweather!" I leapt on the spot, still not stirring Orton.

It was Jon Monkhouse retiring to his bunk. Noticing me licking at Orton's bleeding ears, he was shocked.

"What the devil have you done to Orton?" he bellowed.

Me? I was assisting the poor chap in the absence of sober men!

His shouting woke all those in need of sleep. He flung me from the man's bunk and inspected the damage. The astounded crew bounded from their bunks to see what all the fuss was about.

There was Orton, as naked as the day he was born. This was enough to shock, but my good self sitting on Orton's chest licking at his wounded ears sent gasps through the gathering!

"What's goin' on?" asked my Isaac pushing through the crowd to Orton's bunk.

"That blasted cat has bitten a piece out of each of Orton's ears!" barked Jon Monkhouse.

What? I was astounded that this misunderstanding would see me blamed for such an atrocious crime! I could do little but sit on the bunk, looking as innocent as was possible.

"He wouldn't do any such a thing!" yelled Isaac above the booing of the assembled crowd.

"No, not Fairweather!" my other boys chimed in.

"How then, do you explain me catching this wretched animal in the act?" he challenged them.

"Hear! Hear!" cried the other men, appalled that I had done such a misdeed to an unconscious man.

Jon Monkhouse hissed at me. The other men joined in and I ran for my life to a corner where I could hide out of reach. They had it in for me!

"Get him!" Jon motioned to the men off in my fleeing direction.

"It's over the side for him!" They rushed to my corner and I pressed myself into my hiding place as far as I could.

Hands reached in to grab me! I was doomed! Paralysed with fear!

"Fairweather did not do this!" yelled Doctor Bill Perry, the surgeon's mate, just as my Isaac grabbed me in an attempt to protect.

All eyes turned to the young man, Doctor Monkhouse's assistant. I cowered still in my corner under Isaac's grip, he afraid to produce me from my hide, lest I be thrown into the sea.

"The cat did not bite Orton's ears!" Bill Perry confirmed, dabbing at the wounds with a cloth.

"I say he did!" yelled Jon Monkhouse. "I saw him at it!" Mumbling broke out among the men, not knowing whom to believe.

Bill Perry took control of the standoff. "Fetch Doctor Monkhouse!" he ordered of Will Howson who was closest the gangway. He took off at speed.

"Well?" Jon Monkhouse defied. "What evidence is there that the cat is not to blame when I saw 'im standing over 'im lickin' his ears with my own two eyes?" he challenged.

"The wounds to his ears are not bites, Mister Monkhouse. They are cuts from a knife!" said Doctor Orton.

All gasped in horror. Isaac deemed it safe to drag me out of my corner and holding me tightly, I hid my face under his arm for I did not believe myself to be out of the woods yet! I could see how it would have looked to Jon Monkhouse upon discovering me in situ!

"Ridiculous! I saw the cat at 'im!" defended Jon Monkhouse.

The men were quiet awaiting the outcome.

"I reiterate, Mister Monkhouse, the ears have not been bitten by a cat or any other animal! Perhaps Fairweather was attempting to assist Orton's ears from bleeding him to death?" I popped my head up upon hearing the absolute truth!

"Fairweather would do that if a man were injured!" swore my Isaac.

"Hear! Hear!" agreed my boys and a number of the crew. Just then, Doctor Monkhouse appeared with his medical bag, Will Howson following.

"What the devil goes on here? I am summoned to attend a man with bitten ears in the middle of the night? And what is he doing here with not a stitch of clothing?" He was appalled at his disturbance just as much as the far-fetched story Will Howson had told him!

Bill Perry gave the doctor his findings and upon close inspection Doctor Monkhouse confirmed that indeed Orton's ears had not been bitten but cut, a large piece out of each!

"I don't believe it, William!" Jon Monkhouse pleaded with his brother the surgeon.

"It is true, Jon, this is the work of a malicious man!" Doctor Monkhouse confirmed.

Jon remained resolute. "Bah!" he stomped. His brother the doctor rolled his eyes at his argumentative kin.

"Does the cat have blood on his face?" challenged the good doctor.

"No, sir! Only a little on his whiskers from licking at him, I think," supported my Isaac.

"Jon, if the cat had bitten Orton's ears she would be covered in his blood! Take a look at the wounds. There are no teeth marks! These wounds are that of a sharp knife!" He pointed out to all who listened intently, so ready were they to have me blamed!

Now a man was suspected and I was off the hook. Jon Monkhouse knew that Saunders and Magra were going below to wreak mischief upon the man but still suspected me!

"Doctor Perry, gather some men to carry the poor wretch to my quarters for stitches. He is drunk enough to feel nothing! He is oblivious!" Doctor Monkhouse ordered, angry as much at his brother's arguments, as his being disturbed from his sleep.

The boys helped Doctor Perry carry the still unconscious Orton away as Lieutenant Hicks turned up to ascertain the disturbance, he being the lieutenant-on-call that evening.

"What goes, young Isaac?" he enquired, the men disbursing to their beds.

Isaac explained the shocking attack and my suspicion in the event, then my proven innocence.

"Very well, I shall report this to the captain on the morrow. Do we have a suspect?" asked Lieutenant Hicks.

"No, sir, it has only just been established that Fairweather was not to blame," reported Isaac officiously.

The lieutenant patted my head.

"I will make my inquiries now, before the captain has to deal with this in the morning." With that, Lieutenant Hicks turned on his heel to discover the truth while the crime was still fresh.

My Isaac and I followed him, keen to assist.

The rest of the men did not sleep well for the remainder of the night knowing a cutter of ears was in their midst and much gossip about who the culprit could be was bandied about.

Isaac and I followed Lieutenant Hicks on deck marching about with his hands behind his back. I jumped in his way to gain his attention but he was single minded and I did not have the rapport with him that I had with my captain. He paid me little attention.

His detective ways, however, did point him in the direction of the sleeping Saunders and Magra. He leaned forward to smell their rum-soaked breath and made his own deduction that these two, being the only drunkards on deck, would implicate them! Jon Monkhouse, however drunk, had discovered the crime and Lieutenant Hicks doubted the man's involvement.

I pawed at the sleeping Magra knowing that my Isaac would read my gestures.

"Fairweather seems to think James Magra is the offender, sir!" Isaac deduced.

"Don't be silly, Isaac. Fairweather could not possibly identify the criminal just by pawing at his clothing." Isaac and I decided our help was useless and had to merely hold hope that the lieutenant would discover it for himself.

He kicked at the sleeping drunks.

"What?" mumbled Patrick Saunders, his eyes still closed, and not knowing who had disturbed him.

"Get up, Saunders!" ordered the lieutenant, leaving no doubt that he was indeed the Commanding Officer. "And wake James Magra while you're down there!"

Saunders leapt to his feet and kicked at Magra until he, too, realised he was in the presence of the lieutenant and stood staggering.

"Yes, Lieutenant?" They stood at attention.

"There has been a crime against Richard Orton. Do either of you know anything about it?" He eyed them curiously to determine their response.

Magra spoke up first. "No, sir, been here drinkin' rum with Saunders and Jon Monkhouse." He was too quick to reply given his condition.

Saunders shuffled somewhat but denied any knowledge. Isaac looked at me as a witness and I did not disappoint. I strolled to the offensive Magra and bit him squarely on the leg!

"Ouch!" Magra kicked me hard, knocking the wind from my frame!

"You see, Lieutenant? Fairweather knows who cut Orton's ears!" Before the Lieutenant could reply, Saunders drew in a gasp of disbelief. He knew that he and Magra were the perpetrators of Orton's loss of clothing, but he had passed out drunk and slept through Magra's evil attack on Orton's ears. He looked at Magra knowingly but said nothing, for fear of implicating himself in the crime, however partially.

"Go below and consider yourselves off duty and confined to quarters until the captain deals with you at sunrise," ordered Lieutenant Hicks.

They marched off together silently, but Isaac and I knew they would discuss this much as Saunders seemed to be innocent of the brutality.

The lieutenant continued to ask those on deck working during the night if they knew anything of the attack but none had heard of it until the lieutenant explained.

Isaac and I retired to his bunk, well away from Magra and Saunders. He insisted I stay with him to ensure that we slept the rest of this shift without incident.

The next morning of the 23rd day of May, the captain rose early to be greeted by the view of a large protected bay and ordered the ship rounded into it for a landing.

Lieutenant Hicks had been in conference with Lieutenant Gore on the events of the night watch. They approached the captain, telling all, just as Isaac and I arrived to meet them.

The captain called for the culprits to be brought on deck and assembled the crew once the ship was at anchor.

By now, Orton was dressed, up and about, and had been apprised of the misdeeds to his person from Jon Monkhouse and his brother the good Doctor Monkhouse, who had stitched his ears while he lay dead drunk. He was angry and he knew who might have done it, but said nothing until summoned by the captain in front of his attackers.

"Well, Orton? Do you have any knowledge of who your attacker may be?" barked the captain, incensed at such a crime.

"I was drinking with Saunders, Magra and Jon Monkhouse last night. That's all I remember, Captain," he admitted.

"Jon Monkhouse found you bleeding and naked in your cot. He is not to blame. He thinks the cat may have bitten your ears, but we doubt this theory as the wounds were inflicted by a knife," explained the captain. "Jon Monkhouse has admitted to seeing you, Magra, on deck brandishing a knife with mischief in mind." The captain had interviewed Jon Monkhouse himself, in an attempt to gather the facts!

"Well, Saunders? Magra? Do you have anything to add?" He prompted them for the truth believing that he would not get it.

"But we know nothing, sir!" Saunders pleaded, innocent of the cutting of Orton's ears, but not completely blameless. "We were drunk and sleeping on deck."

I coughed aloud. Saunders was not sure if Magra had done it but he was protecting him all the same.

Lieutenant Hicks interrupted. "Captain, if I may?" he whispered.

The captain nodded for him to interject. The lieutenant whispered his findings. "It is reputed that Magra has cut Orton's clothes off him on one or two occasions. Both while they were drinking. It is said that once Magra threatened to kill him." The captain was unsure how best to proceed, except to ask Orton if this were true.

"I cannot say, sir." Orton knew it was Magra, but as they had to work together on the ship and he was not about to tempt death by confirming what the captain had been told. Magra would most certainly ensure that Orton met an untimely demise if he told all!

The captain was sure that he would get no further with this inquisition.

"Very well!" said the captain after some pause to think. "I look upon such proceedings as highly dangerous on such voyages as this, and the greatest insult that could be offered to my authority on this ship, as I have always been ready to hear and fairly redress every complaint that has been made against any person!"

The crew stood ready to hear the punishment and hoped it severe as they all valued the captain's justice and wished to sleep well without fearing for their ears!

"Midshipman Patrick Saunders!" he called. "I demote you to Able Seaman for your part in this crime. I have no proof but by reason of your state and whereabouts, and I suspect you."

Saunders was shocked and I could see that all Able Seamen alike would ensure that he was punished in their own way!

"Able Seaman James Magra!" the captain called. "You are relieved of duty and confined to quarters. Again, I have no real proof that you were a part of this crime but I suspect you." He turned to the crew.

"I offer a reward for any information further to this to despatch the criminals. Should any man have something to offer it will be accepted with the utmost discretion. If there is any repercussion to Orton the victim, or Jon Monkhouse who is clearly innocent, I will deal with it in the harshest of possible manners." With that, the captain dismissed the men.

Isaac picked me up and tucked me under his arm. "Well, Fairweather? I know that you saw all but there would be mutiny if the captain believed the cat!" I was much miffed but saw his point.

Yet another time that I wished the ability to speak and be heard! Needless to say, the men slept with one eye open when encamped with Magra and Saunders! It was an unsettling event!

The next day, the captain took a boat around the bay and Mister Banks and the gents with Tupia as guide were well pleased to be out and about on land once again.

They saw smoky fires and rowed to where they had seen them, but by the time they landed the Aborigines had fled into the sparse woods. Here they found ten fires in a circle each with cockles cooking.

There were pieces of bark the length and breadth of a man and Tupia deduced that these were their beds. No huts were found, yet the ground was so long-trodden that Tupia considered that they slept in the open and were indeed "poor" people.

More tracks of strange animals were found but none had been seen.

The soil was dry and sandy and the wood not good, but Mister Banks was pleased to find mangroves, a sand-dwelling tree that grows on the shore of the lagoon, its roots and lower trunk flooded when the tide is high.

In them, however, he discovered nests of ants that were green and bit him with a passion, for disturbing them. Another friend of the mangrove were hairy green caterpillars. They grouped themselves together, some twenty or thirty upon one leaf. As Mister Banks could not help but touch them, he found that their prickles stung like a nettle!

With his samples and Mister Parkinson's drawings, he returned to the ship a happier man, for they had collected new species here; some that were not found in Botany Bay.

After the pink unction was applied to his ant bites and caterpillar pricks, Mister Banks shot some bustard birds and we ate of them for dinner, thanks to our butcher and cook! They were the largest birds we had seen to date in this Australia. Three or four were enough to feed the entire crew at fifteen pound each! Mister Banks and the gents thought them the tastiest birds we had eaten since leaving England. I could not have agreed more! They made a nice change from fish, and the captain named this bay Bustard Bay in their honour.

We sailed from Bustard Bay the next morning at daybreak.

The captain ordered the casks of orange and lemon juices sent on board in England to be tapped and tasted.

Mister Banks had instructions from the senders, Doctors Hulmes and Fothergill of England, on how they were to be used in the prevention of scurvy. Even though they were evaporated essences and quite tart, they were further evaporated over heat in the galley and doled out to the crew, as we had not collected any new fruits or vegetables in this Australia so far.

In travelling close to the land, we began to see islands to our starboard side. These were lush with the familiar palm trees of Polynesia. They kept the surf and swell away from the mainland and led us to calmer waters.

The sandy shoals became a difficulty, though, and the captain ordered vigil from the topmast as we slowly crept through the maze of shallows hoping not to be beached or landlocked, and have to turn the ship around to escape. We crossed the Tropic of Capricorn and the captain named a prominent cape after it.

When we came to anchor in shallow water on the 26th day of May, the captain sent the boats to sound the depths ahead. We were at a low tide and could see the sandy bottom from the deck.

Mister Banks and the gents fished from the cabin windows but it was so shallow that no fish were caught. Mister Banks could see movement in the water and persevered with his hook and line. He managed to pull up a crab of size, which had held fast to his bait with its claws. With that the men continued fishing for them and brought some number aboard. Some of them were brown and plain but a new species of a brilliant blue colour was highly prized and investigated!

Chester, Lady, and I watched as the catch shuffled their legs sideways all over the deck in a bid to escape.

"Rather attractive colouring, Lady? They remind me of Madam's fine china back at home with their royal blue backs and their white bellies," I said in passing as we watched.

"You are right, Fairweather. Mister Banks has china just like it back in England!" She admired them from a distance.

"They are merely crab!" Chester puffed. "Not a fine dining setting!" He was not an admirer of English plate-ware. With that, he poked his nose at one and without delay its claw found his beezer and attached itself with a crunching sound.

"Yike!" Chester leapt about with the sizeable crab attached to his snout. Lady and I laughed not a little as Mister Banks came to the rescue, prizing the claw open to release Chester's nose.

"That will teach you to mock the finer things, Chester!" I said, chuckling heartily.

"Hurrumph!" said the hound, rubbing his troubled snout along some rope in the vain hope it would ease his pain. With that, we left Mister Banks to his crabbing.

The captain was keen to find water for the casks, so as soon as the tide lifted the ship higher than the sandy bottom, we kept moving forward, passing many inlets, but with the lieutenants sounding the bottom in the boats ahead; he was finding them too shallow for an anchorage. We passed by Keppel Island with only two feet of water to spare under the ship!

As much as we were gaining north with good winds, this kind of sailing kept all the crew on watch for shallows and taunted the captain.

On the morning we passed Cape Townshend, we found ourselves amongst many islands in the shallowest part of the channel. The captain kept the small boats out full time to sound the way and we managed to stay afloat.

The islands we passed were inhabited and the Aborigines came down to the sandy beaches to see our giant canoe! They had canoes with outriggers much more like the Polynesians but they did not venture out to us for fear.

We anchored in what the captain named Thirsty Bay. It looked as if we might collect water there.

The dogs and I joined Mister Banks and the gents on a mission to the beach. Chester and Lady were keen to stretch their legs and I found that the shore-bound exercise helped me sleep better at night.

The dogs were busy chasing a cloud of coloured butterflies whilst I nosed around on shore amongst the mangroves.

I noticed a movement out of the corner of my eye and whipped my head around to ascertain it. I could see a strange looking animal with the head of a frog but no legs. Its body was that of a fish! But it was not in the water! How odd!

I sat for some time and having trained the Fairweather eye for the likes of them, found them leaping and skipping all through the mud and rocks by way of their dorsal fins. Mister Banks noticed my observations and sauntered over, wondering what had my attention.

"Why, Fairweather, this is a strange phenomenon! A fish that skips over the mud!" He addressed me, as he would have one of the scientists, so I felt rather important having found the thing. He caught one of the fast-moving fish in a net and picked it up for examination.

"What shall we call it, Fairweather?" I was honoured.

"A mud skipper, me thinks! Well done, cat!" he announced. And there it was, my first discovery!

I was beaming with pride as the gentry came to witness this odd creature. Mister Parkinson drew it and the rest watched its comical advances among the mud and rocks.

Mister Banks reported my findings to the captain that evening and I was congratulated privately when alone with him and his charts. A proud moment for my good self!

"Thirsty Bay has left us just so, Fairweather. No water for the gathering. We move on tomorrow," he announced, attending to his log.

With the boats sounding ahead, we went out of the channel and around the next few islands. The surf broke upon a reef, which we followed in deeper water. We weaved our way back along the coastline still looking for a watering place and found ourselves within a passage between the mainland and islands. The captain named it Whitsunday Passage, as we discovered it on the day that the church celebrates the Pentecostal Festival of that name back in good old England. He named the islands that lay in the Whitsunday Passage: the Cumberlands, in honour of His Royal Highness, Prince William, the Duke of Cumberland. He was a younger son of King George, and the captain was sure that the king would find this favourable.

Through the passage we sailed with plenty of water under us and out into wider waters. The surf still crashed on the reef to our starboard side but the shoals became fewer and the sailing quicker.

The captain was beginning to have trouble with his compass. It wandered aimlessly around the dial at times and confused his bearings. Upon heated discussion in the Great Cabin, the consensus was that the earth upon the mainland and surrounding islands must carry much iron, affecting the compass magnetically. He named one such large island after this phenomenon, Magnetic Island, as the compass needle swung violently upon passing it.

Cape Grafton, Dunk Island, and Trinity Bay came and went as the captain looked for an anchorage with fresh water. The channel of deep water began to narrow and the captain had our men out sounding yet again for an anchorage.

We were in deep water and should not have had to worry, but at eleven bells on the night of the 10th of June, the *Endeavour* struck a reef and held fast. These reefs were submerged coral and the worst kind to have hit, for they were sharp and had a grinding ability that did not meet well with the wooden bottom of our ship!

The captain leapt into action!

I ran for the safety of the longboat, but it was taken from me as all boats were manned to sound the depth around the ship.

Into the rigging I went!

I looked down to see the prow of the *Endeavour* fast upon the coral and rock, the swell battering against her, tipping the men off their feet until they felt for the conditions and adapted.

The captain looked over the side to see her sheathing boards adrift around her and by midnight the false keel had come away.

The depth sounders reported that we had three to four fathoms depth on the starboard side but merely three to four feet on the port side, this being where the ship was struck!

The *Endeavour*'s head was lying to the northeast. We were stuck on the south-eastern edge of a coral reef with deep water astern. The tide was high and it was now or never if the captain was to heave the ship off the reef!

"Bring in the sails, men!" was the order.

Calmly, he despatched the men to task even though this was the direst of situations! If the ship was not released soon, while the weather was calm, she could be smashed to pieces upon the reef! Every man was up and ready for action, as all knew that we could sink after coming off the reef and letting the water into the gaping hole!

"Cable and anchor into the longboat, men! Man the capstan and winch! We'll try to haul her off before the tide runs out!" Alas, no amount of heaving would loosen her from the reef.

"Man two of the pumps!" came the next order, after the lieutenants had been below to ascertain the amount of water coming in. It was little considering the damage as the coral was stuck fast within the hole, and the two pumps kept up with the water initially. They were manned in fifteen-minute shifts to ensure the strongest hands were employed in their service.

"Lighten the ship, lieutenants!" came the order. They knew what to do. Employing all available hands the crew dumped the decayed stores over the side, our four-pound guns, iron and stone ballast, casks, hoops, staves, oil jars, anything of weight to ease the ship and float her higher above the water.

The tide began to fall and the two pumps could handle the water pouring in to the ship.

By the afternoon of the 11th the weather had remained calm but with the tide coming back in again the rush was on to free the ship before she could take on more water. I stayed up in the rigging as I was of no use in this crisis.

"Take the two bower anchors out! One on the starboard quarter and the other right astern!" Immediately his words were out, men scurried to the task.

"Put blocks and tackles on the cables! Bring the falls in abaft! And heave tight!" Every muscle strained under the instructions. Mere men were hoping to defy the sea and hold the weight of the enormous ship! It seemed an impossible task!

By five in the afternoon, the tide began to rise and two more pumps were sent for as the ship began taking on more water than the two pumps could remove. One of the pumps was broken, but the three kept the water at bay. By nine at night the water was overtaking the pumps when the ship righted herself on the tide. The Captain was alarmed to learn that the ship had three feet and nine inches of water in her hull!

"We risk immediate destruction here, lieutenants!" the captain admitted quietly. "The *Endeavour* will grind herself to pieces on this reef if we are not successful." He pondered as the wide-eyed lieutenants kept quiet. "We will be forced upon this barren shore with no hope of rescue! If we do get her off this reef we will sink before making to shore this being seven or eight leagues away!" The lieutenant did not know what to say. They could only listen and hope their captain had an answer.

"We risk all, sirs, but we cannot stay here and do nought!" The captain was now resolved to make every attempt to save the *Endeavour* and her crew!

"All men not on the pumps heave on the capstan and windlass! This is it, men! Show no weakness!" he ordered passionately. They pulled till their arms burned in pain. Even the gentry joined the push to save us! No man wanted to die here!

Pushing and pulling for an hour or so, the *Endeavour* floated finally and they hove off into deeper water.

The men were exhausted but the trouble was only beginning. The sea rushed in to the hole in the ship now unblocked by the coral, and the three pumps struggled to keep the water out.

The captain set Midshipman Jonathon Monkhouse to plug the leak with a heavy sail. Jon Monkhouse had done this "fothering" before on another ship. He smeared oakum and manure and wool from the sheep onto a spare sail. He then tied ropes to the sail, throwing the ropes over the side to the men in the longboat. The men caught them and slung them under the ship, dragging the sail forward by them, to the place where the leak stood. The sail was tied off on the deck to keep it in place. The sail plugged the hole by the weight of the water against it and the oakum, wool and manure stuck it in place, bunging up the hole!

The captain was much pleased with Jon Monkhouse's efforts as the water coming in was now minimal and only one pump was required to keep it out. We were free of the reef and not taking on too much water that could not be handled!

Jon Monkhouse was congratulated accordingly.

The crisis was not over. We were afloat but amid rocks and shoals and had to inch the *Endeavour* through deep water with accuracy to find a place to anchor.

The land we had passed so far in this area did not seem to hold any such place. Over the following few days every man went without sleep. Food and water were brought to them by the ever-sturdy John Thompson to keep up their strength in this dangerous manoeuvre.

Little by little, the captain edged the ship around a point and into a bay and we anchored alongside a river and beach. Mercifully, it was the perfect place to beach the ship and fix her; timbers and fresh water was abundant!

As the main anchor was dropped and the ropes and anchors that hauled us off the reef were stowed, the men collapsed wherever they could to sleep off their worst nightmare!

The captain left them to it, knowing that they had indeed performed a miracle. The captain and lieutenants sat on the aft deck wearily but without asking what was next. Rest was needed. I climbed down from my perch and sat by my captain, proud of what he had achieved against the odds.

"Fairweather," he acknowledged me, fatigued to the end. "I see you survived the crush of activity?" I purred as he petted me. "Fairweather," he repeated. "Had it not been for 'fair weather' we would have lost all, my friend," he mumbled, trailing off into sleep.

The decks were the quietest I had ever seen them. Not a man was standing as our captain had safely and expertly gotten them to a safe anchorage close to shore, and the exhaustion had caught up with one and all.

Chester and Lady had been locked in Mister Banks's cabin all this time to keep them out of the way. They were released onto the deck now and joined me.

"Spot of bother, what?" Chester asked stupidly.

"Clearly, dumb hound, you are not up to date on the affairs of the ship for the last few days!" I hissed at him.

"Well, Lady and I have been confined!" he woofed, taking umbrage.

"I am too tired from merely keeping out of the way and watching this debacle to give you an update, Chester! Can you not see that we have been through the mill?" I chastised him.

"Yes, the ship looks a shambles. What occurred?" he asked keenly, having been left out of the loop for days.

"Oh, all right! The short version only! We struck a reef, holed the ship, nearly sunk and drowned! There! Are you happy?" My eyes were closing, sitting next to my dozing captain.

"Woof!" he exclaimed.

Lady was disturbed.

"This news is significant, Fairweather! I did hear a ruckus! Are all hands safe and well? We seem to be in a nice spot for some repairs! Why is everyone asleep and all quiet?" His infernal questions and idiotic observations were getting on my nerves.

"Go, foul beast, to a corner as far away from me as possible and leave me to my captain. When we are all up and about, I shall fill you in on the details."

"Come, Chester, leave the boy to his duty with the captain." Lady sensibly got the churlish Chester out of the reach of a snout-slapping from yours truly! They sauntered away I knew not where and in the quiet of the afternoon with not a sound on board, I slept, as did the entire company.

CHAPTER 31

U p and about early the next day, the captain assembled the crew and praised their efforts.

"In justice to the ship's company I must say that no men ever behaved better than they have done on this occasion, animated by the behaviour of the gentlemen on board, every man seemed to have a just sense of the danger we were in and exerted himself to the very utmost."

Lieutenant Gore led the way. "Well done one and all!" he applauded. A cheer went up from the tired men. "Now to work again, and have us repaired to get us home." Another cheer and all were ready for their orders, knowing that their captain's swift thinking had saved their lives.

A foul wind came upon us and it was the consensus of the men that had it done so when we were stuck on the reef, we would no doubt have been smashed to pieces there and then.

The captain was not happy with our mooring at the mouth of the newly named Endeavour River. We were too exposed to the wind, so he sent the boats ahead into the river itself to find a more sheltered site. He edged us in and beached the *Endeavour* head first on the sand, in a favourable spot so we may get the stores off the ship and onto land with ease.

This beaching kept the tides below the hole in the ship to stop more water coming in. He had the men erect tents, one for the sick, of which there were eight or nine, and one for the stores to be emptied to lighten the ship.

A forge was set up for the armourer Robert Taylor to make nails. Carpenter John Satterley's tools and equipment were taken ashore. The men constructed a raft to use as a platform for the work on the Endeavour's hole.

It was the 17th day of June 1770 and we were safe.

The captain went on the raft with John Satterley to inspect the damage to the ship. Her injuries were worse than first thought. Part of the false keel had gone, but not enough to sink her. On the starboard side, the coral had torn through four planks and damaged three more. The coral had sawn through it as if done by the hand of a man with an axe, not a splinter was there! A piece of coral was stuck in the hole with the oakum and wool gathering sand and pebbles. This had helped the fothering sail to do its work well!

"Good luck hath saved us, Mister Satterley!" said the captain, quite astonished that we were not sunk.

"Seems so, Captain!" agreed John Satterley scratching his head, as confused at our safety as the captain. "I will lay out the needs to the others and we will be mending her as fast as we can, sir." They came back on board to be greeted by Mister Banks.

"What say you, Captain?" he asked, readying himself for a trip inland.

"We are lucky, Mister Banks. It will take some time, but I cannot see why we will not sail her again." With that, Mister Banks assembled his usual posse and made for the land to collect specimens. Chester, Lady, and I took a turn with him onshore. Nothing of natives had been seen so far, and as their way was to run in fear we did not feel that our safety was at risk.

We found an Aboriginal camp that had been abandoned for some six months. The shore of our beach was sandy and barren and that of the river was overgrown with mangroves. It was hilly inland and the going a little rough.

We sighted the elusive animal that had made odd tracks in the land all the way up this coastline. I must say it was a strange creature. A little like a deer upon the face, and the colour of a mouse, but it sat on powerful hind legs and bounced along with the help of its strong tail.

The gents were well pleased to have finally seen the new animal and they were plentiful but mysterious, as they hopped away from us skittishly and at speed, bounding high over the long grass. Mister Banks could not hold any in the sights of his musket so he had Chester and Lady off after them. Chester barked and scared most of them off, but Lady took a more stealthy approach and managed to round up a small one and bring it back.

"Well done, Lady!" said Mister Banks.

Chester was a bit miffed that he had not gotten the specimen but for all his barking it served him right! The gents set out to examine this creature upon our return to the ship, not having a name for it as yet.

Fresh water was found coming from a stream on the other side of the river. This place, whilst a little barren, held enough for us to stay for the repairs to the ship.

The fish were difficult to catch, as a few days had hauled nothing. The men were sent to shoot pigeon and this kept us going for some time.

Each time they went ashore, they saw the elusive hopping animal but so swift were they that none could shoot them. Chester and Lady were kept from chasing them as some were as big as the dogs themselves and Mister Banks feared his hounds would be injured, having seen them fight with each other using their powerful back legs to easily harm.

On one trip we saw a cluster of mounds that ants had made, some as tall as a man.

"These remind me of the Rune Stones on the Plains of Upsal in Sweden," Doctor Solander commented.

"Yes, they do have a Druid appearance," Mister Banks interjected. I did not understand this reference and saw them as little more than towers in my way of other things.

The humble magpie sounded like two women chatting over the garden fence. Magpies are of the crow genus, I am told, and are of a black and white colour. I chased them as I would any bird, but when nesting they were fierce defenders. They swooped us to keep us clear of their young, snapping their beaks as if to peck. I left them to their families, as I did not wish to lose an eye!

Mister Banks came running to the captain, having forgotten that he was keeping some of his plant specimens in the bread room. This was flooded by the leakage and had now subsided, so he claimed as many hands as the captain would allow, removing his samples from the sopping bread room and laying them out to dry again in the sun. Some had perished and this made him unhappy though it could not be helped.

Most of the crew had spent their time emptying the *Endeavour* of everything of weight to keep her damaged parts above the tide level. Empty casks were lashed to the bottom to keep her afloat when the tide came in.

The captain sent the men out with the nets but they only caught twenty to thirty pounds of fish, which was given to the sick. Mister Banks found a sea of kale, a type of wild cabbage, growing up in the country and all hands were employed in harvesting it for the men to get their greens.

The men reported seeing animals like small hares, and one had seen the native dog. Thinking it was a wolf, he tried to shoot it but missed and it ran from him.

By the end of June the fishing had become more plentiful when the nets were cast in just the right places and there was enough fish and wild cabbage for all hands.

On the 1st day of July, the repairs to the ship were nearing completion and the captain went up into the country to establish a route through the shoals north. Try as he might, every path he saw was littered with shallows that came to dead ends. He had lost faith in getting out of this place.

Two days later he sent Master Robert Molyneux out in the pinnace to establish a route for us. He found no such way out of here. This was now his full-time duty and he travelled far and wide in all directions to find a course out of the Endeavour River to deep water.

One night at high tide the *Endeavour* floated for some time and we hauled off the shore a little to ensure she stayed afloat. I looked over the side to see a long tree trunk with gnarly bark sitting alongside the ship. I thought I may have taken liberties with the rum when I saw the thing move of its own accord!

"Chester! There is a log moving below the ship!" Chester came to where I stood and looked over.

"Haaahaha!" He laughed uncontrollably.

"What is the meaning of this merriment?" I asked impatiently, seeing what I thought were eyes on the front of the log.

"That is a crocodile, you ninny! Nasty creature. Eats cats. Large jaws. Snap a cat in two with one bite!" he said in his pompous blasé manner.

"How can it survive on cats when I have seen none here?" I demanded.

"Ah other small rodents suit its appetite just as well." He remained nonchalant.

"Rodents? I am no such thing. I will have you!" I was incensed.

"Did I say you were a rodent?" Chester challenged.

"No, but you implied it, foul beast!" I claimed.

"Will you two stop arguing?" Lady chastened.

"But…" said Chester.

"But…" said I.

"No buts! This is a crocodile. It would eat a man! Least of all a cat or dog! We must be wary of them, as they will strike on land and in water. They are a danger to us all. Now be quiet!" And that was that!

When stirring Lady's ire, it is wise to cease and desist! Chester and I eyed each other purposefully. Boredom wreaked havoc on the ship for us four-legged types. I had heard the pigs and sheep niggling each other many times of late. We agreed to terminate such petty arguments.

Every party that went ashore reported the sighting of animals that none of us had seen before. They even stumped Mister Banks and he had seen and knew all of the animals to be found about the islands and many countries he had visited.

There was a strange laughter that was thought to be the Aborigines having a fine old time! Until we noticed that none had so much as a smile on their faces, yet this wretched laughter taunted us daily!

Mister Banks finally saw that it came from a bird!

We all felt a little embarrassed as we realised our mistake. Mister Banks knew them to be a new species of kingfisher and until he could ascertain their tribal name from the Aboriginal people he hoped to meet, they remained unnamed.

On one of Master Molyneux's attempts to find the way out of our anchorage he caught a curious creature. Huge turtle! Three of them, weighing some seven hundred and ninety one pounds, and they were brought aboard the pinnace and trafficked back to the ship where Mister Banks examined them.

John Thompson and Henry Jeffs were then put to the task of removing the shell and cooking the meat. Once the shell was removed the meat was very tender and we all agreed that this was a good change to the diet!

Aboriginal fires were seen up in the country, but each time the gents went to find them, they had abandoned their cooking and ran away.

The captain, too, was getting frustrated with the inability to interview the natives. On one expedition, a sailor from a party sent to find food was separated from the others and came upon a family of

Aborigines on the other side of the bay. They were spearing fish from a canoe but were distracted by the sight of the *Endeavour*, half in and half out of the water and the noises coming from the crew mending her. They took no notice of him and he saw them as closely as anyone had so far.

For the very first time, two Aborigines paddled across the bay and came close enough to the ship to take some of our trinkets. They paddled away, gathering another two natives and came back to land on the beach.

Tupia convinced them with gestures to lay down their spears, as they did not understand his Tahitian language. The captain and Mister Banks approached the four, being careful not to come between them and their weapons. They sat upon the beach to show a peaceful indication. Chester, Lady, and I watched from the deck, not wanting to frighten them when the captain and gents were finally establishing contact with the natives.

The kingfisher's laughter was heard amongst the afternoon trees. Tupia gestured to the Aborigines as to what they were called.

"Kookaburra!" they said in their harsh tone.

"Kookaburra?" Tupia asked, making flapping motions and copying the call, to ensure he was asking the right thing. They laughed at his silliness, but confirmed the bird was known as a "kookaburra." This was exciting for the captain and the gents and they continued their lessons handing trinkets over each time the Aborigines answered a question successfully.

As the afternoon progressed, a herd of the mysterious jumping animals gathered on the other side of the river to forage for food. Tupia pointed at them, and motioned for the Aboriginal word for them, by holding his hands closely in front of his chest and jumping along the sand.

This humoured the Aborigines as much as his other gestures and they were enjoying themselves. "Kangaroo!" they spat, laughing. Again, Tupia pointed at the herd and jumped to be sure that he had the right word. "Kangaroo!" they laughed.

Mister Banks wrote down every word, and then gestured to the crew to bring the dogs ashore. Chester and Lady were presented to them, and Tupia asked if they had a word for the native dog. So alike were they to our proud dogs that this was easy for them to answer.

"Tingo!" They reached out and patted the pair. "Dingo!" some said.

Mister Banks was unsure and asked Tupia to have them say it again.

"Did they say Tingo? Or Dingo?" Mister Banks asked of Tupia. He merely shrugged as the coarseness of their speech made the word sound either way.

Mister Banks wrote down "dingo" as the word of choice and was happy that now the native dog had a name. He was most pleased to invite the Aborigines for dinner with us.

They declined, however, and hopped along the sand mocking Tupia and his "kangaroo" and off they paddled with their trinkets to the other side of the river to join their family.

That evening Mister Banks wrote of the event in his diary along with Tupia and the captain and a fine brandy.

"Excellent progress today, Captain!" He strutted about, pleased with himself and Tupia who was at hand.

"Yes, Mister Banks. Fine work, Tupia!" He praised the fellow who had done all the hard work.

Mister Banks ignored him.

"They are a dark native, are they not? And I wonder what the markings mean painted on their skin? Some had red markings on the body and the one had white on the breast and upper lip. Perhaps he was a leader? Their hair is black but not woolly like the Polynesians, but somewhat curly, however. They have lively eyes and white even teeth, do they not? And they repeated some of our words with ease, me thinks!" He prattled on as if talking to himself.

"Mister Banks, I have yet to find us a way out of this place and get us home. Your talk of the Aborigine is riveting but I must consult my charts before I may sleep." This was enough to keep Banks quiet and him off to consult anyone who would listen. Tupia and he took their leave, wishing the captain a good night.

The natives came back the next day while the crew were busy loading the dried stores and collecting rocks for ballast. The captain and Mister Banks interviewed them again without much success, as their language was completely new to us. Gestures were all that we could use, and this entertained the Aborigines.

A new man had been added to the group and Mister Banks could not help but inspect his nose. It had a hole through it as big as a man's finger and a bone through the hole. On closer inspection all of the Aborigines had these holes but only one man had the bone in it. Mister Banks could only conjecture that the piercing had a cultural significance, as they still could not be understood.

The men kept bringing turtle back from their fishing trips so we all ate very well. The Aboriginal people came to look at us regularly and seemed to enjoy our gifts. With each visit Mister Banks tried to follow them back to their camp but they made it quite clear to him that they did not want his company!

Mister Gore finally managed to shoot a large kangaroo and brought it back to be examined. It was as big as a dog and gathered much attention from the scientists. None had ever seen anything like it. The dogs and I inspected it. It had furry short bristled hair of a mousey grey colour and ears like a rabbit! Its forearms were short and only used for eating. The strong back legs and even stronger tail were to propel it along in a jumping fashion of some seven to eight feet in one bound!

Mister Banks likened it to a gerbua found in Egypt, but I knew not of this.

The captain and gents dined upon its meat after the scientists had finished their investigations. John Thompson cooked it and I stayed around the kitchen for some scraps and can confirm that it was fine eating of little fat, perhaps from all that jumping!

Every day was spent on or off the ship preparing her to sail, and the gents eagerly gathering and storing their botanical finds.

When the repairs were nearing completion, a group of ten Aborigines came on board the ship with great purpose. They left their dingo pack on shore. They wanted the turtles we had caught of which eight or nine lay upon our deck.

Turtle was a great delicacy for them, and as they could not hope to catch them from their flimsy canoes, they only caught them when the female turtles came ashore to lay eggs in the sand.

So prized was such a catch that they asked for them, but Mister Banks refused to hand them over. They began to drag them toward the gangway without permission to take them back to their village! Mister Banks intervened but an Aborigine stamped his feet and pushed Mister Banks back! Try as they may, no one was letting this catch off the ship. They gave up and paddled to shore in their canoes, angry that we would not give them the catch!

The Aborigines began gathering clumps of long dry grass very quickly and muttering to each other.

There was a small fire on the beach on which our pitch kettle was boiling, the pitch being kept hot to paint the ship's repaired timbers.

The natives plunged the tufts of grass into the flames and set fire to the entire outer edges of the camp!

The long grass caught fire easily and threatened the few things we had out to dry on the beach, clothes and linen that were not packed away on the ship yet!

Mister Banks's tent was in the line of fire, and he called for the crew to help those on shore to put out the fire by any means!

Chester and Lady fretted, and I hid, while the men were stamping and throwing buckets of water, only just to kept it at bay for long enough to drag the tent down to the safety of the water's edge!

Our sow and her piglets were more difficult to move. She had just given birth to them and would not move away!

Chester barked at her to frighten her enough to move but she stood fast. Mister Spöring grabbed at her ears and pulled her squealing to the safety of the shoreline, then ran back for the piglets, the flames edging ever closer! He managed to save all but one, which burnt to death! I made a note to call on her later to express my regret for her sad loss.

The captain was most upset having shown such good intentions to these people!

They were now running from the scene of their crime and the captain took off after them with a musket loaded with small shot!

One of the Aborigines turned on him and he shot him, harming him only enough to scare them all off! His trail left a little blood behind, on the linen that the native had run across on the beach.

All the while, I thought I was well hidden in the grass behind a rock assessing the unfolding event, but one of the dingo savages caught me by the scruff, and carted me galloping in the same direction as the Aborigines!

I would be a snack for the dingo tribe! Chester and Lady were witness to this foul play and barked with horrendous tone to call all to arms for their Fairweather!

I flopped about dangling from the evil dingo's mouth, unable to defend myself or cause harm to the kidnapper!

The other dingoes followed him knowing that they could tear me from limb to limb and all taste a piece of my fresh flesh. With much barking, Chester heralded the call and Mister Banks aimed skilfully for the offending dingo!

A blast and a jolt released me from the dingo; such was the accuracy of the shot from Mister Banks!

I floundered about on the wet sand for only a moment before leaping to my feet. No sooner had I steadied to run like the wind than another foul dingo scooped me up in a similar fashion!

The scruff of my neck was beginning to hurt like the dickens. The dingo teeth were sharp and for a second time, well into my neck!

I could not look back in hope, but wondered if Mister Banks's aim was now on this second kidnapper. I heard no shot though and death felt somehow imminent!

Without warning, the dingo dropped me! What luck!

Again, I flopped about the sand as I was released on the run! I heard a familiar "woof!" but I did not look back, as I wasted no time in righting myself and running up the nearest tree, only to look down and see Chester in a brawl with the felon!

Teeth bared and barking, Chester bit the fiend squarely on the neck and shook him with a might that I did not know him to possess!

The dingo lay there on the sand lifelessly, his neck broken!

The rest of the pack ran off with the Aborigines. Chester motioned for me to come down and we walked slowly toward the longboat, my neck aching from the grip of teeth, and Chester spitting dingo fur as we trudged along the sand.

"Chester! My most heartfelt thanks to you, my friend!" I rasped, my throat swelling from the assault.

"Think nothing of it, Fairweather. The men did not see you snatched for the second time. I was your only hope," he admitted, unusually modestly. He said nothing more and we caught up with Lady to return to the ship.

My Isaac and the boys witnessed the rescue and patted Chester heartily whilst rowing us back to the ship to seek medical attention.

The captain and Mister Banks had pursued the Aborigines for about a mile until they met an old man who carried a spear with no point. This was apparently a sign of peace and the old man sat down to show this.

He motioned that the felonious fire starters wished to be forgiven and wanted to come back to the ship. He indicated that they would not set fire to our camp again, so the captain gave them all some musket balls as much a gift as a threat!

They came back but did not go back onto the ship. The captain made it clear they were not invited, so they had to be content to watch the ship being painted with the hot pitch left over from their fiery attack.

Isaac took Chester and I to see Doctor Monkhouse.

"The cat will be quiet for a few days, his throat has some swelling, but he is lucky if he escaped from the clutches of the dingoes twice!" He looked at Isaac wondering if his story was altogether true.

"It happened as I said, sir. Will and the others witnessed it, too." The other boys all nodded that Isaac spoke the truth.

"The dog is well. Take them for a refreshment." The doctor eyed us for the signs of lies, as we left his quarters.

Chester, Lady, and I retired to the Great Cabin.

Isaac and the lads went off to report the incident to Mister Banks and the captain upon their return.

Lady was the first to speak to her unusually quiet partner. "Chester, dear, what a noble and yet dangerous feat!" she praised. "You saved the boy!"

"Yes, yes, thank you, Lady. Fairweather, are you quite alright?" he asked vaguely.

"Considering all? Yes, dear hound, and again I must say you are the hero of the day! I would have been evenly distributed inside dingoes by now, had it not been for your bravery! And not here to speak of it either!" I was having a little trouble speaking but the raspy whisper was heard.

Chester merely looked out the Great Cabin window as if concerned with other matters.

"Are you well dear?" Lady asked of him.

"Yes, my dear, but one cannot help being a little weary and ponderous after such an ordeal. I am merely tired from the struggle, and having killed a fellow canine sits unwell with me." This brooding side of Chester was new to me.

I wondered at the fellow's thinking, considering he spiritedly hunted all manner of animals for Mister Banks, yet felt uneasy about killing of his own species. I took him from that moment on to be of a deeper character than I had thought!

The captain, lieutenants and misters Banks and Spöring came rushing into the Great Cabin not long after, Mister Banks dithering over Chester to a fault.

"Brave dog, Chester!" He admired his hound with a good solid slapping on the back and a scratch behind the ears, the universal sign of a job well done to the canine world!

My captain having heard the story picked me up from my favourite chair and tucked me under his arm. I flinched not a little as he stroked my head and neck. After precariously dangling from several dingo mouths, I was a little sensitive! He understood, thankfully, and ceased his painful stroking.

"Well, Fairweather! You have escaped the clutches of death yet again. I am certain the rumour that cats have nine lives is based in truth!" He chuckled.

Mister Banks agreed.

"Fine dog, Mister Banks. The cat and I are indebted," he congratulated.

Chester sat a little more proudly now! It was a good thing that he was well praised, allowing him to forget his murderous ponderings. I would not lightly forget him for it. He had saved me from a hideous death!

The Aborigines went back to their camp in the evening, but their fires could be seen that night, as they had burned most of an entire hillock. Mister Banks considered that lighting fires must be their way of maintaining their land. We all thought it probable.

By the 20th day of July, the ship was stowed and ready to sail.

Master Molyneux had tirelessly searched mile after mile for safe passage from this place but with no luck. Shoals blocked the way out to the north, or the surf smashed against the coral reefs to the east. The captain wished to trackback the way we had come but the winds were not in our favour. We would have to wait.

The days passed with the men gathering greens, fishing, and making ropes.

Lieutenant Gore shot the largest kangaroo to date at some eighty pounds!

On the 28th day of July, the carpenters had finished caulking the ship and she was keen to sail, having been tested on high tide by edging her into the channel. Not much water came into the hold, only one inch per hour and with the newly fixed pumps, the captain deemed her fit to voyage home, as long as a route could be found.

As we were about to sail and the last-minute work was being completed, I nosed around curiously on the shoreline and spotted a large hollow log. Poking my nose into the darkness I was confronted with a familiar hissing. Upon straining my neck to ascertain what was inside I felt the sting of a sharp claw across my beezer! I snapped my body backwards bumping my head on the roof of the log.

"Who is in there?" I demanded from a safe distance.

The reply was only a low growl.

Feeling that I had the right to confront my attacker I crept around to the rear of the log and spied a recognizable tail! It was a dark grey and short of bristle, which could have been anything in this new land of ours, but I had an inkling it was of the feline variety! I crept covertly toward the tail and gave it a sharp bite.

"Reeeeoooowwwwww!" came the desired effect! A cat shot out of the other end of the log and ran up the nearest tree.

"By Jove, you are a cat!" I yelled up at it in disbelief!

I had not seen another of my species since Tahiti and wondered why I had not seen them here, if they were indeed native to the land. The grey fellow stayed in the tree looking keenly down at me with wide yellow eyes. I licked my nose where the skin had been scratched.

"Come down from there at once and state your name!" I commanded.

"I weell not come down until you agree to a truce!" said the cat with an unfamiliar accent.

"You scratched me first!" I argued. "I was merely defending myself with that nip to your tail!"

"Zat was more zan a neep!" he replied, inspecting the damage.

"A neep?" I quizzed.

"A neep! Eediot! You said you neeped my tail!" Rather a cheeky reply, considering he was avoiding me by sitting in a tree!

"I will have you know that I am not an idiot and that you will come down at once or I shall come up there and force you down!" I threatened.

"You are zee sheep's cat?" he asked, confusing me.

"The sheep?" I mocked him. "Sheep do not possess cats!"

"Non! Non! Ze cat from ze boat!" he rephrased.

"Ah the ship's cat?" I asked him to clarify.

"Oui! Zee sheep's cat!" He was confusing me. I was neither "wee" nor did I belong to a "sheep!"

"Well, speak properly you blot! I can barely understand you! Now extract yourself from that blasted tree! All this yelling back and forth is confusing and may attract the attention of the dingoes!" I warned.

"A truce, zen?" he insisted.

"Yes, yes! Alright!" I complied. He slid down the tree deftly, looking about skittishly.

"You are a feline!" I was overjoyed.

"A félin?" It sounded close enough to what I was asking so I nodded. "I am a sheep's cat also!" He stood proudly, but his eyes darted from their sockets in all directions.

"For the last time, 'sheep' do not own cats!" I knew this for a fact and the fellow required straightening out on this point.

"Sheep! Boat! Same zing!" he snapped back rudely at my inability to understand him.

"It is not the same thing in the English language, sir! But I shall not argue further with you on the subject. We are wasting time and our ship sails soon! Are you indigenous to this country? Are there more of you hiding? I have not seen any of you in all our time here!" I asked keenly.

"Indigène?" Non, non! I am French!" he bloated. "I am ze only cat here since my landing in June 1768." I was astounded!

"1768? It is currently 1770! You have been here alone for two years? This does not make any sense as we Englishmen were the first to discover this Australia! How did you get here?" was the obvious question.

He puffed himself up, ready to educate me, but still looking about for dingoes. I, too, was becoming a little nervous. We agreed that our introductions and stories would be best conducted in the tree above. We both climbed to a comfortable branch and sat low to avoid detection.

"I am Fairweather of the Bark *Endeavour* out of England and captained by Lieutenant James Cook." I introduced myself.

"I am François of ze frigate *Boudeuse* out of France, by Capitaine Nicolas Pierre Duclos-Guyot. Our expedition leader was Louis-Antoine, Count de Bougainville."

"Bougainville?" I asked, searching the grey matter for this familiar name. "Ah, Mister Banks mentioned of him when we were in Tierra del Fuego!"

The grey chap sported a rather worn collar with his name upon it along with the name "Bougainville."

"I 'ave too been zere!" Surprise crossed our faces as we realised we were kindred sailors on a similar adventure!

"Tell me all, François, leave nothing out!" I was so happy to have a fellow feline and mariner in my midst and I wished to hear how he got to this Australia.

He began as if he had been saving this story for someone to ask of it, and finally two years on, he had his chance.

"We set sail from Nantes, France on 15th of November 1766 wis' two sheeps. I was on ze frigate *Boudeuse*, capitained by Nicolas Pierre Duclos-Guyot. Ze second sheep was for ze stores, ze Étoile, wis' my friend Rene as sheep's cat, and captained by François Chenard de la Giraudais. Ze Étoile was slower and left separately, to join us in Rio de Janeiro later."

"I must interrupt here, François. The word for the boat is 'ship,' not 'sheep'! Tidy up this word as you are confusing me," I demanded.

"Sheep…sheep…shep…ship!" He had mastered it. I was most pleased and begged him continue.

"Louis-Antoine, Compte de Bougainville was our expedition leader. He 'ad French government backing to circumnavigate ze world and discover ze great Souzern Continent."

"Souzern?" His accent was bothersome!

"Zis place! Souzern!" He was angering at my insolence.

"Ah, you mean 'southern'! Yes, but we discovered it! It is now known as Australia!" I said proudly. He ignored me and prattled on obviously having no one to talk to since his landing here. I let him resume.

"Like your Mister Banks, Spöring and Doctor Solander, we too had a botaneste and docteur in Philibert Çommerson and 'is valet Jean Barét until ze scandal in Tahiti…"

"Tahiti?" I asked. "We have been there, too! Do you know the cats there? One in particular I took a liking to. Her name was Kitchen?" I quizzed. He took absolutely no notice of my question and continued his tale as if he had practiced long and hard for this moment. I let him be.

"I weell get to Tahiti later! Our astronomer was Pierre-Antoine Véron, like your Mister Charles Green. Our writers and 'istorians were Louis-Antoine Starot de Saint-Germain and a fellow wis' only one name, Michau. Ze surgeons, Louis-Claude Laporte and François Vives looked after ze men."

"I say old boy, enough with the French names. One does get the general picture and you are most observant to know of our dignitaries."

"I 'ave been watching you for some time," he admitted.

"And you have waited until our departure date to come forward?" I was a little miffed that my fellow feline had not made himself known to me!

"I was not sure of your intentions 'ere, Fairweazer. I did not know if ze English ate cats," he explained. I took umbrage at the mispronunciation of my name, as I had inflected the correct French accent into his name as a matter of courtesy.

"I understand but we English do not partake of cat!" I was piqued, but he was obviously concerned for his own skin and I begged he continue.

"You were manned much like the *Endeavour*, yes?" I attempted to clarify.

"Oui!" said François.

"Wee?" I quizzed unable to understand his thick French accent. I could see nothing small in the vicinity to warrant the word "wee!"

"Non, 'oui', it means 'yes' in your English," he explained hurriedly in an attempt to blurt out as many facts as possible with one breath!

"Well, say 'yes' if you mean 'yes' old bean! I am an Englishman!" I scolded, having none of this French business wherever I could help it.

"Oui…err…yes, Fairweazer," he complied.

"Although Monsieur Bougainville was in charge of ze voyage, he was not a sailing man and Capitaine Duclos-Guyot was in charge of ze ship. On ze 17th of November 1767, after only sailing two days, we 'ad a big storm, breaking two of our masts and forcing us to make repairs in Brest until we sailed again on ze 5th of December." He took a breath.

"Yes, storms are treacherous, but we have been lucky," I confirmed. Again he went on with his story with no acknowledgement of my comments.

"Monsieur Bougainville had settled ze Falkland Islands at 'is own expense in 1763, but England was jealous, and Spain feared zat ze French ownership of ze Falkland Islands would become a rear base for France to attack and steal 'er Peruvian gold. Monsieur Bougainville was ordered by ze French government to evacuate 'is colonists and sell ze islands to the Spanish. Ze King of Spain paid 'im six hundred and zree zousand pounds for ze Falkland Islands at a meeting in Montevideo."

"Yes, we passed the Falkland Islands but did not make land there." I may as well have been talking to myself. He was not listening and frowned at my interruptions.

"We finally met up wis' ze Spanish ships, ze Esmerelda and Liebre and we zree set sail on ze 28th of February 1767 for ze Falklands. Ze islands were handed over on ze 1st of April 1767. Bougainville's settlers were allowed to stay under Spanish rule or return to France. Ten volunteered to sail wis' us, replacing ze sick and ze zree deserters who ran away in Montevideo. Ze Spanish ships left us on ze 27th of April and we waited at Port Louis for the Étoile to catch up wis' us. Ze Étoile had not shown up by ze end of May, so we sailed on ze 2nd of June to our second selected rendezvous, Rio de Janeiro. We anchored zere on ze 21st of June where we found ze Étoile waiting for us.

"Ah Rio de Janeiro! We too have been there!" I chirped in. "My memories of that place are not fond. We were delayed by the port authorities and shot at on our way out!"

"Zey shot at you?" His first response since starting his story.

"Yes! They…" I was immediately interrupted for the continuation of his story. I merely sighed and listened.

"Francis Nicolas Buet de Kemper, the Étoile's chaplain had been murdered on shore while zey waited zere for us!" he gasped.

"Brutes!" I agreed.

"Oui…err…yes," he continued. "At first, we were welcomed by ze Portuguese viceroy but after a few days fights broke out between our crew on shore leave and ze local Portuguese. Monsieur Bougainville zought it wise for us to leave for Montevideo. Our sheeps…err…ships, left Rio de Janeiro on ze 15th of July 1767. Ze Étoile was taking on water and was much slower than our frigate ze *Boudeuse* and often we had to wait for the Étoile to catch up wis' us. Monsieur Bougainville left us in Montevideo to attend to some business in Buenos Aires and when he returned, he found zat ze Étoile 'ad been badly damaged by another ship dragging anchor in a severe storm and 'itting it. The bowsprit was gone and a zere was a hole in ze bow taking on water. Ze port of Montevideo did not 'ave ze facilities to repair ze Étoile. He sailed it to Ensenada de Baragan to a refitting yard where he anchored it waiting permission for repairs. Permission took one monse, verrry slow!"

"Monse?" I dared to ask.

"Yes, monse, thirty days, sometimes thirty one, February twenty eight or nine!" he snapped.

"You mean month!" I declared. François shook his head as if I were some kind of dullard.

"Ze cargo was removed from ze Étoile and ze repairs were made, zen she was reloaded and left for Montevideo on ze 31st of October and landing on ze 3rd of November. Finally, we left on ze 14th of November, a full year since we 'ad left France!"

"Some serious delays, old chap!" I noted.

"Yes, and zen on our passage past Patagonia the Étoile was damaged again in a storm!" The pitch of his voice becoming feverish with excitement.

"We entered ze Straits Magellan on ze 5th of December."

"I am familiar with the Straits, but we took the Straits Lemaire instead of Magellan so do spare me your place names as I do not know the area," I requested.

"Oui…er…yes, Fairweazer. The year 1768 did not start well for us. We were snowed in wis' gale winds and rain. It was below freezing and we suffered much. Eventually on ze 25th of January 1768 after two attempts to leave, ze weazer changed and we rounded ze Twelve Apostle Rocks and into ze Pacific Ocean!" He was chuffed, as one would be after such a harrowing passage.

"We zen passed by many islands, the Tuamotus. Monsieur Bougainville took possession of zem for France, wis'out landing. We sailed norz and found ze Polynesian Island of Moorea, anchoring on ze east coast of ze northern part of ze island."

"I am well versed in Tahiti which is Moorea's neighbouring island!" I volunteered. He still kept to his train of thought without asking of my experiences, as if he were running out of time. I must admit I was wondering when he would finish as the ship was due to leave at any time.

"We were not welcomed so well by ze islanders, but Monsieur Bougainville promised to be gone wi'sin eighteen days, so a peace was found."

"Funny that!" I exclaimed. "We were treated with kindness by the natives. Sometimes there was the odd scuffle but nothing our good captain could not fix!"

He ignored me yet again.

"We made a building close to a stream for ze sick," he continued.

"Sick?" I quizzed.

"Ze scurvy, Fairweazer! You must know of zis being a sheep's cat!" I ignored his mispronunciation and defended our anti-scurvy practise.

"No, François, our men are all hale and healthy due to the taking of fresh fruit and vegetables as ordered by the captain!" I bragged.

"Zsst! Zsst!" he waived a paw, not believing me for a second.

"Don't you mean Pfft! Pfft!?" I asked.

"Non! Zsst! Zsst!" Each one to their own, I concluded.

He continued. "We drew water for ze shee…ship!"

I nodded approval as he went on.

"Our soldiers guarded ze camp for ze natives were zieves!" I understood his misspoken "thieves." I had correctly deduced that the chap could not pronounce "th" and left him to it.

"The men collected wood and Monsieur Çommerson and 'is valet Jean Barét, collected specimens. It was 'ere zat Jean Barét on ze first visit to the island was surrounded by ze natives who cried out zat he was a woman!"

I was riveted.

"One native chief was even attracted to her! When ze capitaine found out, she explained zat she was a woman of twenty-six, an orphan from Burgundy. After the loss of a lawsuit and penniless, she was forced to disguise herself and work as a valet. The Bougainville expedition piqued her curiosity and she joined our botanist Çommerson as his valet onboard ze *Boudeuse*. When zis scandal was revealed she was confined to ze shee…ship!" At least he was trying with the word. "Her true name was Jeanne Barét, not Jean!"

"Sounds the same to me!" I interrupted.

"Non, Jean is like your John, and Jeanne is more a feminine name." I was educated.

"Ze capitaine promised to protect 'er from ze men and to help her procure a pardon from France for 'er debts upon our return."

"What a difficulty it must have been for her!" I commented.

"Yes, Fairweazer, she was most brave to attempt zis, no?" he agreed.

"From now, I am forever astounded at the strength of womenfolk!" I concluded my comments on the subject and begged he continue.

"Men gazered crops to cure ze sick of 'zeir scurvy and zen strong winds blew on ze 12th of April losing our anchors and cables. We were lucky to not be driven on to ze coral. On ze 13th three natives had been killed or wounded and ze chiefs were verrry angry. The capitaine put four soldiers in irons to show zat someone would be punished, and gave ze chiefs many gifts. All was forgiven. Chief Eriti persuaded our capitaine to take a native wis' us. 'Aotourou' was 'is name."

"We too have a Tahitian native on board the *Endeavour*. His name is Tupia and his servant Tiata…" Again my own story took a back seat to his.

"Monsieur Bougainville erected a sign on a tree near ze beach and buried a bottle wis' a message in it for future travellers. We called it Nouvelle Cythère and claimed it for France!" He bloated.

"Now here you are mistaken, François!" I interjected. "The Tahitis as they are now known, is an English discovery and possession of recent date!"

"Non! Non! Fairweazer it is you who are misguided! We were zere before you English and it is called Nouvelle Cythère!" he demanded.

"Incorrect, sir!" I bristled patriotically. "England owns Tahiti!"

"Silly, Fairweazer!" He laughed. "Ze whole area is now known as French Polynesia! Hence, it is French!" He emphasised, giving me that look as if I were missing some grey matter.

"Captain Cook made claim to Tahiti!" I argued.

"I will 'ave none of zis! We French were 'ere before you Englishmen!" he proclaimed.

"We will see, François." I gave in for the sake of expedition of the story. "No doubt our governments will work it out for ownership."

"Yes, but France will own Nouvelle Cythère!" He stood firm.

"May we continue with the story?" I was watching the ship making ready and we had not much time.

He nodded, so as to continue his chronicle.

"Ze *Étoile* sailed norzerly on ze 14th of April and us on ze *Boudeuse* ze next day. We were 'eaded for ze Great Souzern Continent. Continuing west, on ze 3rd of May we discovered islands naming zem the Manu'a Group and claimed zem for France. On ze 5th of May, we saw Tutuila, zen Upolu, but we did not land as ze weazer did not permit and we sailed on, claiming zem for France. Passing Espiritu Santo Island, we entered ze strait separating it from Malekula Island and hoped to discover ze Great Souzern Continent."

Here he became quite animated and almost hysterical.

"By ze 3rd of June 1768, we 'eared ze sound of breakers and fired our canons to warn ze *Étoile*. A reef wis' 'uge breaking surf kept us from going any furzer west to ze Great Souzern Continent. Ze captain named zis reef Bougainville Reef after our leader, and we stood off it until morning. Capitaine Duclos-Guyot ordered that ze last goat and ze dog be eaten for dinner zat night and ze rats I 'ad captured were kept and cooked!

"Yes, I am well aware that men find the odd rat palatable when in need. Your stocks must have been very low!" I commented.

He fidgeted agitatedly for me to cease my interruptions so as he could continue his story.

"Oui, Fairweazer!" He forgot himself but I let it go. "I was next on ze menu! I was ze last animal alive on ze ships! Rene must 'ave been eaten too as I 'ad not 'eard from 'im for some days between ze two ships!" He cried.

"What?" I was agog.

"Oui! I, François de Beaujolais of Lyon France, ze vineyard félin was to be eaten! And by ze capitaines, no less! And poor Rene! 'Ad I known of zis plan I could 'ave got word to 'im and 'e could 'ave jumped wiz moi!" He was bursting with agitation!

I could only sit stunned at this news and await the next flurry from him.

"Oui! I was as shocked as you! Horreur de mon coeur et âme! " He was so upset he had reverted to his native tongue! "Étant mangé par les capitaines!" He nearly fell out of the tree!

"English, dear boy!" I ordered. "I do not understand you in this vital part of your history!

"Oui, horror of my 'eart and soul! Being eaten by the capitaines! Or somesing like zat!" He translated.

"I can well imagine!" I agreed whole-heartedly. He had slipped into a stupor and I had to urge him to continue for a change.

"Pray tell, what next François?" I implored.

"I jumped from ze ship when no one was looking!" My eyes leapt from their sockets!

"Into the sea?" I asked incredulously.

"Oui, Eediot! Into ze sea! I was not going to be dinner! De toutes les questions stupides!" He scolded me.

I got the gist and did not require a translation.

"So, how did you get here?" I asked stupidly.

"I swam 'ere! Imbécile!" I was not enjoying his tirades but the story held more importance.

"I was battered by ze surf but determined to 'ead for land, which 'ad been seen from ze ship moments before I jumped!"

I watched the horror on his face as he described his ordeal.

"I was tumbled and beaten on the coral, and 'ad to swim a verrry long way to land. I paddled and paddled but the land did not seem to get any closer. I must 'ave fainted from 'ow you say? Épuisement?... ex...exhaust..." he paused.

"Exhaustion old boy!" I was captivated!

"Oui...er yes!" I was glad his English was back on track.

"And?" I grew impatient.

"I woke up on ze beach a few miles from 'ere, alone and sick. I hid myself in the 'ills and Nugal-Warra's caves norse-east of 'ere, where ze Guugu Yimithirr tribe draw art on its walls. Zey did not know I was zere for some time." He took a breather and relaxed a little.

"Good Lord, François! I am hardly able to comment! You have been here for nearly two years! Alone? No other cats to keep you company?"

"None, alone I was." He drifted into a melancholy and stared off into the distance.

"I detected no cats here during our stay! If you had been watching us for some time, why did you not come forward?" I asked.

"I repeat, I was not sure whezer you English eat cat!" he reminded me.

"Well, that has now been established," I confirmed.

"I 'ave waited and waited but I 'ave not seen the *Boudeuse* and Étoile since, nor any ozer ship." His melancholy returning. "Zen one day I came down to ze river and zere you were!" He brightened somewhat.

"How then have you survived all this time?" I wondered.

"Ze trees kept me from ze dingo packs and zey could not reach me in ze sacred caves as I 'id high up in zem. I 'ad to be vigilant when ze 'unters were about. Again, ze trees 'id me well."

"But what of food, François?" I asked obviously.

"I 'unted ze local bush animals at night until one day I was seen in ze Nugal-Warra cave by ze cave painters. Zey 'ad never seen any'sing such as me before. Zat is 'ow I know zere are no félins 'ere. I disappeared into a hole in ze cave wall before zey could catch me. Zey returned wis ze whole tribe and ze painters drew my shape on ze wall. No one believed zey 'ad seen such a 'sing and 'zey decided I was a spirit only seen sometimes and never when ze Aborigène were around. Zey left bark out wiz food on it for me daily from 'zen on. I would only come out to eat it when no one was zere. Zis was lucky for me, no?" he asked.

"A most desirable outcome considering the circumstances!" I commented.

"A what?" he said, confused.

"Never mind, François," I said. "Lucky for you, yes!"

I was keen to learn more but was rudely interrupted by a familiar barking below us.

"Stop that barking foul hound!" I yelled down at Chester who had sought out François's scent and barked furiously at the tree. François was afraid and became one with the branch we were atop.

"Who is that up there? I smell a blasted cat and it is not you!" he demanded.

"Chester! This is François from the Bougainville expedition! Allow us to come down and I will update you!" I yelled at him.

"There is no time to bring me up to date, you blot! The *Endeavour* sails as soon as the winds favour and we must all be on the ship. I was sent to find you! And here you are passing the time of day with an unknown feline? You never cease to annoy!" he growled.

"But this fellow is a significant find! He has been marooned here for two years alone!" I explained as I shimmed down the tree expecting François to follow.

"I am not coming down, Fairweazer! Zat is a dog!" He had every right to be afraid, I supposed.

"It is safe, François! This is Chester of the Bark *Endeavour*. Mister Banks's chief hound and my very good friend! He will not harm you, will you, Chester?" I shot him a look.

"Come down, friend of Fairweather. If he says so, I shall not harm you," Chester woofed impatiently.

François shimmed down the tree nervously and stood as still as a statue while Chester sniffed him all over. Satisfied that François was indeed a cat he sat as Lady approached.

"There you are, dear!" she was relieved. "And who is your friend?" Lady was much better mannered than Chester at all times.

I explained briefly, and then Chester puffed himself up. "Well, say your goodbyes, old thing. The ship sails at any time now and we must be ready!" He was dutiful to the end.

"But what of François? We cannot leave him here! We must rescue him and take him with us!" I decided. François's eyes widened, thinking he might make it back to France, an idea he had no doubt dismissed long ago and given his situation.

"Fairweather! I will not allow another bothersome cat on board my ship!" he protested.

"Your ship? The captain and the gents would see it differently, given that he has a collar with Bougainville's mark upon it!" I argued.

"Fairweather is correct, dear, Mister Banks would be most pleased to see him," Lady added.

"Hurrumph!" Chester objected, but knew that Lady and I were right. "Well, get a move on then, all of you! We must away to the last longboat and back to the ship." He was not as thrilled as I to have another cat on board but he knew I was right, and that his master would be pleased.

We raced off to the beach at speed as my Isaac was preparing the longboat to leave with a full cargo of wild cabbage for the trip ahead. He looked at us running towards him and tilted his head curiously.

"Am I seeing double Fairweather? Or have you found a cat here?" He was shocked at the sight of François, knowing that cats were not native to this land. He bent down to inspect his collar.

"François!" he blurted. "A friend for Fairweather!" He shouted to the other boys. He looked closer at the collar. "Bougainville?" he uttered. He was speechless when the other boys joined us.

"What's wrong, Isaac?" asked Will Howson. "Have you seen a ghost?"

"I may as well have! This is Bougainville's cat, lads!" he was stunned.

"Bougainville? The Frenchman? But he didn't land here!" scoffed Will, all knowingly. "Let me see…"

As he and Isaac sat on their haunches, the other boys looked down to see for themselves. I sat dusting a gnat from my paw nonchalantly, being the discoverer of said fellow.

"He's right!" said Will Howson as the boys took their turns in checking the collar for themselves.

"Blimey! How'd he get here?" Isaac asked me. Unfortunately, as always when something warranted a good explanation, I was unable to convey the story to him, and such a good story it was!

"Captain'll be miffed if the French landed here before us!" said Will, not knowing that François had swum here.

"Good point, Will! We better be off and tell him." Isaac motioned for the boys to collect the dogs and François and I and off we sped, the boys rowing hard, to the *Endeavour*.

Isaac usually carried me up the rope ladder but he had François under his arm, so Will Howson tucked me under and scurried up the rope with the other boys.

Isaac was off like a shot to the Great Cabin to tell the captain and gents of his find, while Will dropped me unceremoniously on the deck and I had to make my own way down there. I would have taken umbrage but François was a discovery of some monument, and must be reported to the captain immediately.

As I sauntered into the room, the gents had already gathered with the captain and were taking their turn to look at François's collar.

"Indeed, gentlemen!" Mister Banks spouted. "So, Bougainville has been here before us?" He was displeased.

"It seems so, Mister Banks," said the captain downheartedly.

I was not in a position to enlighten, even by signs to my captain, as he was not alone and our banter was always unaccompanied for fear that the gents and crew might think the captain daft.

"Bougainville?" they all said one by one, inspecting François's collar.

"I heard he had returned without sighting Australia," said Lieutenant Gore.

"As did I," agreed Lieutenant Hicks.

"It cannot be possible, lieutenants, if we have François, ship's cat of the frigate *Boudeuse* in our midst!" boasted Mister Banks. "Where did you find him, Isaac?" he turned to the lad, as I took my place on the captain's chair to oversee the doings.

"On the beach with Fairweather, Mister Banks, sir." Isaac was well pleased with his discovery.

"If they could talk, they would have splendid tales to tell each other!" the captain said and everyone laughed. "And François would be capable of enlightening us all of the French movements." The laughter continued.

French landing before us? Pffft! The cowards fled at the first sign of a reef! I said to myself as François was petted and marvelled at upon the map table of the Great Cabin.

"François looks a little thin. Have the cook find him some victuals!" ordered Mister Banks of Tupia's servant Tiata.

Off he scurried keenly, still waiting for his turn to pat François. He returned promptly with my plate from the good and worthy John Thompson! And loaded with goodness, it was!

Again, this found yours truly a little peeved, but the poor brute had not partaken of a good ship's dinner in some time, so I let it be. Tiata placed my plate in front of François and he gorged himself appropriately on a fine English meal. Sitting on the chart table he licked his paws to clean his face as Tiata petted him softly.

"Tupia!" beckoned the captain. "Your young boy here seems quite taken with François. I charge him with his welfare," the captain ordered. The beam on Tiata's face was unmistakeable as that of pure joy to have a pet to tend!

I did not know if a member of his French crew had tended François but I gave him a nod to convince him that this was indeed a good idea. Tiata would no doubt be his sponsor, much like my Isaac was to me. I would show him around later, when the novelty had expired and he would soon find his feet aboard the *Endeavour*.

As the gents and officers left the Great Cabin, Tiata took François to sleep with him. I was of that inclination so I snoozed as the captain pottered around.

I caught up with my captain, tending his diary again on the night of the 4th day of August. He was sick of being stuck in what was now known as "cooktown." He had little to say but "Laying in port spends time to no purpose, consumes our provisions of which we are very short in many articles, and we have yet a long passage to make to the East Indies through an unknown and perhaps dangerous sea, these circumstances considered, makes me very anxious of getting to sea!"

I felt for the man as his frustration had grown with each passing day, waiting for the winds to favour us, and now he doubted he could get us home.

He petted me while examining his charts, pitifully fearing his claiming of Australia for King George to be too late!

He was heading us for the new route known as Torres Strait, discovered by Luis Váez de Torres, a Spanish sailor who was the first to successfully sail through the strait, in late 1606. He guessed that this strait lay between the East Indies and our Australia.

He intended us to go this way as far as the northern tip of Australia would take us, and on to the East Indies to the first outpost of civilization, Dutch Batavia.

"So, you have a new friend and comrade, Fairweather? Bougainville's very own cat, no less. This should amuse you?" He quizzed with some maudlin, as if a man beaten to the important discovery of this Australia. I clawed his hand resting on the map, drawing a small amount of blood.

"Ouch, Fairweather! Why this attack on my person? Are you jealous of François?" He wrongly determined. I licked my paw and marked the map at Bougainville Reef where François had deserted his ship. I leapt upon the spot, there on the map table and "meowed" at him, to convince him that an alert was required. Then I walked the route they would have taken to avoid the surf. The captain was curious.

"Did you speak with this, François?" he asked quietly as the gents had not yet retired for the night but were readying for bed and would hear him.

I nodded.

"Did Bougainville land here before us?" he ventured.

I shook my head. The captain's eyes darted from their sockets.

"How did François get here, then?" he asked suspiciously.

I jumped from the map table to the floor and began a swimming motion.

"He abandoned ship?" asked the captain, hoping it was true.

I nodded.

"Excellent news, Fairweather! This shall remain our secret!" He looked about him for listeners as he lifted me back onto the map table and poured us both a refreshment of the brandy kind.

He sat back as I lapped at my saucer and toasted me as his saviour for the new land of the king, as if beating the French to this new land was amongst his highest priorities. I was delighted and napped with him for the night.

CHAPTER 32

As if by magic, the next day saw favourable breezes and the captain ordered us under way, slowly and cautiously following the pinnace with Master Molyneux in it, sounding the depths and signalling the shoals.

However, the wind shifted and we were stuck surrounded by shoals as the tide ran out, forcing us to lay anchored in the deepest water.

The next day, the winds persisted in the wrong direction for us and we made no progress. The pinnace went back and forth to the reef to bring in as many turtles and fish as we could hold.

During the night, the *Endeavour* was dragging on her anchor and straight for the shoals. Most of our other anchors had been thrown into the sea when we were holed. The last remaining sheet anchor was put into service stopping us from running aground.

With this beating wind and the tides running in the same direction the men were forced to take down the sails. It was a restless night for all. In the morning, the captain climbed to the topmast on the low tide and found no way out of here in any direction.

Master Molyneux's only recommendation was to go back south the way we had come in but the captain was not sure that this was even more dangerous than trying to push north. He was very tired, and had not slept for days keeping a watch for an opening in the breakers on the reef and keeping the *Endeavour* from bottoming on the sandy shoals.

On the high tides, the captain inched us through the deeper channels passing Cape Bedford with some hope. But again, the reef and shoals surrounded us so that the captain named the next point, Cape Flattery, for lulling us into a sense we would escape the reef.

We passed at Point Lookout and the captain took us to within a reasonable distance of Lizard Island, taking the longboat to shore and walking to the highest peak to ascertain the waters between several other islands.

Although the weather was hazy, he was of the opinion, studying the surf, that indeed there was a break in the reef. He could not be sure but he knew what he must do.

He edged our way slowly past Eagle Island, Master Molyneux going ashore to discover that the Aboriginal people must visit this island as turtle shells were discarded here and there.

We awaited his return with the news that a narrow channel ran between Lizard and Eagle islands but Master Molyneux deemed it dangerous. The captain knew we must take this route by some inward knowledge, and the certainty that following the mainland would find us land locked with merely three months of provisions on board.

We hoisted sail and edged our way through on the 13th day of August with Master Molyneux in the pinnace ahead. The passage was but a mile wide and the swell of the surf was still there, and while the waves did not break about us, the thunderous crash of them upon the reefs on each side of us was enough to frighten the strongest seaman!

We inched our way through tentatively and were now out in the open sea and free of the shoals and fears among us!

A rousing cheer came up for the captain upon Master Molyneux's return to the ship and much congratulating and backslapping occurred.

We headed north at speed leaving the reef and all its wonders to its own business for the while. The rollers we were sailing ensured us that no reefs were near and for the first time in some three months we were completely out of sight of dry land.

The heavy sea made the *Endeavour* leak a little more but on report, no more than nine inches every hour and no more than one pump could discharge back into the sea. This was looked upon as a light evil compared to our being stuck on Australia's shores with no hope of seeing home.

We were headed for New Guinea and Torres Strait, supposing the strait lay between it and Australia. Again, the intrepid explorer, he could have stayed well clear of the mainland but would miss the opportunity to chart it for future captains, and discover the northernmost point of Australia.

Mister Banks was unimpressed with this menacing potential manoeuvre and stormed in on the captain when he had first heard of his plans. Chester and Lady were in tow, as was Mister Spöring and

Tupia, his avid disciples. I was already seated with the man he sought, along with the lieutenants and Master Molyneux.

"Have we not had enough of this reef problem, Captain?" he begged.

"There is a channel through between this Australia and New Guinea and I intend to investigate," said the captain resolutely. Nodding came from the others who agreed with the captain.

"A reef such as I now speak is a thing scarcely known in Europe or indeed anywhere but in these seas. It is a wall of coral rock rising almost perpendicularly out of the unfathomable ocean, always covered at high water commonly seven or eight feet, and generally bare at low water; the large waves of the vast ocean meeting with so sudden a resistance make here a most terrible surf breaking mountainously high, especially when as in our case the general trade wind blows directly upon it. We dare not go through it, Captain?" Mister Banks was a dither and explaining to the captain the facts about reefs that he already well knew.

"Mister Banks!" he sounded. "Have I prohibited you from your discoveries?"

"No, Captain, but…" he pleaded, Mister Spöring pulling at his coat tails as if to egg him on.

"Then I will hear nought of it, Mister Banks!" A voice rarely raised coming from the captain. "We enter through the first available gap in the reef and hug the land to find this Torres Strait, charting to the northern tip of Australia as we go!"

The lieutenants and Master Molyneux looked at each other, knowing the captain to be right in doing so, but afraid all the same. This looking about was not lost on the captain.

"Have any of us forgotten the spirit of our orders from the Royal Society?" he barked, angered by this doubt.

"No, sir!" came the cry from the lieutenants in unison with Master Molyneux, for they were sure to wish a command of their own such as their captain's someday, and must follow the man blindly into anything to ensure their success. He had not led them astray thus far and had been the model of good sense.

"I do not wish to proceed in this manner!" Mister Banks blustered, stamping his foot! Mister Spöring and Tupia had the good sense to be quiet.

"Then Mister Banks, I will be most pleased to land you on the nearest shore on the morrow, so that you may await a cruising ship to take you comfortably back to England!" Mister Banks gasped. Mister Spöring coughed and backed away, bowing to where Tupia stood out of harm's way.

"You wouldn't dare!" coughed Mister Banks, his voice had somewhat of that girlish tone, as he nervously fidgeted with his kerchief.

The captain stood and leaned forward on his desk engaging the eye of his botanist.

"Oh, but you are mistaken, Mister Banks! Any more challenges to my authority or intentions will be treated as mutinous and those responsible will be put ashore at the earliest possible convenience!" He warned through gnashing teeth.

Tupia and Mister Spöring had the good sense to bow and back out of the Great Cabin.

Mister Banks shrivelled under the captain's glare.

"As you wish it, Captain!" His girlishness still evident. "I will not be pleased should you be mistaken on this course you take, and I may have to report you to the Royal Society should we make it home at all!" He wanted the last word, and turning on his heel with a fluster so that the captain could not chastise him further he strutted off in a huff.

"Come, Chester! Come, Lady!" he snapped. Chester and Lady gave me an odd look and went with their master.

The captain turned to the lieutenants and Master Molyneux, who were now his greatest allies, knowing that the captain would indeed put them off the ship should they protest, or they would be tried for mutiny when we finally got back to England.

"We will carry on to look for Torres Strait." He was still seething but managed to remain calm. "Master Molyneux will arrange the pinnace and yawl to sound us when the tide and winds are right."

"Yes, Captain!" came the reply, not a doubt to be heard.

The lieutenants and Master Molyneux left and went about their duties and I was alone with my captain. I jumped to the table that he was still leaning across as if to relay my support for his aims.

"Fairweather, be off with you!" He swiped me across the table and I landed on the floor below. There I was holding out the paw of advocacy and he tossed me, ignoring my intention! I was not a little miffed!

I stood tall and walked from the room, not turning back to acknowledge his apology. I would not hold it against him as he had much upon his mind, but for now I was wounded and left him to himself. A previously unseen temper in him was duly noted for the future.

I located François the next morning taking breakfast in the Great Cabin. Tiata had permission from the captain but I thought it a little rude as I was always supped in the galley! As I entered, the captain shot me an apologetic glance and I nodded to him that all was forgiven.

"Ah François, there you are, old boy. How did you sleep?" I asked casually.

"I slept like I 'ave not slept in two years! No dingoes or natives to disturb me, and a nice boy to keep me warm! Magnifique!" He licked his paws and washed after his meal.

"You will show me around the ship?" he asked.

"Yes of course, follow me, dear boy," I prompted casually.

We inspected every nook and cranny and I told him of this and that. He always had a story of his own to compare with our ship's construction and use. It seemed that in his opinion, his French ship, the *Boudeuse*, was better in all manner of ways than the *Endeavour*, and I grew tired of his bragging.

"François!" I turned on him. "If the *Boudeuse* was a better ship then why are you not still on it?" I snapped.

He had been successfully put in his place.

"I just make ze observation, Fairweather. I do not belittle 'zis fine ship who saved me." He backed down and took further instruction from me without incident.

My main aim was to establish him as a crewman as I did not intend him to laze about whilst I tended my duties. He, too, would be catching mice and ridding the stores of vermin if I had my way!

"I am good at 'zis, 'ow you say? Mousing?" He boasted. I doubted very much that he could out-mouse yours truly but I let him have a go at it. I waited by the gangway and he came back from the stores empty mouthed.

"What of this mousing talent of yours, François?" I asked nonchalantly.

"Zere are no mice 'ere in ze stores!" he argued.

"That, my dear François, is because I have them eradicated to a point where my work is now manageable. I leave a few happy hidden couples to reproduce. Not until they become a pest do I gather them for our grateful cook, John Thompson." I buffed a claw and grinned with pride.

"Ah, you are smart, Fairweazer!" he praised appropriately.

"Off to the galley to meet our good and kind staff," I urged. He followed me, receiving petting and chin scratching from whomever we passed.

Henry Jeffs and John Thompson were preparing turtle, of which we had gathered much and threw a large piece to François and a small morsel to me.

"Ah this is the famous cat of Bougainville, Fairweather?" He threw him another scrap, but this time none for me! I was piqued!

"Be careful, he might do you out of a job!" He laughed. "Never 'eard of two cats on a ship. Captain might chuck you off! Gettin' a bit fat and lazy there, Fairweather!" Henry Jeffs joined in the laughter. I was mortified. My closest comrades! Not only overfeeding the fellow but also belittling my position in front of him!

"I 'sink you are safe 'ere, Fairweather," François mumbled, chewing down the best parts of the turtle. "I wish only to go to Dutch Batavia to join a French ship." He swallowed.

That might all be very well, but the captain and crew did not know this and no doubt expected him to sail back to England with us! I would have to be careful with this fellow! He and I progressed to the deck to visit with Chester and Lady.

Passing the boys, Isaac said, "Fairweather! Showing François around the ship?" I shot him a nasty glance that made him chuckle. "Oh, I see! Jealous of the attention the French cat's gettin'?" He nudged young Isaac Manly.

"Don't worry, Fairweather," droned young Isaac dumbly. "I'll make sure you're looked after." He probably remembered the comfort I gave him when he was new to the ship and cried almost every night. Good lad, that!

We marched on finding Chester and Lady lazing on the foredeck under the stars.

"Ah, there you are, foul cats!" gloated Chester.

"Leave off with the insults, Chester, you know you are my dearest friend!" I chastened.

"You are friends wiz' ze dogs?" François was aghast.

"Why of course, old thing! We are the best of friends, comrades to the end!" I was proud of my affiliation with the canine species. "After all, we must work together for the good of the ship!"

"Impossible!" he bristled as Chester growled a little.

"Not at all, François! The canine, while awkward and dumb at times, is quite a useful fellow!" I chuckled at Chester's expense.

"Foul beast!" Chester sniped at me.

"Stop that, you two!" Lady injected. "You both know we are companions and fellow crewmates. Do not lead François astray!" she chided.

"Yes, dear," mumbled Chester.

"Yes, Lady," I added.

"Well, if Fairweazer says so, you are my friends also! I am François de Beaujolais from Lyon, France and I am very 'appy to meet you bose." He bowed reverently. Chester's head cocked sideways, not understanding François's accent, but he got the gist.

"Are you going to be as annoying to me as this foul Fairweather?" Chester asked, toying with me.

"Non, non, I am a guest and I am at your service!" François bowed again.

Chester was noticeably impressed. "Fairweather, you should take a leaf out of this chap's book. He knows his place in the order of things!"

"Pffft! Chester!" I scolded, and just as there was about to be a rather public argument and a bit of hissing and growling, the order came from Lieutenant Hicks. The brothers Littleboy rushed to us and took Chester and Lady off to Mister Banks's cabin where they would be out of the way.

The winds had changed and we were drifting toward another reef in the dark! François heard the sound of the waves and began to shake in anticipation of the ship slamming into the coral and rocks. This being when he had jumped from his own ship, I saw him visibly shaken.

"Calm down, dear boy!" The captain will have the ship under control.

"Nous descendrons un ce récif!" he cried, lapsing into his native tongue.

"Stop it! You are hysterical! I cannot understand you!" I snarled.

"We will be sinking on zis reef!" he shrieked his interpretation.

"I must attend my captain! Find a place to hide out of the way of the men and their duties!" I charged off and left him there. No time for hysterics!

The captain was on deck with the lieutenants. I joined them in the rigging out of the way.

"We are being carried by the waves, sir! We are but a mile from the reef!" said Lieutenant Gore a little nervously.

The sun was rising and we could see breaking surf as far north and south as the eye could see. Mister Banks appeared on deck.

"I told you we should steer clear of the reefs!" he cried.

"Mister Banks! Do not press my patience at this time!" the captain ordered.

"But…" he attempted.

"Be gone!" barked the captain, leaving no room for argument.

"We have no hope of anchoring, Captain! The winds will not allow!" yelled Lieutenant Hicks trying to be heard over the savage surf.

Ever closer we came, the heaving sea and blasting wind pointing us right for the thunderous reef!

"We are only eighty or one hundred feet from it, sir!" shouted Lieutenant Gore.

Mister Banks ran around the ship, nervously wishing us all a quick and painless death! I would have swiped at him from my post in the rigging but he was not within reach!

All of a sudden, the wind altered and so little that the lieutenants missed it, but our Captain smelled the land and knew what to do.

"The wind has changed all but a little, lieutenants! We have a puff from the land! Point her up into the north, trim the sails and make haste!" he ordered.

The lieutenants knew what to do. The yawl, longboat, and pinnace were deployed. Two large "sweeps" or oars were put through the gun ports aft of the ship and the men pulled at them with all their might against the wind and the sea. The faint breeze from the land only lasted a short time but with the help of the oarsmen held us off the reef!

We edged further north, the men in the boats keeping the ship from disaster for many hours. The land wind having dropped we were still only a short distance from the reef!

Suddenly, Master Molyneux had found an opening in the reef about two hundred yards ahead of us, no wider than the length of our ship, and he sounded forward of the ship to the captain's relief.

The little land wind joined us again. Master Molyneux tried to guide us into the gap, but the tide was rushing out against us and we could not push the ship through. The tide merely carried us further away from the reef to safety within one quarter of a mile of it.

Through his eyeglass, the captain spotted another opening about a mile to the westward and knew what he must do!

Day was dawning and the tide had reversed by the time we made for this break in the reef. With a favourable wind and all hands to the sheets, we plummeted through the narrow gap racing at speed on the tide flooding through and into calm waters!

"The shoals we have avoided are a relief to see!" shouted the captain to the crew. All let up a rousing cheer!

There and then he decided. "Lieutenants! We will continue tomorrow, keeping the mainland within view!" They understood the order, knowing it was easier to navigate the calmer shoals than keeping the ship from smashing against the reef in open waters.

"Aye, Captain!" came the call, in unison from all.

"Let the consequences be what they will!" decided the captain.

For some time, I feared that François had jumped overboard as he had once before, as I could not find hide nor hair of him. I called but to no avail. Eventually, I found him cowering in a corner of the Great Cabin.

"Descendons-nous?" asked François, eyes wide with fear.

"What are you talking about?" I asked calmly, knowing that our captain had saved us all yet again, however close the call.

"Do we go down?" He shivered.

"Go down?" I asked.

"Ze sheep, eediot! Does ze sheep go down?" He hissed at me.

"I will not have you refer to me as an idiot, sir! And I will not answer your question until you have sworn that you will cease and desist in this manner!" I took advantage of his fright to establish some regard for the Fairweather position.

He was petrified but managed to nod his consent.

"We are safe, François, the ship is not holed, nor is it smashed against the reef. Our captain has yet again saved the day. We are anchored in calm waters!" I boasted.

He huffed and puffed, as he had been holding his breath thinking we would sink.

"Your captain…a good man…" was all he could manage.

"Absolutely, dear boy!" I verified with not a doubt in my mind.

He calmed eventually and we kept out of the way while the men went ashore to find water and wood. Mister Banks was now in possession of his faculties and pretended he had been very brave. He rallied the gents to join him on a botanical excursion on the morrow.

Later that evening in the Great Cabin, I found the captain relaying his belief that this Australia does not link to New Guinea and that we should prove it to the world by sailing around the tip of Australia using the shallows and shoals.

The lieutenants were in agreement but Mister Banks and the gents said nought. It was a standoff between the lieutenants and the gents, and I believed it would continue whilst ever we sailed in these dangerous conditions.

When all but the captain and I were left quite alone he read his entry in the log to me quietly.

"Such are the vicissitudes attending this kind of service and must always attend an unknown navigation. Was it not from the pleasure which naturally results to a man from being the first discoverer, even was it nothing more than sands and shoals, this service would be insupportable, especially in far distant parts like this, short of provisions and almost also every other necessity." He sighed, continuing his log entry.

"The world will hardly admit of an excuse for a man leaving a coast he has unexplored, he has once discovered. If dangers are his excuse, he is then charged with timorousness and want of perseverance and at once pronounced the unfittest man in the world to be employed as a discoverer."

"If, on the other hand, he boldly encounters all the dangers and obstacles he meets and is unfortunate enough not to succeed, he is then charged with temerity and want of conduct."

"The former of these aspersions cannot with justice be laid to my charge and if I am fortunate enough to surmount all the dangers we may meet, the latter will never be brought in question."

"I must own I have engaged more among the islands and shoals upon this coast than may be thought with prudence I ought to have done with a single ship and every other thing considered, but if I had not, I should not have been able to give any better account of the one half of it than if we had never seen it."

I agreed he had a point as he thus ended his log entry. Either brave and fortuitous in discovery, or cautious and finding nothing! He was damned if he did and damned if he did not!

He noted the date: the 17th day of August 1770. He charted and named our entry point Providential Chanel, and the area Port Weymouth.

Swallowing a large swill of brandy straight from a bottle, he retired after the lieutenants gave the all clear that we were safely at anchor. I snoozed on the captain's chair for what little night there was left.

The next morning at first light with the ship clambering with activity I sauntered up to the deck to find Chester and Lady, recently having been released from Mister Banks's cabin, where they were always secured during times of crisis. They were getting ready for a landing with Mister Banks and the gents as arranged.

"Close call, what?" I interrupted.

"We could only hear it, Fairweather! Was it two or three times that we nearly smashed upon the reef? It was confusing!" Chester wanted the unadulterated story. Lady, too, was keen having heard Mister Banks's death wishes to one and all. The coward, I thought!

"We were certainly in peril several times from one thing or another, the wind, the flood tides, all very frantic measures were taken and the men were quite remarkable but yes, we nearly smashed upon the reef and some eight to ten leagues from land. We would all have perished," I reported.

"'T'was nussing!" François spat from behind me. I turned to see him saunter up and sit comfortably in on the conversation.

"Nothing?" I gaped.

"Oui, err…yes! Of course, nussing!" he said.

"It did not sound like nothing!" Chester blustered.

"François! I left you cowering like a cornered mouse when the danger began!" I was appalled at his blasé behaviour in light of his hysterics at the time.

Chester and Lady looked at each other.

"I was not cowering! It was you who was so frightened that I 'ad to comfort you!" he lied boldly.

"What? François! You were positively shivering!" I was aghast.

"Non, non! I merely felt a little cold! You, my friend, were afraid!" he continued.

"You? Fairweather? Brave ship's cat? Afraid?" Chester was in shock.

"I was absolutely not! I ran to assist my captain!" I said in my defence.

"You ran away to 'ide!" François continued this appalling lie.

"You hid? Fairweather! I cannot believe it!" said Lady sadly.

"You! François! Are a liar of the highest order! How dare you besmirch my good name to my closest friends!" I challenged.

"It 'ees not I who lies, Fairweazer! It 'ees jou!" he accused, nonchalant in this outrageous fabrication.

"This is positively the last straw, François! You have been welcomed on this ship by one and all and now you conjure up this ridiculous story?" I was outraged.

"Where was Fairweather hiding François?" Chester examined suspiciously.

"In a corner of ze Great Cabin!" he convinced Chester.

"Fairweather, you coward!" Chester accused.

"This is a blatant fabrication, Chester, Lady! I would do no such thing and you know it!" I attempted to win them round.

"Hmm..!" Chester was not convinced.

"François, you fiendish liar, be gone with you at once to a place where I cannot see you. You are a prevaricating pest!" I ordered in my defence.

"I shall do no such 'sing!" He turned to Chester. "'E was crying like a leetle girl, afraid to come out!" He intended to incriminate me further!

"François, you most foul fibber! This behaviour of yours is appalling! You have eaten from my plate, seduced my cook and butcher, and now you accuse me of cowardice to my face and my friends?" I was furious.

"Jealous of François, are you?" asked Chester.

"I most certainly am not!" I shot back at him.

"I merely speak ze truse, Fairweazer, it is nussing to be ashamed of!" He crowed as if to comfort me.

"What!?" I blubbered, stupefied by the hide of my accuser!

My eyes blackened and my fur stood to attention. Without hesitation I swiped my extended claw across François's treacherous face, catching his eye! He reeled and fell to the deck.

Lady ran to his aid. "Fairweather! What have you done?"

"You foul beast!" Chester said hurtfully.

"My face! My eye!" François cried.

I stood firm and would have not a second more of this rot!

Will Howson saw me attack the brute and came over quickly to scoop me up.

"Rotten cat! What are you doing to François?" He threw me down the gangway to my Isaac who was thankfully standing there to catch me, albeit awkwardly.

"Your cat just attacked François!" accused Will.

Isaac grappled with my flailing limbs and having sorted me out, carried me to his bunk.

"What are you doing attacking the French cat, Fairweather?" he asked of me.

I was stung hard and mortified at what had just occurred. I could not explain this treachery to Isaac and was at his mercy. He merely shook his head.

"The captain will hear of this!" And with that, he left me alone.

Will Howson passed me sitting on Isaac's bed and shot me a nasty look.

"See what you did? Now, I have to take him to the surgeon!" He spat at me, holding the blighted François who beamed mischievously at my plight.

Chester and Lady followed him down to Doctor Monkhouse's quarters, and as they passed I distinctly heard a threatening growl emanate from Chester's throat.

Lady merely "tsk tsk-ed" at me.

I was appalled! Shunned by my friends who believed this perfidious pest's lies! And then my Isaac, who always stood by me, believing me of a wrongdoing when the evil François deserved the slap I had inflicted! The captain would be informed!

I climbed into my Isaac's duffle bag, a familiar place I had not visited since my boarding the ship. I could do nought but sit there in shock! Word would race around the ship and I would be forever infamous as the beast that harmed Bougainville's cat! True, he had it coming, but how was I supposed to defend the Fairweather honour?

I could hear a feline cry coming from the Doctor Monkhouse's vicinity and imagined the worst! The surgeon was no doubt stitching the fiend's eye! Had I blinded François? Would the captain punish me, as he would had one of the crew did such a thing? Would I be put off the ship somewhere in a hideous land, never to see my friends and crewmen again? And what of my home? Would I ever see it again?

I felt the tears of regret moisten my eyes. I knew not of my fate, so I stayed in my hide for two days without food or water. My Isaac knew I was there as he slept on his duffle bag but did not let on of my presence. I stroked at his hair at night for comfort but he brushed my paw away irritably.

I heard talk of François and heard him chatting genially with Chester and Lady as they passed my duffle bag, but I dare not come out for fear of recrimination. Sooner or later I would have to face the consequences but the Fairweather heart was heavy and I did not have the fortitude to venture out yet.

Within another night in my hide, and calm seas felt around me, I ventured out, as my midsection was empty.

I crept cautiously so as not to awaken the crew and loitered around the galley hoping my good friends John and Henry were onsite. All was quiet and my plate was emptied, no doubt by the felonious François. I was bereft!

There was nothing for it but to hunt the odd mouse in the stores. Quietly, I crept by the sleeping crew and down to where my domain lay. I sniffed around for a while and located a stray, not of the happy couple variety and with heavy heart I ate him. I found a place to sleep and deemed it best to stay there for the night.

Misters Banks and Spöring came down to the stores to put away two large jars containing sea snakes they had caught and preserved. I meowed but they both shot me a contemptuous glare.

"He should be ashamed of himself, Mister Spöring!" said Mister Banks in passing. I slept for a while.

Upon waking, and thinking that I could not possibly feel any lower, I decided to head for the Great Cabin in the hope that my captain would understand.

Every soul I passed either commented on my presence to the negative or merely ignored me. I stopped in at the galley for a morsel or two.

"Fairweather! I don't feel much like it, but I should feed you I s'pose," said John Thompson as if I were some kind of pest.

He put down some leftover scraps from dinner the night before; things that the men would not eat. My plate smelled of François and I felt spurned by my good friend the cook. I ate of it as hunger drove me to it but it was unpalatable and was obviously meant to be.

"There he is, Isaac!" said Will Howson as I approached him in passing.

"Where've you been, Fairweather?" He picked me up and a glimmer of hope fell upon me. Perhaps my Isaac was still my friend. "Taking you to the captain and he's cross with you!" The traitorous boy entered the Great Cabin and dumped me unceremoniously on the map table.

The captain was busy with Mister Banks and the lieutenants.

"The tide here runs immensely strong, Captain!" said Mister Banks.

The captain nodded as they looked out the windows.

Mister Banks continued his observation. "Yes, and we look upon it as a good omen: so strong a stream must in all probability have an outlet by which we could get out either on the south or north side of New Guinea. The smoothness of the water, however, plainly indicates that the reef continues between us and the ocean."

"You are correct, Mister Banks," the captain replied. I was much pleased that he was in better spirits since our brush with the reef several days ago and the lieutenants seemed buoyant as regarded our position.

"I shall not be reporting you to the Royal Society for you have saved us yet again. I gather we will forget our little disagreement then?" Mister Banks hoped.

"As you wish, Mister Banks. I do not expect a repeat performance." The captain eyed him purposefully.

"Of course not, James," he said familiarly, bowing. "You have my word."

I was glad that they had patched things up between them and the captain would not be reported.

I looked about waiting for my captain to see me there and spotted François sitting on the captain's chair! And to boot, wearing an eye patch not unlike that of Turkel's back in England! He eyed me smugly knowing that he sat in my very own position in the Great Cabin. I was incensed!

"Ah, Fairweather," the captain spotted me. "Leave us men." He dismissed all but François and they loitered out, leaving us alone.

"I had Isaac stitch a patch for François's eye. Doctor Monkhouse assures me he will regain his sight," the captain informed me nonchalantly. I thought I might be spared yet!

"This is a punishable offence, Fairweather!" He growled. "What possessed you?" He was disappointed in me.

I had no possible way of telling him what had occurred and François knew it! He rested his head on his paws to watch with satisfaction as I was chastised.

"Your behaviour on my ship has thus far been commendable, but as I cannot lash nor cane you, I will have you put off at the next port. François will take your place." He was resolute!

François was smug.

I bowed my head and backed out of the Great Cabin, my heart broken! I was to be evicted from my post and the ship in some awful strange place! Stripped of my station! My good deeds forgotten! Never to see my home again!

I sought out Chester and Lady on deck.

"There you are, Fairweather. You have been hiding from your fate, I suspect?" Chester was almost mortified by my existence! Lady gave me a sorrowful look but said nought. She was completely disenchanted with me.

"Chester, dear friend, Lady, my supporter, I have been ordered off the ship at the next port," I said grimly.

"I am sorry, dear, but you did a bad thing. Like the crewmen, we must all get along," she said sadly.

"Poor form, Fairweather. I would have defended you but this unprovoked attack on poor François is too much!" was all Chester said, ignoring me further.

That was that!

My heart sunk to a new low and the pit of my stomach ached!

My eyes filled with tears but I turned from Chester and Lady and walked with my head lowered to the gangway. The stores were my destination and the place I realised I must stay until we reached some wretched port where I would be evicted.

My captain, my boys, my friends had all taken the side of the wretch François and he had taken my place!

That night I lay in the captain's private store where he kept his best port, brandy and prized possessions.

I could hear Master Molyneux and lieutenants Hicks and Gore in the boats sounding the channels ahead of the ship.

I was too sad to be on deck and of some assistance. I found a sack with some tobacco that was sparingly doled out to the crew on special occasions. It was soft enough to allow sleep, and with heavy heart and the words of recrimination echoing in my ears, I dozed fitfully, tossing and turning for some time.

It was during the night that I heard footfall of a familiar type. I was well hidden high upon the tobacco sack and comfortable enough to be quiet.

It was the foul François!

What was he doing down here when he had my captain's chair to sleep on and the entire crew's favour?

He bumped into a few things having only the sight of one eye, and with it no sense of distance, but he headed straight for the barrel of port.

Pawing at the tap just enough to allow a drizzle he lay on his back and gulped the trickling port! The barbarian!

I watched as he slowly emptied what I calculated was half of the contents and then he fumbled to turn off the tap. He licked up a little spillage and laid there, eyes swimming drunk as a sailor as they say!

A plan began to form in the Fairweather brain!

I waited patiently until the foul François had drunk himself to sleep laying paws up on his back. I leapt from the sack and ran for the door. I did not disturb him. Off I went at speed to seek out Chester and Lady. They were asleep in Mister Banks's cabin.

"Pssst!" I hissed at them. Chester lifted his head.

"What do you want, foolish cat?" he whispered harshly at me. "Can you not see we are sleeping?"

Mister Banks was snoring noisily enough and rolled himself over.

"You must follow me at once, Chester!" I whispered back urgently.

"Are you mad? I will do no such thing!" "But this is dire and you must witness it!" I whispered louder.

Lady stirred and chastised me. "Be quiet, Fairweather, or you will wake Mister Banks."

"You fiendish pestilence, be off with you!" Chester snapped harshly.

"I will jump on the sleeping Banks and scratch him sorely if you do not come at once!" I hissed.

He got up, untangling those long legs and told Lady to stay there.

"I knew you had gone mad with the François incident, but threatening to scratch Mister Banks? This only proves to confirm your lunacy!" he said outside the door.

"Follow me! And quickly!" I urged.

"Where are we going, you loony feline?" He was grumpy from his rude awakening.

"Hush, Chester, you will see!" I ran at speed for the stores.

Chester slipped and slid trying to keep up with me, and it made him all the more cranky.

"Slow down!" he panted.

"Catch up!" I retorted.

We reached the gangway to the stores and came to a halt. I turned to him as he panted.

"Now, catch your breath and be quiet. I wish you to stand outside the captain's private stores and not breathe a word. You must merely listen," I instructed.

He was growling the guttural growl of an upset hound.

"Shhhh! He will hear you!" I whispered, looking about wide-eyed.

"You have without doubt gone completely daft! Who will hear me?" He was losing his patience.

"François will hear you and I do not wish him to. Now just sit quietly by the door and listen," I instructed.

He had no choice but to comply as his newfound friend François was mentioned. No doubt he incorrectly thought I was up to no good! I made for the doorway and begged he take a peek at the sprawled drunken François.

This got his attention and he sat still to listen.

I sauntered into the captain's stores.

"Ah, François!" I said loudly. "There you are!"

"Allo? Who 'ees 'ere?" He slurred, not moving from his position paws aloft and on his back under the port tap.

"What are you up to?" I said purposefully.

"Fairweazzzzer!" he slurred. "Mon ami! Come drink wis me! It is ze captain's finest port!"

"I am well aware of the contents of the barrel, François. Should you be drinking it?" I baited him.

"Non, but no one weel find out weel 'zey silly cat!" he bragged.

"And why is that François?" I lured him once again.

"Becaussse, no one weel believe you, eediot!" he hiccupped. "Ze whole sheep 'sinks you are a coward for 'itting François de Beaujolais of Lyon, France across ze face!" he bragged, laughing.

"Yes, I am aware of that, my friend," I said pretending to lap at the puddle of the captain's port still left on the floor.

I heard Chester "Hurrumph" and shot him a look as to quiet him. He could see us between the hinges on the doorway and still held me in contempt.

"Do you recall why I hit you, François?" I laughed along with him.

"Oui!" He laughed. "I told ze dogs you were a coward, 'iding in ze Great Cabin, when ze sheep…err…ship, was about to smash upon ze reef! I lied to 'zem!" He chortled away happily. "Eediot dogs!" He laughed heartily.

I heard Chester gasp audibly and I glared at him, as there was more to unfold.

"And why did you lie, François? Telling Chester and Lady that I was a shrivelling coward?" I prompted, pretending to be amused.

"I was…'ow you say…embarrassed?" He chortled. "I was 'ze one shivering wis' cowardice but I did not want it known to anyone," he admitted, laughing at my misfortune.

"And why not, François?" I lapped at the puddle, catching Chester's widened eye at the gap between the door and its frame.

"Better for you to be a coward 'ere than moi!" He chuckled. "I would be put off ze sheep in ze next port, and to be honnête…er… you would say honest?" I nodded. "I quite like 'zis sheep! Everyone 'ere treat moi wis kindness!" He rolled about the floor laughing and then expected me to turn on the port tap for his leisure. I poured it on to be sure, all over him with a gush! Honest? He said! This fellow did not have an honest bone in his body!

"There you are, François, the best of the captain's port for you!" I chuckled. He laughed along with me, soaked in the captain's finest, until Chester burst through the door eyes wide with anger. Lady had caught up with him and witnessed the key moments of the conversation through the hinge gap above Chester.

"François, you beast!" Chester blustered. I turned off the tap to the port barrel and let François lick the contents from his stomach awkwardly, as cats will do. I stood back and held my head high as Chester and Lady questioned the felonious François further.

"You did this, François?" Chester asked angrily.

"What?" François was clever and although drunk, knew to whom he was speaking.

"This foul misdeed, naming our Fairweather as a coward?" Chester probed.

"I know not of wheech you speak, Chester!" drooled François, consumed by alcohol and trying his best to lie his way out of Chester's accusation.

He began to sing! "Fairweather is an imbecile! Fairweather is an imbecile! La la la la la!" As if it were a lilt he knew well!

"I will ask that you cease this foul singing, sir!" Chester growled.

"Chester?" I asked. "Did you hear enough to expunge the Fairweather reputation?"

"I did, indeed," he confirmed.

"Zsst! Zis means nussing to moi! Your friends 'ere witnessed your attack upon moi and you can do nussing to prove 'uzerwise!" He gloated in the knowing that I had been found guilty for no reason, and then attempted to sleep! The gall!

Chester was filled with rage having been duped by a cat! And a French one at that!

"Do not dismiss me, sir! I can see now that Fairweather was right in slapping you! The chap has shown you nothing but kindness and you accuse him of the foulest crime of cowardice?" He turned to me, Lady flanking him.

"I should have known you better, Fairweather. I think I speak for Lady, and I offer you my most sincere apologies." He bowed and Lady followed suit.

"I confess your rejection of my actions and reasons cut me to the core. I have never been so outcast and destitute, but the truth is out. I am innocent," I reconciled.

François rolled to his side and found yet another puddle of the captain's port and eyes closed began licking more of it.

"That will be enough for you, François!" Chester snarled. He picked François up by the scruff of his neck with his powerful jaws and turned to the door.

"Where are you going, Chester?" He obviously had a plan.

"Captain," he mumbled, his mouth full of François.

"But we will not be able to explain François's crime!" I had a point.

Chester spat out the felonious feline and he crumpled in a drunken heap on the still port-soaked floor. Smelling it he smiled and closed his eyes, licking his damp paws.

Chester pondered for a moment and then his eyes widened with a plan. "Lady and I will awaken the captain and bring him to this spot to witness this for himself. I am sure that you will be vindicated when he sees what François has been up to!"

"Yes, yes Chester, this is a most favourable plan! I will go to the other stores and hide, however, as the captain may consider that I have set François up for it, being as my stock is so low with one and all," I decided.

"Yes, dear boy," Lady admitted. "We do not want you in any further trouble. It is best that you be absent. Trust us to make our point," she insisted.

I heard Chester and Lady's paws skidding on the decking at speed to the captain's cabin. I crept into the botanist's stores, next-door, and hid among the jars of specimens. I scratched at a familiar knothole in the wall between the stores and could see the foul François still lapping where he lay.

I heard Chester and Lady barking wildly above me, and the footsteps of a number of men. Down the gangway they sped and toward the scene of the crime. They passed my hide in the botanist's stores, Chester and Lady in the lead. They had managed to summon Mister Banks and the captain! Even the lieutenants were bringing up the rear!

"What in the name of all that is good and fair are we doing down here?" Mister Banks asked of his dogs.

The captain and the lieutenants merely kept up, panting for the outcome.

Peering through my knothole, I was not disappointed. The men came to an abrupt halt behind the barking dogs in the doorway of the captain's stores.

Chester and Lady had not let me down. The captain, Mister Banks and the lieutenants jockeyed for position! All gasped audibly at what they could see!

"My port!!!" was all the captain could manage, shaking the barrel to determine the loss.

"Chester? Lady? Is this what you have had us see?" he quizzed the dogs. They barked in unison and sniffed at the port barrel, then sniffed at the foul François, his tongue floundering from his mouth and appearing to be quite asleep whilst doing so.

"This cat is drunk!" squealed Mister Banks.

"And on my good port, it seems!" said the captain, bending down to François to sniff the evidence.

"Where is Fairweather?" asked the captain, expecting that I had something to do with François's predicament. I gasped under my breath, as my captain doubted me. Chester and Lady looked at each other bewildered as if not to know.

"They know not of Fairweather's whereabouts," Mister Banks confirmed.

The captain picked François up by the scruff of his wretched neck and held him aloft. "Drunk! On my reserve port! Half of it gone!" he roared, shaking the demon to rouse him from sleep. "He is positively stupefied!"

The captain asked Mister Banks to consult his dogs as to my involvement.

"Did Fairweather have anything to do with this?" asked Mister Banks of his dogs.

All were keen for their response, and they bowed their heads to the negative. I was most pleased!

The captain stormed out with the intoxicated François, and all and sundry followed him. It was my guess that they were making for the Great Cabin to hold conference over François's misdemeanour.

I snuck my way through the galley and past the bunks without being discovered and into Lieutenant Hicks's cabin, which lay directly under the Great Cabin where I would be able to hear all.

"Boys!" summoned the captain as he heard them clambering outside. "Fetch Fairweather!" he ordered.

They scurried off to search the ship for my presence.

I could detect a concerned tone in my captain's voice. Perhaps he thought that in my shame I might have deserted the ship. I was heartened to hear of this, and deemed it wise to make myself available to the boys' search.

I sauntered from Lieutenant Hicks's room and was clutched in the gangway not far from the Great Cabin by my very own Isaac.

Lieutenant Gore was sent with Master Molyneux to attend to the ever-present shoals.

My Isaac, in the midst of the gents, lieutenants and my boys, unceremoniously plopped me down on the map table. Mister Banks and my good friends Chester and Lady had done their work. My captain wished to speak with me alone so as our secret communications would not be witnessed.

"Leave us, men," ordered the captain and he closed the Great Cabin door as they left.

François was laid out on the floor awkwardly as he was so drunk he was incapable of moving. The captain sat at the map table and held my eye.

"Fairweather. Did you have any part in François's drinking a large portion of my best port?" he asked firmly.

I sat tall and shook my head, holding his gaze. I had certainly not discouraged François, but it was not my initial doing. I felt I could answer to the negative with good conscience.

"You have been shunned for your attack on this cat. Are you certain you have not set him up for this, in your own way as retribution?" I was a little saddened that he doubted my character but kept to the point. Again, I shook my head.

He stood and paced. I watched him keenly for the next instalment. I was not disappointed!

"I believe you, Fairweather. Now I feel it imperative to ask you and you must be perfectly honest with me." He sat again and leaned in to me to express the gravity of the question. "Has this François sullied your good name on this ship?" That was it! I had hoped with all my heart that I would be asked of this! I nodded gravely and bowed my head in disappointment.

"Ha! I knew you not to be the perpetrator!" the captain mused. I nodded purposefully, a tear welling in each eye.

"I knew it! I knew you would not attack without reason!" he beamed. "François deserved your anger?" I nodded yet again.

He sat back in his chair and we both observed the cataleptic criminal lying listlessly.

The captain scratched at his chin.

"I shall have a word with the gents and the boys and the word will travel that you have been wronged," he decided. "As for François, it will be he and not you who is put ashore at the next harbour."

His hand came down upon the map table in anger, frightening me not a little!

"I should never have doubted you, Fairweather!" he reprimanded himself.

I stood tall and he stroked me from head to tail, which I accepted gratefully.

"I am most sorry to you for this humiliation!"

He stood and called for the gents and boys who were all waiting outside the Great Cabin door to hear of the outcome. They marched in purposefully, Chester and Lady sitting by the map table supportive of yours truly.

"I have gotten to the bottom of this crime." The gents and boys looked keenly at each other, knowing the captain to have only been alone with the drunken François, and I as suspected felon. I imagined they were curious as to how the captain could have communicated with me. He ignored the sceptical faces and made his explanation brief so as not to bring doubt upon his sanity.

"François is to be put off the ship at the next port of call. Fairweather is innocent of all charges. He is to be treated with the respect he has deserved. Thank you, men, you may go about your business." Thus ended the episode there and then leaving no room for argument.

I had been redeemed! François was uncovered as the criminal he was!

The gents and boys seemed well pleased and all gave me an apologetic pat as they left.

Mister Banks stayed behind with the dogs. Chester and Lady both put their front paws up on the map table and licked me happily.

"Leave off, you two!" I hissed. "We will discuss this later."

Mister Banks pulled them down from the map table by their collars as their behaviour was indeed inappropriate, but he too seemed pleased with the outcome in favour of the Fairweather variety of feline.

CHAPTER 33

The following days were spent navigating around the scattered islands that lay off the northern point of Australia. Some were inhabited and Aborigines came down to the shore as we passed, holding their spears. A musket shot of two made them disappear before they could board their canoes and come out to us.

The captain was bent on getting us to the Dutch outpost of Batavia.

François was not to be found and I was indeed happy to know him in hiding.

While I had been in exile, the captain had named Cape Grenville after George Grenville who whilst treasurer of the Navy and a politician, had passed the act forcing the prompt and speedy payment of sailors upon their return from voyages, and the payment of support for their families whilst they were at sea. A friend he had in all sailors!

Between this cape and Bolt Head lay a bay and it was christened Temple Bay, after Henry Temple, second Viscount Palmerston, who was on the board of trade in 1765 and appointed Lord of the Admiralty in 1766.

We passed some higher islands and the captain dubbed them Sir Charles Hardy's Isles, after the admiral of that name.

Another group of islands passed us, the Home Islands, and six of these were named after crewmen Orton, Gore, Hicks, Perry, Harvey and Clerke. The men were always much pleased to leave their name and mark behind them for history!

Then again, he saw an island group covered in birds and simply named them Bird Isles.

Then for no apparent reason a group of low islands were named the Boydong Cays.

One did not always understand the captain's mind!

The East Islets saw many shoals again with inhabitants and empty turtle shells upon the beaches. The captain set the pinnace to try and catch turtle but the men only returned with one. It must not have been the season for the turtle to come ashore to lay its eggs.

By the 20th day of August 1770, we had all but run out of this Australia, having reached the northernmost point of mainland. I knew not of François's whereabouts but he had lain low since the aforementioned despicable incident.

John Thompson and Henry Jeffs welcomed my appetite when word had reached them that I had been innocent all this time. My plate was glistening and stacked with the best portions of food that they could purvey. I ate heartily to eliminate the aftertaste of mouse in my mouth. I was concerned, however, that François had not shown his face in the galley to dine. My only conclusion was that the fiend was eating my "happy couples" in the stores below. This was not acceptable! I had not only to maintain my profession on the *Endeavour*, as one and only mouser, but also keep the blighter alive until he could be banished from my ship!

I ventured below in an attempt to alleviate my suspicions.

"François!" I called.

Nothing.

"François, old thing!" I reiterated easily so as to lure him out.

Nothing.

"François de Beaujolais of Lyon, France!" I pronounced boldly!

"Oui?" I heard but a whisper from the hold.

"Announce your whereabouts immediately!" I demanded.

He crept out of the coal room, black as soot and rather gaunt.

"I have not seen you for some time, François," I voiced concern.

"I am unwelcome 'ere…" He trailed off sadly.

"It is your own doing, sir!" I said strongly. "But you must eat and toilet away from the hold." I was plain in my direction.

"Ze men will 'iss at me!" he cowered.

"And so they should, François! I will attempt to conciliate them in your favour." I was more than generous.

"Con…what?" He demanded as if I were a peasant.

"Ease them to your presence, François!" I explained harshly. "It is not in your interest to bristle me further, nor shall I come again to see to your welfare, should you not be more amenable!" I threatened.

He gazed at me quizzically not knowing his English. I had to make it clear and simple for this fiendish fool.

"Be nice to me or I shall not look out for you in the future!" I pressed.

"Oui, Fairweazer. I am sorry for all ze trouble I 'ave caused you," he said obediently.

"Have you been eating of the mice in the hold?" I asked, ignoring his apology and sounding his situation on the subject.

"Oui, Fairweather," he admitted coyly, knowing my position on the welfare of the population.

"Stop it at once or I will not have a function on this ship!" I scolded.

"But I am 'ungry!" he cried. "And Monsieurs Thompson and Jeffs 'it me wis a broom when I went to the galley for foods!"

I felt a sense of satisfaction in my belly, imagining them swiping at this criminal upon hearing of my innocence.

One may well ask why I did not wish him dead, for all the trouble he had caused me, but Fairweather is a fair fellow and the welfare of this chap must take some importance.

"Come with me at once!" I ordered of him. I could barely stand his whimpering further.

We made our way to the galley and all we passed were impressed with my benevolence, they too imagining I should have pushed him overboard by this time!

"Ah, Fairweather! What ya' doin' with that wretch?" John Thompson looked up from preparing fish. Henry Jeffs and Thomas Matthews came from the mess upon hearing of my mention. John put down a plate of fish scraps for me.

"François, eat your fill." I stepped aside and let him through.

"Well, I never seen anythin' like that!" laughed John Thompson. "These two shouldn't be friends after what happened?" he ventured to Henry and Thomas.

"No, odd that!" Henry Jeffs agreed.

"Fine cat, our Fairweather, makin' sure the ratbag still eats till the captain kicks 'im off!" praised Thomas Matthews, stroking my fur while François scarfed down my meal.

François stood back, my plate emptied, and cleaned himself. I gave a grin to my cook and he fetched more fish for my empty plate so that I did not miss out!

"I'd swear that cat is human," mumbled John, then going about his business.

François and I ventured up onto the deck to find the captain and lieutenants busily navigating the numerous islands off the northernmost point of Australia.

"This coast is littered with islands and shoals. It is a geographical mess," remarked the captain in conference with his men. "We will keep the pinnace and yawl out sounding ahead," he ordered. The lieutenants went off to carry out the order.

"What are you two doing together?" The captain noticed us sauntering by, heading for'ard.

As I was trotting proudly ahead and François cowered behind me, the captain got the gist of my position. I vowed to confirm it with him later in the Great Cabin, bringing François with me. For now, I was on the lookout for Chester and Lady, finding them sunning themselves on the gents' deck.

"Ah, Fairweather..." Chester did not see François behind me at first. "What is this criminal doing here with you? Should he not be locked in the farthest reaches of the ship without food nor hope?" Chester was remarkably unimpressed by his presence.

"Now, dear..." chided Lady. "I am sure Fairweather has the best of intentions." She was always most impartial.

"Blast you, Fairweather! How can you loiter with this foul wretch after his crimes against you?" Chester growled, eyeing François with intent.

"I am a fair chap as my name implies, dear boy. I have been vindicated and now must see to the fellow's wellbeing until he can be eventually banished from the ship." I shot François a withering glance so that he would not forget his place. After all, I was being more than fair!

"Ah you have fallen for some kind of trickery from this François!" He did not understand and resorted to his own theory.

"No dear boy, I am merely extending the hand of forgiveness and kindness even though the foul blot has done me wrong." Again, with the harsh glare for François's sake.

He sullied forward and cleared his throat. "I 'ave made my apology to Fairweazer, and you too must accept it!" François demanded.

"You cheeky brute!" Chester was infuriated. "I will accept nothing from you. In fact, I may very well creep up upon you when you least expect and throw you overboard myself!" he warned.

"You would not!" François dared.

"You underestimate me, sir! My friend has suffered much from your stupidity and I will be pleased to avenge him should it suit me!" Chester left no room for argument.

"Thank you, Chester, but I shall manage this pest, knowing that I can call on you in future if the need be apparent." I bowed.

Lady was impressed with my humanity and smiled at me.

The boys were busy in the rigging but my Isaac saw us all together and ventured down to ascertain the situation. As with everyone I had encountered since my exile, he too found my presence with François confusing.

"Want me to chuck him over the side, Fairweather?" He asked, wiping tar from his hands.

I stood in front of François so as to defend.

"Odd cat, you are." He left us to his chores.

"There it is, François!" I said. "I shall ensure your safety, but only on the condition that you behave yourself accordingly as a guest upon this ship. My friends have made their point clearly," I warned.

"Oui, Fairweazer," he replied meekly. I had his assurance but was not so naïve as to believe this chap for a moment! I would have to be vigilant with him as his nature was not that of a true gentleman!

On the 22nd day of August, we approached the very tip of Australia. From the masthead one could see across the thin point of land, to the sea on the other side. The captain still wished the pinnace and yawl ahead of us sounding around the various islands we had to navigate. He named these York Islands and the peak of Australia, Cape York after the Duke of York as we rounded it.

We came to anchor under an island, and the captain and gents, Chester, Lady, and I, went ashore with armed Marines to climb to the highest peak looking for the passage the captain had guessed was ahead of us.

We met with three Aborigines who blocked our way to a landing on the beach. It was not known whether they intended to assist or challenge us, so musket shot was fired into the air to disperse them.

The gents botanised, bringing back new plants not before seen.

We climbed the barren hill and saw the strait that the captain had sought. It was deep and wide and as far as the eye could see! Yet again, and beyond the doubts of certain gentlemen and crewmen, he was correct in his observations of the land and sea to calculate that this strait was indeed there!

The captain addressed the gathering. "Having satisfied myself of the great probability of a passage, through which I intend going with the ship, and therefore may land no more upon this eastern coast of Australia, and on the western side I can make no new discovery, the honour of which belongs to the Dutch navigators; but the eastern coast from the latitude of thirty-eight degrees south down to this place, I am confident was never seen or visited by any European before us, and notwithstanding I have in the name of His Majesty taken possession of several places upon this coast."

"I now, once more, hoist English colours and in the name of His Majesty King George the Third, taking possession of the whole eastern coast by the name of New South Wales, together with all the bays, harbours, rivers, and islands situated upon the said coast." With that, Lieutenant Gore stabbed the English flag into the barren ground. Following this came three rousing cheers.

He ordered three volleys of shots to mark the occasion, and the same three shots were returned by those upon the ship.

The captain named this island Possession Island and the island on the other side of the strait Prince of Wales Island.

We returned to the ship and were under way immediately, the captain wishing to use the high tide to have us through the narrow channel.

That evening, I invited François to the Great Cabin with me. The captain was alone.

"Fairweather, I found the strait!" He was keen to brag, not looking up. "I am naming it 'Endeavour Strait' on my charts as we speak. It proves geographically that this Australia and New Guinea are two separate lands, something that was supposed but never proven. I have merely cleared up a doubtful point." He was a modest fellow when it came to his capabilities, but I could tell that he was mightily chuffed at this discovery.

He lifted his head and spotted François with me.

"Ah, yes, we must discuss this questionable alliance between the two of you." He motioned for me to attend my usual position on his chair while he paced.

"You are pardoning this cat's behaviour?" He looked at François cowering in the very same corner he had occupied during the storm. I shivered at the sight but was resolved and nodded so.

"As you wish, but watch your back. He seems a menace!" The captain shot François a stern look. "I will not suffer such behaviour on my ship, be it man or beast, and I will not wait for a civilized port should François step out of line! He is your charge, Fairweather."

I felt no need to say more to the shivering François. My point had been made several times, and by my every comrade.

We both settled for the night. I lay on the captain's chair, and François on the floor where I believed him to belong for now.

The next morning, François sauntered off to the galley to find food, his belly being his only concern.

I went up on deck to join the captain who was enjoying the gentle rolling of the Arafura Sea, which signalled open water.

We were on our way home to England and steering away from this Australia. The men became buoyant. The sick became well and the melancholy looked gay.

The talk for days was of their homes and what they had missed. Roast beef seemed to have been the ultimate sacrifice for an adventure at sea! I admitted that the sound of it made my mouth water and I longed a little for England.

To take our minds off our stomachs, even though it was not over the evening brandy, Mister Banks gave his findings of Australia as we sailed gently.

"Having now, I believe, passed through between New Holland, or Australia as I shall call it here, and New Guinea, we have an open sea to the westward thanks to our captain's excellent navigational skills." The gentlemanly applause was forthcoming.

"I much wished indeed to have had better opportunities to observe the people, as they differ so much from the account of William Dampier's. For those not familiar with the man I shall give him his due.

"In 1699, Dampier sailed on the *Roebuck*, where he explored the western coast of Australia from Shark Bay north to King Sound, some nine hundred miles. He described the land as low and sandy with no fresh water and few animals. He noted what we now call the kangaroo, and said thus of the natives. 'The inhabitants are the most miserable wretches in the universe!' Of the country, he said 'The only pleasure I had had in this voyage was the satisfaction of discovering the most barren spot on the face of the earth!'"This may be true of his account of that Western Coast of Australia, but in my opinion he only saw the worst of the country. It is indeed barren but holds more to the inland." The captain and gents nodded their approval.

"For the whole length of the coast we have sailed there was a sameness, sandy and light soil with thin grass and a few trees scattered here and there. The banks of the bays were clothed with thick mangroves sometimes a mile or so inland. The soil under these was rank mud. The valleys between the hills where water runs down had much undergrowth but were steep and narrow. "Water was scarce there but we were in the height of the dry season. There would be plenty in the rainy season, which was evident by the channels cut through the country even though dry at the time we saw them. "The soil was so barren that it would not afford cultivation to yield any support for man. We had been so long at sea with scanty fresh provisions that we ate everything we could lay our hands upon; Indian kale, and a sort of purslane or pigweed were in tolerable plenty. Other plants we ate were a kind of bean that tasted very bad, a kind of parsley and something resembling spinach. I have given them botanical names and taken samples as I believe that they have never been seen before." He was rather chuffed with his discoveries.

"Fruits were even fewer. To the south, a kind of heart cherry only the stone was soft and it had a mild acidic flavour. Northward a kind of fig growing from a tree, and wild plantains. All the fruits were so full of seeds that they had little or no pulp and eating them was but an unprofitable business. "The trees were middling to large in size and of very hard wood, that our carpenters complained that it damaged their tools! Palms were of three different sorts. The first which grew southward had leaves pleated like a fan. The cabbage of these small but exquisitely sweet, and the nuts in abundance were a good food for our hogs. The second was much like the West Indies cabbage tree, not as sweet as the other sort but more plentiful. The third was more northern, much smaller and like a fern. It produced no fruit but a nut; the hulls of which we found plentiful near the Aborigine's fires. Gentlemen, I believe you sampled them but suffered a hearty fit of vomiting?"

"Oh, yes, Mister Banks!" came Doctor Solander nearly greening from the thought if it!

"The hogs did not suffer from them and ate of them heartily without initial effect until one week later they all came down with extreme indigestions, two of which died, but the rest were saved although with difficulty."

"Other useful plants we saw none, except two we found yielding a gum resin in abundance. Dampier mentioned it in his travels. One blood red and the other a bright yellow with a sweet smell, samples of which I have and no doubt a chemist might be able to determine a use for it."

"For animal life, I shall say no more than that we had some time ago learnt to eat any species that came in our way. A hawk or crow was to us as delicate and perhaps better relished than a partridge or pheasant back in England. If it was not salted for storage and fresh, it was a delicacy. Even shags and seagulls did not taste rank to us wanting of fresh flesh. No doubt if we had fresh beef or mutton, we would have spurned the sea fowl."

"Quadrupeds we saw but a few and caught even less. The natives called the largest of these the 'Kangaroo.' It is different to any animal I have ever heard or read of. The largest we shot weighed eighty-four pounds. It is easily distinguished from all other animals by the singular property of hopping upon only its hind legs carrying its forearms close to its chest. In this manner, however, it hops so fast that in the rocky bad ground where it is commonly found it easily outpaced my greyhound Chester! The natives called another a 'Quoll' and it is the size of a polecat of a light brown and spotted with white on the back and is white under the belly. The third was a 'Possum' of medium size, greyish brown in colour with a long bushy tail. Bats were many, small and large. Our people saw wolves and the Aborigine call them 'Dingo.' "Birds were of several species: seagulls, shags, gannets, boobies and pelicans of enormous size, the latter so shy that we never got one of them, as were the cranes of which we saw several large and some beautiful species. In the rivers were ducks in large flocks but they were hard to get. On the beaches there were curlews and many small beach birds. The land birds were crows, and parrots and parakeets most beautiful. White cockatoos, pigeons, beautiful doves, bustards and many others that did not at all resemble those of Europe. "Insects were few; ants and mosquitoes. The mosquitoes did not trouble us much as we were only a little time wherever they gathered. The ants, however, made amends for the mosquitoes. One sort was as green as a leaf and built their nests in trees. Such nests were sometimes as big as a man's head. They bent the leaves together and glued them with a whitish papery substance. Some of the leaves were enormous and they banded together to bend them into the place they wished, while others were employed fastening the glue. If we accidently shook the tree the nest would disintegrate and the ants fell upon us, stinging us with a vengeful disposition, their sting as painful as a bee! Another sort of ant was black and lived in their hollowed-out branches of a tree, yet the tree still flourished! When we first discovered them, we were collecting branches and when disturbed by us our hands were covered with legions of them stinging us intolerably! Experience taught us to be more careful for the future. A third type of ant nested inside the root of a plant that grew on the bark of trees and was much smaller, though they still stung us when disturbed. The fourth type was a minute white ant with superior architecture employed for their nests. Some were suspended from a tree, where others stood upright from the ground, some as tall as six feet! The outside was thick clay and when broken open showed their passages underground heading for the trees nearby. I admired this country's ants as superior to any I have seen!

"The sea made some amends for the barrenness of the land. Fish were plentiful and we could haul the net and catch fifty to one hundred in one tide! There were various kinds and most delicate to the palate. The stingrays we caught were coarser but more filling for our bellies. To the northward when we became entangled with the reef the area was plenty with turtle. The weather though was most boisterous and our boats could not row as fast as the turtle could swim, so we got but a few, but they were excellent and so large that a single turtle served the entire ship!"

I licked my lips, as this was always my favourite part, Mister Banks talking of the native foodstuffs! I let him continue even though my stomach rumbled audibly.

"The giant clam supplied us with some ten or fifteen pounds of meat, a rather strong taste but very wholesome and relished by all. On different parts of the coast, we found good oysters and the shells of good-sized lobster and crab, although it was never our fortune to catch them."

"Upon the whole, New Holland, or New South Wales, or Australia, however it may become was a barren country, not so bad that between the productions of the sea and land anyone who became shipwrecked here could support themselves. Thanks to the captain and crew we were not, however!" Mister Banks nodded his gratitude in the captain's direction.

"Undoubtedly a longer stay there, visiting different parts would discover more. This immense tract of land, being considerably larger than all of Europe is thinly inhabited. Most of the time the natives ran from us.

"Whatever the reason for this scarcity of people in such a large continent is difficult to guess, unless it is the barrenness of the soil and scarcity of fresh water, or that they have many wars and consequent casualties."Their customs were nearly the same along the entire coast we sailed and though we only had connection with them at Stingray Bay, their colour, weapons and how to use them, being naked and painting themselves, the sameness of their houses, their netting and knitting which I have seen nowhere else, was all new to us.

"The men were remarkably short and slender, their medium being five feet and six inches. What their absolute colour is, is difficult to say, as they were so completely covered with dirt, which seemed to have stuck to their hides from the day of their birth without once having attempted to remove it; I did try by spitting upon my finger and rubbing, but it altered the colour very little, which resembled that of chocolate. Their beards were bushy, black and thick. Their hair was as lank as Europeans but some as crisp and curly as the South Sea Islanders. They were all lean, light and active; their countenance was not without expression but their voices were shrill and effeminate."They wore no clothes but an ornament consisting of a bone of five or six inches in length worn through a large hole between the nostrils as wide as a man's finger, so that when in place it completely blocked both nostrils, making their speech scarcely intelligible. They had necklaces made of shells, four or five small cords round the upper arm, and a string tied around the waist that was either made of human hair or that of the beast they called kangaroo. They painted themselves red or white."For food, they depended highly upon the sea but not completely. Of land animals, they probably ate everything that they could kill which does not amount to any large number; every species here being shy and highly cautious."The only vegetable we saw them use were yams; small but sweet. We never did find the plants that produced them, but the Aborigines knew where to find them regardless. They ate of the pandanus, a kind of fruit resembling a pineapple. The fruit of another palm was so unwholesome that our crew who were forewarned ate but suffered violently. Even our hogs whose constitution was as strong as those of the Aborigine, died after eating them. It could only be guessed that they have a method of cooking them by which their poisonous quality was destroyed."We observed that some held the leaves of an herb constantly in their mouth which they chewed on as a European chews tobacco, or an East Indian chews betel. We did not discover what is was but unlike betel it did not stain their teeth or lips."I believe they wander the country in search of food in a nomadic manner, deserting their crude huts for the next place with a source of food. Others coming along will inhabit their huts in the same manner. They kept a fire alight in their huts, possibly to ward off mosquitoes, and so small were the dwellings that no more than three or four people could huddle in them. We saw many places in the bush where they had slept with no shelter at all, other than a few bushes and long grass, to keep them from the wind."The only furniture we saw belonging to these houses were oblong vessels made of bark for fetching water from springs. We supposed that the women carried these in their wanderings, while the men carried their lances and struck at animals or fish that they may happen upon. Besides these, they all seemed to carry a net the size of a cabbage, containing some of their body paint, some fish hooks and lines, shells, points of darts and resin, and their ornaments."A stone made sharp at the edge and a wooden mallet were the only things we saw that had been formed by art; the use of these we supposed to be in making the notches in the bark of high trees, which they climb for reasons unknown to us, but perhaps to stalk prey from above or hunt birds who have roosted for the night. They made their fish hooks from shells and their lines were well twisted and made of some vegetable."The many fires burning the ground we think were intended to flush out the Kangaroo, as these were afraid to go over places newly burnt. They get fire very expeditiously using two sticks; both being dry and soft, one must be round and eight or nine inches long and the other sharpened at one end pressing it upon the other and turning it with the palm of their hands, often shifting their hands down quickly to increase the pressure. In this manner, they will get a fire within two minutes and when possessed of the smallest spark, increase it in a way truly wonderful! We often admired a man running along shore who seemed to carry nothing in his hands, and yet as he ran, stooping down every fifty or one hundred yards, produced smoke and fire among the driftwood in an instant!"Their weapons were lances from eight to fourteen feet in length, made of cane of a bulrush, straight and light. The point was made of hardwood or stingray barbs, and sometimes of broken bits of shells held together on the tip with resin which would break off in a wound and certain to heal with great difficulty."They had a flat throwing stick which they balanced and threw with the greatest ease imaginable, but for the most part they had no defensive weapons and when we approached they shunned us, giving up their area, and running away as fast as they could."To the southward their canoes were little more than a piece of bark tied together in pleats at the ends and in the middle small bows of wood which carried one or two people. In the middle of some canoes was a fire set upon a bed of seaweed, perhaps to give the fisherman the opportunity of cooking his fish the moment it was caught. Northward the canoes were hollowed out of a tree trunk and fitted with an outrigger."Of their language, I can say very little as our acquaintance with them was so short in duration that we did not have much time to speak with them. Most of our conversations were conducted in signs. We have made a list of some words we were all in agreement of meaning and I will include it in my findings for the Royal Society," he concluded breathlessly.

"Ah, Mister Banks, most informative. No doubt the powers that be, back in England, will send forth more ships to Australia thanks to your reports, this land now belonging to His Majesty!" said the Captain with pride.

With that, the gentlemen and crew who had listened in, went about their duties. I joined the captain at the bittacle as he checked the compass. He was keen to get the men home now that he had gone above and beyond his call of duty. The shoals remained an ever-constant threat even though we were in clear sea, so the watch was ever vigilant.

Some of the muddied waters had turned out not to be shallows or mud at all. They were shoals of a stringed type of algae floating upon the surface of the sea. Mister Banks examined them under his microscope confirming them not to be an animal by burning a sample and the smell was that of a plant. The gathering of them were as long as the eye could see from shore, sometimes miles, and they clung together in tidal streams for as wide as fifty to one hundred feet! Manoel Pereira from Rio de Janeiro, volunteered his knowledge of such a natural curiosity. He said that at St Salvador on the Coast of Brazil where the Portuguese have a whale fishery, he had often seen vast quantities of it taken out of the stomachs of whales. They must have ingested it while swimming through these long rivulets of "sea sawdust" as the men were now calling it.

By the 29th of August, we had sighted south-western New Guinea. Smoke from fires and groves of coconut trees ensured that it was inhabited but the water here was as muddy as the Thames at Gravesend, and we dare not go closer than we could sound with the pinnace and yawl still out in front of us wary of shallows.

It had become intolerably hot and the men dispensed of their clothing as best they could without indecency, their reddening bare skin blistering in the sun. I preferred to find some shade with Chester and Lady as my fur had moulted to a point coming north, but not nearly enough to cool the skin. Wisps of it still fouled the ropes and the boys were set to gathering it, but I wished to have shed much sooner in this heat. Unfortunately, nothing could be done to expedite the process!

On the 3rd of September, the captain attempted to land on the coast of New Guinea, finding that the *Endeavour* had to keep off land by five or six miles for fear of running aground in the ever-present and vast shallows of this place.

The pinnace set off for shore. Mister Banks reported that these natives were the size and colour of the Aborigines we had seen in Australia but with close-cropped fuzzy hair. Some appeared lighter than others and Mister Banks assumed they had coloured their bodies with a whitish pigment.

Our party were admiring the coconuts, plantains and breadfruit for harvest when the natives attacked without warning! Musket shot was fired, allowing our men to board the pinnace and thankfully return to the ship without incident!

The captain decided to be well rid of this New Guinea and we made sail for the island of Timor. New Guinea had, after all, been circumnavigated by the Spanish and the Dutch, as the captain's maps had names upon it in both of these languages. He would find nothing new here and the risk was great!

The water deepened and open sea birds were soon seen. Boobies were caught among the rigging, the first of these birds we had seen! They were fine eating, and a surety of open sea! Mister Banks and the gents kept us in booby meat for some time! I was an avid fan!

The captain doubted the maps he had, as islands popped up from time to time and in no specific chart or order, and certainly not where they were geographically supposed to be. He could not help the incompetence of previous navigators to chart as well as he! He believed that the previous discoveries and charts of some of the coasts and islands were purposefully in error to trick the English or other explorers so that they may not make claim to new lands.

Not altogether sporting, I thought, as respect would no doubt be given to the established owners of the land in good time.

Tiata had been taking good care of François as he was ordered to do. I felt that he did not mind, as my boys had never really taken a keen liking to the lad, nor the felonious François. They were somewhat outcasts and François was indeed in need of one friend.

The rest of the crew had never really forgiven him for his attack upon my good name. I greeted him when encountered but with all of my good intentions considered, he remained distant. I imagined he had fancied himself taking over my position, and was unhappy that he had been thwarted.

Chester, Lady, and I continued to be lethargic in the heat until Timor was sighted.

On the 10th day of September, we sighted high land in the distance. Some disbelievers amongst the crew thought the sighting to be merely low clouds upon the horizon, but the captain stood firm that this was Timor and as we neared, it was plain to see that this was indeed land!

The next day, two large sharks were caught and the entire company dined heartily, including François and I in the galley. I asked him of his movements of late. He was still maudlin and mumbled something about not wishing to be put out in Timor as he wolfed down his shark uncouthly. I left him to his foul mood and checked the decks for my friends Chester and Lady. They were not in attendance after dining as usual and I thought it odd, as we always enjoyed the evening skies when clear.

I sought them out below and found them in Mister Banks's cabin, Chester lying sleepily on the decking and Lady at attention by his side.

"Chester, what are you doing down here on such a fine evening when cool breezes blow?" I inquired.

He did not answer, closing his eyes and sighing.

"He is not well, dear," explained Lady, licking his forehead affectionately.

"What is it, Chester? Have you eaten something rotten?" I speculated sincerely.

"No, I have not," he droned, no life to his voice.

"Mister Banks has determined that he suffers from nostalgia, Fairweather," Lady explained.

I had heard of this some time ago when the order to sail home had been given. The men suffered from it as they thought of their homes and families and it depressed their feelings and energy.

Doctor Monkhouse had been summoned to some of them but they soon cheered when we got under sail and left Australia behind us.

Mister Banks had determined the cause and the good doctor confirmed that there was little physically wrong with them, it was an overwhelming sadness.

"Come now, old hound! There are fires on the island, dear boy, you know how we enjoy the sight!" I invited him.

"The croakers on board say we are in for the westerly monsoon," he moaned pitifully.

"Croakers? Monsoon?" I quizzed not knowing to what he was referring.

He merely moaned and rolled himself away from me, not bothering with my questions.

"'Croakers' are those who are naysayers on the ship, finding fault with everything. The 'westerly monsoon' is a seasonally bad wind and against us if we wish to get home," explained Lady.

"I see. Chester seems to suffer terribly with maudlin," I agreed.

"The captain seems to think that the wind will die down, Chester. No more than two days of it, he expects," I tried to cheer.

"Hurrumph. I long to chase rabbit through the fields of England and eat from my fine china bowl. Leave me alone," came the pathetic response.

Surely enough, as predicted, the "westerly monsoon" reported by the "croakers" was nothing more than the usual turn of fresh weather for the predicted two days.

Chester began to cheer and I worked mightily hard to goad him out of Mister Banks's cabin, but to no avail. He was staying put. Depression had got a hold of him. I attempted to soothe but it did not help him.

Quite suddenly one night there was a commotion on the decks above. Lady and I ran to the gangway to ascertain the problem. Chester would not follow.

We were greeted with a beautiful sight. It must have been ten in the evening and not only were the fires from Timor glowing in the hills, but a strange phenomenon appeared above the horizon.

It was a dull reddish light reaching in the sky above the land. It moved and shaped a curtain draping in the sky, and I can only liken it to Madam's drawing room curtain in a breeze back at my home. Through it passed rays of a brighter coloured light directly upwards, as if a lamp had been held behind the curtain. They appeared and vanished right before our eyes.

All were on deck and mesmerised by the beauty!

Lady went to fetch Chester who we deemed should not miss this wondrous sight. He came up loping as if he were woken from the dead, poor pooch!

"What is this, Fairweather? I have never seen anything more beautiful!" His spirits were finally raised.

"I know not, Chester, but beautiful it is." I wondered at the oddity of nature.

Some of our "croakers" were frightened as it was their first sighting, but Mister Banks explained it.

"This is likened to the Aurora Borealis, or 'polar lights' seen in the Arctic and Antarctic regions, but are entirely without that trembling or vibratory motion observed in that phenomenon. This is Aurora Australis, or the 'southern lights' found more equatorially but still a rarity at this latitude."

I was glad there was no trembling or vibrations with this variety! One could only guess how that would have felt!

We sat for some time admiring the lights in the sky and the equally bright fires on Timor Island and by midnight most had gone below to sleep.

François joined us on deck when all but the necessary crew were still on duty. He said nought but we were happy for him to join us as long as he was quiet.

"Chester, old thing," I addressed him as we lay on the deck watching the lights of land and sky.

"Yes, Fairweather." He could not take his eyes off the spectacle.

"Good to have you back amongst the land of the living, old boy," I whispered.

"Thank you, dear friend, I was lost for a while but your encouragement buoyed me and this night has certainly done the trick." He was a happy hound.

We fell asleep on the deck watching the show.

I looked in on my captain the following morning. He was ponderous and spoke to the two lieutenants. "I am strongly importuned by some of my officers to go to the Dutch settlement at Concordia on this island for refreshments, but this I refuse to comply with, knowing that the Dutch look upon all Europeans with a jealous eye that come among these islands and our necessities are not so great to oblige me to put into a place where I might expect to be but indifferently treated."

"Yes sir, on to Batavia, then?" Lieutenant Hicks asked.

"Yes, our supplies are low but we are making good time and distance." He was satisfied with his decision.

Many of the men had become ill on this leg with the heat and poor state of the stores. The fresh seabirds that Mister Banks shot, and fish that the crew provided were all that was keeping us going other than the dried stores still intact after our holing off the reef. The animals on deck were depleted and the men could see sheep and cows grazing on this land but a few miles away!

The captain was resolved to stay off, but by morning of the 17th of September with the crew feeling at a new low as we were within touching distance of Timor and its shores of plenty, the captain put the ship in between Rote Island and Timor and sent Lieutenant Gore in the pinnace to see if there was a suitable place to anchor and find refreshment.

He returned with the bad news that we could not anchor there but that a leeward shore on the island of Savu ahead held a bay more suitable. We carried on to Savu with the winds favourable. The men were most pleased to hear of a landing!

As we approached, we saw horsemen on the shore wearing European colours complete with blue jackets, white waistcoats and lacquered hats. It was all the men could do to stay on the ship and not jump for shore so homesick were they, but this was not an English settlement. These people were Malay and the Timorese had spoken only of the natives, Portuguese and Dutch being on Savu.

We rounded into a shallow bay hoisting the English colours from the topmast. Surely as the captain thought, the Dutch colours were flown from the town, and three guns fired.

We anchored one mile from the shore and Lieutenant Gore was again sent ashore to find that this was a Dutch settlement. They had flown their colours on the beach as the lieutenant landed. He was not arrested but escorted by a shabby guard of natives to the king of the island, Raja Madocho Lomi Djara. He was a fat fellow with much body hair, the latter not being a trait of the usual native islanders. Mister Gore lied about our ship, and told the raja that the *Endeavour* was a "man o' war" and we had been at sea for some time, our sick requiring fresh food.

The captain did not want to share the real purpose of our voyage and the discoveries we had made.

The raja was happy to provide but needed permission from the Dutch East India Company for approval. A message was dispatched and answered by the agent himself, Johan Christopher Lange, a Saxon of German descent.

The raja and Lange came on board the ship.

Chester, Lady, François and I sat at the galley gangway watching the doings. The gents wined and dined them as best we could, with English mutton prepared by John Thompson, and much alcohol, with the promise that on the morrow, there would be buffaloes, hogs, chickens, sheep and fruits available for us to purchase at an agreed price.

"I 'ope ze price is not a cat!" gasped François, fearing for his skin. "I do not 'sink I will like zis place."

"Agreed, François, but if a cat is what they seek you will be said cat!" I decreed. "Since your eye has healed and our food has fattened you up, you do look more fetching than I," I goaded him.

"Zssst! Fairweazer! I will not go!" he said promptly as if he would have a choice in the matter. "I would run away and 'ide in ze woods. I 'ave done it before, you will remember."

He had a point there, but we all awaited the going rate for provisions with anticipation. Chester hushed us firmly, straining his ear for the demands.

The first request from the raja was for an English sheep similar to that which he was dining upon. It was our last one, but it was handed over to assure our provisions would be forthcoming the next day.

Lange asked for a spyglass, which was handed over all but hesitantly being a prized possession.

The final request was shockingly unexpected! The raja had taken a liking to the English dogs we had on board, none of their native dogs being of that type, so fine and regal!

I gasped in horror as Mister Banks offered Chester to the raja!

Chester's head shot helplessly in my direction!

"I have two dogs and one will be yours if we are provisioned well," he called Chester.

"Chester, no!" I whispered hoarsely. My friend went forward to his master dutifully standing proud, but the look in his eye directed exactly at me was one of fear and foreboding!

Lady panted nervously. "Fairweather! We cannot allow this!" she whispered to me, petrified to the bone!

I, too, had turned ashen and felt the dryness of mouth that can only be likened to sand on the palate!

François giggled and I offered to slap him again should he continue! The rude pest had no sense of honour!

"I like this dog!" the raja squealed, clapping his hands. "He will mate with my native dogs and make regal babies!"

"We will make provisions available to you at this price," said Herr Lange with a distinct accent I had never before heard. He was a harsh-looking chap, very direct and to the point.

As shocked as the men were, the alcohol flowed freely with three cheers for the raja.

As they were about to leave, and the Marines were on parade on deck, the raja requested they exercise and Sergeant Edgcumbe ordered them to fire three rounds. The raja was impressed!

Mister Banks ordered the Littleboys to fetch Chester's lead! I was panicked!

The drunken raja and Lange left us, accompanied by Doctor Solander and Mister Banks with Chester tethered but looking behind him for some kind of reprieve!

They landed on shore and heard the salute of five guns from our ship. They walked through the town with them and sampled some sweet palm wine, but returned without Chester!

It was more than merely I who was flabbergasted at what had just occurred!

The men began to mumble their disapproval of this situation having become attached to the dogs, even though it meant fresh provisions!

"Mister Banks! I am well aware that you esteem your hounds highly. Why give the male to this raja with no assurance that he will provide?" the captain asked as I bounded through the gathered men to find out what of Chester's fate. It had all occurred so quickly!

"The health of the men is at stake, Captain. We need the supplies to continue. This may be our only chance," Mister Banks said sadly.

"An honourable gesture, sir. It must not sit well that you have parted with him." The captain credited Mister Banks, but he did not answer as all could see that his eyes were welling gloomily. He called for Lady, who dutifully appeared and retired with him below.

"Well, at least it was not a cat 'e wanted!" François annoyingly announced upon catching up with me.

"François, you most foul feline! I am astounded at your lack of regret! This is a crewman and my dearest friend who has been given to this fat raja! I ought to slap you silly at this time!" I turned with my tail in the air and left him to seek out Lady in Mister Banks's cabin.

Mister Banks was in the Great Cabin partaking of a large brandy to numb his grief so I crept into his cabin where Lady sat crying softly.

"I will not carry on without him, Fairweather. I shall join him in the morning and stay behind." Her sorrow was great and I felt as overwhelmed as she!

"There must be something we can do!" I begged of her.

"No dear, if Mister Banks has given him as a gift to save the men from starvation, Chester will have resigned himself to his fate bravely. We cannot hope for his return." She bowed her head in the deepest of sorrows. Curling herself into a ball on her stool, she cried softly.

"I will think of something, Lady!" I licked her tears away; my own tears would have to dry in due course.

The Great Cabin was now abuzz with the gents and this development, and the hope that it brought us on the morrow.

Mister Banks silently drank his brandy, hoping he would be capable of sleep, having donated his faithful friend.

He retired from the group to his cabin with a parting speech. "This land abounds in buffalo, sheep, hogs, and fowl, all of which the next day should be driven down to the beach and we might buy any quantity of them. My gift of the dog should assure this," he said, dully walking from the room.

I sought out François who was lazing on the deck without a care in the world, while the crew discussed this turn of events.

"François, we must rescue Chester!" I demanded.

"Zsst! I will not endanger myself for a dog!" he callously replied, blasé to a fault.

"You will help me release Chester tomorrow or I shall have the captain put you out here in Savu!" I commanded.

"You would not dare! I am a fellow feline!" he argued.

"Oh, be sure of this, François; I would trade you in a heartbeat for my friend Chester!" I warned.

"Hmm…" he pondered. I could see his mind working, knowing that I had much influence with the captain. "You 'ave a plan?" he asked finally, resolved to helping me whether he liked it or not.

"I do not, François. We will sit here all night, devising one if we have to!" I was determined.

François yawned and began to get comfortable but the look I gave him was that of an offended Fairweather and not to be taken lightly! He stayed awake and listened to my bevy of plans and having nutted out something of a plot we slept fitfully until dawn.

The men assembled on deck to accompany the captain, misters Banks and Spöring and Doctor Solander, who understood the Dutch language. Seaman John Dozey who was Brazilian by birth, and could speak Portuguese, joined them.

My plan was for François and I to go ashore undetected. We darted for the longboat, before the men could board and hid under the seat in the bow. In the haze of feet, and wobbling of the boat as they boarded, we were successful in securing our passage to the shore.

François began to wriggle uncomfortably as my Isaac, Will Howson, and the brothers Littleboy rowed.

"Be still, François! We will be detected and sent back to the ship!" I commanded. He obeyed and I felt us land on the sand.

"Captain, I see no stock awaiting us on shore!" said Doctor Solander.

"Yes, Doctor, the absence has not escaped me," the captain said impatiently.

"Have we been duped out of our gifts and kindnesses?" asked Mister Spöring.

"And my dog?" Mister Banks was upset.

"This may be so, but I will thank you to reserve your judgement until we meet with the raja and Herr Lange for an explanation," ordered the captain wisely.

I turned to François. "Wait until everyone has left the longboat and we will follow them, but out of sight."

The captain and gents marched through the town led by a furious Mister Banks, to what they thought was the Royal Palace but was in fact the town hall.

François and I darted hither and yon, strategically keeping up with them.

They rather luckily found the raja and Herr Lange there at the town hall.

I could not see Chester. This was not a good sign as the raja could have locked him up anywhere upon the island!

"I do not see 'ze dog!" François stated the obvious.

"Nor I." I was worried.

François and I hid behind the door as the captain addressed the crooks. "I have come for the purchase of the livestock you promised us and I find no such thing upon the beach as discussed!"

"It is my fault, Captain," said Herr Lange abruptly. "With so much drinking last night I was not well 'zis morning, and unable to assemble 'zem for you." He explained in his heavy Germanic accent. His eyes darted in all directions, giving suspicion that he was lying.

"I should like to settle on a price for the stock so that we may procure them now and be on our way." The captain was getting impatient.

I looked keenly at every corner but could not see Chester!

Herr Lange became evasive. "Ze Governor of Timor in Concordia has instructed me by letter to allow provisions for you at ze going price, but 'zat you must be on your way in 'ze minimum time. You will have to arrange a price wiz' 'ze natives 'zemselves, Captain. 'Zey wish to be paid in cash directly." Again, with the eyes fidgeting in their sockets.

"I will have a word with my colleagues, Herr Lange," said the captain.

François and I crept undetected toward the rear of a large statue to hear the conference.

"I fear this is a ruse, Mister Banks," the captain whispered.

"I agree, Captain. They perpetrate a deception. I feel that the talk of last evening was merely the alcohol they consumed, and was big talk with no intention of supplying us. My guess is that Herr Lange makes a cash commission from the sale of the stock!" He, too, whispered.

The gents gasped, as this was scandalous!

The captain was furious!

"The evening is fast upon us, gentlemen. I wish to purchase a hog and some rice, and someone to cook for us as we will miss dinner on board." The captain made up this request to allow him more time to negotiate and smooth relations with the raja and Herr Lange.

"If you can eat victuals prepared by my subjects, I will do the honour of entertaining you!" The spirited raja clapped his hands and the arrangements began.

"To the palace!" he ordered.

The captain sent the brothers Littleboy to the ship to procure alcohol to accompany the meal and the party made their way to the raja's palace, François and I in hot pursuit.

The palace was ornate in the typical native manner and the fat raja had many servants dithering about him.

"François! This may be our only chance to find Chester!" I hissed quietly.

"Yes, 'ze men sit down for a good smelling dinner!" He sniffed the air, hoping he would partake.

"We are not here to eat, François!" I snapped him back into my train of thought. We must away and find him while they are so busy," I urged.

"If we must." François sulked as he could only think of his stomach and clearly did not hold the urgency of the situation as I had. Honour and comradeship were traits he did not possess.

Mats were laid out upon the floor for the gents to take rest in anticipation of the meal. François and I stayed in our hide until the food came.

By dusk, thirty-six palm baskets arrived, half containing cooked rice and half boiled pork. A soup made from the water the pork was boiled in was served in earthenware bowls.

The men were directed to a hole in the ground filled with water so they could wash their hands and then directed to their mats to wait for the raja to sit down first.

An awkward silence ensued until the raja explained that it was not a tradition for him to eat meat with his guests. They sat, but the raja also did not partake of alcohol, either, as was his custom to be more sober than his visitors.

While they were busy chatting and admiring the good food, I gave the word!

"Run, François!" But the fool had nodded off!

I prodded him and we sped for the door unseen.

Once outside, it was clear that the villagers were dining in their own homes, so the streets were relatively deserted.

I did not know where to start, but earlier I had seen an area where livestock was kept as we crept through town. I deemed it best to start with the locals.

We arrived at the enclosure to find the very beasts the captain was attempting to purchase. They were hale, hearty, and plentiful and I had to agree that Herr Lange must have had no intention of parting with them unless he could make a commission from the sale, as Mister Banks had conjectured.

I consulted the bullock closest to me. "Have you seen a rather stylish dog by the name of Chester, sir?" He looked stupidly at me.

"Dogs not kept here. Over there." He pointed his horns in the direction of a hut that was divided into stalls for each animal.

"Thank you, sir." It pays to be polite, even to the common bullock.

"Come, François!" I ordered.

"I fear 'zere is more 'zan one dog in 'zis hut, Fairweazer!" François whispered as we approached.

"Shh! They will hear us!" I hissed at him. Too late!

A horrid barking began with one, and then many, and the local hounds had detected our scent.

I could not hear a familiar woof above the din!

I strained my eyes to see Chester's familiar face behind the gate of the last partition.

There he was lying listlessly on the ground and uninterested in joining the native dogs at barking. Our scent must not have reached his nose. I ran further down the enclosure in the hope that his senses would pique. François brought up the rear.

"I see 'im!" François announced as if he was the first.

"Yes, yes, François! We must get his attention! He lies there like the dead."

With a leap unforeseen from the fat François, he mounted the gate and down into the common area of the dog pen he landed with relative ease! I was a little stunned by his agility to say the least!

"Chester!" He hissed at his gate. Chester's head came up like a shot from a musket!

"François!" Chester whispered. I could see his eyes popping from their sockets!

"Where is Fairweather?" he asked quickly, knowing that François would not have sought to rescue him without my urging.

"Fairweazer is at ze fence," explained François and I saw Chester look right at me even though it was getting darker by the minute.

The native dogs persisted and their barking took on a mightier note now that François and I had been seen and smelled. They strained at their gates with what can only have been a keen sense to eat of us both!

"Quiet!" Chester barked in a monstrous tone leaving no room for argument. They ceased. I, too, leapt the fence and joined François in front of Chester's confines.

"Fairweather!" he said joyously. "What are you doing here? I thought I would never see you again!" he blubbered.

"Be silent, dear friend. We are here to rescue you. Can you jump the fence as François and I have?" I pleaded.

"Yes, I believe so, but I am locked in this stall!" He lost faith.

"Yes, that is a problem," I mused.

"Pssst!" came a voice. We all stood deathly still as we imagined that we had been caught. I could see no one.

"Pssst!" It came again.

"Who is it?" I demanded bravely.

"I am Mantu. I am in the pen next to yours!" it whispered harshly.

I was impressed with this native's grasp of our language.

I approached his gate and introduced myself.

"You are from the ship?" he asked.

"Zsst! Of course, we are! You do not 'sink we would be 'ere on this 'orrible island by choice?" François mocked.

Mantu was not impressed with this rudeness.

I led François out of hearing distance. "François, you fool, leave this to me please!"

We returned to Mantu's gate.

"Yes, sir, we are from the English ship the *Endeavour*. Please take no insult from François here; he is a little touched in the head, if you get my meaning. I am here to rescue my good and deserving friend, Chester, and take him back with us," I explained. "Do you by chance have any hints as to how we might get him out of this pen?" I was polite to a fault knowing that good manners are always the correct way to start a thing!

"You want to go with these cats?" Mantu asked of Chester.

"I do, Mantu!" Chester prayed.

"Look in the corner of your stall under the bedding. There is a hole leading you to the rear of the complex." Chester turned and pulled back his bedding and found it!

"What ho!" Chester exclaimed.

"Why, Mantu! You cunning devil!" I kidded with him.

"There are holes in each stall, Fairweather. You do not think we are so stupid as to stay in these confines? We, too, like the freedom of the town when all have gone to sleep!" He chuckled. Then he took on a more serious tone. "Tell no one!"

"You have my word, Mantu!" I confirmed.

"Chester! Be gone before the guards make their patrol," Mantu advised. "They make the rounds upon the hour."

The agile Chester climbed through the hole and all of a sudden he was outside the fence around the front of the stalls where we had been earlier. The female dogs began to whine as news of Chester's leaving had gone from pen to pen.

"They are sad not to have the honour of mothering Chester's regal babies," Mantu explained. "Be quiet, women!" he ordered. They settled as François and I leapt over the fence and joined Chester outside.

"François! Fairweather!" He licked us enthusiastically. "You came for me!" He exclaimed incredulously.

"Zsst! It was nussing! Do not lick me, eediot!" François spat, as if it had been his plan and not mine. I let it go for now as it was not the time to clear up who did what!

Chester ceased his licking and addressed me.

"How are we going to get back to the ship unseen?" Chester had come to his senses and wanted in on the arrangements.

"I have not thought that far ahead, Chester! This easy rescue of yours thanks to Mantu was unexpected!" I bowed to Mantu and he bid us farewell.

"We must get back to the festivities to determine when the captain and gents are returning to the ship!" I declared.

"Festivities? Do the captain and gentlemen dine with the Raja?" Chester inquired annoyingly.

"Yes, Chester, now be quiet! François, come! To the palace and with much stealth!" I shot off with François while Chester thanked Mantu and caught up quickly.

We crept swiftly from building to hut, and hut to building, and made it back to the party just in time for its end. The captain and gents were shaking hands with Herr Lange and assembling at the front of the palace.

"We will land in the morning to trade for our supplies Herr Lange," the captain confirmed what could only have been an arrangement made over the dinner victuals.

"Yes, yes!" he dismissed us drunkenly. "I will see you in 'ze morning, captain. Goodnight, gentlemen!" He sang stupidly.

Our party were making their way to the longboat.

"Quickly! We must get there before them," I advised, and we ran without fear of discovery to the longboat before our party could see us.

"François and I in the bow of the boat!" I ordered. "Chester, you will tuck yourself as small as possible and hide under the first seat back from us. The gents will sit there and you may not be noticed. We can only hope. Now quickly, into position before they arrive!"

With that we all took our spots as the captain, gents, and crewmen arrived full of pork and gossip about the validity of Herr Lange's promise to provide all upon the morrow.

The captain did not believe him but had to trust him nonetheless.

Misters Banks and Spöring sat for'ard on the seat that was Chester's hiding place. From where François and I were well hidden, I could see the two with their feet out in front of them, full of the raja's pork.

I deemed they would probably not tuck their feet under them and detect Chester, as their condition would rely upon their extended legs to ease their full stomachs. I was correct in part until we were nearly to the *Endeavour* and Mister Banks shifted his weight to prepare for disembarking the longboat.

"What is this package under our seat, Mister Spöring?" He kicked at Chester who yelped at once.

Mister Banks struggled to look down between his legs and find his lost pooch!

"Chester!" he squealed.

"What?" yelled the captain.

Chester scrambled to get to his feet in the usual leggy fashion. Mister Banks pulled him up by his collar.

"My Chester!" He warmly greeted his lost chum. Much ear scratching was forthcoming and Chester licking Mister Banks's face in sheer joy that he was not lost on this island.

"How did this dog get out of the raja's confinement and onto the longboat?" asked the captain, not believing his eyes.

I deemed it wise to peer out from my hide in the bow and caught the captain's eye.

"Ah I see!" The captain had the entire company on board confused as only he could see me. I came out and advised François to do the same, just as the longboat came alongside the *Endeavour*.

"That cat!" came the chorus.

"Fairweather? François? After you…" advised the captain abruptly as the lines were thrown to the Littleboys to secure the longboat alongside. Up the rope ladder we clambered and assembled on the deck to await our outcome.

Chester came up under the secure arm of Richard the elder Littleboy.

"Eediot dog, Chester! We could 'ave crept up later, when no one was 'ere! It is your fault we are in trouble!" chastised François in his usual offensive manner.

"It is not his fault, François! He is bigger than us and a risk to stow under a longboat seat but we had no choice in the matter!" I reprimanded. "He is now safe amongst us and let that be the end of it!"

"Had Mister Banks kept still your plan would have worked, Fairweather, but I would have been discovered on board later regardless. I am difficult to hide." Chester admitted to his size even though he had remained still and as small a bundle as possible on the ride back in the longboat.

"Shh! Later comrades. The captain cometh!" I warned. François seemed rather chuffed to be called a comrade and assumed he was back in my good books.

"Well. This is a fine mess, Fairweather!" he noted, knowing my involvement would have been paramount.

The gents and crew all gathered round as Chester's return spread quickly amongst the crew.

The captain continued. "The Raja thinks he has a new breeding hound to elevate the genes in his dogs! This being one of the conditions of our being supplied on the morrow!" He was angry. "Should this missing hound be found out by morning we will not be replenished!" He had enough to deal with, with the lying Herr Lange without jeopardising the relationship he had fostered with the raja!

"What will you have me do with them, Mister Banks?" asked the captain of his botanist, knowing well the answer but keeping up his dutifully strict appearance.

"Fairweather and François should be congratulated! Chester is back amongst us!" he came forward and scratched each of us under the chin.

"And what of our trade relations, Mister Banks?" asked the concerned captain.

"You have said it yourself, Captain; if we are not provided with out stores by morning we will be on our way to Batavia and to the devil with Herr Lange!" Mister Banks spoke out of turn, revealing the conversation he had had with the captain in private earlier.

The captain could do nought but agree now that his intentions were revealed.

"Three cheers for the Captain!" Mister Banks sought, hoping it would soften the captain to his illegally returned hound. The cheer went up!

"Three cheers for Fairweather and François!" Mister Banks encouraged, as we were Chester's saviours, even though the Banks had freely given of his own hound!

A louder cheer came forth! François puffed himself up as he was cheered, and honoured by those who had previously condemned him.

"I can see that one and all are delighted with the return of the dog. Let us hope that it is not discovered by morning and that we are provisioned as requested." The captain could not hope to fight this overwhelming satisfaction.

Mister Banks took Chester down to his cabin where Lady had lied listlessly since his donation, missing her mate, as one would. I followed him, with the somewhat altered François bringing up the rear.

When Chester appeared at Mister Banks's cabin door, Lady became buoyant and welcomed home her partner with much licking and tail wagging!

Peace had been restored! The hounds and my heart were filled with goodness!

François and I watched as they cavorted lovingly for each other's company.

"You see, François? Honour and chivalry are lauded among the English and you have experienced gratitude for your assistance with Chester's rescue!" I encouraged.

"I am beginning to see 'ze fruits of goodness, Fairweazer!" He grinned from ear to ear. "'Zey are 'appy, no?" he asked me, as if it was not evident.

"Yes, François. You have done a good deed today," I congratulated.

"Vivent longtemps l'honneur!" he said in his native French.

"Whatever that means I am sure you mean well," I replied.

"Long live honour! Let us go to ze galley and celebrate wis' some food?" Again, with the stomach first, but I did have to agree with him, the whole salvage operation had made me ravenous.

"Onward, François!" I was right behind him.

A ship is a small community if I have not already mentioned.

By the time François and I had appeared in the galley, the leftover mutton from the evening before was piled high on not one, but two proper plates and we both ate heartily.

"Cats are an oddity," was all John Thompson could say, leaving us to our supper. A good night's sleep was all that remained and we both hoped Chester's absence from the raja's palace would not jeopardise tomorrow's provisioning.

CHAPTER 34

The raja must have slept late the next morning as the captain's party rowed ashore to find only one native chap and one dismal buffalo. It must have been starved to be so lean. The native wanted five guineas for it and the captain argued that it was overpriced and offered three.

A message of the captain's dissatisfaction was sent to Herr Lange and the return response was that we were not permitted to trade except for the going price. If the buffalo was five guineas, then the buffalo was five guineas. He would not budge. This confirmed to the captain that Herr Lange was pocketing a handsome profit from the natives for such poor trade.

Soon a large mob of militia descended upon the beach, some one hundred men sporting muskets and lances and headed by a stranger; a white man who spoke only Portuguese and was Herr Lange's assistant.

Seaman John Dozey translated his orders to the captain. "He says the king has ordered that we leave after this day. We are no longer welcome here, to trade or otherwise, sir."

"Hmm…" the captain scratched his chin, noticing an old raja standing on the beach. The captain had presented him with an eyeglass earlier that morning upon landing. He now gave him an old broadsword, which he promptly brandished wildly over the Portuguese militia who retreated at once.

The gathered natives came forward to resume trade, driving buffalo, sheep, hogs and chicken, and bringing a large quantity of the island's syrup. The captain was obliged to pay ten guineas for two very lean bullocks, not weighing more than one hundred and sixty pounds each, but after this the price came down and the quality of offerings improved.

Buffaloes went for a musket each and guineas were asked for the rest. Soon the Captain had purchased everything we needed and rushed a load back to the ship, ordering the other boats to come ashore quickly and retrieve our purchases before the king, the raja or Herr Lange could intervene.

The moment all the livestock was on board, the captain ordered anchors weighed early and made sail without delay, ignoring an invitation by Herr Lange to come ashore for more trade.

The captain had bought more than expected, thanks to the obliging old raja, and the *Endeavour* was crowded with animals and their fodder.

We made good progress south, out of sight of Sumbawa, Bali and Java, so as to catch the easterly winds to hurry us home.

"Spot of good relations by the captain, Chester? And your absence was not discovered before we left!" I found him on deck happily herding the animals.

"Oh, Fairweather, I could not be more happy than to be back with the ship. Thank you for coming for me." He beamed.

"François helped me," I said, chuckling.

"Yes, I know, dear friend." He too smirked.

"Under duress at first, but he got the hang of it and now values fellowship!" I explained.

"Indeed!" Chester was quite shocked.

"'Ow are you feeling now, silly dog?" François appeared.

"Fellowship, Fairweather? Me thinks he is still a rude menace." Chester nudged me.

"His manners may take some time to develop." I laughed.

"I am grateful to you for releasing me, François." Chester bowed.

"It was nussing. My plan was good and Fairweather 'elped me a little," François bragged.

"François! This fibbing must stop!" I protested. "Remember, it was you who said 'long live honour'?"

"Zsst!" François waived at me.

"You mean pffft?" I argued.

"Non, zsst!" he persisted.

"Stop this infernal disagreement, you two foul cats!" Chester demanded. "I am trying to be thankful to you!"

"Yes, well we all know whose plan it was, do we not?" I asked.

"Yes, Fairweather, I knew it to be yours and I am equally grateful to both of you." And that was that.

The men were happy and healthy with our new provisions, although most of the hen eggs the captain had purchased were rotten. We had procured nine buffaloes of some three hundred pounds each. The six sheep were Bengal sheep that the Dutch had imported from Calcutta; they were covered in hair instead of wool with large hanging ears and resembled our English goats. Their meat was the worst mutton we had ever eaten, whilst tender, very tasteless. Our three hogs were the fattest we had ever seen. I was looking forward to pork and knew the meat would be sweet, as the hogs' diet consisted of rice husks and palm syrup dissolved in water! We had thirty dozen fowls, mainly game breed and large, but with small eggs. A few limes, and some cocoa-nuts, a little garlic, and several hundred gallons of palm syrup completed our stores.

A few days out of Savu, large albacore tuna leapt about the ship. They were as large a fish as I had seen, more like the size of a dolphin! The crew baited some large hooks and let long lines out.

After a time, they brought the lines in and only the strongest of men could lift the giant fish into the ship by jagging them with a gaff.

John Thompson filleted them and cut the meat into portions for the entire crew. Tuna was a dark flesh but I found it very palatable and keenly went back with François for seconds. Even Chester and Lady, who were not fond of fish, found it appealed to their taste.

Flying fish were again seen in abundance and I spent much time watching them as we caught the easterly monsoon winds. Man o' war birds, gannets and boobies flocked about the sails but few could land as we picked up speed.

Mister Banks had made his report on Savu for the Royal Society and in the Great Cabin one night, sharing his findings with all who assembled there for a brandy. Most of Mister Banks's findings were gathered through long chats with Herr Lange before relations with him had soured.

"Herr Lange was free in his discussions with me, hence I do believe him to have not deceived in what he told me. I will now pass on what I have discovered. The information regarding the other islands in this neighbourhood was little more than to confirm that the Dutch confine their spice production to particular islands. "The little island of Savu appears to be of great importance to the Dutch East India Company.

It has three good harbours, and five principalities governed each by their own raja or king.

"The hills gently slope and were planted with thick groves of the fan palm, a most stately pillar known for its straightness and beauty. Their produce was profuse in fruit and sugar and their fronds used to thatch their houses, make baskets, umbrellas, hats, cups, and tobacco pipes. Of course, the palm wine produced was of fine quality and the syrup delicious! They even use it to fatten the cattle!

"The spring crops we did not see but I imagined the hills would be truly picturesque covered in maize, millet, and indigo, which apparently covers every inch of the ground around the palms when in season."The production of Savu is of every kind, animal, vegetable, herbs and fruits. Herr Lange told me that the cinnamon that grew there merely as a curiosity and not the genuine stuff, but the Dutch had always been so careful not to trust any spices out of their islands, that I believe Herr Lange to have deceived me. I cannot confirm this, as we were not permitted to see the crops for ourselves."Herr Lange told me that when the Portuguese first came to this island there were horses upon it. Again, I doubted his word, but regardless, horses were abundant, small but brisk and nimble. There were a vast plenty of dogs, cats, rats and pigeons. The people ate of them all except the rats."

My head shot up along with a meaningful look from Chester and Lady. That anyone would eat us was always a shock!

Mister Banks continued. "Fish there were in short supply and little valued by the islanders. They were only caught when one has business to attend by the seaside."

"Firewood was scarce but I did see a contraption which could well be used in England to make the better use of our wood! It was a burrow dug into the ground of about two yards and open at each end. A small fire was set at the broad end and the opposite end acted as a flue. Circular holes were dug over the burrow and large earthenware pots set into the holes to cook. It was marvellous to see how small a quantity of fire was required to keep all the pots boiling! I am certain this method has been suggested at home but our countrymen are loathe to change." Mister Banks was quite passionate on this cooking method, but as no one else had seen it in action he did not receive the excitement he was looking for. He continued less excitedly.

"The men of Savu were a middling size, but the women were remarkably short and squat but they were all of an even brown colour. Their hair was lank and black; the men wore theirs long and fastened it atop their heads with a comb, the women tied theirs behind in a kind of club that was not very becoming.

"Both sexes were swathed in a kind of blue and white clouded cotton which they make themselves. Their arms and legs were kept bare and the women wore silk handkerchiefs over their hair. They both eradicated the hair from their armpits, a custom in these hot climates for cleanliness. The men also plucked out their beards, as I saw some of the better sorts carrying a pair of silver pincers hanging around their necks for the purpose, and I asked Herr Lange of this, which he explained."

The gents cringed and rubbed at their shaved faces, knowing this method must have hurt like the dickens!

"They wore ornaments around their necks; the better sort of gold, but chiefly made of plaited wire. They wore beads also, but the women had the largest quantity and wore theirs around their waists. The younger boys wore spirals of brass around their uppers arms and the wealthier men ivory rings in the same manner. "They all chewed betel, making what teeth they had black and worn away to stumps and they smoke tobacco rolled in palm leaf, the total of the two causing their breath to smell horribly. "Their houses were well built on posts some three or four feet above the ground with a loft that Herr Lange told me was for the women. "The shortness of our stay and the few opportunities Herr Lange gave us to go among the people gave us no time to investigate their arts or manufactures. How they police their villages I cannot say, but the populace was well behaved.

"Herr Lange told me their religion is an absurd kind of paganism, every man choosing his own god and mode of worshipping him. The Dutch boast of many converts to Christianity but I cannot confirm this as I saw not one clergyman nor church. "The Dutch gift the rajas heavily to ensure the peace and giving of their produce and Herr Lange oversees this arrangement by touring the island regularly. "I would have wished to learn more but for the restrictions upon our movements but I can only hope the Royal Society accepts my report of this Savu." He concluded, looking disappointedly at the captain.

"Considering the time and limitations, Mister Banks, you have reported much and I am sure that England will be impressed." The captain cheered him somewhat as the meeting ended.

We headed northward in the last days of August, as the captain was keen to have us through the Sunda Strait leading us to Batavia.

The captain's charts were more accurate now that we were in the Timor Sea. Whoever had made the maps was not hiding points, capes, islands or whole continents from the English in these well-sailed waters!

The captain's charting days were now officially nearing an end and he was more relaxed than I had seen him for some time, concentrating on the preparation of letters to the English Admiralty to be sent from Batavia.

On the 30th day of September, we were nearing the area where the Sunda Strait would appear. The captain thought that it would be no more than a day or two and we would be anchored in Batavia, the capital of the East Indies and the Dutch East India Company's headquarters, where he intended to have the *Endeavour* fully repaired for the last leg home. He gathered as many of the officers', petty officers' and seamen's log books and personal journals so that he may include these in his package of letters to the Admiralty, and to keep the Dutch from finding out our travels to date and important discoveries for England. The captain securely locked them all away until he had his chance to dispatch them.

Having had favouring currents and winds, we overshot Java Head, and Princes Island, the entrance to the Sunda Strait. The charts were correct but he had not taken the westerly current into account.

We turned about and headed in the right direction sighting the two islands in due course. We rounded Princes Island and were now sailing the Sunda Strait between Java and Sumatra.

Krakatoa Island, with its steaming volcano high in the cloudless sky, was breathtaking as we passed it!

Two ships came into view and were heading out to sea just off Point Anger. They were Dutch East India ships, and a small Dutch packet boat accompanied them whilst on duty delivering and collecting mail.

Our suspicious captain thought it would be more likely to have been a reporting boat to check on who and what was sailing toward Batavia. Lieutenant Hicks was sent in a boat to ask of the latest news.

"The Dutch had much to tell, Captain!" Lieutenant Hicks was excited. "The *Swallow* had been here two years ago!"

All thought this was good news as a fellow Englishman was welcomed in the port. I remembered that the *Swallow* was the sister ship of Turkel's *Dolphin* voyage and took great interest although no more had been said about her.

"One of the Dutch ships is bound for Cochin on the West Coast of India and the other for Ceylon. Their captains received me very politely and told me some European news!" The gents and men gathered round to hear. "The government in England is in the utmost disorder! The people are demonstrating against the king, crying up and down the streets 'down with King George'!"

The gents gasped in horror of such a thing!

"There is more! The Americans refuse to pay taxes of any kind and in consequence a large force both of sea and land forces is being sent there!"

"Good Lord! What has the world come to in our absence?" Mister Banks muttered.

"The party of Polanders who had been forced into a late election by the Russians interfering, had asked assistance of the Grand Seignior, who had granted it, in consequence of which the Russians had sent twenty sailing, and a large army by land to besiege Constantinople!"

I had no idea of which they spoke and upon consultation with Chester and Lady, was no more likely to know what this news referred to.

Chester called it "politics," and deemed that we canines and felines need not delve into it, as it was the affairs of men. I was happy to hear that I need not learn of it, as it sounded awfully complicated and unnecessary to our immediate and current position.

"It is imperative we purchase an English newspaper the moment we land, Captain!" Mister Banks piped up. "These developments are scandalous and we must be caught up by the time we make England!"

"Yes, I agree, Mister Banks, but for now Lieutenant Hicks, how goes the passage to Batavia?" he asked, concerned with the here and now.

"In relation to our present circumstances they told me that our passage to Batavia was likely to be very tedious, as we should have a strong current constantly against us and at this time of the year, calms and light breezes were the only weather we can expect," reported Lieutenant Hicks.

"Very well," the captain accepted.

We crawled through the Sunda Strait curling around Sangiang Island, or as the Dutch and English called it, "Thwart The Way Island," as it lay right in the middle of the strait.

Native proas came around us selling all manner of tantalizing goods but would not accept any currency but Spanish dollars, and the prices were said to be outrageous so we declined.

We rounded Bantam Point into the Java Sea, and passed Tunda Island finding the current very strong against us.

Day and night all could not sleep nor tend their duties effectively as the excitement of Batavia was upon us, but the going was slow and we had to anchor many times just to keep from going backwards!

Tidung Island found us anchored for the night and much sea sawdust around us. The current drifted us during the night and found us dangerously near a ledge of rocks on the island the next morning! The captain set to sailing us off it but only slow progress was made, and the crew on edge as yet another potential disaster was thwarted.

We finally made past Rambung Island and saw Edam Island in the distance some six miles. The captain knew this to be the way to Batavia Road and our anchorage, and the course was beaconed and signed in an efficient manner.

As we put into the harbour, we noticed other European ships. From one of the closer ships came a boat with a few crewmen and an officer, boarding us to inquire who we were and what we were doing in Batavia.

The captain told them little but our name and that we were English and they left us. He was determined to keep our mission a secret from those who could steal our discoveries!

Mister Banks came forward as we passed close to the ships leaving Batavia. "The crew, Captain! They are but spectres! Pale as ghosts! This is no good omen of the healthiness of the country we are arrived at!" Mister Banks reported.

"No, they look unwell, do they not? Fetch Doctor Monkhouse. He may shed some light." Mister Banks was off in a shot, returning quickly with the good doctor.

"Their countenance does not bode well, Captain. If these men have been here for some time, it is a sign of an unhealthy port. We must take every precaution, and warn the men to do the same. Who knows what diseases lay here?" reported Doctor Monkhouse.

It was true, the men we could see were grey looking and our men looked rosy and fleshy in comparison to the thin pale men. The crew jeered and hooted at their sickly counterparts as we passed them.

As the lieutenants guided us into the busy port of Batavia Road, we saw the ship *Harcourt*, an Indiaman from England, two English country ships, thirteen large Dutch ships and a number of small vessels.

As soon as we anchored on this 11th day of October 1770, the captain sent Lieutenant Hicks ashore to acquaint the governor of our arrival.

I found the captain busy in the Great Cabin making a secure package with a copy of his journal and his charts of the Pacific, Australia, and New Zealand. He included two letters to the Royal Society, one from Mister Green and one from his own hand.

He read aloud to me his section giving praise to the officers and crew.

"They have gone through the fatigues and dangers of the whole voyage with that cheerfulness and alertness that will always do honour to British seamen." He looked to me for approval and I nodded so.

I wished that Chester, Lady, and I could be noted also, but I feared the Royal Society would think the captain had gone mad if we were included in his commendations. My captain must have known my thoughts.

"Do not fret, Fairweather." He scratched me under the chin. "It is enough that I know you have acted in the interest of the *Endeavour* and along with your canine friends you have all been a credit to your position. I will not forget it."

I was pleased to be honoured by him even though none of the English authorities would understand, or perhaps ever know.

Just then a flurry of lieutenants and gents came to the Great Cabin and interrupted my proud moment. A port authority was sent on board with comprehensive forms for the captain to explain and report our journey. The Dutch were suspicious of every ship attending their port!

The captain refused to lay down any information other than that we were called the *Endeavour*, belonged to His Majesty King George the Third, and had come from England as he had done so before.

The port authority pressed him for more information but he stood firm!

The governor general pestered the captain from his quarters by the shore, but even given the knowledge that a garrison of twelve hundred soldiers marched in his square every day, the captain would give no further information, governor general or not!

He immediately arranged a conference with the carpenter from the Dutch dockyard, and after taking a look at the ship the carpenter reported her damage, and what needed to be repaired for the journey home.

The ship was very leaky, taking in six to twelve inches of water per hour via the main keel, which was wounded in many places from our brush with the reef. The false keel was gone beyond the midships. She was wounded on her port side under the main channel where the captain imagined the greatest leak was. One pump on the port side was useless, the others decayed. Otherwise, the masts, yards, boats and the rest of the hull were in good condition.

Permission from the Dutch governor for these repairs would have to be sought, so the captain sent a letter to him laying out our requirements. All the captain could do now was await permission to haul the *Endeavour* ashore, allowing the repairs to be carried out. The refusal of information from the captain about our ship slowed the process however.

The stench of Batavia was about the ship constantly!

The city streets had canals, some as much as one hundred feet across, running into one stream for one half a mile before they empty into the sea. The stream was gated and closed at night, but during the day it allowed small craft to enter from Batavia Bay. At the gate stood the Custom House where the duty is paid on imported or exported goods. One must have a permit to enter.

The anchorage of the bay was known as Batavia Road and the dome of the great church is seen from it. One must anchor one or two miles from the shore as a mud bank prevented closer positioning. Anchors would bury themselves so deeply here in the mud that all ships moor with but one small anchor so that when leaving it was no great loss to have to cut it free.

The Dutch East India Company, knowing that all ships that stop here need provisioning have set the refreshments, stores and sea provisions at a very high price. The commodore of the company provides the fresh water to foreigners, pledging that it will keep sweet at sea, but the locals tell that this is not so. It was a moot argument, as all needed water, no matter the cost or quality.

The captain and Doctor Monkhouse held a meeting with all of the crew before anyone was allowed ashore.

"This Batavia is criss-crossed with canals, and the houses are in close proximity along them. The canals are in disrepair and full of every kind of human and animal waste!" The crew looked unworried but the doctor continued. "You must all be watchful of rotted foods, the drinking water, and bad hygiene in this town. We have all seen the pale and sickly leave here unwell on their ships as we approached. You all taunted them. You may very well become just as sick as them! Take good care, men! We will be here for some time whilst repairs are undertaken." The captain was pleased with the doctor's speech and allowed those who wished to go ashore, to take their leave.

Mister Banks and Doctor Solander took their servants and Tupia and stayed in a hotel, which was the custom for seagoing dignitaries.

Tupia had become bilious, refusing to take any medicines, and stayed on the ship with Tiata.

The gents found that the hotel prices were double what the local men would have paid and the food dreadful compared to the fare of our good John Thompson.

I deemed it wise to stay on board with good food and hygiene, until Mister Banks hired a small house in town for the gents some days later. They took their belongings and Chester and Lady, so I joined them on the first night to ascertain their whereabouts should I wish to visit them.

One must know where to go to find one's friends in a strange town!

It was a charming cottage in the township, but far from private were the gents, as every Dutchman who walked by their house, knowing they were back from a long voyage, came running into their house to ask what they had to sell. It was assumed that those on a ship so long at sea would have gathered items to vend in Batavia.

Word eventually got around that Mister Banks and the gents were merely boring English sightseers and had nothing of merit from their travels, thus ceasing the interruptions. Mister Banks was not about to tell of our discoveries!

I returned to the ship and kept council with my captain.

"I have had an introduction to the governor general today." He spoke to me as his only companion in the Great Cabin. "We shall have everything we require for repairs and permission to ground the ship on Onrust Island for the carpenters to properly see to her bottom." Finally, the captain was pleased with this arrangement and stayed on board the ship other than for these vital visits with officials.

We received beef and fresh greens on board to feed the already ailing men. Those who had been ashore were poorly. Lieutenant Hicks was ill, but had been so since he left England with consumption, a disease that attacks the lungs, and had caused him to cough on and off for the entire voyage. The sultry weather conditions in Batavia had worsened his ailment.

Mister Green, too, had become unwell.

Tupia somewhat recovered from his recent bout of scurvy, after sufficient freshly prepared food but it was confirmed that this Batavia was indeed bad for the health!

Mister Banks sent for Tupia, and his boy Tiata, who was all this time perfectly well and going mad being confined to the ship to attend Tupia. I joined them on their trip to Mister Banks's house. Tiata dragged François with him although François had voiced his wish to join a French ship in Batavia as soon as one arrived.

As we wandered through Batavia to find Mister Banks, I took the lead as I had been there previously. Tupia was in awe and Tiata danced, as we walked, neither having ever seen the likes of such a city!

"Houses, carriages, streets, everything!" Tupia marvelled. "They are sights which I had often heard described but never well understood!"

"I look upon them all with more than wonder!" squealed Tiata, clutching the displeased François tightly. The numberless novelties, which diverted his attention from one to the other, caused him to trip about the streets examining everything to the best of his abilities.

One of Tupia's first observations was the various types of European dress which he saw worn by different people. He told Mister Banks when we arrived at his house, and he immediately arranged for south sea cloth to be tailored to Tupia's taste.

"Mister Banks! This is a wonderful place!" Tupia paraded around the cottage in his fine new clothes. "May I request more sensible dress for young Tiata?" he asked respectfully.

"Why, of course, Tupia. We cannot have the boy treated badly for not fitting in with the latest fashion of a seagoing fellow!" And with that Tiata delightedly wore the clothes of a young English servant in keeping with his post.

Mister Banks had secured what he thought was good local food. It tasted well and looked to be healthy. The water that it was washed and cooked in, however, was contaminated and made them all sick.

Tupia had already suffered with a touch of scurvy, since our long leg here without his usual diet of fresh vegetables, but now he worsened from the water-born diseases and the heat. Tiata caught cold and an infection of the lungs. Mister Banks, his servants, James Roberts and Peter Briscoe, and Doctor Solander were all in the beginnings of various local ailments. Dysentery and malaria were the town favourites but with so many men from various countries using Batavia as a stopover, who knew what contagions were afoot?

On those days that Mister Banks felt well enough to walk about, he set off examining the town. As so many of our men were sick and unable to explore for themselves, his reports to the captain upon each return entertained the men and we learned much of Batavia from him.

Batavia was the capital of the Dutch Dominions in India and said to be the finest town possessed by the Europeans in the area. It laid on a plain under hills and mountains some forty miles inland and several rivers here emptied themselves into the sea.

Up in the hills the country was healthier and vegetable crops thrived there where the people even had some colour to their faces. The town doctors often sent the sick there to recover from their town borne illnesses.

Stone walls surrounded Batavia Township with few guns for protection. Mister Banks had seen the whole town from atop a high building and deemed it not as large as it felt walking about it.

There was a castle providing apartments for the governor and the council of India, and large stores kept the Dutch East India's goods. Large cannon protected the castle, and the guns frightened the Indians so much that law and order was simple.

Forts dotted the country some twenty miles out of the main town with poor defences, though their few guns kept the natives in check.

The Chinese lived here too in a quarter to themselves. They had staged a rebellion of some sorts and the best-protected Dutch houses with some eight guns each had levelled the Chinese houses to the ground during the melee. They had to rebuild. Few of them knew how to use firearms but their threat remained, as they were masters of their own weapons, lances, swords, and daggers. Mister Banks found out little more of the rebellion, as with most of his trips to the town his illness would flare up and find him returning to the ship, then to his house for rest.

The streets were broad and lined with trees. The canals followed every street, hoping to bring a coolness with so much water, but in Mister Banks's opinion those stagnant foul-smelling waters merely reflected the hot sun and made the climate more humid.

He saw dead animals stranded in the shallows; one such buffalo had rotted there for one week before heavy rain carried it away. This ignorance of dead beasts in the canals was most likely to have contributed to the illnesses so rife here. It was told that from any one-hundred soldiers arriving here from Europe, fifty would die in one year, and the rest would be in hospitals from their sicknesses contracted here.

Some of the houses were large and well built; one big room with spindly furniture. The Malays packed into shanties within the town.

The public buildings were old and shabby but the new church, the dome of which we saw from the sea, was as fine as any English church.

As for the sea, Batavia was well protected as one could not get within half a mile of the harbour's entrance without running aground. The highest walls and strongest guns of the castle protected the only channel in to the Batavia Road.

Around the harbour lay several islands. Edam was a penal colony for those criminals not worthy of death. Onrust was for the heaving down and repair of ships and all of the best tradesmen worked there.

It was said that the Dutch kept a great fleet here ready for any invasion of Batavia, but Mister Banks found that those he did see were in a poor state of repair and largely unmanned. The better Dutch ships were deployed to Ceylon and the coast for trade.

Inland from the capital the houses were built among uncleared trees. So many and thick were they that they allowed little fresh breeze from the harbour, and lightning during storms favoured this area, striking at the many of the trees. The prolific lightning damaged several ships during our stay. A bolt of lightning nearby the *Endeavour*, once struck down our own sentry! He was lucky to live!

The rest of the land Mister Banks had the opportunity to survey was boggy and unwholesome, completing the picture of a stinking sultry uncomfortable existence.

The church graveyard appeared to hold more bodies than the town!

There were different breeds of cattle and sheep here. Not like our English fare. They were thin and tasted unwell. The Dutch ate of their own breed of cattle, the Chinese of theirs and the natives, some of both as and when they could afford it.

There were wild horses and cattle in the hills and plentiful deer and hogs most often shot by the Portuguese to sell.

In the mountains, there were tigers and rhinoceros. I had not heard of them but Chester set me straight about going to look for them. His knowledge of them was that they were large and would eat me. I refrained, of course.

Large lizards called iguana, some up to five feet long and as thick as a man's thigh were caught in the wild areas and provided very good meat. Having seen one that Mister Banks had purchased I decided against a tasting. Ugly creature as it was, I deemed it could not possibly have tasted well!

Fowls, ducks, and geese were plentiful but lean and dry to the taste. Mister Banks suspected that the general health of the animals was due to poor feed and the stinking water.

Rice and corn and a vast variety of kidney beans and lentils were grown, and along with the plentiful supply of vegetables from the hills, there was much variety in the diet. Sugar was grown here and a fine "arrack" brewed from its huge canes. The native also made an excellent range of palm wines.

All manner of fruits were available at markets, some we knew well and others native to the area. The men tried them all as fruit helped their sick stomachs.

The Dutch grew pepper, cloves, and nutmeg and although the Malays enjoy them, the Dutch had put a high price on them, making them a rare treat.

The Malays sold and burned certain dried flowers to make the air more fragrant. Different types would waft past the ship on occasion, masking the stench of the town for a moment.

There were very few native Javanese. Most of the people there were from all corners of the world and the language was a mixed kind of Malay.

The women wore their hair piled high upon their heads and Arabian jasmine adorned it. All Malays bathed in the river daily. Their teeth were blackened by the constant chewing of the betel nut.

I spent many long hours in Mister Banks's cottage learning of all things Batavian. Chester, Lady, and I were riveted by his knowledge.

François, however, skulked about the small cottage wanting more to spend his time with the possibility of French cats at the nearest inn. I advised against this after Mister Banks's descriptions of the place, and Doctor Monkhouse's speech about the local fare, but he merely gave me the usual "Zsst!" and left us for the nearest tavern.

"I think that you should accompany him, Fairweather," said Lady with care. "He is not a likeable chap and may get himself into trouble."

"To be honest, Lady, I would hope it so, and then we can be well rid of him!" I dared to say.

"Woof!" said Chester in full agreement. "I have not liked him from the beginning. He is shifty, a liar, and not to be trusted."

"Chester!" Lady reprimanded.

"It is true, is it not?" he barked back.

"Be that as it may, I believe it is the right thing to do. Off you go, Fairweather, and be safe," she finished.

There was nothing more for it, so I bid Chester and Lady a fine farewell for the time being and hastened after François, catching him up in the street.

"François!" I called as he ran at speed for the local tavern.

The bustle of this shipping town was like my England but with all manner of Europeans walking this way and that, and speaking several different languages. I was afraid I might lose him in the rush of feet so I hastened to his side.

"François!" I puffed. "Slow down!"

"Keep up, Fairweazer! I am keen to find 'ze French!"

"French? But there are no French ships here!" I argued sensibly.

"Per'aps not, but 'zere may be French cats!"

I could not dispute his reasoning, and kept up with him until the familiar sounds of drunken sailors piqued our interest.

The inn was full to overflowing and the men drank in the streets talking of their travels as the odd scuffle broke out.

It was unlike the inn back in England; ruffians gathered here in my opinion. This was lost on François and he headed for the rear of the Pork-a-Knuckle Tavern, smelling the Dutch wares and ready for council with foreign cats.

I, personally, would have skulked with due care, but François boldly pranced up the rear alleyway to the usual stairway area, filled with empty crates, that may or may not have entertained the odd cat.

"François, come back and be more careful!" He did not hear me.

I watched as a nuisance of large felines came from all corners of the alley and cornered François. I was not about to go and rescue him until I could hear the reason for their attack, so I lay in wait for a clue.

François, in his usual uncouthness, took umbrage.

"'Ow dare you! Get out of my way! I smell pork and wish to see 'ze cook!" he challenged, unaware of the danger he was in.

"You will see the cook if I allow you to see him!" the leader of the pack yelled coarsely. "Who are you?" he said only a light Dutch accent, almost as refined as English.

"I am François, formerly of 'ze French ship *Boudeuse* under Captain Bougainville! Now I sail wis' 'ze English *Endeavour* under Captain Cook, which 'as just landed 'ere." He stood proud of his seagoing history.

I counted no less than six pale cats that laughed inexplicably as the leader stepped forward.

"Bougainville's cat?" Their large blonde-coloured leader challenged.

"'Ze very same!" François stood proudly. "And you are?" he asked brashly.

"Kurt Van Der Sharp." He coolly polished his claws.

"And 'zis rabble?" François boldly showed now fear, smelling the pork knuckles roasting from the inn.

"Hans the Henchman, Deadly Dieter, Fritz the Feral, Max the Mauler, Killer Kristian and Gustav Gutterman." Van Der Sharp threatened.

"I am pleased to meet 'wis you but you are in my way of foods!" François was again with the stomach first and foremost, and no manners to speak of.

"Bougainville did not come here with a cat!" said Van Der Sharp offhandedly.

The others gasped, as did I within! François was in for some trouble!

"'Zat is because I was 'srown from the *Boudeuse* in a great sea and washed ashore in a country undiscovered." François lied like the fiend he was, but he was unaware that his skin was on the line in this instance.

"Oh?" teased Van Der Sharp.

"Oui! Now be out of my way!" François stood firm.

"I heard from the very mouths of the crew of the *Boudeuse* that Bougainville's cat jumped ship for fear he would be eaten!" Van Der Sharp again nonchalantly buffed at a claw.

A more audible gasp was heard from the pack!

"Err…" François had to think quickly. "Zat was not moi!" he balked innocently. "You 'ave me mistaken wis' ano'zer cat!"

"I think not! You match the description of the *Boudeuse* cat, and her crew who were here in Batavia some time ago, only mentioned one French cat! A deserter, Gustav?" Van Der Sharp bragged in his knowledge of the comings and goings of the port.

Gustav the informant nodded his confirmation of Van Der Sharp's revelation.

The cats stepped forward unexpectedly, surrounding François!

With this information, François was done for, in my opinion. I had to be forthcoming to save his skin. I strode in amongst the group as casually as was possible.

"Ah François my friend!" I interrupted hopefully.

"Who are you?" asked the petulant Van Der Sharp, hoping for a fight and expecting only one victim.

"I am Fairweather of the *Endeavour*, just in from a long voyage of discovery out of England!" I gloated, knowing that the affairs of cats would not interfere with the captain's wishes not to let humans know of our travels. After all we could not tell them!

"What business do you have with this coward?" he asked cautiously, not knowing me in the slightest.

"Mijnheer Van Der Sharp is it?" He nodded, aware of my good manners to address him as "mister" in his native tongue, as I had heard it uttered in the street.

"I am here with my friend François here, from the *Endeavour*, as he says, and we are in town to sample the local fare," I said as bravely as I could with the other cats now stepping further forward and breathing down my neck.

"I am looking for 'ze food I smell and some company of French cats!" interrupted François rudely.

"There are no French cats here!" Van Der Sharp barked at François. "Do you know of this *Endeavour*, Gustav?" yelled the leader to his informant.

"Ya, Kurt!" Gustav saluted obediently. "It is an English ship back from some sort of fact-finding mission in the Pacific." Gustav's English was rather good, too, for a Dutchman.

I was impressed that this fellow knew the purpose of our mission even before the Dutch officials knew of it!

Cats will be cats and curiosity their principle!

"Alright, Fairweather. You and this coward are not welcome here. Now I suggest you move on before we kill you both." He was blasé with his threat, as he must have thought he could make light work of us both, and to be honest we were outnumbered considerably by rough-looking Dutch-Batavian cats with evil names!

"You would not dare!" scoffed François stupidly.

"François! Cease at once!" I hissed, herding him away slowly.

"Oh, dare I would, François! You are the cat who abandoned the French ship *Boudeuse*!" Van Der Sharp said knowingly.

"How does he know this?" I whispered to François, somewhat shocked at the level of knowledge this chap possessed.

'I do not know. Perhaps my men mentioned 'ze incident when 'zey stopped 'ere." He dismissed me with a wave of his paw.

"We do not take a liking to deserters here and you, Fairweather, are just as guilty for knowing this coward!" Van Der Sharp judged.

"But I was to be eaten!" pleaded François pathetically.

I took umbrage. "Now, just a moment Mijnheer Van Der Sharp! Whatever François's crimes were, we are merely tourists here, on our way back to England after some repairs, and we mean no harm to you. Leave us about our scrounging for a sample of the fine-smelling pork that brought us here and we will be on our way."

"No! This is our tavern and you and this stain upon sea-going cats have been warned." He turned his back on us and nodded for the other cats to close in ominously.

"Turkel told me the Dutch were a rough lot! We must go, François!" I took a chance and just loudly enough, slipped in my friend Turkel's name, as I knew that the *Dolphin* had been here, too. It might either endear me to this Dutchman, or it might make him dislike me more depending on whether they had met and become friends or enemies.

"Turkel?" François asked me stupidly.

"I will explain Turkel to you later! Now be quiet and move back slowly," I advised as this could have gone either way. With each step we took backwards, the gang crept forward, not letting us out of the alley.

"Turkel?" Van Der Sharp's head snapped back to me. "Of the *Dolphin*?" His eyes became narrow with suspicion, searching the grey matter for the connection.

François and I continued edging away.

"Halt!" Van Der Sharp shouted hoarsely! I could not determine whether this was a good thing or not!

He sauntered forward and right up to my face until I could smell his breath!

"You know Turkel of the *Dolphin*?" he growled, turning my stomach to gravy, but I showed no fear for the moment.

"Why, yes, we are comrades! It is on his advice that I am the *Endeavour*'s crewman!" I did not wish to be too brash until I determined his stance on my connection to Turkel.

It seemed to be an age of tension, waiting for the upshot, and François was getting annoyingly fidgety.

"Stop it at once, François!" I hissed, as Mijnheer Van Der Sharp was making up his mind.

"Fairweather?" motioned Van Der Sharp, pausing for effect.

I bristled ready to fight or run!

"Call me Kurt! Any friend of Turkel's is a friend of mine!" He was unexpectedly jolly and patted me roughly on the back. "Come, we will eat!" With that, the gang stood at ease and the threat was no more!

My stomach gathered its parts!

"What ho! My friend!" I was so relieved I could think of nothing else to say. "I say, old thing, you had me worried there for a moment!" I revealed as we trotted off together.

"You should have been worried! We were about to kill you both!" He laughed, making me uneasy. "How is Turkel, the old swine? It has been some time since I have seen him!"

"I am sure he is well! I have been at sea for more than two years but I can report that he was hale and healthy when we last spoke back in England over a catnip or two!"

"Excellent! Excellent!" He sent the other cats to whine at the rear door of the inn until a huge plate of pig scraps came forward from the kitchen hand.

Along with that came a large bowl of catnip!

"Hans looks after us, as we keep the rats from the tavern. It is a big job for us. This town has become very dirty," Kurt explained.

"A noble profession, Kurt! I, too, am friend of my cook and butcher on the ship for my hunting skills," I bragged.

"As a fine ship's cat should! Eat! Drink! Fairweather!" instructed Kurt. I turned to see François frozen in the alley where we had left him.

Max the Mauler stood in his way and would not let him through.

"Fairweazer! Can you 'elp me?" he pleaded, seeing the food he so pined for.

I turned to Kurt. "He is harmless, Kurt. We rescued him from Australia and he has been with us since. A rude pest and a ninny but tolerable to a point," I explained.

"Ah, you found the Australia? Our Dutchman Abel Tasman found Van Diemen's Land and some have spoken of the western coast." He was suitably proud.

"Yes, we discovered the eastern coast. It is vast and unfriendly but now England's property," I ventured.

"Fairweazer!" came François's cry. "I am 'ungry, too!"

Max the Mauler was not letting François pass and he was beginning to sound pathetic, which did not stand him in good stead with these tough Dutch cats!

"Do not let him through, Max," Kurt ordered. "He is not welcome here."

He turned to me. "Friend of Turkel's or not, Fairweather, I will not entertain cowards!" He had his principles.

"Go back to the ship, François!" I ordered. He sniffed the air hopelessly and left for the ship.

I supped with Kurt and the gang on the most sumptuous pork I had ever tasted. We drank a little too much catnip, telling tales of sea-going cats and chaps, and he was riveted to my stories so far of our journey. Thanks to my mention of Turkel, I now had Dutch friends, which would be useful if we were to be here for some time.

"Your colouring is unusually pale and distinguished," I complimented of all the gang.

"Batavian cats have bred this way and are not found anywhere else but here!" he puffed up.

"I find it fetching, Kurt, very strong, and I note that your eyes are all blue!" I admired.

"It is our nature to be handsome!" he gloated, the rest of the group admiring each other.

One can never do too much buttering up where tough Dutch cats are concerned!

"I must get back to my captain, Kurt. It has been a fine evening and your food, drink and company have been most welcome to a weary sea traveller." I thanked him.

"Come whenever you like, Fairweather!" He turned as I strode away.

Then I received a call from Max the Mauler. "Do not bring that idiot François with you!" he warned.

Kurt nodded and I knew François would never be welcome here!

I went back to the ship after welcoming Kurt's promise of protection whilst I was in town. Not all cats would know of Turkel and I was warned about running into the wrong types. As I sauntered back, my belly full of pork and catnip, I felt at ease here for the first time.

As I boarded the *Endeavour*, François was waiting for me and pounced as if to attack.

"You eediot! You did not defend me from 'zis rabble! I smell catnip and pork on your person!" He was livid!

"I tried my best, François, but you have made your bed and you must now lie in it!" I waived him away.

"What bed? I do not wish to lie down!" he scoffed, thinking me drunk.

"It is an old saying, François. How could I defend your honour when you were so rude to our hosts?" I asked him. "Honestly! You do not have a charming bone in your body! And now you are not welcome there."

"Zsst! I am 'ze most charming of all 'ze cats, as I am French!" He tried to defend, using his nationality as an excuse.

"What rot, François! Your rudeness was the reason you were shunned. Not to mention your position as a ship's deserter!" I was nothing if honest.

He had no retort.

"'Ow was 'ze pork?" he simpered.

"It was most succulently cooked, and the catnip accompaniment was indeed a tasty brew!" I bragged.

"I will find my own inn and my own pork and catnip, and friends. You will see!" He sauntered off, "Zsst-ing" at everything he passed.

I retired to the Great Cabin to sleep with my stomach full from the Pork-A-Knuckle Tavern, thinking myself lucky on more than one occasion to have known the famous Turkel.

CHAPTER 35

No longer had a week passed since our anchoring in Batavia than more men fell ill from the reeking, disease-filled air that hung over the city.

The men who were well were sent ashore to erect tents for the sick to recover and receive treatment on land. Those who had been stricken by dysentery or malaria were thus kept from infecting the few hale hands we had left on board.

The captain had ordered and received two live oxen, one hundred and fifty gallons of arrack, the strong Batavian rum, three barrels of tar, and one barrel of pitch for our repair work.

The next day, Lieutenant Hicks was sent ashore to recover in the tents as his consumption had worsened.

Over the following days all who were well unrigged the ship ready for her repairs. It was slow going with so few healthy hands, but the Dutch governor was in no rush to move us to Onrust Island either, so the captain deemed that we would just have to do our best.

Mister Banks and the gents in town began to feel the effects of the unwholesome climate; their appetites and spirits were low.

Tupia and Tiata were ailing most of all and Mister Banks began to fear for Tupia's life, as the stubborn chap would not take any of the medicines he was offered to relieve him. He asked to be moved back to the ship where the food was stable and the air fresher than in this rotting town. Tiata joined him but both were low in morale.

I suggested to François that he tend to Tiata as the boy had looked after him since his joining us in Australia. Typically of François, he did so, but under sufferance, as I believed him now to be the most selfish and insufferable bore I had ever met! He had not a thought for anyone other than himself, and he failed to endear himself to anyone except the poor young Tiata, who thought François's companionship was his own idea! Indeed, he had to be pushed to tend to the youngster and I deemed it a serious lack of character!

After a long and tiresome wait we were granted permission to haul alongside one of the wharves at Kuypers, in order to relieve the ship of her stores for her beaching and careening at Onrust Island, so that the Dutch carpenters could attend her bottom. They made it well known that only they could repair the ship; our carpenters and riggers could do nought but stand back and watch. It was the rule here in Batavia and obey it we must!

On the morning of the 25th of October, the captain arranged for his package of letters and maps bound for England to be sent with the ship Kronenburg, captained by Commodore Fredrick Kelger, who together with another ship was sailing immediately for Cape Horn where they would wait for the remainder of their fleet. The package would then be sent on to England.

The captain despatched it tentatively when the commodore's young aide came calling, as it must reach the Royal Society intact, or others could claim this proof of our mission!

Day by day, the tents seemed to fill with our ailing men. Mister Banks himself finally succumbed to the local diseases, coming down with a tertian; malarial fits of fever, making him delirious and so weak he had to crawl down the stairs of his cottage!

I visited daily as Chester and Lady worried for their master and I thought it a good idea to keep their spirits up with tales I had heard from Kurt and his gang.

I travelled between the ship and Mister Banks's house, visiting the Pork-A-Knuckle nightly to hear the stories of the many men who passed through Batavia.

François hissed at me every night as I left the ship, knowing where I was off to and that he could not attend.

Kurt elaborated on many of the sailors and Navy men that the captain had spoken of, and his stories put their mention in context and made sense of many of the captain's prior comments.

While we waited for the Europeans to stock their mended ships with pepper and vacate our upcoming position at Onrust Island, the captain set the few well men to overhauling the rigging, making rope and repairing sails.

François had taken to going into the town every night in search of an inn that would feed and entertain him. Kurt had ensured that the word had gotten around that François was a ship's deserter and he returned each night shunned, hungry, and friendless. He was eating from rubbish bins rather than admit he had been turned away from the taverns. He became ill himself and expected someone to look after him! No one volunteered.

Poor Doctor Monkhouse had tended so many of our sick by now that he too had become so ill, that we feared for his life.

I visited François who had taken my favourite spot in the Great Cabin to recover from his ills.

"What of your condition, François?" I asked, knowing he would whine on dramatically of it.

"I am so sick, Fairweazer!" he cried, lifting his head from my bed. "You must fetch 'ze doctor for me!" He languished back on the pillow.

"For goodness's sake, François! You have brought this on yourself!" I chided him.

"I 'ave not! I am inflicted wiz' 'zese Batavian diseases! Fetch 'ze doctor for me!" he moaned.

"I will do no such thing! You have merely eaten something rotten from the rubbish in town! You will live!" I diagnosed.

"'Zis may be so but I need 'ze doctor! My stomach! My 'ead!" He groaned with finality.

"Oh, alright I shall fetch him for you," I submitted painfully.

He was not going to let up until I brought Doctor Monkhouse to his side.

I walked in on the doctor who was sitting in his chair taking of medicine.

"Ah, Fairweather, I believe I have come down with what ails the men." He sounded dreadful and was as pale as paper.

I jumped to his desk and rubbed my cheek against his hand, which was clutching his head in pain and fever. My attempt to comfort was greeted with a pat and I sat to receive it. His hand became heavy and still upon my back, and his head dropped to the desk with a thud!

I jumped to release myself and pushed my ear to his neck in an effort to hear his pulse, as I had seen him do on many occasions with the men he treated.

I detected nothing! No movement at all!

I ran at speed for the captain who was on deck and had just received word that we could finally transport the ship to Onrust Island for the work to begin upon her beaching.

He was mightily excited and was giving orders left and right. I meowed insistently at his feet but he ignored me!

He must be informed if there was to be any hope for Doctor Monkhouse!

I leapt to the rigging and jumped to his hat, tipping it off and landing squarely on his shoulder sinking my claws in so as not to fall and fail to get his attention.

"Fairweather, you nit!" He shrugged me to the ground. "That hurt like the dickens!" He complained, rubbing the afflicted spot.

I meowed so loudly that he could not ignore me, and ran to the gangway whilst I had his attention. He followed, knowing me to never interrupt him unless there was good reason! I rushed to Doctor Monkhouse's cabin and when we arrived, he pushed past me to check for the good doctor's vital signs of life!

"It is too late, Fairweather! The doctor is dead!" He gasped. My head fell with grief. I was the last to speak with him.

"Isaac! Will! Anyone!" he yelled. He lifted the doctor to his bed and laid him there carefully. I jumped to his head and stroked it, purring, as I could see that his eyes were open! I was unsure of the captain's diagnosis, as opened eyes seemed to me a sign of life!

The captain closed the doctor's eyes and drew a fresh clean sheet over his body when Will came rushing to the door.

"Fetch Doctor Perry!" ordered the captain.

Will took one look at the sheet over the doctor's head, knowing what it meant, and rushed to find Doctor Monkhouse's assistant. They both returned and I was placed on the doctor's desk so that Doctor Perry could examine him.

He folded back the sheet and checked the doctor for a pulse, his head on the doctor's chest listening for his heart sounds.

"He is dead, Captain. By the sweat and fever on his brow I suspect he is a victim of this Batavia," reported the surgeon's mate.

The captain shook his head as Doctor Bill Perry recovered Doctor Monkhouse with the sheet. Men had gathered outside the doctor's quarters and bowed their heads upon hearing this dreadful news.

"We will bury him in Batavia before we move the ship. Make the arrangements, Doctor Perry." Everyone felt the pall of death as the sick had taken their toll on our good doctor.

I walked with the captain back to the Great Cabin and as he removed his hat and looked out the window at the stinking city he whispered a few words to the Almighty.

I bowed my head with respect when the noxious sound of François's voice interrupted the prayers.

"Where is 'ze doctor, Fairweazer?" he demanded. "I am so unwell!" He feigned a collapse.

"Doctor Monkhouse is dead, you foul blot!" I growled.

"Dead?" His head shot up.

"Dead!" I confirmed, thinking this news would silence the fool.

"But I need 'im to see to my great sickness!" he whined.

"François!" I could hardly contain my anger. "The man is dead! Have you no respect?" I was flabbergasted at his foolish selfishness.

"I suppose it is sad," he admitted. "Can you fetch his assistant for me now?" He asked unconscionably! I could not slap him, as the captain would be witness, so it was a verbal lashing he was going to receive.

"François! Get up from my bed at once and take your hideous countenance from my sight before I scratch you to within an inch of your life!" I threatened.

"You would not dare!" he said carefully, knowing the Fairweather to be even-tempered unless provoked, and the captain to be present.

"When you least expect it, you foul fiend! I have killed before!" I added, referring to my fatal fight with Muto'i in Tahiti, which although accidental to a point, was a surety in truth.

"You 'ave?" François was shocked!

"Check with Chester and Lady when we next see them. I do not have the time for you at this moment. Our good doctor is dead and all you can think of is your own silly illness, the onset of which is rotten garbage! Get out!" I pointed for him to leave the Great Cabin immediately.

"I will not!" he defied me.

"Oh, you will, or I shall lull the captain from the room and return to finish you off!" I growled so gutturally that it did not merit argument!

He was suitably silenced.

The captain sent word to Mister Banks's house of the funeral for the good doctor, but he was unable to attend, as he had become so unwell himself.

Late in the afternoon of this 7th day of November 1770, after Doctor Monkhouse was put to rest in the Batavian ground, word came to the captain that Onrust Island was now free of the European ships, and we could transport the *Endeavour* there for the work to begin.

The entire company, sick or well, came back on the ship, all but Mister Banks's party, and were well pleased to be away from this Batavia and looking forward to the somewhat fresher airs of Onrust Island.

The captain officially appointed Doctor William Perry, the surgeon's assistant, to take Doctor Monkhouse's place. By now, several men each day were falling ill, which made Doctor Monkhouse's loss more cruelly felt, but Doctor Perry was an equally skilled physician and now in high demand!

John Ravenhill, our elderly sail maker, did not think Batavia's diseases would affect him if he was drunk every day, and it seemed to work in his favour thus far! Strangely, his excess drinking did not affect his skills, only his speech, which slurred constantly making him difficult to understand. I liked him, as his age always guaranteed a good sea-going story or two, when he was not completely passed out where he had taken his last drink for the evening.

A few days after Doctor Monkhouse's funeral, we were successfully beached on Onrust Island, not far from Batavia Road but far enough not to smell the rancidness of the disease-ridden town, and receive the much-wanted fresh sea airs.

The ship was towed to the beach and the Batavian carpenter's slaves heaved the port side of the ship keel and it was discovered that her bottom was in worse condition than first imagined. I watched from the edge of the deck as the captain, lieutenants Hicks and Gore, and the carpenters assembled on the sand, all scratching their chins quietly at first.

"'Tis a wonder you made it this far, Captain!" said Lars, the Batavian carpenter finally.

"It seems so, Lars!" the captain stared incredulously at the *Endeavour*'s injuries.

The false keel was gone to within twenty feet of the stern, the main keel was damaged in many places, especially under the main channel near the keel where two planks, six feet in length were within one eighth of an inch of being cut through. The worms had gotten well in amongst her timbers and many parts were eaten away. The slaves got to work immediately to bail the water out of the hold and the skilled tradesmen got to work under the instruction of the talented Lars.

The captain and John Satterley looked on daily, as the costly repairs were under way.

"I had suggested to the governor of Batavia that we do this work ourselves to save the expense of Lars and his chaps, John, but at the rate the men are falling ill we could only spare but twenty at a stretch."

"I agree, Captain. I'll say this much: their work is of a fine quality," praised John Satterley, our own carpenter. This pleased the captain and the labour continued.

François soon became well after purging the rotted food he had eaten, but he still annoyed me constantly for an invitation to the Pork-A-Knuckle Tavern with Kurt and his men.

From our long discussion in the alley at night it seemed that Kurt knew every cat in Batavia and who was in town and for how long. His men were of the highest order in this city of taverns, and a word from Kurt was the difference between good treatment and a cat's undoing!

François was in the latter category and no amount of my pleading his case made any difference as Kurt and his men had made up their minds, quite rightly, that François was a cad. I could not argue the fact for fear of losing my status amongst these local and influential chaps, an admirable position thanks to the well-known Turkel, and my own achievements at sea, of which word was spreading through the town.

My safety was assured at every turn!

Word reached us a few days later that a French ship had docked, and François was keen to learn of her, whether she had come to Batavia on the way to a distant exotic port, or was merely stopping by to trade, repair, and restock to return to France.

I went with François to see this ship and make my own determinations. We came in to town with the boys in the longboat fetching supplies for the ship's refit. At this important stage of her repairs, the *Endeavour* asked constantly for more fittings than we were prepared for and the boys were sent daily on errands to find the right pieces for her reconstruction.

All the way to the designated dock, François strutted purposefully, spouting the names of French sailors he knew, dead or alive!

"'Zey may be on 'zis stupendous French ship and bound for riches and wealths!" he bragged incessantly, hardly watching where he was going.

"François, if you are not careful, I will lose track of you, or you might take a wrong turn to this gargantuan French ship of yours!" I pleaded for my own safety, if not his.

"Or she may be capitained by Bougainville 'imself, having 'eard that I am in Batavia; and 'e has come to rescue me from 'zis 'orrible town!" There was no end to the imagination and self-absorption of this François!

When we approached the designated dock, all we found was a tattered old supply ship flying the French East India flag.

"This is your grand French ship, François?" I chuckled.

"Rouillé?" François read her name, almost too appalled to repeat it.

"What of its name?" I probed, not understanding his horror.

"It is 'ow you say in English?" he thought for a moment, and I was all ears.

"Rusty!" he announced.

I howled with laughter as anything metal was covered in the orange stuff. "Rusty? It most certainly is!" I could hardly pull myself together.

"Stop 'zat laughing, Fairweazer! She may be a spy ship and supposed to look like 'zis for 'ze secret French business!" he fabricated.

"Oh, please!" I cackled uncontrollably.

"You never know!" he said doubtfully.

"She looks like a supply ship; a rusty one at that!" I tried to hold back my mirth. "They almost always have cats. I suggest we board her, François, find the chap in question and enquire as to her purpose." The few crew upon her took no notice of our boarding, merely lolling about with little more to do than drink.

We found the scoundrel down below, face down in a bowl of ale.

The motley feline opened one eye as we approached, his tongue hanging loosely from his mouth. He gathered the thing back into the parent vessel and slurred.

"Who are you?" he asked.

"François de Beaujolais of Lyon, France, formerly of 'ze *Boudeuse* and *Étoile* and now of 'ze *Endeavour*." He carried out his long-winded introduction.

"Fairweather of the Bark *Endeavour*," I said more simply.

"Bark?" The chap chuckled. "Is 'zat to mean your ship is a dog? Woof! Woof!" He lolled about sniggering.

"A 'bark' sir, is a category of ship, like a frigate or a sloop. She has from three to five masts, all of them square-rigged except the after mast, which is fore-and-aft rigged. Any sea-going cat worth his salt would know this!" I took umbrage and was sickening of French cats.

"Ah 'zat is what 'ze 'bark' means!" François, too, was enlightened. I deemed that all French cats must be ninnies.

"Back to the introductions! Who are you and what is your purpose here in Batavia?" I asked the Frenchman as he stood with some drunken difficulty.

"Pierre is my name and 'zis sheep is 'ze Rouillé. Last of 'ze French East India Company sheeps, dropping off Dutch crewmen 'ere before leaving for France to be recommissioned," he said, bored with the introductory process and turning back to finish off his ale. "What do you want?" he asked.

François was excited. "I wish passage back to France wiz' you!"

"I could not be more delighted if you would take him with you!" I was never so keen to be rid of a fellow feline and would plead his case to this Pierre! "He is a fine crewman and mouser and we would miss him ever so, but I know him to wish to return to France at the earliest possible convenience!" I talked François up to this Pierre, but he was a simple fellow and did not well understand English.

"It is true, I will be missed by 'ze men of 'ze *Endeavour* but I wish to get back to my 'ome," François boasted, not really needing me to help him in the least.

"I suppose you can come, but stay out of my way. We leave 'zis afternoon when 'ze cook returns wis' 'ze rations."

François looked at me briefly and ran at speed to the *Endeavour*, no doubt to bid his farewells. I turned to Pierre and at no time had I ever meant to thank a fellow more than right at this moment!

"Thank you, Pierre! I wish you safe sailing and fair winds!" I strolled back to the ship, admiring Batavia in a new and delighted way, thankful that the French had sent one last ship to this hideous town to rid the *Endeavour* of François. The world could not have been a happier place!

I strode along the canals taking my time.

François was off to France sooner than I could have hoped! Those Batavian canals smelled like English rose gardens to a heartened Fairweather!

As I made my way slowly to the ship, skipping now and then, I heard a familiar voice, but it did not sound well.

"Tyau mate oee! Tyau mate oee!" It was a deathly call. I rushed on board the longboat going out to the *Endeavour*.

I arrived to find Tiata's dysentery had worsened!

"What is he saying, Lady?" I begged, hurrying to her side as she sat by the ailing boy with Chester.

"It is Tahitian, Fairweather. 'My friends, I am dying!' he says." Lady licked his tears. He repeated the words deliriously full of fever!

François appeared as we kept Tiata company, to bid us a blasé farewell.

"Toodle-poo! As you English would say! I am off to France!" he declared.

"That would be 'toodle-ooh' you blighter, and I cannot fathom your leaving when Tiata is so ill!" I swiped at him but he flinched at the last moment and I regretfully missed my aim.

"I cannot 'elp it if 'ze boy is sick! Toodle-poo! Toodle-poo! Toodle-poo!" he sang, just to annoy me. Chester growled a guttural warning as if to ready himself for attack.

"Leave him, Chester," I warned. "He is not worth the trouble. Believe me!"

"It is not the done thing to abandon one's boy when he is so mightily struck down!" Chester argued.

"We will take good care of him, Chester!" I assured him. "Be off with you blighted, François!" I crawled up under the arm of the ailing boy and rested my head on his chest, both for comfort and to hear of his beating heart.

"Yes, be gone, foul blot! May you have lightning and storms all the way back to France!" Chester growled. This was harsh stuff from Chester. One did not wish bad weather on even the worst of caddish crewmen!

"Zsst!" François hissed and flicked his tail and that was the last we saw of him, jumping to the longboat for shore.

A collected sigh of relief came from Chester, Lady, and I!

Doctor Perry came to look in on Tiata but knew not to wish us away as the boy was receiving comfort from his friends. I looked up at him.

"It does not look good, Fairweather," he diagnosed grimly.

I laid my head back on the boy's chest as the doctor left. Tiata let out one last cry.

"Tyau mate oee!" His voice trailed off at the end as his heart stopped.

"He is gone, Lady, Chester." I rubbed my face against Tiata's cheek. Lady licked his forehead, and Chester bowed his head in sadness.

Tupia came rushing in as if knowing that his boy had died. He cried out to his gods as the tears wet his cheeks. The ruckus caused the captain to attend and seeing Tiata's lifeless body sent for Doctor Perry to confirm his death.

"On this 9th day of November 1770, I will list the boy's death in my log. May his gods be kind to him in death, as he was a good boy in life," announced the captain.

Tupia was inconsolable and went to the deck to wail his name toward the sky for as long as he could speak! He, too, was sick from the dysentery.

Word was sent to Mister Banks and the gents and as ill as they were they came to Onrust Island to see to Tiata's funeral rites as dictated by Tupia. Tiata's life was short, so Tupia instructed that his body need only be laid out on the ground for a short time.

Our carpenter John Satterley placed a makeshift burial platform upon the beach next to the ship like the ones we had seen in Tahiti. Tupia dressed Tiata in his favourite English clothes, leaving shells he had gathered by his side. When Tiata had lain there long enough and Tupia had prayed over his body he was then buried on Onrust Island.

Once the ritual was complete, Mister Banks asked the captain for a word in private.

As always, I managed to be within hearing distance.

"I believe that Tupia will be next, Captain," Mister Banks said with some authority. "He has lost his companion in Tiata and I believe his deep bereavement will worsen his ailment."

"I see, Mister Banks. What do you suggest?" the captain asked, wanting to help all of our sick, but they were falling so fast from their ills that one could not be favoured over another.

"I will send for him to join me at the house on the morrow. I am arranging the purchase of two Malay women for Doctor Solander and myself. Our own illnesses having taken a turn for the worse and I have rightly decided that as women they might look after us better than the male slaves have done so far. Lazy fellows! Besides, the fairer sex being more considerate and caring we should at least be in better hands. Tupia will join us," Mister Banks informed.

That evening, I looked in on Tupia.

He lay feverishly on the examination table in Doctor Monkhouse's old cabin to keep him from infecting any more of the crew. His illness was such that Doctor Perry could not determine whether it was dysentery or malaria.

"These native Tahitians seem so much more prone to the illnesses of other countries, sir," he told the captain. "They have no such diseases on their own islands and this Batavian sickness is harsh upon their bodies!"

"Yes, and he has lost his attendant. His sadness is great and cannot be helping him to recover." The captain passed on Mister Banks's theory.

"True, sir. I cannot cheer him," admitted Doctor Perry, as they covered him with more blankets and left him alone with his chills. He moaned inconsolably so I did as I had done with Tiata two days earlier and crept under his arm to aid and comfort.

His moaning subsided and he petted me for a while before his heart sounds stopped. I pushed at his hand but it flopped to the side of the bed. I called loudly to the captain. By now he knew my cries, and my current enlistment as aide to the dying, so that once I called it meant there was no hope!

He returned with Doctor Perry who confirmed his death and sent Will Howson ashore to inform Mister Banks.

The burial arrangements were the same for Tupia as we had done for Tiata.

Mister Banks dressed the man in his finest English clothes and collected the shells himself to place around the still standing platform John Satterley had constructed for Tiata.

The captain gave a similar speech, calling on Tupia's gods to be good to him and afterwards Mister Banks left for town as Doctor Solander had worsened.

I went with his party to check in on Chester and Lady. They were both saddened by the deaths of Tiata and Tupia within days of one another and I found their spirits difficult to lift.

I tried my best, reminding them of the awful François and his timely departure but nothing piqued their interest.

Mister Banks sent for a local doctor the next day to see if he could help Doctor Solander. He was a small, thin Malay chap named Doctor Jaggi, and carried an oversized bag of medical supplies.

"I apply sinapisms to his feets and legs to draw 'da fever down from he head but I do not believe he will live through 'da night," he diagnosed.

"Sinapisms, Chester?" I asked.

"Mustard plasters. A medicinal plaster made with a paste mixture of powdered black mustard, flour, and water. The limbs are wrapped in cloth over the applied paste. It is a primitive remedy but may be his only hope," Chester explained.

Doctor Jaggi wrapped strips of cloth covered in the foul-smelling brew and placed them here and there on Doctor Solander. He said he could do no more until morning.

As sick as Mister Banks was, he sat up with Doctor Solander all night and by morning he appeared to be better than anyone had hoped!

Doctor Jaggi looked in on them the next morning, quite satisfied with himself, and advised that the fresher air of a country house would serve them better than the wretched rancid town, so they resolved to move when a suitable house could be found.

By the 13th of November, the port side of the *Endeavour*'s repair was finished, and to an excellent standard owing to the superior workmanship of the Dutch tradesmen.

She was then careened to her starboard side and it was found that there was very little damage on that side, and soon the work was finished.

Two days later, the captain transported the ship from Onrust Island to nearby Cooper's Island and moored her at the wharf to begin restocking her and taking on coal and ballast.

New pumps arrived from Batavia and were fitted by the Dutchmen.

The number of sick had reduced us to only twelve healthy hands, and the going was slow to rig the ship and bring the stores on board.

Mister Banks had secured his city landlord's country house by the banks of a briskly running river and well open to sea breezes. Mister Spöring joined them and the captain sent one of his servants and a crewman to tend to all of their needs as they all attempted to recover from their ailments.

The captain had now taken ill on board the ship, and when Mister Banks was informed, he sent the captain's servant back to care for him.

The captain, however, refused to lie down and convalesce as he was employed daily with the rigging and supplying for our journey home. My captain was a stubborn man and wanted us away from Batavia as soon as possible so that our crew and gentry could recuperate from their varied maladies.

At night I comforted him as with Tiata and Tupia and I believe that it helped to fight his fevers for every morning that we awoke he became better and I was pleased to be of assistance!

By the end of November, the westerly monsoon arrived and along with the heavy rain, more mosquitoes to bring disease and discomfort from their bites. With the rain came loud frogs and I enjoyed chasing them when invited along with the captain, who went looking in on Mister Banks and the gents at his country house.

I refrained from eating them as I had it on good advice from Chester and Lady that some frogs are poisonous!

Sport was all I could make of them.

Doctor Solander had recovered enough to walk about but Mister Banks still suffered daily in the afternoon, his fevers and fits only eased by attending his bed for a few hours, after which he became more himself.

Doctor Jaggi was convinced it was still the badness of the air and suggested that Mister Banks be "bled" frequently to purge the frequency of his attacks.

This did not sound well to me and I was somewhat horrified to see it done!

Doctor Jaggi used a scalpel to open a vein in Mister Banks's forearm and used a heated cup over the wound to suck out the blood quickly. He carefully measured and caught the blood, then disposed of it.

As I showed not a little panic at this method, Chester and Lady, aware of such medicinal cures, assured me that Mister Banks would not bleed to death as I had thought!

In early December, Doctor Solander's fever returned and his decline was swift. Doctor Jaggi was back on the job and returned him to good health with his plasters and bleedings.

I had become somewhat of the ship's nurse, comforting those who fell ill. I did not see much of Kurt and his gang during this time of poor health amongst my crew. My mission was to care for the sick!

The captain was still not himself but he battled on bravely, to have us away from Batavia as soon as possible, and set for home.

By the 8th of December we were fully stocked and the sick were all back on board.

The captain raised the anchor and took the run into the stinking Batavia Road mooring to finish the ship off there. Scraping and repainting her timbers were among the multitude of little things that required work for the homeward leg of our journey. The captain wished us to look our best when returning home to England!

For the next few weeks, a number of ships weighed in during our stay. The *Earl of Elgin* was an English East India Company ship from Madras bound for China. The East India Company ships were known as "Indiamen," and primarily for the carriage of goods.

The *Elgin* had lost her passage and had put in to Batavia to wait the next favourable season.

There was also the *Phoenix*, under Captain Black, an English country ship from Bencoolen.

The captain dined with his fellow captains but only briefly as he wished us on our way as quickly as possible having watched our men falling ill in such great numbers.

My boys' youth and strength kept them well and they found new friends amongst the crew of these ships; fellows their own age with as many exciting tales to tell around the table at the Pork-A-Knuckle Tavern with a tankard of ale or rum.

On the nights they were permitted to attend the town, I joined them to visit my friend Kurt and his chaps. Unfortunately, all I could discuss was our sick and dying, which did not cheer the group in the least!

"For this reason, we have not become attached to people of this town. They suffer and die regularly and our affections are wasted upon them!" Kurt cold-heartedly explained.

I did understand his reasoning, though, having attachments to our crew and feeling my heavy heart when they departed.

While the last of the work continued, Mister Green's servant, John Reynolds, died of the dysentery on the 18th day of December 1770.

After the usual burial and ceremonies were performed, I joined the captain that night attending his charts and smartening up his own belongings ready for the long journey home.

"Fairweather, old friend," he said, wearily polishing his copper beaker.

I jumped to the table where his log and charts were scattered untidily. He had been working hard this night.

"I intend to leave this God-forsaken place on the eve of Christmas. It will do the morale of the men well," he informed me. "We are all but done here, so make your farewells and be ready for leaving. The winds and currents favour us for departure on that day." I cannot express to my public my relief at my captain's statement!

He had been so busy refitting the ship that no one knew when we would leave this place!

The men were officially informed the next day. The sick felt better and the well were positively jubilant!

Mister Banks and the gents made their arrangements to vacate the country house and rejoin the ship.

The men said their goodbyes to any womenfolk they had befriended.

Word had been out that we had buried eight men in all here from Batavia's ills. The Dutch thought it good odds when most ships lost all their crewmen on extended stays here!

We had so many still ill over the months here that the captain put out word of recruitment for nineteen men to sail back on the *Endeavour* to England.

All of the successful applicants were English and glad to have passage home from this stinking hellhole. One of these was Charles Praval, who became a draftsman and copyist once the captain knew of his talent during his interview.

Mister Banks employed a nineteenth man. He was evidently Eurasian of Dutch and Javanese ancestry. His name was Alexander. Just Alexander, he had no surname. He was hired as an extra servant for the voyage back to England and although Mister Banks would not admit it, he was there to replace the beloved and sadly missed Tupia.

It was my turn to take my leave. I followed the boys to the Pork-A-Knuckle Tavern on the night before the 24th of December to bid my farewells to Kurt and the fellows.

"What ho, chaps! 'Tis I, Fairweather!" I hollered up the alley to alert them that friend, not foe approacheth!

"Ah, Fairweather, rumour has it that you leave tomorrow?" Kurt asked.

"How did you know this? It has just been decided this day!" I was suitably impressed with his knowledge of the doings in the port!

"I have my means, Fairweather!" He grinned, not giving away his source but inviting me to sit, and gathering his lads together for a hearty farewell.

The usual howl went up and the kitchen hand was forthcoming with that tasty pork I was going to miss! A double helping for the exiting Fairweather! I was then presented with the finest, but strongest catnip! Kurt had been keeping it for my departure, knowing as he did, more than I about when that would occur!

"Kurt, my friend!" I slurred, full of the good stuff!

"Yes, Fairweather," he replied.

"I am eternally grateful for your friendship in this rotten town!" I praised him.

"Rotten?" he said, annoyed. The gang were not impressed.

"I mean no harm, my friends. I merely refer to the sickness and deaths that have become my crewmen," I retracted hurriedly.

"We understand kameraad!" Kurt said as his men nodded.

"Kameraad?" I asked stupidly, as had I thought it through, it sounded similar and would have made perfect sense, but for my catnip intoxication.

"Comrade!" Kurt confirmed in English.

"Ah! You consider me a comrade? But you are not seagoing cats?" I stretched the friendship.

"You are mistaken, Fairweather! We have all sailed for the Dutch East India Company and found ourselves in similar circumstances as you. This is why we have settled in this alley. We are not cowards but we embrace our lives and wish to live peacefully here," he admitted.

"I do not judge you, chaps! It is a fine lifestyle, this Pork-A-Knuckle Tavern is decidedly where I would wish to retire should the mood take me," I admitted. "I would find such a place, and your company, an admirable end to my voyages!" I hoped they would accept my findings.

"To Fairweather! Safe voyage home, kameraad! You are most welcome to return!" Kurt toasted.

"Fairweather!" shouted the men.

"Thank you, my friends! Now I must make my way back to the ship to be ready for our departure on the morrow." I would rather have stayed with all this camaraderie but knew I would need to be at my best the next morning!

I walked out of the alley with barely a look back. I had had a little more catnip than I should have on the eve of our departure. I straggled hither and yon in fine spirits, losing my way somewhat, but caring little, knowing that with the dawn came our departure and the promise of home!

I traversed a small bridge over a canal of which I was unfamiliar and began to worry that I may have strayed too far from the path in my silliness and in the dark.

The next thing I felt was a small arm under my midsection lifting me from my footing!

It squeezed as I writhed and secured me with a deathly grip!

I could not scratch it, nor moved my limbs, as the very breath from my chest was compressed from my body!

With what I thought would be my last words I howled before I believed I would die!

My eyes closed and lost consciousness, falling limp over the shoulder of the thing that had caught me.

I woke in a strange place! A shanty of sorts, no bigger than a ship's cabin and without windows. It was very sparsely furnished, and poorly decorated with dirt for a floor. It smelled of cooked fish and rancid habits.

I was alone.

My breathing was shallow and my ribs ached. The demon that had taken me prisoner must have been a mighty beast as I laboured to get to my feet.

I looked about and saw no one in the general vicinity but I heard many voices outside the structure, none of which were speaking my language.

Needless to say, I was panicked! Had I missed the *Endeavour*'s departure? Was I in a strange town, or even country?

I calmed a little as the Malay language drifted to the Fairweather ear. Even though I did not understand it, I was familiar with its intonation, as I had heard Mister Banks's women speak in this way.

I presumed, albeit hopefully, that I was still in Batavia, in the Malay shanty area, but this remained to be seen.

The flimsy iron door rattled as it was being unlocked and I hid behind the only fixture, a rudimentary cooking stove with a pot upon it. In walked a Malay boy no more than seven or eight years of age. I feared that the monster that had grabbed me was after him.

"Kucing!" he yelled, with a grin from one ear to the other. I wished I had the gift of human speech to warn him of the monster outside the door who had kidnapped me! This young boy must have saved me from it, but I shivered behind the pot even though it was simmering with some kind of meal, the smell of which made my stomach turn.

"Kucing!" he said again quietly as to lure me out of my hiding place. He turned and locked his door and I felt a little more at ease. He crouched down to my level.

"Kucing," he said softly.

I tilted my head in wonder at this young boy's word.

"Cat?" he translated quietly. I nodded, but kept my eye out for the monster that had grabbed me.

"Ing-il-ish cat?" he asked, not so well versed in my language. I nodded again, hoping he would be the protector of all English cats from brutes who would abscond with the likes of me!

"I frend of yoo! Kucing! Frend!" He grinned again.

Ah, "friend," I thought. He must have rescued me from the heavy-handed kidnapper!

I came out from behind his simmering dinner, my tail aloft, and walked around him rubbing myself upon his body gratefully. He seemed to enjoy this. The boy petted me lovingly, however, I had my ship to return to, and this was doing me no good. I so wished to speak to the lad.

A rattle came from the young boy's door and I feared it might be the brute after me!

"Berani!" came an elderly man's voice. I cowered even though the chap sounded somewhat too feeble to have abducted me in such a fashion as to damage me so!

"Kakek!" the boy replied, keen to see the beast and unlocked the door! I hid behind the stove yet again!

A small aged chap with a walking stick stood in the doorway. I hoped that they both spoke some English.

The boy pointed to me. "A cat!"

The old man nodded and I felt some relief although one never knows the strength of the aged, and he could well have been the beast, however unlikely!

"Kakek! Err…Grandfather!" he yelled excitedly. All was clear! It was a relative of the child! I was safe for the moment.

"We must speek Eng-il-ish so the cat will understand Kakek… err…Grandfather," he implored.

"Yes, Berani. He a nice-looking cat. Where yoo find him?" asked Grandfather. I rightly assumed that Berani was the boy's name.

"On da bridge near here! I catched him," he said proudly. I was confused. This small boy was the beast? The brute that nearly squeezed the very life from me?

I bristled somewhat! This small boy squeezed me half to death!

I found myself not so fond of him after all.

"I will keep him and call him 'Kucing'!" he announced.

"Why Kucing? It is Malay name for cat, is it not?" asked the old man.

"Yes, Grandfather. It just make it easy for me. Chicken is call Ayam. Fish is call Ikan. Dog is call Anjing. My name, Berani, mean 'brave', so cat will be Kucing! See? I learn Ing-il-ish at same time! It easy for me!" Berani explained.

But I was not here for a lesson in Malay; I must away to my ship! I scanned the small space for an opening but other than his locked door the boy had none but a small covered pipe for a chimney above his stove, and I could not get up there, let alone fit through it!

"Where is Anjing, Grandfather?"

Dog? The boy has a dog?

I thought his mention of it had been purely an example of his language skills! I hoped it was far away as its presence at the moment was not ideal!

"He wait outside. Smell cat and want to come in." Grandfather chuckled.

I froze! I was not in the mood for introductions, especially with an unknown dog!

I saw an overly large snout poke itself under the door and puffs of dust go up as he sniffed the Fairweather scent long and hard. Anjing leant against the shanty door wagging his tail, and from the noise it made I gathered it was a rather sizeable tail!

"Go away, Anjing!" yelled the boy. The dog whimpered and left.

"You my Kucing now!" he sai,d doling out some of the foul-smelling brew from the stove for me. I sniffed it and winced.

"It only greens but we have fish next day!" He was excited, pushing the tin plate toward me, along with a cup of water.

I lapped at it as if grateful but it tasted as bad as it smelled. The water was more to my need to wash the last effects of catnip from my system. I had to get out of here! And a clear head was integral!

I was not sure of the time or even the day, as my unconsciousness could have been long and the *Endeavour* may already have left without me!

I was all a dither when the grandfather and Berani readied themselves for bed. After extinguishing their fire, they unrolled two mats and laid down, the boy grabbing me and hugged me to himself for comfort.

I wriggled not a little but not enough to invite that death grip of his, as I needed to stay alert. He began to squeeze so I ceased writhing and lay there for a moment.

Thinking was the thing to do!

I did not know how far I was from the Pork-A-Knuckle Tavern but I imagined I had not gone far. I had no way out of the shanty. I decided I had but one chance and that was to howl as loudly as possible to attract someone's attention.

Hopefully that of Kurt and the lads!

I took a long large breath quietly in, and without thought for Berani's hearing, let out an ear-piercing howl! The boy jumped from his bed! Even Grandfather shot up rather more deftly than I would have imagined!

"What was dat, Kucing?" he was shocked and rubbed at the ear I had deafened.

"Dis cat mad!" uttered Grandfather in fright.

"It okay, Grandfather. He maybe had bad dream." Berani petted me.

Just for good measure I let out another, wailing well above the other sounds of the Batavian night.

I could do nought now but wait.

I sat peaceably enough by the door while the boy and his grandfather settled back to sleep. I heard the boy sob a little but was not in the mood to comfort him.

"It be okay Berani. He get used to you soon," Grandfather reassured him.

Just as I was hoping I would not have to get used to Berani I heard a low meow outside the rear of the shanty. Was it Kurt? I could not tell! I had never heard him meow before!

"Kurt?" I called.

"Yes!" he answered. "I have Chester with me."

I was ecstatic!

"Woof!" came the loudest bark I had ever heard.

"Woof! Woof!"

Anjing!

Hopefully, Kurt and Chester had the lads along, as by the sound of that "woof" Anjing was enormous!

I could do nothing but let them hatch their plan, assuming they had one!

Berani and Grandfather woke, as Anjing was always their warning of any trouble.

"What is it, Grandfather?" Berani was afraid.

"I go see." Grandfather went to the door, grabbing up his large stick and unlocking the door. I could see my chance!

"Do not let Kucing out!" he squealed.

Too late! I bolted with the dust flying behind me! I jumped to a crate and then took one leap to the roof of the shanty.

"Fairweather! Stay up there! This dog is huge!" warned Chester.

I looked down to see the brown and black coat of what I first thought was a horse! It had a head the size of a bucket, a body as wide as a water barrel and was as tall as Grandfather and Berani who were now outside!

Chester was going to be up against it!

Fortunately, Anjing was chained to a post but he strained at it so powerfully upon spotting Chester and Kurt's gang that the thing splintered into two pieces, releasing the beast!

The dogs faced each other in a standoff!

"Is this silly dog your friend, Kurt?" asked Anjing menacingly.

"Why, yes, he is!" Kurt said rather casually, assuming that Anjing would back down.

"Then he is mine to kill!" Anjing ran on the spot, stirring up dirt, before gaining momentum and leaping toward Chester!

Chester steadied himself for the attack but for all his strength the brute's huge head hit him amidships causing him to yelp and roll a number of times!

He was up in an instant, teeth bared against his massive attacker!

They both stood on hind legs, their paws on each other's shoulders, writhing, growling and snapping at each other. Although Anjing was powerful, Chester being the more agile of the two deflected Anjing's huge slathering jaws with a slap of his sharp snout across the brute's face. The sound of their jaws colliding with such force was sickening and I feared fatally for Chester!

Berani ran to come between the dogs but the wise grandfather stopped him for fear he would be bitten. They could do nothing but watch.

Kurt jumped to the roof where I surveyed the scene. The odds did not look good for Chester!

"Do not fear for your friend, Fairweather. My men are at the ready." He tried to comfort me but I could not see Chester making it out of this fight with his life!

Sooner or later those colossal jaws would connect with Chester's neck and it would snap like a twig!

I could not sit there on the roof and do nothing!

I steadied to pounce but Kurt stopped me!

"Wait!" he said with authority. "Attack!" he ordered loudly.

Just as he stopped me from jumping on the hound, Kurt's men hurtled at the huge dog's hind quarters and sunk their claws into him with such might that Anjing leapt in the air snapping at his behind.

Hans, Dieter, Fritz, Max, Kristian and Gustav curled their well-planted claws into the target!

Anjing yelped like the dickens, unable to reach behind him and detach the attackers!

"Stay here!" ordered Kurt, jumping down from the roof.

"Bite!" ordered Kurt. As one, the gang sank their teeth into the flesh of the fiend.

Anjing could do nought but run as fast as he could hoping to shake free his attackers!

"Release!" called Kurt. The team let go of the whimpering Anjing as he loped away to lick at his wounds somewhere.

Grandfather came at Chester with his stick but knowing me to be safe on the roof, Chester took off like a shot.

"I will meet you at the tavern!" he called to me as he ran off into the night.

Kurt jumped back to the roof knowing his men would meet him back at the Pork-A-Knuckle.

"I suggest we go and meet Chester and the boys for a catnip or two after that!" Kurt was enjoying himself.

I did not know that Chester knew of the Port-A-Knuckle!

I was confused and concerned.

"If it is the boy that worries you, he will not catch you. We can jump from roof to roof here, the shanties are all so close, all the way to the tavern!" Kurt knew his way around.

I thought it prudent to have one drink with my rescuers and knowing Chester to be there, I agreed.

Indeed, we jumped from one shanty to another until the Pork-A-Knuckle appeared. The gang were sitting together recalling their brawl with Anjing and laughing over catnip.

Chester sat quietly, panting from the strain.

"Well done, men!" Kurt praised as we approached. "Are you all in one piece?" He asked, chuckling, knowing that his men were well trained and would not have been hurt.

"Ya!" They nodded, chuckling in concert.

"A drink for Fairweather and Chester!" he ordered.

I slurped it down to calm the nerves.

"Are you hurt, Chester?" I asked, worried for him.

"I will live." He lapped gratefully at his drink as the kitchen hand placed it in front of him.

"I cannot thank you enough for my rescue!" I nodded to each chap. They nodded back as was the cats' way.

"You are lucky. Anjing is the toughest hound in all Batavia!" he informed.

"He certainly is a large fellow!" I admitted, my heart still pounding.

"A Rottweiler, no less!" said Chester.

"A what?" I asked stupidly.

"A large German breed of dog, brought here for hunting, usually belonging to butchers," said Chester quietly.

"He is correct. The boy's grandfather was a butcher here before he got too old, but they keep him for protection," Kurt explained. "When I first heard your howl and rushed to your predicament, I felt the need for your friend Chester's help with him."

I was confused. "How did you get Chester off the *Endeavour*? She sails at dawn tomorrow! All but my boys are on board!" I thought.

"Chester was here at the Pork-A-Knuckle, dining with your gentlemen, when the Fairweather howl came upon the wind." He laughed heartily.

"Yes, I heard you! Damned screeching! I could hardly miss it!" He cursed, although fondly. "Mister Banks decided to join the boys at the infamous Pork-A-Knuckle when he heard that they were attending. The gents came, too. We took the pinnace after you left with them in the longboat."

"Is Lady with you?" I asked.

"No, she deemed this jaunt to be men's business and stayed behind." Chester panted.

"I am relieved! Are the gents still here? And the boys?" I asked, straining to see them through the kitchen.

"Yes, and we will be leaving with them now for the ship and staying there!" Chester insisted.

"I thank you again, fellows! If you are ever in England, I am at your service," I praised them all.

Chester noticed Mister Banks getting ready to leave the tavern. "Get moving, Fairweather. Our men are leaving. We will miss the longboat," Chester ordered.

I quickened with him to catch up to the gents, running past the lads.

"What is Fairweather doing here with you, Chester?" Mister Banks asked casually. "Strange cat that, what chaps? Gets around a bit, does he not?" The gents agreed.

"He came with us, sir," explained my Isaac, bringing up the rear as our party approached the dock.

We rowed out to the *Endeavour*, Chester and I silently, as the boys chattered on filled with ale.

The gents followed in the pinnace and all were boarded for the last time.

Chester went below slowly and quietly.

The men lolled about the deck so I followed my friend to Mister Banks's cabin. By the time I reached it, Chester was lying exhausted on the floor with Lady licking his face.

"Chester!" I was glad to see my rescuer.

"He can hardly breathe, Fairweather. Nor talk well. What happened?" Lady was deeply concerned.

"Chester, old thing, are you injured?" I asked.

"Of course, I am, you twit!" He coughed, flinching. "Did you not see the size of that dog?" He whispered hoarsely instead.

"Yes, he was a monster! A Rottweiler, Lady!" I conveyed the enormity of our foe.

"Bigger than our young Isaac on all fours!" was the only comparison I could successfully make!

"You fought a Rottweiler, Chester?" Lady was shocked! "What for?" He had not yet informed her.

"This fool cat." He puffed breathlessly. "Got into more trouble."

"Don't speak, I shall fetch Doctor Perry to see to you." She glared at me and left to find the doctor. It was not long before Lady came back with the doctor and Mister Banks.

"Chester, my boy, what has become of you?" Mister Banks pushed Doctor Perry through to attend him. He felt him all over and checked where Chester winced in pain.

His findings were worse than I thought, though none too surprising, having witnessed the fight.

"He has broken ribs on his right side, and his jaw is also broken to the left side," deduced Doctor Perry.

We all gasped in horror!

"He will heal but must be kept quiet and given only mashed food as he cannot chew. He may walk around but he will lie down when it pains him," diagnosed the doctor.

"Chester! How did this happen to you? You were with me at the tavern. I saw you go off but only for a moment!" Mister Banks was inconsolable!

"This severity of damage could only have been inflicted by something larger than him, Mister Banks," noted Doctor Perry.

We all knew but could not inform!

"A horse, perhaps?" Mister Banks suggested.

"A horse would not break a dog's ribs or jaw, Mister Banks. Horses are not that aggressive," the doctor reflected.

"No, you are correct, Doctor Perry. A man, perhaps?" Mister Banks put forward.

"Perhaps, but I think it more likely to be a larger dog." The good doctor guessed it!

Chester whispered a "woof" to confirm the doctor's notion.

"A bigger dog than Chester?" asked Mister Banks incredulously.

"I have seen them around the town, Mister Banks. The Rottweiler breed is popular here," he confirmed.

Chester gave another quiet "woof" and established the culprit.

"A Rottweiler? It is a wonder he survived!" Both men were surprised that Chester got off lightly, although Chester himself did not feel so lucky in this, his time of pain.

Mister Banks and Doctor Perry left the room, Lady sitting dutifully beside Chester should they be needed again.

Lady turned to me the moment they were gone.

"Now, Fairweather, you may explain to me exactly what happened to poor Chester!" She was angry with me, so I related the story.

"I understand that he acted for you, Fairweather, but mark my words, he will not save you again if I have anything to do with it! You are to stay out of trouble! You two are testing my patience! Friendship or not! I will not have either of you injured. We are on our way home with not long to sail. Try to behave so that we may all arrive home safely!"

And with that, her harsh words were not lost on either of us, as Lady was not usually one to chasten!

There was nothing more to say but a heartfelt apology from yours truly.

Lady curled up beside Chester on her stool, her head near his so she could monitor his breathing. I slid up under his paw, my head resting softly on his chest so as not to cause him further pain, so that I may hear his heart sounds. I had done this with many of the sick men, but never to my best friend.

It held a sad significance and my cheeks wet with tears.

"No snivelling, you ninny," whispered Chester softly.

"Yes, Chester. And I was never here in this embrace with you. It would be considered soppy and unmanly by one and all," I suggested.

"Agreed," he whispered wearily.

We slept.

CHAPTER 36

By morning the news of Able Seamen Timothy Reardon's and John Woodworth's deaths overnight had reached us all. The captain delayed our sailing by one day.

It was the 25th of December 1771, and he thought it necessary to honour the dead. Their burial was effected in Batavia as the last-minute adjustments were being made to the ship and the new seamen were briefed and getting to know the ship and her crew.

The captain had nicknamed the *Endeavour*, his "hospital ship," with upwards of forty men stricken with malaria, dysentery, or both.

Our aged sail maker, John Ravenhill was still the only man to have not suffered any ills and he proudly maintained it was his heavy drinking that protected him!

On this Christmas Day, our third at sea, the captain had made his farewells to the governor and gentlemen he had met during our stay, and Mister Banks and the Gents had arrived on board, along with the last of the provisions.

We ate a hearty Christmas fare prepared by the always-diligent company in the galley. Henry Jeffs had prepared the roast beef from the first of our felled oxen. John Thompson supplied us with Yorkshire pudding and all the trimmings for those who could eat. Sad to say that there were not many who felt like eating such a fine feast as their sickness put them off their food to such an extent!

It was not the usual Christmas in the mess with half the crew bedridden! Scarce of company, it was! The captain carried on regardless; he blessed the sick and toasted our pending journey, wishing our families well in wait of our return.

On the 26th Day of December 1771, we finally raised anchor.

The *Elgin* Indiaman saluted us with three cheers and thirteen guns, and soon after, the garrison, with fourteen guns, both of which we returned as was the done thing.

Batavia was behind us, and every man on board thanked the Almighty God! However, the wind shifted and we were forced to lie at anchor near Edam Island, just out of the mouth of the bay until the next morning when the winds were more favourable and we made out to sea.

To have fresh sea airs in the lungs! We had all missed it so!

Chester was improving by the day with John Thompson mincing his food so he may swallow it without using his broken jaw. He walked the decks for his toilet but lay resting on blankets in Mister Banks's cabin most of the time as was Doctor Perry's orders. Lady stayed by his side continually, assuring his comfort as best she could.

Unfortunate to say, but no one missed François and we gathered he was on his way back to France. I doubted whether I could have tolerated him further.

No soft spot had he made in any of our hearts!

As we sailed, even in the open waters, mosquitoes troubled the crew and they especially had a taste for Mister Banks.

"Captain!" He came running into the Great Cabin tangled in netting and tripping forth. Both of us looked up from the charts at such a silly sight. "These mosquitoes increase in number and bother us all to distraction!" He shouted in frustration.

"Nonsense, Mister Banks! We are away from stagnant waters and in fresh sea airs!" The captain dismissed him, swatting at the odd beastie of said type inhabiting the area.

Mister Banks turned on his heel in a huff. "My aim is to find out why they are so many and where they are coming from!"

"So be it." The captain mumbled under his breath. He was grateful that Mister Banks had taken his leave so quickly, but also pleased that someone was looking into the infestation.

We had all noticed them.

Mister Banks enlisted the gents and scientists in looking for the answer.

"Still water is where they breed. Look for still water! It could be a bucket or a puddle somewhere!" Mister Banks set them to the task.

Doctor Solander happened to be standing near the scuttle cask that had been filled from the hold that morning. He rushed to Mister Banks.

"I have found that our drinking water holds the larvae of the mosquito and in this humid weather they are hatching at an alarming rate!" He reported to Mister Banks. They hurried to the captain with this news.

"We will have to filter the entire water supply through your mosquito netting, Mister Banks." The captain sent for two of the new crewmen, James Campbell and William Burn turned up, keen to flush the drinking water of such pests.

"But my netting protects me!" Mister Banks protested.

"It will protect you more if we eradicate the pests at the source, will it not?" he said sternly.

"Yes, of course, Captain." He could not argue with such sensibility.

Campbell and Burn rounded up enough of the crew to strain the little grubs from the water in the hold and flushed them from the netting into the sea.

This relieved the mosquito problem almost immediately and Mister Banks felt highly of himself for solving the problem. The captain conveyed his gratitude to the gents and Mister Banks was able to stow his netting.

Doctor Perry kept vigil over the sick, ordering a section of the mess to be cordoned off with sheets for the unhealthy to sleep separately from the well and neither to disturb the others.

He called it the "sick bay."

He looked in on the ever-improving Chester when he could. John Thompson had been keeping broth for him, from the boiled meats, and serving him fish when Chester could make it to the galley, as was much the diet of the crew.

The ever-changing currents and fickle winds in the Sunda Strait slowed our progress yet again.

We made for Princes Island. The captain had heard we might get fresh fruits and vegetables there, as well as fish and fowl, for our ailing men. By the 6th day of January, we were anchored on the south-eastern side of Princes Island.

The captain went ashore to procure water from the natives. On mandatory closer inspection, it was good water this time, not riddled with mosquito grubs.

The natives were as easy to do business with as Europeans and the captain secured enough turtle for all hands that night. It was a pleasant change from the salt meat and fish we had been eating for a few days.

The natives brought fowls, fish, monkeys, and small deer for us to purchase with Spanish dollars, which was the only currency they would accept. We bought turtles but they were not as tasty as the ones we caught off New Holland. The seawater must have been more pure there to breed such fine catches as we had enjoyed!

Mister Banks's new servant Alexander had discovered in speaking with the locals, that there was a town along shore to the westward of our anchorage. Mister Banks, the gents and lieutenants took a walk there to find an old settlement on one side of the river and paid some local chaps to row them across it to a new part of the town where the kings and noblemen lived. They showed them around happily. Most of the people, though, had shut up their houses to tend their rice crops.

Chester, Lady, and I wished we could have accompanied them as it sounded like a pleasant visit, but Chester was still ailing and not up to the long walk.

The party arrived back late in the afternoon having hired a small sailing ship to bring them back to us. Mister Banks had his usual report of the island for the captain and as always I sat in. He would always learn much on even the shortest of jaunts.

"Princes Island was formerly much visited by ships of many nations but especially the English. Of late, we had forsaken it as it was reported that the water here was brackish. We did not find it so, simply by filling the casks further up the brook. The captain promised the king we would report their good water when we got back to England, thus encouraging sailors to bring their trade back to the island."

Mister Banks nodded gratefully to the captain and continued.

"The Island lies in the western mouth of the Sunda Straits, woody but without any hills. "Green turtle was the locals' trade but if out of season one would only dine lightly. Fowls, monkeys, and small deer were available. Cheap fish and vegetables pleased us and we purchased as much as was not rotten. "The natives here were Javanese and their raja received orders from the sultan of Bantam. Their customs were much like those in Batavia. They were much more jealous of their women and when seen by us, they would run and hide them in the woods.

"We had arrived during a custom of 'fasting.' No one would eat nor even chew their betel until sunset, but they would trade actively with us for exorbitant profit!"Their town had some three hundred houses, but a great part of the town was in ruins. The houses were built on stilts four or five feet above the ground. The walls and floors were made of bamboo and thatched with palm leaves. "They had smaller houses situated in their crops so they could stay and protect them from monkeys and birds before the harvest. "The people were agreeable and their language differed from Batavian Malays. It was told they spoke Javanese Mountain Malay." He thus ended briefly, not having learned any more than this.

In the evening I coaxed Chester to join us as the gents were going ashore.

It was discovered that a native had stolen an axe from one of our men. Mister Banks sent Alexander to report this theft to the King of Princes Island, who promised it would be returned in the morning. Indeed, it was, as the culprit did not wish to be punished!

Mister Banks suffered a relapse of his Batavian illness, gathering that his busy day and the harshness of the sun had set it off. He rested with Chester for a few days and his further account of the area was not forthcoming.

The captain resolved to sail on the 14th day of January but the winds were so light we were delayed.

Finally, we woke on the 16th day and already at sea, with only the sky and water in sight.

The men continued to ail and some to worsen as we awaited the trade winds to carry us out of our light airs. The increase in the slow fevers, delirium, and purging was thought to perhaps have come from the Princes Island water supply. The water was treated with lime juice to purify it and the decks were swabbed thoroughly with vinegar.

She was a clean ship but it did not seem to help the sick. They worsened with every passing day!

I held council with my captain as he set our course for Southern Africa.

"We sail for Capetown, rounding the Cape of Good Hope." He pointed it out on the map for me.

I wondered why we were not going back the way we had come, ever since we left Australia. I placed my paw on the route I imagined would return us to England, as the captain's route seemed to be taking us further away, his map being flat. I did not understand and he could see my confusion. He rolled the map into a cylinder shape to show me that the world is round, and it was only then that I understood "circumnavigation," a word that had been bandied about often during our voyage.

We were circling the world! I was much relieved that indeed our path would lead us right back to England where we started!

"These light airs do us no favours," the captain mused. Lieutenants Hicks and Gore joined us with news that two Dutch ships approached, going our way and showing their colours. We all went on deck to see them pass us swiftly.

"As sure as our ship might be, she is too slow to outsail even a Dutchman!" Mister Banks laughed, choosing unwisely to bristle the captain.

"The *Endeavour* has done what she is supposed to do, Mister Banks! If she were faster, we would not have made the discoveries we have enjoyed! She will have us home safely I should add, and I would prefer that a gratitude of her be forthcoming in future!" The captain turned and left him to think long and hard about spouting future derogatory comments on this, our fine ship.

I hissed at him as I followed my captain back to the Great Cabin.

"Infernal chap. Would not know a good ship if it up and bit him…" the captain mumbled as he sat before his maps.

We continued with little wind but made good progress considering it.

On the morning of the 24th of January, Corporal John Truslove of our Marine Corp died of the flux. We buried him at sea with the now usual sadness and reverence. He would be heavily missed as an esteemed member of our crew, and the captain told it so in delivering his speech upon his committal to the sea. Sergeant Edgcumbe paid tribute to him being his next in command. It was a sad and sorry Marine Corp that attended their posts that day.

The crew had just gotten back to their tasks after all this death when the next day Mister Banks came running to the deck.

"Captain! Captain!" He was hysterical. All who could rushed to his aid.

"What is it?" the captain droned, used to Mister Banks's panic attacks.

"My clerk! Mister Spöring!" Mister Banks choked. "He is dead!" He spluttered, sobbing like a child and falling faintly into Doctor Solander's arms.

The captain rallied quickly. This was not merely one of Mister Banks's tantrums.

"He did not come on deck for the corporal's funeral! He was too ill! I just this moment found him in his bunk! Dead!" Mister Banks cried.

"We will attend to him, Mister Banks," soothed the captain.

"I have known him long, Captain," said Doctor Solander, holding Mister Banks up. "He would not wish to be buried at sea. I believe he would appreciate a burial back in England."

Mister Banks renewed his howling for his dead companion.

"I cannot have a rotting corpse on the ship, Solander! Please take Mister Banks below for a brandy where I will meet you in a moment," the captain ordered.

Doctor Perry came forward. "I can preserve him. The weather is still very humid so I must act at once before he begins to decay."

"I will advise you when I have made my decision," said the captain, leaving for the Great Cabin to address the issue at hand.

The dogs and I followed the captain below to comfort Mister Banks in his time of great sorrow.

Mister Spöring had been his assistant and closest companion. Mister Banks, in his currently ill condition, would not be easily calmed. Doctor Solander had helped him to a seat in the Great Cabin and poured him a sizeable swill. He could hardly hold his beaker for his weakness and grief.

The good doctor helped him choke down the calming brew.

"Captain!" he spat, sobbing louder. "I believe that Mister Spöring desired to be transported home for a proper burial in the family plot, should he meet his maker." He sobbed. "I insist his wishes be honoured!"

"Mister Banks…" the captain found this a difficult subject, as it was not the done thing at sea. "We have a long way to sail yet and I do not believe the body of Mister Spöring would be still intact when we arrive in England." He almost pleaded. "We have no room for a dead man, and should he rot, the ship will become diseased, and an unbearable smell will permeate every nook."

"I want him transported home!" Mister Banks was inconsolable, but stubborn in his grief.

"Doctor Perry feels that it is possible if he is preserved. I will allow it on one condition," warned the captain. "If he shows the slightest decay, we will bury him at sea. I am not an undertaker and this is not a funeral parlour!" He was cross with himself for giving in to such a proposal.

Mister Banks slid off his chair and fell at the captain's feet. "I bow to you in thanks, good Captain!" He bawled. I could see that the captain was suitably embarrassed. He backed away properly and left it at that.

"Fetch Doctor Perry!" the captain ordered. My Isaac appeared promptly with the man.

"Prepare Mister Spöring as you would a specimen for preservation, Doctor, only better!" He turned to leave the Great Cabin but forewarned. "If the men dispute this unusual behest in great numbers, I will have to review my decision."

The doctor had Mister Spöring's body sent to the stores where the preserving liquids and suitable cloth could be found, and he was promptly treated and wrapped for storage back to England.

Where to keep him out of the way was the next problem!

The specimen storage room was the only answer as it was airtight and no bugs or vermin would get to his body. I managed to get a look at Mister Spöring before the door was sealed shut and his body looked like that of an Egyptian mummy that I had seen in one of Mister Banks's books. It was an odd sight!

Some of the crew began to mutter that they too would like to be buried at home and took umbrage that Mister Spöring was treated better than they. Others thought it bad luck to be carrying a dead body on the ship. The talk settled after a good dinner and rum rations for all, sick or well. A few stalwarts still bellyached on deck that night as I went below to find my captain.

"Still moaning up there, are they, Fairweather?" he asked of me. I nodded.

"Only those that moan upon every little thing?" he ventured. I nodded.

"It will pass," he said hopefully.

Two days passed without death nor incident until it was discovered that John Ravenhill, our elderly sail maker, had died in his sleep. All his talk of the drink keeping him from the ills of Batavia had served him well, but he finally died of his age of seventy or eighty years on the 27th January 1771. He was buried at sea with the usual kind words for his family back at home, and the offering of his soul to God.

The able seamen all let up a cheer, pointed subtly at the captain, for his "proper" sea burial!

On the very same day, Mister Sidney Parkinson, the natural history painter to Mister Banks, was found dead in his cabin slumped over his drawings. His purging from the flux had taken his life, much like the symptoms had the rest of our dead.

Those still purging took this as a bad omen for their own lives!

Mister Banks, again bereft, insisted that Doctor Perry embalm Mister Parkinson and transport him back to England. The captain gave in to his pleadings but instilled the same warnings as with Mister Spöring's remains.

Two days later, on the 29th day of January 1771, Mister Charles Green our astronomer from the Royal Society, who had been in bad health for a longer time than any other, collapsed dead in the Great Cabin right in front of us all!

Mister Banks shrieked in horror!

"Captain! What is to become of us?" he sobbed.

"I can but hope that we live to return to England," said the captain numbly.

"Mister Green should be taken back home for his burial also!" Mister Banks insisted, snivelling into his kerchief.

"Very well, Mister Banks," agreed the captain, if only to appease him.

He called for Doctor Perry to embalm yet another gent.

The specimen room was filling with dead gents!

The captain and remaining gents took their loss badly and after the funereal kind words and commitment of their souls to God, they drank our best brandy in an attempt to cheer. It was futile. All the drinking managed was to depress the captain and incite Mister Banks into sobbing. I knew him to be at a loss for his gentlemen, but feared he sobbed more for his own skin, as he too had contracted the purgings of the flux!

Upon pondering the deaths, I would like to say that I would miss them all equally, but Mister Spöring never had the time of day for the Fairweather of the species, yet John Ravenhill had endeared himself to me as a funny old drunkard, Mister Parkinson was always kind to me, and Mister Green always enlightening. I found myself in an odd spot with my thoughts being uneven toward the deceased!

Those troublesome few, who wished to murmur their discontent about the gents' superior treatment over the ordinary seamen, did so around the scuttle cask after each of the services.

They were now deliberate in converting others to their views and a growing number of men had gone from caring little of how the dead were treated, to speaking up against the gents at such gatherings.

I feared this was not the end of the thing!

The doctor's "sick bay" was filling with stricken men!

The next day, the 30th day of January 1770, Able Seaman Francis Haite and Samuel Moody of the carpenter's crew both died, having succumbed to the flux.

The captain prepared for them the now usual burial at sea. This caused the mood among the sick to degenerate, and the well to despair for their lives and that of their crewmates.

The two were buried at sea and the talk amongst the men worsened and grew. The disgruntled crewmen had had enough! The scuttlebutt was rife with chatter by the evening of this last two's burial!

I hovered around it to ascertain the gist.

"Dunno 'bout you lot but I've had enough of this stowin' dead gents on the ship," mumbled Archie Wolfe, the troublemaking Scot. He was sick himself and weak, but not too weak to incite unrest!

"Tis the code 'o the sea! For ye to die in it? Be buried in it!" agreed his pal and fellow Scotsman. He too was sick of the same diseases but where there was Archie Wolfe, there was always James Nicholson, in for trouble.

"Hear! Hear!" agreed the rest.

"Tis bad luck, havin' the dead aboard!" said someone.

"We'll be lucky to get 'ome!" cursed another.

"Somethin' terrible might 'appen to us!" one warned.

"I say we chuck 'em off!" suggested Wolfe.

"Yeah! We can give 'em a proper sea burial!" coughed Nicholson.

"'E's right! We'll dump 'em into the sea like the rest o' the men!" Archie Wolfe decided.

"The only thing for it, I say! Treat everyone the same!" one agreed.

"Yeah!" They all mumbled resolutely.

None of this sounded good to me!

It was a heated discussion, and I could go as far as to say it was mutinous talk!

I knew the captain to be unhappy with the deceased gents stowed in the hold but if these men took it upon themselves to throw the gents overboard without permission they could very well be punished!

The "cat" had not seen the light of day for some time, but I believed it to be coming out of retirement soon if this was not reported to the captain!

I hurried below to engage him but found him asleep on his maps. I jumped to his desk upsetting his ink and papers.

His head rose enough to see my mishap, and with his finest brandy on board he swatted me to the floor with a "Damn you, Fairweather!" and returned to his sleeping position without even cleaning it up!

The other lieutenants!

I hurried to their cabins, one after the other only to be ignored!

I had forgotten that I did not hold a similar understanding relationship with them as I did with my captain. They merely hissed at me as a pesky mad cat!

The boys!

I tried to wake them but to no avail! They had been lamenting the recent deaths over their rum rations and could not be roused!

Chester and Lady!

I was off to Mister Banks's cabin and he was awake but ill. He shooed me off to let the ailing Chester sleep, and he to read, taking his mind off his sickness.

I was thwarted in any attempt to stop my fellows from their felony!

I scarpered back to the deck to ascertain the progress of the insurgent's intent.

They had dissipated!

They were going about their business as if I had only imagined their complaining, yet not ten or so minutes had passed! I breathed a much-needed sigh of relief, imagining that they had seen sense to cease from carrying out their threats.

All talk perhaps? Yes, that was it! Mere talk!

I went down to the galley for a midnight snack that John Thompson had started putting out for me. The men were so ill that there was an excess of food some nights, and Chester, Lady and I reaped the benefits.

I made a mental note to watch my waistline, however, as we still had much sailing to do. The port of Capetown lay ahead and the potential for a vermin infestation was always a threat.

A fat Fairweather would be of no use to anyone!

As I supped peacefully, shadows appeared descending the darkened gangway!

My head bolted to attention!

I squinted in the dim light, recognising the very chaps who were grumbling on deck earlier. Following them were a few willing accomplices from the Batavian intake, and I knew this to be a disaster in the making!

I had already tried to rouse the officials to no avail so I was forced to only bear witness!

One by one the rigid bodies of the gents were hauled up the gangway as quietly as if they were ghosts!

I ran by the first of them and jumped to the rigging to see one of them thrown unceremoniously over the side of the ship!

A large splash accompanied it, but was not heard, for the newly rolling seas we were now traversing was also splashing against the ship!

I ran back down as the second body was coming up.

I had to rouse Chester!

He would at least be able to bark for Mister Banks's attention and I knew him to still be awake.

"Chester!" I hissed as I ran to the cabin doorway.

He did not stir!

Mister Banks was ready to swat me with a book but did not aim well, so I ducked as it whizzed past my head.

"I have told you to get out, damnable cat! Can you not see we are sick in this room?" He yelled loudly enough to rouse Chester and Lady.

"Chester!" I hissed again, hoping the Banks would not find another book too quickly as my head rounded the doorway.

"What do you want, foul cat?" he groaned. "Mister Banks is right, be off!" He turned and went back to his sleeping.

Thankfully, Lady knew my pestering was not for sheer fun. "What is it?" she asked sleepily.

I looked behind me and the third body was going up the gangway. It would be too late if someone did not intervene soon!

"Lady, you must get Mister Banks to the deck immediately!" I howled, caring little for the noise I was making.

"Quiet! Foul Fairweather!" Another book aimed for my head had hit the doorway.

"Mister Banks has terrible pain from the flux and is in no mood for a trip to the deck!" Lady chastened.

I looked back down the gangway and all was quiet.

I was too late!

"The men have thrown the gents' bodies over the side of the ship!" I spluttered, avoiding another book.

"What?" She bolted out the door and looked around. There was no one in sight.

"And yes, they have gone to their bunks. We are too late!" I spoke up before she could tell me I was imagining it.

"Come to the stores with me and I will prove it to you!" I demanded.

She followed me. "As incredible as I find your story, my dear, I fear you have been dreaming. Perhaps you have a fever?" The matriarch in her was coming out.

"Pffft!" I dismissed this line of questioning. She should know me by now.

"Look!" I pointed out the opened specimen cabin door and she went in, her nose to the ground, sniffing for the embalmed gents only to find a bare floor where they had once laid one atop the other!

"Fairweather! Mister Banks will be furious! I dare not think what the captain will do!"

She ran, with me trailing behind for Mister Banks's cabin.

She woofed loudly at him and circled a few times, whining to signify her distress!

"What is it, Lady?" he asked tiredly. "Can it not wait until morning? My pain is subsiding and I may finally get some sleep if that cat leaves us all alone!"

"I must leave him to rest, Fairweather. He is most unwell and I fear for his life. Do you know who threw the bodies over the side?" she asked, settling next to Chester who was still sleeping soundly.

"Yes, of course! I know my men! Why do you ask?" I was dumbstruck that no one would come to my aid when such a callous crime had been committed!

"If they have been thrown over the side, there is nothing we can do about it now," she said resignedly. "We can report this in the morning." My guess was that she was suffering from chagrin at her mate and master being so ill.

"But Lady…!" I begged.

She shushed me and nosed the door closed, shutting me out of the cabin!

I did not sleep that night!

I could do nought but wait for the morning when Lady might help me report the incident and I could point out those responsible. I sat in the Great Cabin fidgeting terribly.

As the sky lightened, the captain roused from his brandy stupor. He had ink all over one side of his face as he looked into his mirror whilst washing.

"Where did this come from?" he looked in horror.

I appeared in his doorway skittishly from lack of sleep.

He rubbed at the black spot until the skin was raw.

"Why do I suspect you had something to do with this?" he asked of me.

What luck! He did not remember the incident!

I took full advantage and looked away in denial.

"Hmm…!" was all he could muster, as no evidence was apparent to him, yet his suspicions were correct. I was not about to admit to it considering that he had not only ignored me at the time, but also swiped me from his desk at that!

He was blissfully unaware of what had occurred in the night and in no rush to straighten up and wash so I went to scratch at Mister Banks's cabin door.

No one stirred. I scratched again!

Lady roused and lifted the door latch with her nose.

"Lady, we must report the men to the captain!" I spluttered. Mister Banks roused and was looking a little rosier.

"You again! I threw several perfectly fine books at you from memory, blasted cat!" He was about to shove me out when Lady began barking. Not in her highest of spirits but enough to pique the now fully conscious Banks. Chester, too, rose to the occasion. He refrained from barking as he normally would in concert with Lady, favouring his ribs, but snuffled and puffed a little, hearing the alert in her tone.

"What is it, Lady?" Mister Banks asked keenly, and about time, too, I thought!

She circled and fidgeted as he dressed enough to be seen in public.

"What is all this?" asked Chester.

I explained my interruption of the previous night and he was aghast, or as much as he could be with a broken jaw. His eyes popped from their sockets and would not return. He, too, began circling, to get to the specimen storage cabin suite.

"Damned painful, broken ribs, Fairweather," he said in passing, and panting.

"Yes, dear mutt, I can imagine," I agreed, pacing the hallway.

Mister Banks was finally ready and set the dogs to leading the way. I followed up the rear just in case Mister Banks had a spare book in a secret pocket somewhere on his person, and felt the need to launch it at yours truly!

The dogs led him to the opened door of the small specimen hold.

A shriek of hideous intemperance echoed throughout the stores!

Those from the deck above came running to find out who was being maliciously murdered!

"Get the captain!" was all that came from the befuddled Banks. He walked in and out checking that he indeed was in the correct storage room of the hold.

"Where are the bodies of my comrades?" he asked me.

I flinched, waiting for a tome of merit to clip my ear but none was forthcoming. It was safe to say that Mister Banks did not have any stray books upon his person.

He set the dogs to finding them, thinking that perhaps they had been moved. Lady knew of their fate but still dutifully sniffed every room in the stores to obey her master. Chester sniffed along with her, knowing it was a fruitless search but for the same reason, he did his duty.

The captain appeared on the scene, his ink-blackened face still evident despite his efforts to scrub it clean. He had laid in it all night, hence its stubbornness to be removed. The skin, however, was visibly raw on the affected side from his attempts.

"What is wrong with your face, Captain?" asked Mister Banks off subject but visibly shaken by his appearance.

The captain looked sternly at me. "Nothing, Mister Banks." He dismissed his question. "What is wrong down here in the hold would be more to the point?" he snapped.

"The bodies of the embalmed gents?" Mister Banks started out as calmly as he could.

"What of them, Mister Banks?" the captain asked coldly.

"Have they been moved at your request from the specimen room?" Mister Banks's tone ascended slightly.

"No. I have not ordered it so." The captain was puzzled.

"Ahhhhhh!" Mister Banks shrieked in that womanly way that was his.

The captain pushed Mister Banks aside and looked into the specimen room for himself.

"They are not in here, Mister Banks! Did you request them moved?" the captain asked.

"No, I did notttt!" Mister Banks wailed.

"Then where are they?" the captain asked dumbly. All was quiet for a moment. The dogs and I knew where they were but could not convey the explanation.

"How did you know that they were gone from here?" His eyes became steely. He knew something was amiss.

"The dogs!" Mister Banks bawled. "They alerted me!"

"That they were missing?" The captain tried to make sense of it.

"Yessss!" His wailing continued.

"How did the dogs know?" the captain asked. Then a resolution passed across his face, and none too soon I must say!

"Fairweather!" the captain spat.

I stood to attention.

His face contorted as he remembered me trying to wake him during the night; the ink and paper incident came to mind as he touched his keenly sore face. He dared not let Mister Banks think he may have been warned had it not been for his consumption of brandy!

"Yes!" Mister Banks squealed. "Fairweather came to my cabin last night upsetting me terribly and rattling the dogs!"

Of course, Mister Banks had his own knowing relationship with his hounds, but not to the extent that the captain and I kept our counsel.

"Did you see what happened to the gents?" Mister Banks knelt down to my eye line quizzically as if I would open my mouth to speak.

Overwhelmingly, I felt the need to hiss, spit, and slap him as only this opportunity might ever afford me, especially following the tossing of the books, but curbed it for the greater good. I looked dumbly at the captain instead and winked an eye unbeknownst to all but he and I.

"Mister Banks, the cat cannot speak." He pulled him to his feet as if he were quite mad. Chester and Lady knew differently.

Having heard the ruckus, the lieutenants were both on hand by now asking what they could, in a small space that needed no more humans than we already had!

"Lieutenants! Did you order the moving of the dead gents' bodies?" was the captain's obvious next line of questioning.

"No, sir," they confirmed, confused.

"Ahhhhhh!" Mister Banks cried with renewed passion.

The captain knew that I knew what had become of the gents, but needed to get me alone to determine the answer.

He set the lieutenants to order a search of the entire ship to start the proceedings.

Doctor Perry arrived on the scene in just the nick of time, as Mister Banks was about to fall from a conniption.

"Doctor Perry! Take Mister Banks and his hounds to his cabin and administer a potion or brandy to relieve him," he ordered.

Then all clear was upon us.

"Fairweather! Where are the gents?" he asked purposefully.

I began to walk and gestured for him to follow. Up the gangway I went with him staunchly behind me. Up and up we trod, passing the now searching crewmen, and whether they were in the know or not, they were not about to confess. Those who were guilty showed it in their faces as I paused to give them a nasty stare in passing!

We arrived on the deck and I walked calmly to the starboard side where the gents had been dispatched over the side. I looked purposefully down into the briny deep long enough for the captain to get the gist.

He gasped audibly but none knew why except those below, who were pretending to search for the gents as ordered but knowing exactly where they were!

The captain thought for a moment, of the disgruntled crewmen, and the rumours of their discontent over the gents' receiving a homeland burial.

"Have any of the crew sent them over the side?" he asked quietly. I nodded only once to save him from embarrassment should someone see us conversing in this manner.

We both stood looking down into the ocean for what seemed an eternity, but may only have been a few seconds.

He stood, adjusted his waistcoat and trousers and yelled for his lieutenants. They were there within an instant having ordered all available hands to the search.

"Have you found the missing gentlemen?" the captain asked with concern to mask his knowing.

"No, sir! The ship seems devoid of them! We do not understand it!" said Lieutenant Gore definitively.

"Cease the search, lieutenants! There has been a transgression!" ordered the captain.

Mister Banks came storming up the gangway wanting answers for the cessation of the investigation.

The captain raised his hand to Mister Banks and there were no words required for him to understand the need to be quiet and wait.

Mister Banks shook visibly and sniffled into his kerchief with Doctor Perry by his side, ready for another fit should he take one.

The captain gathered the authorities together.

"I believe that the gentlemen's bodies have been pitched into the sea," he stated confidently.

"Ohhhhhhh! Ahhhhhh!" Mister banks wailed. "Who would do such an evil atrocious thing?"

"I warned you, Mister Banks! The men were not keen to have the gents' bodies onboard! The right and proper disposal of them on a ship is to commit them to the sea!" he explained harshly.

"You tolerate this crime?" Mister Banks asked the captain dubiously.

"I do not, but I doubt we will find any who will admit to it! And none who would regret it! The superstitions of the crew are a powerful force and I am not surprised that they acted upon it!" he barked.

"What???" Mister Banks was furious. "Begin an investigation at once! I demand it! Those responsible must be severely punished!" He sobbed again, imagining his friends being dumped into the sea by an angry rabble!

"I will not, Mister Banks!" the captain insisted. "These men have to sail us home successfully. If enough of them were displeased with the storage of dead men in the hold, to the point where they took it upon themselves to dispatch them to the deep, then there is little I can do about it! Whilst this behaviour is abhorrent, if I lock them up, who will sail the ship?"

"Surely you jest, Captain! My colleagues have been thrown into the sea like unwanted garbage! I will launch my own investigation!" he growled; his tears replaced with resolution.

"That is enough, Mister Banks!" the captain shouted. All stopped and looked our way as such a heated tone from our captain was rarely heard.

"I am the captain of this ship and you will not supersede me! The matter will be brought to the entire company's attention and that will be all I intend to do about it!"

He turned to the lieutenants, his face reddened where it was not black!

"Assemble the entire company on deck!" he barked unintentionally at lieutenants Gore and Hicks. "Fetch me from the Great Cabin when they are ready."

He turned on his heel but Mister Banks gave chase.

"You will not let this crime go unpunished, Captain!" he screamed. "I will report this to the navy and the Royal Society!" The captain continued along the deck toward the gangway, ignoring the screaming botanist. "I will report you to the king!"

That was it! The captain turned and slapped Mister Banks squarely across his face!

"Ahhhhhh!" he flinched, holding his cheek. "How dare you!" He was furious and held up his arm to strike back but paused as the steely eye of the captain met his.

"It is ill advised for you to hit me, Mister Banks," the captain warned between gnashed teeth.

Mister Banks arm was poised and still as their eyes met!

"I will lock you up for the rest of the journey and have you tried for assaulting an officer, in the courts upon our return!" the captain threatened.

Mister Banks lowered his arm. "You would not dare! You hit me! I would have you charged!" he countered.

The captain turned.

"Did anyone here witness my hitting Mister Banks?" he shouted to the witnesses.

Without pause for doubt, they all shook their heads to the negative!

The captain was on their side and they in turn would be loyal to him. Most of them believed Mister Banks had had it coming for some time, and revelled in their captain's attack upon him.

The captain went on his way to the Great Cabin, leaving Mister Banks embarrassed. I joined him in awe!

"Blasted Banks!" He thumped his fist down on the map table and then stood, looking out the cabin windows pondering his actions. I rubbed against his leg.

"Yes, I know he deserved it, but it is not the done thing for a captain to strike a man. And of all men, Joseph blasted Banks!" he lamented.

The lieutenants appeared, letting the captain know that the men were assembled and ready for him.

He straightened himself, splashed some water on his reddened face and walked up the gangway.

Standing above the men on the foredeck, he addressed them.

They were keen to listen.

"Crew of the *Endeavour*! This is a dark hour for us all. Some of you have taken it upon yourselves to dispatch the bodies of the deceased gentlemen over the side of the ship!" He paced.

Word had reached every corner of the ship and even those bedridden had risen for this speech.

"I do not condone your actions in taking this matter upon yourselves! You have put me in a predicament." The crew took in an audible breath, hoping for leniency.

"Those of you who perpetrated the crime, and those of you who pardon it are equally guilty." The men looked about at one another, not knowing their fate.

"I have chosen to avoid an investigation, upon the proviso that should discontent raise its ugly head in future, that a spokesman for it can be elected by you to bring the problem directly to me!" The crowd breathed a collective sigh!

"This incident will not be shown in the records and I trust you will not begrudge the taking of your rum rations for this day?"

All heads shook, as they knew that they were getting off easy.

"I expect you will be more forthcoming in future?" he asked.

Nodding came from all!

Mister Banks stood astounded as the captain let them off almost unpunished.

"Do you have anything further to add, Mister Banks?" The captain put him on the spot.

"No, Captain, I do not!" He gnashed his teeth in frustration, wringing his hands in anger.

"Back to your duties or your beds, whichever the case may be!" he so ordered.

There was much chatter amongst the crew that day!

Those who did it felt obliged to accept the day without rations as they could have been found out and punished severely.

Those who knew who did it wanted to congratulate them but kept it for another time.

Those who knew nothing of it were keen to find out the details but waited for a better moment.

All accepted the lack of rum, as their captain had followed the code of the sea.

Ironically, that very afternoon, seamen Archibald Wolfe and James Nicholson died, as if punished for inciting those who had thrown the gents into the deep, along with carpenter's mate Benjamin Jordan who was in on the crime. The flux had taken them, too. Their bodies were rightly committed to the sea and the men settled back into their routines. There was much whispering of the morning's events.

A renewed respect was unspoken for the captain!

We finally picked up the trade wind, which helped to raise the spirits of the surviving sick, who were still battling on.

Those still in service of their duties found a renewed strength to sail the *Endeavour* short-handedly.

Chester, Lady, and I sat on deck at dusk discussing the controversial nature of the events of the day but we all came to an agreement that perhaps the captain did the correct thing, as the men we relied upon to have us home would now go to any lengths for their captain.

We lay snoozing in the sun when we noted Henry Jeffs come on deck. He had been preparing meat for the evening dinner as always. He spoke quietly with the captain and they both went below.

"I had best run along and find out what gives," I said to the hounds, leaving them momentarily. "It is almost dinner time!" My stomach never failed me when it came to meal times.

I went below to the galley to find the captain and Henry Jeffs standing over the good and deserving cook John Thompson's dead body!

My grief was complete!

John Thompson! My dear friend and consummate ship's cook!

My reason for being on the *Endeavour* in the first instant as he needed a mouser!

My employer and companion!

I was bereft. The tears came without a thought for who might see me weep! I could not stand to see his lifeless body there on the galley floor. Sick as he was, he kept the crew fed right to his end!

I needed my chums and walked numbly to the deck to inform Chester and Lady. They, too, were heartbroken, as the always-cheery chap, ever devoted to his work, had given our stomachs many fine reasons to rejoice his life.

I sobbed into Lady's chest, wetting her fur, but she knew us to have enjoyed a close relationship and understood my grief.

The captain ordered one last burial at sea for that day of the 31st of January 1771, and as much as I wished to sulk in the Great Cabin for my loss, I stood proudly in the rigging and watched as John Thompson's body splashed into the sea.

The captain spoke well of him and appointed Able Seaman Joseph Childs, an Irishman, to take over his position of ship's cook.

I went below to the galley later that night to find Henry Jeffs silently crying alone over a haunch of bullock. I rubbed against his leg and he threw me a scrap.

"Yes, I will miss him, too, Fairweather," he whispered. I stood by until he had finished his work and then we both sat on the floor in front of the oven, pondering life and death, until sleep came.

CHAPTER 37

I grieved for some days at the loss of my cook.

John Thompson's servant, Tom Matthews, was showing Joseph Childs around the galley and along with Henry Jeffs, both were bringing the man up to master his new role.

I refrained from food for my mourning period, for which the poor chap took as my not liking my offerings. His first night of mastery saw me snub one dish after another in his attempt to please me, and I must say the food looked tasty but I wished to honour my lost employer.

"What's wrong with Fairweather?" Joseph Childs asked Tom Matthews.

"Dunno. Dogs like the food well enough. My guess is he's just missin' old John Thompson." Tom Matthews had it right.

These deaths were taking a toll on my appetite.

Daniel Roberts, the gunner's servant died on the 2nd day in February 1771.

John Thurman, the sailmaker's assistant, died the next day on the 3rd.

John Bootie, our midshipman died, and our bosun John Gathrey, both on the 4th. Samuel Evans, bosun's mate was promoted to John Gathrey's position upon his death. He was ordered to conduct a survey of the stores to keep him busy, and report to the captain as to what we may need in Capetown.

The trade winds endured but ever so slowly in comparison to the rate of the dying men.

By the 6th day of February Jonathan Monkhouse, our dead surgeon's brother, succumbed to the flux and death. Although he had falsely accused me of biting Orton's ears at what seemed an eternity ago, I did admire him for "fothering" the ship when she hit the reef.

I could not believe the rate at which we were losing the men!

More concerning was the much-reduced sense of loss that the crew and even I were feeling. At first, each death was a tragedy! By now, each death whilst equally disastrous was looked upon as just another casualty of the dreaded Batavian diseases!

I still felt guilty that I mourned for one over another. I knew every crewman but I had several special relationships with some above others.

The men felt it too, me thinks.

Around the scuttle cask it had become more like a daily obituary than a passing of the time during one's pause from duty!

We sighted another Dutch ship flying her colours and again we were outsailed, but this time Mister Banks had the good sense to refrain from comment!

We had been a few days without a death and the men were beginning to think that the fresh trade winds we were enjoying were finally flushing the hideousness of Batavia from every corner of the ship, until the 12th day of February when our carpenter John Satterley died from the flux.

Again, as an esteemed and enriching member of the crew he was honoured at his burial. The captain appointed George Nowell in his place but despaired that we only had George and one other carpenter left on board!

The captain similarly employed George to surveying the carpenter's stores for a report of what we might need in Capetown.

It was of great importance for those who had been promoted to replace the dead, to know of our requirements for the next port.

It was also important to keep the men busy as the death toll continued!

On the 14th, Able Seaman Alexander Lindsay, who we had taken on board in Batavia, died. The captain knew that the man had spent some time prior in India and may have come aboard sick.

Doctor Perry had lost track of the means in which some died.

It was recorded so as the flux, rather than attempt to find another cause. They all suffered in the same way no matter where it had been contracted and which disease it was.

The next day, Private Daniel Preston, one of our Marines, fell to the disease.

The morale of the remaining men was so low that even the captain's attempts to keep them busy could not cheer them sufficiently.

The mood upon the ship was now dire.

Those who were still bedridden calmly awaited their death.

Those still able, performed their duties but with no great joy.

We finally had some six days without tragedy! One would think that this cessation would have lifted the hearts, but the deaths had touched everyone in one way or another.

By the time Alexander Simpson, able seaman, died on the 21st of February 1771, we were still only half way across the Indian Ocean with what the captain estimated to be another month before we made Capetown!

The men had taken to drinking heavily to soothe their sorrows.

I was restless that evening when Mister Banks had taken ill again, bringing Chester and Lady to his cabin for company while he suffered.

I took up with Doctor Perry to see to the sick. It was the good and noble thing to do!

As we prepared to do the rounds after taking a breath of fresh air, we came upon the officer on watch who was sitting, head in hands nursing a blackened eye!

"Did you fall, young man?" asked the doctor, checking the damage to see that nothing was serious.

"No, Tom Rossiter punched me fair in the eye and left me! I didn't even get to punch him right back! He's drunk!" he grumbled.

I knew the culprit as he had been lashed twelve times for stealing rum from the spirit cask some ages ago. He liked the drink and with the captain raising the rations in this time of grief, Thomas Rossiter was not one to pass it up!

So keen was he that in fact I had seen him taking of a dead man's rations before the deceased could be scratched off the list!

"Who is Tom Rossiter?" asked the doctor, unsure of the guilty party.

"Drummer of the Marines. He's lurking about down below with intent," warned the officer.

"Come, Fairweather! Point him out!" ordered Doctor Perry. I was impressed.

He knew me to be a chap of honour and not the average cat!

With pride I took the lead!

"Shhhh!" ordered the Doctor as we quietly descended below. I knew to be quiet but the good doctor was new to the Fairweather strategies so I let it go for now.

We could hear a thumping and moaning from the "sick bay." I snuck under the sheet dividing the area, while Doctor Perry peaked around it.

We saw the maliciously drunk Tom Rossiter beating on one of the sickest men there!

Doctor Perry cleared his throat as if to approach without knowing he was there.

Rossiter took off through the cordoned section hoping he had not been seen.

The doctor and I surveyed the culprit's damage. Not one, but four of the men had been beaten by the evil Rossiter! Sick they were, but blind and mute they were not!

They were happy to give the name of their attacker, as they were suffering enough from their ills without a beating to boot!

Doctor Perry tended their wounds although minor, but Thomas Rossiter was in for it! The doctor was a man to reckon with when tending his sick!

Late as it was, the doctor marched to the captain's cabin with me in tow and knocked furiously.

"What is it?" the captain asked, already in his bed.

"It is I, Doctor Perry, Captain! We must speak at once!" he begged.

The captain opened the cabin door and came out into the Great Cabin in his night clothes.

"You wake me for what?" the captain asked, irritated but knowing the good doctor would not be without cause. Seeing me with him made him all the more curious after the result of having ignored me on the last occasion of my interrupting his sleep!

"Thomas Rossiter, sir! Drummer of the Marine Corp…" he started.

"Yes, I know who he is!" the captain interrupted impatiently.

"He has assaulted the officer on watch, and beaten several of the men in the 'sick bay' as they lay on their bunks!" the doctor reported with gusto.

"Good Lord!" shouted the captain.

He raced to the lieutenants' quarters hoping to find one of them dressed for the occasion and not in their bed clothes.

Hicks was asleep but Lieutenant Gore was reading by a dim lamp.

"What is it, Captain?" said Lieutenant Gore upon his door being flung open.

"Wake Sergeant Edgcumbe!" the captain ordered. "I must dress!"

"Yes, sir!" Mister Gore hurried to the sergeant's quarters.

The doctor and I waited while the captain dressed quickly. Lieutenant Gore returned with a hastily dressed sergeant.

"Doctor Perry, tell the sergeant and Lieutenant Gore!" The captain was irate!

Doctor Perry told the story and the sergeant marched out of the Great Cabin without the need for orders from the captain.

He knew what to do.

He roused Privates Henry Paul and William Wilshire.

"Yes, sir!" They threw on their uniforms when requested. Marines had no sense of time when their sergeant came beckoning in the middle of the night!

He relayed the complaint and the three of them went off into the ship to track down the malicious Rossiter.

The captain, Doctor Perry, and Lieutenant Gore who had fetched the "cat," were headed for the deck. The Marines soon appeared with the now staggering Rossiter; Henry Paul and Bill Wilshire had a hand under each of his arms.

"What? What did I do wrong?" he pleaded, slurring from the liquor.

The captain reminded him of his crime.

"It wasn't me. Must have been someone else!" he denied.

"Your assault has been witnessed," explained the captain. "It is bad enough that you have attacked the officer on watch! But beating the sick? I am appalled! They suffer enough!"

The captain turned to Lieutenant Gore. "Twelve of your best and make them sting!" He ordered. Rossiter was taken to the deck and lashed harshly.

He was spurned, and over the following days every man aboard cursed him for such a cowardly act!

Order was eventually restored and we enjoyed a few more days without a death and hoped again that it would continue.

Our hopes were dashed when Manoel Pereira and Peter Morgan died on the 27th day of February 1771. Peter Morgan had come on board sick in Batavia and never recovered. They were being prepared for their sea burial when the final blow came.

Henry Jeffs, my butcher, was found dead in his bunk!

My despair was complete! My strong but quiet butcher had succumbed to this meanest of maladies, taking all three men in one day!

He was quickly prepared and joined the other two for their committal to the sea. The captain, as always, spoke well of all of them in death but my heart broke for my butcher.

Again, I swore off my food for the mandatory mourning period, and sulked in the Great Cabin with a fearsome case of maudlin.

We had finally experienced some fresh gales but their help in moving us along was hindered by their damaging of our foretopsail. Gales required more hands than we had and no one could reef it in time. The fresh winds had their benefits, however, and seemed to blow the last of the dysentery from the ship!

By the 4th day of March, and with no more deaths, some of the men thought they sighted land to the northward. This was dismissed until daylight the next day when we saw that we were but five miles from Point Natal off the African coast. This point appeared on the chart to be the mouth of St Johns River and the captain noted it.

Two days later, the Agulhas Current had us two miles south and west even though we had been sailing east and north! We had to sail against it to reach the Cape of Good Hope.

Finally, by the 13th day of March 1771, we rounded Cape Agulhas, the southernmost point of Africa.

Upon rounding it, we sailed on to Table Bay where Capetown lay the next morning.

The wind blew so strong from the bay that we were forced to hold off outside it until it dropped.

We could see sixteen ships anchored at the Capetown Road: eight Dutch, three Danes and four French of which there was a frigate and three store ships.

There was one English East Indiaman, the *Admiral Pocock*, homeward bound from Bombay. She saluted us with eleven guns and we returned the compliment with nine guns of our own. Her Captain Riddle and some of his crew rowed out and came aboard us that evening with the gift of a basket of fruit, and the two captains discussed their travels into the night.

In the morning, we were able to get under sail and stood in the Capetown Road where a Dutch boat came out to us with the master attendant and some gentlemen, to guide us to our proper anchorage.

We saluted and the same number of guns returned from on shore! This gave us our welcome!

The captain went ashore to see the governor who promised us all that we could want. He sent us a surgeon to examine the men and upon his word that they were not contagious to the townsfolk, gave us the all clear to come ashore.

The captain's next care was to find a house ashore to lodge the remainder of our sick.

He sent Doctor Perry to find the correct lodging. He secured a boarding house with fresh airs and a good diet and proceeded ashore with the twenty-eight sick men to tend them.

Sadly, it was all too late for Able Seaman Richard Thomas, one of our Batavian chaps, and on the 15th of March 1771, he died and was soon buried ashore.

Fresh meat and greens were got on board for the rest of the crew. The captain set about writing letters to the Admiralty and Royal Society, as Captain Riddle was taking his ship back to England and agreed to deliver them. She would certainly beat us home, and the captain was sure that the authorities would be pleased to hear from us after so long at sea!

Capetown was a busy port and the *Holton* under Captain Smith, another English Indiaman from Bengal, anchored, saluting us with eleven guns, which we returned.

I always enjoyed this greeting as it was loud and hearty and gave us all a sense that we Englishmen had not been forgotten!

The *Holton*'s stay in India had lost between thirty and forty men to the dysentery sickness, and had a good many down with scurvy!

Upon counselling with my captain when receiving this news, he was most proud.

"Fairweather, these ships have more sick in twelve months at sea than we have had in near three times as long! The length of our voyage is uncommon and I am sure our men will exaggerate our experiences, ensuring that such lengthy voyages will always be thought of as hazardous to the highest degree, but I am more than happy with our death rate so relatively low!"

I must say that when comparing with other ships we had fared well, but I felt that one death was as bad as many, hardly avoidable under the circumstances, but disagreeable all the same. The captain seemed of similar opinion that a suitable cure for dysentery, or flux, and malaria, would do well in such climates as Batavia as it was impossible to water and victual a ship without contracting those diseases from the food, water, or conditions.

On the 16th day of March, Captain Riddle sailed the *Admiral Pocock* out of Capetown and back to England. We saluted her and she returned the compliment.

The next day, as the crew were watering and stocking the *Endeavour*, mending her sails and tending the repairs, Doctor Solander came down with the illness that seemed to have killed our men.

The surgeon was sent for and it appeared that he had a complaint somewhat dissimilar to the usual flux. It only affected his lower stomach, but the pain and fever were harsh. I looked in on him but he was most contrary and not in the mood for company.

Mister Banks set up house in town with his servants to tend to the doctor's health.

The *Holton* left Capetown on the 20th and again the firing of guns and their return were most amicable, and reminded us there indeed was an England!

The men were coming and going from the ship as and when they were able.

This Capetown was indeed a healthier city than Batavia but equally, if not more, cosmopolitan. So many ships camped here from all parts of the world during their ventures at sea.

Lieutenant Gore climbed to the summit of Table Mountain with one of the seamen and brought back many plants for Mister Banks to botanize.

Lieutenant Hicks was to join him but he was still too ill, surviving both malaria and dysentery, but the consumption had a fatal grip on his lungs and he feared he had not long to live!

Mister Banks returned from his usual fact-finding jaunts, and although limited by his attending Doctor Solander, was full of information and his reports in the Great Cabin over a brandy resumed.

Capetown was another Dutch settlement, and I could not help but think the Dutch an intrepid type, finding and settling so many places we seemed to visit.

Mister Banks began.

"One thousand or so neatly built brick and thatched houses settled at the base of Table Mountain on the edge of Table Bay. Again, the roads were lined with canals and rows of oak trees. These drained much better than their Batavian counterparts, ensuring a cleaner town.

"The Dutch here were all directly from Holland and the womenfolk the best housekeepers imaginable, and great child bearers! I go so far as to say that if I were inclined for a wife, I would have best suited myself here!"

I did not ever imagine that Mister Banks would be the type to take a wife, let alone consider it!

"The governor of Capetown, Ryk Tulbagh, had established the colony's first library and a botany collection in the East India Company gardens, which also housed a menagerie of rare beasts and birds rarely or never seen in Europe. He was an aged but learned man and much to my taste, so I plan to spend much time with him whilst we were here."

The captain nodded his approval.

"The climate was hot but the winds that came down from the hills had such violence that it carried sand, filling the eyes and mouth and blowing into the houses as dust. It was thought by some physicians that this sand cured consumption, as the malady was scarcely known there. In fact, diseases brought from Europe were said to be cured here, but those from the Indies not so easily."

I had it on good authority that none of our sick felt any better in capetown so far!

"The Dutch produce was first rate, wheat and hops, cattle and sheep of the highest standard. The milk from the cows made a fine butter and perfect cheese. Goats aplenty, poultry and wild game abound. Fine European vegetables and the fruits of the Indies completed the diet.

"Their vineyards produced great quantities of wine. Madeira and frontignac, fortified wines, were being produced here, not to my taste, but somewhat like the French and Portuguese sweet white wines. Now famous in Europe, 'Constantia' was made at a vineyard not ten miles from Capetown and exported to Europe!"

Mister Banks kept his roaming to a minimum as measles broke out in the town at the time of our arrival. He reported to us daily when his frail health allowed it.

"The sandy ground gave no hope to trees for some miles around the town. I spoke to the locals and discovered it to be a barren country, the Dutch settling some two thousand miles inland looking for fertile places to plant or raise cattle. Horse drawn land carriages took supplies to the outreaching settlements. "The 'Khoikhoi' were the natives of the land. The Europeans called them the 'Hottentot' people and even though they were already practicing agriculture in the Capetown region, they were expelled from their lands as the Dutch took their farms over."

Mister Banks was bitterly disappointed not to see them but their lands were four days' journey away. Some were servants of Dutch farmers and Mister Banks saw a few of them.

"They were the colour of soot, but partly owing to the great measure of dirt that seemed ingrained in their skin. Their hair curled in rings like that of a Persian lamb skin but in long ringlets. They wore sheepskin with a leather flap over their privies for decency. Some wore sandals but most were bare of feet, and they were nimble and highly active. Their language articulated a 'click' or 'cluck' with their tongues at regular intervals during their speech. They danced wildly and smoked tobacco mixed with hemp leaves. They did not tolerate the demon drink well, and when consuming it, they would inevitably drink to excess. "Some of the other tribes were able to melt and prepare copper, making plates to adorn their foreheads. Others knew how to melt iron and produce better knives than the Dutch could sell them!

"Their chief people who had cattle of their own further into the country wore the skins of lions, tigers and zebras, which they knew how to hunt, and avoid!"

Thus ended Mister Banks's fact-finding mission as he lapsed into one of his fevers and stayed on board until he was well enough to return to his lodgings in town with Chester and Lady.

On the 30th day of March, the *Duke of Gloucester*, an English East India Ship from China under Captain Lauder, came in to the Capetown Road.

Our guns were exchanged as happily as always and the captains met and spoke into the night.

My captain was always secretive about our discovery of Australia! He wished to keep it quiet until we returned to England so that he could see how impressed the king would be! He always remained guarded with other captains and officials!

Doctor Solander recovered somewhat the next day but was weakened by his illness and had no energy for wandering Capetown.

I took my leave with the captain on the last day of March. He had decided to dine ashore unusually and found a fine inn not too far from the ship.

All kinds wandered here and there in the town. The slaves were Malay and brought from Batavia to tend the Europeans. I kept watch for small Malay boys as a matter of previous inconvenience!

The inn we visited was an English affair and the captain sat down to as good and fat beef as he had ever eaten, and was promised by the vendor that our supply of ship's beef would be of the same high quality!

I dutifully went to the rear of the inn while he dined, to make any acquaintance I might find there. Among the usual crates and rubbish receptacles I did not find the customary gang of cats. I thought this odd and widened my search. Poking around further I jumped to a crate and looked behind it.

"Reeeeoooowwwww!" A scratch to my beezer took me aback!

I could not see a cat in the dark behind the crate, but knew it to be there by the sting on my nose! I licked at it and a little blood had been drawn! Wretch!

"Who is in there?" I demanded. "Come out at once and show yourself! You have injured me!"

"I will do no such thing and if you come back here again, I will scratch you even harder!" a female voice warned me!

"Madam!" I softened a little.

"Do not 'madam' me! Be away with you or suffer terribly!" she hissed.

"Are you alone back there?" I ventured.

"No, there are many of us and waiting to pounce upon you. Get away from here!" she spat harshly.

I could hear no one else but the faint "mew" of the youngster of my species!

I edged my nose over the crate but was whacked yet again and on the same spot! Again, I wailed like the dickens!

"Madam, I mean you no harm. If you would refrain from injuring me we may talk a little," I tried.

"You are English?" she asked.

"Why, yes! And of no dread demeanour!" I pledged.

Just then I felt razor-sharp teeth sink into my tail from behind! I jumped backwards preparing to attack the assailant only to find a wee kitten hanging from my flicking tail, intent on staying attached there!

"Humphrey!" screeched the madam. I scatted him with a paw and grabbed him by the scruff before he could run off.

I said nought as my mouth was full of Humphrey but made my way around the back of the crate to find "madam" with a litter of similar wee villains.

"Humphrey, I told you to stay with me!" Madam scolded.

I spate him out and he nuzzled into his mother's belly with the other kittens.

"Thank you, sir," she said more civilly. Something about this group was not quite right but I could not put my finger on it.

"It is a pleasure, I think!" I checked and my tail was still in one piece although stinging a little from the bite. "He has quite the bite on him, the small Humphrey!"

"Yes, but he must learn to keep it to himself until he is grown!" she admonished the little devil.

"I am Fairweather of the Bark *Endeavour*, on my way back to England," I introduced myself, still puzzled by their appearance.

"My name is Nombeko," she said briefly, herding her litter. "My partner is James, an English cat, just left on the *Holton*."

"Ah yes, the *Holton*, she has just left for England?" I commented, in the know.

The kittens had settled a little as they fed on mother's milk, allowing us to talk more freely.

"Yes." A tear came to her eye. "He will be at sea for some months."

"Fear not, Nombeko, the English are the finest sailors in the world and he will return to you in no time at all!" I attempted to cheer but I was still unsure what was missing from this gathering.

"I suppose so," she said sadly.

I gathered that this mother had her hands full with the six kittens I counted in all, and perhaps wished her mate had stayed to help her.

"One cannot stop a feline when the seagoing urge takes him. I left my home behind to do just that." I tried to comfort but it was to no avail.

Just then, I stumbled upon the thing that disturbed me!

"Nombeko! Your offspring have no tails!" I was aghast. The feline's finest feature was missing from her brood!

"I have no tail also!" she defended haughtily. "We are of the Manx breed and are highly esteemed!"

"Manx? I have never heard tell of it," I said dumbly.

"According to legend, the Manx came from the Spanish Armada. Legend has it that the cats originally went on board a Spanish ship in the Far East. The cats on the ship swam ashore and became an established breed. We are considered exotic here in Capetown and I am a descendant of the Manx belonging to a most highly regarded family," she explained.

"But no tail! Do you not feel at a loss?" I put it as gently as possible but she took umbrage as expected.

"Far from it, sir! The features one does not have can sometimes afford them more respect than those who do!" She had a point there!

"I cannot help but agree with you, Nombeko, but I always understood tails to be a necessity to any feline." I was not making myself as agreeable as I should.

"Nonsense!" she scolded. "Now if you continue to harp on the subject, I would bid you leave!" She was hurt.

"I shall cease but for one question. Does your partner James possess a tail?" I was curious, as I thought that a fitting English ship's cat should have one, or perhaps be bullied and taunted!

"Yes, he does, but my kittens have not inherited it, all but Humphrey." She pointed it out as the youngster nuzzled.

"Ah, yes, the cheeky youngster who bit at my tail!" I looked closely at Humphrey suckling away and his tail was in fine order.

"He is troublesome, but he meant you no harm, sir." She softened as she surveyed her kittens at rest.

"You have met Humphrey. The others are female and true tailless Manx: 'Helder' which is Afrikaan for 'bright', Soet meaning 'sweet', Bietjie 'little', Omgee 'caring', Mooi 'pretty'."

"They are impressive names Nombeko, but why Humphrey for the lad? Is it not an English name?" I quizzed.

"I promised James to name the boy Humphrey as he takes after his father. It is a family name." She was not all that impressed with her pledge, perhaps favouring something more local, and equally as exotic as her girls' names.

"Children, this is Mister Fairweather," she introduced me but they continued suckling as if unaware of me.

"Are there other cats here behind the inn?" I asked.

"No, we are alone," she said.

"I shall be right back."

I scooted to the inn door and wailed the cry of the hungry cat!

A rather short but round chap appeared in the doorway, a half-chewed cigar hanging from the corner of his mouth and stained yellow fingers from smoking it.

"You want food, cat?" he asked, his breath reeking of smoke.

He waddled away in search of what leftovers he perhaps had not eaten himself, judging from his size!

I was correct!

The plate held little but I thought it might nourish Nombeko at the very least. I scooped up one mouthful after another and took them to her.

"Fairweather! You are a kind fellow. I have not eaten all day." She thanked me.

"I can only imagine that nursing your brood would be hungry work!" I commented.

Just then she got up, shaking the little ones free so she could eat my offering.

"It is little, but from the looks of the kitchen hand, scraps have padded his own figure!" I chuckled.

Nombeko thought it funny, too.

Unfortunately, her break from feeding her litter caused them to scatter in all directions. I was concerned for their safety and began herding them back toward the crate.

"Thank you, Fairweather," he said, scoffing down the food as if she might never eat again.

"You little blighters!" I swore.

No sooner had I rounded up one than another would slip away!

Humphrey was the worst! He was a cunning upstart, no doubt the product of his English blood, and I took a liking to him readily.

Nombeko finished her meal while I wrestled with the kittens playfully. I would not admit it to another soul but I was quite enjoying their playfulness, the odd nip from those little teeth aside.

"Fairweather!" I heard my captain's voice. I leapt to attention as he approached but he had already seen me frolicking with the kittens.

"So this is what you get up to when in port?" He laughed.

I gave him a steely glare as it was not my usual form, but knew that he would not tell of my antics.

It was the code between us.

"I request your presence back at the ship," he asked, his voice playful and somewhat silly as he bent down to stroke Nombeko and her wayward waifs.

"A fine little family you have, Madam," he said softly. "Come, Fairweather." He shuffled me along. "Rare cats, the Manx!" he said in passing, obliging me to rub his leg for his wealth of such things feline!

I was a little concerned that he had seen a softer side to yours truly, but knowing him to be a family man with sons of his own I imagined he could see the benefits that a bit of childish play could have upon the spirit.

In fact, I was feeling quite chirpy from my gambol with the kittens, and thought I might visit as often as I could, Nombeko being on her own and all.

Dark dense fog hazes came upon us, and white clouds gathered over Table Mountain, a sign of approaching gales.

Surely enough, we were kept aboard by the winds.

By the 2nd day of April, the *Duke of Gloucester* saluted us and departed for England. She had not been in Capetown long.

Such was this busy port.

I visited Nombeko daily, bringing food to her from the inn, and played hide and seek with her kittens. They were growing quickly and becoming more mischievous by the day. I doubt that Nombeko was terribly impressed with my antics in the alley with her brood, but as it gave her a break from the rigours of motherhood she allowed me some license with them.

One evening back at the ship, Mister Banks came to the ship with Chester and Lady, barging into the Great Cabin all a fluster!

"Captain! There is rumour that a French ship is travelling soon toward Australia by way of Abel Tasman's route. She may discover our Cook Straits!" he blustered.

"Is she on her way there now?" quizzed the captain, knowing that rumours were never to be trusted.

"I do not know, Captain. I have merely heard it said in passing at the inn with some of the French sailors! We must find out her whereabouts!" His voice became shrill.

"True that should the French publish any of their findings of Australia before we can return to England, the results would be dire, but if she is on her way there now, and we are returning home, we will no doubt be the first to lay claim to this Australia," the captain thought it out sensibly.

"But Captain! Our discoveries! I will not have the French take credit for our findings!" Mister Banks wailed.

"Mister Banks!" he scolded, stopping the botanist in his tracks as it were. "What would you have me do? Hunt down the French ship and attack her?"

"Err…Yes!" he replied, not sure of himself, but suitably selfish with his discoveries to date.

"The French would be well provisioned and judging by the state of the ships here in Capetown, well-armed. They would most certainly outdo us and any altercation would no doubt cause an international incident!" the captain chided.

"Yes, I understand the implications, Captain, but our years of work!" Mister Banks was going to be difficult on this subject.

"All being well I should have us back in England sometime in July. The French cannot hope to reach Australia before such time and even then they would have to chart it as we have done. We will be home and our findings published before they can set foot on our Australia!" The captain had to be firm. He was not about to go looking for trouble on the strength of a French rumour!

"Very well, Captain. Have us home as soon as possible!" ordered Mister Banks, turning on his heel and leaving us alone.

"As if I am not doing so, Fairweather!" He turned, cross with his botanist but deeming it best to let him think he had the run of the ship as he was still mourning the loss of his gentlemen terribly.

I sighed in concert with him and he knew me to understand his frustration.

The captain set about employing new people from Capetown to assist us on the voyage home.

Nine men were required and I sat in the rigging as the captain tended the Muster book upon each man's entry.

I took an interest at these employments as each seaman had to give his history and although some were little qualified, the captain would retain them if he gathered them to be of good temperament and character.

Others wished to see England and had much sailing experience, making them a must to employ!

"Turkel Hanson, sir!" the next in line piped up.

"Turkel?" I hoped the captain would accept this man as he looked hale and strong and had the name of my former benefactor!

I wondered of Turkel for some time and hoped he would still be around when we reached England. I would have much to tell!

The ships came and went as the captain put the fresh men to work, painting the ship and tending her rigging.

Eleven of our sick were brought back on board much recovered, however we had lost seaman John Lorrain from Batavia on the 4th April 1771, and on the 7th Able Seaman John Dozey. By the 11th, the captain began to provision the ship so I took it we were to sail soon.

The captain went ashore on the evening of the 13th of April to take his leave of the governor, and gather Mister Banks and his cronies, wishing to sail on the morrow.

I went off to the inn as I had nightly to say my farewells to Nombeko and her little family. I found them in their usual hide behind the crate all tucking in to a large bowl of scraps.

"Madam! You have weaned the little ones from the breast?" I asked respectfully.

"Yes, Fairweather, and the kitchen hand discovered us out here due to your nightly howl for food! He has promised to nourish us! I am so grateful to you!" she said, watching her young ones nibble at solid food for the first time.

I was used to seeing most of them tailless but something was amiss around this bowl!

"Humphrey!" I gasped. "Where is the little blighter and his fine tail?" I misspoke for which I received a reproachful eye from Nombeko regarding this tail versus no tail business.

She was not at all concerned for him!

"He is trying to hunt mice in the alley," she laughed. "He is having some trouble without the direction of his father. He amuses us with his attempts but fails miserably to catch them." The little ladies of the brood all giggled.

"I shall instruct him!" I offered, only too pleased to be of assistance, as my father had taught me well all that time ago in the alley outside my home.

"Thank you, Fairweather. You will find him out there somewhere. He never stops trying." She motioned toward the entrance to the alley.

"Hah! I see his problem." I turned to find him running from one side of the alley to the other in pursuit of a small mouse, but right at the entrance, a most dangerous and unsuitable spot!

"Humphrey!" I called, but he would not come.

I ran up and scruffed him.

"Hey!" he protested as I carried him back to the safety of the end of the alley.

I set him down.

"Why did you do that, Mister Fairweather? I nearly had him!" he grumbled, albeit respectfully.

"You were not even close, Humphrey!" I laughed.

"Not funny, Mister Fairweather!" he sulked. "I have tried all day!"

"Well, let me instruct you on the finer art of mousing, young Humphrey," I offered.

"Would you?" he was keen.

"Of course! I sail for England soon but have the evening to devote to your education."

He danced a little jig and then he sat dutifully for his lesson, eyes wide in the hope of success.

"Now, you must keep away from the entrance to the alley," I started.

"Why?" he asked.

"People walk there," I explained.

"Why?" he asked again.

"Because that is what people do," I told him.

"Why?" he asked annoyingly.

"They walk from hither to yon and if you are seen, you may be stolen away by a young boy or injured by a passerby," I explained in more length, hoping to appease his quizzical nature.

"Why?" he was at it again, and I became annoyed as we had little time and he was wasting it.

"Stop that! 'Why' is neither here nor there! I am trying to teach you to catch mice! Now merely listen to what I tell you as we only have this night to bring you up to speed!" I chastised him.

He sniffled a little, trying not to cry and I would have softened but for the urgency of the matter!

"Pluck up, young Humphrey, and do not interrupt!" I began.

I told him of the dangers of the alley entrance and begged he chose as old a mouse as possible within the alley as they were not quite so fleet of foot as the youngsters!

I instructed him to herd it toward the rear so that he may corner it easily, and to be quick at it, as they are still fast to run even when aged.

He got the gist and I set him to it, watching with his mother and the girls.

Humphrey poked around as I explained to the little females what a good mouser must do. After all, females could very well make good ship's cats if they set their minds to such a thing!

I had never heard of one but it was not out of the question and I told Nombeko, who was none too keen for her girls to go off on ships, but she knew the desire to perhaps be in the blood from their English father, and otherwise it would do them well to be able to provide should they have their own family one day.

Humphrey skulked well enough as he found his prey, but he pounced too quickly and the old mouse shot out of his way, leaving Humphrey in full flight to bang his head against the alley wall. His sisters laughed uncontrollably and Nombeko tried hard to control her own mirth.

"Humphrey!" I called. He trudged over to me, downhearted at missing his mouse, not to mention bumping his head.

"Leave of you girls! I was trying!" he hissed at his sisters.

"Take no notice boy." I shot the girls a stern look and they ceased their giggling.

"Now, when you have spotted your prey, you must creep ever closer before you pounce, to narrow the gap between you and your mouse, and then leap upon him before he smells or sees you." I pointed out the flaw in his technique.

"Righto, Mister Fairweather!" he said very Englishly and off he went for another go at it.

He skulked about where he had seen the elderly mouse disappear and spotted him in no time.

He looked back at me and I nodded my approval of his "creeping" timing.

He crept with great ease and stood still when the mouse looked around, avoiding his detection.

Closer and closer he came and then he leapt to his prey coming down on the mouse perfectly!

"Bravo, Humphrey!" I yelled.

Humphrey took the old mouse into his mouth and returned to where we all sat watching.

Nombeko and her girls were now quietly impressed.

"What do I do with him now?" muffled Humphrey, his mouth filled with mouse.

"Why, you eat him!" I said reproachfully.

"Ick!" he spat, the mouse escaping.

"Go and get him back!" I chastised.

"Why?" He started this again and I had to put a stop to it before it became a habit.

"Never mind 'why'. You must eat him now you have caught him," I instructed in the correct manner.

"But I can have scraps from the kitchen. Why must I eat an icky mouse?" He was painfully persistent.

"Humphrey, you may not always have the luxury of scraps from the kitchen. You are lucky until now to have your mother and I to provide for you, but if you wish to earn your keep, either in the home or upon a ship, you may have to eat them to sustain you in lean times. After all, it is what we felines do!"

"You have eaten mice, Mister Fairweather?" he asked.

"Yes, boy, and rats! As big as you!" I explained.

"Rats?" he asked unknowingly.

"Yes, a larger rodent of the same species, but you will have to grow somewhat before taking on a rat!" I chuckled and ruffled his fur playfully. "Now go and get that mouse!" I demanded.

Humphrey returned with his mouse and played with the poor old thing, his sisters joining in, until it died of fright and old age.

"Now you must teach your sisters what I have taught you," I ventured, hoping Nombeko would not be angry with me.

"Yes, you will all learn from Humphrey," she confirmed.

I was rather proud of her modern thinking, that females should learn to mouse!

"And you will all listen to me very carefully!" Humphrey spouted, puffing himself up with self-importance.

I suspected he was going to enjoy having it over his sisters for a while!

"Thank you, Fairweather," said Nombeko as I straightened myself up to leave her.

"It has been my pleasure, Madam. I have enjoyed your youngsters and now I bid you farewell." I bowed.

"Don't go, Mister Fairweather!" cried the children, no doubt feeling I was abandoning them as their father had done.

"You will do well here. Learn from your brother and always be respectful to your mother! My ship awaits! Your father will be back soon!" I yelled back at them as they looked at after me.

I would miss them, but the *Endeavour* waits for no one and I must report for duty!

Back at the ship, I weighed in on the captain.

"Been out with the adopted family again?" he asked, as we were alone.

I sniffed a little and he understood.

"I miss my boys, too, Fairweather. I look forward to seeing them soon. How they must have grown!" he said with some melancholy.

The captain sat up late and described Capetown for his log, him content in the knowing he would see his youngsters soon. I slept. My gloom in already yearning for my adopted family was not to be had on this night, the eve of our last leg home. I must be robust for the morning.

CHAPTER 38

I awoke to find the captain and all hands hard at it early! Chester and Lady were back on board with Mister Banks's party. I must get up to speed on the doings!

As I entered the conversation with lieutenants Gore and Hicks on deck, the captain was in two minds.

"I would like to have awaited the English ships due here anytime now, but a favourable breeze has got up and I believe we should get under sail. Your thoughts, lieutenants?" he asked.

"I say we sail while the going is good, sir," said Lieutenant Hicks, coughing dreadfully.

"I, too, believe we should take advantage of the good conditions," agreed Lieutenant Gore.

"Up anchor then, men!" the captain ordered cheerily on the 16th day of April 1771, knowing that this was our passage home.

The moment was not lost on the crew and they hopped to it happily!

I perched myself somewhat out of the way and watched as all hands worked to have us under way and out of the bay.

The Dutch *Castle* saluted us with thirteen guns, which we returned as was customary.

As we passed the *Europa*, an East Indiaman just arrived from Bengal, we exchanged eleven guns with her.

Doctor Perry appeared quite suddenly as the captain and lieutenants were watching our progress.

"Excuse me, Captain." He bowed. "I realise that this is an inopportune time to do so, but I must report the death of Master Molyneux."

One could have knocked us all down with a sigh!

"The *Endeavour*'s Master? Master Molyneux? How could this be?" asked the captain, not aware that he had even been unwell.

"It came upon him very sudden, Captain, and his drinking exacerbated his death," explained the doctor.

"A young man of good parts but had unfortunately given himself up to extravagancy and intemperance which brought on disorders that put a period to his life," mused the captain sadly.

"Yes, sir, precisely," confirmed Doctor Perry.

The captain removed his hat and lowered his head in reverence but he had a ship to sail. "We shall lay up out of the bay under Robben Island to affect his burial in deep water. Make it so, lieutenants."

He turned to the doctor and quietly whispered his fears for Lieutenant Hicks's illness as the chap coughed his orders to the men.

"There is nothing I can do for him. He has done well to have survived this long, having left England with the consumption!" admitted Doctor Perry.

Mister Banks came down from the gentlemen's deck where he and the dogs were perched for our departure.

The gents deck had become a lonely place since we had lost most of them!

"What ho! Jolly good to be off home, what?" he said, cheerfully approaching.

"Not quite, Mister Banks," said the captain sadly. "Master Molyneux has passed this day."

"Oh, goodness, not another! I did not know him to be ill!" His cheer turned to regret.

"It was sudden and swift, Mister Banks," explained Doctor Perry.

"I suppose it favourable that he did not suffer long," Mister Banks said solemnly. "What are your plans, Captain?" he asked.

"We will anchor off Robben Island for his burial," explained the captain.

"Excellent!" Mister Banks said inappropriately. "We shall go ashore and examine the place!"

"We will not!" spat the captain. "It is a Dutch penal colony for those not sentenced to death! They are employed in the East India's service digging for limestone. According to reports, a Danish ship that had lost a large proportion of her crew to sickness, came into the harbour and asked for assistance from the governor. She was refused and went to Robben Island, sending her boats ashore and overpowering the guards, taking on board as many criminals as she required to navigate the ship home! The Dutch are now very careful with this island!" warned the captain.

"Yes, but we are English! Supposing they allow us ashore? We may procure more supplies!" Mister Banks argued, knowing full well our stocks were complete but his curiosity getting the better of him.

"It is said to abound with fresh garden produce," the captain conceded. "I will allow a boat to attempt a landing, but be warned, Mister Banks; I have heard tell that the Dutch have been known to kidnap our fine English sailors from Capetown, and bring them to this island as prisoners until they are needed to sail the Dutch East India's ships!"

"The wretches! This is most unsporting and the governor should be informed!" He spat.

"I believe that the governor knows of it and chooses to ignore it for the good of the company. Our English sailors are the best and they know it!" the captain explained.

"But this is criminal!" Mister Banks argued.

"Yes, it is! It is why they defend it so, especially from we Englishmen, but I am not about to return to the Capetown road and launch a one-man attack on the governor over it! It is a matter for the English government to investigate!" He stood firm.

"Well! I shall make it known to the correct people upon our return!" Mister Banks blustered.

Mister Banks and Doctor Solander, now the only "gents" left, took the longboat with Lieutenant Gore and a few able seamen.

We watched as they approached the shore and heard the Dutch warn them that they land at her peril!

Six soldiers with muskets paraded on the beach and Lieutenant Gore determined it was not worth the risk, returning with a sulky Mister Banks but a relieved Doctor Solander!

"Did you see that, Captain?" Mister Banks huffed as he clambered aboard the ship.

Doctor Solander merely fidgeted and was glad to be back on the ship.

"Of course, Mister Banks. It was as I suspected," said the captain fittingly. "The Dutch would not wish us to discover English seamen locked in their prisons as slaves to the East India Company!"

"Hurrumph!" he grumbled, knowing he had wasted his time, returned empty handed, and that the captain as usual was right! He strode off to the gents' deck with Doctor Solander, grumbling harshly about the report he would make upon our return.

"We may have been able to rescue some of them had we landed," Lieutenant Gore was sorely disappointed.

"True, Lieutenant Gore, but Mister Banks will have more luck with his diplomatic and political connections back in England than we, merely taking a few of our subjects and risking an incident."

"Yes, Captain. I must admit we should not risk all so close to home," Lieutenant Gore agreed.

"Quite right," said the captain, putting an end to the subject.

We stayed at anchor off Robben Island that afternoon to bury Master Molyneux with military honours and a fine speech from the captain. His body was committed to the deep with the customary thoughts for his loved ones.

There was little time to mourn; the captain was on a mission to have us home!

We put to sea at once with a fair breeze to hurry us along!

I held council with my captain that evening over the charts.

"We will put in at Saint Helena," he reported to me pointing out a small island in the middle of the vast Atlantic Ocean.

We were not far from the African continent when the great rolling of the sea from the south began in earnest.

The winds blew us in the right direction and the weather warmed, as we got up to speed.

The captain was pleased with our progress and employed the spare men to repairing the small boats and sails, and exercising the great guns and small arms.

I had duties to attend!

I must rid the ship of any new mice brought on board with the fresh stores in Capetown. The little blighters quite often came aboard in the foodstuffs unaware of their potential journey. I was to rid us of them, for this was my purpose for now, freshly out of port.

Down into the stores I went and rounded up a half dozen or so rather swiftly. They were not native to the *Endeavour*, and with their tails in my mouth purposefully, I presented them to Joseph Childs, our new cook, who had taken on his new role with gusto, and was deserving of my attention!

"Arr! Fairweather! Ship's mouser! I am mightily glad to see 'ye!" He blustered in his Irish brogue. "And with 'ye a fair compliment of vermin! I've noticed a good few of 'em down in the stores meself!

Good lad!" He took them from me and threw them out of the nearest porthole.

"Seems he's back to his old self," commented Tom Matthews who was cutting meat for the evening fare.

"Rightly, too!" said Joseph Childs, throwing me a morsel for my trouble. "Tis 'is job!" he reminded me.

By the end of April, the captain announced that we had crossed the line of Greenwich, the initial meridian crossed when we left England!

We had now circumnavigated the globe and were making good distance!

Refreshments were made available to all and a feeling of accomplishment roused the men who had begun our journey in England.

Those who had come aboard later enjoyed the spirit of the occasion regardless of their length of service with us.

I was kept busy for most of our two-thousand-mile passage with assorted vermin plentiful in the hold. Capetown had hidden its pests well in our grain and fresh stores and Joe Childs chided me repeatedly for not attending their riddance, although as many as I would capture and present to him, all the more were still hidden down there.

Samuel Evans, the new bosun, had taken possession of John Gathrey's old cabin, being the last before the stores. He, too, complained of the plague that seemed to have overrun my station.

Capetown! I damned it as I scurried from one store to another capturing the little beasties in no small numbers daily!

I was busy and saw little rest with my canine chums!

By the 1st day of May 1771, Saint Helena was sighted and the captain mightily pleased to have covered nearly two thousand miles since Capetown in so short a time!

I had all but ridden the hold of the Capetown plague and with the warmer weather producing more of them than ever, was exhausted by the time I had the numbers down to a manageable group of English mice to keep my position intact.

Joe Childs and Tom Matthews had me back in their good books and had reported it so to the captain who was much pleased with me.

As we approached the Saint Helena road near its capital Jamestown's fortress, we were amazed at the dazzling show of ships anchored there!

His Majesty's *Portland*, no less than twelve English East Indiamen their naval escort the *Swallow*! Turkel had told of the old sloop as part of his voyage!

The captain became suspicious with this turnout of so many ships and consulted the lieutenants to discuss his fears.

"From the magnitude of this fleet I worry that England may be at war!" he declared.

"True, Captain. It is a prodigious turnout of our ships!" coughed Lieutenant Hicks, mopping at his fevered brow.

"I will have a message to the *Portland* immediately to ascertain the doings, Captain!" said Lieutenant Gore off at a run to round up a boat and party.

Misters Banks and Doctor Solander joined the conversation and gave their opinions, wanted or not.

"If we are at war, it would be with Spain!" concluded Mister Banks.

"And how do you know this?" asked the captain gravely.

"I have heard tell of English war potential with Spain while we were in Capetown," he said, buffing at his fingernails.

"And you did not inform me?" the captain was incredulous.

"I thought it merely a rumour and did not wish to bother you with it," he said dismissively.

"Rumour or not, Mister Banks! It is important to our voyage to be apprised of any potential risk of attack on our leg home! I am aghast that you should deem it wise to keep this to yourself!" he blustered, and rightly so!

"Well, now you know. Therefore, I have done my duty." Mister Banks backpedalled, knowing he had done the wrong thing.

"But Mister Banks!" The captain was still mortified by his omission of such an important rumour. "We have travelled nearly two thousand miles since Capetown and all the while risked potential attack from any number of Spanish ships that may have been patrolling the very waters we sailed! I would have wished to know this in advance to arm us as substantially as possible and to keep added watch! This oversight of yours disturbs me so, but I shall await an answer from Lieutenant Gore upon his return from the *Portland*."

The captain was furious with his botanist and Doctor Solander and all who heard it merely stood with mouths agape at this news, knowing its effects could not only risk our lives on the way home to

England, but dampen the good news of our findings, as war would pale our significance!

We waited for what seemed like an age, but soon Lieutenant Gore's party returned with word that war with Spain was merely a rumour at this time, but Captain Elliot of the Portland had been dispensed from England to convoy the English ships home as a precaution, should there be a breach with Spain.

The captain had to take this advice as truth as the *Portland* was fresh out of England and would hold the most updated news, but the *Portland*'s deployment for the safety of the English ships should not be taken lightly.

Captain Elliot had sent over some stores for the officers, which were fresh cheeses and wine from London and were well received!

We all breathed a sigh of relief that war had not been proclaimed with Spain at this time, especially Mister Banks, but he was not to be let off the hook for his blunder in not informing the captain earlier. Not many could hear but Chester, Lady, and I who were in close vicinity.

"Mister Banks." The captain motioned him to come close enough to whisper. "If I find that you are concealing vital information to this ship, her crew and her safety, I shall throw you overboard myself!" he hissed.

Mister Banks reeled and dusted his nose with his ruffled perfumed sleeve to avoid being seen as red as a beet with eyes bulging!

He could do nought under the captain's threat but nod and take his leave!

Mister Banks knew that our good captain held the safety of this voyage at his highest priority and if he had endangered the *Endeavour*, the captain would most certainly dispatch him into the sea!

He bustled off to the gents' deck with Chester and Lady, still reddened by the captain's threat.

"We will overhaul the rigging and sails quickly, lieutenants! I intend us to sail with the convoy under the Portland's protection back to England. The fleet is well armed," he so ordered, remembering that we had disposed of our big guns overboard at our mishap with the reef to lighten the *Endeavour* and sail her off!

We would be easy pickings for an enemy should any country embrace war, and our secret findings for England may fall into the wrong hands!

The lieutenants agreed it was a safe measure, for dissent between Spain and England could erupt at any time and leave us alone and vulnerable on our passage home.

Upon hearing of this news, Mister Banks put together a botanising party to cover as much land as he could in one day.

On his return, he wished to give his report but the captain was busy in talks with Captain Elliot from the *Portland* and the other captains of the English Indiamen whom he intended us to sail with back to England.

The captains rallied to visit each of the ships and arranged to dine at the Duck and Bucket Inn located near James Fort, upon James Bay not far from Jamestown in James Valley! I deemed that there was little thought given to naming places here, and much "James-ing" on this wee Saint Helena. I was unfamiliar with the chap but he must have been an important "James"! Perhaps a prior king of some sort!

I decided to join the captain at his meeting at the inn, hoping to eagerly make the acquaintance of any English ship's cats similarly employed as I.

He arranged to have his clothing freshly washed and pressed to meet with his comrades and I must say we both looked rather dapper as we alighted the ship and strolled to the tavern.

I was not disappointed! It seemed that every captain at the meeting was dressed for the occasion. Unfortunately, my captain looked a little shabby in his well-worn uniform; he wore it proudly if only to prove that we had been gainfully employed at sea for such a long time, compared to the crisp, fresh dress of his peers who were just out of England.

To my delight, each captain had been escorted by his companion feline!

I counted no less than thirteen other cats, being the twelve from the Indiamen and one from the *Swallow*!

They were perched on the window ledge of the kitchen at the rear of the inn as I approached.

Unusual, that!

Not lurking about in the alley amongst the scraps and rubbish!

Right there in the kitchen window they were allowed!

"What ho, lads!" I greeted cheerfully.

They snubbed me at first thinking me one of the local rabble but I soon attempted to remedy that!

"'Tis I, Fairweather of the Bark *Endeavour*!" I introduced myself pompously.

"You are not!" came a cockney accent from one of the Indiamen. "'E's three feet tall, black as night and e's got fearsome fangs!"

They all laughed at me thinking me an imposter!

"Nay, he is not, for I am he!" I scoffed loudly as they attempted to ignore me.

"Scat, common rabble! This ledge is only for the 'saluted sovereign's' ship's cats!" spat one of the better-spoken chaps.

They all went about their chitchat and snubbed me!

Common rabble?

I was incensed!

"How dare you, sir! I resent your tone and the implication that I am not whom I tell you I am! Again…" I bowed. "Fairweather of the Bark *Endeavour* at your service! I am a 'salted slobbering' ship's cat or whatever you called it!" I announced.

One and all burst into laughter at my mispronunciation of the term.

"Oh 'e's 'salted' alright!" said one.

"And 'slobberin'!" joked the others.

"Ah give it a rest, Guv'nor! You're no such thing as the fine Fairweather! I seen him and he rightly is as big as told and black, wif' steely eyes and the growl of a lion!" The rest of the group were impressed with this lying fiend's story!

I was having none of it!

"I have never laid eyes upon you, sir! How can you profess to know me?" I asked convincingly.

"B'cause, you ain't Fairweather, that's 'ow! I seen 'im on a dark night and he tried to kill me and 'is size was such that I 'ad to beg for me life! No match for the likes of 'im I ever saw!" lied the fiend, while the rest of the gathering gasped at the thought of such a beast.

"I swear, upon my sailor's soul, that I am indeed Fairweather of the Bark Endeavour and you sir are a liar and a coward!" I hissed.

"That will be enough of that sir!" warned the well-spoken chap. "We hardly believe that you are he. This Fairweather is a legend amongst ship's cats and you sir, are a mere chump! Now be off and leave us to our own!"

"But…" I was shunned!

They were to have nothing more to do with me!

I could hardly pick a fight with thirteen ship-worthy cats!

I was greatly outnumbered!

There was nothing for it but to saunter off, head held high so as not to let them feel they had got the better of me.

They sniggered as I haughtily plodded down the alley to the street.

I sat at the corner moping for a moment. Then I remembered what the well-spoken chap had called me. A legend? I was a "legend amongst ship's cats?"

Jolly good, I thought!

How on earth had they gotten word of me? Legend or not?

I mused as I spied Misters Banks and Doctor Solander strolling toward the inn with Chester and Lady.

A plan came to mind! I would give them "chump!"

"I have heard of this Duck and Bucket, Daniel. Shall we enter and peruse the menu?" Mister Banks asked, approaching my corner of the alley, back at Doctor Solander trailing behind.

I steadied myself for the correct timing and jumped out in front of Mister Banks's descending foot so that he would trip over me just at the correct moment!

He caught me amidships but I was braced for the impact and it only winded me for a second!

Forward, he stumbled oafishly, for my presence was only shortly in his way before I regrouped my limbs and was back at the corner of the alley, seated casually.

"Fairweather!" he shouted at me. "Blasted cat! Forever under foot!" He straightened and gathered himself, rubbing sorely at his turned ankle. "Help me inside, Daniel!" He hurried Doctor Solander to his aid.

As suspected, the chaps on the ledge of the kitchen window heard the ruckus and the name of "Fairweather" uttered loudly! It had the desired effect and every feline for miles would have heard it!

Doctor Solander reefed his shoulder under Mister Banks's affected side and staggered him into the Duck and Bucket to be seated and fed, ordering a rather large brandy for each of them.

I merely sat near the end of the alley, buffing my claws, and awaited the call of the disbelievers to the Fairweather personage!

The incident had the desired effect. Necks strained on the kitchen sill and as I glanced over my shoulder minutely, I saw every determined eye at my rear!

I buffed at a claw, as an envoy for the group approached me.

It was the well-spoken chap!

"I say..." he started.

I held up a paw dismissively, and then went back to my manicure.

"Fairweather?" the chap asked, looking back at his cronies, who were egging him on and straining their ears for the gist.

I merely continued to buff and ignore him!

Chester and Lady approached at the perfect moment.

"Fairweather! There you are!" exclaimed my pally pooch. "What was that business with tripping Mister Banks?" He was incensed with my behaviour, he not being up to speed with the alley doings to date.

"Hush hound!" I demanded.

Chester and Lady looked oddly at each other as the envoy ran off to the ledge to report what he had heard.

"Forgive me, Chester, Lady," I whispered. "My peers are on the ledge and do not believe that I am 'the legend,' Fairweather of the Bark *Endeavour*. I had to create a disturbance for my name to be uttered out loud by someone other than my good self. Mister Banks just happened to be in the right place at the right time. I apologize for my rudeness, but it was well placed for effect," I explained quietly.

Chester and Lady looked up the alley and saw the group of ship's cats to which I referred.

I still had my back to them in contempt!

"Legend?" Chester was almost bursting to laugh, and Lady confined herself to a grin.

"Yes, 'legend'!" I hissed quietly.

"You?" Chester could barely contain his mirth.

"Yes, evil hound. Apparently, I am not only a legend, but am three feet tall, black as night, and I possess fearsome fangs! Not to mention, that I should not be confronted for fear of a feline's life!" I grinned.

"Who told you that?" Chester asked.

"My seagoing pals on the ledge!" I gestured over my shoulder. "They are of the English ships we are joining to convoy home."

I could see the cogs turning in Chester's mind. He was counting the cats and trying to digest my meaning.

All of a sudden, his eyes bulged and he understood all.

Lady, of course, was well ahead of him.

"Fairweather!" she spoke loudly, nudging Chester to play along with the gag. "Please spare Chester! His impertinence is the product of a little too much brandy with Mister Banks!" She emphasised the latter's name, knowing full well that any discerning English cat would know of her renowned master.

She lowered her head in a display of false restraint.

Cats were one thing on a ship, but rarely dogs, and as the latter were well known for chasing the former, Lady's begging for mercy from me was impressive to say the least!

An audible gasp came from the ledge and much mumbling followed.

"Very well, Lady!" I replied, keen to contribute to the ruse at hand. "I shall spare him this once! Chester!"

He bowed now, knowing what I was trying to achieve.

"Do not let it happen again or I shall punish you severely! Now sit! And stay!" I commanded, buffing again at that well-polished claw, whilst Chester sat obediently and Lady by his side.

"Yes, Fairweather!" his emphasis was on my name and almost too loud to be believable, but I let it go for now.

The envoy was returning, his tail down and his belly close to the ground should I attack.

Chester and Lady were enjoying this as much as I!

"Oh, thank you, merciful Fairweather!" Chester was bunging it on well!

"Ahem," came the envoy, from my rear.

I whipped my head around and the chap stopped dead in his tracks, fear oozing from every pore.

"What is the meaning of this?" I asked, as Chester and Lady growled at the unfamiliar cat as if to protect their most prized possession.

"Shall I kill him, Fairweather?" Chester was keen.

"No, Chester. Not yet. I shall see what he wants. Stay tuned." I turned and sat before the cowering envoy, aloof to a fault.

"Mister Fairweather?" he asked quietly, his eyes large and full of fear.

"Hmm?" I looked at him squarely as he withered.

I intended to draw this out, rubbing it in to its full potential.

"You wish to speak with me?" I oozed.

Chester growled gutturally to ensure a full intimidation.

The cat quaked visibly!

"Err…Mister Fairweather, I have come to convey our humblest apologies regarding our treatment of your fine self back at the ledge. Err…please…"

I held up a halting paw.

"Enough!" I growled, as much like a lion as I imagined one to sound.

I turned to Chester and Lady. "Shall I let him live, comrades?"

"I suppose so, Fairweather. He has not harmed you in any way, has he?" Chester's gaze was determined and one to be feared.

"No, I am untouched, so to speak." I stared down this fellow. "My physical self is intact, but I am wounded to be rejected so!"

"We are all so very sorry, sir! And bid you join us on the ledge?" He was still unsure of his safety.

"Lead on good, fellow!" I announced leniently. "Come, Chester and Lady."

"The dogs, Mister Fairweather?" he asked reservedly.

"Do I detect a discriminatory tone, sir?" I asked threateningly, hardening my gaze.

"No, no! Err…It is just not the done thing." He fumbled awkwardly.

My trifling with this chap's fear had turned to a note of disgust! I would certainly not want the company of any feline who would spurn another species!

"To skin you from head to toe would be 'the done thing'!" I chastened severely. "I prefer the company of dogs to those who would be prejudiced!" I turned to shun this bigot.

He came close to me so the others would not hear him. "I have been told not to return to the ledge without your company, Mister Fairweather. What should I do?"

"Come, Chester and Lady!" I sang loudly for effect. "The cats on the ledge wish us to partake in a spot of friendship!" I now found myself rubbing in a rather different message – that my pals meant more to me than a dozen ships cats!

The effect was not lost on any who had heard me!

Chester and Lady stood proudly and the ship's cats fidgeted on the ledge as we approached. The haughty chap ran ahead to warn his comrades of my high standards. As I approached with my entourage, they gathered themselves and sat tall before me.

"What ho, fellows?" I sang. "Sit by me, Chester and Lady," I respectfully requested.

Each cat bristled from the presence of two canines but none could move for fear they might attack. Neither did any one attempt to leave the ledge, as should one be the first to leave, the others would construe their cowardice!

I had a captive audience either way!

The well-spoken chap pounced to the ledge to join his peers. They looked down upon us, but now their demeanour had altogether changed.

"Ere, guv'nor…ah…we're sorry we…ah…" started the cockney fellow.

"Did not believe who I am?" I interrupted, hurrying things along a bit.

"Yeh, we 'eard tell stories of 'ya for ages…" He trailed off, not wishing to insult a cat with two greyhounds as his closest companions.

"I shall attempt to inform. For a second time, I am Fairweather of the Bark *Endeavour* under Captain James Cook. These are my comrades, Chester and Lady, the companions of our botanist Mister Joseph Banks." We bowed together.

The cats all looked at me, and each other, unsure of how to proceed.

"I say, old thing!" came the well-spoken chap. "We are honoured to meet you!" he laughed, trying to brush over my recent humiliation.

"You were not honoured to meet me initially! The term 'common rabble' comes to mind!" I accused, buffing once again at that nonchalant claw.

Chester and Lady growled a low and threatening presence.

"But Mister Fairweather…" He began before I cut him off.

"But nothing, my good man! You spurned me as an imposter! This is bad enough! But you then held yourselves above me as unequal to you! I go further and accuse you of bias toward my comrades Chester and Lady, merely for being dogs!" I glowered at them as my hounds increased the volume and intensity of their contemptuous growl.

"On behalf of us all here, I offer you my humblest apologies. Will you join us for catnip? And perhaps a chat?" I could not help but feel that he still thought better of himself than I could tolerate.

"And what of my comrades?" I quizzed, eyeing him purposefully.

"Ah…yes, dogs…" Try as he might, he could not hide his disrespect for my chums.

I refused to waste another moment!

"I am not in the habit of tolerating such prejudices, sir! I wish you good evening! Come, Chester, Lady! We will return to the ship. Upon my return to England, Turkel will hear of this!"

"The Turkel?" someone said hesitantly. "Of the Seaman's Rest?"

They all looked at each other in fear.

I was somewhat surprised that every one of them knew the famous fellow but it was all the more to my advantage!

"The very same!" I growled threateningly. "A personal friend of mine!"

They stood as I turned my back to them, Chester and Lady falling in behind me as I began to walk toward the street.

"Mister Fairweather!" came the group beckoning.

I ignored them and kept my aplomb as I walked in concert with Chester and Lady, just in time to be welcomed by my captain, who was returning to the ship.

"Ah, Fairweather! Chester! Lady! Good evening!" He was a little tipsy having attended his fellow captains in more than a few toasts.

I could hear the gasp from the thirteen on the ledge.

Clearly, their captains were not in the habit of wishing them a "good evening!"

"Wait for me, chaps!" came a tiddly Mister Banks favouring his injured ankle but rushing to our sides regardless.

He patted his dogs and scratched me under the chin.

"No hard feelings, Fairweather?" he begged of me.

I rubbed myself against his leg in forgiveness looking up the alley to find the thirteen looking back at me longing for such respect from not only dogs, but their own people in kind!

We all waited for Doctor Solander to catch up and walked back to the ship together.

"I say, Fairweather!" Chester could barely contain himself as we approached the Great Cabin for a late-night nip with the captain and gents. "That was remarkable! Jolly good form, old thing!"

"Yes, Fairweather, dear! I am so very proud of you!" said Lady lovingly.

"I have learned much on this voyage. There was a time when I would have begged such cats to accept me. Having now met so many different types, and in such different circumstances, I felt unease amongst such bigots, be they ship's cats or not!"

"I am astounded that you took our favour! There you were! With thirteen ship's cats at your disposal! Invited to sup and all! I doubt whether you could have found a more perfect reason to disown us, but no! You gave those blighters what for! And came back to the ship with us!" Chester could hardly believe what he had seen, feeling the need to describe the scene out loud to convince himself!

"I believe you may have risen above such bias, now that you are a well-travelled feline, Fairweather!" said Lady proudly.

"Yes, Chester! Fear not! You did not dream it! I have spurned my own in your favour!" I laughed, lapping at the brandy Mister Banks had produced for us all.

"And I am impressed, old thing!" He garbled, lapping loudly at his brandy.

We sat and enjoyed Mister Banks's report of St Helena, warmed by the brandy and each other's company!

"We rode our borrowed horses around the entire island, being only forty-ish miles squared. Judging from the burnt rocks I found, this island is vastly volcanic and is the summit of an immense mountain having risen out of the sea." I could not fathom this but believed him all the same.

"Jamestown was founded in 1659 by the English East India Company and named after James, Duke of York. James Fort was built within a month on James Bay and houses were built further up the James Valley." All this James-ing yet again! I thought we had finished James-ing some time ago but I let him continue with his history lesson.

"In 1673, the Dutch East India Company forcibly took the island, before English troops restored the island to English East India Company control ruled by England."

"Yes, yes, Mister Banks. We are aware of the history of the place," the captain injected impatiently. Mister Banks frowned but continued with his findings.

"We climbed the highest peak and looked down at the town situated in Chapel Valley which resembles a large trench, its sides as barren as its sea cliffs. The valleys green as they become more inland, and there the residents tend sparse plantations. It is worth noting that this peak we climbed was where Nevil Maskelyne was dispatched from England in 1761 to observe the last Transit of Venus prior to our own. As we know, they had bad weather and therefore incomplete findings, but he developed his distance of the method of determining longitude using the position of the moon, which became known as the lunar distance method."

Mister Banks was digressing and the captain set him right with a stern "Yes, yes, Mister Banks! St Helena, if you please!"

He complied. "The town's houses are ill built and the market house and church are in ruins. The white inhabitants are mainly English, serving the ships with refreshments. Shamefully in their laziness, they have not cultivated the fertile soil that is ideal for fruits and vegetables. None of the ships seem to be able to procure these here, excepting that I have heard Captain Elliot was furnished by order of the governor from his own garden!" Mister Banks "hurrumphed" at this favouritism and all agreed that the Englishmen here lacked verve in propagating their own supplies in such a fruitful environment.

"The plant life is mainly of European species, no doubt brought here by the ships, and thriving in the temperate climate. Yams are the chief supply for their numerous slaves who hail from most parts of the world, a miserable race worn out by the severity of the punishments of which they frequently complained. I was disgraced to be an Englishman as I heard of our countrymen's cruelty and inhumanity to these slaves." Mister Banks took of his brandy, shaking his head and mumbling his desire to report this mistreatment to the authorities upon our return to England.

The captain agreed, but urged him to continue in his findings, as the hour was late.

"Among the native products is ebony. The dense black wood I saw was of fine colour and the hardness of iron, but the trees that produced it here were all but extinct and no one remembers when they had become so. Fish abound, and of all varieties."

The captain interrupted. "Excellent. We shall have some aboard on the morrow." He looked to my Isaac, who was patiently attending, to arrange it so.

Mister Banks frowned upon any intrusion to his accounts, but he continued without taking issue, as supplies must be acquired and the captain informed.

"There are few insects, but rats and mice are rife." Mister Banks looked at me, as did the captain, to remind me that I must be vigilant of an infestation, as if I required prompting!

This annoyed me, as they should know me well by now!

I turned my head in pique, but continued to listen.

Mister Banks was brief and we were all relieved. Upon serving up another brandy, however he chose to muse. All of us fidgeted wearily but politely gave him our ear.

"Upon creation and evolution, I am confounded. Here we are at this tiny island some two thousand miles from the easternmost coast of the Americas and one thousand miles from the Africas, surrounded by sea. For my part, I confess I feel more wonder in the finding of a little snail on the top of the ridges of St Helena, than in finding people upon any other part of the globe. The seed of a thistle supported by its down, the insect by its weak, and the bird by its more able wing, may tempt the dangers of the sea, but of these how many millions must perish for one who arrives at the distance of so many miles from the place of its rest; it appears indeed far more difficult to account for the passage of one individual, than to believe the destruction of all that ever may have been by their ill fate hurried into such an attempt." Mister Banks peered out the window, pondering botany and life.

The rest of us had tired and the captain lost patience, taking Mister Banks's pause to spare us all more of the same.

"Yes, well thank you, Mister Banks, for your wealth of St Helena." He concluded the meeting.

Each bid their goodnights and I was alone with my captain. He mopped his brow as if Mister Banks account had exhausted him terribly, brief as it was for a change, but hard work on the ear all the same.

He had other things to concern him with our stay short upon this St Helena, and he directed his attention to yours truly to lighten his burden as he prepared for bed.

"So you finally got to meet with other ship's cats?" He ruffled my fur playfully, referring to our mutual Duck and Bucket visit.

I stood to my full height and snubbed the air.

"It did not go as well as you wished, this meeting?" he asked, knowing I should have been truly happy to talk to such similar fellows.

I shook my head.

"You came out of the alley with the dogs. Were you shunned?" he quizzed, rubbing his chin in an attempt to remember the circumstances of our meeting.

I nodded.

"And you favoured the hounds to the company of your peers?" He looked at me keenly.

Again, I nodded.

He petted me avidly in admiration.

"Well, blow me down! A fine Englishman you have turned out to be!" He poured himself a final brandy and held it high.

"To Fairweather!" he whispered as usual, so as not to arouse suspicion that he was indeed talking to his ship's cat and enjoying a lighter moment.

He filled my saucer with the stuff and I pondered the true meaning of my status.

I decided it was more desirable to honour one's ship-bound comrades who stood with me as one, than a loose gathering of snobs who only accepted their own kind, to wit said cats at the Duck and Bucket.

A friend they did not have in the "legend" that is Fairweather!

I slept there in the Great Cabin within the warmth of the friendships I had acquired, having sailed around the world with men, dogs, and honour, even though I had only just realised it!

CHAPTER 39

The next morning, a local chap from Jamestown came out to the ship selling maps. The captain, as always, was keen to procure the latest as the young man laid them out on his map table in the Great Cabin. He looked them over and took on a supercilious grin.

"I shall decline the purchase of these," he said uncommonly to Lieutenant Gore who was standing by.

"Why, Captain?" asked the lieutenant.

"They are my maps!" he said with pride. "My parcel from Batavia must have reached the Royal Society as they have already been printed and distributed for maritime use!"

"Good Lord!" said Lieutenant Gore, enthusiastically. "That was quick!"

"Yes, and I the author will save my money for other things!" quipped the captain, unusually pleased with himself.

"What goes, Captain?" Mister Banks always appeared when there was a discovery of any kind and this was no exception to his rule.

How he managed to materialize every time, I still did not fathom. A fifth or sixth sense, as they say, perhaps!

"My maps, Mister Banks! This chap is offering to sell them to me!" he explained, holding out one for Mister Banks's perusal.

He studied them long and hard as the vendor scratched his head in confusion, thinking the captain an eccentric loony of some kind; this sea-wearied man on a beaten old ship claiming to have drawn the very maps he was trading!

"You are correct, Captain! I believe these to be your drawings. They are unmistakable! But what if they have been stolen and reproduced elsewhere?" asked Mister Banks, always the sceptic.

"Then I can only hope these are English maps that this chap is vending!" The captain would not be put off.

"Tell me, young man, have the other English captains here purchased copies of these?" he asked of the map merchant.

"Um…Yes." He was unsure where this admission would take him.

"Do you know who produced them?" he quizzed.

"…Err…no." He was cautious.

"Excellent! Be off, I have the originals!" He ordered, grinning from ear to ear! For now, it was enough that his peers had paid good money for copies of his very own maps!

"Blasted Dutch might have absconded with your package out of Batavia!" Mister Banks added, ever aware of the sinister.

"Only time will tell, Mister Banks. For now, my maps are in circulation and I am pleased," he said cheerfully, putting the subject to rest.

Lieutenant Gore and Mister Banks shook the captain's hand heartily, and my Isaac stood proudly in the knowing that he had contributed in no small manner, with his charting and taking of measurements along the way, taught of course by one of the best!

It was a busy time here with so many English ships around us. The following day, the comings and goings of the captains and their messengers was dizzying!

I stayed tuned in the Great Cabin watching the endless parade of nosing officials, not wishing to tour the other ships nor meet with my pompous peers in the process!

The captain got word that the fleet was convoying on the morrow. Much was to be done to enable us to leave with them.

I went up on deck to watch the work in progress.

In my surveillance, I spotted the familiar shape of a cat, and not just any cat; the well-spoken chap from the Duck and Bucket!

He was trying to attract my attention from the *Portland*, which was nearest moored to us, and head of the potential fleet.

"I say!" came the call, his head bobbing up and down and side-to-side to catch my eye. "Mister Fairweather! 'Tis I, Montague of the *Portland*! I met you at the Duck and Bucket!"

I kept my position and nonchalantly nodded in recognition, going back to my vigil over the works.

"Mister Fairweather! A word?" he hollered, trying desperately to gain my interest.

I merely turned to the men and ignored him.

"Please, sir! I beg your company!" he pleaded. I must say I was enjoying this!

He did not seem the type to enjoy begging anything so I dragged his discomfort out for a while!

"My company? I am rather busy at the moment," I replied offhandedly.

"I shall take little of your time!" he bellowed hopefully.

Just then, his own captain scatted him for wailing so!

I had obviously earned more respect from my crewmates than he, as should I choose to holler it was clearly for good reason and quite acceptable!

I viewed him out of the corner of my eye, creeping along the deck back to his hollering position.

"Sir!" He kept it brief this time.

"Oh, if you must!" I said impatiently. "Come over on the next trip." He beamed and left his spot for the longboat that had been ferrying supplies and notes between the *Portland* to the *Endeavour* all morning.

I did not have to wait long when he came aboard tentatively, clearly not knowing whether he would be well received by man, dog or Fairweather!

I would go so far as to say that he skulked, and as a well-bred fellow, it did not suit him!

He approached my supervisory position with care.

"Err…How do you do, Mister Fairweather? Montague of the *Portland* at your service." He bowed reverently.

He was eyeing the dogs, which had seen him come aboard and approached menacingly.

"Montague, is it?" I yawned wearily. "I am sure that I have introduced myself prior to this occasion!" A note of sarcasm began in earnest, as I referred to the evening before when the ship's cats spurned me so.

"Err…Yes! Yes! I do recall. Tell me…am I safe here?" He fidgeted madly as the dogs sat to flank me.

"Why, I am not absolutely sure!" I toyed. "Chester? Lady? Is this 'Montague' of the *Portland* safe here on the *Endeavour*?" It was probably poor form but I relished my position and mockery oozed from my every pore.

Chester and Lady were enjoying his discomfort as much as I!

"Hmm…" Chester paused for an awkward silence. "Define safe!" he asked of me eventually.

"Well…Am I likely to fight him to the death?…Or are you and Lady keen to eat him?…Or will the captain throw him into the deep?… Something like that?" I quizzed Chester playfully.

"Oh, well…any of those predicaments are likely, Fairweather! After all, he is a complete cad and is quite alone!" Chester threatened.

Montague began to tremble uncontrollably!

I thought it best to put the poor fool out of his misery.

"I believe that I will spare you, Monty, old thing!" I said benevolently.

"Monty…? But…" He was incensed as if the shortening of his name was a sore point, but then he was at my mercy and had to swallow it down as I saw fit!

"Yes, Monty. That is your name, is it not?" I bothered him shamelessly.

He cleared his throat as if a fur ball had gotten wedged in there somewhere!

All he could do was nod.

I deemed it time to be fair.

"How goes the *Portland*?" I changed the subject.

"Oh, quite well, and we sail on the morrow! Together!" He was so grateful for the change in the direction of the conversation that he expelled his answer boisterous with relief!

"Chester, Lady, shall I give this chap a tour of the *Endeavour*?" I asked them as my advisors.

"I suppose it is the polite thing to do, Fairweather, but I recall our not being good enough for this chap on this last eve!" Chester could little resist a jab at him in compensation.

"My humblest apologies, Mister Chester, Madam Lady." He bowed, knowing they could snap his neck at any time!

"If Fairweather forgives your poor form, then I suppose we must," said Chester resolvedly.

"Oh, thank you, sir, madam." He bowed.

"Off we go then, Monty, old thing, tiddly-um!" I sang happily, knowing I had this chap where I wanted him.

I started forward and he followed compliantly, relieved that the dogs were not coming with us below.

I pointed out this and that.

Our poor old ship having travelled further than this "Monty" could ever have dreamed, he was suitably impressed with her condition when I told him where we had been.

"Yes, my captain much admires your captain's fortitude!" he admitted.

"Do not forget the crew, Monty! Not to mention the gents and dogs and my good self! We are none without the others!"

I reminded him that it takes more than one man to sail a ship!

"Err…yes! Forgive my omission!" he begged.

I ignored him as we strolled to the stores.

He sniffed about, sensing that the odd mouse may have eluded my detection, and no doubt hoping that he could find fault with me.

I left him to his investigations and sat casually, awaiting his comments.

"Err…Mister Fairweather…" He was having trouble speaking his mind.

"Spit it out, man!" I scolded.

"There are quite a few mice in your hold…" he started, unsure of the consequences.

"And your point is, Monty?" I asked playfully.

"Do you need some help in eradicating them?" he asked, pleased with himself, and all too ready to do me some injustice!

"Spare me, my good man!" I spat back at him. "They are here for a reason!"

He looked vacantly at me as if I were quite mad!

"They are?" he was confused.

"They are, indeed! Do you not spare the odd happy couple to ensure the breed?" I asked poignantly.

"What for?" he boasted. Clearly his ship's stores were void of vermin.

"Why, for leaner times, my dear Monty!" I buffed at that all too familiar claw.

"I do not understand you, sir! It is our duty to rid the hold of mice and rats!" he postured proudly.

Noticeably, he did not possess the intelligence of the Fairweather brain!

"And Monty, old thing, how many times have you rid the ship of vermin completely, only to be threatened with being tossed off at the next possible port?" I had him here! My superior knowledge outdid him, and well.

"Err…Whatever do you mean?" He expected me to fall for such a ruse.

"In my travels around the globe, old Monty, it has been my method to ensure the safety of a good breeding pair of mice. When the food is scarce, they come in handy when the cook chooses rightly enough to feed the men and not the ship's cat! Not to mention that when the chips are down, and one's favour is in doubt, a mouthful of mice heartens even the staunchest feline disbeliever! I cannot believe you are not aware of this integral strategy!" I scoffed.

Monty's slightly smaller brain was visibly trying its best to digest what I had announced!

His eyes widened as my words penetrated finally.

"Fairweather! Jolly good tip that, old thing! It is brilliant!" he announced, and then remembered himself. "Err…do you mind if I call you Fairweather? After all, we are equal in rank?" He stuttered.

"If you wish Monty!" I said cordially. "This rank business may be a debateable thing however! I have clearly been at sea longer than you! And my mousing is obviously far superior for it!" I insisted he keep his place in the order of things, after all, he had been such a snobbish bore at the inn, and I did not want him getting above himself.

"Of course, Fairweather!" he said, trying my name on for size without his customary "Mister."

"Do you mind if I pass your mousing tips on to my colleagues? Your modus operandi is impressive!"

"I cannot see why not, Monty, as long as you mention my name as author of whatever it is you called it!" I did not wish him taking credit for my own techniques! Even if they were "modus operandi!" The meaning of which I noted to ask Chester later.

"Well, Monty, old thing, the stores are coming aboard and I must check them for additions to the Fairweather population," I said dismissively.

"Yes, yes, Fairweather! I too will have to get back to the *Portland* on the next longboat. If the provisions are arriving, I have certain mice to kill! Not all of them though 'eh?" He nudged me chummily.

I let it go for now.

The men began busily bringing stores down to the hold so I briskly ran for the gangway and motioned Montague to do the same. As we reached the deck, our longboat was being despatched to the *Portland* with a message and Monty would have to be on it, as I heard the captain say that this was the last longboat off the *Endeavour* for the day.

Monty scurried to the longboat with a "Tootle-ooh! I shall see you at the Seaman's Rest upon our return!" he shouted, as if we were now the best of friends.

Chester came up behind me. "I am glad he has gone!" he growled.

"Now, now Chester! Monty isn't all bad if one keeps him in his place," I retorted.

"The chap is a blatherskite and I am glad to see the end of him! For a moment there I thought you were going to invite him to join us on the leg home!" Chester complained.

"Blatherskite? Chester! What kind of word is that?" I scoffed, watching the longboat return to the *Portland* happily.

"Blatherskite! A braggart!" Chester replied but I was still none the wiser and took on that curious demeanour.

"A windbag you ninny!" Chester spat.

"Ah yes! That he was! That reminds me Chester, what is a 'modus operandi'?" I asked inanely.

"It is a technique or method of approaching a thing," he explained.

Chester was always the one to ask of such topics!

I put the word into the context Monty had used it, and was pleased that he had not been attempting to insult me with it. I was satisfied with this and retired for the evening as we had a big day ahead of us.

Upon rising early to the sounds of the *Endeavour*'s crew attending her every need, Chester and Lady came for me.

The *Portland*'s captain had given the word for us to unmoor!

We were off!

It was the 4th day of May 1771 and I went to the cathead with the dogs as we sailed out of the Jamestown Road with a flotilla of thirteen fine English ships, their sails flapping in the sturdy breeze, crisp and white for the most, but ours a little tainted from our near on three years at sea!

It was a sight to end all with our little ship surrounded by much larger ones, and the noise of their captains, lieutenants and men shouting orders to their subordinates. Even though we were the smallest of this fleet, I felt that we were the most important ship that England would see coming up the Thames when we finally arrived!

Chester and Lady thought so, too!

The captain was proudly on deck with lieutenants Gore and Hicks, even though the poor Hicks's consumption had worsened and we feared for his life, he was not about to stay below when such a magnificent fleet was to be witnessed!

We all milled about the captain as he steered, drinking in the significance of this our last leg, and home, our next port!

We were off for England! The crew were robust!

I was not sure how I felt about this, though, as we were at sea and I now had the time to ponder.

On the one paw, I missed my palatial home and my mother, not to mention the chaps back at the Seaman's Rest Inn, where my lust for adventure began in earnest.

On the other, I had had the time of my life, whether in danger or delight, at sea with my men!

But we were thousands of miles from England yet, and I deemed it an inappropriate time to think of such things.

Mister Banks interrupted my musings and joined us for this visual treat.

"Ah, the *Endeavour*! She certainly sails worse than any one of the fleet!" He blustered as we lagged only just behind the rest.

"Mister Banks! Have I not mentioned my distaste for your negative comments regarding our ship? She takes us home and well!" yelled the captain for all to hear.

The entire crew let up a cheer, Chester and Lady woofed, and I howled. No doubt the cacophony carried upon the wind behind us, and the fleet would be wondering what the devil was doing back on the *Endeavour*!

Mister Banks was quieted yet again and the captain stood proudly even though we would doubtless lose sight of the fleet eventually, as they powered home under full sail!

We were a thing of beauty! Our sturdy little ship amongst the pride of the English fleet!

By the following morning, the ships were ahead of us but only just.

They had close reefed their sails to keep us in their company, and three days into our leg we were abreast the head ship, the *Portland*! I hoped that Monty was miffed!

Flying fish and birds were about and the weather pleasant enough for the captain to exercise the men their small arms.

On the 10th day of May, the little volcanic Island of Ascension came into view there alone in the midst of the Atlantic, much like St Helena.

The captain sent signal to the *Portland* that we would not be anchoring there. Mister Banks was unimpressed, as he wished to sight a cactus of some kind that was known to grow there but had not been botanised.

The captain would have none of his begging. He had to be satisfied with going below and preparing his works for the Royal Society.

Soon after, Captain Elliot himself came aboard us on the *Portland*'s longboat and our captain presented him with a box containing a letter to the Admiralty, the *Endeavour*'s common log books and some of the officers' journals.

Very important stuff!

It was clear to our captain that the fleet wished to hurry along and as we sailed so much heavier than they, so he bid Captain Elliot farewell with strict instructions on the delivery and importance of his charge, and with a promise to meet in England sometime after we arrived.

The favourable breeze continued and we still managed to keep up with them in the days that followed!

The captain found every opportunity to remind Mister Banks of our *Endeavour*'s spectacular progress, and he deserved it after his endless droning about her ability!

On the 15th day of May, the captain announced that an eclipse of the sun would be observed.

Some of the men feared this as the sky grew dark and with it the weather turned to a misty rain. An eerie evening experience was felt even though it was the midst of the day!

Those who thought the world would end, pottered carefully about the decks hoping for the sun to return before they would meet their maker.

The captain tried to explain that an eclipse was a common phenomenon but those naysayers would have none of it until the sun broke free of its shadow and beamed through the mist, cloaking us in a magical light!

Everyone enjoyed the radiance, and a silence in pondering the wonders of the universe!

Mister Banks continued to sieve the sea, bringing small sharks, a bonito fish weighing near twenty pounds, and spotting the familiar Portuguese man o' war floating natively on the surface of the sea.

The fleet remained in our company and our convoy gave us a feeling of belonging that we had missed by sailing alone in uncharted waters!

The men heartened for each of their reasons; be it family or loved ones, or even a good pint of beer at their local inn!

By the 19th day of May our favourable winds had dropped and the entire fleet was becalmed, even us of the *Endeavour*, all bobbing in concert around the surface of the sea.

Mister Banks was invited to the *Portland* to dine with Captain Elliot and he was taking the dogs, so I joined them to see how my new chum Monty was doing.

"Welcome, welcome!" came Captain Elliot as we boarded his ship.

The dogs were not entirely welcome but the crew tethered them on deck, with one of the younger lads fetching them some rather tasty looking food and a bowl of water.

Monty was on hand.

"Greetings, Fairweather! I am pleased to have you aboard!" he said cheerily.

"Why thank you, Monty!" I was dismissive as the *Portland* was enormous compared to my *Endeavour*! I tried not to seem overwhelmed but she was as clean and shiny as a new penny! As I had heard the captain mumble when he could not be heard.

"This is the fourth ship of the name *Portland*, launched at Sheerness in 1770 and she has fifty guns!" Monty tried to impress. "We had a typhoid fever epidemic within weeks of entering service, poor hygiene in the galley, but she is clear of the disease and back in service. Come, sir, we will inspect the hold!" he said eagerly.

We passed a multitude of finely dressed sailors going about their businesses.

The kitchen was spacious and two cooks with their servants were frantically preparing a feast in honour of our Mister Banks.

As we passed, a china saucer of duck scraps appeared in front of us!

I had not tasted duck on a saucer since my home in England!

It reminded me of the fine china that Madam's maids served to me in my youth!

Monty tucked in and polished off the offering in no time.

I declined the duck, as Monty's mention of the *Portland*'s galley as a source of typhoid fever prevented me from partaking.

I knew not of such a disease, but so late in our voyage and with so many deaths already, I did not wish to transmit it to my men back at the *Endeavour*!

Wisdom here was essential and I hoped Mister Banks would be prudent should he hopefully be in possession of these facts!

"Off to the stores!" cried Monty excitedly.

Down and down we went through innumerable decks and past many cabins holding all sorts of chaps and their goods.

The hold of the *Portland* was bigger than I imagined, carrying stores of monumental proportion. Being a trading ship, she was stacked to the timbers with cargo bound for England. This mass of stores was much work for one cat and I held a new appreciation for this Montague, although I was loathe admitting it to him.

"I have been employing your strategy here, Fairweather! All clear but a few 'happy couples,' as you called them!" he boasted proudly.

"Well done old boy! This will ensure your passage!" I applauded his good works.

We ambled back to the deck to see the *Endeavour*'s longboat coming back for us well before the designated time!

My Isaac came rushing on board, calling for Mister Banks. This could not be good news! I rushed after him to a palatial gentlemen's dining room. He was about to dine.

"Captain Elliot, sir!" he bowed apologetically. "Mister Banks!" He addressed them in the correct order. "Captain Cook asks if the *Portland*'s surgeon could come to the *Endeavour* and take a look at Lieutenant Hicks! He is very poorly!" he asked politely but with haste.

"I knew it would come to this eventually!" interjected Mister Banks. "Chap has had consumption since we left England. He has been worsening of late!"

Captain Elliot motioned to his servant to run and fetch their Doctor Carret.

I did not even bid my goodbyes to Monty, as such word required instant action on my part!

Within an instant we were all on the longboat, Mister Banks and Captain Elliot without their dinner, and off at speed to the *Endeavour*!

Chester and Lady gathered with me as I came aboard. We were not of importance to the situation, but we stood on deck for news of our lieutenant.

When the captain and Mister Banks returned to the deck finally, to farewell Captain Elliot and his surgeon, it was clear that Lieutenant Hicks was to remain in bed for the remainder of the voyage home.

Doctor Carret instructed our new cook, Joseph Childs, to ensure Lieutenant Hicks had hot broth fresh from the galley at every opportunity.

Mister Banks had missed his dinner and took a left-over portion to the Great Cabin in conference with the captain. When I had meowed enough to be given my own offering, I was glad of a safe plate from my own ship.

I ambled back to the Great Cabin to be greeted by Chester and Lady who attended Mister Banks in his brandy with the captain.

They spoke of Lieutenant Hicks, for their fears for his life had been examined on more than one occasion.

"I have a certain feeling that this will be the last time we see Lieutenant Hicks on deck," said Lady intuitively.

"Yes, he most certainly will be in bed until we land," said Chester in passing.

"No, it is more than that dear..." she said vaguely.

With this presentiment we slept fitfully there in the Great Cabin, the *Endeavour* still without a breeze, and Lady's words resounding in our ears.

The following days saw the fleet in tolerable breezes one minute and then stalled and becalmed in the next.

It was a frustrating time for my captain as he longed to be home now and we were ever so close!

The *Portland* threw out a new kind of casting net that we had not ever seen, much like a retractable umbrella. Curious, the captain and Mister Banks accompanied by Doctor Solander went across in the longboat to ascertain its design.

The captain was most impressed that it could hold as much as one hundred and fifty men could haul in. He wished one for our ship, but as misfortune would have it, parts of our forge had been ditched over the side on the reef at Australia, and one could not be duplicated on board.

The *Endeavour* was used to such light airs as we had encountered, and at one point we were ahead of the lead ship!

"You see, Mister Banks! She heads the fleet in these doldrums!" The captain could not help but rub his nose in all of his previous comments regarding the accomplishment of the *Endeavour*!

It was a fine moment and not lost on anyone on board!

Grins from ear to ear were forthcoming and even a little strutting about was displayed by some of the chaps!

By the following day, we had gotten somewhat too far ahead of the fleet, and the captain enjoyed ordering our sails close-reefed so the other ships could catch up!

Again, Mister Banks was reminded of our accomplishment!

Mister Banks had had enough of his taunting, and during a calm spot went off with alone to dine with Captain Elliot yet again.

He came back with the report of a common old English "House Martin" bird that flew about the gentlemen's dining cabin! This meant that the poor thing had either sailed entirely upon the *Portland* since England, or that we were indeed close to home!

Most preferred to think the latter!

The wind picked up and during a hazy rain, the last of the fleet overtook us.

Overnight, we had lost sight of them, and they were not seen the next morning.

The captain was not concerned as we had finally picked up the trade wind and it would not be long before we would see them in England!

Mister Banks had come forward early and voiced his concern that the ships had sailed on without us, but the captain dismissed him with a wave of his hand. After all, the captain knew his way home and it had merely been a stroke of luck that we could have convoyed with other ships out of St Helena Island!

I sat on deck with him and my Isaac at the wheel and the fresh wind in my whiskers lapping up the moment as Mister Banks was dismissed.

CHAPTER 40

By the next morning of the 26th of May 1771, and I still at the wheel with my captain and Isaac having coasted us all night, he finally tired of it.

"Isaac, go and see if Lieutenant Hicks is up to a stint at the wheel. I am sure it would cheer him now that we have picked up speed," he dispatched Isaac happily.

It was some time before Isaac returned with his head lowered, sniffling a little.

"Doctor Perry wishes to report that Lieutenant Hicks has died." He bawled, uncaring that his emotions were seen.

"Oh! No!" said the captain, thinking that Lieutenant Hicks may have been on the mend since his bed confinement.

He motioned to my Isaac to take the helm and he rushed to Lieutenant Hicks's cabin door, and I with him.

Doctor Perry was in attendance.

"He has died, Captain. The consumption has finally taken its toll," said the doctor sadly.

"It was my hope that he sees England again. And so close…" said the captain, trailing off and taking his lifeless hand.

I jumped to his chest and sat on him in consolation and sadness!

The captain knew me to be fond of him and let me be, knowing I meant well.

"Have him prepared for immediate burial at sea with full honours!" the captain ordered, leaving Doctor Perry to his duty.

I followed my captain to the Great Cabin and as it was unattended he poured himself a stiff brandy.

"I have but one lieutenant left, Fairweather! Poor Hicks left England with his disease, and it could be said that he has been dying ever since!" He poured another brandy.

"I believe Batavia put the last nail in his coffin!" He slammed the glass down in anger and poured himself another.

"Damn it!" He swallowed the beaker in one gulp.

I knew his pain and felt awfully for him, having lost so many of his comrades, and now Lieutenant Hicks; he, himself, still only officially a lieutenant but still the captain of this voyage to the end.

He poured me a bowl of the good stuff and I lapped at it with vigour!

Benevolence was required!

I grieved and angered with him as one!

No sooner had I licked the bowl clean than he was rifling about for his notes in the Great Cabin desk.

He was on a mission!

He found the list he was looking for, and proceeded at speed for the deck, where Lieutenant Hicks was prepared for his sea burial.

All were in place, as by now, they were well practiced in death and interment!

He began solemnly.

"I commit Lieutenant Zachary Hicks to the sea, so close to England it is a tragedy; a fine lieutenant and committed leader! May the Almighty accept him and may his family be comforted in the knowing of him to have sailed with honour on one of the finest voyages known to England!" The captain shed a tear.

"Three cheers for the lieutenant!" someone called as Lieutenant Hicks's body was committed to the deep.

A roar came up from the lowest to the highest of rank, with this hopefully our last death; each and every soul having taken it as so that we would now all return to England.

We thought that the Batavian diseases had already taken our last man!

Now, so close to our destination any one of us could be in doubt!

The men began to disperse to their duties when the captain hailed them back.

Producing his piece of paper, he called them to order as the weather appeared as it would change and all hands would be to the sheets.

"I take this opportunity earlier than I should, men!" he announced.

They shuffled a little.

"Settle down now. I know we are soon to disembark in our mother England!" he quieted the crew.

"Lieutenant Hicks's death has dashed our hopes of a final leg without incident. At this time, I urge each of you to be grateful for your survival, and mindful that we still have long to sail. To improve the spirits, I ask Lieutenant Gore to serve double rations of rum for all!" The required cheer went up!

"I have some announcements to make!" he quieted, as the crew were well pleased to stand around for announcements if rum were to accompany them!

When young Isaac Manly had doled out the rations, and all had settled, the captain consulted his list.

"Master Charles Clerke, Master's Mate, please come forward!" the captain began.

"You are to be promoted to the rank of lieutenant effective immediately." Lieutenant Clerke was surprised but none of the crew doubted his cheerful attendance to all of his duties and thought the captain fair in promoting him.

The customary three cheers went up for the fellow and the captain now had another fine lieutenant in the absence of Hicks.

"Lieutenant Gore? Please accept your promotion from third to second lieutenant!" He shook the man's hand heartily in his diligent service.

"Isaac Smith, please come forward!" Isaac complied, removing his hat. I held my breath, as I knew my Isaac to be a good and deserving lad!

"Isaac Smith, for your attention to the charts: drawings, surveys and plans, of which you have become expert, I promote you to master's mate!" Three cheers went up and most heartily from my boys!

I meowed aloud and Chester and Lady woofed in concert!

Spirits were beginning to fortify as the rum and promotions encouraged the men!

"I have drawn up recommendations for our return. They will be presented to the Navy board with my highest commendations," he continued.

"Mister Richard Pickersgill, Master, you are deserving of a lieutenant's position!" Pickersgill was quite astounded as were the rest of the men. Whilst he had performed admirably, I thought him still to this day a pompous and irritating chap. Ever since the incident with Mister Banks and the bugs he and Edward Terrell had shamelessly bullied the younger boys. He just knew when to do so in a manner that always appeared innocent!

I did not meow aloud, nor did the crew cheer quite so vehemently, for this fellow's potential promotion.

I made a note to myself to check the Muster book for his name, and avoid any ship he commanded.

The captain continued.

"Mister Richard Orton, our clerk, and Mister Francis Wilkinson, master's mate; wish to have places in our Custom House or other such Public Office and I shall recommend them accordingly." The cheers continued.

Poor Mister Orton still sported mangled ears from his run in with the drunken James Magra all that time ago.

Along with Mister Wilkinson, they had clearly decided not to sail again. No doubt they had their reasons.

Some could take it and others could not!

"Mister Richard Hutchins, bosun's mate, is well deserving of a bosun's warrant and I shall put it forward upon our return!" More cheering and rum!

"Sergeant Edgcumbe, step forward!" He did so humbly. "I cannot promote you as you are a Marine, but it will be with my strongest urging that you receive a promotion within the Marine Service!" Much cheering followed this hard-working man's mention, especially from his fellow soldiers!

"Finally, young Isaac Manly, step up!" The entire crew cheered in advance as the enormous young fellow lumbered forward respectfully.

Young Isaac had not an enemy on the ship as his sheer size but gentle nature endeared him to one and all.

"I shall inform the Naval Office of your outstanding character and they will award you upon my suggestion!" the captain announced.

"Thank you, Captain!" said the huge lad, a tear coming to his eye.

Only a confidently large boy would allow such a show of gratitude in front of his fellows at sea!

I was duly proud of his progress from his position as the youngest boy of twelve years to his well-earned status, not to mention his monumental size!

"As for the rest of you here, I personally commend you, especially those who have sailed from our beginnings. We have seen much, learned much, and all should stand tall as the *Endeavour*'s crew on this auspicious, history making voyage!"

"To the captain!" yelled the newly appointed Lieutenant Clerke.

"The captain!" came an uproar! Whether they be glad to be so close to home, pleased with their new positions, full of rum, or merely proud of our voyage, it was a boisterous cheer to be sure!

Chester howled and Lady woofed, and I rubbed against my captain's leg.

"Oh! In all this cheer, you slipped my mind," he said out loud as the applause subsided.

"An oversight has occurred, men!" shouted the captain above the remaining revellers.

All stood to attention, wondering what the captain referred.

"I would be remiss in the most terrible manner if I did not promote one of the finest members of our crew!" They scanned each man as the captain consulted his list.

"Fairweather of the Bark *Endeavour*! Step up where all can see you!" called the captain as I milled around his feet.

A brouhaha broke out as I leapt to the longboat as requested.

Cheering and waving, and much hearty laughing surrounded me!

Lieutenant Gore handed the captain a fresh beaker of rum.

"For your tireless service to the *Endeavour* stores, your vigilance as a fine lookout, your tireless care of the downtrodden and my personal assistant in charting the world, I promote you to…" He could not decide a station for me.

"He should be a captain!" someone yelled from the crowd.

"Yeah!" came the shout from the unified men.

"Captain Fairweather in His Majesty's Service, it is!" My captain held his beaker aloft to toast my new position.

The entire company followed suit.

"Captain Fairweather!" up went the cheer.

I was embarrassed for a moment.

A flush filled my cheeks. It was a good thing my fur covered it!

I stood proudly and accepted my appointment, this being a ruffle on my head from my captain.

Chester and Lady stood by proudly with Mister Banks as he too ruffled my fur.

A procession gathered and one by one each and every man filed by me to scratch my chin.

"He's our lucky cat!" yelled young Isaac Manly remembering my sitting on the cathead for the first time as we left England.

"For luck!" they all said as they ruffled me in turns.

Last was my Isaac. Who rubbed a little more vigorously than most.

"Good thing I brought you aboard, 'eh chum?" he whispered.

I would have gotten on board somehow! But my Isaac was to be complimented for his hand in it. He merely expedited the inevitable, so I let him have his moment as the captain congratulated him for his fine choice of mousers back in England so long ago!

Lieutenant Gore was happy in the knowing that he had survived much, and sat back to watch the show!

Mister Banks looked a little miffed and it was not lost on the captain.

"May I make my recommendations that Chester and Lady be promoted?" he asked, taking another rum from Lieutenant Clerke, and seeing the happiness of Mister Banks.

"Why, Captain! That would be generous of you! They have been fine companions and vigilant workers!" beamed Mister Banks.

"Lord Chester!" sang the captain!

Mister Banks scratched behind his ears as Chester stood proudly accepting his title.

"Lady…err…Lady!" The captain had not thought out her title efficiently.

Everyone laughed but I knew how much she meant to this voyage, Chester and my good self!

"Lady Lady" was a stretch and a mouthful too, but it stuck.

By this time, the men were ready to toast to anyone and anything, the rum flowing freely and the captain in good spirits!

"Now back to work, men!" he finally slurred as they all tottered to their posts.

I scanned the horizon in the hope that our good weather would continue as none were sober enough to handle the ship should a gale ensue. Clear weather seemed the forecast.

As the men fumbled about the ship, I leapt down from the longboat to chat with my hounds.

"Well, Chester! Or what was that? Ah yes, Lord Muck!" I mocked playfully. "That was a bit of fun, what?"

"Yes, Captain Chump!" He sparred back at me.

"Now, you two!" chided Lady.

"A mere bit of jesting is all it was, um…Lady Lady!" I giggled at the double use of her title and her given name.

Chester giggled along with me.

"Can we cease and desist, you childish pair? My name is simply Lady and that is all that is required." She was always humble and thought it all a silly game at that.

"I beg to differ, Madam!" I proclaimed in an elegant tone. "A fine Lady you are! You would agree, Chester?"

"Of course, my dear Captain Fairweather!" he agreed.

"Thank you, Lord Chester!" I bowed.

"Oh, for goodness's sake, you two!" She had tired of our shenanigans and strode off for a rest.

Chester and I lolled about on the foredeck watching the men stagger to and from their tasks.

I must admit I was quite fond of my new title! After all, one does not make captain at any old whim and fancy!

I tried it on in my mind and wondered if the boys back at the inn would believe it if I told them I had been made captain of the Bark *Endeavour*.

Smiling a little at my budding boastfulness, I dozed off in the afternoon sun, knowing I would have trouble convincing them.

By the 30th of May, we were in a full-blown Atlantic gale. The ship pitched and yawed and a new main topmast sail was required when the mended one finally failed us.

Our calm weather had broken and the men cursed the wind and swell as if we had had calm sea for near on three years!

As it subsided, gulf weed was seen all around the ship and Mister Banks hauled much of it aboard filled with all manner of hidden sea life. He took to his botanising as even now, out in the Atlantic Sea off the coast of Africa in well-sailed waters, he discovered new and uncategorised species.

The seas had calmed by mid-June and the breezes lightened.

To avoid boredom, the captain and lieutenants exercised the men in their small arms.

A small sloop came into view but we quickly outsailed her and it was on to England!

On the morning of the 16th of June, we came upon a Portuguese ship from Rio de Janeiro bound for Lisbon.

The captains came within shouting distance but both ships were in a rush and we left her to her business.

The next day, we saw another two ships but they were very far away and we were now in favourable strong winds and making good time!

A few days later, we saw three New England schooners ahead of us. Upon nearing them, the captain sent a boat over with lieutenants Gore and Clerke aboard. We learned they were a fleet from Rhode Island of the Americas, out on a whale fishing expedition.

The captain was still concerned with the earlier rumour of wars, but the master of the whaling fleet confirmed that there was peace in Europe, and disputes in America had been calmed.

We purchased four large albacore tunas from them and left them to their business, as the captain was keener than ever to have us home.

Needless to say, our tuna dinner was afforded for all hands and deliciously prepared by Joe Childs and his assistant.

Another ship was sighted in the distance the following day and the next, a fleet of thirteen, which the captain deemed to be the English East India fleet, with whom we had sailed from Saint Helena.

We all felt rather proud that we had caught up with them!

Chester and I watched them in the distance.

"All this traffic is unusual after sailing alone for so long," he said in passing.

"I agree, Lord Chester. We have sailed with no one other than Tahitian and Maori canoes. It brings the excitement of England closer though, what?" I replied hopefully.

"Time will tell, Captain Fairweather! The men are troubled with the state of the rigging," he noticed.

"I have spoken to the captain and he only wishes for sensible weather to see us home in one piece," I reported.

There was not much more for it. The entire ship's company knew the dear old *Endeavour* was showing her fatigue from our expedition, but nothing would help us now but good luck!

This was not to be, as a squall attacked us on the 22nd of June tearing the topgallant sails. They were hauled down when the wind retired and no effort was spared in mending them. This lack of sail power sent the fleet well ahead of us and they were out of sight overnight.

Tempers frayed over the following days. It seemed that every man found fault at regular intervals in someone or over something.

Fights broke out, nothing lethal, but disconcerting even so!

The captain was uncommonly terse, too, now, and to add to the dissent on board, some part of the *Endeavour* failed daily and required repair.

It was clear to him she would hobble home, but not in good shape, and he would have preferred her to sparkle upon her return!

He knew the men would hearten when they sighted England but could not accurately say when that would be. He merely hoped they would refrain from killing each other in the process!

Rainy squalls now set in making the going rough.

More and more pieces of the ship fell into disrepair; mending was constant.

The *captain* tried to lift the men's spirits by doling out the liquor more freely but this only resulted in more fighting!

Things were grim!

By the 3rd of July, we had six ships in sight but not close enough for us to identify.

Chester was laying low with Lady a little unwell in Mister Banks's cabin.

I kept to myself in the Great Cabin as the captain came in and out with his lieutenants, cursing the rigging and sails for their inability to stay in one piece for this last leg.

Mister Banks would have complained to the captain over the state of the ship, as was his usual way, but by now he knew only to diarise his thoughts on the performance of our little ship.

I overheard him speaking it out loud from his cabin and as he walked into the Great Cabin with Chester.

I let a stray claw clip his shin!

"Damn you, foul cat!" he rubbed at it sorely.

"Was that entirely necessary, Captain Foul?" asked Chester derisively.

"Why, yes, Lord Blot! He speaketh most foul of my ship!" I defended my captain's position on these things.

"I advise you to let it go, Fairweather. Mister Banks's temper frays as we approach England with nary a sail nor rig in one piece!" he warned.

"I shall do nothing of the sort, Chester! The captain has voiced his opinion of his bellyaching, and I as co-captain, cannot let such whining occur!" I expressed my obligation according to my new rank. "And whilst I am at it, I will not have you griping about our *Endeavour* either!"

"You speak above yourself, my good man! I should nip you through your blasted neck!" He showed me his rear as he swaggered pompously.

"Lord Mongrel! You wart on dog-dom! It is you, sir, who should come down off your high horse!" I let him have it!

I was in no mood for this with my captain, stomping impatiently about the Great Cabin!

"Lord Mongrel? Why, you impertinent blot on the seascape! Come here and let me at you!" He growled as I backed myself into a cautious corner.

"Cease this bickering!" called Lady breathlessly from Mister Banks's cabin.

"Quiet, Lady! I have a dread feline to devour!" Cchastened Chester in return.

"You would dare harm a hair on my good self, cowardly hound? I am the captain! I would have you flogged!" I bickered.

"You! Ha! You would have to catch me first, you deranged dimwit! Flogging? Ha!" laughed Chester to himself.

"Fear me, Chester! I am your sworn enemy as of this juncture! The captain will hear of this!" I warned.

"And how will you articulate your complaint, you reprehensible rat? Hand signals? Ha!" He spat as if he had me there!

"Chester! Leave it alone!" groaned Lady.

"I will not! He threatens me, my dear woman!" argued Chester.

"Why, yes! I do converse with my captain so!" I confirmed. "And be warned that communications between the captain and I are quite clear!"

"Pfft!" Chester dismissed. He left me there in the Great Cabin.

"I will have nothing more of you, you pernicious prat!" He was off to the gangway with finality.

"You will rue the day! You and your big words! Be off with you!" I called behind him.

"Pfft!" he finished.

"You have upset him, dear," Lady said softly.

"Him? He has upset me!" I argued.

"You must not squabble. Everyone is on edge at the moment. Go and make friends with him," she advised quietly.

"I will not, dear Lady! He can come to me!" I defied.

"You are good companions and should rally at a time like this!" she advised.

"He is a blockheaded blowhard! He can sulk on deck as he should!" I concluded.

"I must sleep, Fairweather. Please assure me you will mend your friendship with him," she begged wearily.

I sensed a yearning in her voice but could not put my finger on it. I left her to rest with a "Good day!" and plodded to the kitchen for some refreshments.

Chester and I avoided each other for the rest of the day.

I was too proud to go begging his pardon, and of course he too was not about to ask for my absolution!

We dined separately and he retired early to his cabin with Mister Banks and Lady whilst I stood in the Great Cabin to be a comfort to my captain.

"Fairweather, old boy," he addressed me thoughtfully. "Tense times at sea?"

I jumped to the map table where he had flopped down with a sigh and a brandy.

I nodded to him sadly for I did not particularly relish the disagreement with my pal Chester when we were soon to make England and go our own way.

"Where are the dogs?" he quizzed. I stuck my nose in the air with the contempt I held for Chester.

"Ah, there is trouble between you?" He was correct as usual.

I nodded.

"There is trouble all over the ship, Fairweather." He was disappointed that hostilities arose between all manner of chums and cohorts, and so close to home!

He decanted a share of his brandy into a nearby saucer and placed it on the table for me to join him.

I lapped gratefully of it as my tiff with Chester hurt me sorely and the more I thought of it, the more determined I was to mend my rift with him on the morrow.

The captain and I dozed off right there in the Great Cabin with enough brandy to soothe us both.

I woke with a start sometime in the dead of night to a yelp. I thought it was Lady but dismissed it as a bad dream and went back to sleep.

Early the next morning Mister Banks came running from his cabin gasping for enough breath to speak!

The captain and I woke from the very positions in which we had gone to sleep.

"What is it, Mister Banks?" the captain asked of the reddening fellow.

"My dog! Lady!" He choked back his breath and tears streaked down his face.

Chester plodded hopelessly after Mister Banks from his cabin, with his head bowed in a manner I had not seen before!

"What about her?" the captain urged as Mister Banks sobbed uncontrollably.

I jumped to attention on seeing my chum so downtrodden.

"She is dead!" Mister Banks wailed.

I rushed to Chester's side.

"Tell me it is not true!" I begged of him.

"I cannot, Fairweather!" He was overwrought!

"But Chester!" He shook his head as if to confirm her demise.

I was speechless!

I ran into the cabin where she lay on her stool and nudged her with my nose, expecting her to lift her head and say, "Good morning, Fairweather."

She did not move!

I went to where her head lay and put my keen ear to her nose to hear for breathing; not even a whisper!

To her chest for the heart sounds?

Nothing!

Her eyes were closed as if to sleep and a calm expression graced her face, as I had not seen before.

I was shocked to the core!

"Chester!" was all I could utter.

He wore an empty expression, so forsaken that it made him weak and unable to speak. His eyes welled with tears unashamedly. He sat hunched over next to Mister Banks who was crying on the captain's shoulder.

"I heard her cry out in the night but dismissed it as a dream she may have had!" he whimpered.

So I had not dreamt her last yelp!

It was her dying breath!

I was ashamed to have not assisted her, but not so much as Chester who was utterly lost!

Mister Banks blubbered inconsolably as the captain comforted him.

I went to Chester and wriggled up under his befallen chin.

He spoke not a word.

His chest heaved with a sobbing kind of sigh, and he and I sat as one, our grief too deep for words!

My Isaac came running at the captain's request. He stood gaping at the Great Cabin door not able to see what had struck us so.

"What is it, Captain?" my Isaac asked concernedly.

"Fetch lieutenants Gore and Clerke. Mister Banks's bitch, Lady, she has died in the night," he explained calmly, but it set Mister Banks into hysterics, as if he had heard those words for the first time!

Isaac took off at speed as Chester leaned further forward against me in total anguish, his tears wetting my fur.

Mister Banks picked Lady up as if she were a fallen child. He hugged her to his chest, her limp head resting on his shoulder like a loved one!

The lieutenants rushed through the doorway and on seeing the limp body of Lady, understood what had occurred. Lieutenant Gore instructed my Isaac to bring Doctor Perry to the scene.

"Shall I take her, Mister Banks?" he offered respectfully.

"No!" Mister Banks would not let her go, turning from us all and burying his head into her fur to sob his sorrow!

Doctor Perry arrived but Mister Banks would not release his hold upon her. He examined the temperature of one of her lifeless limbs and merely shook his head, as she was, obviously to him, dead, and many hours before!

"I am dreadfully sorry, Mister Banks." He tried to convey his condolences but Mister Banks was frozen in despair.

He patted Chester thoughtfully on the head, knowing him to be her dedicated companion but Chester felt nothing.

"Thank you, Doctor," said the captain dutifully.

"Lieutenant Clerke, prepare the men for a burial," he ordered. "That is, if Mister Banks wishes it," he added.

Mister Banks nodded his approval and the lieutenant and my Isaac left to assemble the men.

"Would you prepare Lady's body, Doctor Perry?" He motioned for Mister Banks to release her.

The doctor took her reverently to wrap her in cloth for the service.

Poor Mister Banks had held her for the last time!

Chester started after her but Mister Banks held him back.

"She is gone, Chester," he said, still sobbing.

Chester sat and hung his head as before.

I could do nought!

I do not think I had ever felt quite so powerless!

The loss Chester must have felt, and poor Mister Banks, but most of all my own complete emptiness in the loss of my matriarch!

She had been as a mother to me!

Those who knew Mister Banks and believed him to not possess a soft spot for anyone changed their minds upon witnessing his grief.

The captain and assembled men who had known Lady from our beginnings to be a gentle and faithful hound, assembled for her committal to the sea.

Chester and Mister Banks stood together as the captain said a few words.

"This day of the 4th of July 1771, to the deep I commit this fine crewmember. As Chester and Mister Banks mourn her loss, we ask the Almighty to take her to his side." It was a fine eulogy, and with it she was sent splashing to the deep.

"She will be missed gambolling through the Lincolnshire landscape from whence we came," said Mister Banks sadly.

He snivelled into his kerchief trying awfully hard to maintain some dignity but he was bereaved to the point of not caring who saw him sob and howl!

We all watched as Lady's body sunk wistfully out of sight into the deep blue.

"I will never forget her, Chester. It has been a privilege to know her and a blessing to call her my exquisite friend," I declared, choking back a sob.

Chester plodded sadly back to Mister Banks's cabin.

He was destroyed!

His spirit and will to exist vanished!

I, too, found the going tough as a part of my heart had been taken on this day!

I went to him to attempt my best to cheer.

"Chester, I am very sorry for your loss. We all loved her," I offered.

"Blast you, Fairweather!" he growled unexpectedly. "No one loved her as I." He bared his teeth and bristled in contempt!

With a snap of his jaw, he chased me out of the cabin!

I had to move fast as I was unsure of his intent! I had not seen this side of him before.

As I ran toward the gangway, I turned briefly to find that he no longer gave chase. It was clear that he wished to be alone with his memories of his mate.

I wished sorely to console him but his temper was plainly not one to be tested at this time!

I went solemnly to the cathead and pondered the delicacy of existence!

In a moment, one's life can be snatched away without the luxury of goodbyes and last tender moments!

It was a cruel old world to take such a kind soul, and as the wind whipped around me, ruffling my whiskers, I felt as fragile and alone as I had ever felt before!

I settled myself into a corner to examine the evening stars.

I was not sure what possessed one to look at the sky when contemplative, but that night I stared at them and wondered much on many things.

The next morning, I saw a ship in the distance and the captain joined me at the cathead with a scratch under my chin as a condolence of some kind.

He said it was a small Dutch galleon and that he would be speaking to her when we neared.

Yelling back and forth when she finally came within range, the captain found she was bound for Riga in Latvia and we moved on.

The usual running of the ship had resumed all too quickly, and thoughts of Lady would be kept to ourselves, as was the way of the sea.

Mister Banks busied himself with the various, more familiar sea life around the ship, as the distance to home decreased. The shearwaters and gannets had returned. He pulled up his own mackerel from a large shoal we sailed through; it was enough for the whole company's dinner!

He swept the depths constantly for crabs and seaweed in a bid to distract himself from his melancholy.

Chester was not seen on deck for days!

As we neared England the traffic increased. The captain bid his good wishes to a passing brig out of Boston; her most recent stop in Gibraltar and now bound for Falmouth in England. She being faster than us would see her in England much sooner than we could travel.

The next day saw us signal another brig travelling against us, out of Liverpool, England, and bound for Porto in Portugal.

By my reckoning it was time to raise my cheerless chum from his mourning, so I went down to Mister Banks's cabin and tentatively greeted the door.

"Chester? Old chum? Old pal of mine?" I whispered.

A rustle and a groan was all that came from the room.

"Chester!" I spoke a little louder this time and with feeling.

"What do you want?" came the exhausted cry.

"There are ships, Chester! And possibly news!" I tried to cajole his interest.

"Perhaps England soon!" I added.

"Go away…" His voice tapered off.

"Chester, I know how you must feel but you must rally, old thing!" I pleaded.

"Pfft!" came the official response.

Then I heard a familiar "Ahoy" from the captain and deemed it wise to investigate.

"Another ship cometh, Chester!" I attempted to arouse his curiosity.

"Oh, all right..." he forfeited.

I peeked around the cabin corner and saw him lying on Lady's stool, perhaps as a comfort to smell her presence.

His legs disentangled and he lurched to his feet awkwardly.

"Um...err...Fairweather?" he garbled, his mouth dry.

"Chester! Have you not taken of water all these days you have been mourning herein?" I asked, concerned for his health.

"Um...no," he admitted.

"What about food?" I demanded.

"Err...no."

"You fool dog! To what purpose was this omission?" I asked sternly.

"I had no appetite nor thirst, Fairweather! I am bereft without Lady!" The tears began to well in his eyes.

I ignored them.

"Come, Lord Chester! It is off with you to seek out Joe Childs for some victuals!" I prescribed.

"But you said there was a ship!" he argued.

"Not before you have partaken of food and drink!" I commanded.

"Now hurry up with you before we miss something of vital importance on deck!" I nipped impatiently at his heels as he sauntered wearily to the gangway.

"Ah! There you are, Chester!" said Joe as we approached the galley. "Been savin' your plate! 'Bout time you came up for a feed!"

He placed a laden offering in front of my chum.

It seemed that all of a sudden, the last few days of hunger had caught up with him as the smell of good meat awoke the senses!

He devoured the good stuff with a few well-placed gulps and as he slurped at the water bowl I could hear the familiar cries of our crew pulling us up to another ship!

"Later, Chester!" I sprinted for the gangway to see another brig beside us.

Chester was behind me having regained his senses.

Chester and I sidled up to our masters to hear the discourse. The captain was pleased to see me knowing I had pulled Chester out of his funk, and Mister Banks rubbed Chester's ears with joy!

Upon the captain introducing himself and our little ship to his counterpart across the water, there was a note of shock amongst her officers.

"We are from London and bound for the Grenadines in the Caribbean Sea. We are only three days sail from the Scilly Isles off the southern English coast," her captain informed.

"Then we are close now!" called our captain back to the men!

"You say the *Endeavour*? Under Captain Cook?" asked the brig's captain suspiciously.

His crew looked upon us wide eyed, as if we were ghosts!

"I am he and this is the *Endeavour* out of England returning with discoveries for the king!" confirmed our captain proudly.

"But no accounts had been received from you in England, and wagers are held that you were lost!" said the brig's captain.

Every soul on our ship staggered with confusion and the captain was furious!

"Lost? But I sent a package from Batavia with letters and maps for England!" he blustered.

"They have not been received! But we are pleased to see you in one piece!" the other captain shouted back, but I saw on his face the look of disbelief that we not only still existed, but clearly we were much worse for the wear!

"Thank you, Captain, and God speed!" shouted our captain, ordering Lieutenant Gore to steer us for home.

"I look forward to your findings upon my return to England! Cheerio-oh!" signalled the captain of the brig as she veered away from us.

"Damnable blighters!" he cursed, for he now knew that the English had not produced the maps he had been offered for purchase back in Capetown! Indeed, it seemed that his package of letters sent from Batavia had not reached England at all! Mister Banks had been right!

"I knew it!" Mister Banks hissed.

"My blasted letters and maps were not delivered by the Dutch!" sputtered the captain.

"I told you this might happen back in Capetown. One cannot entrust such important documents to another party, least of all from another country!" said Mister Banks, disappointed that we had been deemed "lost" so easily.

The captain and Mister Banks went below to the Great Cabin for a spot of brandy upon hearing this awful news.

Chester and I joined them.

They cursed and squabbled for hours about the politics of countries versus the good of the people and the laws of the sea.

"This is boring me, Chester," I yawned.

"I, too, am not in the mood, Fairweather," he agreed, and we both dawdled to the deck for a whiff of fresh airs.

"Chester, old friend…" I began when we were settled out of the way.

"Yes?" he attended.

"I have omitted to offer my proper condolences to you. I am awfully sorry for the loss you have experienced. Lady was closer to me than my own mother and will be sadly missed." A tear welled in my eye but I overcame for the sake of my pooch.

"Thank you, Fairweather. Nothing shall be the same without her," he admitted, looking longingly out to sea.

I waited hopefully for an apology from him for his harsh attack on my person when I looked in on him soon after her death, but as his grief was all so fresh in the mind, I did not press him for it.

Chester continued to muse at the seascape until a familiar sight interrupted his reflections.

Land!

Chester bolted all over the ship, barking at the crew and pointing his nose at the snippet of earth to our northeast.

"Land!" came the cry!

The captain came on deck with his eyeglass and announced that the Scilly Isles was what Chester had seen.

A chuffed Chester rejoined me on the gents' deck with Mister Banks looking longingly at English ground, but the isles were not our destination and we watched them disappear on the horizon.

"Well done, Chester!" I praised. "Trust you to spot the 'Scilly Isles'!" I chuckled.

"What are you chortling about?" he thought me no doubt a ninny.

"Scilly Isles! If you take away the 'c', you have the 'Silly Isles'. No doubt you would find those!" I teased.

"Thank you, F. I aim to please!" he said grandly.

"F?" I scolded.

"Yes, your initial…F! For Fairweather!" He thought himself very clever.

"Cease this immediately or you will 'F' for Find yourself without an 'F' for Friend!" I admonished.

"And you, dear feline, will find yourself looking 'Scilly' hanging from my mouth as I parade your scrawny self around the deck by your scruff!" he threatened.

"Ah Chester! It is good to have you back among the land of the living!" I laughed heartily.

"It is good to be back, my friend," he chortled.

We relaxed on the deck that afternoon trying to remember England and finding it a little difficult after so long at sea.

Young Nick, whose keen eye had found New Zealand, burst the silence with a hale and hearty "Land Ho!"

"Excellent!" bellowed the captain. "England! Rum for all!"

A cheer roused every corner of the ship as the *Endeavour* was abandoned for a toast.

"It is Lizard Point! We are home!" shouted the captain, consulting his charts.

It was the 10th day of July 1771 and my captain's whole demeanour changed. His shoulders relaxed and his neck loosened. He was now able to sail his ship without charting or mapping his course for the first time in near on three years!

Hearty hand-shaking began all over the ship, whether they be new or old to the *Endeavour*. Those who had been with us long were the happiest, but those who had joined us later in the voyage were still mindful of what we veterans had all been through.

"Have us home, young Isaac!" the captain ordered the boy cheerfully. "I am going below to prepare my letters and pack my belongings."

"Wait, Captain!" said Mister Banks. "I shall join you!"

"Yes! Yes! Mister Banks! The ship is in good hands. Come, gentlemen. I had saved some of my best brandy for this very occasion!" He motioned to Doctor Solander, lieutenants Gore and Clerke, and Sergeant Edgcumbe who were the most senior of all the ranks.

Chester and I followed along, as we knew this to be a momentous occasion.

From the Great Cabin we could hear the joy in the crew who had swallowed their rum ration and got back to sailing the *Endeavour*! Ditties were sung, and thus I had not heard before:

Up aloft, amid the rigging
Swiftly blows the fav'ring gale,
Strong as springtime in its blossom,
Filling out each bending sail,
And the waves we leave behind us
Seem to murmur as they rise;
We have tarried here to bear you
To the land you dearly prize.
Rolling home, rolling home,
Rolling home across the sea,
Rolling home to dear old England
Rolling home, dear land to thee.

Now, it takes all hands to man the capstan,
Mister see your cables clear!
Soon you'll be sailing homeward bound sir,
And for the channel you will steer.
See your sheets and crew lines free sir,
all your buntlines overhauled;
Are the sheerpoles and gear all ready?
Soon for New England we will steer.
Rolling home, rolling home,
Rolling home across the sea,
Rolling home to dear old England
Rolling home, dear land to thee.

Full ten thousand miles behind us,
And a thousand miles before,
Ancient ocean waves to waft us
To the well-remembered shore.
Newborn breezes swell to send us
To our childhood welcome skies,
To the glow of friendly faces
And the glance of loving eyes.
Rolling home, rolling home,
Rolling home across the sea,
Rolling home to dear old England
Rolling home, dear land to thee.

Every man knew this tune and the chorus in particular rang out as loud as all could sing!

Chester and I howled in time with the men and a cacophony was begun.

T'was busy and joyful aboard the ship!

"Well, Mister Banks?" the captain addressed his botanist. "This wreck of a ship has gotten us home!" He laughed heartily, for nothing Mister Banks could say about his *Endeavour* now would cause him any antagonism.

"Yes, I will give you that, Captain! She has been a hale and sturdy ship, and with the most commendable captain it has been my honour to assist." He slapped the captain heartily on the back.

A fine botanist he might be, but the captain did not press the point that Mister Banks did not "assist" in any way. That he was not a seaworthy chap was not lost upon any of us.

"To those who cannot be here to see us home!" toasted the captain when all the beakers were full of the best!

"Our fallen comrades!"

"Hear! Hear!" roused the gents.

A drop of the captain's finest made its way to a bowl for Chester and I to share.

"To Lady!" I saluted.

"To Lady! She would have given anything to see England again!" Chester welled a tear.

"She is with us in spirit, Chester. Never forget it," I said proudly but sadly.

We shook ourselves to rid the melancholy and returned to the deck to watch the coastal towns come into view.

I do not hesitate to say that Chester and I stayed awake for every landmark on the following days, sailing in the English Channel. The water was calm and the sun ablaze as the wind came at our heel.

We passed The Lizard, England's southernmost point hugging the coast like a long-lost friend.

Cornwall, Plymouth, Start Point, Portland, The Isle of Wight, all passed with what seemed the wink of an eye.

The white cliffs of Sussex Seven Sisters and Beachy Head loomed as tall as any we had seen on our journey.

People who had seen us approaching from their coastal homes rushed out to point to their children and wave frantically at us.

It was comforting to know that England had not forgotten the *Endeavour*.

The shoreline rushed by us and with each spot, what seemed to be the entire town's folk came to the cliffs and shores to watch us sail gracefully home.

Our *Endeavour* sailed one hundred and ninety seven miles in two days and nights, albeit in terrible disrepair, but she did us proud!

The men were as keen to see home as the captain and no effort was spared. Between their last watches the men jumped and waved hysterically to those on land who greeted us.

By day we saw them; by night their lanterns showed us their many.

At such and important time no one slept!

On the 13th day of July 1771, the *Endeavour* rounded Dungeness, and word had somehow preceded us, for the crowd cheered as we slipped by. At three in the afternoon, the captain set the *Endeavour* to anchor in the Downs, at Deal.

The pilot boat came out to us at once!

"John Hudson, Captain." He shook the captain's hand vigorously. "I'll be takin' her up the Thames to Gallion's Reach. Well done, sir!" he said.

"Look after her," said the captain meekly, taking one last look around.

"Oh, I will!" comforted John Hudson.

Lieutenants Gore, Clerke, and the crew were staying aboard to sail her up the Thames River under the pilot's guidance.

The captain turned to them; now at a stand still, for the last time he would see them as a group. "My thanks, men! You will be honoured with me! I shall ensure it so!"

The captain shook the lieutenants' hands heartily even though they would be catching up at the Admiralty Office in the coming weeks.

The moment was not lost on any of them.

They had endured much and discovered more!

Chester looked at me longingly as Mister Banks tethered him to join him in alighting the ship. He knew he would return to his home with Mister Banks, but that I had abandoned my home in favour of the sea, and did not have any immediate plans.

"Chester, fear not!" I said as Mister Banks assembled with the captain and Doctor Solander, all carrying light luggage. "I will find my way somehow! Be it home or to the Seaman's Rest Inn!"

Chester yowled pitifully and both the captain and Mister Banks knew we would miss each other once separated.

My Isaac held the longboat for the captain and gents to take them ashore. Mister Banks and Doctor Solander boarded first as Isaac steadied the boat.

"Isaac!" The captain yelled down to him as he tossed him his duffle.

"Captain?" answered my lad.

"Do you have any particular plans for your cat?"hHe asked.

"Err…no! I hadn't thought past bringing him aboard!" said Isaac, scratching his head.

"May I take him?" enquired the captain.

My head bolted up as if I had been slapped!

Chester woofed!

Mister Banks laughed.

Doctor Solander shook his head.

"What?" he chided his gents. "He is a memento of our journey!" was the captain's excuse for his sentimentality.

"Fairweather's the *Endeavour*'s cat, so e's yours if you wish it!" Isaac called back. "Besides, me mother wouldn't be happy, me bringin' home another cat! Far as I can remember she's already got two of 'em!" he yelled.

"Woof!" cried Chester, getting the gist.

I imagined the captain had some kind of plan for me but I knew not what.

With that the captain lifted my tensed frame under his arm and climbed down to the longboat with me. I looked up at his face sitting there, ever so loyal and determined.

He winked at me subtly. Was I dreaming? Or was he taking me with him to wherever he lived? I did not know. All I knew was that I was leaving my *Endeavour* with the party heading for the beach!

I had no time to say my farewells and my destination was quite out of my hands!

"There!" exclaimed Mister Banks. "A coach awaits!"

I looked back at my crew who had ingratiated themselves to me without question, and then to my Isaac at the oars, for confirmation that I would be safe. He nodded in the most positive sense.

"What does this mean, Chester?" I asked of him.

"You are off to the captain's home!" he exclaimed.

I was a little lost! The captain's home? Chester woofed his approval and I relaxed a little. We reached the shore and as I had done many times before in strange and unfamiliar places, I leapt to the dry sand.

"England!" Chester announced as he leapt from the longboat. "My paws are home!"

"Quite right!" I said enthusiastically, but not knowing what was in store for me.

People had gathered and milled around to get a look at the captain and gentlemen of the *Endeavour*.

The women waved and the men lined up to shake the captain's hand.

I must say I was much impressed with how quickly word had gotten around that we were back!

I was still under the captain's arm and received much petting from the children.

With no further ado, we all boarded the carriage that had been sent for us by the Royal Society. Even they knew we were home and no doubt eagerly awaited Mister Banks's reports!

It was a long carriage ride of some seven or so hours.

The captain and company said little to each other as Chester and I watched the towns and countryside race by us.

As London loomed, it became a blur of civilization and a touch of fear took me!

"Chester, I shall miss the sea! This London sprawls large and worrisome," I admitted, troubled with the sheer size and pace of the place, as our carriage rattled hastily along the streets filled with homes and businesses of all kinds.

Even in the wee hours of a Sunday morning the place was abuzz with folk!

"You will get used to it, especially now that you are to live with the captain. You will have a home close to Mister Banks's house and I can visit you with him!" He attempted to allay my fears.

"I suppose," I said vacantly while the unfamiliar passed our carriage at speed.

Chester announced we were nearing Piccadilly and our carriage stopped abruptly.

I remembered this place as mentioned on the dock nearly three years ago, when the disbelieving Charles and Reginald wagered with Robert that we would fail.

Our timing here could not have made me happier than to witness the pompous Reginald and Charles dancing ridiculously in a circle, holding fifty guineas on their hats!

Off to the side was the winner of the bet, Robert, laughing hysterically as he had most surely won a hundred guineas! I alone knew what this was, but it stumped the captain and left Mister Banks and Doctor Solander scratching their heads.

"What gives, Fairweather?" Chester asked as I chuckled to myself.

"T'was a wager I witnessed before we left England, Chester. The men making ninnies of themselves wagered we would not return, and now I have the pleasure of seeing them make utter fools of themselves!" I was well pleased as the crowd gathered there laughed heartily at the ridiculous pair.

As we alighted the coach, the gathered crowd shifted their interest when Robert declared, "There is the chap now! Well done, Cook!"

The crowd cheered and embarrassed my modest captain but Mister Banks in his inimitable form took a bow for him.

"Well, chaps! We go our separate ways. It has been my honour!" bowed Mister Banks to the captain and Doctor Solander. "I reside in New Burlington Street, chaps, and would be honoured to entertain you there at any time. I am off to the Royal Society to report!" They exchanged addresses and the sentiment was returned. They gathered their things to depart for their respective homes.

"Chester!" I hollered as he walked off with Mister Banks. "I will see you at the Seaman's Rest at the soonest instance!"

"Where is it?" he yelled.

"Deptford Docks, London! Look for the big ships!" I informed.

"Righto!"

My chum was leaving me and to see him saunter off with Mister Banks for his home saddened me so!

We had been inseparable, but I knew I would see him somehow. If I had travelled around the globe for nearly three years, I was sure that I could find one silly dog in London!

"Well, Fairweather." The captain sighed as the crowd dissipated. "It is too early in the morning to go straight to my home but I will send a note to my wife Elizabeth of our return." He scribbled out a note, telling her we would be along soon.

"Mister Stephens, the Secretary of the Admiralty, is our next stop." People stared as they watched this tall and regal man talking mindlessly to a cat!

I felt I would never be free of such prejudices, but there was nought I could do. The relationship between a captain and his cat was indeed a special thing. Others would always think it odd.

He set me down and we walked together quietly. I kept close to him for fear of being accosted by passing feet. We approached a grand old building and a chap waiting impatiently outside.

"Cook!" said Mister Stephens as we approached. "And a cat!" He looked down at me grinning superciliously.

"Mister Stephens. Good morning. I was not expecting you to be waiting for me," the captain said, somewhat surprised.

"Ever since I received word of your return I have been glued to this very spot! Your arrival is the talk of London as I must say, we had thought you lost!" He shook the captain's hand enthusiastically.

"I apologize for our tardy return but we present with significant discoveries for the king. Mister Banks has gone straight to the Royal Society with his findings and herewith I deliver you the Bark *Endeavour*. She has been a sturdy ship and a credit to England!" he said with pride.

"I anticipate your charts and maps and we will meet more comprehensively when you have settled back at home. I shall not delay you after such a long voyage. No doubt your family awaits. Well done, James!" Mister Stephens shook the captain's hand again and kindly let us depart without delay.

We walked at pace down the Strand and Fleet Street, past St Paul's Cathedral, through the bustling city and made for the Mile End Road.

Upon seeing their father coming down the road, the captain's two boys of eight and seven years ran headlong into his clutches as I watched the cheerful reunion.

"James! Nathaniel! You have grown so!" He rustled their hair playfully.

Elizabeth stood in the doorway and in greeting they embraced long and lovingly.

"James," she said through tears of joy. "I thought you lost!"

"Elizabeth," he replied, welling up himself. "What of Eliza and Joseph?" he asked, looking up the hall to see their happy faces.

Elizabeth held my captain's hands and delivered the awful news. "Eliza died this past April of age four, and George died just after you left barely three weeks old."

"I am so sorry I could not be here for you, my dear," the captain wiped away a bereaved tear.

"And who is this?" Elizabeth asked cheerfully, changing the subject as her boys discovered me hiding behind the captain's things.

"This is Fairweather! Ship's cat of the *Endeavour* and fine mouser!" he introduced me proudly.

"Well, we could certainly use a good mouser. The summer has seen them in my kitchen in droves!" she welcomed me warmly.

The boys petted me happily. "Can we keep him father?" They pleaded.

"So much as a cat such as Fairweather can be kept, yes! But if he wanders off from time to time, fear not. He has the sea in his heart, boys!" Not a truer word could my captain have said. He knew me well.

As the captain, Elizabeth and their boys supped and chatted, I was given a hearty plate of Madam Cook's finest and appreciated it so that I rubbed the madam's leg.

She petted me and we became instant friends.

A knock came to the front door as the meal was coming to an end. The captain and I went to investigate. He was handed an envelope. He opened it on his way back to the dining room and I sat in the corner to hear of its content.

"It is from Mister Banks," he said offhandedly, thinking it a mere cheery-oh. His eyes widened and an enormous grin graced his face as he read and reread it.

"What is it dear?" asked Madam Cook.

"I have been made captain on Mister Banks's recommendation to the Earl of Sandwich! He has rushed it through the Admiralty Office upon hearing of our return!" he informed happily.

"Good for Mister Banks! Congratulations, dear!" Madam Cook was delighted.

"There you are, Fairweather! I, too, am now a captain!" He said to me knowingly, as he had promoted me to the title long before he himself had it!

He sought out the decanter of brandy and poured two glasses and a saucer to celebrate.

"Why a saucer of brandy, James?" she asked confusedly.

"It is Fairweather's," the captain responded as if all cats consumed the stuff!

"Brandy for a cat?" she asked, a little concerned.

"Fairweather, or should I say Captain Fairweather, is no ordinary cat!" he explained.

I am certain that Madam Cook took a cautious view of her husband's sanity, but as the boys began to laugh and chant "Captain Fairweather!" she could do nought but join in the merriment. I lapped at my plate unconcerned with the jollity at my expense as my captain knew what was what, and that was all that mattered!

Madam Cook sent the boys to bed and the captain scooped me up to bid them goodnight, thinking I might enjoy a warm comfortable young boy's bed. Indeed, I would eventually but I was not ready to retire, as I had wondered whether the chaps would be at the inn this evening.

I wriggled and resisted his grip until he set me down.

I gave him a knowing look and strolled off to the window ledge.

"Ah, the Seaman's Rest, is it?" he asked after me. I nodded.

I waited on the sill for him to give me permission.

"You need not ask my consent, Captain Fairweather! I shall leave the window open for your return." And with that, I jumped to the street.

I made my way to the Deptford Docks.

I could hear the ruckus almost from my outset. It sounded like much was doing in the dock area. When I arrived, I noticed many changes. The ships were more and larger and the docks full of them from all parts. With the growth that had occurred, there were a few more inns well placed along the riverside but I knew the Seaman's Rest and headed straight for it.

As I approached, I could hear the familiar sounds of some of my crewmate's voices. I had heard them for so long that they were unmistakable. The *Endeavour* must have reached Gallion's Reach already and her crew decided wisely that a familiar watering place was required before heading to their homes. As I looked in the window, every sailor in the inn was transfixed by our men telling stories of our voyage.

"Oy!" came a familiar sound. "You! What 'ya doin' at that window?"

It was Slim!

"Bandit?" He addressed me with my former name coming closer for a better look.

"It is I, home from my voyage!" I announced.

"'Ere come and see the lads, they're all 'ere!" He was as scrawny as ever and just as annoying. "Bandit's 'ere! Bandit's 'ere! Back from the dead!" He sprinted up the alley to announce my arrival.

I followed him happily.

Every cat on the high window ledge looked down at me as if they had seen a ghost! My friends were all there, along with a few new additions.

"Bandit?" asked Badger, his eyes wide. "You have returned with your men of the *Endeavour*?"

"Yes, Badger, but my name is now Fairweather! A name given to me onboard the very same ship!" I instructed proudly.

Rubbish-Bin-Bob sat chewing some mutton fat and merely eyed me as if I would steal it from him.

"Fairweather? Are you mad? He is a legend! A myth! Told in stories from ships docked here from all parts of the world! No one here has ever seen him!" He eyed me suspiciously.

"And I am he! We are one and the same!" I defended.

"'Ya lyin' begger!" Slim spat at me.

"I speak the truth, lads!" I stood firm. "The *Endeavour* has just docked, and I with it!"

I leapt to the ledge to confirm my existence.

"Hey! Fairweather!" came a cry from Joe Childs, my cook. "You've come for a wee nip, have 'ya? Come 'ere! I'll give 'ya some of me ale!"

I looked as my feline friends and the new fellows gaped in awe!

I leapt nonchalantly to the main inn as men made way for me to drink with my fellows.

As Joe Childs poured me a saucer of ale and the rest of my crewmen watched the faces of their fellow sailors, I could see the look of shock on my pals' faces.

With that the entire crew held up their tankards of ale. "To Fairweather! Finest ship's cat!"

I bowed and made my way back to the ledge and nimbly leapt back into position.

I buffed at that all too familiar claw as the faces of my feline friends continued to stare dumbstruck!

"You are he!" announced Badger, as if meeting me for the first time.

"It's 'im! Well, I'll be blowed! It's 'im! It's 'im! Bandit's Fairweather!" he spluttered annoyingly.

"Oh, be quiet Slim! We have just established that!" Badger chided.

A familiar shape came out of the shadows.

Turkel!

"Of course, it is! Fairweather! Welcome home and well done, my boy!" he said quietly, as was his way.

"Turkel! It has been done! Terra Australis Incognita is a secret no more!" I said proudly.

"And you survived!" he added.

"More than that Turkel, lads! I revelled in it from the moment we departed England."

Badger interrupted, "Catnip for all!" And with that Rubbish-Bin-Bob and Slim assembled for the all-too-familiar bowl.

"I apologize sincerely for doubting you, but with your new name you can see where the confusion lay?" Badger backed up respectfully. "Drink, Fairweather, old friend and then tell us of your journey!"

"I prefer brandy or rum thank you, Badger! But do not let me keep you from the catnip." I politely refused him.

"Brandy and rum eh? Fine ship's cat you certainly are! Asking for the best!" he answered.

Turkel pushed a saucer of rum toward me that he had been sipping by himself.

"Here lad," he invited me to share. I lapped at it with him until a familiar "woof" came from the alley!

"Lord Chester!" I greeted him from my lofty spot.

"Captain Fairweather!" He yoo-hooed.

"A dog!" Slim screeched. Every cat tensed at the thought.

"You know this mongrel?" Badger snobbishly asked, knowing that the ledge could not be reached by the average hound.

"How dare you, sir!" I hissed. "This fine chap is my closest friend! If you are to discriminate, I shall leave you forthwith!" I warned.

"No!" thundered Turkel. "Bring him up. He will drink with us as he is as welcome as Fairweather himself." He left no room for argument.

"Righto, Turkel," Badger said warily.

"Come, dear friend! Join us for a dram!" I invited, rubbing it in.

I turned to the cats. "I am appalled by this lack of tolerance between species, Badger! You will make him feel right at home!" I chastened, as this kind of behaviour embarrassed me.

With that, the agile Chester leapt to the ledge as if he possessed all the characteristics of the finest feline form.

"Proud of you, my boy," said Turkel quietly.

It was everything I could have imagined of a hero's welcome!

Badger sat impressed as Chester and I spoke long of our voyage.

Slim interrupted persistently for more details.

Turkel merely fixed his gaze and remembered his own journey with a touch of melancholy.

The night was a mixture of revelling and remembering, and rousing tales came easily.

The other cats retired to the alley one by one until only Turkel, Chester, and I were left.

"I knew you had it in you, Fairweather," he said knowingly.

"Thank you, Turkel, and I remembered you fondly as I sailed entirely around the globe! You are known in many of the ports I visited and my knowing of you assisted me in more than one spot of trouble!" I confided.

"Yes, he spoke of you fondly and often!" added Chester, full of rum and looking quite the ninny on the cat ledge of the inn. I cared not. He was with me!

"I suppose you will go to sea again?" Turkel asked. The sea and his age had beaten him, and he would clearly never sail again. Chester was as keen as Turkel to hear my views.

"That is a good question and one I am loathe to answer so soon after returning, but I have seen many things and made many fond friends." I nudged my pal Chester fondly.

"I cannot think of a single thing I would rather have done! My crewmates and their antics? My love for a Tahitian girl? The funny old gents? Chester and Lady, may her soul rest! That special bond between cat and canine? And my magnificent captain? I would trade none of it!" I concluded.

Turkel nodded his final approval of my summing up. He went off to sleep somewhere, bidding us a goodnight.

I leapt to the alley with Chester and we wandered slowly back to the captain's house.

"I leave you here and it's off to Mister Banks with me. Toodle-oo!" slurred a comical Chester from a little too much rum.

I leapt happily to my captain's opened window, pausing to look back at the London skyline and the masts of tall ships in the distance.

I wondered where they would be headed?

But for now, I knew that at last a comfortable bed and a warm boy awaited me!

THE END